CONTENTS

BOOK THREE

His Freedom

BOOK FOUR

His Start in Life

INTRODUCTION

On an early page of *Clayhanger* may be read four words which represent both the excellence and the limitation of Arnold Bennett's approach to the Novel. Those words refer to 'the interestingness of existence'. Other novelists had shown passion, humour, great invention, and art. They had exalted the courage and endurance of mankind, or had demurely ridiculed the snobberies and meannesses of decaying baronets and interfering aunts, or had sighed over young love, Vanity Fair, or the inadequacy of goodness of heart. Nobody since Defoe, whose interest in facts was insatiable, had found the spectacle of life, kindly and warmly seen, as engrossing as Bennett did.

He had learned this approach, in part, from the French realists and George Moore, who was a disciple of the French realists; but by the time he wrote *The Old Wives' Tale* he had found a way to bring his own English humour into association with a capacity for regarding facts. Although he stood apart from the persons and events of his narrative, he also entered cordially into their feelings. He did this, not with ardour, but with benevolence. He was interested in everything, as boys are interested in machinery. He did not wish to participate; he observed. But he observed imaginatively, putting himself into the minds of simple people and raising them from the ordinary to the unique.

The Old Wives' Tale was his great triumph in this exercise; for he followed 'those two girls' as individuals rather than types or instances, and carried both through their middle years to the pathos of age and death. If you remember, the inspiration for this book had come from sight in a Paris restaurant of one old woman whom he immediately pictured as having been once young and perhaps beautiful. *The Old Wives' Tale*, therefore, was in its beginnings uncalculated. Plan, which is the artist's supplement to inspiration, legitimately followed; but the book was first seen in a flash of vision.

When *The Old Wives' Tale* and its successor, *Clayhanger*, were published, it was usual for reviewers of the last Edwardian years to refer to Bennett's method as 'meticulous', by which the reviewers meant minute in detail. *Clayhanger* is much more minute than *The Old Wives' Tale*, the reason being that this successor was quite differently conceived, and was intended by the author to contain a rather close commentary on the life of the Potteries as it was affected by local development as well as external affairs. The central figure was to be Edwin Clayhanger; but behind him and about him and through his eyes was to be seen a district which 'is characterized by a perhaps excessive provincialism'.

Where *The Old Wives' Tale* had been about two old women who had once been girls growing up from laughing youth to maturity, *Clayhanger* and its sequels were to be about (*a*) a boy growing up; (*b*) a girl growing up; and (*c*) the two growing old together. The three books were seen as a trilogy; but if *The Old Wives' Tale* had not been written, and had not established a reputation, the trilogy might have remained 'in the dark backward and abysm of time'. Arnold Bennett was not primarily a sociologist. He was a creative writer absorbed in 'the interestingness of existence'.

It must not be thought that he was trying to repeat a great popular success. On its publication *The Old Wives' Tale* had a sale, I believe, of fewer than six thousand copies, which even in 1908 was far from being large. No American publisher would take it for the United States market until George Doran bought a thousand copies in sheets and one American bookseller, George Melcher, became actively partisan, with excellent results. No, the thought of the Clayhanger trilogy arose from Bennett's surprised discovery that men expected him to continue upon the grand scale of whole lifetimes. He enters quietly in his *Journal* saying nothing of his surprise – that 'I saw Pinker [his agent] on Tuesday, who had got an offer from Methuen of £300, £350, and £400, on account of next three books.' *Clayhanger* was the first of those books; the £300 one. He planned to begin writing it on 1 January 1910.

On 19 November 1909 he wrote, still in the *Journal*, 'Yesterday I finished making a list of all social, political, and artistic events, which I thought possibly useful for my novel between 1872 and 1882. Tedious bore, for a trifling ultimate result in the book. But necessary. Today in the forest (of Fontainebleau) I practically arranged most of the construction of the first part of the novel. Still lacking a title for it. If I thought an ironic title would do, I would call it "A thoughtful young man". But the public is so damned slow in the uptake.' By 3 December he had decided on *Clayhanger*; and at 9.45 on the morning of Wednesday, 5 January 1910, he began the actual writing, at the Royal York Hotel, Brighton, managed at that time by the celebrated Harry Preston.

A General Election was in full swing. He was much perturbed about it, about 'Tory lies' and a discovery in himself of 'the symptoms of crass Toryism'. He was also writing for *The English Review*, under Ford Madox Hueffer, and *The Nation*, under H. W. Massingham, as well as for his old loves, *The New Age* and *T.P.'s Weekly*. Nevertheless, he finished the first part of *Clayhanger*, 42,000 words, by 7 February, and found it more 'coloured' and variegated than he had expected. A later chapter was 'a bit dull'; while by the middle of March he was in a panic about the book : 'I was frightened by a lot of extraordinary praise of *The Old Wives' Tale* that I have recently had. I was afraid *Clayhanger* was miles inferior to it.' However, the book was finished at 3 p.m. on

3 June; and as a single volume, apart from all question of its sequels, it increased the author's fame, which had become prodigious.

I must briefly refer to those sequels at this point. *Hilda Lessways,* which attempts to give a comparable picture of Edwin Clayhanger's beloved, proved a disappointment, not because it contains less veracious detail, but because that detail was recorded by Bennett from observation, and because scenes which in *Clayhanger* hold the romantic charm of the unsolved become almost mechanical keys to what has baffled and enchanted the young Edwin. Charm is gone; the Five Towns are in abeyance; emotion has been lowered.

If emotion is lowered in *Hilda Lessways,* it rises again, harshly and grimly, in the concluding volume, *These Twain,* where Edwin Clayhanger is led to question, in 'terrible gloom', the justification of all life. The interestingness of existence has been, for a time, forgotten; and Clayhanger, lying close to his wife in the dark, 'perceived that the conflict between his individuality and hers could never cease. . . . Hilda had divined nothing. She never did divine the tortures which she inflicted in his heart.'

I cannot believe that the conflict dwelt upon in *These Twain* was foreseen when the early pages of *Clayhanger* were written. It was a conflict in which Bennett himself was engaged. War had come upon the world; all the decencies of civilization had been outraged. *These Twain* was written in wartime, six years after *Clayhanger*. It was written with the same sincerity, the same integrity; but war and the lapse of time had been fatal to continuity of mood, and Bennett's delight in the interestingness of existence had suffered eclipse. He had become a stoic.

These are some of the reasons why *Clayhanger* alone of the three books can be compared with *The Old Wives' Tale*. It was a picture of that way of life amid which he had grown up, so that the lesser characters, with their mannerisms and turns of speech, constantly add verisimilitude to the narrative. The scene was not an imaginary scene; Bennett went to the trouble of taking the walk Edwin takes at the beginning of the book, and he could at all moments call before his eyes the familiar streets and squares renamed in his pages. Memory reinforced all his imaginings; for although Edwin was not himself, and the Clayhangers were not the Bennetts (but rather, perhaps, the Orgreaves), he was at home in Bursley as he was at home nowhere else. What happened there happened, as it were, within himself. When he wrote of Bursley, he was a god, to whom all things were known.

The historical perspective of *Clayhanger*, though he found the preparations to ensure its accuracy a tedious bore, was an immense help to his conception; for he was stimulated by something of which nobody, he said, perceived the interest – 'this interchange of activities, this ebb and flow of money, this sluggish rise and fall of reputations and fortunes, stretching out of one century into another and towards a third'. He himself perceived the interest: it lay within the very spectacle through the ingenuous eyes of Edwin, it became fascinating. He wrote the book steadily, as was his wont, day by day, with almost Trollopean regularity; but while he wrote he was moved and amused and sometimes deeply stirred by what he imagined.

Clayhanger is a very honest and sagacious book; but it is much more than honest and sagacious. It is the portrait of a civilization, and, cumulatively, the revelation of a young man belonging to that civilization and apart from it, growing from page to page, overawed by his tremendous father, struggling for independence, making and keeping his friends, learning to think, falling in love, and with what is called in Chapter VI 'the old basis of "decency"' showing what young men were really like in and out of the Five Towns at the end of the Victorian age.

Here, too, is the majestic Auntie Hamps, whose latter days are splendidly shown in *These Twain*. Here is Mr Shushions, the old man whose outstanding characteristic is his immense age. It is a beautiful sketch. Here are Edwin's sister Maggie, the Orgreaves family, the strange and inexplicable Hilda, Big James the printer's foreman, and many more. Above all is Darius Clayhanger, Edwin's father, with whom his struggle in Darius's health and sickness produces not only torment but the reserves of character which make Edwin's development clear to us. Darius is a great figure; not a type such as commoner novelists have drawn, but one in the rigour of authority whose effect on others, son, daughter, and friends, is such as to quicken a reader's pulse. Bennett remains calm before Darius. He is still the god, creating a man. If, therefore, *Clayhanger* contained nothing more than Darius it would be destined to live, as it is doing, out of its own age into another and towards a third. It has the still further claim that it testifies to the interestingness of existence.

1953   FRANK SWINNERTON

BOOK ONE : HIS VOCATION

I

Edwin Clayhanger stood on the steep-sloping, red-bricked canal bridge, in the valley between Bursley and its suburb Hillport. In that neighbourhood the Knype and Mersey canal formed the western boundary of the industrialism of the Five Towns. To the east rose pitheads, chimneys, and kilns, tier above tier, dim in their own mists. To the west, Hillport Fields, grimed but possessing authentic hedgerows and winding paths, mounted broadly up to the sharp ridge on which stood Hillport Church, a landmark. Beyond the ridge, and partly protected by it from the driving smoke of the Five Towns, lay the fine and ancient Tory borough of Oldcastle, from whose historic Middle School Edwin Clayhanger was now walking home. The fine and ancient Tory borough provided education for the whole of the Five Towns, but the relentless ignorance of its prejudices had blighted the district. A hundred years earlier the canal had only been obtained after a vicious Parliamentary fight between industry and the fine ancient borough, which saw in canals a menace to its importance as a centre of traffic. Fifty years earlier the fine and ancient borough had succeeded in forcing the greatest railway line in England to run through unpopulated country five miles off instead of through the Five Towns, because it loathed the mere conception of a railway. And now, people are inquiring why the Five Towns, with a railway system special to itself, is characterized by a perhaps excessive provincialism. These interesting details have everything to do with the history of Edwin Clayhanger, as they have everything to do with the history of each of the two hundred thousand souls in the Five Towns. Oldcastle guessed not the vast influences of its sublime stupidity.

It was a breezy Friday in July 1872. The canal, which ran north and south, reflected a blue and white sky. Towards the bridge from the north came a long narrow canal-boat roofed with tarpaulins; and towards the bridge from the south came a similar craft, sluggishly creeping. The towing-path was a morass of sticky brown mud, for in the way of rain that year was breaking the records of a century and a half. Thirty yards in front of each boat an unhappy skeleton of a horse floundered its best in the quagmire. The honest endeavour of one of the animals received a frequent tonic from a bare-legged girl of seven who heartily curled a whip about its crooked large-jointed legs. The ragged and filthy child danced in the rich mud round the horse's flanks with the simple joy of one who had been rewarded for good behaviour by the unrestricted use of a whip for the first time.

II

Edwin, with his elbows on the stone parapet of the bridge, stared uninterested at the spectacle of the child, the whip, and the skeleton. He was not insensible to the piquancy of the pageant of life, but his mind was preoccupied with grave and heavy matters. He had left school that day, and what his eyes saw as he leaned on the bridge was not a willing beast and a gladdened infant, but the puzzling world and the advance guard of its problems bearing down on him. Slim, gawky, untidy, fair, with his worn black-braided clothes, and slung over his shoulders in a bursting satchel the last load of his school-books, and on his bright, rough hair a shapeless cap whose lining protruded behind, he had the extraordinary wistful look of innocence and simplicity which marks most boys of sixteen. It seemed rather a shame, it seemed even tragic, that this naïve, simple creature, with his straight-forward and friendly eyes so eager to believe appearances, this creature immaculate of worldly experience, must soon be transformed into a man, wary, incredulous, detracting. Older eyes might have wept at the simplicity of those eyes.

This picture of Edwin as a wistful innocent would have made Edwin laugh. He had been seven years at school, and considered himself a hardened sort of brute, free of illusions. And he sometimes thought that he could judge the world better than most neighbouring mortals.

'Hello! The Sunday!' he murmured, without turning his eyes.

Another boy, a little younger and shorter, and clothed in a superior untidiness, had somehow got on to the bridge, and was leaning with his back against the parapet which supported Edwin's elbows. His eyes were franker and simpler even than the eyes of Edwin, and his lips seemed to be permanently parted in a good-humoured smile. His name was Charlie Orgreave, but at school he was invariably called 'the Sunday' – not 'Sunday', but 'the Sunday' – and nobody could authoritatively explain how he had come by the nickname. Its origin was lost in the prehistoric ages of his childhood. He and Edwin had been chums for several years. They had not sworn fearful oaths of loyalty; they did not constitute a secret society; they had not even pricked forearms and written certain words in blood; for these rites are only performed at Harrow, and possibly at the Oldcastle High School, which imitates Harrow. Their fellowship meant chiefly that they spent a great deal of time together, instinctively and unconsciously enjoying each other's mere presence, and that in public arguments they always reinforced each other, whatever the degree of intellectual dishonesty thereby necessitated.

'I'll bet you mine gets to the bridge first,' said the Sunday. With an ingenious movement of the shoulders he arranged himself so that the parapet should bear the weight of his satchel.

Edwin Clayhanger slowly turned round, and perceived that the object which the Sunday had appropriated as 'his' was the other canal-boat, advancing from the south.

'Horse or boat?' asked Edwin.

'Boat's nose, of course,' said the Sunday.

'Well,' said Edwin, having surveyed the unconscious competitors, and counting on the aid of the whipping child, 'I don't mind laying you five.'

'That be damned for a tale!' protested the Sunday. 'We said we'd never bet less than ten – you know that.'

'Yes, but –' Edwin hesitatingly drawled.

'But what?'

'All right. Ten,' Edwin agreed. 'But it's not fair. You've got a rare start on me.'

'Rats!' said the Sunday, with finality. In the pronunciation of this word the difference between his accent and Edwin's came out clear. The Sunday's accent was less local; there was a hint of a short 'e' sound in the 'a', and a briskness about the consonants, that Edwin could never have compassed. The Sunday's accent was as carelessly superior as his clothes. Evidently the Sunday had someone at home who had not learnt the art of speech in the Five Towns.

III

He began to outline a scheme, in which perpendicular expectoration figured, for accurately deciding the winner, and a complicated argument might have ensued about this, had it not soon become apparent that Edwin's boat was going to be handsomely beaten, despite the joyous efforts of the little child. The horse that would die but would not give up, was only saved from total subsidence at every step by his indomitable if aged spirit. Edwin handed over the ten marbles even before the other boat had arrived at the bridge.

'Here,' he said. 'And you may as well have these, too,' adding five more to the ten, all he possessed. They were not the paltry marble of today, plaything of infants, but the majestic 'rinker', black with white spots, the king of marbles in an era when whole populations practised the game. Edwin looked at them half regretfully as they lay in the Sunday's hands. They seemed prodigious wealth in those hands, and he felt somewhat as a condemned man might feel who bequeaths his jewels on the scaffold. Then there was a rattle, and a tumour grew out larger on the Sunday's thigh.

The winning boat, long preceded by its horse, crawled under the bridge and passed northwards to the sea, laden with crates of earthen-ware. And then the loser, with the little girl's father and mother and her brothers and sisters, and her kitchen, drawing-room, and bedroom, and her smoking chimney and her memories and all that was hers, in the stern of it, slid beneath the boys' downturned faces while the whip cracked away beyond the bridge. They could see, between the whitened tarpaulins, that the deep belly of the craft was filled with clay.

'Where does that there clay come from?' asked Edwin. For not merely was he honestly struck by a sudden new curiosity, but it was meet for him to behave like a man now, and to ask manly questions.

'Runcorn,' said the Sunday scornfully. 'Can't you see it painted all over the boat?'

'Why do they bring clay all the way from Runcorn?'

'They don't bring it from Runcorn. They bring it from Cornwall. It comes round by sea – see?' He laughed.

'Who told you?' Edwin roughly demanded.

'Anybody knows that!' said the Sunday grandly, but always main-taining his gay smile.

'Seems devilish funny to me,' Edwin murmured, after reflection, 'that they should bring clay all that roundabout way just to make crocks of it here. Why should they choose just *this* place to make crocks in? I always understood –'

'Oh! Come *on*!' the Sunday cut him short. 'It's blessed well one o'clock and after!'

IV

They climbed the long bank from the canal up to the Manor Farm, at which high point their roads diverged, one path leading direct to Bleakridge where Orgreave lived, and the other zigzagging down through neglected pasturage into Bursley proper. Usually they parted here without a word, taking pride in such Spartan taciturnity, and they would doubtless have done the same this morning also, though it were fiftyfold their last walk together as two schoolboys. But an incident inter-vened. 'Hold on!' cried the Sunday.

To the south of them, a mile and a half off, in the wreathing mist of the Cauldon Bar ironworks, there was a yellow gleam that even the capricious sunlight could not kill, and then two rivers of fire sprang from the gleam and ran in a thousand delicate and lovely hues down the side of a mountain of refuse. They were emptying a few tons of molten slag at the Cauldon Bar Ironworks. The two rivers hung slowly dying in the mists of smoke. They reddened and faded, and you thought they had vanished, and you could see them yet, and then they escaped the

16

baffled eye, unless a cloud aided them for a moment against the sun; and their ephemeral but enchanting beauty had expired for ever.

'Now!' said Edwin sharply.

'One minute ten seconds,' said the Sunday, who had snatched out his watch, an inestimable contrivance with a centre seconds hand. 'By Jove! That was a good 'un.'

A moment later two smaller boys, both laden with satchels, appeared over the brow from the canal.

'Let's wait a jiff,' said the Sunday to Edwin, and as the smaller boys showed no hurry he bawled out to them across the intervening cinder-waste : 'Run!' They ran. They were his younger brothers, Johnnie and Jimmie. 'Take this and hook it!' he commanded, passing the strap of his satchel over his head as they came up. In fatalistic silence they obeyed the smiling tyrant.

'What are you going to do?' Edwin asked.

'I'm coming down your way a bit.'

'But I thought you said you were peckish.'

'I shall eat three slices of beef instead of my usual brace,' said the Sunday carelessly.

Edwin was touched. And the Sunday was touched, because he knew he had touched Edwin. After all, this was a solemn occasion. But neither would overtly admit that its solemnity had affected him. Hence, first one and then the other began to skim stones with vicious force over the surface of the largest of the three ponds that gave interest to the Manor Farm. When they had thus proved to themselves that the day differed in no manner from any other breaking-up day, they went forward.

On their left were two pitheads whose double wheels revolved rapidly in smooth silence, and the puffing engine-house and all the trucks and gear of a large ironstone mine. On their right was the astonishing farm, with barns and ricks and cornfields complete, seemingly quite unaware of its forlorn oddness in that foul arena of manufacture. In front, on a little hill in the vast valley, was spread out the Indian-red architecture of Bursley – tall chimneys and rounded ovens, schools, the new scarlet market, the grey tower of the old church, the high spire of the evangelical church, the low spire of the church of genuflexions, and the crimson chapels, and rows of little red houses with amber chimney-pots, and the gold angel of the blackened Town Hall topping the whole. The sedate reddish browns and reds of the composition, all netted in flowing scarves of smoke, harmonized exquisitely with the chill blues of the chequered sky. Beauty was achieved, and none saw it.

The boys descended without a word through the brick-strewn pastures, where a horse or two cropped the short grass. At the railway bridge, which carried a branch mineral line over the path, they exchanged a brief volley of words with the working-lads who always played pitch-and-toss there in the dinner-hour; and the Sunday added to the collection of shawds and stones lodged on the under ledges of the low iron girders. A strange boy, he had sworn to put ten thousand stones on those ledges before he died, or perish in the attempt. Hence Edwin sometimes called him 'Old Perish-in-the-attempt'. A little farther on the open gates of a manufactory disclosed six men playing the noble game of rinkers on a smooth patch of ground near the weighing machine. These six men were Messieurs Ford, Carter, and Udall, the three partners owning the works, and three of their employees. They were celebrated marble-players, and the boys stayed to watch them as, bending with one knee almost touching the earth, they shot the rinkers from their stubby thumbs with a cannon-like force and precision that no boy could ever hope to equal. 'By gum!' mumbled Edwin involuntarily, when an impossible shot was accomplished; and the bearded shooter, pleased by this tribute from youth, twisted his white apron into a still narrower ring round his waist. Yet Edwin was not thinking about the game. He was thinking about a battle that lay before him, and how he would be weakened in the fight by the fact that in the last school examination, Charlie Orgreave, younger than himself by a year, had ousted him from the second place in the school. The report in his pocket said : 'Position in class next term : third'; whereas he had been second since the beginning of the year. There would of course be no 'next term' for him, but the report remained. A youth who has come to grips with that powerful enemy, his father, cannot afford to be handicapped by even such a trifle as a report entirely irrelevant to the struggle.

Suddenly Charlie Orgreave gave a curt nod, and departed, in nonchalant good-humour, doubtless considering that to accompany his chum any farther would be to be guilty of girlish sentimentality. And Edwin nodded with equal curtness and made off slowly into the maze of Bursley. The thought in his heart was : 'I'm on my own now. I've got to face it now, by myself.' And he felt that not merely his father, but the leagued universe, was against him.

CHAPTER 2 : *The Flame*

I

The various agencies which society has placed at the disposal of a parent had been at work on Edwin in one way or another for at least a decade, in order to equip him for just this very day when he should step into the world. The moment must therefore be regarded as dramatic, the first crucial moment of an experiment long and elaborately prepared. Knowledge was admittedly the armour and the weapon of one about to try conclusions with the world, and many people for many years had been engaged in providing Edwin with knowledge. He had received, in fact, 'a good education' – or even, as some said, 'a thoroughly sound education'; assuredly as complete an equipment of knowledge as could be obtained in the county, for the curriculum of the Oldcastle High School was less in accord with common sense than that of the Middle School.

He knew, however, nothing of natural history, and in particular of himself, of the mechanism of the body and mind, through which his soul had to express and fulfil itself. Not one word of information about either physiology or psychology had ever been breathed to him, nor had it ever occurred to anyone around him that such information was needful. And as no one had tried to explain to him the mysteries which he carried about with him inside that fair skin of his, so no one had tried to explain to him the mysteries by which he was hemmed in, either mystically through religion, or rationally through philosophy. Never in chapel or at Sunday school had a difficulty been genuinely faced. And as for philosophy, he had not the slightest conception of what it meant. He imagined that a philosopher was one who made the best of a bad job, and he had never heard the word used in any other sense. He had great potential intellectual curiosity, but nobody had thought to stimulate it by even casually telling him that the finest minds of humanity had been trying to systematize the mysteries for quite twenty-five centuries. Of physical science he had been taught nothing save a grotesque perversion to the effect that gravity was a force which drew things towards the centre of the earth. In the matter of chemistry it had been practically demonstrated to him scores of times, so that he should never forget this grand basic truth, that sodium and potassium may be relied upon to fizz flamingly about on a surface of water. Of geology he was perfectly ignorant, though he lived in a district whose whole livelihood depended on the scientific use of geological knowledge, and though the existence of

Oldcastle itself was due to a freak of the earth's crust which geologists call a 'fault'.

II

Geography had been one of his strong points. He was aware of the rivers of Asia in their order, and of the principal products of Uruguay; and he could name the capitals of nearly all the United States. But he had never been instructed for five minutes in the geography of his native country, of which he knew neither the boundaries nor the rivers nor the terrene characteristics. He could have drawn a map of the Orinoco, but he could not have found the Trent in a day's march; he did not even know where his drinking-water came from. That geographical considerations are the cause of all history had never been hinted to him, nor that history bears immediately upon modern life and bore on his own life. For him history hung unsupported and unsupporting in the air. In the course of his school career he had several times approached the nineteenth century, but it seemed to him that for administrative reasons he was always being dragged back again to the Middle Ages. Once his form had 'got' as far as the infancy of his own father, and concerning this period he had learnt that 'great dissatisfaction prevailed among the labouring classes, who were led to believe by mischievous demagogues', etc. But the next term he was recoiling round Henry the Eighth, who 'was a skilful warrior and politician', but 'unfortunate in his domestic relations'; and so to Elizabeth, than whom 'few sovereigns have been so much belied, but her character comes out unscathed after the closest examination'. History indeed resolved itself into a series of more or less sanguinary events arbitrarily grouped under the names of persons who had to be identified with the assistance of numbers. Neither of the development of national life, nor of the clash of nations, did he really know anything that was not inessential and anecdotic. He could not remember the clauses of Magna Carta, but he knew eternally that it was signed at a place amusingly called Runnymede. And the one fact engraved on his memory about the battle of Waterloo was that it was fought on a Sunday.

And as he had acquired absolutely nothing about political economy or about logic, and was therefore at the mercy of the first agreeable sophistry that might take his fancy by storm, his unfitness to commence the business of being a citizen almost reached perfection.

III

For his personal enjoyment of the earth and air and sun and stars, and of society and solitude, no preparation had been made, or dreamt of. The sentiment of nature had never been encouraged in him, or even mentioned. He knew not how to look at a landscape nor at a sky. Of plants and trees he was as exquisitely ignorant as of astronomy. It had not occurred to him to wonder why the days are longer in summer, and he vaguely supposed that the cold of winter was due to an increased distance of the earth from the sun. Still, he had learnt that Saturn had a ring, and sometimes he unconsciously looked for it in the firmament, as for a tea-tray.

Of art, and the arts, he had been taught nothing. He had never seen a great picture or statue, nor heard great orchestral or solo music; and he had no idea that architecture was an art and emotional, though it moved him in a very peculiar fashion. Of the art of English literature, or of any other literature, he had likewise been taught nothing. But he knew the meaning of a few obsolete words in a few plays of Shakespeare. He had not learnt how to express himself orally in any language, but through hard drilling he was so genuinely erudite in accidence and syntax that he could parse and analyse with superb assurance the most magnificent sentences of Milton, Virgil, and Racine. This skill, together with an equal skill in utilizing the elementary properties of numbers and geometrical figures, was the most brilliant achievement of his long apprenticeship.

And now his education was finished. It had cost his father twenty-eight shillings a term, or four guineas a year, and no trouble. In younger days his father had spent more money and far more personal attention on the upbringing of a dog. His father had enjoyed success with dogs through treating them as individuals. But it had not happened to him, nor to anybody in authority, to treat Edwin as an individual. Nevertheless it must not be assumed that Edwin's father was a callous and conscience-less brute, and Edwin a martyr of neglect. Old Clayhanger was, on the contrary, an average upright and respectable parent who had given his son a thoroughly sound education, and Edwin had had the good fortune to receive that thoroughly sound education, as a preliminary to entering the world.

IV

He was very far from realizing the imperfections of his equipment for the grand entry; but still he was not without uneasiness. In particular the conversation incident to the canal-boat wager was disturbing him. It amazed him, as he reflected, that he should have remained, to such an advanced age, in a state of ignorance concerning the origin of the clay from which the 'crocks' of his native district were manufactured. That the Sunday should have been able to inform him did not cause him any shame, for he guessed from the peculiar eager tone of voice in which the facts had been delivered, that the Sunday was merely retailing some knowledge recently acquired by chance. He knew all the Sunday's tones of voice; and he also was well aware that the Sunday's brain was not on the whole better stored than his own. Further, the Sunday was satisfied with his bit of accidental knowledge. Edwin was not. Edwin wanted to know why, if the clay for making earthenware was not got in the Five Towns, the Five Towns had become the great seat of the manufacture. Why were not pots made in the South, where the clay came from? He could not think of any answer to this enigma, nor any means of arriving by himself at an answer. The feeling was that he ought to have been able to arrive at the answer as at the answer to an equation.

He did not definitely blame his education; he did not think clearly about the thing at all. But, as a woman with a vague discomfort dimly fears cancer, so he dimly feared that there might be something fundamentally unsound in this sound education of his. And he had remorse for all the shirking that he had been guilty of during all his years at school. He shook his head solemnly at the immense and nearly universal shirking that continually went on. He could only acquit three or four boys, among the hundreds he had known, of the shameful sin. And all that he could say in favour of himself was that there were many worse than Edwin Clayhanger. Not merely the boys, but the masters, were sinners. Only two masters could he unreservedly respect as having acted conscientiously up to their pretensions, and one of these was an unpleasant brute. All the cleverness, the ingenuities, the fakes, the insincerities, the incapacities, the vanities, and the dishonesties of the rest stood revealed to him, and he judged them by the mere essential force of character alone. A schoolmaster might as well attempt to deceive God as a boy who is watching him every day with the inhuman eye of youth.

'All this must end now!' he said to himself, meaning all that could be included in the word 'shirk'.

v

He was splendidly serious. He was as splendidly serious as a reformer. By a single urgent act of thought he would have made himself a man, and changed imperfection into perfection. He desired – and there was real passion in his desire – to do his best, to exhaust himself in doing his best, in living according to his conscience. He did not know of what he was capable, nor what he could achieve. Achievement was not the matter of his desire; but endeavour, honest and terrific endeavour. He admitted to himself his shortcomings, and he did not underestimate the difficulties that lay before him; but he said, thinking of his father: 'Surely he'll see I mean business! Surely he's bound to give in when he sees how much in earnest I am!' He was convinced, almost, that passionate faith could move mountainous fathers.

'I'll show 'em!' he muttered.

And he meant that he would show the world. . . . He was honouring the world; he was paying the finest homage to it. In that head of his a flame burnt that was like an altar-fire, a miraculous and beautiful phenomenon, than which nothing is more miraculous nor more beautiful over the whole earth. Whence had it suddenly sprung, that flame? After years of muddy inefficiency, of contentedness with the second-rate and the dishonest, that flame astoundingly bursts forth, from a hidden, unheeded spark that none had ever thought to blow upon. It bursts forth out of a damp jungle of careless habits and negligence that could not possibly have fed it. There is little to encourage it. The very architecture of the streets shows that environment has done naught for it : ragged brickwork, walls finished anyhow with saggars and slag; narrow uneven alleys leading to higgledy-piggledy workshops and kilns; cottages transformed into factories and factories into cottages, clumsily, hastily, because nothing matters so long as 'it will do'; everywhere something forced to fulfil, badly, the function of something else; in brief, the reign of the slovenly makeshift, shameless, filthy, and picturesque. Edwin himself seemed no tabernacle for that singular flame. He was not merely untidy and dirty – at his age such defects might have excited in a sane observer uneasiness by their absence; but his gestures and his gait were untidy. He did not mind how he walked. All his sprawling limbs were saying : 'What does it matter, so long as we get there? The angle of the slatternly bag across his shoulders was an insult to the flame. And yet the flame burned with serene and terrible pureness.

It was surprising that no one saw it passing along the mean, black, smoke-palled streets that huddle about St Luke's Church. Sundry experienced and fat old women were standing or sitting at their cottage doors, one or two smoking cutties. But even they, who in childbed and at gravesides had been at the very core of life for long years, they, who saw more than most, could only see a fresh lad passing along, with fair hair and a clear complexion, and gawky knees and elbows, a fierce, rapt expression on his straightforward, good-natured face. Some knew that it was 'Clayhanger's lad', a nice-behaved young gentleman, and the spitten image of his poor mother. They all knew what a lad is – the feel of his young skin under his 'duds', the capricious freedom of his movements, his sudden madnesses and shoutings and tendernesses, and the exceeding power of his unconscious wistful charm. They could divine all that in a glance. But they could not see the mysterious and holy flame of the desire for self-protection blazing within that tousled head. And if Edwin had suspected that anybody could indeed perceive it, he would have whipped it out for shame, though the repudiation had meant everlasting death. Such is youth in the Five Towns, if not elsewhere.

23

CHAPTER 3 : *Entry into the World*

I

Edwin came steeply out of the cinder-strewn back streets by Woodisun Bank [hill] into Duck Square, nearly at the junction of Trafalgar Road and Wedgwood Street. A few yards down Woodisun Bank, cocks and hens were scurrying with necks horizontal, from all quarters, and were even flying, to the call of a little old woman who threw grain from the top step of her perch. On the level of the narrow pavement stood an immense constable, clad in white trousers, with a gun under his arm for the killing of mad dogs; he was talking to the woman, and their two heads were exactly at the same height. On a pair of small double gates near the old woman's cottage were painted the words, 'Steam Printing Works. No admittance except on business'. And from as far as Duck Square could be heard the puff-puff which proved the use of steam in this works to which idlers and mere pleasure-seekers were forbidden access.

Duck Square was one of the oldest, if the least imposing, of all the public places in Bursley. It had no traffic across it, being only a sloping rectangle, like a vacant lot, with Trafalgar Road and Wedgwood Street for its exterior sides, and no outlet on its inner sides. The buildings on those inner sides were low and humble, and, as it were, withdrawn from the world, the chief of them being the ancient Duck Inn, where the handbellringers used to meet. But Duck Square looked out upon the very birth of Trafalgar Road, that wide, straight thoroughfare, whose name dates it, which had been invented in the lifetime of a few then living, to unite Bursley with Hanbridge. It also looked out upon the birth of several old pack-horse roads which Trafalgar Road had supplanted. One of these was Woodisun Bank, that wound slowly up hill and down dale, apparently always choosing the longest and hardest route, to Hanbridge; and another was Aboukir Street, formerly known as Warm Lane, that reached Hanbridge in a manner equally difficult and unhurried. At the junction of Trafalgar Road and Aboukir Street stood the Dragon Hotel, once the great posting-house of the town, from which all roads started. Duck Square had watched coaches and wagons stop at and start from the Dragon Hotel for hundreds of years. It had seen the Dragon rebuilt in brick and stone, with fine bay windows on each storey, in early Georgian times, and it had seen even the new structure become old and assume the dignity of age. Duck Square could remember strings of pack-mules driven by women, 'trapesing' in zigzags down Woodisun Bank and Warm Lane, and occasionally falling, with awful smashes of the crockery they carried, in the deep, slippery, scarce passable mire of the first slants into the alley. Duck Square had witnessed the slow declension of these roads into mere streets, and slum streets at that, and the death of all mules, and the disappearance of all coaches and all neighing and prancing and whipcracking romance; while Trafalgar Road, simply because it was straight and broad and easily graded, flourished with toll-bars and a couple of pair-horsed trams that ran on lines. And many people were proud of those cushioned trams; but perhaps they had never known that coachdrivers used to tell each other about the state of the turn at the bottom of Warm Lane (since absurdly renamed in honour of an Egyptian battle), and that Woodisun Bank (now unnoticed save by doubtful characters, policemen, and schoolboys) was once regularly 'taken' by four horses at a canter. The history of human manners is crunched and embedded in the very macadam of that part of the borough, and the burguesses unheedingly tread it down every day and talk gloomily about the ugly smoky prose of industrial manufacture. And yet the Dragon Hotel, safely surviving all revolutions by the mighty virtue and attraction of ale, stands before them to remind them of the interestingness of existence.

II

At the southern corner of Trafalgar Road and Wedgwood Street, with Duck Square facing it, the Dragon Hotel and Warm Lane to its right, and Woodisun Bank creeping inconspicuously down to its left, stood a three-storey building consisting of house and shop, the frontage being in Wedgwood Street. Over the double-windowed shop was a discreet signboard in gilt letters, 'D. Clayhanger, Printer and Stationer', but above the first floor was a later and much larger sign, with the single word, 'Steam-printing'. All the brickwork of the façade was painted yellow, and had obviously been painted yellow many times; the woodwork of the plate-glass windows was a very dark green approaching black. The upper windows were stumpy, almost square, some dirty and some clean and curtained, with prominent sills and architraves. The line of the projecting spouting at the base of the roof was slightly curved through subsidence; at either end of the roof-ridge rose twin chimneys each with three salmon-coloured chimney-pots. The gigantic word 'Steam-printing' could be seen from the windows of the Dragon, from the porch of the big Wesleyan chapel higher up the slope, from the Conservative Club and the playground at the top of the slope; and as for Duck Square itself, it could see little else. The left-hand shop window was alluringly set out with the lighter apparatus of writing and reading, and showed incidentally several rosy pictures of ideal English maidens; that to the right was grim and heavy with ledgers, inks, and variegated specimens of steam-printing.

III

In the wedge-shaped doorway between the windows stood two men, one middle-aged and one old, one bareheaded and the other with a beaver hat, engaged in conversation. They were talking easily, pleasantly, with free gestures, the younger looking down in deferential smiles at the elder, and the elder looking up benignantly at the younger. You could see that, having begun with a business matter, they had quitted it for a topic of the hour. But business none the less went forward, the shop functioned, the presses behind the shop were being driven by steam as advertised; a customer emerged, and was curtly nodded at by the proprietor as he squeezed past; a girl with a small flannel apron over a large cotton apron went timidly into the shop. The trickling, calm commerce of a provincial town was proceeding, bit being added to bit and item to item, until at the week's end a series of apparent nothings had swollen into the livelihood of near half a score of people. And nobody perceived how interesting it was, this interchange of activities, this ebb and flow of money, this sluggish rise and fall of reputations and fortunes, stretching out one century into another and towards a third! Printing had been done at that corner, though not by steam, since the time of the French Revolution. Bibles and illustrated herbals had been laboriously produced by hand at that corner, and hawked on the backs of asses all over the county; and nobody heard romance in the puffing of the hidden steam-engine multiplying catalogues and billheads on the self-same spot at the rate of hundreds an hour.

The younger and bigger of the two men chatting in the doorway was Darius Clayhanger, Edwin's father, and the first printer to introduce steam into Bursley. His age was then under forty-five, but he looked more. He was dressed in black, with an ample shirt-front and a narrow black cravat tied in an angular bow; the wristbands were almost tight on the wrists, and, owing to the shortness of the alpaca coat-sleeves, they were very visible even as Darius Clayhanger stood, with his two hands deep in the horizontal pockets of his 'full-fall' trousers. They were not precisely dirty, these wristbands, nor was the shirt-front, nor the turned-down pointed collar, but all the linen looked as though it would scarcely be wearable the next day. Clayhanger's linen invariably looked like that, not dirty and not clean; and further, he appeared to wear eternally the same suit, ever on the point of being done for and never being done for. The trousers always had marked transverse creases; the waistcoat always showed shiningly the outline of every article in the pockets thereof, and it always had a few stains down the front (and never more than a few), and the lowest button insecure. The coat, faintly discoloured round the collar and fretted at the cuffs, fitted him easily and loosely like the character of an old crony; it was as if it had grown up with him, and had expanded with his girth. His head was a little bald on the top, but there was still a great deal of mixed brown and greyish hair at the back and the sides, and the moustache, hanging straight down with an effect recalling the mouth of a seal, was plenteous and defiant – a moustache of character, contradicting the full placidity of the badly shaved chin. Darius Clayhanger had a habit, when reflective or fierce, of biting with his upper teeth as far down as he could on the lower lip; this trick added emphasis to the moustache. He stood, his feet in their clumsy boots planted firmly about sixteen inches apart, his elbows sticking out, and his head bent sideways, listening to and answering his companion with mien now eager, now roguish, now distinctly respectful.

The older man, Mr Shushions, was apparently very old. He was one of those men of whom one says in conclusion that they are very old. He seemed to be so fully occupied all the time in conducting those physical operations which we perform without thinking of them, that each in his case became a feat. He balanced himself on his legs with conscious craft; he directed carefully his shaking and gnarled hand to his beard in order to stroke it. When he collected his thoughts into a sentence and uttered it in his weak, quavering voice, he did something wonderful; he listened closely, as though to an imperfectly acquired foreign language; and when he was not otherwise employed, he gave attention to the serious business of breathing. He wore a black silk stock, in a style even more antique than his remarkable headgear, and his trousers were very tight. He had survived into another and a more fortunate age than his own.

IV

Edwin, his heavy bag on his shoulders, found the doorway blocked by these two. He hesitated with a diffident, charming smile, feeling, as he often did in front of his father, that he ought to apologize for his existence, and yet fiercely calling himself as ass for such a sentiment. Darius Clayhanger nodded at him carelessly, but not without a surprising benevolence, over his shoulder.

'This is him,' said Darius briefly.

Edwin was startled to catch a note of pride in his father's voice.

Little Mr Shushions turned slowly and looked up at Edwin's face (for he was shorter even than the boy), and gradually acquainted himself with the fact that Edwin was the son of his father.

'Is this thy son, Darius?' he asked; and his ancient eyes were shining.

Edwin had scarcely ever heard anyone address his father by his Christian name.

Darius nodded; and then, seeing the old man's hand creeping out towards him, Edwin pulled off his cap and took the hand, and was struck by the hot, smooth brittleness of the skin and the earnest tremulous weakness of the caressing grasp. Edwin had never seen Mr Shushions before.

'Nay, nay, my boy,' trembled the old man, 'don't bare thy head to me . . . not to me ! I'm one o' th' ould sort. Eh, I'm rare glad to see thee !' He kept Edwin's hand, and stared long at him, with his withered face transfigured by solemn emotion. Slowly he turned towards Darius, and pulled himself together. 'Thou'st begotten a fine lad, Darius ! . . . a fine, honest lad !'

'So – so !' said Darius gruffly, whom Edwin was amazed to see in a state of agitation similar to that of Mr Shushions.

The men gazed at each other; Edwin looked at the ground and other unresponsive objects.

'Edwin,' his father said abruptly, 'run and ask Big James for th' proof of that Primitive Methodist hymn-paper; there's a good lad.'

And Edwin hastened through the shadowy shop as if loosed from a captivity, and in passing threw his satchel down on a bale of goods.

v

He comprehended nothing of the encounter; neither as to the origin of the old man's status in his father's esteem, nor as to the cause of his father's strange emotion. He regarded the old man impatiently as an aged simpleton, probably over pious, certainly connected with the Primitive Methodists. His father had said 'There's a good lad' almost cajolingly. And this was odd; for, though nobody could be more persuasively agreeable than his father when he chose, the occasions when he cared to exert his charm, especially over his children, were infrequent and getting more so. Edwin also saw something symbolically ominous in his being sent direct to the printing office. It was no affair of his to go to the printing office. He particularly did not want to go to the printing office.

However, he met Big James, with flowing beard and flowing apron, crossing the yard. Big James was brushing crumbs from the beard.

'Father wants the proof of some hymn-paper – I don't know what,' he said. 'I was just coming –'

'So was I, Mister Edwin,' replied Big James in his magnificent voice, and with his curious humorous smile. And he held up a sheet of paper in his immense hand, and strode majestically on towards the shop.

Here was another detail that struck the boy. Always Big James had

28

addressed him as 'Master Edwin' or 'Master Clayhanger'. Now it was 'Mister'. He had left school. Big James was, of course, aware of that, and Big James had enough finesse and enough gentle malice to change instantly the 'master' to 'mister'. Edwin was scarcely sure if Big James was not laughing at him. He could not help thinking that Big James had begun so promptly to call him 'mister' because the foreman compositor expected that the son of the house would at once begin to take a share in the business. He could not help thinking that his father must have so informed Big James. And all this vaguely disturbed Edwin, and reminded him of his impending battle and of the complex forces marshalled against him. And his hand, wandering in his pockets, touched that unfortunate report which stated that he had lost one place during the term.

VI

He lingered in the blue-paved yard, across which cloud-shadows swept continually, and then Big James came back and spectacularly ascended the flight of wooden steps to the printing office, and disappeared. Edwin knew that he must return to the shop to remove his bag, for his father would assuredly reprimand him if he found it where it had been untidily left. He sidled, just like an animal, to the doorway, and then slipped up to the counter, behind the great mahogany case of 'artists' materials'. His father and the old man were within the shop now, and Edwin overheard that they were discussing a topic that had lately been rife in religious circles, namely, Sir Henry Thompson's ingenious device for scientifically testing the efficacy of prayer – known as the 'Prayer Gauge'. The scheme was to take certain hospitals and to pray for the patients in particular wards, leaving other wards unprayed for, and then to tabulate and issue the results.

Mr Shushions profoundly resented the employment of such a dodge; the mere idea of it shocked him, as being blasphemous; and Darius Clayhanger deferentially and feelingly agreed with him, though Edwin had at least heard his father refer to the topic with the amused and noncommittal impartiality of a man who only went to chapel when he specially felt like going.

'I've preached in the pulpits o' our Connexion,' said Mr Shushions with solemn, quavering emotion, 'for over fifty year, as *you* know. But I'd ne'er gi' out another text if Primitives had ought to do wi' such a flouting o' th' Almighty. Nay, I'd go down to my grave dumb afore God!'

He had already been upset by news of a movement that was on foot for deferring Anniversary Sermons from August to September, so that people should be more free to go away for a holiday, and collections be

29

more fruitful. What! Put off God's ordinance, to enable chapel-members to go 'a-wakesing'! Monstrous! Yet September was tried, in spite of Mr Shushions, and when even September would not work satisfactorily, God's ordinance was shifted boldly to May, in order to catch people and their pockets well before the demoralization incident to holidays.

Edwin thought that his father and the mysterious old man would talk for ever, and timorously he exposed himself to obtain possession of his satchel, hoping to escape unseen. But Mr Shushions saw him, and called him, and took his hand again.

'Eh, my boy,' he said, feebly shaking the hand, 'I do pray as you'll grow up to be worthy o' your father. That's all as I pray for.'

Edwin had never considered his father as an exemplar. He was a just and merciful judge of his father, against whom he had a thousand grievances. And in his heart he resentfully despised Mr Shushions, and decided again that he was a simpleton, and not a very tactful one. But then he saw a round yellow tear slowly form in the red rim of the old man's eye and run crookedly down that wrinkled cheek. And his impatient scorn expired. The mere sight of him, Edwin, had brought the old man to weeping! And the tear was so genuine, so convincing, so majestic that it induced in Edwin a blank humility. He was astounded, mystified; but he was also humbled. He himself was never told, and he never learnt, the explanation of that epic tear.

CHAPTER 4 : *The Child-Man*

I

The origin of the tear on the aged cheek of Mr Shushions went back about forty years, and was embedded in the infancy of Darius Clayhanger.

The earliest memory of Darius Clayhanger had to do with the capital letters Q.W. and S. Even as the first steam-printer in Bursley, even as the father of a son who had received a thorough sound middle-class education, he never noticed a capital Q. W. or S. without recalling the Widow Susan's school, where he had wonderingly learnt the significance of those complicated characters. The school consisted of the entire ground floor of her cottage, namely, one room, of which the far corner was occupied by a tiny winding staircase that led to the ancient widow's bedchamber. The furniture comprised a few low forms for scholars, a table, and a chair; and there were some brilliant coloured prints on the whitewashed walls. At this school Darius acquired a knowledge of the alphabet, and from the alphabet passed to Reading-Made-Easy, and then to the Bible. He made such progress that the widow soon singled him out for honour. He was allowed the high and envied privilege of raking the ashes from under the fireplace and carrying them to the ash-pit, which ash-pit was vast and lofty, being the joint production of many cottages. To reach the summit of the ash-pit, and thence to fling backwards down its steep sides all assailants who challenged your supremacy, was a precious joy. The battles of the ash-pit, however, were not battles of giants, as no children had leisure for ash-carrying after the age of seven. A still greater honour accorded to Darius was permission to sit, during lessons, on the topmost visible step of the winding stair. The widow Susan, having taught Darius to read brilliantly, taught him to knit, and he would knit stockings for his father, mother, and sister.

At the age of seven, his education being complete, he was summoned into the world. It is true that he could neither write nor deal with the multiplication table; but there were always night-schools which studious adults of seven and upwards might attend if business permitted. Further, there was the Sunday school, which Darius had joyously frequented since the age of three, and which he had no intention of leaving. As he grew older the Sunday school became more and more enchanting to him. Sunday morning was the morning which he lived for during six days; it was the morning when his hair was brushed and combed, and perfumed with a delightful oil, whose particular fragrance he remembered throughout his life. At Sunday school he was petted and caressed. His success at Sunday school was shining. He passed over the heads of bigger boys, and at the age of six he was in the Bible class.

Upon hearing that Darius was going out into the world, the superintendent of the Sunday school, a grave whiskered young man of perhaps thirty, led him one morning out of the body of the Primitive Methodist Chapel which served as schoolroom before and after chapel service, up into the deserted gallery of the chapel, and there seated him on a stair, and knelt on the stair below him, and caressed his head, and called him a good boy, and presented him with an old, battered Bible. This volume was the most valuable thing that Darius had ever possessed. He ran all the way home with it, half suffocated by his triumph. Sunday-school prizes had not then been invented. The young superintendent of the Sunday school was Mr Shushions.

II

The man Darius was first taken to work by his mother. It was the winter of 1835, January. They passed through the market-place of the town of Turnhill, where they lived. Turnhill lies a couple of miles north of Bursley. One side of the market-place was barricaded with stacks of coal,

31

and the other with loaves of a species of rye and straw bread. This coal and these loaves were being served out by meticulous and haughty officials, all invisibly braided with red-tape, to a crowd of shivering, moaning, and weeping wretches, men, women, and children – the basis of the population of Turnhill. Although they were all endeavouring to make a noise, they made scarcely any noise, from mere lack of strength. Nothing could be heard, under the implacable bright sky, but faint ghosts of sound, as though people were sighing and crying from within the vacuum of a huge glass bell.

The next morning, at half past five, Darius began his career in earnest. He was 'mould-runner' to a 'muffin-maker', a muffin being not a comestible but a small plate, fashioned by its maker on a mould. The business of Darius was to run as hard as he could with the mould, and a newly created plate adhering thereto, into the drying-stove. This 'stove' was a room lined with shelves, and having a red-hot stove and stove-pipe in the middle. As no man of seven could reach the upper shelves, a pair of steps was provided for Darius, and up these he had to scamper. Each mould with its plate had to be leaned carefully against the wall, and if the soft clay of a new-born plate was damaged, Darius was knocked down. The atmosphere outside the stove was chill, but owing to the heat of the stove, Darius was obliged to work half naked. His sweat ran down his cheeks, and down his chest, and down his back, making white channels, and lastly it soaked his hair.

When there were no moulds to be sprinted into the drying-stove, and no moulds to be carried less rapidly out, Darius was engaged in clay-wedging. That is to say, he took a piece of raw clay weighing more than himself, cut it in two with a wire, raised one half above his head and crashed it down with all his force upon the other half, and he repeated the process until the clay was thoroughly soft and even in texture. At a later period it was discovered that hydraulic machinery could perform this operation more easily and more effectually than the brawny arms of a man of seven. At eight o'clock in the evening Darius was told that he had done enough for that day, and that he must arrive at five sharp the next morning to light the fire, before his master the muffin-maker began to work. When he inquired how he was to light the fire his master kicked him jovially on the thigh and suggested that he should ask another mould-runner. His master was not a bad man at heart, it was said, but on Tuesdays, after Sunday and Saint Monday, masters were apt to be capricious.

Darius reached home at a quarter to nine, having eaten nothing but bread all day. Somehow he had lapsed into the child again. His mother took him on her knee, and wrapped her sacking apron round his ragged clothes, and cried over him and cried into his supper of porridge.

and undressed him and put him to bed. But he could not sleep easily because he was afraid of being late the next morning.

III

And the next morning, wandering about the yards of the manufactory in a storm of icy sleet a little before five o'clock, he learnt from a more experienced companion that nobody would provide him with kindling for his fire, that on the contrary everybody who happened to be on the place at that hour would unite to prevent him from getting kindling, and that he must steal it or expect to be thrashed before six o'clock. Near them a vast kiln of ware in process of firing showed a white flaming glow at each of its mouths in the black winter darkness. Darius's mentor crept up to the archway of the great hovel which protected the kiln, and pointed like a conspirator to the figure of the guardian fireman dozing near his monster. The boy had the handle-less remains of an old spade, and with it he crept into the hovel, dangerously abstracted fire from one of the scorching mouths, and fled therewith, and the firemen never stirred. Then Darius, to whom the mentor kindly lent his spade, attempted to do the same, but being inexpert woke the fireman, who held him spellbound by his roaring voice and then flung him like a sack of potatoes bodily into the slush of the yard, and the spade after him. Happily the mentor, whose stove was now alight, lent fire to Darius, so that Darius's stove too was cheerfully burning when his master came. And Darius was too excited to feel fatigue.

By six o'clock on Saturday night Darius had earned a shilling for his week's work. But he could only possess himself of the shilling by going to a magnificent public-house with his master the muffin-maker. This was the first time that he had ever been inside a public-house. The place was crowded with men, women, and children eating the most lovely hot rolls and drinking beer, in an atmosphere exquisitely warm. And behind a high counter a stout jolly man was counting piles and piles and piles of silver. Darius's master, in company with other boys' masters, gave this stout man four sovereigns to change, and it was an hour before he changed them. Meanwhile Darius was instructed that he must eat a roll like the rest, together with cheese. Never had he tasted anything so luscious. He had a match with his mentor, as to which of them could spin out his roll the longer, honestly chewing all the time; and he won. Someone gave him half a glass of beer. At half past seven he received his shilling, which consisted of a sixpenny-piece and four pennies; and, leaving the gay public-house, pushed his way through a crowd of tearful women with babies in their arms at the doors, and went home. And such was the attraction of the Sunday school that he was there the next morning, with scented hair, two minutes before the opening.

33

IV

In about a year Darius's increasing knowledge of the world enabled him to rise in it. He became a handle-maker in another manufactory, and also he went about with the pride of one who could form the letters of the alphabet with a pen. In his new work he had to put a bit of clay between two moulds and then force the top mould on to the bottom one by means of his stomach, which it was necessary to press downwards and at the same time to wriggle with a peculiar movement. The workman to whom he was assigned, his new 'master', attached these handles, with strange rapid skill, to beer-mugs. For Darius the labour was much lighter than that of mould-running and claywedging, and the pay was somewhat higher. But there were minor disadvantages. He descended by twenty steps to his toil, and worked in a long cellar which never received any air except by way of the steps and a passage, and never any daylight at all. Its sole illumination was a stove used for drying. The 'throwers'' and the 'turners'' rooms were also subterranean dungeons. When in full activity all these stinking cellars were full of men, boys, and young women, working close together in a hot twilight. Certain boys were trained contrabandists of beer, and beer came as steadily into the dungeons as though it had been laid on by a main pipe. It was not honourable, even on the part of a young woman, to refuse beer, particularly when the beer happened to arrive in the late afternoon. On such occasions young men and women would often entirely omit to go home of a night, and seasoned men of the world aged eight, on descending into the dungeons early the next morning, would have a full view of pandemonium, and they would witness during the day salutary scenes of remorse, and proofs of the existence of a profound belief in the homeopathic properties of beer.

But perhaps the worst drawback of Darius's new position was the long and irregular hours, due partly to the influences of Saint Monday and of the scenes above indicated but not described, and partly to the fact that the employees were on piece-work and entirely unhampered by grandmotherly legislation. The result was that six days' work was generally done in four. And as the younger the workman the earlier he had to start in the morning, Darius saw scarcely enough of his bed. It was not of course to be expected that a self-supporting man of the world should rigorously confine himself to an eight-hour day or even a twelve-hour day, but Darius's day would sometimes stretch to eighteen and nineteen hours : which on hygienic ground could not be unreservedly defended.

V

One Tuesday evening his master, after three days of debauch, ordered him to be at work at three o'clock the next morning. He quickly and even eagerly agreed, for he was already intimate with his master's rope-lash. He reached home at ten o'clock on an autumn night, and went to bed and to sleep. He woke up with a start, in the dark. There was no watch or clock in the house, from which nearly all the furniture had gradually vanished, but he knew it must be already after three o'clock; and he sprang up and rushed out. Of course he had not undressed; his life was too strenuous for mere formalities. The stars shone above him as he ran along, wondering whether after all, though late, he could by unprecedented effort make the ordained number of handles before his master tumbled into the cellar at five o'clock.

When he had run a mile he met some sewage men on their rounds, who in reply to his question told him that the hour was half after midnight. He dared not risk a return to home and bed, for within two and a half hours he must be at work. He wandered aimlessly over the surface of the earth until he came to a tile-works, more or less unenclosed, whose primitive ovens showed a glare. He ventured within, and in spite of himself sat down on the ground near one of those heavenly ovens. And then he wanted to get up again, for he could feel the strong breath of his enemy, sleep. But he could not get up. In a state of terror he yielded himself to his enemy. Shameful cowardice on the part of a man now aged nine! God, however, is merciful, and sent to him an angel in the guise of a night-watchman, who kicked him into wakefulness and off the place. He ran on limping, beneath the stellar systems, and reached his work at half past four o'clock.

Although he had never felt so exhausted in his long life, he set to work with fury. Useless! When his master arrived he had scarcely got through the preliminaries. He dully faced his master in the narrow stifling cellar, lit by candles impailed on nails and already peopled by the dim figures of boys, girls, and a few men. His master was of taciturn habit and merely told him to kneel down. He knelt. Two bigger boys turned hastily from their work to snatch a glimpse of the affair. The master moved to the back of the cellar and took from a box a piece of rope an inch thick and clogged with clay. At the same moment a companion offered him, in silence, a tin with a slim neck, out of which he drank deep; it contained a pint of porter owing on loan from the previous day. When the master came in due course with the rope to do justice upon the sluggard he found the lad fallen forward and breathing heavily and regularly. Darius had gone to sleep. He was awakened with

35

some violence, but the public opinion of the dungeon saved him from a torn shirt and a bloody back.

This was Darius's last day on a pot-bank. The next morning he and his went in procession to the Bastille, as the place was called. His father, having been too prominent and too independent in a strike, had been black-listed by every manufacturer in the district : and Darius, though nine, could not keep the family.

CHAPTER 5 : *Mr Shushions's Tear Explained*

I

The Bastille was on the top of a hill about a couple of miles long, and the journey thither was much lengthened by the desire of the family to avoid the main road. They were all intensely ashamed; Darius was ashamed to tears, and did not know why; even his little sister wept and had to be carried, not because she was shoeless and had had nothing to eat, but because she was going to the Ba-ba-bastille; she had no notion what the place was. It proved to be the largest building that Darius had even seen; and indeed it was the largest in the district; they stood against its steep sides like flies against a kennel. Then there was rattling of key-bunches, and the rasping voices of sour officials, who did not inquire if they would like a meal after their stroll. And they were put into a cellar and stripped and washed and dressed in other people's clothes, and then separated, amid tears. And Darius was pitched into a large crowd of other boys, all clothed like himself. He now understood the reason for shame; it was because he could have no distinctive clothes of his own, because he had somehow lost his identity. All the boys had a sullen, furtive glance, and when they spoke it was in whispers.

In the low room where the boys were assembled there fell a silence, and Darius heard someone whisper that the celebrated boy who had run away and been caught would be flogged before supper. Down the long room ran a long table. Someone brought in three candles in tin candlesticks and set them near the end of this table. Then somebody else brought in a pickled birch-rod, dripping with the salt water from which it had been taken, and also a small square table. Then came some officials, and a clergyman, and then, surpassing the rest in majesty, the governor of the Bastille, a terrible man. The governor made a speech about the crime of running away from the Bastille, and when he had spoken for a fair time, the clergyman talked in the same sense; and then a captured tiger, dressed like a boy, with darting fierce eyes, was dragged in by two men, and laid face down on the square table, and four boys were commanded to step forward and hold tightly the four members of this tiger. And, his clothes having previously been removed as far as his waist, his breeches were next pulled down his legs. Then the rod was raised and it descended swishing, and blood began to flow; but far more startling than the blood were the shrill screams of the tiger; they were so loud and deafening that the spectators could safely converse under their shelter. The boys in charge of the victim had to cling hard and grind their teeth in the effort to keep him prone. As the blows succeeded each other, Darius became more and more ashamed. The physical spectacle did not sicken nor horrify him, for he was a man of wide experience; but he had never before seen flogging by lawful authority. Flogging in the workshop was different, a private if sanguinary affair between free human beings. This ritualistic and cold-blooded torture was infinitely more appalling in its humiliation. The screaming grew feebler, then ceased; then the blows ceased, and the unconscious infant (cured of being a tiger) was carried away leaving a trail of red drops along the floor.

II

After this, supper was prepared on the long table, and the clergyman called down upon it the blessing of God, and enjoined the boys to be thankful, and departed in company with the governor. Darius, who had not tasted all day, could not eat. The flogging had not nauseated him, but the bread and the skilly revolted his pampered tastes. Never had he, with all his experience, seen or smelt anything so foully disgusting. When supper was completed, a minor official interceded with the Almighty in various ways for ten minutes, and at last the boys were marched upstairs to bed. They all slept in one room. The night also could be set down in words, but must not be, lest the setting-down should be disastrous . . .

Darius knew that he was ruined; he knew that he was a workhouse boy for evermore, and that the bright freedom of sixteen hours a day in a cellar was lost to him for evermore. He was now a prisoner, branded, hopeless. He would never be able to withstand the influences that had closed around him and upon him. He supposed that he should become desperate, become a tiger, and then . . .

III

But the following afternoon he was forcibly reclothed in his own beautiful and beloved rags, and was pushed out of the Bastille, and there he saw his pale father and his mother, and his little sister, and another man. And his mother was on her knees in the cold autumn sunshine,

37

and hysterically clasping the knees of the man, and weeping; and the man was trying to raise her, and the man was weeping too. Darius wept. The man was Mr Shushions. Somehow, in a way that Darius comprehended not, Mr Shushions had saved them. Mr Shushions, in a beaver tall-hat and with an apron rolled round his waist under his coat, escorted them back to their house, into which some fresh furniture had been brought. And Darius knew that a situation was waiting for his father. And further, Mr Shushions, by his immense mysterious power, found a superb situation for Darius himself as a printer's devil. All this because Mr Shushions, as superintendent of a Sunday school, was emotionally interested in the queer, harsh boy who had there picked up the art of writing so quickly.

Such was the origin of the tear that ran down Mr Shushions's cheek when he beheld Edwin, well-nourished, well-dressed, and intelligent, the son of Darius the successful steam-printer. Mr Shushions's tear was the tear of the creator looking upon his creation and marvelling at it. Mr Shushions loved Darius as only the benefactor can love the benefited. He had been out of the district for over thirty years, and, having returned there to die, the wonder of what he had accomplished by merely saving a lad from the certain perdition of a prolonged stay in the workhouse, struck him blindingly in the face and dazzled him.

Darius had never spoken to a soul of his night in the Bastille. All his infancy was his own fearful secret. His life, seen whole, had been a miracle. But none knew that except himself and Mr Shushions. Assuredly Edwin never even faintly suspected it. To Edwin Mr Shushions was nothing but a feeble and tedious old man.

CHAPTER 6 : *In the House*

I

To return to Edwin. On that Friday afternoon of the breaking-up he was, in the local phrase, at a loose end. That is, he had no task, no programme, and no definite desires. Not knowing, when he started out in the morning, whether school would formally end before or after the dinner-hour, he had taken his dinner with him, as usual, and had eaten it at Oldcastle. Thus, though the family dinner had not begun when he reached home, he had no share in it, partly because he was not hungry, and partly because he was shy about having left school. The fact that he had left school affected him as he was affected by the wearing of a new suit for the first time, or by the cutting of his hair after a prolonged

38

neglect of the barber. It inspired him with a wish to avoid his kind, and especially his sisters, Maggie and Clara. Clara might make some facetious remark. Edwin could never forget the Red Indian glee with which Clara had danced round him when for the first time – and quite unprepared for the exquisite shock – she had seen him in long trousers. There was also his father. He wanted to have a plain talk with his father – he knew that he would not be at peace until he had had that talk – and yet in spite of himself he had carefully kept out of his father's way during all the afternoon, save for a moment when, strolling with affected nonchalance up to Darius's private desk in the shop, he had dropped thereon his school report, and strolled off again.

Towards six o'clock he was in his bedroom, an attic with a floor very much more spacious than its ceiling, and a window that commanded the slope of Trafalgar Road towards Bleakridge. It had been his room, his castle, his sanctuary, for at least ten years, since before his mother's death of cancer. He did not know that he loved it, with all its inconveniences and makeshifts; but he did love it, and he was jealous for it; no one should lay a hand on it to rearrange what he had once arranged. His sisters knew this; the middle-aged servant knew it; even his father, with a curt laugh, would humorously acquiesce in the theory of the sacredness of Edwin's bedroom. As for Edwin, he saw nothing extraordinary in his attitude concerning his bedroom; and he could not understand, and he somewhat resented, that the household should perceive anything comic in it. He never went near his sisters' bedroom, never wished to go near it, never thought about it.

II

Now he sat idly on the patchwork counterpane of his bed and gazed at the sky. He was feeling a little happier, a little less unsettled, for his stomach was empty and his mind had begun to fix itself with pleasure on the images of hot toast and jam. He 'wanted his tea': the manner in which he glanced at his old silver watch proved that. He wished only that before six o'clock struck he could settle upon the necessary changes in his bedroom. A beautiful schooner, which for over a year, with all sails spread, had awaited the breeze in a low dark corner to the right of the window, would assuredly have to be dismissed to the small, empty attic. Once that schooner had thrilled him; the slight rake of its masts and the knotted reality of its rigging had thrilled him; and to navigate it had promised the most delicious sensations conceivable. Now, one moment it was a toy as silly as a doll, and the next moment it thrilled him once more, and he could believe again its promises of bliss – and then he knew that it was for ever a vain toy, and he was sad, and his sadness was pleasure. He had already stacked most of his school-books in the

39

other attic. He would need a table and a lamp; he knew not for what precise purpose; but a table and a lamp were necessary to the continuance of his self-respect. The only question was, Should he remodel his bedroom, or should he demand the other attic, and plant his flag in it and rule over it in addition to his bedroom? Had he the initiative and the energy to carry out such an enterprise? He was not able to make up his mind. And, moreover, he could not decide anything until after that plain talk with his father.

His sister Clara's high voice sounded outside, on the landing, or half-way up the attic stairs.

'Ed-*win*! Ed-*win*!'

'What's up?' he called in answer, rising with a nervous start. The door of the room was unlatched.

'You're mighty mysterious in your bedroom,' said Clara's voice behind the door.

'Come in! Come in! Why don't you come in?' he replied, with good-natured impatience. But somehow he could not speak in a natural tone. The mere fact that he had left school that day and that the world awaited him, and that everybody in the house knew this, rendered him self-conscious.

III

Clara entered, with a curious sidelong movement, half-winning and half-serpentine. She was aged fourteen, a very fair and very slight girl, with a thin face and thin lips, and extraordinarily slender hands; in general appearance fragile. She wore a semi-circular comb on the crown of her head, and her abundant hair hung over her shoulders in two tight pigtails. Edwin considered that Clara was harsh and capricious; he had much fault to find with her; but nevertheless the sight of her usually affected him pleasurably (of course without his knowing it), for he never for long sat definitely in adverse judgement upon her. Her gestures had a charm for him which he felt but did not realize. And this charm was similar to his own charm. But nothing would have so surprised him as to learn that he himself had any charm at all. He would have laughed, and been ashamed – to hear that his gestures and the play of his features had an ingratiating, awkward, and wistful grace; he would have tried to cure that.

'Father wants you,' said Clara, her hand on the handle of the thin attic-door hung with odd garments.

Edwin's heart fell instantly, and all the agreeable images of tea vanished from his mind. His father must have read the school report and perceived that Edwin had been beaten by Charlie Orgreave, a boy younger than himself!

40

'Did he send you up for me?' Edwin asked.

'No,' said Clara, frowning. 'But I heard him calling out for you all over. So Maggie told me to run up. Not that I expect any *thanks*.' She put her head forward a little.

The episode, and Clara's tone, showed clearly the nature and force of the paternal authority in the house. It was an authority with the gift of getting its commands anticipated.

'All right! I'm coming,' said Edwin superiorly.

'I know what you want,' Clara said teasingly as she turned towards the passage.

'What do I want?'

'You want the empty attic all to yourself, and a fine state it would be in a month, my word!'

'How do you know I want the empty attic?' Edwin repelled the on-slaught; but he was considerably taken aback. It was a mystery to him how those girls, and Clara in particular, got wind of his ideas before he had even formulated them definitely to himself. It was also a mystery to him how they could be so tremendously interested in matters which did not concern them.

'You never mind!' Clara gibed, with a smile that was malicious, but charmingly malicious. 'I know!'

She had merely seen him staring into the empty attic, and from that brief spectacle she had by divination constructed all his plans.

IV

The Clayhanger sitting-room, which served as both dining-room and drawing-room, according to the more primitive practices of those days, was over one half of the shop, and looked on Duck Square. Owing to its northern aspect it scarcely ever saw the sun. The furniture followed the universal fashion of horse-hair, mahogany, and wool embroidery. There was a piano, with a high back – fretted wood over silk pleated in rays from the centre; a bookcase whose lower part was a cupboard; a sofa; and a large leather easy-chair which did not match the rest of the room. The easy-chair had its back to the window and its front legs a little towards the fireplace, so that Mr Clayhanger could read his newspaper with facility in daytime. At night the light fell a little awkwardly from the central chandelier, and Mr Clayhanger, if he happened to be read-ing, would continually shift his chair an inch or two to left or right, backwards or forwards, and would also continually glance up at the chandelier, as if accusing it of not doing its best. A common sight in the sitting-room was Mr Clayhanger balanced on a chair, the table having been pushed away, screwing the newest burner into the chandelier. When he was seated in his easy-chair the piano could not be played,

because there was not sufficient space for the stool between the piano
and his chair; nor could the fire be made up without disturbing him,
because the japanned coal-box was on the same side of the hearth-rug
as the chair. Thus, when the fire languished and Mr Clayhanger neglected it, the children had either to ask permission to step over his legs,
or suggest that he should attend to the fire himself. Occasionally, when
he was in one of his gay moods, he would humorously impede the efforts
of the firemaker with his feet, and if the firemaker was Clara or Edwin,
the child would tickle him, which brought him to his senses and forced
him to shout : 'None o' that ! None o' that !'

The position of Mr Clayhanger's easy-chair – a detail apparently
trifling – was in reality a strongly influencing factor in the family life,
for it meant that the father's presence obsessed the room. And it could
not be altered, for it depended on the window; the window was too
small to be quite efficient. When the children reflected upon the history
of their childhood they saw one important aspect of it as a long series of
detached hours spent in the sitting-room, in a state of desire to do something that could not be done without disturbing father, and in a state of
indecision whether or not to disturb him. If by chance, as sometimes
occurred, he chose to sit on the sofa, which was unobtrusive in the corner
away from the window, between the fireplace and the door, the room
was instantly changed into something larger, freer, and less incon-
venient.

V

As the hour was approaching six, Edwin, on the way downstairs, looked
in at the sitting-room for his father; but Darius was not there.

'Where's father?' he demanded.

'I don't know, I'm sure,' said Maggie, at the sewing-machine. Maggie
was aged twenty; dark, rather stout, with an expression at once benevolent and worried. She rarely seemed to belong to the same generation
as her brother and sister. She consorted on equal terms with married
women, and talked seriously of the same things as they did. Mr Clayhanger treated her somewhat differently from the other two. Yet, though
he would often bid them accept her authority, he would now and then
impair that authority by roughly 'dressing her down' at the meal-table.
She was a capable girl; she had much less firmness, and much more
good-nature, than she seemed to have. She could not assert herself
adequately. She 'managed' very well; indeed she had 'done wonders in
filling the place of the mother who had died when Clara was four and
Edwin six, and she herself only ten. Responsibility, apprehension, and
strained effort had printed their marks on her features. But the majority
of acquaintances were more impressed by her good intention than by

42

her capacity; they would call her 'a nice thing'. The discerning minority, while saying with admiring conviction that she was 'a very fine girl', would regret that somehow she had not the faculty of 'making the best of herself', of 'putting her best foot foremost'. And would they not heartily stand up for her with the superficial majority!

A thin, grey-haired, dreamy-eyed woman hurried into the room, bearing a noisy tray and followed by Clara with a white cloth. This was Mrs Nixon, the domestic staff of the Clayhanger household for years. Clara and Mrs Nixon swept Maggie's sewing materials from the corner of the table on to a chair, put Maggie's flower-glasses on to the ledge of the bookcase, folded up the green cloth, and began rapidly to lay the tea. Simultaneously Maggie, glancing at the clock, closed up her sewing-machine, and deposited her work in a basket. Clara, leaving the table, stooped to pick up the bits of cotton and white stuff that littered the carpet. The clock struck six.

'Now, sharply!' she exclaimed curtly to Edwin, who stood hesitatingly with his hands in his pockets. 'Can't you help Maggie to push that sewing-machine into the corner?'

'What on earth's up?' he inquired vaguely, but starting forward to help Maggie.

'*She'll* be here in a minute,' said Maggie, almost under her breath, as she fitted on the cover of the sewing-machine.

'Who?' asked Edwin. 'Oh! Auntie! I'd almost forgotten it was her night.'

'As if anyone could forget!' murmured Clara, with sarcastic unbelief.

By this time the table was completely set.

VI

Edwin wondered mildly, as he often wondered, at the extremely bitter tone in which Clara always referred to their Aunt Clara Hamps – when Mr Hamps was not there. Even Maggie's private attitude to Auntie Clara was scarcely more Christian. Mrs Hamps was the widowed younger sister of their mother, and she had taken a certain share in the supervision of Darius Clayhanger's domestic affairs after the death of Mrs Clayhanger. This latter fact might account, partially but not wholly, for the intense and steady dislike in which she was held by Maggie, Clara, and Mrs Nixon. Clara hated her own name because she had been 'called after' her auntie. Mr Clayhanger 'got on' excellently with his sister-in-law. He 'thought highly' of her, and was indeed proud to have her for a relative. In their father's presence the girls never showed their dislike of Mrs Hamps; it was a secret pleasure shared between them and Mrs Nixon, and only disclosed to Edwin bacause the girls were indifferent to what Edwin might think. They casually despised him for somehow liking his auntie, for not seeing through her wiles; but they could count on his loyalty to themselves.

'Are you ready for tea, or aren't you?' Clara asked him. She frequently spoke to him as if she was the elder instead of the younger.

'Yes,' he said. 'But I must find father.'

He went off, but did not find his father in the shop, and after a few futile minutes he returned upstairs. Mrs Nixon preceded him, carrying the tea-urn, and she told him that his father had sent word into the kitchen that they were not to 'wait tea' for him.

CHAPTER 7 : *Auntie Hamps*

I

Mrs Hamps had splendidly arrived. The atmosphere of the sitting-room was changed. Maggie, smiling, wore her second-best black silk apron. Clara, smiling and laughing, wore a clean long white pinafore. Mrs Nixon, with her dreamy eyes less vacant than usual, greeted Mrs Hamps effusively, and effusively gave humble thanks for kind inquiries after her health. A stranger might have thought that these women were strongly attached to one another by ties of affection and respect. Edwin never understood how his sisters, especially Maggie, could practise such vast and eternal hypocrisy with his aunt. As for him, his aunt acted on him now, as generally, like a tonic. Some effluence from her quickened him. He put away the worry in connexion with his father, and gave himself up to the physical pleasures of tea.

Aunt Clara was a handsome woman. She had been called – but not by men whose manners and code she would have approved – 'a damned fine woman'. Her age was about forty, which at that period, in a woman's habit of mind, was the equivalent of about fifty today. Her latest photograph was considered to be very successful. It showed her standing behind a velvet chair and leaning her large but still shapely bust slightly over the chair. Her forearms, ruffled and braceleted, lay along the fringed back of the chair, and from one negligent hand depended a rose. A heavy curtain came downwards out of nothing into the picture, and the end of it lay coiled and draped on the seat of the chair. The great dress was of slate-coloured silk, with sleeves tight to the elbow, and thence, from a ribbon-bow, broadening to a wide triangular climax that revealed quantities of lace at the wrists. The pointed ends of the sleeves were picked out with squares of velvet. A short and highly ornamental fringed and looped flounce waved grandly out behind from

44

the waist to the level of the knees; and the stomacher recalled the orna-
mentation of the flounce; and both the stomacher and flounce gave
contrasting value to the severe plainness of the skirt, designed to empha-
size the quality of the silk. Round the neck was a lace collarette to match
the furniture of the wrists, and the broad ends of the collarette were
crossed on the bosom and held by a large jet brooch. Above that you
saw a fine regular face, with a firm hard mouth and a very straight nose
and dark eyebrows; small ears weighted with heavy jet ear-rings.

The photograph could not render the clear perfection of Aunt Clara's
rosy skin; she had the colour and the flashing eye of a girl. But it did
justice to her really magnificent black hair. This hair was all her own,
and the coiffure seemed as ample as a judge's wig. From the low forehead the hair was parted exactly in the middle for about two inches;
then plaited bands crossed and recrossed the scalp in profusion, forming
behind a pattern exceedingly complicated, and down either side of the
head, now behind the ear, now hiding it, now resting on the shoulders,
now hanging clear of them, fell long multitudinous glossy curls. These
curls – one of them in the photograph reached as far as the stomacher
– could not have been surpassed in Bursley.

She was a woman of terrific vitality. Her dead sister had been nothing in comparison with her. She had a glorious digestion, and was the
envy of her brother-in-law – who suffered much from biliousness –
because she could eat with perfect impunity hot buttered toast and raw
celery in large quantities. Further, she had independent means, and no
children to cause anxieties. Yet she was always, as the phrase went,
'bearing up', or, as another phrase went, 'leaning hard'. Frances Ridley
Havergal was her favourite author, and Frances Ridley Havergal's little
book *Lean Hard*, was kept on her dressing-table. (The girls, however,
averred that she never opened it.) Aunt Clara's spiritual life must be
imagined as a continual, almost physical leaning on Christ. Nevertheless she never complained, and she was seldom depressed. Her desire, and
her achievement, was to be bright, to take everything cheerfully, to
look obstinately on the best side of things, and to instil this religion into
others.

II

Thus, when it was announced that father had been called out un-
expectedly, leaving an order that they were not to wait for him, she
said gaily that they had better be obedient and begin, though it would
have been more agreeable to wait for father. And she said how beautiful
the tea was, and how beautiful the toast, and how beautiful the straw-
berry-jam, and how beautiful the pikelets. She would herself pour some
hot water into the slop basin, and put a pikelet on a plate thereon,

covered, to keep warm for father. She would not hear a word about the toast being a little hard, and when Maggie in her curious quiet way 'stuck her out' that the toast was in fact hard, she said that that precise degree of hardness was the degree which she, for herself, preferred. Then she talked of jams, and mentioned gooseberry-jam, whereupon Clara privately put her tongue out, with the quickness of a snake, to signal to Maggie.

'Ours isn't good this year,' said Maggie.

'I told auntie we weren't so set up with it, a fortnight ago,' said Clara simply, like a little angel.

'Did you, dear?' Mrs Hamps exclaimed, with great surprise, almost with shocked surprise. 'I'm sure it's beautiful. I was quite looking forward to tasting it; quite! I know what your gooseberry-jam is.'

'Would you like to try it now?' Maggie suggested. 'But we've warned you.'

'Oh, I don't want to trouble you *now*. We're all so cosy here. Any time –'

'No trouble, Auntie,' said Clara, with her most captivating and innocent smile.

'Well, if you talk about "warning" me, of course I must insist on having some,' said Auntie Clara.

Clara jumped up, passed behind Mrs Hamps, making a contemptuous face at those curls as she did so, and ran gracefully down to the kitchen.

'Here,' she said crossly to Mrs Nixon. 'A pot of that gooseberry, please. A small one will do. She knows it's short of sugar, and so she's determined to try it, just out of spite; and nothing will stop her.'

Clara returned smiling to the tea-table, and Maggie neatly unsealed the jam; and Auntie Clara, with a face beaming with pleasurable anticipation, helped herself circumspectly to a spoonful.

'Beautiful!' she murmured.

'Don't you think it's a bit tart?' Maggie asked.

'Oh no!' protestingly.

'*Don't* you?' asked Clara, with an air of delighted deferential astonishment.

'Oh *no*!' Mrs Hamps repeated. 'It's beautiful!' She did not smack her lips over it, because she would have considered it unladylike to smack her lips, but by less offensive gestures she sought to convey her unbounded pleasure in the jam. 'How much sugar did you put in?' she inquired after a while. 'Half and half?'

'Yes,' said Maggie.

'They do say gooseberries were a tiny bit sour this year, owing to the weather,' said Mrs Hamps reflectively.

Clara kicked Edwin under the table, as it were viciously, but her

46

delightful innocent smile, directed vaguely upon Mrs Hamps, did not relax. Such duplicity passed Edwin's comprehension; it seemed to him purposeless. Yet he could not quite deny that there might be a certain sting, a certain insinuation, in his auntie's last remark.

III

Then Mr Clayhanger entered, blowing forth a long breath as if trying to repulse the oppressive heat of the July afternoon. He came straight to the table, with a slightly preoccupied air, quickly, his arms motionless at his sides, and slanting a little outwards. Mr Clayhanger always walked like this, with motionless arms so that in spite of a rather clumsy and heavy step, the upper part of him appeared to glide along. He shook hands genially with Auntie Clara, greeting her almost as grandiosely as she greeted him, putting on for a moment the grand manner, not without dignity. Each admired the other. Each often said that the other was 'wonderful'. Each undoubtedly flattered the other, made a fuss of the other. Mr Clayhanger's admiration was the greater. The bitterest thing that Edwin had ever heard Maggie say was 'It's something to be thankful for that she's his deceased wife's sister!' And she had said the bitter thing with such quiet bitterness! Edwin had not instantly perceived the point of it.

Darius Clayhanger then sat down, with a thud, snatched at the cup of tea which Maggie had placed before him, and drank half of it with a considerable indrawing noise. No one asked where or why he had been detained; it was not etiquette to do so. If father had been 'called away', or had 'had to go away', or was 'kept somewhere', the details were out of reference allowed to remain in mystery, respected by curiosity. . . . 'Father – business' . . . All business was sacred. He himself had inculcated this attitude.

In a short silence the sound of the bell that the carman rang before the tram started for Hanbridge floated in through the open window.

'There's the tram!' observed Auntie Clara, apparently with warm and special interest in the phenomena of the tram. Then another little silence.

'Auntie,' said Clara, writhing about youthfully on her chair. 'Can't ye sit still a bit?' the father asked, interrupting her roughly, but with good humour. 'Ye'll be falling off th' chair in a minute.'

Clara blushed swiftly, and stopped.

'Yes, love?' Auntie Clara encouraged her. It was as if Auntie Clara had said: 'Your dear father is of course quite right, more than right, to insist on your sitting properly at table. However, do not take the correction too much to heart. I sympathize with all your difficulties.'

'I was only going to ask you,' Clara went on, in a weaker, stammering voice, 'if you knew that Edwin's left school today.' Her archness had deserted her.

'Mischievous little thing !' thought Edwin. 'Why must she deliberately go and draw attention to that?' And he too blushed, feeling as if he owed an apology to the company for having left school.

'Oh yes!' said Auntie Clara with eager benevolence. 'I've got something to say about that to my nephew.'

Mr Clayhanger searched in a pocket of his alpaca, and drew forth an open envelope.

'Here's the lad's report, Auntie,' said he. 'Happen ye'd like to look at it.'

'I should indeed !' she replied fervently. 'I'm sure it's a very good one.'

IV

She took the paper, and assumed her spectacles.

'Conduct – Excellent,' she read, poring with enthusiasm over the document. And she read again : 'Conduct – Excellent.' Then she went down the list of subjects, declaiming the number of marks for each; and at the end she read : 'Position in class next term : Third. Splendid, Eddy !' she exclaimed.

'I thought you were second,' said Clara, in her sharp manner.

Edwin blushed again, and hesitated.

'Eh? What's that? What's that?' his father demanded. 'I didn't notice that. Third?'

'Charlie Orgreave beat me in the examination,' Edwin muttered.

'Well, that's a pretty how d'ye do !' said his father. 'Going down one ! Ye ought to ha' been first instead of third. And would ha' been, happen, if ye'd pegged at it.'

'Now I won't have that? I won't have it !' Auntie Clara protested, laughingly showing her fine teeth and gazing first at Darius, and then at Edwin, from under her spectacles, her head being thrown back and the curls hanging far behind. 'No one shall say that Edwin doesn't work, not even his father, while his auntie's about! Because I know he does work! And besides, he hasn't gone down. It says, "position *next term*" – not this term. You were still second today, weren't you, my boy?'

'I suppose so. Yes,' Edwin answered, pulling himself together.

'Well ! There you are !' Auntie Clara's voice rang triumphantly. She was opening her purse. 'And *there* you are !' she repeated, popping half a sovereign down in front of him. 'That's a little present from your auntie on your leaving school.'

'Oh, Auntie !' he cried feebly.

'Oh !' cried Clara, genuinely startled.

Mrs Hamps was sometimes thus astoundingly munificent. It was she

48

who had given the schooner to Edwin. And her presents of elaborately enveloped and costly toilet soap on the birthdays of the children, and at Christmas, were massive. Yet Clara always maintained that she was the meanest old thing imaginable. And Maggie had once said that she knew that Auntie Clara made her servant eat dripping instead of butter. To give inferior food to a servant was to Maggie the unforgivable in parsimony.

'Well,' Mr Clayhanger warningly inquired, 'what do you say to your aunt?'

'Thank you, Auntie,' Edwin sheepishly responded, fingering the coin.

It was a princely sum. And she had stuck up for him famously in the matter of the report. Strange that his father should not have read the report with sufficient attention to remark the fall to third place! Anyway, that aspect of the affair was now safely over, and it seemed to him that he had not lost much prestige by it. He would still be able to argue with his father on terms not too unequal, he hoped.

<h1 style="text-align:center">v</h1>

As the tea drew to an end, and the plates of toast, bread and butter, and tea-cake grew emptier, and the slop-basin filled, and only Maggie's flowers remained fresh and immaculate amid the untidy débris of the meal; and as Edwin and Clara became gradually indifferent to jam, and then inimical to it; and as the sounds of the street took on the softer quality of summer evening, and the first filmy shades of twilight gathered imperceptibly in the corners of the room, and Mr Clayhanger performed the eructations which signified that he had enough; so Mrs Hamps prepared herself for one of her classic outbursts of feeling.

'Well!' she said at last, putting her spoon to the left of her cup as a final indication that seriously she would drink no more. And she gave a great sigh. 'School over! And the only son going out into the world! How time flies!' And she gave another great sigh, implying an immense melancholy due to this vision of the reality of things. Then she remembered her courage, and the device of leaning hard, and all her philosophy.

'But it's all for the best!' she broke forth in a new brave tone. 'Everything is ordered for the best. We must never forget that! And I'm quite sure that Edwin will be a very great credit to us all, with help from above.'

She proceeded powerfully in this strain. She brought in God, Christ, and even the Holy Spirit. She mentioned the dangers of the world, and the disguises of the devil, and the unspeakable advantages of a good home, and the special goodness of Mr Clayhanger and of Maggie, yes, and of her little Clara; and the pride which they all had in Edwin, and the unique opportunities which he had of doing good, by example, and also, soon, by precept, for others younger than himself would begin to look up to him; and again her personal pride in him, and her sure faith in him; and what a solemn hour it was . . .

Nothing could stop her. The girls loathed these exhibitions. Maggie always looked at the table during their progress, and she felt as though she had done something wrong and was ashamed of it. Clara not merely felt like a criminal – she felt like an unrepentant criminal; she blushed, she glanced nervously about the room, and all the time she repeated steadily in her heart a highly obscene word which she had heard at school. This unspoken word, hurled soundlessly but savagely at her aunt in that innocent heart, afforded much comfort to Clara in the affliction. Even Edwin, who was more lenient in all ways than his sisters, profoundly deplored these moralizings of his aunt. They filled him with a desire to run fast and far, to be alone at sea, or to be deep somewhere in the bosom of the earth. He could not understand this side of his auntie's individuality. But there was no delivery from Mrs Hamps. The only person who could possibly have delivered them seemed to enjoy the sinister thraldom. Mr Clayhanger listened with appreciative and admiring nods; he appeared to be quite sincere. And Edwin could not understand his father either. 'How simple father must be !' he thought vaguely. Whereas Clara fatalistically dismissed her father's attitude as only one more of the preposterously unreasonable phenomena which she was constantly meeting in life; and she persevered grimly with her obscene word.

VI

'Eh !' said Mrs Hamps enthusiastically, after a trifling pause. 'It does me good when I think what a *help* you'll be to your father in the business, with that clever head of yours.'

She gazed at him fondly.

Now this was Edwin's chance. He did not wish to be any help at all to his father in the business. He had other plans for himself. He had never mentioned them before, because his father had never talked to him about his future career, apparently assuming that he would go into the business. He had been waiting for his father to begin. 'Surely,' he had said to himself, 'father's bound to speak to me sometime about what I'm going to do, and when he does I shall just tell him.' But his father never had begun; and by timidity, negligence, and perhaps ill-luck, Edwin had thus arrived at his last day at school with the supreme question not merely unsolved but unattacked. Oh, he blamed himself ! Any ordinary boy (he thought) would have discussed such a question naturally long ago. After all, it was not a crime, it was no cause for shame, to wish not to be a printer. Yet he was ashamed! Absurd! He blamed himself. But he also blamed his father. Now, however, in responding to his auntie's remark, he could remedy all the past by simply and boldly stating that he did not want to follow his father. It would be unpleasant, of course, but the worst shock would be over in a moment, like the drawing of a tooth. He had merely to utter certain words. He must utter them. They were perfectly easy to say, and they were also of the greatest urgency. 'I don't want to be a printer.' He mumbled them over in his mind. 'I don't want to be a printer.' What could it matter to his father whether he was a printer or not? Seconds, minutes, seemed to pass. He knew that if he was so inconceivably craven as to remain silent, his self-respect would never recover from the blow. Then, in response to Mrs Hamps's prediction about his usefulness to his father in the business, he said, with a false-jaunty, unconvinced, unconvincing air –

'Well, that remains to be seen.'

This was all he could accomplish. It seemed as if he had looked death itself in the face, and drawn away.

'Remains to be *seen*?' Auntie Clara repeated, with a hint of startled pain, due to this levity.

He was mute. No one suspected, as he sat there, so boyish, wistful, and uneasily squirming, that he was agonized to the very centre of his being. All the time in his sweating soul, he kept trying to persuade himself : 'I've given them a hint, anyhow! I've given them a hint, anyhow!'

'Them' included everybody at the table.

VII

Mr Clayhanger, completely ignoring Edwin's reply to his aunt and her somewhat shocked repetition of it, turned suddenly towards his son and said, in a manner friendly but serious, a manner that assumed everything, a manner that begged the question, unconscious even that there was a question –

'I shall be out the better part o' tomorrow. I want ye to be sure to be in the shop all afternoon – I'll tell you what for downstairs.' It was characteristic of him thus to make a mystery of business in front of the women.

Edwin felt the net closing about him. Then he thought of one of those 'posers' which often present themselves to youths of his age.

'But tomorrow's Saturday,' he said, perhaps perkily. 'What about the Bible class?'

Six months previously a young minister of the Wesleyan Circuit, to whom Heaven had denied both a sense of humour and a sense of honour, had committed the infamy of starting a Bible class for big boys on Saturday afternoons. This outrage had appalled and disgusted the boyhood of Wesleyanism in Bursley. Their afternoon for games, their only fair afternoon in the desert of the week, to be filched from them and used against them for such an odious purpose as a Bible class! Not only Sunday school on Sunday afternoon, but a Bible class on Saturday afternoon! It was incredible. It was unbearable. It was gross tyranny, and nothing else. Nevertheless the young minister had his way, by dint of meanly calling upon parents and invoking their help. The scurvy worm actually got together a class of twelve to fifteen boys, to the end of securing their eternal welfare. And they had to attend the class, though they swore they never would, and they had to sing hymns, and they had to kneel and listen to prayers, and they had to listen to the most intolerable tedium; and to take notes of it. All this, while the sun was shining, or the rain was raining, on fields and streets and open spaces and ponds!

Edwin had been trapped in the snare. His father, after only three words from the young minister, had yielded up his son like a burnt sacrifice – and with a casual nonchalance that utterly confounded Edwin. In vain Edwin had pointed out to his elders that a Saturday afternoon of confinement must be bad for his health. His attention had been directed to his eternal health. In vain he had pointed out that on wet Saturday afternoons he frequently worked at his home-lessons, which therefore might suffer under the régime of a Bible class. His attention had been directed to the peace which passeth understanding. So he had been beaten, and was secretly twitted by Clara as an abject victim. Hence it was with a keen and peculiar feeling of triumph, of hopelessly cornering the inscrutable generation which a few months ago had cornered him, that he demanded, perhaps perkily: 'What about the Bible class?'

'There'll be no more Bible classing,' said his father, with a mild but slightly sardonic smile, as who should say: 'I'm ready to make all allowances for youth; but I must get you to understand, as gently as I can, that you can't keep on going to Bible classes for ever and ever.'

Mrs Hamps said –

'It won't be as if you were at school. But I do hope you won't neglect to study your Bible. Eh, but I do hope you'll always find time for that, to your dying day!'

'Oh – but I say –' Edwin began, and stopped.

He was beaten by the mere effrontery of the replies. His father and his aunt (the latter of whom at any rate was a firm and confessed religionist, who had been responsible for converting Mr Clayhanger from Primitive Methodism to Wesleyan Methodism) did not trouble to defend their new position by argument. They made no effort to reconcile it with their position of a few months back, when the importance of heavenly welfare far exceeded the importance of any conceivable earthly welfare. The fact was that they had no argument. If God took precedence of knowledge and of health, he took precedence of a peddling shop! That was unanswerable.

VIII

Edwin was dashed. His faith in humanity was dashed. These elders were not sincere. And as Mrs Hamps continued to embroider the original theme of her exhortation about the Bible, Edwin looked at her stealthily, and the doubt crossed his mind whether that majestic and vital woman was ever sincere about anything, even to herself – whether the whole of her daily existence, from her getting-up to her down-lying, was not a grandiose pretence.

Not that he had the least desire to cling to the Bible class, even as an alternative to the shop! No! He was much relieved to be rid of the Bible class. What overset him was the crude illogicality of the new decree, and the shameless tacit admission of previous insincerity.

Two hours later, as he stood idly at the window of his bedroom, watching the gas lamps of Trafalgar Road wax brighter in the last glooms of twilight, he was still occupied with the sham and the unreason and the lack of scruple suddenly revealed in the life of the elder generation. Unconsciously imitating a trick of his father's when annoyed but calm, he nodded his head several times, and with his tongue against his teeth made the noise which in writing is represented by 'tut-tut'. Yet somehow he had always known that it would be so. At bottom, he was only pretending to himself to be shocked and outraged.

His plans were no further advanced; indeed they were put back, for this Saturday afternoon vigil in the shop would be in some sort a symbolic temporary defeat for him. Why had he not spoken out clearly? Why was he always like a baby in the presence of his father? The future was all askew for him. He had forgotten his tremendous serious resolves. The touch of the half-sovereign in his pocket, was comforting in a universe of discomfort.

CHAPTER 8 : *In the Shop*

I

'Here, lad!' said his father to Edwin, as soon as he had scraped up the last crumbs of cheese from his plate at the end of dinner on the following day.

Edwin rose obediently and followed him out of the room. Having waited at the top of the stairs until his father had reached the foot, he leaned forward as far as he could with one hand on the rail and the other pressing against the wall, swooped down to the mat at the bottom, without touching a single step on the way, and made a rocket-like noise with his mouth. He had no other manner of descending the staircase, unless he happened to be in disgrace. His father went straight to the desk in the corner behind the account-book window, assumed his spectacles, and lifted the lid of the desk.

'Here!' he said, in a low voice. 'Mr Enoch Peake is stepping in this afternoon to look at this here.' He displayed the proof, an unusually elaborate wedding card, which announced the marriage of Mr Enoch Peake with Mrs Louisa Loggerheads. 'Ye know him as I mean?'

'Yes,' said Edwin. 'The stout man. The Cocknage Gardens man.'

'That's him. Well, ye'll tell him I've been called away. Tell him who ye are. Not but what he'll know. Tell him I think it might be better' – Darius's thick finger ran along a line of print – 'if we put "widow of the late Simon Loggerheads Esquire", instead of "Esq." See? Otherwise it's all right. Tell him I say as otherwise it's all right. And ask him if he'll have it printed in silver, and how many he wants, and show him this sample envelope. Now, d'ye understand?'

'Yes,' said Edwin, in a tone to convey, not disrespectfully, that there was nothing to understand. Curious, how his father had the air of bracing all his intellect as if to a problem!

'Then ye'll take it to Big James, and he can start Chawner on it. Th' job's promised for Monday forenoon.'

'Will Big James be working?' asked Edwin, for it was Saturday afternoon, when, though the shop remained open, the printing office was closed.

'They're all on overtime,' said Mr Clayhanger; and then he added, in a voice still lower, and with a surreptitious glance at Miss Ingamells, the shop-woman, who was stolidly enfolding newspapers in wrappers at the opposite counter. 'See to it yourself now. He won't want to talk to

54

her about a thing like that. Tell him I told you specially. Just let me see how well ye can do it.'

'Right!' said Edwin; and to himself, superciliously : 'It might be life and death.'

'We ought to be doing a lot o' business wi' Enoch Peake, later on,' Mr Clayhanger finished, in a whisper.

'I see,' said Edwin, impressed, perceiving that he had perhaps been supercilious too soon.

Mr Clayhanger returned his spectacles to their case, and taking his hat from its customary hook behind him, over the job-files, consulted his watch and passed around the counter to go. Then he stopped.

'I'm going to Manchester,' he murmured confidentially. 'To see if I can pick up a machine as I've heard of.'

Edwin was flattered. At the dinner-table Mr Clayhanger had only vouchsafed that he had a train to catch and would probably not be in till late at night.

The next moment he glimpsed Darius through the window, his arms motionless by his sides and sticking slightly out; hurrying in the sunshine along Wedgwood Street in the direction of Shawport station.

II

So this was business! It was not the business he desired and meant to have; and he was uneasy at the extent to which he was already entangled in it; but it was rather amusing, and his father had really been very friendly. He felt a sense of importance.

Soon afterwards Clara ran into the shop to speak to Miss Ingamells. The two chatted and giggled together.

'Father's gone to Manchester,' he found opportunity to say to Clara as she was leaving.

'Why aren't you doing those prizes he told you to do?' retorted Clara, and vanished. She wanted none of Edwin's superior airs.

During dinner Mr Clayhanger had instructed his son to go through the Sunday school prize stock and make an inventory of it.

This injunction from the child Clara, which Miss Ingamells had certainly overheard, prevented him, as an independent man, from beginning his work for at least ten minutes. He whistled, opened his father's desk, and stared vacantly into it, examined the pen-nib case in detail, and tore off two leaves from the date calendar so that it should be ready for Monday. He had a great scorn for Miss Ingamells, who was a personable if somewhat heavy creature of twenty-eight, because she kept company with a young man. He had caught them arm-in-arm and practically hugging each other, one Sunday afternoon in the street. He could see naught but silliness in that kind of thing.

The entrance of a customer caused him to turn abruptly to the high shelves where the books were kept. He was glad that the customer was not Enoch Peake, the expectation of whose arrival made him curiously nervous. He placed the step-ladder against the shelves, climbed up, and began to finger volumes and parcels of volumes. The dust was incredible. The disorder filled him with contempt. It was astounding that his father could tolerate such disorder; no doubt the whole shop was in the same condition. 'Thirteen Archie's Old Desk', he read on a parcel, but when he opened the parcel he found seven *From Jest to Earnest*. Hence he had to undo every parcel. However, the work was easy. He first wrote the inventory in pencil, then he copied it in ink; then he folded it, and wrote very carefully on the back, because his father had a mania for endorsing documents in the legal manner : 'Inventory of Sunday school prize stock'. And after an instant's hesitation he added his own initials. Then he began to tie up and restore the parcels and the single volumes. None of all this literature had any charm for him. He possessed five or six such books, all gilt and chromatic, which had been awarded to him at Sunday school, 'suitably inscribed', for doing nothing in particular; and he regarded them without exception as frauds upon boyhood. However, Clara had always enjoyed reading them. But lying flat on one of the top shelves he discovered, nearly at the end of his task, an oblong tome which did interest him : *Cazenove's Architectural Views of European Capitals, with descriptive letterpress.* It had an old-fashioned look, and was probably some relic of his father's predecessor in the establishment. Another example of the lack of order which prevailed !

III

He took the volume to the retreat of the desk, and there turned over its pages of coloured illustrations. At first his interest in them, and in the letterpress, was less instinctive than deliberate. He said to himself : 'Now, if there is anything in me, I ought really to be interested in this, and I must be interested in it.' And he was. He glanced carelessly at the clock, which was hung above the shelves of exercise-books and note-books, exactly opposite the door. A quarter past four. The afternoon was quietly passing and he had not found it too tedious. In the background of the task which (he considered) he had accomplished with extraordinary efficiency, his senses noted faintly the continual trickle of customers, all of whom were infallibly drawn to Miss Ingamells's counter by her mere watchful and receptive appearance. He had heard phrases and ends of phrases, such as : 'No, we haven't anything smaller', 'A camel-hair brush', 'Gum but not glue', 'Very sorry, sir. I'll speak firmly to the paper boy', and the sound of coins dragged along the counter, the sound of the testing of half a sovereign, the opening and shutting of the till-drawer; and occasionally Miss Ingamells exclaiming to herself upon the stupidity of customers after a customer had gone; and once Miss Ingamells crossing angrily to fix the door ajar which some heedless customer had closed : 'Did they suppose that people didn't want air like other people?' And now it was a quarter past four. Undoubtedly he had a peculiar, and pleasant, feeling of importance. In another half-minute he glanced at the clock again, and it was a quarter to five.

What hypnotism attracted him towards the artists' materials cabinet which stood magnificent, complicated, and complete in the middle of the shop, like a monument? His father, after one infantile disastrous raid, had absolutely forbidden any visitation of that cabinet, with its glass case of assorted paints, crayons, brushes, and pencils, and its innumerable long drawers full of paper and cards and wondrous perfectly equipped boxes, and T-squares and set-squares, with a hundred other contrivances. But of course the order had now ceased to have force. Edwin had left school; and, if he was not a man, he was certainly not a boy. He began to open the drawers, at first gingerly, then boldly; after all it was no business of Miss Ingamells's ! And, to be just, Miss Ingamells made no sort of pretence that it was any business of of hers. She proceeded with her own business. Edwin opened a rather large wooden water-colour box. It was marked five and sixpence. It seemed to comprise everything needed for the production of the most entrancing and majestic architectural views, and as Edwin took out its upper case and discovered still further marvellous devices and apparatus in its basement beneath, he dimly but passionately saw, in his heart, bright masterpieces that ought to be the fruit of that box. There was a key to it. He must have it. He would have given all that he possessed for it, if necessary.

IV

'Miss Ingamells,' he said : and, as she did not look up immediately, 'I say, Miss Ingamells! How much does father take off in the shilling to auntie when she buys anything?'

'Don't ask *me*, Master Edwin,' said Ingamells; '*I* don't know. How should I know?'

'Well, then,' he muttered, 'I shall pay full price for it – that's all.' He could not wait, and he wanted to be on the safe side.

Miss Ingamells gave him change for his half-sovereign in a strictly impartial manner, to indicate that she accepted no responsibility. And the squaring of Edwin's shoulders conveyed to Miss Ingamells that he advised her to keep carefully within her own sphere, and not to make impertinent inquiries about the origin of the half-sovereign, which he could see intrigued her acutely. He now owned the box; it was not a box of colours, but a box of enchantment. He had had colour-boxes before, but nothing to compare with this, nothing that could have seemed magical to anybody wiser than a very small boy. Then he bought some cartridge-paper; he considered that cartridge-paper would be enough for preliminary experiments.

V

It was while he was paying for the cartridge-paper – he being, as was indeed proper, on the customers' side of the counter – that a heavy loutish boy in an apron entered the shop, blushing. Edwin turned away. This was Miss Ingamells's affair.

'If ye please, Mester Peake's sent me. He canna come in this afternoon – he's got a bit o' ratting on – and will Mester Clayhanger step across to th' Dragon tonight after eight, with that there peeper [paper] as he knows on?'

At the name of Peake, Edwin started. He had utterly forgotten the matter.

'Master Edwin,' said Miss Ingamells dryly. 'You know all about that, don't you?' Clearly she resented that he knew all about that while she didn't.

'Oh! Yes.' Edwin stammered. 'What did you say?'

It was his first piece of real business.

'If you please, Mester Peake sent me . . .' The messenger blundered through his message again word for word.

'Very well. I'll attend to it,' said Edwin, as nonchalantly as he could.

Nevertheless he was at a loss what to do, simple though the situation might have seemed to a person with an experience of business longer than Edwin's. Just as three hours previously his father had appeared to be bracing all his intellect to a problem that struck Edwin as entirely simple, so now Edwin seemed to be bracing all his intellect to another aspect of the same problem. Time, revenging his father! . . . What! Go across to the Dragon and in cold blood demand Mr Enoch Peake, and then parley with Mr Enoch Peake as one man with another! He had never been inside the Dragon. He had been brought up in the belief that the Dragon was a place of sin. The Dragon was included in the generic term 'gin-palace', and quite probably in the Siamese-twin term 'gaming-saloon'. Moreover, to discuss business with Mr Enoch Peake. . . . Mr Enoch Peake was as mysterious to Edwin as, say, a Chinese mandarin! Still, business was business, and something would have to be done. He did not know what. Ought he to go to the Dragon? His father had not foreseen the possibility of this development. He instantly decided one fundamental; he would not consult Miss Ingamells; no, nor even

Maggie! There remained only Big James. He went across to see Big James, who was calmly smoking a pipe on the little landing at the top of the steps leading to the printing office.

Big James showed no astonishment.

'You come along o' me to the Dragon tonight, young sir, at eight o'clock, or as soon after as makes no matter, and I'll see as you see Mr Enoch Peake. I shall be coming up Woodisun Bank at eight o'clock, or as soon after as makes no matter. You be waiting for me at the back gates there, and I'll see as you see Mr Enoch Peake.'

'Are you going to the Dragon?'

'Am I going to the Dragon, young sir!' exclaimed Big James, in his majestic voice.

CHAPTER 9 : *The Town*

I

James Yarlett was worthy of his nickname. He stood six feet four and a half inches in height, and his girth was proportionate; he had enormous hands and feet, large features, and a magnificent long dark brown beard; owing to his beard his necktie was never seen. But the most magnificent thing about him was his bass voice, acknowledged to be the finest bass in the town, and one of the finest even in Hanbridge, where, in his earlier prime, James had lived as a 'news comp' on the *Staffordshire Signal*. He was now a 'jobbing comp' in Bursley, because Bursley was his native town and because he preferred jobbing. He made the fourth and heaviest member of the celebrated Bursley Male Glee Party, the other three being Arthur Smallrice, an old man with a striking falsetto voice, Abraham Harracles, and Jos Rawnpike (pronounced Rampick). These men were accustomed to fame, and Big James was the king of them, though the mildest. They sang at dinners, free-and-easies, concerts, and Martinmas tea-meetings. They sang for the glory, and when there was no demand for their services, they sang to themselves, for the sake of singing. Each of them was a star in some church or chapel choir. And except Arthur Smallrice, they all shared a certain elasticity of religious opinion. Big James, for example, had varied in ten years from Wesleyan, through Old Church, to Roman Catholic up at Bleakridge. It all depended on niceties in the treatment accorded to him, and on the choice of anthems. Moreover, he liked a change.

He was what his superiors called 'a very superior man'. Owing to the more careful enunciation required in singing, he had lost a great deal of the Five Towns accent, and one cannot be a compositor for a quarter of a century without insensibly acquiring an education and a store of knowledge far excelling the ordinary. His manner was gentle, and perhaps somewhat pompous, as is common with very big men; but you could never be sure whether an extremely subdued humour did not underlie his pomposity. He was a bachelor, aged forty-five, and lived quietly with a married sister at the bottom of Woodisun Bank, near the National Schools. The wonder was that, with all his advantages, he had not more deeply impressed himself upon Bursley as an individuality, and not merely as a voice. But he seemed never to seek to do so. He was without ambition; and, though curiously careful sometimes about preserving his own dignity, and beyond question sensitive by temperament, he showed marked respect, and even humility, to the worldly-successful. Despite his bigness and simplicity there was something small about him which came out in odd trifling details. Thus it was characteristic of Big James to ask Edwin to be waiting for him at the back gates in Woodisun Bank when he might just as easily have met him at the side door by the closed shop in Wedgwood Street.

Edwin, who from mere pride had said nothing to his sisters about the impending visit to the Dragon, was a little surprised and dashed to see Big James in broadcloth and a high hat; for he had not dreamed of changing his own everyday suit, nor had it occurred to him that the Dragon was a temple of ceremoniousness. Big James looked enormous. The wide lapel of his shining frock-coat was buttoned high up under his beard and curved downwards for a distance of considerably more than a yard to his knees : it was a heroic frock-coat. The sleeves were wide, but narrowing at the wrists, and the white wristbands were very tight. The trousers fell in ample folds on the uppers of the gigantic boots. Big James had a way of sticking out his chest and throwing his head back which would have projected the tip of his beard ten inches forth from his body, had the beard been stiff; but the soft silkiness of the beard frustrated this spectacular phenomenon, which would have been very interesting to witness.

II

The pair stepped across Trafalgar Road together, Edwin, though he tried to be sedate, nothing but a frisking morsel by the side of the vast monument. Compared with the architectural grandeur of Mr Yarlett, his thin, supple, free-moving limbs had an almost pathetic appearance of ephemeral fragility.

Big James directed himself to the archway leading to the Dragon stables, and there he saw an ostler or oddman. Edwin, feeling the imminence of an ordeal, surreptitiously explored a pocket to be sure that the proof of the wedding card was safely there.

The ostler raised his reddish eyebrows to Big James. Big James jerked his head to one side, indicating apparently the entire Dragon, and simultaneously conveying a query. The ostler paused immobile an instant and then shook his insignificant turnip-pate. Big James turned away. No word had been spoken; nevertheless, the men had exchanged a dialogue which might be thus put into words –

'I wasn't thinking to see ye so soon,' from the ostler.

'Then nobody of any importance has yet gone into the assembly room?' from Big James.

'Nobody worth speaking of, and won't, for a while,' from the other.

'Then I'll take a turn,' from Big James.

The latter now looked down at Edwin, and addressed him in words –

'Seemingly we're too soon, Mr Edwin. What do you say to a turn round the town – playground way? I doubted we should be too soon.'

Edwin showed alacrity. As a schoolboy it had been definitely forbidden to him to go out at night; and unless sent on a special and hurried errand, he had scarcely seen the physiognomy of the streets after eight o'clock. He had never seen the playground in the evening. And this evening the town did not seem like the same town; it had become a new and mysterious town of adventure. And yet Edwin was not fifty yards away from his own bedroom.

They ascended Duck Bank together, Edwin proud to be with a celebrity of the calibre of Big James, and Big James calmly satisfied to show himself thus formally with his master's son. It appeared almost incredible that those two immortals, so diverse, had issued from the womb practically alike; that a few brief years on the earth had given Big James such a tremendous physical advantage. Several hours' daily submission to the exact regularities of lines of type and to the unvarying demands of minutely adjusted machines in motion had stamped Big James's body and mind with the delicate and quasi-finicking preciseness which characterizes all compositors and printers; and the continual monotonous performance of similar tasks that employed his faculties while never absorbing or straining them, had soothed and dulled the fever of life in him to a beneficent calm, a calm refined and beautified by the pleasurable exercise of song. Big James had seldom known a violent emotion. He had craved nothing, sought for nothing, and lost nothing.

Edwin, like Big James in progress from everlasting to everlasting, was all inchoate, unformed, undisciplined, and burning with capricious fires; all expectant, eager, reluctant, tingling, timid, innocently and wistfully audacious. By taking the boy's hand, Big James might have poetically symbolized their relation.

61

III

'Are you going to sing tonight at the Dragon, Mr Yarlett?' asked Edwin. He lengthened his step to Big James's, controlled his ardent body, and tried to remember that he was a man with a man.

'I am, young sir,' said Big James. 'There is a party of us.'

'Is it the Male Glee Party?' Edwin pursued.

'Yes, Mr Edwin.'

'Then Mr Smallrice will be there?'

'He will, Mr Edwin.'

'Why can Mr Smallrice sing such high notes?'

Big James slowly shook his head, as Edwin looked up at him. 'I tell you what it is, young sir. It's a gift, that's what it is, same as I can sing low.'

'But Mr Smallrice is very old, isn't he?'

'There's a parrot in a cage over at the Duck, there, as is eighty-five years old, and that's proved by record kept, young sir.'

'No!' protested Edwin's incredulity politely.

'By record kept,' said Big James.

'Do you often sing at the Dragon, Mr Yarlett?'

'Time was,' said Big James, 'when some of us used to sing there every night, Sundays excepted, and concerts and whatnot excepted. Aye! For hours and hours every night. And still do sometimes.'

'After your work?'

'After our work. Aye! And often till dawn in summer. One o'clock, two o'clock, half past two o'clock, every night. But now they say that this new Licensing Act will close every public-house in this town at eleven o'clock, and a straight-up eleven at that! ...'

'But what do you do it for?'

'What do we do it for? We do it to pass the time and the glass, young sir. Not as I should like you think as I ever drank, Mr Edwin. One quart of ale I take every night, and have ever done; no more, no less.'

'But' – Edwin's rapid, breaking voice interrupted eagerly the deep majestic tones – 'aren't you tired the next day? I should be!'

'Never' said Big James. 'I get up from my bed as fresh as a daisy at six sharp. And I've known the nights when my bed ne'er saw me.'

'You must be strong, Mr Yarlett, my word!' Edwin exclaimed. These revelations of the habits and prowess of Big James astounded him. He had never suspected that such things went on in the town.

'Aye! Middling!'

'I suppose it's a free-and-easy at the Dragon tonight, Mr Yarlett?'

'In a manner of speaking,' said Big James.

'I wish I could stay for it.'

'And why not?' Big James suggested, and looked down at Edwin with half-humorous incertitude.

Edwin shrugged his shoulders superiorly, indicating by instinct, in spite of himself, that possibly Big James was trespassing over the social line that divided them. And yet Big James's father would have condescended to Edwin's grandfather. Only, Edwin now belonged to the employing class, whilst Big James belonged to the employed. Already Edwin, whose father had been thrashed by workmen whom a compositor would hesitate to call skilled – already Edwin had the mien natural to a ruler, and Big James, with dignified deference, would submit unresentingly to his attitude. It was the subtlest thing. It was not that Edwin obscurely objected to the suggestion of his being present at the free-and-easy; it was that he objected (but nicely, and with good nature) to any assumption of Big James's right to influence him towards an act that his father would not approve. Instead of saying, 'Why not?' Big James ought to have said : 'Nobody but you can decide that, as your father's away.' James ought to have been strictly impartial.

IV

'Well,' said Big James, when they arrived at the playground, which lay north of the covered Meat Market or Shambles, 'it looks as if they hadn't been able to make a start yet at the Blood Tub.' His tone was marked by a calm, grand disdain, as of one entertainer talking about another.

The Blood Tub, otherwise known as Snaggs's, was the centre of nocturnal pleasure in Bursley. It stood almost on the very spot where the jawbone of a whale had once lain, as a supreme natural curiosity. It represented the softened manners which had developed out of the old medievalism of the century. It had supplanted the bear-pit and the cock-pit. It corresponded somewhat with the ideals symbolized by the new Town Hall. In the tiny odorous beerhouses of all the undulating, twisting, reddish streets that surrounded the contiguous open spaces of Duck Bank, the playground, the market-place, and St Luke's Square, the folk no longer discussed eagerly what chance on Sunday morning the municipal bear would have against five dogs. They had progressed as far as a free library, boxing-gloves, rabbit-coursing, and the Blood Tub.

This last was a theatre with wooden sides and a canvas roof, and it would hold quite a crowd of people. In front of it was a platform, and an orchestra, lighted by oil flares that, as Big James and Edwin approached, were gaining strength in the twilight. Leaning against the platform was a blackboard on which was chalked the announcement of two plays : *The Forty Thieves* (author unstated) and Cruikshank's *The Bottle*. The orchestra, after terrific concussions, fell silent, and then a troupe of players in costume, cramped on the narrow trestle boards, performed a sample scene from *The Forty Thieves*, just to give the crowd in front an idea of the wonders of this powerful work. And four thieves passed and repassed behind the screen hiding the doors, and reappeared nine times as four fresh thieves until the tale of forty was complete. And then old Hammerad, the beloved clown who played the drum (and whose wife kept a barber's shop in Buck Row and shaved for a penny), left his drum and did two minutes' stiff clowning, and then the orchestra burst forth again, and the brazen voice of old Snaggs (in his moleskin waist-coat) easily rode the storm, adjuring the folk to walk up and walk up : which some of the folk did do. And lastly the band played 'God Save the Queen,' and the players, followed by old Snaggs, processionally entered the booth.

'I lay they come out again,' said Big James, with grim blandness.

'Why?' asked Edwin. He was absolutely new to the scene.

'I lay they haven't got twenty couple inside,' said Big James.

And in less than a minute the troupe did indeed emerge, and old Snaggs expostulated with a dilatory public, respectfully but firmly. It had been a queer year for Mr Snaggs. Rain had ruined the Wakes; rain had ruined everything; rain had nearly ruined him. July was obviously not a month in which a self-respecting theatre ought to be open, but Mr Snaggs had got to the point of catching at straws. He stated that in order to prove his absolute *bona fides* the troupe would now give a scene from that world-renowned and unique drama, *The Bottle*, after which the performance really would commence, since he could not as a gentle-man keep his kind patrons within waiting any longer. His habit, which emphasized itself as he grew older, was to treat the staring crowd in front of his booth like a family of nephews and nieces. The device was quite useless, for the public's stolidity was impregnable. It touched the heroic. No more granitic and crass stolidity could have been dis-covered in England. The crowd stood; it exercised no other function of existence. It just stood, and there it would stand until convinced that the gratis part of the spectacle was positively at an end.

v

With a ceremonious gesture signifying that he assumed the young sir's consent, Big James turned away. He had displayed to Edwin the poverty and the futility of the Blood Tub. Edwin would perhaps have liked to stay. The scenes enacted on the outer platform were certainly tinged with the ridiculous, but they were the first histrionics that he had ever witnessed; and he could not help thinking, hoping, in spite of his com-mon sense, that within the booth all was different, miraculously trans-

64

formed into the grand and the impressive. Left to himself, he would surely have preferred an evening at the Blood Tub to a business interview with Mr Enoch Peake at the Dragon. But naturally he had to scorn the Blood Tub with a scorn equal to the massive and silent scorn of Big James. And on the whole he considered that he was behaving as a man with another man rather well. He sought by depreciatory remarks to keep the conversation at its proper adult level.

Big James led him through the market-place, where a few vegetable, tripe, and gingerbread stalls – relics of the day's market – were still attracting customers in the twilight. These slatternly and picturesque groups, beneath their flickering yellow flares were encamped at the gigantic foot of the Town Hall porch as at the foot of a precipice. The monstrous black walls of the Town Hall rose and were merged in gloom; and the spire of the Town Hall, on whose summit stood a gold angel holding a gold crown, rose right into the heavens and was there lost. It was marvellous that this town, by adding stone by stone, had upreared this monument which, in expressing the secret nobility of its ideals, dwarfed the town. On every side of it the beerhouses, full of a dulled, savage ecstasy of life, gleamed brighter than the shops. Big James led Edwin down through the mysteries of the Crock Yard and up along the Bugg's Gutter, and so back to the Dragon.

CHAPTER 10 : *Free and Easy*

I

When Edwin, shyly, followed Big James into the assembly room of the Dragon, it already held a fair sprinkling of men, and newcomers continued to drop in. They were soberly and respectably clothed, though a few had knotted handkerchiefs round their necks instead of collars and ties. The occasion was a jollity of the Bursley Mutual Burial Club. This Club, a singular example of that dogged private co-operative enterprise which so sharply distinguishes English corporate life from the corporate life of other European countries, had lustily survived from a period when men were far less sure of a decent burial than they were then, in the very prosperous early seventies. It had helped to maintain the barbaric fashion of ostentatiously expensive funerals, out of which undertakers and beer-sellers made vast sums; but it had also provided a basis of common endeavour and of fellowship. And its respectability was intense, and at the same time broadminded. To be an established subscriber to the Burial Club was evidence of good character and of social spirit. The periodic jollities of this company of men whose professed aim was to bury each other, had a high reputation for excellence. Up till a year previously they had always been held at the Duck, in Duck Square, opposite; but Mr Enoch Peake, Chairman of the Club, had by persistent and relentless chicane, triumphing over immense influences, changed their venue to the Dragon, whose landlady, Mrs Louisa Loggerheads, he was then courting. (It must be stated that Mrs Louisa's name contained no slur of cantankerousness; it is merely the local word for a harmless plant, the knapweed.) He had now won Mrs Loggerheads, after being a widower thrice, and with her the second best 'house' in the town.

There were long benches down the room, with forms on either side of them. Big James, not without pomp, escorted a blushing Edwin to the end of one of these tables, near a small raised platform that occupied the extremity of the room. Over this platform was printed a legend : 'As a bird is known by its note –'; and over the legend was a full-rigged ship in a glass case, and a pair of antlers. The walls of the room were dark brown, the ceiling grey with soot of various sorts, and the floor tiled red and-black and sanded. Smoke rose in spirals from about a score of churchwarden pipes and as many cutties, which were charged from tin pouches, and lighted by spills of newspaper from the three double gas-jets that hung down over the benches. Two middle-aged women, one in black and the other checked, served beer, porter, and stout in mugs, and gin in glasses, passing in and out through a side door. The company talked little, and it had not yet begun seriously to drink; but, sprawled about in attitudes of restful abeyance, it was smoking religiously, and the flat noise of solemn expectorations punctuated the minutes. Edwin was easily the youngest person present – the average age appeared to be about fifty – but nobody's curiosity seemed to be much stirred by his odd arrival, and he ceased gradually to blush. When, however, one of the women paused before him in silent question, and he had to explain that he required no drink because he had only called for a moment about a matter of business, he blushed again vigorously.

II

Then Mr Enoch Peake appeared. He was a short, stout old man, with fat hands, a red, minutely wrinkled face, and very small eyes. Greeted with the respect due to the owner of Cocknage Gardens, a sporting resort where all the best foot-racing and rabbit-coursing took place, he accepted it in somnolent indifference, and immediately took off his coat and sat down in cotton shirt-sleeves. Then he pulled out a red handkerchief and his tobacco-box, and set them on the table. Big James motioned to Edwin.

'Evening, Mr Peake,' said Big James, crossing the floor, 'and here's a young gent wishful for two words with you.'

Mr Peake stared vacantly.

'Young Mr Clayhanger,' explained Big James.

'It's about this card,' Edwin began, in a whisper, drawing the wedding card sheepishly from his pocket. 'Father had to go to Manchester,' he added, when he had finished.

Mr Enoch Peake seized the card in both hands, and examined it; and Edwin could hear his heavy breathing.

Mrs Louisa Loggerheads, a comfortable, smiling administrative woman of fifty, showed herself at the service-door, and nodded with dignity to a few of the habitués.

'Missis is at door,' said Big James to Mr Peake.

'Is her?' muttered Mr Peake, not interrupting his examination of the card.

One of the serving-women, having removed Mr Peake's coat, brought a new churchwarden, filled it, and carefully directed the tip towards his tight little mouth : the lips closed on it. Then she lighted a spill and applied it to the distant bowl, and the mouth puffed; and then the woman deposited the bowl cautiously on the bench. Lastly, she came with a small glass of sloe gin. Mr Peake did not move.

At length Mr Peake withdrew the pipe from his mouth, and after an interval said –

'Aye !'

He continued to stare at the card, now held in one hand.

'And is it to be printed in silver?' Edwin asked.

Mr Peake took a few more puffs.

'Aye !'

When he had stared further for a long time at the card, his hand moved slowly with it towards Edwin, and Edwin resumed possession of it.

Mrs Louisa Loggerheads had now vanished.

'Missis has gone,' said Big James.

'Has her?' muttered Mr Peake.

Edwin rose to leave, though unwillingly; but Big James asked him in polite reproach whether he should not stay for the first song. He nodded, encouraged; and sat down. He did not know that the uppermost idea in Big James's mind for an hour past had been that Edwin would hear him sing.

Mr Peake lifted his glass, held it from him, approached his lips towards it, and emptied it at a draught. He then glanced round and said thickly – 'Gentlemen all, Mester Smallrice, Mester Harracles, Mester

Rampick, and Mester Yarlett will now oblige with one o' th' ould favourites.'

There was some applause, a few coats were removed, and Mr Peake fixed himself in a contemplative attitude.

III

Messrs Arthur Smallrice, Abraham Harracles, Jos Rawnpike, and James Yarlett rose, stepped heavily on to the little platform, and stood in a line with their hands in their pockets. 'As a bird is known by its note –' was hidden by the rampart of their shoulders. They had no music. They knew the music; they had sung it a thousand times. They knew precisely the effects which they wished to produce, and the means of production. They worked together like an inspired machine. Mr Arthur Smallrice gave a rapid glance into a corner, and from the corner a concertina spoke – one short note. Then began, with no hesitating shuffling preliminaries nor mute consultations, the singing of that classic quartet, justly celebrated from Hull to Wigan and from Northallerton to Lichfield, 'Loud Ocean's Roar'. The thing was performed with absolute assurance and perfection. Mr Arthur Smallrice did the yapping of the short waves on the foam-veiled rocks, and Big James in fullest grandeur did the long and mighty rolling of the deep. It was majestic, terrific, and overwhelming. Many bars before the close Edwin was thrilled, as by an exquisite and vast revelation. He tingled from head to foot. He had never heard any singing like it, or any singing in any way comparable to it. He had never guessed that song held such possibilities of emotion. The pure and fine essential qualities of the voices, the dizzying harmonies, the fugal calls and responses, the strange relief of the unisons, and above all the free, natural mien of the singers, proudly aware that they were producing something beautiful that could not be produced more beautifully, conscious of unchallenged supremacy – all this enfevered him to an unprecedented and self-astonished enthusiasm.

He murmured under his breath, as 'Loud Ocean's Roar' died away and the little voices of the street supervened : 'By Gad! By Gad!'

The applause was generous. Edwin stamped and clapped with childlike violence and fury. Mr Peake slowly and regularly thumped one fist on the bench, puffing the while. Glasses and mugs could be seen, but not heard, dancing. Mr Arthur Smallrice, Mr Abraham Harracles, Mr Jos Rawnpike, and Mr James Yarlett, entirely inattentive to the acclamations, stepped heavily from the platform and sat down. When Edwin caught Big James's eye he clapped again, reanimating the general approval, and Big James gazed at him with bland satisfaction. Mr Enoch Peake was now, save for the rise and fall of his great chest, as immobile and brooding as an Indian god.

IV

Edwin did not depart. He reflected that, even if his father should come home earlier than the last train and prove curious, it would be impossible for him to know the exact moment at which his son had been able to have speech with Mr Enoch Peake on the important matter of business. For aught his father could ever guess he might have been prevented from obtaining the attention of the chairman of the proceedings until, say, eleven o'clock. Also, he meant to present his conduct to his father in the light of an enterprising and fearless action showing a marked aptitude for affairs. Mr Enoch Peake, whom his father was anxious to flatter, had desired his father's company at the Dragon, and, to save the situation, Edwin had courageously gone instead : that was it.

Besides, he would have stayed in any case. His mind was elevated above the fear of consequences.

There was some concertina-playing, with a realistic imitation of church bells borne on the wind from a distance; and then the Bursley Prize Handbell Ringers (or Campanologists) produced a whole family of real bells from under a form, and the ostler and the two women arranged a special table, and the campanologists fixed their bells on it and themselves round it, and performed a selection of Scotch and Irish airs, without once deceiving themselves as to the precise note which a chosen bell would emit when duly shaken.

Singular as was this feat, it was far less so than a young man's performance on the ophicleide, a serpentine instrument that coiled round and about its player, and when breathed into persuasively gave forth prodigious brassy sounds that resembled the night-noises of beasts of prey. This item roused the Indian god from his umbilical contemplations, and as the young ophicleide player, somewhat breathless, passed down the room with his brazen creature in his arms, Mr Enoch Peake pulled him by the jacket-tail.

'Eh !' said Mr Enoch Peake. 'Is that the ophicleide as thy father used to play at th' owd church?'

'Yes, Mr Peake,' said the young man, with bright respect.

Mr Peake dropped his eyes again, and when the young man had gone, he murmured, to his stomach –

'I well knowed it were th' ophicleide as his father used to play at th' owd church;' And suddenly starting up, he continued hoarsely, 'Gentlemen all, Mr James Yarlett will now kindly oblige with "The Miller of the Dee".' And one of the women relighted his pipe and served him with beer.

V

Big James's rendering of 'The Miller of the Dee' had been renowned in the Five Towns since 1852. It was classical, hallowed. It was the only possible rendering of 'The Miller of the Dee'. If the greatest bass in the world had come incognito to Bursley and sung 'The Miller of the Dee', people would have said, 'Ah! But ye should hear Big James sing it!' It suited Big James. The sentiments of the song were his sentiments; he expressed them with natural simplicity; but at the same time they underwent a certain refinement at his hands; for even when he sang at his loudest Big James was refined, natty, and restrained. His instinctive gentlemanliness was invincible and all-pervading. And the real beauty and enormous power of his magnificent voice saved him by its mere distinction from the charge of being finicking. The simple sound of the voice gave pleasure. And the simple production of that sound was Big James's deepest joy. Amid all the expected loud applause the giant looked naïvely for Edwin's boyish mad enthusiasm, and felt it; and was thrilled, and very glad that he had brought Edwin. As for Edwin, Edwin was humbled that he should have been so blind to what Big James was. He had always regarded Big James as a dull, decent, somewhat peculiar fellow in a dirty apron, who was his father's foreman. He had actually talked once to Big James of the wonderful way in which Maggie and Clara sang, and Big James had been properly respectful. But the singing of Maggie and Clara was less than nothing, the crudest amateurism, compared to these public performances of Big James's. Even the accompanying concertina was far more cleverly handled than the Clayhanger piano had ever been handled. Yes, Edwin was humbled. And he had a great wish to be able to do something brilliantly himself – he knew not what. The intoxication of the desire for glory was upon him as he sat amid those shirt-sleeved men, near the brooding Indian god, under a crawling bluish canopy of smoke, gazing absently at the legend : 'As the bird is known by its note –'.

After an interval, during which Mr Enoch Peake was roused more than once, a man with a Lancashire accent recited a poem entitled 'The Patent Hairbrushing Machine', the rotary hairbrush being at that time an exceedingly piquant novelty that had only been heard of in the barbers' shops of the Five Towns, though travellers to Manchester could boast that they had sat under it. As the principle of the new machine was easily grasped, and the sensations induced by it easily imagined, the recitation had a success which was indicated by slappings of thighs and great blowings-off of mirth. But Mr Enoch Peake preserved his tranquillity throughout it, and immediately it was over he announced with haste –

'Gentlemen all, Miss Florence Simcox – or shall us say Mrs Offlow, wife of the gentleman who has just obliged – the champion female clog-dancer of the Midlands, will now oblige.'

VI

These words put every man whom they surprised into a state of unusual animation; and they surprised most of the company. It may be doubted whether a female clog-dancer had ever footed it in Bursley. Several public-houses possessed local champions – of a street, of a village – but these were emphatically not women. Enoch Peake had arranged this daring item in the course of his afternoon's business at Cocknage Gardens, Mr Offlow being an expert in ratting terriers, and Mrs Offlow happening to be on a tour with her husband through the realms of her championship, a tour which mingled the varying advantages derivable from terriers, recitations, and clogs. The affair was therefore respectable beyond cavil.

Nevertheless when Florence shone suddenly at the service-door, the shortness of her red-and-black velvet skirts, and the undeniable complete visibility of her rounded calves produced an uneasy and agreeable impression that Enoch Peake, for a chairman of the Mutual Burial Club, had gone rather far, superbly far, and that his moral ascendancy over Louisa Loggerheads must indeed be truly astonishing. Louisa now stood gravely behind the dancer, in the shadow of the doorway, and the contrast between her and Florence was in every way striking enough to prove what a wonderful and mysterious man Enoch Peake was. Florence was accustomed to audiences. She was a pretty, doll-like woman, if inclined to amplitude; but the smile between those shaking golden ringlets had neither the modesty nor the false modesty nor the docility that Bursley was accustomed to think proper to the face of woman. It could have stared down any man in the place, except perhaps Mr Peake.

The gestures of Mr Offlow, and her gestures, as he arranged and prepared the surface of the little square dancing-board that was her throne, showed that he was the husband of Florence Simcox rather than she the wife of Offlow the reciter and dog-fancier. Further, it was his rôle to play the concertina to her: he had had to learn the concertina – possibly a secret humiliation for one whose judgement in terriers was not excelled in many public-houses.

VII

She danced; and the service-doorway showed a vista of open-mouthed scullions. There was no sound in the room, save the concertina and the champion clogs. Every eye was fixed on those clogs; even the little eyes of Mr Peake quitted the button of his waistcoat and burned like diamond points on those clogs. Florence herself chiefly gazed on those clogs, but occasionally her nonchalant petulant gaze would wander up and down her bare arms and across her bosom. At intervals, with her ringed fingers she would lift the short skirt – a nothing, an imperceptibility, half an inch, with glance downcast; and the effect was profound, recondite, inexplicable. Her style was not that of a male clog-dancer, but it was indubitably clog-dancing, full of marvels to the connoisseur, and to the profane naught but a highly complicated series of wooden noises. Florence's face began to perspire. Then the concertina ceased playing – so that an undistracted attention might be given to the supremely difficult figures of the dance.

And thus was rendered back to the people in the charming form of beauty that which the instinct of the artist had taken from the sordid ugliness of the people. The clog, the very emblem of the servitude and the squalor of brutalized populations, was changed, on the light feet of this favourite, into the medium of grace. Few of these men but at some time of their lives had worn the clog, had clattered in it through winter's slush, and through the freezing darkness before dawn, to the manufactory and the mill and the mine, whence after a day of labour under discipline more than military, they had clattered back to their little candle-lighted homes. One of the slatterns behind the doorway actually stood in clogs to watch the dancer. The clog meant everything that was harsh, foul, and desolating; it summoned images of misery and disgust. Yet on those feet that had never worn it seriously, it became the magic instrument of pleasure, waking dulled wits and forgotten aspirations, putting upon everybody an enchantment . . . And then, suddenly, the dancer threw up one foot as high as her head and brought two clogs down together like a double mallet on the board, and stood still. It was over.

Mrs Louisa Loggerheads turned nervously away, pushing her servants in front of her. And when the society of mutual buriers had recovered from the startling shameless insolence of that last high kick, it gave the rein to its panting excitement, and roared and stamped. Edwin was staggered. The blood swept into his face, a hot tide. He was ravished, but he was also staggered. He did not know what to think of Florence, the champion female clog-dancer. He felt that she was wondrous; he felt that he could have gazed at her all night; but he felt that she had put him under the necessity of reconsidering some of his fundamental opinions. For example, he was obliged to admit within himself a lessening of scorn for the attitude towards each other of Miss Ingamells and her young man. He saw those things in a new light. And he reflected, dazzled by the unforeseen chances of existence : 'Yesterday I was at school – and today I see this !' He was so preoccupied by his own intimate sensations that the idea of applauding never occurred to him, until he perceived his conspicuousness in not applauding, whereupon he clapped self-consciously.

VIII

Miss Florence Simcox, somewhat breathless, tripped away, with simulated coyness and many curtseys. She had done her task, and as a woman she had to go : this was a gathering of members of the Mutual Burial Club, a masculine company, and not meet for females. The men pulled themselves together, remembering that their proudest quality was a stoic callousness that nothing could overthrow. They refilled pipes, ordered more beer, and resumed the mask of invulnerable solemnity.

'Aye !' muttered Mr Enoch Peake.

Edwin, with a great effort, rose, and walked out. He would have liked to say good night to Big James; he did not deny that he ought to have done so; but he dared not complicate his exit. On the pavement outside, in the warm damp night, a few loitering listeners stood doggedly before an open window, hearkening, their hands deep in their pockets, motionless. And Edwin could hear Mr Enoch Peake : 'Gentlemen all, Mester Arthur Smallrice, Mester Abraham Harracles, Mester Joe Rampick, and Mester James Yarlett –'

CHAPTER 11 : *Son and Father*

I

Later that evening, Edwin sat at a small deal table in the embrasure of the dormer window of the empty attic next to his bedroom. During the interval between tea and the rendezvous with Big James he had formally planted his flag in that room. He had swept it out with a 'long-brush' while Clara stood at the door giggling at the spectacle and telling him that he had no right thus to annex territory in the absence of the overlord. He had mounted a pair of steps, and put a lot of lumber through a trap at the head of the stairs into the loft. And he had got a table, a lamp, and chair. That was all that he needed for the moment. He had gone out to meet Big James with his head quite half-full of this vague attic-project, but the night sights of Bursley, and especially the music at the Dragon, and still more especially the dancing at the Dragon, had almost expelled the attic-project from his head. When he returned unobtrusively into the house and learnt from a disturbed Mrs Nixon, who was sewing in the kitchen, that he was understood to be in his new attic, and that his sisters had gone to bed, the enchantment of the attic had instantly resumed much of its power over him, and he had hurried upstairs fortified with a slice of bread and half a cold sausage. He had eaten the food absently in gulps while staring at the cover of *Cazenove's Architectural Views of European Capitals*, abstracted from the shop without payment. Then he had pinned part of a sheet of cartridge-paper on an old drawing-board which he possessed, and had sat down. For his purpose the paper ought to have been soaked and stretched on the board with paste, but that would have meant a delay of seven or eight hours, and he was not willing to wait. Though he could not concentrate his mind to begin, his mind could not be reconciled to waiting. So he had decided to draw his picture in pencil outline, and then stretch the paper early on Sunday morning; it would dry during chapel. His new box of paints, a cracked T-square, and some india-rubber also lay on the table.

He had chosen 'View of the Cathedral of Notre-Dame, Paris, from the Pont des Arts'. It pleased him by the coloration of the old houses in front of Notre-Dame, and the reflections in the water of the Seine, and the elusive blueness of the twin towers amid the pale grey clouds of a Parisian sky. A romantic scene! He wanted to copy it exactly, to re-create it from beginning to end, to feel the thrill of producing each wonderful effect himself. Yet he sat inactive. He sat and vaguely gazed at the slope of Trafalgar Road with its double row of yellow jewels, beautifully ascending in fire to the ridge of the horizon and there losing itself in the deep and solemn purple of the summer night; and he thought how ugly and commonplace all that was, and how different from all that were the noble capitals of Europe. Scarcely a sound came through the open window; song doubtless still gushed forth at the Dragon, and revellers would not for hours awake the street on their way to the exacerbating atmosphere of home.

II

He had no resolution to take up the pencil. Yet after the Male Glee Party had sung 'Loud Ocean's Roar', he remembered that he had a most clear and distinct impulse to begin drawing architecture at once, and to do something grand and fine, as grand and fine as the singing, something that would thrill people as the singing thrilled. If he had not rushed home instantly it was solely because he had been held back by the stronger desire to hear more music and by the hope of further novel and exciting sensations. But Florence the clog-dancer had easily diverted the seeming-powerful current of his mind. He wanted as much as ever to do wondrous things, and to do them soon, but it appeared to him that he must think out first the enigmatic subject of Florence. Never had he seen any female creature as he saw her, and ephemeral images of her were continually forming and dissolving before him. He could come to no conclusion at all about the subject of Florence. Only his boyish pride was gradually being beaten back by an oncoming idea that up to that very evening he had been a sort of rather silly kid with no eyes in his head.

It was in order to ignore for a time this unsettling and humiliating idea that, finally, he began to copy the outlines of the Parisian scene on his cartridge-paper. He was in no way a skilled draughtsman, but he had dabbled in pencils and colours, and he had lately picked up from a handbook the hint that in blocking out a drawing the first thing to do was to observe what points were vertically under what points, and what points horizontal with what points. He seemed to see the whole secret of draughtsmanship in this priceless counsel, which, indeed, with an elementary knowledge of geometry acquired at school, and the familiarity of his fingers with a pencil, constituted the whole of his technical equipment. All the rest was mere desire. Happily the architectural nature of the subject made it more amenable than, say, a rural landscape to the use of a T-square and common sense. And Edwin considered that he was doing rather well until, quitting measurements and rulings, he arrived at the stage of drawing the detail of the towers. Then at once the dream of perfect accomplishment began to fade at the edges, and the crust of faith to yield ominously. Each stroke was a falling-away from the ideal, a blow to hope.

And suddenly a yawn surprised him, and recalled him to the existence of his body. He thought: 'I can't really be tired. It would be absurd to go to bed.' For his theory had long been that the notions of parents about bedtime were indeed absurd, and that he would be just as thoroughly reposed after three hours' sleep as after ten. And now that he was a man he meant to practise his theory so far as circumstances allowed. He looked at his watch. It was turned half past eleven. A delicious wave of joy and of satisfaction animated him. He had never been up so late, within his recollection, save on a few occasions when even infants were allowed to be up late. He was alone, secreted, master of his time and his activity, his mind charged with novel impressions, and a congenial work in progress. Alone? . . . It was at if he was spiritually alone in the vast solitude of the night. It was as if he could behold the unconscious forms of all humanity, sleeping. This feeling that only he had preserved consciousness and energy, that he was the sole active possessor of the mysterious night, affected him in the most exquisite manner. He had not been so nobly happy in his life. And at the same time he was proud, in a childlike way, of being up so late.

He heard the door being pushed open, and he gave a jump and turned his head. His father stood in the entrance to the attic.

'Hello, father!' he said weakly, ingratiatingly.

'What art doing at this time o' night, lad?' Darius Clayhanger demanded.

Strange to say, the autocrat was not angered by the remarkable sight in front of him. Edwin knew that his father would probably come home from Manchester on the mail train, which would stop to set down a passenger at Shawport by suitable arrangement. And he had expected that his father would go to bed, as usual on such evenings, after having eaten the supper left for him in the sitting-room. His father's bedroom was next door to the sitting-room. Save for Mrs Nixon in a distant nook, Edwin had the attic floor to himself. He ought to have been as safe from intrusion there as in the farthest capital of Europe. His father did not climb the attic stairs once in six months. So that he had regarded himself as secure. Still, he must have positively forgotten the very existence of his father; he must have been 'lost', otherwise he could not but have heard the footsteps on the stairs.

'I was just drawing,' said Edwin, with a little more confidence.

He looked at his father and saw an old man, a man who for him had always been old, generally harsh, often truculent, and seldom indulgent. He saw an ugly, undistinguished, and somewhat vulgar man (far less dignified, for instance, than Big James); a man who had his way by force and scarcely ever by argument; a man whose arguments for or against a given course were simply pitiable, if not despicable. He sometimes indeed thought that there must be a peculiar twist in his father's brain which prevented him from appreciating an adverse point in a debate; he had ceased to expect that his father would listen to reason. Latterly he was always surprised when, as tonight, he caught a glance of mild benevolence on that face; yet he would never fail to respond to such a mood eagerly, without resentment. It might be said that he regarded his father as he regarded the weather, fatalistically. No more than against the weather would he have dreamed of bearing malice against his father, even had such a plan not been unwise and dangerous. He was convinced that his father's interest in him was about the same as the sun's interest in him. His father was nearly always wrapped in business affairs, and seemed to come to the trifling affairs of Edwin with difficulty, as out of an absorbing engrossment.

Assuredly he would have been amazed to know that his father had been thinking of him all the afternoon and evening. But it was so. Darius Clayhanger had been nervous as to the manner in which the boy would

acquit himself in the bit of business which had been confided to him.
It was the boy's first bit of business. Straightforward as it was, the boy
might muddle it, might omit a portion of it, might say the wrong thing,
might forget. Darius hoped for the best, but he was afraid. He saw in his
son an amiable, irresponsible fool. He compared Edwin at sixteen with
himself at the same age. Edwin had never had a care, never suffered a
privation, never been forced to think for himself. (Darius might more
justly have put it – never been allowed to think for himself.) Edwin had
lived in cotton-wool, and knew less of the world than his father had
known at half his years; much less. Darius was sure that Edwin had
never even come near suspecting the miracles which his father had
accomplished : this was true, and not merely was Edwin stupendously
ignorant, and even pettily scornful, of realities, but he was ignorant of
his own ignorance. Education ! . . . Darius snorted. To Darius it seemed
that Edwin's education was like lying down in an orchard in lovely summer and having ripe fruit dropped into your mouth . . . A cocky infant !
A girl ! And yet there was something about Edwin that his father
admired, even respected and envied . . . an occasional gesture, an attitude in walking, an intonation, a smile. Edwin, his own son, had a personal distinction that he himself could never compass. Edwin talked
more correctly than his father. He thought differently from his father.
He had an original grace. In the essence of his being he was superior
to both his father and his sisters. Sometimes when his father saw him
walking along the street, or coming into a room, or uttering some simple
phrase, or shrugging his shoulders, Darius was aware of a faint thrill.
Pride? Perhaps; but he would never have admitted it. An agreeable
perplexity rather – a state of being puzzled how he, so common, had
begotten a creature so subtly aristocratic . . . aristocratic was the word.
And Edwin seemed so young, fragile, innocent, and defenceless.

IV

Darius advanced into the attic.

'What about that matter of Enoch Peake's?' he asked, hoping and
fearing, really anxious for his son. He defended himself against probable
disappointment by preparing to lapse into savage paternal pessimism
and disgust at the futility of an off-spring nursed in luxury.

'Oh! It's all right,' said Edwin eagerly. 'Mr Peake sent word he
couldn't come, and he wanted you to go across to the Dragon this
evening. So I went instead.' It sounded dashingly capable.

He finished the recital, and added that of course Big James had not
been able to proceed with the job.

'And where's the proof?' demanded Darius. His relief expressed
itself in a superficial surliness; but Edwin was not deceived. As his father

gazed mechanically at the proof that Edwin produced hurriedly from his pocket, he added with a negligent air :

'There was a free-and-easy on at the Dragon, father.'

'Was there?' muttered Darius.

Edwin saw that whatever danger existed was now over.

'And I suppose,' said Darius, with assumed grimness, 'if I hadn't happened to ha' seen a light from th' bottom o' th' attic stairs I should never have known aught about all this here?' He indicated the cleansed attic, the table, the lamp, and the apparatus of art.

'Oh yes, you would, father !' Edwin reassured him.

Darius came nearer. They were close together, Edwin twisted on the cane-chair, and his father almost over him. The lamp smelt, and gave off a stuffy warmth; the open window, through which came a wandering air, was a black oblong; the triangular side walls of the dormer shut them intimately in; the house slept.

'What art up to?'

The tone was benignant. Edwin had not been ordered abruptly off to bed, with a reprimand for late hours and silly proceedings generally. He sought the reason in vain. One reason was that Darius Clayhanger had made a grand bargain at Manchester in the purchase of a second-hand printing machine.

'I'm copying this,' he replied slowly, and then all the details tumbled rashly out of his mouth, one after the other. 'Oh, father! I found this book in the shop, packed away on a top shelf, and I want to borrow it. I only want to borrow it. And I've bought this paint-box, out of auntie's half-sovereign. I paid Miss Ingamells the full price. . . . I thought I'd have a go at some of these architecture things.'

Darius glared at the copy.

'Humph !'

'It's only just started, you know.'

'Them prize books – have ye done all that?'

'Yes, father.'

'And put all the prices down, as I told ye?'

'Yes, father.'

Then a pause. Edwin's heart was beating hard.

'I want to do some of these architecture things,' he repeated. No remark from his father. Then he said, fastening his gaze intensely on the table : 'You know, father, what I should really like to be – I should like to be an architect.'

It was out. He had said it.

'Should ye?' said his father, who attached no importance of any kind to this avowal of a preference. 'Well, what you want is a bit o' business training for a start, I'm thinking.'

78

'Oh, of course!' Edwin concurred, with pathetic eagerness, and added a piece of information for his father: 'I'm only sixteen, aren't I?'

'Sixteen ought to ha' been in bed this two hours and more. Off with ye!'

Edwin retired in an extraordinary state of relief and happiness.

CHAPTER 12 : *Machinery*

I

Rather more than a week later, Edwin had so far entered into the life of his father's business that he could fully share the excitement caused by an impending solemnity in the printing office. He was somewhat pleased with himself, and especially with his seriousness. The memory of school was slipping away from him in the most extraordinary manner. His only school-friend, Charlie Orgreave, had departed, with all the multitudinous Orgreaves, for a month in Wales. He might have written to the Sunday; the Sunday might have written to him : but the idea of writing did not occur to either of them; they were both still sufficiently childlike to accept with fatalism all the consequences of parental caprice. Orgreave senior had taken his family to Wales; the boys were thus separated, and there was an end of it. Edwin regretted this, because Orgreave senior happened to be a very successful architect, and hence there were possibilities of getting into an architectural atmosphere. He had never been inside the home of the Sunday, nor the Sunday in his – a schoolboy friendship can flourish in perfect independence of home – but he nervously hoped that on the return of the Orgreave regiment from Wales, something favourable to his ambitions – he knew not what – would come to pass. In the meantime he was conscientiously doing his best to acquire a business training, as his father had suggested. He gave himself with an enthusiasm almost religious to the study of business methods. All the force of his resolve to perfect himself went for the moment into this immediate enterprise, and he was sorry that business methods were not more complex, mysterious, and original than they seemed to be : he was also sorry that his father did not show a greater interest in his industry and progress.

He no longer wanted to 'play' now. He despised play. His unique wish was to work. It struck him as curious and delightful that he really enjoyed work. Work had indeed become play. He could not do enough work to satisfy his appetite. And after the work of the day, scorning all silly notions about exercise and relaxation, he would spend the evening in his beautiful new attic, copying designs, which he would sometimes rise early to finish. He thought he had conquered the gross body, and that it was of no account. Even the desolating failures which his copies invariably proved did not much discourage him; besides, one of them had impressed both Maggie and Clara. He copied with laborious ardour undiminished. And further, he masterfully appropriated Maggie's ticket for the Free Library, pending the preliminaries to the possession of a ticket of his own, to procure a volume on architecture. From timidity, from a singular false shame, he kept this volume in the attic, like a crime; nobody knew what the volume was. Evidence of a strange trait in his character; a trait perhaps not defensible! He argued with himself that having told his father plainly that he wanted to be an architect, he need do nothing else aggressive for the present. He had agreed to the suggestion about business training, and he must be loyal to his agreement. He pointed out to himself how right his father was. At sixteen one could scarcely begin to be an architect; it was too soon; and a good business training would not be out of place in any career or profession.

He was so wrapped up in his days and his nights that he forgot to inquire why earthenware was made in just the Five Towns. He had grown too serious for trifles – and all in about a week! True, he was feeling the temporary excitement of the printing office, which was perhaps expressed boyishly by the printing staff; but he reckoned that his share of it was quite adult, frowningly superior, and in a strictly business sense justifiable and even proper.

II

Darius Clayhanger's printing office was a fine example of the policy of makeshift which governed and still governs the commercial activity of the Five Towns. It consisted of the first floor of a nondescript building which stood at the bottom of the irregularly shaped yard behind the house and shop, and which formed the southern boundary of the Clayhanger premises. The antique building had once been part of an old-fashioned pot-works, but that must have been in the eighteenth century. Kilns and chimneys of all ages, sizes, and tints rose behind it to prove that this part of the town was one of the old manufacturing quarters. The ground floor of the building, entirely inaccessible from Clayhanger's yard, had a separate entrance of its own in an alley that branched off from Woodisun Bank, ran parallel to Wedgwood Street, and stopped abruptly at the back gate of a saddler's workshop. In the narrow entry you were like a creeping animal amid the undergrowth of a forest of chimneys, ovens, and high blank walls. This ground floor had been a stable for many years; it was now, however, a baker's storeroom.

Once there had been an interior staircase leading from the ground floor to the first floor, but it had been suppressed in order to save floor space, and an exterior staircase constructed with its foot in Clayhanger's yard. To meet the requirement of the staircase, one of the first-floor windows had been transformed into a door. Further, as the staircase came against one of the ground-floor windows, and as Clayhanger's predecessor had objected to those alien windows overlooking his yard, and as numerous windows were anyhow unnecessary to a stable, all the ground-floor windows had been closed up with oddments of brick and tile, giving to the wall a very variegated and chequered appearance. Thus the ground floor and the first floor were absolutely divorced, the former having its entrance and light from the public alley, the latter from the private yard.

The first floor had been a printing office for over seventy years. All the machinery in it had had to be manoeuvred up the rickety stairs, or put through one of the windows on either side of the window that had been turned into a door. When Darius Clayhanger, in his audacity, decided to print by steam, many people imagined that he would at last be compelled to rent the ground-floor or to take other premises. But no! The elasticity of the makeshift policy was not yet fully stretched. Darius, in consultation with a jobbing builder, came happily to the conclusion that he could 'manage', that he could 'make things do', by adding to the top of his stairs a little landing for an engine-shed. This was done, and the engine and boiler perched in the air, the shaft of the engine went through the wall; the chimney-pipe of the boiler ran up straight to the level of the roof-ridge, and was stayed with pieces of wire. A new chimney had also been pierced in the middle of the roof, for the uses of a heating stove. The original chimneys had been allowed to fall into decay. Finally, a new large skylight added interest to the roof. In a general way, the building resembled a suit of clothes that had been worn, during four of the seven ages of man, by an untidy husband with a tidy and economical wife, and then given by the wife to a poor relation of a somewhat different figure to finish. All that could be said of it was that it survived and served.

But these considerations occurred to nobody.

III

Edwin, quite unaware that he was an instrument in the hands of his Auntie Clara's Providence, left the shop without due excuse and passed down the long blue-paved yard towards the printing office. He imagined that was being drawn thither simply by his own curiosity – a curiosity, however, which he considered to be justifiable, and even laudable. The yard showed signs that the unusual had lately been happening there. Its brick pavement, in the narrow branch of it that led to the double gates in Woodisun Bank (those gates which said to the casual visitor, 'No Admittance except on Business'), was muddy, littered, and damaged, as though a Juggernaut had passed that way. Ladders reclined against the walls. Moreover, one of the windows of the office had been taken out of its frame, leaving naught but an oblong aperture. Through this aperture Edwin could see the busy, eager forms of his father, Big James, and Chawner. Through this aperture had been lifted, in parts and by the employment of every possible combination of lever and pulley, the printing machine which Darius Clayhanger had so successfully purchased in Manchester on the day of the free-and-easy at the Dragon.

At the top of the flight of steps two apprentices, one nearly 'out of his time', were ministering to the engine, which that morning did not happen to be running. The engine, giving glory to the entire establishment by virtue of the imposing word 'steam', was a crotchety and capricious thing, constant only in its tendency to break down. No more reliance could be placed on it than on a pampered donkey. Sometimes it would run, and sometimes it would not run, but nobody could safely prophesy its moods. Of the several machines it drove but one, the grand cylinder, the last triumph of the ingenuity of man, and even that had to be started by hand before the engine would consent to work it. The staff hated the engine, except during those rare hours when one of its willing moods coincided with a pressure of business. Then, when the steam was sputtering and the smoke smoking and the piston throbbing, and the leathern belt travelling round and round and the complete building a-tremble and a-clatter, and an attendant with clean hands was feeding the sheets at one end of the machine and another attendant with clean hands taking them off at the other, at the rate of twenty copies per sixty seconds – then the staff loved the engine and meditated upon the wonders of their modern civilization. The engine had been known to do its five thousand in an afternoon, and its horse-power was only one.

IV

Edwin could not keep out the printing office. He went inconspicuously and, as it were, by accident up the stone steps, and disappeared into the interior. When you entered the office you were first of all impressed by the multiplicity of odours competing for your attention, the chief among them being those of ink, oil, and paraffin. Despite the fact that the door was open and one window gone, the smell and heat in the office on that warm morning were notable. Old sheets of the *Manchester Examiner* had been pinned over the skylight to keep out the sun, but, as these were torn and rent, the sun was not kept out. Nobody, however, seemed to suffer inconvenience. After the odours, the remarkable feature of the place was the quantity of machinery on its uneven floor. Timid employees had occasionally suggested to Darius that the floor might yield one day and add themselves and all the machinery to the baker's stores below; but Darius knew that floors never did yield.

In the middle of the floor was a huge and heavy heating stove, whose pipe ran straight upwards to the visible roof. The mighty cylinder machine stood to the left hand. Behind was a small, rough-and-ready binding department with guillotine cutting machine, a cardboard-cutting machine, and a perforating machine, trifles by the side of the cylinder, but still each of them formidable masses of metal heavy enough to crush a horse; the cutting machines might have served to illustrate the French Revolution, and the perforating machine the Holy Inquisition.

Then there was what was called in the office the 'old machine', a relic of Clayhanger's predecessor, and at least eighty years old. It was one of those machines whose worn physiognomies, full of character, show at once that they have a history. In construction it carried solidity to an absurd degree. Its pillars were like the piles of a pier. Once, in a historic rat-catching, a rat had got up one of them, and a piece of smouldering brown paper had done what a terrier could not do. The machine at one period in its career had been enlarged, and the neat seaming of the metal was an ecstasy to the eye of a good workman. Long ago, it was known, this machine had printed a Reform newspaper at Stockport. Now, after thus participating in the violent politics of an age heroic and unhappy, it had been put to printing small posters of auctions and tea-meetings. Its movement was double : first that of a handle to bring the bed under the platen, and second, a lever pulled over to make contact between the type and the paper. It still worked perfectly. It was so solid, and it had been so honestly made, that it could never get out of order nor wear away. And, indeed, the conscientiousness and skill of artificers in the eighteenth century are still, through that resistless machine, producing their effect in the twentieth. But it needed a strong hand to bestir its smooth, plum-coloured limbs of metal, and a speed of a hundred an hour meant gentle perspiration. The machine was loved like an animal.

Near this honourable and lumbering survival stood pertly an Empire treadle-machine for printing envelopes and similar trifles. It was new, and full of natty little devices. It worked with the lightness of something unsubstantial. A child could actuate it, and it would print delicately a thousand envelopes an hour. This machine, with the latest purchase, which was away at the other end of the room near the large double-pointed case-rack, completed the tale of machines. That case-rack alone held fifty different founts of type, and there were other case-racks. The lead-rack was nearly as large, and beneath the lead-rack was a rack containing all those 'furnitures' which help to hold a forme of type together without betraying themselves to the reader of the printed sheet. And under the furniture rack was the 'random', full of galleys. Then there was a table with a top of solid stone, upon which the formes were bolted up. And there was the ink-slab, another solidity, upon which the inkrollers were inked. Rollers of various weightiness lay about, and large heavy cans, and many bottles, and metal galleys, and nameless fragments of metal. Everything contributed to the impression of immense ponderosity exceeding the imagination. The fancy of being pinned down by even the lightest of these constructions was excruciating. You moved about in narrow alleys among upstanding, unyielding metallic enormities, and you felt fragile and perilously soft.

V

The only unintimidating phenomena in the crowded place were the lye-brushes, the dusty job-files that hung from the great transverse beams, and the proof-sheets that were scattered about. These printed things showed to what extent Darius Clayhanger's establishment was a channel through which the life of the town had somehow to pass. Auctions, meetings, concerts, sermons, improving lectures, miscellaneous entertainments, programmes, catalogues, deaths, births, marriages, specifications, municipal notices, summonses, demands, receipts, subscription-lists, accounts, rate-forms, lists of voters, jury-lists, inaugurations, closures, bill-heads, handbills, addresses, visiting-cards, society rules, bargain-sales, lost and found notices : traces of all these matters, and more, were to be found in that office; it was impregnated with the human interest; it was dusty with the human interest; its hot smell seemed to you to come off life itself, if the real sentiment and love of life were sufficiently in you. A grand, stuffy, living, seething place, with all its metallic immobility !

VI

Edwin sidled towards the centre of interest, the new machine, which, however, was not a new machine. Darius Clayhanger did not buy more new things than he could help. His delight was to 'pick up' articles that were supposed to be 'as good as new'; occasionally he would even assert that an object bought second-hand was 'better than new', because it had been 'broken in', as if it were a horse. Nevertheless, the latest machine was, for a printing machine, nearly new : its age was four years only. It was a Demy Columbian Press, similar in conception and movement to the historic 'old machine' that had been through the Reform agitation; but how much lighter, how much handier, how much more ingenious and precise in the details of its working! A beautiful edifice, as it stood there, gazed on admiringly by the expert eyes of Darius, in his shirt-sleeves, Big James, in his royally flowing apron, and Chawner, the journeyman compositor, who, with the two apprentices outside, completed the staff! Aided by no mechanic more skilled than a day-labourer, those men had got the machine piecemeal into the office, and had duly erected it. At that day a foreman had to be equal to any-thing.

The machine appeared so majestic there, so solid and immovable, that it might ever have existed where it then was. Who would credit that, less than a fortnight earlier, it had stood equally majestic, solid, and immovable in Manchester? There remained nothing to show how the miracle had been accomplished, except a bandage of ropes round the lower pillars and some pulley-tackle hanging from one of the transverse beams exactly overhead. The situation of the machine in the workshop had been fixed partly by that beam above and partly by the run of the beams that supported the floor. The stout roof-beam enabled the arti-ficers to handle the great masses by means of the tackle; and as for the floor-beams, Darius had so far listened to warnings as to take them into account.

VII

'Take another impress, James,' said Darius. And when he saw Edwin, instead of asking the youth what he was wasting his time there for, he good-humouredly added : 'Just watch this, my lad.' Darius was pleased with himself, his men, and his acquisition. He was in one of his moods when he could charm; he was jolly, and he held up his chin. Two days before, so interested had he been in the Demy Columbian, he had actually gone through a bilious attack while scarcely noticing it! And now the whole complex operation had been brought to a triumphant conclusion.

Big James inserted the sheet of paper, with gentle and fine move-ments. The journeyman turned the handle, and the bed of the machine slid horizontally forward in frictionless, stately silence. And then Big James seized the lever with his hairy arm bared to the elbow, and pulled it over. The delicate process was done with minute and level exactitude; adjusted to the thirty-secondth of an inch, the great masses of metal had brought the paper and the type together and separated them again. In another moment Big James drew out the sheet, and the three men inspected it, each leaning over it. A perfect impression.

'Well,' said Darius, glowing, 'we've had a bit o' luck in getting that up! Never had less trouble! Shows we can do better without those

85

Foundry chaps than with 'em! James, ye can have a quart brought in, if ye'n a mind, but I won't have them apprentices drinking! No, I won't! Mrs Nixon'll give 'em some nettle-beer if they fancy it.'

He was benignant. The inauguration of a new machine deserved solemn recognition, especially on a hot day. It was an event.

'An infant in arms could turn this here,' murmured the journeyman, toying with the handle that moved the bed. It was an exaggeration, but an excusable, poetical exaggeration.

Big James wiped his wrists on his apron.

VIII

Then there was a queer sound of cracking somewhere, vague, faint, and yet formidable. Darius was standing between the machines and the dismantled window, his back to the latter. Big James and the journeyman rushed instinctively from the centre of the floor towards him. In a second the journeyman was on the window-sill.

'What art doing?' Darius demanded roughly but there was no sincerity in his voice.

'Th' floor!' the journeyman excitedly exclaimed.

Big James stood close to the wall.

'And what about th' floor?' Darius challenged him obstinately.

'One o' them beams is agoing,' stammered the journeyman.

'Rubbish!' shouted Darius. But simultaneously he motioned to Edwin to move from the middle of the room, and Edwin obeyed. All four listened, with nerves stretched to the tightest. Darius was biting his lower lip with his upper teeth. His humour had swiftly changed to the savage. Every warning that had been uttered for years past concerning that floor was remembered with startling distinctness. Every impatient reassurance offered by Darius for years past suddenly seemed fatuous and perverse. How could any man in his senses expect the old floor to withstand such a terrific strain as that to which Darius had at last dared to subject it? The floor ought by rights to have given way years ago! His men ought to have declined to obey instructions that were obviously insane. These and similar thoughts visited the minds of Big James and the journeyman.

As for Edwin, his excitement was, on balance, pleasurable. In truth, he could not kill in his mind the hope that the floor would yield. The greatness of the resulting catastrophe fascinated him. He knew that he should be disappointed if the catastrophe did not occur. That it would mean ruinous damage to the extent of hundreds of pounds, and enormous worry, did not influence him. His reason did not influence him, nor his personal danger. He saw a large hook in the wall to which he could cling when the exquisite crash came, and pictured a welter of broken machinery and timber ten feet below him, and the immense pother that the affair would create in the town.

IX

Darius would not lose his belief in his floor. He hugged it in mute fury. He would not climb on to the window-sill, nor tell Big James to do so, nor even Edwin. On the subject of the floor he was religious; he was above the appeal of the intelligence. He had always held passionately that the floor was immovable, and he always would. He had finally convinced himself of its omnipotent strength by the long process of assertion and reassertion. When a voice within him murmured that his belief in the floor had no scientific basis, he strangled the voice. So he remained, motionless, between the window and the machine.

No sound! No slightest sound! No tremor of the machine! But Darius's breathing could be heard after a moment.

He guffawed sneeringly.

'And what next?' he defiantly asked, scowling. 'What's amiss wi' ye all?' He put his hands in his pockets. 'Dun ye mean to tell me as –'

The younger apprentice entered from the engine-shed.

'Get back there!' rolled and thundered the voice of Big James. It was the first word he had spoken, and he did not speak it in frantic, hysteric command, but with a terrible and convincing mildness. The phrase fell on the apprentice like a sandbag, and he vanished.

Darius said nothing. There was another cracking sound, louder, and unmistakably beneath the bed of the machine. And at the same instant a flake of grimy plaster detached itself from the opposite wall and dropped into pale dust on the floor. And still Darius religiously did not move, and Big James would not move. They might have been under a spell. The journeyman jumped down incautiously into the yard.

X

And then Edwin, hardly knowing what he did, and certainly not knowing why he did it, walked quickly out on to the floor, seized the huge hook attached to the lower pulley of the tackle that hung from the roof-beam, pulled up the slack of the rope-bandage on the hind part of the machine, and stuck the hook into it, then walked quickly back. The hauling-rope of the tackle had been carried to the iron ring of a trap-door in the corner near Big James; this trap-door, once the outlet of the interior staircase from the ground-floor, had been nailed down many years previously. Big James dropped to his knees and tightened and knotted the rope. Another and much louder noise of cracking followed, the floor visibly yielded, and the hind-part of the machine visibly sank about a quarter of an inch. But no more. The tackle held. The strain was distributed between the beam above and the beam below, and equilibrium established.

'Out! Lad! Out!' cried Darius feebly, in the wreck, not of his workshop, but of his religion. And Edwin fled down the steps, pushing the mystified apprentices before him, and followed by the men. In the yard the journeyman, entirely self-centred, was hopping about on one leg and cursing.

XI

Darius, Big James, and Edwin stared in the morning sunshine at the aperture of the window and listened.

'Nay!' said Big James, after an eternity. 'He's saved it! He's saved th' old shop! But by gum – by gum –'

Darius turned to Edwin, and tried to say something; and then Edwin saw his father's face working into monstrous angular shaped, and saw the tears spurt out of his eyes, and was clutched convulsively in his father's shirt-sleeved arms. He was very proud, very pleased, but he did not like this embrace; it made him feel ashamed. He thought how Clara would have sniggered about it and caricatured it afterwards, had she witnessed it. And although he had incontestably done something which was very wonderful and very heroic, and which proved in him the most extraordinary presence of mind, he could not honestly glorify himself in his own heart, because it appeared to him that he had acted exactly like an automaton. He blankly marvelled, and thought the situation agreeably thrilling, if somewhat awkward. His father let him go. Then all Edwin's feelings gave place to an immense stupefaction at his father's truly remarkable behaviour. What! His father emotional! He had to begin to revise again his settled views.

CHAPTER 13 : One Result of Courage

I

By the next morning a certain tranquillity was restored.

It was only in this relative calm that the Clayhanger family and its dependants began to realize the intensity of the experience through which they had passed, and, in particular, the strain of waiting for events after the printing office had been abandoned by its denizens. The rumour of what had happened, and of what might have happened, had spread about the premises in an instant, and in another instant all the women had collected in the yard; even Miss Ingamells had betrayed the sacred charge of the shop. Ten people were in the yard, staring at the window aperture on the first floor and listening for ruin. Some time had elapsed before Darius would allow anybody even to mount the steps. Then the baker, the tenant of the ground floor, had had to be fetched. A pleasant, bland man, he had consented in advance to every suggestion; he had practically made Darius a present of the ground floor, if Darius possessed the courage to go into it, or to send others into it. The seat of deliberation had then been transferred to the alley behind. And the jobbing builder and carpenters had been fetched, and there was a palaver of tremendous length and solemnity. For hours nothing definite seemed to happen; no one ate or drank, and the current of life at the corner of Trafalgar Road and Wedgwood Street ceased to flow. Boys and men who had heard of the affair, and who had the divine gift of curiosity, gazed in rapture at the 'No Admittance' notice on the ramshackle double gates in Woodisun Bank. It seemed that they might never be rewarded but their great faith was justified when a hand-cart, bearing several beams three yards long, halted at the gates and was, after a pause, laboriously pushed past them and round the corner into the alley and up the alley. The alley had been crammed to witness the taking of the beams into the baker's storeroom. If the floor above had decided to yield, the noble, negligent carpenters would have been crushed beneath tons of machinery. At length a forest of pillars stood planted on the ground floor amid the baker's lumber; every beam was duly supported, and the experts pronounced that calamity was now inconceivable. Lastly, the tackle on the Demy Columbian had been loosed, and the machine, slightly askew, permitted gently to sink to full rest on the floor : and the result justified the experts.

II

By this time people had started to eat, but informally, as it were apologetically – Passover meals. Evening was at hand. The Clayhangers, later, had met at table. A strange repast! A strange father! The children had difficulty in speaking naturally. And then Mrs Hamps had come, ebulliently thanking God, and conveying the fact that the town was thrilled and standing utterly amazed in admiration before her heroical nephew. And yet she had said ardently that she was in no way amazed at her nephew's coolness; she would have been surprised if he had shown himself even one degree less cool. From a long study of his character she had foreknown infallibly that in such a crisis as had supervened he would behave precisely as he had behaved. This attitude of Auntie Hamps, however, though it reduced the miraculous to the ordinary-expected, did not diminish Clara's ingenuous awe of Edwin. From a mocker, the child had been temporarily transformed into an unwilling hero-worshipper. Mrs Hamps having departed, all the family, including Darius, had retired earlier than usual.

And now, on meeting his father and Big James and Miss Ingamells in the queer peace of the morning, in the relaxation after tension, and in the complete realization of the occurrence, Edwin perceived from the demeanour of all that, by an instinctive action extending over perhaps five seconds of time, he had procured for himself a wondrous and apparently permanent respect. Miss Ingamells, when he went vaguely into the freshly watered shop before breakfast, greeted him in a new tone, and with startling deference asked him what he thought she had better do in regard to the addressing of a certain parcel. Edwin considered this odd; he considered it illogical; and one consequence of Miss Ingamells's quite sincere attitude was that he despised Miss Ingamells for a moral weakling. He knew that he himself was a moral weakling, but he was sure that he could never bend, never crouch, to such a posture as Miss Ingamells's; that she was obviously sincere only increased his secret scorn.

But his father resembled Miss Ingamells. Edwin had not dreamt that mankind, and especially his father, was characterized by such simplicity. And yet, on reflection, had he not always found in his father a peculiar ingenuousness, which he could not but look down upon? His father, whom he met crossing the yard, spoke to him almost as he might have spoken to a junior partner. It was more than odd; it was against nature, as Edwin had conceived nature.

He was so superior and lofty, yet without intending it, that he made no attempt to put himself in his father's place. He, in the exciting moments between the first cracking sound and the second, had had a vision of wrecked machinery and timber in an abyss at his feet. His father had had a vision far more realistic and terrifying. His father had seen the whole course of his printing business brought to a standstill, and all his savings dragged out of him to pay for reconstruction and for new machinery. His father had seen loss of life which might be accounted to his negligence. His father had seen, with that pessimism which may overtake anybody in a crisis, the ruin of a career, the final frustration of his lifelong daring and obstinacy, and the end of everything. And then he had seen his son suddenly walk forth and save the frightful situation. He had always looked down upon that son as helpless, coddled, incapable of initiative or of boldness. He believed himself to be a highly remarkable man, and existence had taught him that remarkable men seldom or never have remarkable sons. Again and again had he noted the tendency of remarkable men to beget gaping and idle fools. Nevertheless, he had intensely desired to be able to be proud of his son. He had intensely desired to be able, when acquaintances should be sincerely enthusiastic about the merits of his son, to pretend, insincerely and with pride only half concealed, that his son was quite an ordinary youth.

Now his desire had been fulfilled; it had been more than fulfilled. The town would chatter about Edwin's presence of mind for a week. Edwin's act would become historic; it already was historic. And not only was the act in itself wonderful and admirable and epoch-making; but it proved that Edwin, despite his blondness, his finickingness, his hesitations, had grit. That was the point : the lad had grit; there was material in the lad of which much could be made. Add to this, the father's mere instinctive gratitude – a gratitude of such unguessed depth that it had prevented him even from being ashamed of having publicly and impulsively embraced his son on the previous morning.

Edwin, in his unconscious egoism, ignored all that.

III

'I've just seen Barlow,' said Darius confidentially to Edwin. Barlow was the baker. 'He's been here afore his rounds. He's willing to sublet me his storeroom – so that'll be all right ! Eh ?'

'Yes,' said Edwin, seeing that his approval was being sought for.

'We must fix that machine plumb again.'

'I suppose the floor's as firm as rocks now ?' Edwin suggested.

'Eh ! Bless ye ! Yes !' said his father, with a trace of kindly impatience.

The policy of makeshift was to continue. The floor having been stayed with oak, the easiest thing and the least immediately expensive thing was to leave matters as they were. When the baker's stores were cleared from his warehouse, Darius could use the spaces between the pillars for lumber of his own; and he could either knock an entrance-way through the wall in the yard, or he could open the nailed-down trap-door and patch the ancient stairway within; or he could do nothing – it would only mean walking out into Woodisun Bank and up the alley each time he wanted access to his lumber !

And yet, after the second cracking sound on the previous day, he had been ready to vow to rent an entirely new and common-sense printing office somewhere else – if only he should be saved from disaster that once ! But he had not quite vowed. And, in any case, a vow to oneself is not a vow to the Virgin. He had escaped from a danger, and the recurrence of the particular danger was impossible. Why, then, commit follies of prudence, when the existing arrangement of things 'would do' ?

IV

That afternoon Darius Clayhanger, with his most mysterious air of business, told Edwin to follow him into the shop. Several hours of miscellaneous consultative pottering had passed between Darius and his compositors round and about the new printing machine, which was once more plumb and ready for action. For considerably over a week Edwin had been on his father's general staff without any definite task or occupation having been assigned to him. His father had been too excitedly preoccupied with the arrival and erection of the machine to bestow due thought upon the activities proper to Edwin in the complex dailiness of the business. Now he meant at any rate to begin to put the boy into a suitable niche. The boy had deserved at least that.

At the desk he opened before him the daily and weekly newspaper-book, and explained its system.

'Let's take the *British Mechanic*,' he said.

And he turned to the page where the title *British Mechanic* was written in red ink. Underneath that title were written the names and addresses of fifteen subscribers to the paper. To the right of the names were thirteen columns, representing a quarter of the year. With his customary laboriousness, Darius described the entire process of distribution. The parcel of papers arrived and was counted, and the name of a subscriber scribbled in an abbreviated form on each copy. Some copies had to be delivered by the errand boy; these were handed to the errand boy, and a tick made against each subscriber in the column for the week : other copies were called for by the subscriber, and as each of these was taken away, similarly a tick had to be made against the name of its subscriber. Some copies were paid for in cash in the shop, some were paid in cash to the office boy, some were paid for monthly, some were paid for quarterly, and some, as Darius said grimly, were never paid for at all. No matter what the method of paying, when a copy was paid for, or thirteen copies were paid for, a crossing tick had to be made in the book for each copy. Thus, for a single quarter of *British Mechanic* nearly two hundred ticks and nearly two hundred crossing ticks had to be made in the book, if the work was properly done. However, it was never properly done – Miss Ingamells being short of leisure and the errand boy utterly unreliable – and Darius wanted it properly done. The total gross profit on a quarter of *British Mechanics* was less than five shillings, and no customers were more exigent and cantankerous than those who bought one pennyworth of goods per week, and had them delivered free, and received three month's credit. Still, that could not be helped. A printer and stationer was compelled by usage to supply papers; and besides, paper subscribers served a purpose as a nucleus of general business.

As with the *British Mechanic*, so with seventeen other weeklies. The daily papers were fewer, but the accountancy they caused was even more elaborate. For monthly magazines there was a separate book with a separate system; here the sums involved were vaster, ranging as high as half a crown.

Darius led Edwin with patient minuteness through the whole labyrinth.

'Now,' he said, 'you're going to have sole charge of all this.'

And he said it benevolently, in the conviction that he was awarding a deserved recompense, with the mien of one who was giving dominion to a faithful steward over ten cities.

'Just look into it carefully yerself, lad,' he said at last, and left Edwin with a mixed parcel of journals upon which to practise.

Before Edwin's eyes flickered hundreds of names, thousands of figures, and tens of thousands of ticks. His heart protested; it protested with loathing. The prospect stretching far in front of him made him feel sick. But something weak and goodnatured in him forced him to smile, and to simulate a subdued ecstasy at receiving this overwhelming proof of his father's confidence in him. As for Darius, Darius was delighted with himself and with his son, and felt that he was behaving as a benignant father should. Edwin had proved his grit, proved that he had that uncommunicable quality, 'character', and had well deserved encouragement.

V

The next morning, in the printing office, Edwin came upon Big James giving a lesson in composing to the younger apprentice, who in theory had 'learned his cases'. Big James held the composing stick in his great left hand, like a matchbox, and with his great right thumb and index picked letter after letter from the case, very slowly in order to display the movement, and dropped them into the stick. In his mild, resonant tones he explained that each letter must be picked up unfalteringly in a particular way, so that it would drop face upward into the stick without any intermediate manipulation. And he explained also that the left hand must be held so that the right hand would have to travel to and fro as little as possible. He was revealing the basic mysteries of his craft, and was happy, making the while the broad series of stock pleasantries which have probably been current in composing rooms since printing was invented. Then he was silent, working more and more quickly, till his right hand could scarcely be followed in its twinklings, and the face of the apprentice duly spread in marvel. When the line was finished he drew out the rule, clapped it down on the top of the last row of letters, and gave the composing stick to the apprentice to essay.

The apprentice began to compose with his feet, his shoulders, his mouth, his eyebrows – with all his body except his hands, which nevertheless travelled spaciously far and wide.

'It's not in seven year, nor in seventy, as you'll learn, young son of a gun!' said Big James.

And, having unsettled the youth to his foundations with a bland thwack across the head, he resumed the composing stick and began again the exposition of the unique smooth movement which is the root of rapid type-setting.

'Here!' said Big James, when the apprentice had behaved worse than ever. 'Us'll ask Mr Edwin to have a go. 'Us'll see what *he*'ll do.'

And Edwin, sheepish, had to comply. He was in pride bound to surpass the apprentice, and did so.

'There!' said Big James. 'What did I tell ye?' He seemed to imply a prophecy that, because Edwin had saved the printing office from destruction two days previously, he would necessarily prove to be a born compositor.

The apprentice deferentially sniggered, and Edwin smiled modestly and awkwardly and departed without having accomplished what he had come to do.

By his own act of cool, nonchalant, unconsidered courage in a crisis, he had, it seemed, definitely proved himself to possess a special aptitude in all branches of the business of printer and stationer. Everybody assumed it. Everybody was pleased. Everybody saw that Providence had been kind to Darius and to his son. The fathers of the town, and the mothers, who liked Edwin's complexion and fair hair, told each other that not every parent was so fortunate as Mr Clayhanger, and what a blessing it was that the old breed was not after all dying out in those newfangled days. Edwin could not escape from the universal assumption. He felt it round him as a net which somehow he had to cut.

CHAPTER 14 : *The Architect*

I

One morning Edwin was busy in the shop with his own private minion, the paper boy, who went in awe of him. But this was not the same Edwin, though people who could only judge by features, and by the length of trousers and sleeves on legs and arms, might have thought that it was the same Edwin enlarged and corrected. Half a year had passed. The month was February, cold. Mr Enoch Peake had not merely married Mrs Louisa Loggerheads, but had died of an apoplexy, leaving behind Cocknage Gardens, a widow, and his name painted in large letters over the word 'Loggerheads' on the lintel of the Dragon. The steam-printer had done the funeral cards, and had gone to the burial of his hopes of business in that quarter. Many funeral cards had come out of the same printing office during the winter, including that of Mr Udall, the great marble-player. It seemed uncanny to Edwin that a marble-player whom he had actually seen playing marbles should do anything so solemn as expire. However, Edwin had perfectly lost all interest in marbles; only once in six months had he thought of them – and that once through a funeral card. Also he was growing used to funeral cards. He would enter an order for funeral cards as nonchalantly as an order for butterscotch labels. But it was not deaths and the spectacle of life as seen from the shop that had made another Edwin of him.

What had changed him was the slow daily influence of a large number of trifling habitual duties none of which fully strained his faculties, and the monotony of them, and the constant watchful conventionality of his deportment with customers. He was still a youth, very youthful, but you had to keep an eye open for his youthfulness if you wished to find it beneath the little man that he had been transformed into. He now took his watch out of his pocket with an absent gesture and look exactly like his father's; and his tones would be a reflection of those of the last important full-sized man with whom he had happened to have been in contact. And though he had not developed into a dandy (finance forbidding), he kept his hair unnaturally straight, and amiably grumbled to Maggie about his collars every fortnight or so. Yes, another Edwin! Yet it might not be assumed that he was growing in discontent, either chronic or acute. On the contrary, malady of discontent troubled him less and less.

To the paper boy he was a real man. The paper boy accepted him with unreserved fatalism, as Edward accepted his father. Thus the boy stood passive while Edwin brought business to a standstill by privately perusing the *Manchester Examiner*. It was Saturday morning, the morning on which the *Examiner* published its renowned Literary Supplement. All the children read eagerly the Literary Supplement; but Edwin, in virtue of his office, got it first. On the first and second pages was the serial story, by George MacDonald, W. Clark Russell, or Mrs Lynn Linton; then followed readable extracts from new books, and on the fourth pages were selected jokes from *Punch*. Edwin somehow always began with the jokes, and in so doing was rather ashamed of his levity. He would skim the jokes, glance at the titles of the new books, and look at the dialogue parts of the serial, while business and the boy waited. There was no hurry then, even though the year had reached 1873, and people were saying that they would soon be at the middle of the seventies; even though the Licensing Act had come into force and publicans were predicting the end of the world. Morning papers were not delivered till ten, eleven, or twelve o'clock in Bursley, and on Saturdays, owing to Edwin's laudable interest in the best periodical literature, they were apt to be delivered later than usual.

II

On this particular morning Edwin was disturbed in his studies by a greater than the paper boy, a greater even than his father. Mr Osmond Orgreave came stamping his cold feet into the shop, the floor of which was still a little damp from the watering that preceded its sweeping. Mr Orgreave, though as far as Edwin knew he had never been in the shop before, went straight to the coke-stove, bent his knees, and began to warm his hands. In this position he opened an interview with Edwin, who dropped the Literary Supplement. Miss Ingamells was momentarily absent.

'Father in?'

'No, sir.'

Edwin did not say where his father was, because he had received general instructions never to 'volunteer information' on that point.

'Where is he?'

'He's out, sir.'

'Oh! Well! Has he left any instructions about those specifications for the Shawport Board School?'

'No, sir, I'm afraid he hasn't. But I can ask in the printing office.'

Mr Orgreave approached the counter, smiling. His face was angular, rather stout, and harsh, with a grey moustache and a short grey beard, and yet his demeanour and his voice had a jocular, youthful quality. And this was not the only contradiction about him. His clothes were extremely elegant and nice in detail – the whiteness of his linen would have struck the most casual observer – but he seemed to be perfectly oblivious of his clothes, indeed, to show carelessness concerning them. His finger-nails were marvellously tended. But he scribbled in pencil on his cuff, and apparently was not offended by a grey mark on his hand due to touching the top of the stove. The idea in Edwin's head was that Mr Orgreave must put on a new suit of clothes once a week, and new linen every day, and take a bath about once an hour. The man had no ceremoniousness. Thus, though he had never previously spoken to Edwin, he made no preliminary pretence of not being sure who Edwin was; he chatted with him as though they were old friends and had parted only the day before; he also chatted with him as though they were equals in age, eminence, and wealth. A strange man!

'Now look here!' he said, as the conversation proceeded, 'those specifications are at the Sytch Chapel. If you could come along with me *now* – I could give them to you and point out one or two things to you, and perhaps Big James could make a start on them this morning. You see it's urgent.'

So he was familiar with Big James.

'Certainly,' said Edwin, excited.

And when he had curtly told the paper boy to do portions of the newspaper job which he had always held the paper boy was absolutely incapable of doing, he sent the boy to find Miss Ingamells, informed her where he was going, and followed Mr Orgreave out of the shop.

III

'Of course you know Charlie's at school in France,' said Mr Orgreave, as they passed along Wedgwood Street in the direction of St Luke's Square. He was really very companionable.

'Er – yes!' Edwin replied, nervously explosive, and buttoning up his tight overcoat with an important business air.

'At least it isn't a school – it's a university. Besançon, you know. They take university students much younger there. Oh! He has a rare time – a rare time. Never writes to you, I suppose?'

'No,' Edwin gave a short laugh.

Mr Orgreave laughed aloud. 'And he wouldn't to us either, if his mother didn't make a fuss about it. But when he does write, we gather there's no place like Besançon.'

'It must be splendid,' Edwin said thoughtfully.

'You and he were great chums, weren't you? I know we used to hear about you every day. His mother used to say that we had Clay-hanger with every meal.' Mr Orgreave again laughed heartily.

Edwin blushed. He was quite startled, and immensely flattered. What on earth could the Sunday have found to tell them every day about *him*? He, Edwin Clayhanger, a subject of conversation in the household of the Orgreaves, that mysterious household which he had never entered but which he had always pictured to himself as being so finely superior! Less than a year ago Charlie Orgreave had been 'the Sunday', had been 'old Perish-in-the-attempt', and now he was a student in Besançon University, unapproachable, extraordinarily romantic; and he, Edwin, remained in his father's shop! He had been aware that Charlie had gone to Besançon University, but he had not realized it effectively till this moment. The realization blew discontent into a flame, which fed on the further perception that evidently the Orgreave family were a gay, jolly crowd of cronies together, not in the least like parents and children; their home life must be something fundamentally different from his.

IV

When they had crossed the windy space of St Luke's Square and reached the top of the Sytch Bank, Mr Orgreave stopped an instant in front of the Sytch Pottery, and pointed to a large window at the south end that was in process of being boarded up.

'At last!' he murmured with disgust. Then he said : 'That's the most beautiful window in Bursley, and perhaps in the Five Towns; and you see what's happening to it.'

Edwin had never heard the word 'beautiful' uttered in quite that tone, except by women, such as Auntie Hamps, about a baby or a valentine or a sermon. But Mr Orgreave was not a woman; he was a man of the world, he was almost *the* man of the world; and the subject of his adjective was a window!

'Why are they boarding it up, Mr Orgreave?' Edwin asked.

'Oh! Ancient lights! Ancient lights!'

Edwin began to snigger. He thought for an instant that Mr Orgreave was being jocular over his head, for he could only connect the phrase 'ancient lights' with the meaner organs of a dead animal, exposed, for example, in tripe shops. However, he saw his ineptitude almost simultaneously with the commission of it, and smothered the snigger in becoming gravity. It was clear that he had something to learn in the phraseology employed by architects.

'I should think,' said Mr Orgreave, 'I should think they've been at law about that window for thirty years, if not more. Well, it's over now, seemingly.' He gazed at the disappearing window. 'What a shame!'

'It is,' said Edwin politely.

Mr Orgreave crossed the road and then stood still to gaze at the façade of the Sytch Pottery. It was a long two-storey building, purest Georgian, of red brick with very elaborate stone facings which contrasted admirably with the austere simplicity of the walls. The porch was lofty, with a majestic flight of steps narrowing to the doors. The ironwork of the basement railings was unusually rich and impressive.

'Ever seen another pot-works like that?' demanded Mr Orgreave, enthusiastically musing.

'No,' said Edwin. Now that the question was put to him, he never *had* seen another pot-works like that.

'There are one or two pretty fine works in the Five Towns,' said Mr Orgreave. 'But there's nothing elsewhere to touch this. I nearly always stop and look at it if I'm passing. Just look at the pointing! The pointing alone. . . .'

Edwin had to readjust his ideas. It had never occurred to him to search for anything fine in Bursley. The fact was, he had never opened his eyes at Bursley. Dozens of times he must have passed the Sytch Pottery, and yet not noticed, not suspected, that it differed from any other pot-works : he who had dreamed of being an architect !

'You don't think much of it?' said Mr Orgreave, moving on. 'People don't.'

'Oh yes! I *do*!' Edwin protested, and with such an air of eager sincerity that Mr Orgreave turned to glance at him. And in truth he did think that the Sytch Pottery was beautiful. He never would have thought so but for the accident of the walk with Mr Orgreave; he might have spent his whole life in the town, and never troubled himself a moment about the Sytch Pottery. Nevertheless he now, by an act of sheer faith, suddenly, miraculously, and genuinely regarded it as an exquisitely beautiful edifice, on a plane with the edifices of the capitals of Europe, and as a feast for discerning eyes. 'I like architecture very much,' he added. And this too was said with such feverish conviction that Mr Orgreave was quite moved.

'I must show you my new Sytch Chapel,' said Mr Orgreave gaily.

'Oh! I should like you to show it me,' said Edwin.

But he was exceedingly perturbed by misgivings. Here was he wanting to be an architect, and he had never observed the Sytch Pottery! Surely that was an absolute proof that he had no vocation for architecture! And yet now he did most passionately admire the Sytch Pottery. And he was proud to be sharing the admiration of the fine, joyous, superior, luxurious, companionable man, Mr Orgreave.

v

They went down the Sytch Bank to the new chapel of which Mr Orgreave, though a churchman, was the architect, in that vague quarter of the world between Bursley and Turnhill. The roof was not on; the scaffolding was extraordinarily interesting and confusing; they bent their heads to pass under low portals; Edwin had the delicious smell of new mortar; they stumbled through sand, mud, cinders, and little pools; they climbed a ladder and stepped over a large block of dressed stone, and Mr Orgreave said –

'This is the gallery we're in, here. You see the scheme of the place now. . . . That hole – only a flue. Now you see what that arch carries – they didn't like it in the plans because they thought it might be mistaken for a church –'

Edwin was receptive.

'Of course it's a very small affair, but it'll cost less per sitting than any other chapel in your circuit, and I fancy it'll look less like a box of bricks.' Mr Orgreave subtly smiled, and Edwin tried to equal his subtlety. 'I must show you the elevation some other time – a bit later.

99

What I've been after in it, is to keep it in character with the street. . . . Hi! Dan, there!' Now Mr Orgreave was calling across the hollow of the chapel to a fat man in corduroys. 'Have you remembered about those blue bricks?'

Perhaps the most captivating phenomenon of all was a little lean-to shed with a real door evidently taken from somewhere else, and a little stove, and a table and a chair. Here Mr Orgreave had a confabulation with the corduroyed man, who was the builder, and they pored over immense sheets of coloured plans that lay on the table, and Mr Orgreave made marks and even sketches on the plans, and the fat man objected to his instructions, and Mr Orgreave insisted, 'Yes, *yes*!' And it seemed to Edwin as though the building of the chapel stood still while Mr Orgreave cogitated and explained; it seemed to Edwin that he was in the creating-chamber. The atmosphere of the shed was inexpressively romantic to him. After the fat man had gone Mr Orgreave took a clothes-brush off a plank that had been roughly nailed on two brackets to the wall, and brushed Edwin's clothes, and Edwin brushed Mr Orgreave, and then Mr Orgreave, having run his hand through the brush, lightly brushed his hair with it. All this was part of Edwin's joy.

'Yes,' he said, 'I think the idea of that arch is splendid.'

'You do?' said Mr Orgreave, quite simply and ingenuously pleased and interested. 'You see – with the lie of the ground as it is –'

That was another point that Edwin ought to have thought of by himself – the lie of the ground – but he had not thought of it. Mr Orgreave went on talking. In the shop he had conveyed the idea that he was tremendously pressed for time; now he had apparently forgotten time.

'I'm afraid I shall have to be off,' said Edwin timidly. And he made a preliminary movement as if to depart.

'And what about those specifications, young man?' asked Mr Orgreave, dryly twinkling. He unlocked a drawer in the rickety table. Edwin had forgotten the specifications as successfully as Mr Orgreave had forgotten time. Throughout the remainder of the day he smelt imaginary mortar.

CHAPTER 15 : *A Decision*

I

The next day being the day of rest, Mrs Nixon arose from her nook at 5.30 a.m. and woke Edwin. She did this from good-nature, and because she could refuse him nothing, and not under any sort of compulsion. Edwin got up at the first call, though he was in no way remarkable for his triumphs over the pillow. Twenty-five minutes later he was crossing Trafalgar Road and entering the schoolyard of the Wesleyan Chapel. And from various quarters of the town, other young men, of ages varying from sixteen to fifty, were converging upon the same point. Black night still reigned above the lamplights that flickered in the wind which precedes the dawn, and the mud was frozen. Not merely had these young men to be afoot and abroad, but they had to be ceremoniously dressed. They could not issue forth in flannels and sweaters, with a towel round the neck, as for a morning plunge in the river. The day was Sunday, though Sunday had not dawned, and the plunge was into the river of intellectual life. Moreover, they were bound by conscience to be prompt. To have arrived late, even five minutes late, would have spoilt the whole effect. It had to be six o'clock or nothing.

The Young Men's Debating Society was a newly formed branch of the multifarious activity of the Wesleyan Methodist Chapel. It met on Sunday because Sunday was the only day that would suit everybody; and at six in the morning for two reasons. The obvious reason was that at any other hour its meetings would clash either with other activities or with the solemnity of Sabbath meals. The obvious reason could not have stood by itself; it was secretly supported by the recondite reason that the preposterous hour of 6 a.m. appealed powerfully to something youthful, perverse, silly, fanatical, and fine in the youths. They discovered the ascetic's joy in robbing themselves of sleep and in catching chills, and in disturbing households and chapel-keepers. They thought it was a great thing to be discussing intellectual topics at an hour when a town that ignorantly scorned intellectuality was snoring in all its heavy brutishness. And it was a great thing. They considered themselves the salt of the earth, or of that part of the earth. And I have an idea that they were.

Edwin had joined this Society partly because he did not possess the art of refusing, partly because the notion of it appealed spectacularly to the martyr in him, and partly because it gave him an excuse for ceasing to attend the afternoon Sunday school, which he loathed. Without such an excuse he could never have told his father that he meant to give up Sunday school. He could never have dared to do so. His father had what Edwin deemed to be a superstitious and hypocritical regard for the Sunday school. Darius never went near the Sunday school, and assuredly in business and in home life he did not practise the precepts inculcated at the Sunday school, and yet he always spoke of the Sunday school with what was to Edwin a ridiculous reverence. Another of those problems in his father's character which Edwin gave up in disgust!

II

The Society met in a small classroom. The secretary, arch ascetic, arrived at 5.45 and lit the fire which the chapel-keeper (a man with no enthusiasm whatever for flagellation, the hairshirt, or intellectuality) had laid but would not get up to light. The chairman of the Society, a little Welshman named Llewellyn Roberts, aged fifty, but a youth because a bachelor, sat on a chair at one side of the incipient fire, and some dozen members sat round the room on forms. A single gas jet flamed from the ceiling. Everybody wore his overcoat, and within the collars of overcoats could be seen glimpses of rich neckties; the hats, some glossy, dotted the hat-rack which ran along two walls. A hymn was sung, and then all knelt, some spreading handkerchiefs on the dusty floor to protect fine trousers, and the chairman invoked the blessing of God on their discussions. The proper mental and emotional atmosphere was now established. The secretary read the minutes of the last meeting, while the chairman surreptitiously poked the fire with a piece of wood from the lower works of a chair, and then the chairman, as he signed the minutes with a pen dipped in an exercise ink-bottle that stood on the narrow mantelpiece, said in his dry voice –

'I call upon our young friend, Mr Edwin Clayhanger, to open the debate, "Is Bishop Colenso, considered as a Biblical commentator, a force for good?" '

'I'm a damned fool!' said Edwin to himself savagely, as he stood on his feet. But to look at his wistful and nervously smiling face, no one would have guessed that he was thus blasphemously swearing in the privacy of his own brain.

He had been entrapped into the situation in which he found himself. It was not until after he had joined the Society that he had learnt of a rule which made it compulsory for every member to speak at every meeting attended, and for every member to open a debate at least once in a year. And this was not all; the use of notes while the orator was 'up' was absolutely forbidden. A drastic Society! It had commended itself to elders by claiming to be a nursery for ready speakers.

III

Edwin had chosen the subject of Bishop Colenso – the ultimate wording of the resolution was not his – because he had been reading about the intellectually adventurous Bishop in the *Manchester Examiner*. And, although eleven years had passed since the publication of the first part of *The Pentateuch and the Book of Joshua Critically examined*, the Colenso question was only just filtering down to the thinking classes of the Five Towns; it was an actuality in the Five Towns, if in abeyance in London. Even Hugh Miller's *The Old Red Sandstone, or New Walks in an Old Field* then over thirty years old, was still being looked upon as dangerously original in the Five Towns in 1873. However, the effect of its disturbing geological evidence that the earth could scarcely have been begun and finished in a little under a week, was happily nullified by the suicide of its author; that pistol-shot had been a striking proof of the literal inspiration of the Bible.

Bishop Colenso had, in Edwin, an ingenuous admirer. Edwin stameringly and hesitatingly gave a preliminary sketch of his life; how he had been censured by Convocation and deposed from his See by his Metropolitan; how the Privy Council had decided that the deposition was null and void; how the ecclesiastical authorities had then circumvented the Privy Council by refusing to pay his salary to the Bishop (which Edwin considered mean); how the Bishop had circumvented the ecclesiastical authorities by appealing to the Master of the Rolls, who ordered the ecclesiastical authorities to pay him his arrears of income with interest thereon, unless they were ready to bring him to trial for heresy; how the said authorities would not bring him to trial for heresy (which Edwin considered to be miserable cowardice on their part); how the Bishop had then been publicly excommunicated, without authority; and how his friends, among whom were some very respectable and powerful people, had made him a present of over three thousand pounds. After this graphic historical survey, Edwin proceeded to the pentateuchal puzzles, and, without pronouncing an opinion thereon, argued that any commentator who was both learned and sincere must be a force for good, as the Bible had nothing to fear from honest inquiry, etc., etc. Five-sixths of his speech was coloured by phrases and modes of thought which he had picked up in the Wesleyan community, and the other sixth belonged to himself. The speech was moderately bad, but not inferior to many other speeches. It was received in absolute silence. This rather surprised Edwin, because the tone in which the leading members of the Society usually spoke to him indicated that (for reasons which he knew not) they regarded him as a very superior intellect indeed; and Edwin was not entirely ashamed of the quality of his speech; in fact, he had feared worse from himself, especially as, since his walk with Mr Orgreave, he had been quite unable to concentrate his thoughts on Bishop Colenso at all, and had been exceedingly unhappy and apprehensive concerning an affair that bore no kind of relation to the Pentateuch.

IV

The chairman began to speak at once. His function was to call upon the speakers in the order arranged, and to sum up before putting the resolution to the vote. But now he produced surprisingly a speech of his own. He reminded the meeting that in 1860 Bishop Colenso had memorialized the Archbishop of Canterbury against compelling natives who had already more than one wife to renounce polygamy as a condition to baptism in the Christian religion; he started that, though there were young men present who were almost infants in arms at that period, he for his part could well remember all the episode, and in particular Bishop Colenso's amazing allegation that he could find no disapproval of polygamy either in the Bible or in the writings of the Ancient Church. He also pointed out that in 1861 Bishop Colenso had argued against the doctrine of Eternal Punishment. He warned the meeting to beware of youthful indiscretions. Everyone there assembled of course meant well, and believed that it was a duty to believe, but all the same . . .

'I shall write father a letter!' said Edwin to himself. The idea came to him in a flash like a divine succour; and it seemed to solve all his difficulties unconnected with the subject of debate.

V

The chairman went on crossing t's and dotting i's. And soon even Edwin perceived that the chairman was diplomatically and tactfully, yet very firmly, bent upon saving the meeting from any possibility of scandalizing itself and the Wesleyan community. Bishop Colenso must not be approved beneath those roofs. Evidently Edwin had been more persuasive than he dreamt of; and daring beyond precedent. He had meant to carry his resolution if he could, whereas, it appeared, he ought to have meant to be defeated, in the true interests of revealed religion. The chairman kept referring to his young friend the proposer's brilliant brains, and to the grave danger that lurked in brilliant brains, and the inability of brilliant brains to atone for lack of experience. The meeting had its cue. Young man after young man arose to snub Bishop Colenso, to hope charitably that Bishop Colenso was sincere, and to insist that no Bishop Colenso should lead *him* to the awful abyss of polygamy, and that no Bishop Colenso should deprive *him* of that unique incentive to righteousness – the doctrine of an everlasting burning hell. Moses was put on his legs again as a serious historian, and the subject of the resolution utterly lost to view. The chairman then remarked that his impartial rôle forbade him to support either side, and the voting showed fourteen against one. They all sang the Doxology, and the chairman pronounced a benediction. The fourteen forgave the one, as one who knew not what he did; but their demeanour rather too patently showed that they were forgiving under difficulty; and that it would be as well that this kind of youthful temerariousness was not practised too often. Edwin, in the language of the district, was 'sneaped'. Wondering what on earth he after all *had* said to raise such an alarm, he nevertheless did not feel resentful, only very depressed – about the debate and about other things. He knew in his heart that for him attendance at the meetings of the Young Men's Debating Society was ridiculous.

VI

He allowed all the rest to precede him from the room. When he was alone he smiled sheepishly, and also disdainfully; he knew that the chasm between himself and the others was a real chasm, and not a figment of his childish diffidence, as he had sometimes suspected it to be. Then he turned the gas out. A beautiful faint silver surged through the window. While the debate was in progress, the sun had been going about its business of the dawn, unperceived.

'I shall write a letter!' he kept saying to himself. 'He'll never let me explain myself properly if I start talking. I shall write a letter. I can write a very good letter, and he'll be bound to take notice of it. He'll never be able to get over my letter.'

In the schoolyard daylight reigned. The debaters had already disappeared. Trafalgar Road and Duck Bank were empty and silent under rosy clouds. Instead of going straight home, Edwin went past the Town Hall and through the Market Place to the Sytch Pottery. Astounding that he had never noticed for himself how beautiful the building was! It was a simply lovely building!

'Yes,' he said, 'I shall write him a letter, and this very day, too! May I be hung, drawn, and quartered if he doesn't have to read my letter tomorrow morning!'

CHAPTER 16 : *The Letter*

I

Then there was roast goose for dinner, and Clara amused herself by making silly facetious faces, furtively, dangerously, under her father's very eyes. The children feared goose for their father, whose digestion was usually unequal to this particular bird. Like many fathers of families in the Five Towns, he had the habit of going forth on Saturday mornings to the butcher's or the poulterer's and buying Sunday's dinner. He was a fairly good judge of a joint, but Maggie considered herself to be his superior in this respect. However, Darius was not prepared to learn from Maggie, and his purchases had to be accepted without criticism. At a given meal Darius would never admit that anything chosen and bought by him was not perfect; but a week afterwards, if the fact was so, he would of his own accord recall imperfections in that which he had asserted to be perfect; and he would do this without any shame, without any apparent sense of inconsistency or weakness. Edwin noticed a similar trait in other grown-up persons, and it astonished him. It astonished him especially in his father, who despite the faults and vulgarities which his fastidious son could find in him, always impressed Edwin as a strong man, a man with the heroic quality of not caring too much what other people thought.

When Edwin saw his father take a second plateful of goose, with the deadly stuffing thereof – Darius simply could not resist it, like most dyspeptics he was somewhat greedy – he foresaw an indisposed and perilous father for the morrow. Which prevision was supported by Clara's pantomimic antics, and even by Maggie's grave and restrained sigh. Still, he had sworn to write and send the letter, and he should do so. A career, a lifetime, was not to be at the mercy of a bilious attack, surely! Such a notion offended logic and proportion, and he scorned it away.

II

The meal proceeded in silence. Darius, as in duty bound, mentioned the sermon, but neither Clara nor Edwin would have anything to do with the sermon, and Maggie had not been to chapel. Clara and Edwin felt themselves free of piety till six o'clock at least, and they doggedly would not respond. And Darius from prudence did not insist, for he had arrived at chapel unthinkably late – during the second chant – and

Clara was capable of audacious remarks upon occasions. The silence grew stolid.

And Edwin wondered what the dinner-table of the Orgreaves was like. And he could smell fresh mortar. And he dreamed of a romantic life – he knew not what kind of life, but something different fundamentally from his own. He suddenly understood, understood with sympathy, the impulse which had made boys run away to sea. He could feel the open sea; he could feel the breath of freedom on his cheek.

He said to himself –

'Why shouldn't I break this ghastly silence by telling father out loud here that he mustn't forget what I told him that night in the attic? I'm going to be an architect. I'm not going to be any blooming printer. I'm going to be an architect. Why haven't I mentioned it before? Why haven't I talked about it all the time? Because I am an ass! Because there is no word for what I am! Damn it! I suppose I'm the person to choose what I'm going to be! I suppose it's my business more than his. Besides, he can't possibly refuse me. If I say flatly that I won't be a printer – he's done. This idea of writing a letter is just like me! Coward! Coward! What's my tongue for? Can't I talk? Isn't he bound to listen? All I have to do is to open my mouth. He's sitting there. I'm sitting here. He can't eat me. I'm in my rights. Now suppose I start on it as soon as Mrs Nixon has brought the pudding and pie in?'

And he waited anxiously to see whether he indeed would be able to make a start after the departure of Mrs Nixon.

III

Hopeless! He could not bring himself to do it. It was strange! It was disgusting! . . . No, he would be compelled to write the letter. Besides, the letter would be more effective. His father could not interrupt a letter by some loud illogical remark. Thus he salved his self-conceit. He also sought relief in reflecting savagely upon the speeches that had been made against him in the debate. He went through them all in his mind. There was the slimy idiot from Baines's (it was in such terms that his thoughts ran) who gloried in never having read a word of Colenso, and called the assembled company to witness that nothing should ever induce him to read such a godless author, . . . going about in the mask of a so-called Bishop. But had any of them read Colenso, except possibly Llewellyn Roberts, who in his Welsh way would pretend ignorance and then come out with a quotation and refer you to the exact page? Edwin himself had read very little of Colenso – and that little only because a customer had ordered the second part of the *Pentateuch* and he had stolen it for a night. Colenso was not in the Free Library. . . . What a world! What a debate! Still, he could not help dwelling with pleasure on Mr Roberts's insistence on the brilliant quality of his brains. Astute as Mr Roberts was, the man was clearly in awe of Edwin's brains! Why? To be honest, Edwin had never been deeply struck by his own brain power. And yet there must be something in it!

'Of course,' he reflected sardonically, 'father doesn't show the faintest interest in the debate. Yet he knew all about it, and that I had to open it.' But he was glad that his father showed no interest in the debate. Clara had mentioned it in the presence of Maggie, with her usual ironic intent, and Edwin had quickly shut her up.

IV

In the afternoon, the sitting-room being made uninhabitable by his father's goose-ridden dozes, he went out for a walk; the weather was cold and fine. When he returned his father also had gone out; the two girls were lolling in the sitting-room. An immense fire, built up by Darius, was just ripe for the beginning of decay, and the room very warm. Clara was at the window, Maggie in Darius's chair reading a novel of Charlotte M. Yonge's. On the table, open, was a bound volume of *The Family Treasury of Sunday Reading*, in which Clara had been perusing 'The Chronicles of the Schönberg-Cotta Family' with feverish interest. Edwin had laughed at her ingenuous absorption in the adventures of the Schönberg-Cotta family, but the fact was that he had found them rather interesting, in spite of himself, while pretending the contrary. There was an atmosphere of high obstinate effort and heroical foreignness about the story which stimulated something secret in him that seldom responded to the provocation of a book; more easily would this secret something respond to a calm evening or a distant prospect, or the silence of early morning when by chance he looked out of his window.

The volume of *The Family Treasury*, though five years old, was a recent acquisition. It had come into the house through the total disappearance of a customer who had left the loose numbers to be bound in 1869. Edwin dropped sideways on to a chair at the table, spread out his feet to the right, pitched his left elbow a long distance to the left, and, his head resting on his left hand, turned over the pages with his right and idly. His eye caught titles such as 'The Door was Shut', 'My Mother's Voice', 'The Heathen Mother', 'The Only Treasure', 'Religion and Business', 'Hope to the End', 'The Child of our Sunday School', 'Satan's Devices', and 'Studies of Christian Life and Character, Hannah More'. Then he saw an article about some architecture in Rome, and he read: 'In the Sistine picture there is the struggle of a great mind to reduce within the possibilities of art a subject that transcends it. That mind would have shown itself to be greater, truer, at least, in its judgement of the capabilities of art, and more reverent to have let it alone'. The seriousness of the whole magazine intimidated him into accepting this pronouncement for a moment, though his brief studies in various encyclopedias had led him to believe that the Sistine Chapel (shown in an illustration in Cazenove) was high beyond any human criticism. His elbow slid on the surface of the table, and in recovering himself he sent *The Family Treasury* on the floor, wrong side up, with a great noise. Maggie did not move. Clara turned and protested sharply against this sacrilege, and Edwin, out of mere caprice, informed her that her precious magazine was the most stinking silly 'pi' [pious] thing that ever was. With haughty and shocked gestures she gathered up the volume and took it out of the room.

'I say, Mag,' Edwin muttered, still leaning his head on his hand, and staring blankly at the wall.

The fire dropped a little in the grate.

'What is it?' asked Maggie, without stirring or looking up.

'Has father said anything to you about me wanting to be an architect?' He spoke with an affectation of dreaminess.

'About you wanting to be an architect?' repeated Maggie in surprise.

'Yes,' said Edwin. He knew perfectly well that his father would never have spoken to Maggie on such a subject. But he wanted to open a conversation.

'No fear!' said Maggie. And added in her kindest, most encouraging, elder-sisterly tone : 'Why?'

'Oh!' He hesitated, drawling, and then he told her a great deal of what was in his mind. And she carefully put the wool-marker in her book and shut it, and listened to him. And the fire dropped and dropped, comfortably. She did not understand him; obviously she thought his desire to be an architect exceedingly odd; but she sympathized. Her attitude was soothing and fortifying. After all (he reflected) Maggie's all right – there's some sense in Maggie. He could 'get on' with Maggie. For a few moments he was happy and hopeful.

'I thought I'd write him a letter,' he said. 'You know how he is to talk to.'

There was a pause.

'What d'ye think?' he questioned.

'I should,' said Maggie.

'Then I shall!' he exclaimed. 'How d'ye think he'll take it?'

'Well,' said Maggie, 'I don't see how he can do aught but take it all right. . . . Depends how you put it, of course.'

'Oh, you leave that to me!' said Edwin, with eager confidence. 'I shall put it all right. You trust me for that!'

V

Clara danced into the room, flowing over with infantile joy. She had been listening to part of the conversation behind the door.

'So he wants to be an architect! Arch-i-tect! Arch-i-tect!' She half-sang the word in a frenzy of ridicule. She really did dance, and waved her arms. Her eyes glittered, as if in rapture. These singular manifestations of her temperament were caused solely by the strangeness of the idea of Edwin wanting to be an architect. The strange sight of him with his hair cut short or in a new neck-tie affected her in a similar manner.

'Clara, go and put your pinafore on this *instant*!' said Maggie. 'You know you oughtn't to leave it off.'

'You needn't be so hoity-toity, miss,' Clara retorted. But she moved to obey. When she reached the door she turned again and gleefully taunted Edwin. 'And it's all because he went for a walk yesterday with Mr Orgreave! I know! I know! You needn't think I didn't see you, because I did! Arch-i-tect! Arch-i-tect!'

She vanished, on all her springs, spitefully graceful.

'You might almost think that infernal kid was right bang off her head,' Edwin muttered crossly. (Still, it was extraordinary how that infernal kid hit on the truth.)

Maggie began to mend the fire.

'Oh well!' murmured Maggie, conveying to Edwin that no importance must be attached to the chit's chittishness.

He went up to the next flight of stairs to his attic. Dust on the table of his work-attic! Shameful dust! He had not used that attic since Christmas, on the miserable plea that winter was cold and there was no fireplace! He blamed himself for his effeminacy. Where had flown his seriousness, his elaborate plans, his high purposes? A touch of winter had frightened them away. Yes, he blamed himself mercilessly. True it was – as that infernal kid had chanted – a casual half-hour with Mr Orgreave was alone responsible for his awakening – at any rate, for his awakening at this particular moment. Still, he was awake – that was the great fact. He was tremendously awake. He had not been asleep; he had only been half-asleep. His intention of becoming an architect had never left him. But, through weakness before his father, through a cowardly desire to avoid disturbance and postpone a crisis, he had let the weeks slide by. Now he was in a groove, in a canyon. He had to get out, and the sooner the better.

A piece of paper, soiled, was pinned on his drawing-board; one or two sketches lay about. He turned the drawing-board over, so that he might use it for a desk on which to write the letter. But he had no habit of writing letters. In the attic was to be found neither ink, pen, paper, nor envelope. He remembered a broken quire of sermon paper in his bedroom; he had used a few sheets of it for notes on Bishop Colenso. These notes had been written in the privacy and warmth of bed, in pencil. But the letter must be done in ink; the letter was too important for pencil; assuredly his father would take exception to pencil. He descended to his sister's room and borrowed Maggie's ink and a pen, and took an envelope, tripping like a thief. Then he sat down to the composition of the letter; but he was obliged to stop almost immediately in order to light the lamp.

VI

This is what he wrote :

'DEAR FATHER, – I dare say you will think it queer me writing you a letter like this, but it is the best thing I can do, and I hope you will excuse me. I dare say you will remember I told you that night when you came home late from Manchester here in the attic that I wanted to be an architect. You replied that what I wanted was business experience. If you say that I have not enough business experience yet, I agree to that, but I want it to be understood that later on, when it is the proper time, I am to be an architect. You know I am very fond of architecture, and I feel that I must be an architect. I feel I shall not be happy in the printing business because I want to be an architect. I am now nearly seventeen. Perhaps it is too soon yet for me to be apprenticed to an architect, and so I can go on learning business habits. But I just want it to be understood. I am quite sure you wish me to be happy in life, and I shan't be happy if I am always regretting that I have not gone in for being an architect. I know I shall like architecture. – Your affectionate son,

EDWIN CLAYHANGER'

Then, as an afterthought, he put the date and his address at the top. He meditated a postcript asking for a reply, but decided that this was unnecessary. As he was addressing the envelope Mrs Nixon called out to him from below to come to tea. He was surprised to find that he had spent over an hour on the letter. He shivered and sneezed.

VII

During tea he felt himself absurdly self-conscious, but nobody seemed to notice his condition. The whole family went to chapel. The letter lay in his pocket, and he might easily have slipped away to the post-office with it, but he had had no opportunity to possess himself of a stamp.

There was no need to send the letter through the post. He might get up early and put it among the morning's letters. He had decided, however, that it must arrive formally by the postman, and he would not alter his decision. Hence, after chapel, he took a match, and, creeping into the shop, procured a crimson stamp from his father's desk. Then he went forth, by the back way, alone into the streets. The adventure was not so hazardous as it seemed and as it felt. Darius was incurious by nature, though he had brief fevers of curiosity. Thus the life of the children was a demoralizing mixture of rigid discipline and freedom. They were permitted nothing, but, as the years passed, they might take nearly anything. There was small chance of Darius discovering his son's excursion.

In crossing the road from chapel Edwin had opined to his father that the frost was breaking. He was now sure of it. The mud, no longer brittle, yielded to pressure, and there was a trace of dampness in the interstices of the pavement bricks. A thin raw mist was visible in huge spheres round the street lamps. The sky was dark. The few people whom he encountered seemed to be out upon mysterious errands, seemed to emerge strangely from one gloom and strangely to vanish into another. In the blind, black façades of the streets the public-houses blazed invitingly with gas; they alone were alive in the weekly death of the town; and they gleamed everywhere, at every corner; the town appeared to consist chiefly of public-houses. He dropped the letter into the box in the market-place; he heard it fall. His heart beat. The deed was now irrevocable. He wondered what Monday held for him. The quiescent melancholy of the town invaded his spirit, and mingled with his own remorseful sorrow for the unstrenuous past, and his apprehensive solicitude about the future. It was not unpleasant, this brooding sadness, half-despondency and half-hope. A man and a woman, arm-in-arm, went by him as he stood unconscious of the conspicuousness under the gas-lamp that lit the post-office. They laughed the smothered laugh of intimacy to see a tall boy standing alone there, with no overcoat, gazing at naught. Edwin turned to go home. It occurred to him that nearly all the people he met were couples, arm-in-arm. And he suddenly thought of Florence, the clog-dancer. He had scarcely thought of her for months. The complexity of the interests of life, and the interweaving of its moods, fatigued his mind into an agreeably grave vacuity.

CHAPTER 17 : *End of a Struggle*

I

It was not one of his official bilious attacks that Darius had on the following day; he only yielded himself up in the complete grand manner when nature absolutely compelled. The goose had not formally beaten him, but neither had he formally beaten the goose. The battle was drawn, and this meant that Darius had a slight headache, a feeling of heavy disgust with the entire polity of the universe, and a disinclination for food. The first and third symptoms he hid as far as possible, from pride, hating bacon. The children knew from his eyes and his guilty gestures that he was not well, but they dared not refer to his condition; they were bound to pretend that the health of their father flourished in the highest perfection. And they were glad that things were no worse.

On the other hand Edwin had a sneezing cold which he could not conceal, and Darius inimically inquired what foolishness he had committed to have brought this on himself. Edwin replied that he knew of no cause for it. A deliberate lie ! He knew that he had contracted a chill while writing a letter to his father in an unwarmed attic, and had intensified the chill by going forth to post the letter without his overcoat in a raw evening mist. Obviously, however, he could not have stated the truth. He was uncomfortable at the breakfast-table, but, after the first few moments, less so than during the disturbed night he had feared to be. His father had neither eaten him, nor jumped down his throat, nor performed any of those unpleasant miraculous feats which fathers usually do perform when infuriated by filial foolishness. The letter therefore had not been utterly disastrous; sometimes a letter would ruin a breakfast, for Mr Clayhanger, with no consideration for the success of meals, always opened his post before bite or sup. He had had the letter, and still he was ready to talk to his son in the ordinary grim tone of a goose-morrow. Which was to the good. Edwin was now convinced that he had done well to write the letter.

II

But as the day passed, Edwin began to ask himself : 'Has he had the letter?' There was no sign of the letter in his father's demeanour, which, while not such as to make it credible that he ever had moods of positive gay roguishness, was almost tolerable, considering his headache and his nausea. Letters occasionally were lost in the post, or delayed. Edwin thought it would be just his usual bad luck if that particular letter, that letter of all letters, should be lost. And the strange thing is that he could not prevent himself from hoping that it indeed was lost. He would prefer it to be lost rather than delayed. He felt that if the postman brought it by the afternoon delivery while he and his father were in the shop together, he should drop down dead. The day continued to pass, and did pass. And the shop was closed. 'He'll speak to me after supper,' said Edwin. But Darius did not speak to him after supper. Darius put on his hat and overcoat and went out, saying no word except to advise the children to be getting to bed, all of them.

As soon as he was gone Edwin took a candle and returned to the shop. He was convinced now that the letter had not been delivered, but he wished to make conviction sure. He opened the desk. His letter was nearly the first document he saw. It looked affrighting, awful. He dared not read it, to see whether its wording was fortunate or unfortunate. He departed, mystified. Upstairs in his bedroom he had a new copy of an English translation of Victor Hugo's *Notre Dame*, which had been ordered by Lawyer Lawton, but could not be called for till the following week, because Lawyer Lawton only called once a fortnight. He had meant to read that book, with due precautions, in bed. But he could not fix attention on it. Impossible for him to follow a single paragraph. He extinguished the candle. Then he heard his father come home. He thought that he scarcely slept all night.

III

The next morning, Tuesday, the girls, between whom and their whispering friend Miss Ingamells something feminine was evidently afoot, left the breakfast-table sooner than usual, not without stifled giggles : upon occasion Maggie would surprisingly meet Clara and Miss Ingamells on their own plane; since Sunday afternoon she had shown no further interest in Edwin's important crisis; she seemed, so far as he could judge, to have fallen back into her customary state of busy apathy.

The man and the young man were alone together. Darius, in his satisfaction at having been delivered so easily from the goose, had taken an extra slice of bacon. Edwin's cold was now fully developed; and Maggie had told him to feed it.

'I suppose you got that letter I wrote you, Father, about me going in for architecture,' said Edwin. Then he blew his nose to hide his confusion. He was rather startled to hear himself saying those bold words. He thought that he was quite calm and in control of his impulses; but it was not so; his nerves were stretched to the utmost.

Darius said nothing. But Edwin could see his face darkening, and his lower lip heavily falling. He glowered, though not at Edwin. With eyes fixed on the window he glowered into vacancy. The pride went out of Edwin's heart.

'So ye'd leave the printing?' muttered Darius, when he had finished masticating. He spoke in a menacing voice thick with ferocious emotion.

'Well —' said Edwin, quaking.

He thought he had never seen his father so ominously intimidating. He was terrorized as he looked at that ugly and dark countenance. He could not say any more. His voice left him. Thus his fear was physical as well as moral. He reflected : 'Well, I expected a row, but I didn't expect it would be as bad as this!' And once more he was completely puzzled and baffled by the enigma of his father.

IV

He did not hold the key, and even had he held it he was too young, too inexperienced, to have used it. As with gathering passion the eyes of Darius assaulted the window-pane, Darius had a painful intense vision of that miracle, his own career. Edwin's grand misfortune was that he was blind to the miracle. Edwin had never seen the little boy in the Bastille. But Darius saw him always, the infant who had begun life at a rope's-end. Every hour of Darius's present existence was really an astounding marvel to Darius. He could not read the newspaper without thinking how wonderful it was that he should be able to read the newspaper. And it was wonderful! It was wonderful that he had three different suits of clothes, none of them with a single hole. It was wonderful that he had three children, all with complete outfits of good clothes. It was wonderful that he never had to think twice about buying coal, and that he could have more food than he needed. It was wonderful that he was not living in a two-roomed cottage. He never came into his house by the side entrance without feeling proud that the door gave on to a preliminary passage and not direct into a living-room; he would never lose the idea that a lobby, however narrow, was the great distinguishing mark of wealth. It was wonderful that he had a piano, and that his girls could play it, and could sing. It was wonderful that he had paid twenty-eight shillings a term for his son's schooling, in addition to book-money. Twenty-eight shillings a term! And once a penny a week was considered enough, and twopence generous! Through sheer splendid wilful pride he had kept his son at school till the lad was sixteen, going on seventeen! Seventeen, not seven! He had had the sort of pride in his son that a man may have in an idle, elegant, and absurdly expensive woman. It even tickled him to hear his son called 'Master Edwin', and then 'Mister Edwin'; just as the fine ceremonious manners of his sister-in-law Mrs Hamps tickled him. His marriage! With all its inevitable disillusions it had been wonderful, incredible. He looked back on it as a miracle. For he had married far above him, and had proved equal to the enormously difficult situation. Never had he made a fool of himself. He often took keen pleasure in speculating upon the demeanour of his father, his mother, his little sister, could they have seen him in his purple and in his grandeur. They were all dead. And those days were fading, fading, gone, with their unutterable, intolerable shame and sadness, intolerable even in memory. And his wife dead too! All that remained was Mr Shushions.

And then his business? Darius's pride in the achievement of his business was simply indescribable. If he had not built up that particular connexion he had built up another one whose sale had enabled him to buy it. And he was waxing yearly. His supremacy as a printer could not be challenged in Bursley. Steam! A double-windowed shop! A foreman to whom alone he paid thirty shillings a week! Four other employees! (Not to mention a domestic servant). . . . How had he done it? He did not know. Certainly he did not credit himself with brilliant faculties. He knew he was not brilliant; he knew that once or twice he had had luck. But he had the greatest confidence in his rough-hewing common sense. The large curves of his career were correctly drawn. His common sense, his slow shrewdness, had been richly justified by events. They had been pitted against foes – and look now at the little boy from the Bastille!

v

To Darius there was no business quite like his own. He admitted that there were businesses much bigger, but they lacked the miraculous quality that his own had. They were not sacred. His was, genuinely. Once, in his triumphant and vain early manhood he had had a fancy for bulldogs; he had bred bulldogs; and one day he had sacrificed even that great delight at the call of his business; and now no one could guess that he knew the difference between a setter and a mastiff.

It was this sacred business (perpetually adored at the secret altar in Darius's heart), this miraculous business, and not another, that Edwin wanted to abandon, with scarcely a word; just casually!

True, Edwin had told him one night that he would like to be an architect. But Darius had attached no importance to the boyish remark. Darius had never even dreamed that Edwin would not go into the business. It would not have occurred to him to conceive such a possibility. And the boy had shown great aptitude. The boy had saved the printing office from disaster. And Darius had proved his satisfaction therein, not by words certainly, but beyond mistaking in his general demeanour towards Edwin. And after all that, a letter – mind you, a letter! – proposing with the most damnable insolent audacity that he

116

should be an architect, because he would not be 'happy' in the printing business; . . . An architect! Why an architect, specially? What in the name of God was there to attract in bricks and mortar? He thought the boy had gone off his head for a space. He could not think of any other explanation. He had not allowed the letter to upset him. By his armour of thick callousness, he had protected the tender places in his soul from being wounded. He had not decided how to phrase his answer to Edwin. He had not even decided whether he would say anything at all, whether it would not be more dignified and impressive to make no remark whatever to Edwin, to let him slowly perceive, by silence, what a lamentable error he had committed.

And here was the boy lightly, cheekily, talking at breakfast about 'going in for architecture'! The armour of callousness was pierced. Darius felt the full force of the letter; and as he suffered, so he became terrible and tyrannic in his suffering. He meant to save his business, to put his business before anything. And he would have his own way. He would impose his will. And he would have treated argument as a final insult. All the heavy, obstinate, relentless force of his individuality was now channelled in one tremendous instinct.

VI

'Well, what?' he growled savagely, as Edwin halted.

In spite of his advanced age Edwin began to cry. Yes, the tears came out of his eyes.

'And now you begin blubbing!' said his father.

'You say naught for six months – and then you start writing letters!' said his father.

'And what's made ye settle on architecting, I'd like to be knowing?' Darius went on.

Edwin was not able to answer this question. He had never put it to himself. Assuredly he could not, at the pistol's point, explain *why* he wanted to be an architect. He did not know. He announced this truth ingenuously –

'I don't know – I –'

'I sh'd think not!' said his father. 'D'ye think architecting 'll be any better than this?' 'This' meant printing.

'I don't know –'

'Ye don't know! Ye don't know!' Darius repeated testily. His testiness was only like foam on the great wave of his resentment.

'Mr Orgreave –' Edwin began. It was unfortunate, because Darius had had a difficulty with Mr Orgreave, who was notoriously somewhat exacting in the matter of prices.

'Don't talk to me about Mester Orgreave!' Darius almost shouted.

Edwin didn't. He said to himself : 'I am lost.'

'What's this business o' mine for, if it isna for you?' asked his father. 'Architecting! There's neither sense nor reason in it! Neither sense nor reason!'

He rose and walked out. Edwin was now sobbing. In a moment his father returned, and stood in the doorway.

'Ye've been doing well, I'll say that, and I've shown it! I was beginning to have hopes of ye!' It was a great deal to say.

He departed.

'Perhaps if I hadn't stopped his damned old machine from going through the floor, he'd have let me off!' Edwin muttered bitterly. 'I've been too good, that's what's the matter with me!'

VII

He saw how fantastic was the whole structure of his hopes. He wondered that he had ever conceived it even wildly possible that his father would consent to architecture as a career! To ask it was to ask absurdly too much of fate. He demolished, with a violent and resentful impulse, the structure of his hopes; stamped on it angrily. He was beaten. What could he do? He could do nothing against his father. He could no more change his father than the course of a river. He was beaten. He saw his case in its true light.

Mrs Nixon entered to clear the table. He turned away to hide his face, and strode passionately off. Two hours elapsed before he appeared in the shop. Nobody asked for him, but Mrs Nixon knew he was in the attic. At noon, Maggie, with a peculiar look, told him that Auntie Hamps had called and that he was to go and have dinner with her at one o'clock, and that his father consented. Obviously, Maggie knew the facts of the day. He was perturbed at the prospect of the visit. But he was glad; he thought he could not have lived through a dinner at the same table as Clara. He guessed that his auntie had been made aware of the situation and wished to talk to him.

VIII

'Your father came to see me in such a state last night!' said Auntie Hamps, after she had dealt with his frightful cold.

Edwin was astonished by the news. Then after all his father had been afraid! . . . After all perhaps he had yielded too soon! If he had held out. . . . If he had not been a baby! . . . But it was too late. The incident was now closed.

Mrs Hamps was kind, but unusually firm in her tone; which reached a sort of benevolent severity.

'Your father had such high hopes of you. *Has* – I should say. He couldn't imagine what on earth possessed you to write such a letter. And I'm sure I can't. I hope you're sorry. If you'd seen your father last night you would be, I'm sure.'

'But look here, Auntie,' Edwin defended himself, sneezing and wiping his nose; and he spoke of his desire. Surely he was entitled to ask, to suggest! A son could not be expected to be exactly like his father. And so on.

No! no! She brushed all that aside. She scarcely listened to it.

'But think of the business! And just think of your father's feelings!'

Edwin spoke no more. He saw that she was absolutely incapable of putting herself in his place. He could not have explained her attitude by saying that she had the vast unconscious cruelty which always goes with a perfect lack of imagination; but this was the explanation. He left her, saddened by the obvious conclusion that his auntie, whom he had always supported against his sisters, was part author of his undoing. She had undoubtedly much strengthened his father against him. He had a gleam of suspicion that his sisters had been right, and he wrong, about Mrs Hamps. Wonderful, the cruel ruthless insight of girls – into some things!

IX

Not till Saturday did the atmosphere of the Clayhanger household resume the normal. But earlier than that Edwin had already lost his resentment. It disappeared with his cold. He could not continue to bear ill-will. He accepted his destiny of immense disappointment. He shouldered it. You may call him weak or you may call him strong. Maggie said nothing to him of the great affair. What could she have said? And the affair was so great that even Clara did not dare to exercise upon it her peculiar faculties of ridicule. It abashed her by its magnitude.

On Saturday Darius said to his son, good-humouredly –

'Canst be trusted to pay wages?'

Edwin smiled.

At one o'clock he went across the yard to the printing office with a little bag of money. The younger apprentice was near the door scrubbing type with potash to cleanse it. The backs of his hands were horribly raw and bleeding with chaps, due to the frequent necessity of washing them in order to serve the machines, and the impossibility of drying them properly. Still, winter was ending now, and he only worked eleven hours a day, in an airy room, instead of nineteen hours in a cellar, like the little boy from the Bastille. He was a fortunate youth. The journeyman stood idle; as often, on Saturdays, the length of the journeyman's apron had been reduced by deliberate tearing during the week from three feet to about a foot – so imperious and sudden was the need for rags in the processes of printing. Big James was folding up his apron. They all saw that Edwin had the bag, and their faces relaxed.

'You're as good as the master now, Mr Edwin,' said Big James with ceremonious politeness and a fine gesture, when Edwin had finished paying.

'Am I?' he rejoined simply.

Everybody knew of the great affair. Big James's words were his gentle intimation to Edwin that everyone knew the great affair was now settled.

That night, for the first time, Edwin could read *Notre Dame* with understanding and pleasure. He plunged with soft joy into the river of the gigantic and formidable narrative. He reflected that after all the sources of happiness were not exhausted.

BOOK TWO: HIS LOVE

CHAPTER I : *The Visit*

I

We now approach the more picturesque part of Edwin's career. Seven years passed. Towards the end of April 1880, on a Saturday morning, Janet Orgreave, second daughter of Osmond Orgreave, the architect, entered the Clayhanger shop.

All night an April shower lasting ten hours had beaten with persistent impetuosity against the window-panes of Bursley, and hence half the town slept ill. But at breakfast-time the clouds had been mysteriously drawn away, the winds had expired, and those drenched streets began to dry under the caressing peace of bright soft sunshine; the sky was pale blue of a delicacy unknown to the intemperate climes of the south. Janet Orgreave, entering the Clayhanger shop, brought into it with her the new morning weather. She also brought into it Edwin's fate, or part of it, but not precisely in the sense commonly understood when the word 'fate' is mentioned between a young man and a young woman.

A youth stood at the left-hand or 'fancy' counter, very nervous. Miss Ingamells (that was) was married and the mother of three children, and had probably forgotten the difference between 'demy' and 'post' octavos; and this youth had taken her place and the place of two unsatisfactory maids in black who had succeeded her. None but males were now employed in the Clayhanger business, and everybody breathed more freely; round, sound oaths were heard where never oaths had been heard before. The young man's name was Stifford, and he was addressed as 'Stiff'. He was a proof of the indiscretion of prophesying about human nature. He had been the paper boy, the minion of Edwin, and universally regarded as unreliable and almost worthless. But at sixteen a change had come over him; he parted his hair in the middle instead of at the side, arrived in the morning at 7.59 instead of 8.5, and seemed to see the earnestness of life. Everyone was glad and relieved, but everyone took the change as a matter of course; the attitude of everyone to the youth was : 'Well, it's not too soon!' No one saw a romantic miracle.

'I suppose you haven't got *The Light of Asia* in stock? began Janet Orgreave, after she had greeted the youth kindly.

'I'm afraid we haven't, Miss,' said Stifford. This was an understatement. He knew beyond fear that *The Light of Asia* was not in stock.

'Oh!' murmured Janet.

'I think you said *The Light of Asia*?'

'Yes. *The Light of Asia*, by Edwin Arnold.' Janet had a persuasive, humane smile.

Stifford was anxious to have the air of obliging this smile, and he turned round to examine a shelf of prize books behind him, well aware that *The Light of Asia* was not among them. He knew *The Light of Asia*, and was proud of his knowledge; that is to say, he knew by visible and tactual evidence that such a book existed, for it had been ordered and supplied as a Christmas present four months previously, soon after its dazzling apparition in the world.

'Yes, by Edwin Arnold – Edwin Arnold,' he muttered learnedly, running his finger along gilded backs.

'It's being talked about a great deal,' said Janet as if to encourage him.

'Yes, it is . . . No, I'm very sorry, we haven't it in stock.' Stifford faced her again, and leaned his hands wide apart on the counter.

'I should like you to order it for me,' said Janet Orgreave in a low voice.

She asked this exactly as though she were asking a personal favour from Stiffford the private individual. Such was Janet's way. She could not help it. People often said that her desire to please, and her methods of pleasing, were unconscious. These people were wrong. She was perfectly conscious and even deliberate in her actions. She liked to please. She could please easily and she could please keenly. Therefore she strove always to please. Sometimes, when she looked in the mirror, and saw that charming, good-natured face with its rich vermilion lips eager to part in a nice, warm, sympathetic smile, she could accuse herself of being too fond of the art of pleasing. For she was a conscientious girl, and her age being twenty-five her soul was at its prime, full, bursting with beautiful impulses towards perfection. Yes, she would accuse herself of being too happy, too content, and would wonder whether she ought not to seek heaven by some austerity of scowling. Janet had everything : a kind disposition, some brains, some beauty, considerable elegance and luxury for her station, fine shoulders at a ball, universal love and esteem.

Stifford, as he gazed diffidently at this fashionable, superior, and yet exquisitely beseeching woman on the other side of the counter, was in a very unpleasant quandary. She had by her magic transformed him into a private individual, and he acutely wanted to earn that smile which she was giving him. But he could not. He was under the obligation to say 'No' to her innocent and delightful request; and yet could he say 'No'? Could he bring himself to desolate her by a refusal? (She had produced in him the illusion that a refusal would indeed desolate her, though she would of course bear it with sweet fortitude.) Business was a barbaric thing at times.

'The fact is, Miss,' he said at length, in his best manner, 'Mr Clayhanger has decided to give up the new book business, I'm verry sorry.'

Had it been another than Janet he would have assuredly said with pride : 'We have decided –'

'Really !' said Janet. 'I see !'

Then Stifford directed his eyes upon a square glazed structure of ebonized wood that had been insinuated and inserted into the opposite corner of the shop, behind the ledger-window. And Janet's eyes followed his.

'I don't know if –' he hesitated.

'Is Mr Clayhanger in?' she demanded, as if wishful to help him in the formulation of his idea, and she added : 'Or Mr Edwin?' Deliciously persuasive !

II

The wooden structure was a lair. It had been constructed to hold Darius Clayhanger; but in practice it generally held Edwin, as his father's schemes for the enlargement of the business carried him abroad more and more. It was a device of Edwin's for privacy; Edwin had planned it and seen the plan executed. The theory was that a person concealed in the structure (called 'the office') was not technically in the shop and must not be disturbed by anyone in the shop. Only persons of authority – Darius and Edwin – had the privilege of the office, and since its occupant could hear every whisper in the shop, it was always for the occupant to decide when events demanded that he should emerge.

On Janet's entrance, Edwin was writing in the daybook : 'April 11th. Turnhill Oddfellows. 400 Contrib. Cards –' He stopped writing. He held himself still like a startled mouse. With satisfaction he observed that the door of the fortress was closed. By putting his nose near the crystal wall he could see, through the minute transparent portions of the patterned glass, without being seen. He watched Janet's graceful gestures, and examined with pleasure the beauties of her half-season toilet; he discerned the modishness of her umbrella handle. His sensations were agreeable and yet disagreeable, for he wished both to remain where he was and to go forth and engage her in brilliant small talk. He had no small talk, except that of the salesman and the tradesman; his tongue knew not freedom; but his fancy dreamed of light, intellectual conversations with fine girls. These dreams of fancy had of late become almost habitual, for the sole reason that he had raised his hat several times to Janet, and once had shaken hands with her and said, 'How d'you do, Miss Orgreave?' in response to her 'How d'you do, Mr Clayhanger?' Osmond Orgreave, in whom had originated their encounter, had cut across the duologue at that point and spoilt it. But Edwin's fancy had continued it, when he was alone late at night, in a very diverting and witty manner. And now, he had her at his disposal; he had only to emerge, and Stiff would deferentially recede, and he could chat with her at ease, starting comfortably from *The Light of Asia.* And yet he dared not; his faint heart told him in loud beats that he could only chat cleverly with a fine girl when absolutely alone in his room, in the dark.

Still, he surveyed her; he added her up; he pronounced, with a touch of conventional male patronage (caught possibly from the Liberal Club), that Janet was indubitably a nice girl and a fine girl. He would not admit that he was afraid of her, and that despite all theoretical argufying, he deemed her above him in rank.

And if he had known the full truth, he might have regretted that he had not caused the lair to be furnished with a trapdoor by means of which the timid could sink into the earth.

The truth was that Janet had called purposely to inspect Edwin at leisure. *The Light of Asia* was a mere poetical pretext. *The Light of Asia* might as easily have been ordered at Hanbridge, where her father and brothers ordered all their books – in fact, more easily. Janet, with all her niceness, with all the reality of her immense good-nature, loved as well as anybody a bit of chicane where a man was concerned. Janet's eyes could twinkle as mischievously as her quiet mother's. Mr Orgreave having in the last eight months been in professional relations with Darius and Edwin, the Orgreave household had been discussing Edwin again. Mr Orgreave spoke of him favourably. Mrs Orgreave said that he looked the right sort of youth, but that he had a peculiar manner. Janet said that she should not be surprised if there were something in him. Janet said also that his sister Clara was an impossible piece of goods, and that his sister Maggie was born an old maid. One of her brothers then said that that was just what was the matter with Edwin too! Mr Orgreave protested that he wasn't so sure of that, and that occasionally Edwin would say things that were really rather good. This stimulated Mrs Orgreave's curiosity, and she suggested that her husband should invite the young man to their house. Whereupon Mr Orgreave pessimistically admitted that he did not think Edwin could be enticed. And Janet, piqued, said, 'If that's all, I'll have him here in a week.' They were an adventurous family, always ready for anything, always on the lookout for new sources of pleasure, full of zest in life. They liked novelties, and hospitality was their chief hobby. They made fun of nearly everybody, but it was not mean fun.

Such, and not *The Light of Asia*, was the cause of Janet's visit.

III

Be it said to Edwin's shame that she would have got no further with the family plot that morning, had it not been for the chivalry of Stifford. Having allowed his eyes to rest on the lair, Stifford allowed his memory to forget the rule of the shop, and left the counter for the door of the lair, determined that Miss Orgreave should see the genuineness of his anxiety to do his utmost for so sympathetic a woman. Edwin, perceiving the intention from his lair, had to choose whether he would go out or be fetched out. Of course he preferred to go out. But he would never have gone out on his own initiative; he would have hesitated until Janet had departed, and he would then have called himself a fool. He regretted, and I too regret, that he was like that; but like that he was.

He emerged with nervous abruptness.

'Oh, how d'you do, Miss Orgreave?' he said; 'I thought it was your voice.' After this he gave a little laugh, which meant nothing, certainly not amusement; it was merely a gawky habit that he had unconsciously adopted. Then he took his handkerchief out of his pocket and put it back again. Stifford fell back and had to pretend that nothing interested him less than the interview which he had precipitated.

'How d'you do, Mr Clayhanger?' said Janet.

They shook hands. Edwin wrung Janet's hand; another gawky habit.

'I was just going to order a book,' said Janet.

'Oh yes! *The Light of Asia*,' said Edwin.

'Have you read it?' Janet asked.

'Yes – that is, a lot of it.'

'Have you?' exclaimed Janet. She was impressed, because really the perusal of verse was not customary in the town. And her delightful features showed generously the full extent to which she was impressed : an honest, ungrudging appreciation of Edwin's studiousness. She said to herself : 'Oh! I must certainly get him to the house.' And Edwin said to himself, 'No mistake, there's something very genuine about this girl.

Edwin said aloud quickly, from an exaggerated apprehensiveness lest she should be rating him too high –

'It was quite an accident that I saw it. I never read that sort of thing – not as a rule.' He laughed again. ·

'Is it worth buying?' Now she appealed to him as an authority. She could not help doing so, and in doing so she was quite honest, for her good-nature had momentarily persuaded her that he was an authority.

'I – I don't know,' Edwin answered, moving his neck as though his collar was not comfortable; but it was comfortable, being at least a size too large. 'It depends, you know. If you read a lot of poetry, it's worth buying. But if you don't, it isn't. It's not Tennyson, you know. See what I mean?'

'Yes, quite!' said Janet, smiling with continued and growing appreciation. The reply struck her as very sagacious. She suddenly saw in a new light her father's hints that there was something in this young man not visible to everybody. She had a tremendous respect for her father's opinion, and now she reproached herself in that she had not attached due importance to what he had said about Edwin. 'How right father always is!' she thought. Her attitude of respect for Edwin was now more securely based upon impartial intelligence than before; it owed less to her weakness for seeing the best in people. As for Edwin, he was saying to himself: 'I wish to the devil I could talk to her without spluttering! Why can't I be natural? Why can't I be glib? Some chaps could.' And Edwin could be, with some chaps.

IV

They were standing close together in the shop, Janet and Edwin, near the cabinet of artists' materials. Janet, after her manner at once frank and reassuring, examined Edwin; she had come on purpose to examine him. She had never been able to decide whether or not he was good-looking, and she could not decide now. But she liked the appeal in his eyes. She did not say to herself that there was an appeal in his eyes; she said that there was 'something in his eyes'. Also he was moderately tall, and he was slim. She said to herself that he must be very well shaped. Beginning at the bottom, his boots were clumsy, his trousers were baggy and even shiny, and they had transverse creases, not to be seen in the trousers of her own mankind; his waistcoat showed plainly the forms of every article in the pockets thereof – watch, penknife, pencil, etc., it was obvious that he never emptied his pockets at night; his collar was bluish-white instead of white, and its size was monstrous; his jacket had 'worked up' at the back of his neck, completely hiding his collar there; the side-pockets of his jacket were weighted and bulged with mysterious goods; his fair hair was rough but not curly; he had a moustache so trifling that one could not be sure whether it was a moustache or whether he had been too busy to think of shaving. Janet received all these facts into her brain, and then carelessly let them all slip out again, in her preoccupation with his eyes. She said they were sad eyes. The mouth, too, was somewhat sad (she thought), but there was a drawing down of the corners of it that seemed to make gentle fun of its sadness. Janet, perhaps out of her good-nature, liked his restless, awkward movements, and the gesture of his hands, of which the articulations were too prominent, and the finger-nails too short.

'Tom reads rather a lot of poetry,' said Janet. 'That's my oldest brother.'

'That *might* justify you,' said Edwin doubtfully.

They both laughed. And as with Janet, so with Edwin, when he laughed, all the kindest and honestest part of him seemed to rise into his face.

'But if you don't supply new books any more?'

'Oh!' Edwin stuttered, blushing slightly. 'That's nothing. I shall be very pleased to get it for you specially, Miss Orgreave. It's father that decided – only last month – that the new book business was more trouble than it's worth. It was – in a way; but I'm sorry, myself, we've given it up, poor as it was. Of course there *are* no book-buyers in this town, especially now old Lawton's dead. But still, what with one thing or another, there was generally some book on order, and I used to see them. Of course there's no money in it. But still . . . Father says that people buy less books than they used to – but he's wrong there.' Edwin spoke with calm certainty. 'I've shown him he's wrong by our order-book, but he wouldn't see it.' Edwin smiled, with a general mild indulgence for fathers.

'Well,' said Janet, 'I'll ask Tom first.'

'No trouble whatever to us to order it for you, I assure you. I can get it down by return of post.'

'It's very good of you,' said Janet, genuinely persuading herself for the moment that Edwin was quite exceeding the usual bounds of complaisance.

She moved to depart.

'Father told me to tell you if I saw you that the glazing will be all finished this morning,' said she.

'Up yonder?' Edwin jerked his head to indicate the south.

And Janet delicately confirmed his assumption with a slight declension of her waving hat.

'Oh! Good!' Edwin murmured.

Janet held out her hand, to be wrung again, and assured him of her gratitude for his offer of taking trouble about the book and he assured her that it would not be trouble but pleasure. He accompanied her to the doorway.

'I think I must come up and have a look at that glazing this afternoon,' he said, as she stood on the pavement.

She nodded, smiling benevolence and appreciation, and departed round the corner in the soft sunshine.

Edwin put on a stern, casual expression for the benefit of Stifford, as who should say: 'What a trial these frivolous girls are to a man immersed in affairs!' But Stifford was not deceived. Safe within his lair, Edwin was conscious of quite a disturbing glow. He smiled to himself – a little self-consciously, though alone. Then he scribbled down in pencil 'Light of Asia. Miss J. Orgreave'.

CHAPTER 2 : *Father and Son after Seven Years*

I

Darius came heavily, and breathing heavily, into the little office.

'Now as all this racketing's over,' he said crossly – he meant by 'racketing' the general election which had just put the Liberal party into power – 'I'll thank ye to see as all that red and blue ink is cleaned off the rollers and slabs, and the types cleaned too. I've told 'em ten times if I've told 'em once, but as far as I can make out, they've done naught to it yet.'

Edwin grunted without looking up.

His father was now a fattish man, and he had aged quite as much as Edwin. Some of his scanty hair was white; the rest was grey. White hair sprouted about his ears; gold gleamed in his mouth; and a pair of spectacles hung insecurely balanced half-way down his nose; his waistcoat seemed to be stretched tightly over a perfectly smooth hemisphere. He had an air of somewhat gross and prosperous untidiness. Except for the teeth, his bodily frame appeared to have fallen into disrepair, as though he had ceased to be interested in it, as though he had been using it for a long time as a mere makeshift lodging. And this impression was more marked at table; he ate exactly as if throwing food to a wild animal concealed somewhere within the hemisphere, an animal which was never seen, but which rumbled threateningly from time to time in its dark dungeon.

Of all this, Edwin had definitely noticed nothing save that his father was 'getting stouter'. To Edwin, Darius was exactly the same father, and for Darius, Edwin was still aged sixteen. They both of them went on living on the assumption that the world had stood still in those seven years between 1873 and 1880. If they had been asked what had happened during those seven years, they would have answered : 'Oh, nothing particular!'

But the world had been whizzing ceaselessly from one miracle into another. Board schools had been opened in Bursley, wondrous affairs, with ventilation; indeed ventilation had been discovered. A Jew had been made Master of the Rolls; spectacle at which England shivered, and then, perceiving no sign of disaster, shrugged its shoulders. Irish members had taught the House of Commons how to talk for twenty-four hours without a pause. The wages of the agricultural labourer had sprung into the air and leaped over the twelve shillings bar into regions of opulence. Moody and Sankey had found and conquered England for Christ. Landseer and Livingstone had died, and the provinces could not decide whether 'Dignity and Impudence' or the penetration of Africa was the more interesting feat. Herbert Spencer had published his *Study of Sociology;* Matthew Arnold his *Literature and Dogma;* and Frederic Farrar his Life of his Lord; but here the provinces had no difficulty in deciding, for they had only heard of the last. Every effort had been made to explain by persuasion and by force to the working man that trade unions were inimical to his true welfare, and none had succeeded, so stupid was he. The British Army had been employed to put reason into the noddle of a town called Northampton which was furious because an atheist had not been elected to Parliament. Pullman cars, *The Pirates of Penzance*, Henry Irving's *Hamlet*, spelling-bees, and Captain Webb's Channel swim had all proved that there were novelties under the sun. Bishops, archbishops, and dissenting ministers had met at Lambeth to inspect the progress of irreligious thought, with intent to arrest it. Princes and dukes had conspired to inaugurate the most singular scheme that ever was, the Kyrle Society – for bringing beauty home to the people by means of decorative art, gardening, and music. The Bulgarian Atrocities had served to give new life to all penny gaffs and blood-tubs. The *Eurydice* and the *Princess Alice* had foundered in order to demonstrate the uncertainty of existence and the courage of the island-race. The *Nineteenth Century* had been started, a little late in the day, and the *Referee.* Ireland had all but died of hunger, but had happily been saved to enjoy the benefits of Coercion. The Young Men's Christian Association had been born again in the splendour of Exeter Hall. Bursley itself had entered on a new career as a chartered borough, with Mayor, alderman, and councillors, all in chains of silver. And among the latest miracles were Northampton's success in sending the atheist to Parliament, the infidelity of the Tay Bridge three days after Christmas, the catastrophe of Majuba Hill, and the discovery that soldiers objected to being flogged into insensibility for a peccadillo.

But, in spite of numerous attempts, nobody had contrived to make England see that her very existence would not be threatened if museums were opened on Sundays, or that Nonconformists might be buried according to their own rites without endangering the constitution.

II

Darius was possibly a little uneasy in his mind about the world. Possibly there had just now begun to form in his mind the conviction, in which most men die, that all was not quite well with the world, and that in particular his native country had contracted a fatal malady since he was a boy.

He was a printer, and yet the General Election had not put sunshine in his heart. And this was strange, for a general election is the brief millennium of printers, especially of steamprinters who for dispatch can beat all rivals. During a general election the question put by a customer to a printer is not, 'How much will it be?' but 'How soon can I have it?' There was no time for haggling about price; and indeed to haggle about price would have been unworthy, seeing that every customer (ordinary business being at a standstill) was engaged in the salvation of England. Darius was a Liberal, but a quiet one, and he was patronized by both political parties – blue and red. As a fact, neither party could have done without him. His printing office had clattered and thundered early and late, and more than once had joined the end of one day's work to the beginning of another; and more than once had Big James with his men and his boy (a regiment increased since 1873) stood like plotters muttering in the yard at five minutes to twelve on Sunday evening, waiting for midnight to sound, and Big James had unlocked the door of the office on the newborn Monday, and work had instantly commenced, to continue till Monday was nearly dead of old age.

Once only had work been interrupted, and that was on a day when, a lot of 'blue jobs' being about, a squad of red fire-eaters had come up the back alley with intent to answer arguments by thwackings and wreckings; but the obstinacy of an oak door had fatigued them. The staff had enjoyed that episode. Every member of it was well paid for overtime. Darius could afford to pay conscientiously. In the printing trade, prices were steadier then than they are now. But already the discovery of competition was following upon the discovery of ventilation. Perhaps Darius sniffed it from a distance, and was disturbed thereby.

III

For though he was a Liberal in addition to being a printer, and he had voted Liberal, and his party had won, yet the General Election had not put sunshine in his heart. No! The tendencies of England worried him. When he read in a paper about the heretical tendencies of Robertson Smith's Biblical articles in the *Encyclopaedia Britannica,* he said to himself that they were of a piece with the rest, and that such things were to be expected in those modern days, and that matters must have come to a pretty pass when even the *Encyclopaedia Britannica* was infected. (Still, he had sold a copy of the new edition.) He was exceedingly bitter against Ireland; and also, in secret, behind Big James's back, against trade unions. When Edwin came home one night and announced that he had joined the Bursley Liberal Club, Darius lost his temper. Yet he was a member of the club himself. He gave no reason for his fury, except that it was foolish for a tradesman to mix himself up with politics. Edwin, however, had developed a sudden interest in politics, and had made certain promises of clerical aid, which promises he kept, saying nothing more to his father. Darius's hero was Sir Robert Peel, simply because Sir Robert Peel had done away with the Corn Laws. Darius had known England before and after the repeal of the Corn Laws, and the difference between the two Englands was so strikingly dramatic to him that he desired no further change. He had only one date – 1846. His cup had been filled then. Never would he forget the scenes of anguishing joy that occurred at midnight the day before the new Act became operative. From that moment he had finished with progress. . . . If Edwin could only have seen those memories, shining in layers deep in his father's heart, and hidden now by all sorts of Pliocene deposits, he would have understood his father better. But Edwin did not see into his father's heart at all, nor even into his head. When he looked at his father he saw nothing but an ugly, stertorous old man (old, that is, to Edwin), with a peculiar and incalculable way of regarding things and a temper of growing capriciousness.

IV

Darius was breathing and fidgeting all over him as he sat bent at the desk. His presence overwhelmed every other physical phenomenon.

'What's this?' asked Darius, picking up the bit of paper on which Edwin had written the memorandum about *The Light of Asia.*

Edwin explained, self-consciously, lamely.

When the barometer of Darius's temper was falling rapidly, there was a sign : a small spot midway on the bridge of his nose turned ivory-white. Edwin glanced upwards now to see if the sign was there, and it was. He flushed slightly and resumed his work.

Then Darius began.

'What did I tell ye?' he shouted. 'What in the name of God's the use o' me telling ye things? Have I told ye not to take any more orders for books, or haven't I? Haven't I said over and over again that I want this shop to be known for wholesale?' he raved.

V

Stifford could hear. Any person who might chance to come into the shop would hear. But Darius cared neither for his own dignity nor for that of his son. He was in a passion. The real truth was that this celibate man, who never took alcohol, enjoyed losing his temper; it was his one outlet; he gave himself up almost luxuriously to a passion; he looked forward to it as some men look forward to brandy. And Edwin had never stopped him by some drastic step. At first, years before, Edwin had said to himself, trembling with resentment in his bedroom, 'The next time, the very next time, he humiliates me like that in front of other people, I'll walk out of his damned house and shop, and I swear I won't come back until he's apologized. I'll bring him to his senses. He can't do without me. Once for all I'll stop it. What! He forces me into his business, and then insults me!'

But Edwin had never done it. Always it was 'the very next time'! Edwin was not capable of doing it. His father had a sort of moral brute-force, against which he could not stand firm. He soon recognized this, with his intellectual candour. Then he had tried to argue with Darius, to 'make him see'! Worse than futile! Argument simply put Darius beside himself. So that in the end Edwin employed silence and secret scorn, as a weapon and as a defence. And somehow without a word he conveyed to Stifford and to Big James precisely what his attitude in these crises was, so that he retained their respect and avoided their pity. The outbursts still wounded him, but he was wonderfully inured.

As he sat writhing under the onslaught, he said to himself, 'By God! If ever I get the chance, I'll pay you out for this some day!' And he meant it. A peep into his mind, then, would have startled Janet Orgreave, Mrs Nixon, and other persons who had a cult for the wistfulness of his appealing eyes.

He steadily maintained silence, and the conflagration burnt itself out.

'Are you going to look after the printing shop, or aren't you?' Darius growled at length.

Edwin rose and went. As he passed through the shop, Stifford, who had in him the raw material of fine manners, glanced down, but not too ostentatiously, at a drawer under the counter.

The printing office was more crowded than ever with men and matter. Some of the composing was now done on the ground floor. The whole organism functioned, but under such difficulties as could not be allowed to continue, even by Darius Clayhanger. Darius had finally recognized that.

'Oh!' said Edwin, in a tone of confidential intimacy to Big James, 'I see they're getting on with the cleaning! Good. Father's beginning to get impatient, you know. It's the bigger cases that had better be done first.'

'Right it is, Mr Edwin!' said Big James. The giant was unchanged. No sign of grey in his hair; and his cheek was smooth, apparently his philosophy put him beyond the touch of time.

'I say, Mr Edwin,' he inquired in his majestic voice. 'When are we going to rearrange all this?' He gazed around.

Edwin laughed. 'Soon,' he said.

'Won't be too soon,' said Big James.

CHAPTER 3 : *The New House*

I

A house stood on a hill. And that hill was Bleakridge, the summit of
the little billow of land between Bursley and Hanbridge. Trafalgar
Road passed over the crest of the billow. Bleakridge was certainly not
more than a hundred feet higher than Bursley; yet people were now
talking a lot about the advantages of living 'up' at Bleakridge, 'above'
the smoke, and 'out' of the town, though it was not more than five
minutes from the Duck Bank. To hear them talking, one might have
fancied that Bleakridge was away in the mountains somewhere. The
new steam-cars would pull you up there in three minutes or so, every
quarter of an hour. It was really the new steam-cars that were to be the
making of Bleakridge as a residential suburb. It had also been predicted
that even Hanbridge men would come to live at Bleakridge now. Land
was changing owners at Bleakridge, and rising in price. Complete streets
of lobbied cottages grew at angles from the main road with the rapidity
of that plant which pushes out strangling branches more quickly than
a man can run. And these lobbied cottages were at once occupied.
Cottage-property in the centre of the town depreciated.

The land fronting the main road was destined not for cottages, but
for residences, semi-detached or detached. Osmond Orgreave had a
good deal of this land under his control. He did not own it, he hawked
it. Like all provincial, and most London, architects, he was a land-broker
in addition to being an architect. Before obtaining a commission to
build a house, he frequently had to create the commission himself by
selling a convenient plot, and then persuading the purchaser that if he
wished to retain the respect of the community he must put on the plot a
house worthy of the plot. The Orgreave family all had expensive tastes,
and it was Osmond Orgreave's task to find most of the money needed
for the satisfaction of those tastes. He always did find it, because the
necessity was upon him, but he did not always find it easily. Janet would
say sometimes, 'We mustn't be so hard on father this month; really, lately
we've never seen him with his cheque-book out of his hand.' Undoubtedly the clothes on Janet's back were partly responsible for the celerity
with which building land at Bleakridge was 'developed', just after the
installation of steam-cars in Trafalgar Road.

II

Mr Orgreave sold a corner plot to Darius. He had had his eye on Darius for a long time before he actually shot him down; but difficulties connected with the paring of estimates for printing had somewhat estranged them. Orgreave had had to smooth out these difficulties, offer to provide a portion of the purchase money on mortgage from another client, produce a plan for a new house that surpassed all records of cheapness, produce a plan for the transforming of Darius's present residence into business premises, talk poetically about the future of printing in the Five Towns, and lastly, demonstrate by digits that Darius would actually save money by becoming a property-owner – he had had to do all this, and more, before Darius would buy.

The two were regular cronies for about a couple of months – that is to say, between the payment of the preliminary deposit and the signing of the contract for building the house. But the contract signed, their relations were once more troubled. Orgreave had nothing to fear, then, and besides, he was using his diplomacy elsewhere. The house went up to an accompaniment of scenes in which only the proprietor was irate. Osmond Orgreave could not be ruffled; he could not be deprived of his air of having done a favour to Darius Clayhanger; his social and moral superiority, his real aloofness, remained absolutely unimpaired. The clear image of him as a fine gentleman was never dulled nor distorted even in the mind of Darius. Nevertheless Darius 'hated the sight' of the house ere the house was roofed in. But this did not diminish his pride in the house. He wished he had never 'set eyes on' Osmond Orgreave. Yes! But the little boy from the Bastille was immensely content at the consequences of having set eyes on Osmond Orgreave. The little boy from the Bastille was achieving the supreme peak of greatness – he was about to live away from business. Soon he would be 'going down to business' of a morning. Soon he would be receiving two separate demand-notes for rates. Soon he would be on a plane with the vainest earthenware manufacturer of them all. Ages ago he had got as far as a house with a lobby to it. Now, it would be a matter of two establishments. Beneath all his discontents, moodiness, temper, and biliousness, lay this profound satisfaction of the little boy from the Bastille.

Moreover, in any case, he would have been obliged to do something heroic, if only to find the room more and more imperiously demanded by his printing business.

III

On the Saturday afternoon of Janet Orgreave's visit to the shop, Edwin went up to Bleakridge to inspect the house, and in particular the coloured 'lights' in the upper squares of the drawing-room and dining-room windows. He had a key to the unpainted front door, and having climbed through various obstacles and ascended an inclined bending plank, he entered and stood in the square hall of the deserted, damp, and inchoate structure.

The house was his father's only in name. In emotional fact it was Edwin's house, because he alone was capable of possessing it by enjoying it. To Darius, to Bursley in general, it was just a nice house, of red brick with terra-cotta facings and red tiles, in the second-Victorian Style, the style that had broken away from Georgian austerity and first-Victorian stucco and smugness, and wandered off vaguely into nothing in particular. To the plebeian in Darius it was of course grandiose, and vast; to Edwin also, in a less degree. But to Edwin it was not a house, it was a work of art, it was an emanation of the soul. He did not realize this. He did not realize how the house had informed his daily existence. All that he knew about himself in relation to the house was that he could not keep away from it. He 'went and had a look at it' nearly every morning before breakfast, when the workmen were fresh and lyrical.

When the news came down to the younger generation that Darius had bought land and meant to build on the land, Edwin had been profoundly moved between apprehension and hope; his condition had been one of simple but intense expectant excitement. He wondered what his own status would be in the great enterprise of house-building. All depended on Mr Orgreave. Would Mr Orgreave, of whom he had seen scarcely anything in seven years, remember that he was intelligently interested in architecture? Or would Mr Orgreave walk right over him and talk exclusively to his father? He had feared, he had had a suspicion, that Mr Orgreave was an inconstant man.

Mr Orgreave had remembered in the handsomest way. When the plans were being discussed, Mr Orgreave with one word, a tone, a glance, had raised Edwin to the consultative level of his father. He had let Darius see that Edwin was in his opinion worthy to take part in discussions, and quite privately he had let Edwin see that Darius must not be treated too seriously. Darius, who really had no interest in ten thousand exquisitely absorbing details, had sometimes even said, with impatience, 'Oh! Settle it how you like, with Edwin.'

Edwin's own suggestions never seemed very brilliant, and Mr Orgreave was always able to prove to him that they were inadvisable; but they were never silly, like most of his father's. And he acquired leading ideas that transformed his whole attitude towards architecture. For example, he had always looked on a house as a front-wall diversified by doors and windows, with rooms behind it. But when Mr Orgreave produced his first notions for the new house Edwin was surprised to find that he had not even sketched the front. He had said, 'We shall be able to see what the elevation looks like when we've decided the plan a bit.' And Edwin saw in a flash that the front of a house was merely the expression of the inside of it, merely a result, almost accidental. And he was astounded and disgusted that he, with his professed love of architecture and his intermittent study of it, had not perceived this obvious truth for himself. He never again looked at a house in the old irrational way.

Then, when examining the preliminary sketch-plan, he had put his finger on a square space and asked what room that twas. 'That isn't a room; that's the hall,' said Mr Orgreave. 'But it's square!' Edwin exclaimed. He thought that in houses (houses to be lived in) the hall or lobby must necessarily be long and narrow. Now suddenly he saw no reason why a hall should not be square. Mr Orgreave had made no further remark about halls at the time, but another day, without any preface, he re-opened the subject to Edwin, in a tone good-naturedly informing, and when he had done Edwin could see that the shape of the hall depended on the shape of the house, and that halls had only been crushed and pulled into something long and narrow because the disposition of houses absolutely demanded this ugly negation of the very idea of a hall. Again, he had to begin to thinking afresh, to see afresh. He conceived a real admiration for Osmond Orgreave; not more for his original and yet common-sense manner of regarding things, than for his aristocratic deportment, his equality to every situation, and his extraordinary skill in keeping his dignity and his distance during encounters with Darius. (At the same time, when Darius would grumble savagely that Osmond Orgreave 'was too clever by half', Edwin could not deny that.) Edwin's sisters got a good deal of Mr Orgreave, through Edwin; he could never keep Mr Orgreave very long to himself. He gave away a great deal of Mr Orgreave's wisdom without mentioning the origin of the gift. Thus occasionally Clara would say cuttingly, 'I know where you've picked that up. You've picked that up from Mr Orgreave.' The young man Benbow to whom the infant Clara had been so queerly engaged, also received from Edwin considerable quantities of Mr Orgreave. But the fellow was only a decent, dull, pushing, successful ass, and quite unable to assimilate Mr Orgreave; Edwin could never comprehend how Clara, so extremely difficult to please, so carping and captious, could mate herself to a fellow like Benbow. She had done so, however; they were recently married. Edwin was glad that that was over; for it had disturbed him in his attentions to the house.

IV

When the house began to 'go up', Edwin lived in an ecstasy of contemplation. I say with deliberateness an 'ecstasy'. He had seen houses go up before; he knew that houses were constructed brick by brick, beam by beam, lath by lath, tile by tile; he knew that they did not build themselves. And yet, in the vagueness of his mind, he had never imaginatively realized that a house was made with hands, and hands that could err. With its exact perpendiculars and horizontals, its geometric regularities, and its Chinese preciseness of fitting, a house had always seemed to him – again in the vagueness of his mind – as something superhuman. The commonest cornice, the most ordinary pillar of a staircase-balustrade – could that have been accomplished in its awful perfection of line and contour by a human being? How easy to believe that it was 'not made with hands'!

But now he saw. He had to see. He saw a hole in the ground, with water at the bottom, and the next moment that hole was a cellar; not an amateur cellar, a hole that would do at a pinch for a cellar, but a professional cellar. He appreciated the brains necessary to put a brick on another brick, with just the right quantity of mortar in between. He thought the house would never get itself done – one brick at a time – and each brick cost a farthing – slow, careful; yes, and even finicking. But soon the bricklayers had to stand on plank-platforms in order to reach the raw top of the wall that was ever rising above them. The measurements, the rulings, the plumbings, the checkings! He was humbled and he was enlightened. He understood that a miracle is only the result of miraculous patience, miraculous nicety, miraculous honesty, miraculous perseverance. He understood that there was no golden and magic secret of building. It was just putting one brick on another and another – but to a hair's breadth. It was just like anything else. For instance, printing! He saw even printing in a new light.

And when the first beams were bridged across two walls . . .

The funny thing was that the men's fingers were thick and clumsy. Never could such fingers pick up a pin! And still they would manoeuvre a hundredweight of timber to a pin's point.

V

He stood at the drawing-room bay window (of which each large pane had been marked with the mystic sign of a white circle by triumphant glaziers) and looked across the enclosed fragment of clayey field that ultimately would be the garden. The house was at the corner of Trafalgar Road and a side-street that had lobbied cottages down its slope. The garden was oblong, with its length parallel to Trafalgar Road, and separated from the pavement only by a high wall. The upper end of the garden was blocked by the first of three new houses which Osmond Orgreave was building in a terrace. These houses had their main fronts on the street; they were quite as commodious as the Clayhangers' but much inferior in garden-space; their bits of flower-plots lay behind them. And away behind their flower-pots, with double entrance-gates in another side street, stretched the grounds of Osmond Orgreave, his house in the sheltered middle thereof. He had got, cheaply, one of the older residential properties of the district, Georgian, of a recognizable style, relic of the days when manufacturers formed a class entirely apart from their operatives; even as far back as 1880 any operative might with luck become an employer. The south-east corner of the Clayhanger garden touched the north-west corner of the domains of Orgreave; for a few feet the two gardens were actually contiguous, with naught but an old untidy thorn hedge between them; this hedge was to be replaced by a wall that would match the topmost of the lobbied cottages which bounded the view of the Clayhangers to the east.

From the bay-window Edwin could see over the hedge, and also through it, onto the croquet lawn of the Orgreaves. Croquet was then in its first avatar; nothing was more dashing than croquet. With rag-balls and home-made mallets the Clayhanger children had imitated croquet in their yard in the seventies. The Orgreaves played real croquet; one of them had shone in a tournament at Buxton. Edwin noticed a figure on the gravel between the lawn and the hedge. He knew it to be Janet, by the crimson frock. But he had no notion that Janet had stationed herself in that quarter with intent to waylay him. He could not have credited her with such a purpose. Nor could his modesty have believed that he was important enough to employ the talent of the Orgreaves for agreeable chicane. The fact was that Janet had been espying him for a quarter of an hour. When at length she waved her hand to him, it did not occur to him to suppose that she was waving her hand to him; he merely wondered what peculiar thing she was doing. Then he blushed as she waved again, and he knew first from the blood in his face that Janet was making a signal; and that it was to himself that the signal was directed : his body had told his mind; this was very odd.

Of course he was obliged to go out; and he went, muttering to himself.

CHAPTER 4 : *The Two Gardens*

I

In the full beauty of the afternoon they stood together, only the scraggy hedge between them, he on grass-tufted clay, and she on orderly gravel.

'Well,' said Janet, earnestly looking at him, 'how do you like the effect of that window, now it's done?'

'Very nice!' he laughed nervously. 'Very nice indeed!'

'Father said it was,' she remarked. 'I do hope Mr Clayhanger will like it too!' And her voice really was charged with sympathetic hope. It was as if she would be saddened and cast down if Darius did not approve the window. It was as if she fervently wished that Darius should not be disappointed with the window. The unskilled spectator might have assumed that anxiety for the success of the window would endanger her sleep at nights. She was perfectly sincere. Her power of emotional sympathy was all-embracing and inexhaustible. If she heard that an acquaintance of one of her acquaintances had lost a relative or broken a limb, she would express genuine deep concern, with a tremor of her honest and kindly voice. And if she heard the next moment that an acquaintance of one of her acquaintances had come into five thousand pounds or affianced himself to a sister-spirit, her eyes would sparkle with heartfelt joy and her hands clasp each other in sheer delight.

'Oh!' said Edwin, touched. 'It'll be all right for the dad. No fear!'

'I haven't seen it yet,' she proceeded. 'In fact I haven't been in your house for such a long time. But I do think it's going to be very nice. All father's houses are so nice, aren't they?'

'Yes,' said Edwin, with that sideways shake of the head that in the vocabulary of his gesture signified, not dissent, but emphatic assent. 'You ought to come and have a look at it.' He could not say less.

'Do you think I could scramble through here?' she indicated the sparse hedge.

'I – I –'

'I know what I'll do. I'll get the steps.' She walked off sedately, and came back with a small pair of steps, which she opened out on the narrow flower-bed under the hedge. Then she picked up her skirt and delicately ascended the rocking ladder till her feet were on a level with the top of the hedge. She smiled charmingly, savouring the harmless escapade, and gazing at Edwin. She put out her free hand, Edwin took it, and she jumped. The steps fell backwards, but she was safe.

'What a good thing mother didn't see me!' she laughed. Her grave, sympathetic, almost handsome face was now alive everywhere with a sort of challenging merriment. She was only pretending that it was a good thing her mother had not seen her : a delicious make-believe. Why, she was as motherly as her mother! In an instant her feet were choosing their way and carrying her with grace and stateliness across the mire of the unformed garden. She was the woman of the world, and Edwin the raw boy. The harmony and dignity of her movements charmed and intimidated Edwin. Compare her to Maggie. . . . That she was hatless added piquancy.

II

They went into the echoing bare house, crunching gravel and dry clay on the dirty, new floors. They were alone together in the house. And all the time Edwin was thinking : 'I've never been through anything like this before. Never been through anything like this!' And he recalled for a second the figure of Florence Simcox, the clog-dancer.

And below these images and reflections in his mind was the thought : 'I haven't known what life *is*! I've been asleep. This is life!'

The upper squares of the drawing-room windows were filled with small leaded diamond-shaped panes of many colours. It was the latest fashion in domestic glazing. The effect was at once rich and gorgeous. She liked it.

'It will be beautiful on this side in the late afternoon,' she murmured. 'What a nice room!'

Their eyes met, and she transmitted to him her joy in his joy at the admirableness of the house.

He nodded. 'By Jove!' he thought. 'She's a splendid girl. There can't be many girls knocking about as fine as she is!'

'And when the garden's full of flowers –!' she breathed in rapture. She was thinking, 'Strange, nice boy! He's so romantic. All he wants is bringing out.'

They wandered to and fro. They went upstairs. They saw the bath-room. They stood on the landing, and the unseen spaces of the house were busy with their echoes. They then entered the room that was to be Edwin's.

'Mine!' he said self-consciously.

'And I see you're having shelves fixed on both sides of the mantel-piece! You're very fond of books, aren't you?' she appealed to him.

'Yes,' he said judicially.

'Aren't they wonderful things?' Her glowing eyes seemed to be expressing gratitude to Shakespeare and all his successors in the dynasty of literature.

'That shelving is between your father and me,' said Edwin. 'The dad doesn't know. It'll go in with the house-fittings. I don't expect the dad will ever notice it.'

'Really!' She laughed, eager to join the innocent conspiracy. 'Father invented an excellent dodge for shelving in the hall at our house,' she added. 'I'm sure he'd like you to come and see it. The dear thing's most absurdly proud of it.'

'I should like to,' Edwin answered diffidently.

'Would you come in some evening and see us? Mother would be delighted. We all should.'

'Very kind of you.' In his diffidence he was now standing on one leg.

'Could you come tonight? ... Or tomorrow night?'

'I'm afraid I couldn't come tonight, *or* tomorrow night,' he answered with firmness. A statement entirely untrue! He had no engagement; he never did have an engagement. But he was frightened, and his spirit sprang away from the idea, like a fawn at a sudden noise in the brake, and stood still.

He did not suspect that the unconscious gruffness of his tone had repulsed her. She blamed herself for a too brusque advance.

'Well, I hope some other time,' she said, mild and benignant.

'Thanks! I'd like to,' he replied more boldly, reassured now that he had heard again the same noise but indefinitely, farther off.

She departed, but by the front door, and hatless and dignified up Trafalgar Road in the delicate sunshine to the next turning. She was less vivacious.

He hoped he had not offended her, because he wanted very much not to go in cold blood to the famed mansion of the Orgreaves – but by some magic to find himself within it one night, at his ease, sharing in brilliant conversation. 'Oh no!' he said to himself. 'She's not offended. A fine girl like that isn't offended for nothing at all!' He had been invited to visit the Orgreaves! He wondered what his father would say, or think. The unexpressed basic idea of the Clayhangers was that the Clayhangers were as good as other folks, be they who they might. Still, the Orgreaves were the Orgreaves. . . . In sheer absence of mind he remounted the muddy stairs.

III

He regarded the shabbiness of his clothes; he had been preoccupied by their defects for about a quarter of an hour; now he examined them in detail, and said to himself, disgusted, that really it was ridiculous for a man about to occupy a house like that to be wearing garments like those. Could he call on the Orgreaves in garments like those? His Sunday suit was not, he felt, in fact much better. It was newer, less tumbled, but scarcely better. His suits did not cost enough. Finance was at the root of the crying scandal of his career as a dandy. The financial question must be reopened and settled anew. He should attack his father. His father was extremely dependent on him now, and must be brought to see reason. (His father who had never seen reason!) But the attack must not be made with the weapon of clothes, for on that subject Darius was utterly unapproachable. Whenever Darius found himself in a conversation about clothes, he gave forth the antique and well-tried witticism that as for him he didn't mind what he wore, because if he was at home everybody knew him and it didn't matter, and if he was away from home nobody knew him and it didn't matter. And he always repeated the saying with gusto, as if it was brand-new and none could possibly have heard it before.

No, Edwin decided that he would have to found his attack on the principle of abstract justice; he would never be able to persuade his father that he lacked any detail truly needful to his happiness. To go into details would be to invite defeat.

Of course it would be a bad season in which to raise the financial question. His father would talk savagely in reply about the enormous expenses of house-building, house-furnishing, and removing – and architects' and lawyers' fees; he would be sure to mention the rapacity of architects and lawyers. Nevertheless Edwin felt that at just this season, and no other, must the attack be offered.

Because the inauguration of the new house was to be for Edwin, in a very deep and spiritual sense, the beginning of the new life! He had settled that. The new house inspired him. It was not paradise. But it was a temple.

You of the younger generation cannot understand that – without imagination. I say that the hot-water system of the new house, simple and primitive as it was, affected and inspired Edwin like a poem. There was a cistern-room, actually a room devoted to nothing but cisterns, and the main cistern was so big that the builders had had to install it before the roof was put on, for it would never have gone through a door. This cistern, by means of a ball-tap, filled itself from the main nearly as quickly as it was emptied. Out of it grew pipes, creeping in secret downwards, between inner walls of the house, penetrating everywhere. One went down to a boiler behind the kitchen-range and filled it, and as the fire that was roasting the joint heated the boiler, the water mounted again magically to the cistern-room and filled another cistern, spherical and sealed, and thence descended, on a third journeying, to the bath and to the lavatory basin in the bathroom. All this was marvellous to

Edwin; it was romantic. What! A room solely for baths! And a huge painted zinc bath! Edwin had never seen such a thing. And a vast porcelain basin, with tiles all round it, in which you could splash! An endless supply of water on the first floor!

At the shop-house, every drop of water on the first floor had to be carried upstairs in jugs and buckets; and every drop of it had to be carried down again. No hot water could be obtained until it had been boiled in a vessel on the fire. Hot water had the value of champagne. to take a warm hip-bath was an immense enterprise of heating, fetching, decanting, and general derangement of the entire house; and at best the bath was not hot; it always lost its virtue on the stairs and landing. And to splash – one of the most voluptuous pleasures in life – was forbidden by the code. Mrs Nixon would actually weep at a splashing. Splashing was immoral. It was as wicked as amorous dalliance in a monastery. In the shop-house godliness was child's play compared to cleanliness.

And the shop-house was so dark! Edwin had never noticed how dark it was until the new house approached completion. The new house was radiant with light. It had always, for Edwin, the somewhat blinding brilliance which filled the sitting-room of the shop-house only when Duck Bank happened to be covered with fresh snow. And there was a dining-room, solely for eating, and a drawing-room. Both these names seemed 'grand' to Edwin, who had never sat in any but a sitting-room. Edwin had never dined; he had merely had dinner. And, having dined, to walk ceremoniously into another room ...! (Odd! After all, his father was a man of tremendous initiative.) Would he and Maggie be able to do the thing naturally? Then there was the square hall – positively a room! That alone impelled him to a new life. When he thought of it all, the reception-rooms, the scientific kitchen, the vast scullery, the four large bedrooms, the bathroom, the three attics, the cistern-room murmurous with water, and the water tirelessly, inexhaustibly coursing up and down behind walls – he thrilled to fine impulses.

He took courage. He braced himself. The seriousness which he had felt on the day of leaving school revisited him. He looked back across the seven years of his life in the world, and condemned them unsparingly. He blamed no one but Edwin. He had forgiven his father for having thwarted his supreme ambition; long ago he had forgiven his father; though, curiously, he had never quite forgiven Mrs Hamps for her share in the catastrophe. He honestly thought he had recovered from the catastrophe undisfigured, even unmarked. He knew not that he would never be the same man again, and that his lightest gesture and his lightest glance were touched with the wistfulness of resignation. He had frankly accepted the fate of a printer. And in business he was convinced, despite his father's capricious complaints, that he had acquitted himself well. In all the details of the business he considered himself superior to his father. And Big James would invariably act on his secret instructions given afterwards to counteract some misguided hasty order of the old man's.

It was the emptiness of the record of his private life that he condemned. What had he done for himself? Nothing large! Nothing heroic and imposing! He had meant to pursue certain definite courses of study, to become the possessor of certain definite groups of books, to continue his drawings and painting, to practise this, that, and the other, to map out all his spare time, to make rules and to keep them – all to the great end of self-perfecting. He had said: 'What does it matter whether I am an architect or a printer, so long as I improve myself to the best of my powers?' He hated young men who talked about improving themselves. He spurned the Young Men's Mutual Improvement Society (which had succeeded the Debating Society – defunct through over-indulgence in early rising). Nevertheless in his heart he was far more enamoured of the idea of improvement than the worst prig of them all. He could never for long escape from the dominance of the idea. He might violently push it away, arguing that it could lead to nothing and was futile and tedious; back it would come! It had always worried him.

And yet he had accomplished nothing. His systems of reading never worked for more than a month at a time. And for several months at a time he simply squandered his spare hours, the hours that were his very own, in a sort of coma of crass stupidity, in which he seemed to be thinking of nothing whatever. He had not made any friends whom he could esteem. He had not won any sort of notice. He was remarkable for nothing. He was not happy. He was not content. He had the consciousness of being a spendthrift of time and of years . . . A fair quantity of miscellaneous reading – that was all he had done. He was not a student. He knew nothing about anything. He had stood still.

Thus he upbraided himself. And against this futility was his courage now braced by the inspiration of the new house, and tightened to a smarting tension by the brief interview with Janet Orgreave. He was going to do several feats at once: tackle his father, develop into a right expert on *some* subject, pursue his painting, and – for the moment this had the chief importance – 'come out of his shell'. He meant to be social, to impress himself on others, to move about, to form connexions, to be Edwin Clayhanger, an individuality in the town – to live. Why had he refused Janet's invitation? Mere silliness. The old self nauseated the new. But the next instant he sought excuses for the old self. . . . Wait a bit! There was time yet.

He was happy in the stress of one immense and complex resolve.

CHAPTER 5 : *Clothes*

I

He heard voices below. And his soul seemed to shrink back, as if into the recesses of the shell from which it had been peeping. His soul was tremendous, in solitude; but even the rumour of society intimidated it. His father and another were walking about the ground floor; the rough voice of his father echoed upwards in all its crudity. He listened for the other voice; it was his Auntie Clara's. Darius too had taken his Saturday afternoon for a leisurely visit to the house, and somehow he must have encountered Mrs Hamps, and brought her with him to view.

Without giving himself time to dissipate his courage in reflection, he walked to the landing, and called down the stairs, 'Hello, Auntie!'

Why should his tone have been self-conscious, forced? He was engaged in no crime. He had told his father where he was going, and his father had not contradicted his remark that even if both of them happened to be out together, the shop would take no harm under the sole care of Stifford for an hour in the quiet of Saturday afternoon.

Mrs Hamps replied, in her coaxing, sweet manner.

'What did ye leave th' front door open for?' his father demanded curtly, and every room in the house heard the question.

'Was it open?' he said lamely.

'Was it open! All Trafalgar Road could have walked in and made themselves at home.'

Edwin stood leaning with his arms on the rail of the landing. Presently the visitors appeared at the foot of the stairs, and Darius climbed carefully, having first shaken the balustrade to make sure that it was genuine, stout, and well-founded. Mrs Hamps followed, the fripperies of her elegant bonnet trembling, and her black gown rustling. Edwin smiled at her, and she returned his smile with usurious interest. There was now a mist of grey in her fine hair.

'Oh, Edwin!' she began, breathing relief on the top stair. 'What a beautiful house! Beautiful! Quite perfect! The latest of everything! Do you know what I've been thinking while your dear father has been showing me all this – So that's the bathroom! Bless us! Hot! Cold! Waste! That cupboard under the lavatory is very handy, but what a snare for a careless servant! Maggie will have to look at it every day, or it'll be used for anything and everything. You tell her what her auntie says . . . I was thinking – if but your mother could have seen it all!'

Father and son said nothing. Auntie Hamps sighed. She was the only person who ever referred to the late Mrs Clayhanger.

The procession moved on from room to room, Darius fingering and grunting, Mrs Hamps discovering in each detail the fine flower of utter perfection, and Edwin strolling loosely in the wake of her curls, her mantle, and her abundant black petticoats. He could detect the odour of her kid gloves; it was a peculiar odour that never escaped him, and it reminded him inevitably of his mother's funeral.

He was glad that they had not arrived during the visit of Janet Orgreave.

In due course Edwin's bedroom was reached, an dhere Auntie Clara's ecstasy was redoubled.

'I'm sure you're very grateful to your father, aren't you, Edwin?' she majestically assumed, when she had admired passionately the window, the door, the pattern of the hearth-tiles, and the spaciousness.

Edwin could not speak. Inquiries of this nature from Mrs Hamps paralysed the tongues of the children. They left nothing to be said. A sheepish grin, preceded by an inward mute curse, was all that Edwin could accomplish. How in heaven's name could the woman talk in that strain? His attitude towards his auntie was assuredly hardening with years.

'What's all this?' questioned his father suddenly, pointing to upright boards that had been fastened to the walls on either side of the mantel-piece, to a height of about three feet.

Then Edwin perceived the clumsiness of his tactics in remaining up-stairs. He ought to have gone downstairs to meet his father and auntie, and left them to go up alone. His father was in an inquisitive mood.

'It's for shelves,' he said.

'Shelves?'

'For my books. It's Mr Orgreave's idea. He says it'll cost less.'

'Cost less! Mr Orgreave's got too many ideas – that's what the matter with him. He'll idea me into the bankruptcy court if he keeps on.'

Edwin would have liked to protest against the savagery of the tone, to inquire firmly why, since shelves were necessary for books and he had books, there need be such a display of illtemper about a few feet of deal plank. The words were ready, the sentences framed in his mind. But he was silent. The door was locked on these words, but it was not Edwin who had turned the key; it was some force within him, over which he had no control.

II

'Now, now father!' intervened Mrs Hamps. 'You know you've said over and over again how glad you are he's so fond of books, and never goes out. There isn't a better boy in Bursley. That I will say, and to his face.' She smiled like an angel at both of them.

'*You* say! *You* say!' Darius remarked curtly, trying to control himself. A few years ago he would never had used such violent demeanour in her presence.

'And how much easier these shelves will be to keep clean than a bookcase! No polishing. Just a rub, and a wipe with a damp cloth now and then. And no dirt underneath. They will do away with four corners, anyhow. That's what I think of – eh, poor Maggie! Keeping all this clean. There'll be work for two women night and day, early and late, and even then – But it's a great blessing to have water on every floor, that it is! And people aren't so particular nowadays as they used to be, I fancy. I fancy that more and more.' Mrs Hamps sighed, cheerfully bearing up.

Without a pause she stepped quickly across to Edwin. He wondered what she was at. She merely straightened down the collar of his coat, which, unknown to him, had treacherously allowed itself to remain turned up behind. It had probably been thus misbehaving itself since before dinner, when he had washed.

'Now, I do like my nephew to be tidy,' said Mrs Hamps affectionately. 'I'm very jealous for my nephew.' She caressed the shoulders of the coat, and Edwin had to stand still and submit. 'Let me see, it's your birthday next month, isn't it?'

'Yes, auntie.'

'Well, I know he hasn't got a lot of money. And I know his father hasn't any money to spare just now – what with all these expenses – the house –'

'Ye may well say it, sister!' Darius growled.

'I saw you the day before yesterday. My nephew didn't see me, but his auntie saw him. Oh, never mind where. And I said to myself, 'I should like my only nephew to have a suit a little better than that when he goes up and down on his father's business. What a change it would be if his old auntie gave him a new suit for a birthday present this year!'

'Oh, auntie.'

She spoke in a lower voice. 'You come and see me tomorrow, and I shall have a little piece of paper in an envelope waiting for you. And you must choose something really good. You've got excellent taste, we all know that. And this will be a new start for you. A new year, and a new start, and we shall see how neat and spruce you'll keep yourself in future, eh?'

III

It was insufferable. But it was fine. Who could deny that Auntie Clara was not an extraordinary, an original, and generous woman? What a masterly reproof to both father and son. Perhaps not delicately administered. Yet Auntie Clara had lavished all the delicacy of her nature on the administering!

To Edwin, it seemed like an act of God in his favour. It seemed to set a divine seal on his resolutions. It was the most astonishing and apposite piece of luck that had ever happened to him. When he had lamely thanked the benefactor, he slipped away as soon as he could. Already he could feel the crinkling of the five-pound note in his hand. Five pounds! He had never had a suit that cost more than fifty shillings. He slipped away. A great resolve was upon him. Shillitoe closed at four o'clock on Saturday afternoons. There was just time. He hurried down Trafalgar Road in a dream. And when he had climbed Duck Bank he turned to the left, and without stopping he burst into Shillitoe's. Not from eagerness to enter Shillitoe's, but because if he had hesitated he might never have entered at all : he might have slunk away to the old, undistinguished tailor in St Luke's Square. Shillitoe was the stylish tailor. Shillitoe made no display of goods, scorning such paltry devices. Shillitoe had wire blinds across the lower part of his window, and on the blinds, in gold, 'Gentlemen's tailor and outfitter. Breeches-maker'. Above the blind could be seen a few green cardboard boxes. Shillitoe made breeches for men who hunted. Shillitoe's lowest price for a suit was notoriously four guineas. Shillitoe's was the resort of the fashionable youth of the town and district. It was a terrific adventure for Edwin to enter Shillitoe's. His nervousness was painful. He seemed to have a vague idea that Shillitoe might sneer at him. However, he went in. The shop was empty. He closed the door, as he might have closed the door of a dentist's. He said to himself, 'Well, I'm here!' He wondered what his father would say on hearing that he had been to Shillitoe's. And what would Clara have said, had she been at home? Then Shillitoe in person came forward from the cutting-out room and Shillitoe's tone and demeanour reassured him.

CHAPTER 6 : *Janet Loses her Bet*

I

Accident – that is to say, a chance somewhat more fortuitous than the common hazards which we group together and call existence – pushed Edwin into the next stage of his career. As, on one afternoon in late June, he was turning the corner of Trafalgar Road to enter the shop, he surprisingly encountered Charlie Orgreave, whom he had not seen for several years. And when he saw this figure, at once fashionably and carelessly dressed, his first thought was one of deep satisfaction that he was wearing his new Shillitoe suit of clothes. He had scarcely worn the suit at all, but that afternoon his father had sent him over to Hanbridge about a large order from Bostocks, the recently established drapers there whose extravagant advertising had shocked and pained the commerce of the Five Town. Darius had told him to 'titivate himself', a most startling injunction from Darius, and thus the new costly suit had been, as it were, officially blessed and henceforth could not be condemned.

'How do, Teddy?' Charlie greeted him. 'I've just been in to see you at your shop.'

Edwin paused.

'Hello! The Sunday!' he said quietly. And he kept thinking, as his eyes noted details of Charlie's raiment, 'It's a bit of luck I've got these clothes on.' And he was in fact rather sorry that Charlie probably paid no real attention to clothes. The new suit had caused Edwin to look at everybody's clothes, had caused him to walk differently, and to put his shoulders back, and to change the style of his collars; had made a different man of Edwin.

'Come in, will you?' Edwin suggested.

They went into the shop together. Stifford smiled at them both, as if to felicitate them on the chance which had brought them together.

'Come in here,' said Edwin, indicating the small office.

'The lion's den, eh?' observed the Sunday.

He, as much as Edwin, was a little tongue-tied and nervous.

'Sit down, will you?' said Edwin, shutting the door. 'No, take the arm-chair. I'll absquatulate on the desk. I'd no idea you were down. When did you come?'

'Last night, last train. Just a freak, you know.'

149

II

They were within a foot of each other in the ebonized cubicle. Edwin's legs were swinging a few inches away from the armchair. His hat was at the back of his head, and Charlie's hat was at the back of Charlie's head. This was their sole point of resemblance. As Edwin surreptitiously examined the youth who had once been his intimate friend, he experienced the half-sneering awe of the provincial for the provincial who has become a Londoner. Charlie was changed; even his accent was changed. He and Edwin belonged to utterly different worlds now. They seldom saw the same scenes or thought the same things. But of course they were obliged by loyalty to the past to pretend that nothing was changed.

'You've not altered much,' said Edwin.

And indeed, when Charlie smiled, he was almost precisely the old Sunday, despite his metropolitan mannerisms. And there was nothing whatever in his figure or deportment to show that he had lived for several years in France and could chatter in a language whose verbs had our conjugations. After all he was less formidable than Edwin might have anticipated.

'*You* have, anyhow,' said Charlie.

Edwin grinned self-consciously.

'I suppose you've got this place practically in your own hands now,' said Charlie. 'I wish *I* was on my own, I can tell you that.'

An instinctive gesture from Edwin made Charlie lower his voice in the middle of a sentence. The cubicle had the appearance, but not the reality, of being private.

'Don't you make any mistake,' Edwin murmured. He, who depended on his aunt's generosity for clothes, the practical ruler of the place! Still he was glad that Charlie supposed that he ruled, even though the supposition might be mere small-talk. 'You're in that hospital, aren't you?'

'Bart's.'

'Bart's, is it? Yes, I remember. I expect you aren't thinking of settling down here?'

Charlie was about to reply in accents of disdain: 'Not me!' But his natural politeness stayed his tongue. 'I hardly think so,' he said. 'Too much competition here. So there is everywhere, for the matter of that.' The disillusions of the young doctor were already upon Charlie. And yet people may be found who will assert that in those days there was no competition, that competition has been invented during the past ten years.

'*You* needn't worry about competition,' said Edwin.

'Why not?'

'Why not, man! Nothing could ever stop you from getting patients – with that smile! You'll simply walk straight into anything you want.'

'You think so?' Charlie affected an ironic incredulity, but he was pleased. He had met the same theory in London.

'Well, you didn't suppose degrees and things had anything to do with it, did you?' said Edwin, smiling a little superiorly. He felt, with pleasure, that he was still older than the Sunday; and it pleased him also to be able thus to utilize ideas which he had formed from observation but which by diffidence and lack of opportunity he had never expressed. 'All a patient wants is to be smiled at in the right way,' he continued, growing bolder. 'Just look at 'em!'

'Look at who?'

'The doctors here.' He dropped his voice further. 'Do you know why the dad's gone to Heve?'

'Gone to Heve, has he? Left old Who-is-it?'

'Yes. I don't say Heve isn't clever, but it's his look that does the trick for him.'

'You seem to go about noticing things. Any charge?'

Edwin blushed and laughed. Their nervousness was dissipated. Each was reassured of the old basis of 'decency' in the other.

III

'Look here,' said Charlie. 'I can't stop now.'

'Hold on a bit.'

'I only called to tell you that you've simply *got* to come up tonight.'

'Come up where?'

'To our place. You've simply *got* to.'

The secret fact was that Edwin had once more been under discussion in the house of the Orgreaves. And Osmond Orgreave had lent Janet a shilling so that she might bet Charlie a shilling that he could not succeed in bringing Edwin to the house. The understanding was that if Janet won, her father was to take sixpence of the gain. Janet herself had failed to lure Edwin into the house. He was so easy to approach and so difficult to catch. Janet was slightly piqued.

As for Edwin, he was postponing the execution of all his good resolutions until he should be installed in the new house. He could not achieve highly difficult tasks under conditions of expectancy and derangement. The whole Clayhanger premises were in a suppressed state of being packed up. In a week the removal would occur. Until the removal was over and the new order was established. Edwin felt that he could still conscientiously allow his timidity to govern him, and so he had remained in his shell. The sole herald of the new order was the new suit.

'Oh! I can't come – not tonight.'

'Why not?'

'We're so busy.'

'Bosh to that!'

'Some other night.'

'No. I'm going back tomorrow. Must. Now look here, old man, come on. I shall be very disappointed if you don't.'

Edwin wondered why he could not accept and be done with it, instead of persisting in a sequence of insincere and even lying hesitations. But he could not.

'That's all right,' said Charlie, as if clinching the affair. Then he lowered his voice to a scarce audible confidential whisper. 'Fine girl staying up there just now!' His eyes sparkled.

'Oh! At your place?' Edwin adopted the same cautious tone. Stifford, outside, strained his ears – in vain. The magic word 'girl' had in an instant thrown the shop into agitation. The shop was no longer provincial; it became part of the universal.

'Yes. Haven't you seen her about?'

'No. Who is she?'

'Oh! Friend of Janet's. Hilda Lessways, her name is. I don't know much of her myself.'

'Bit of all right, is she?' Edwin tried in a whisper to be a man of vast experience and settled views. He tried to whisper as though he whispered about women every day of his life. He thought that these Londoners were terrific on the subject of women, and he did his best to reach their level. He succeeded so well that Charlie, who, as a man, knew more of London than of the provinces, thought that after all London was nothing in comparison to the seeming-quiet provinces. Charlie leaned back in his chair, drew down the corners of his mouth, nodded his head knowingly, and then quite spoiled the desired effect of doggishness by his delightfully candid smile. Neither of them had the least intention of disrespect towards the fine girl who was on their lips.

IV

Edwin said to himself : 'Is it possible that he has come down specially to see this Hilda?' He thought enviously of Charlie as a free bird of the air.

'What's she like?' Edwin inquired

'You come up and see,' Charlie retorted.

'Not tonight,' said the fawn, in spite of Edwin.

'You come tonight, or I perish in the attempt,' said Charlie, in his natural voice. The phrase from their schooldays made them both laugh again. They were now apparently as intimate as ever they had been.

'All right,' said Edwin. 'I'll come.'

'Sure?'

'Yes.'

'Come for a sort of supper at eight.'

'Oh!' Edwin drew back. 'Supper? I didn't – Suppose I come after supper for a bit?'

'Suppose you don't!' Charlie snorted, sticking his chin out. 'I'm off now. Must.'

They stood a moment together at the door of the shop, in the declining warmth of the summer afternoon, mutually satisfied.

'So-long!'

'So-long!'

The Sunday elegantly departed. Edwin had given his word, and he felt as he might have felt had surgeons just tied him to the operating-table. Nevertheless he was not ill-pleased with his own demeanour in front of Charlie. And he liked Charlie as much as ever. He should rely on Charlie as a support during this adventure into the worldly regions peopled by fine girls. He pictured this Hilda as being more romantic and strange than Janet Orgreave; he pictured her as mysteriously superior. And he was afraid of his own image of her.

At tea in the dismantled sitting-room, though he was going out to supper, he ate quite as much tea as usual, from sheer poltroonery. He said as casually as he could –

'By the way, Charlie Orgreave called this afternoon.'

'Did he?' said Maggie.

'He's off back to London to-morrow. He would have me slip up there tonight to see him.'

'And shall you?'

'I think so,' said Edwin, with an appearance of indecision. 'I may as well.'

It was the first time that there had ever been question of him visiting a private house, except his aunt's, at night. To him the moment marked an epoch, the inception of freedom; but the phlegmatic Maggie showed no sign of excitement – ('Clara would have gone into a fit!' he reflected) – and his father only asked a casual question about Charlie.

CHAPTER 7 : *Lane End House*

I

Here was another of those impressive square halls, on the other side
of the suddenly opened door of Lane End House. But Edwin was now
getting accustomed to square halls. Nevertheless he quaked as he stood
on the threshold. An absurd young man! He wondered whether he
would ever experience the sensation of feeling authentically grown-up.
Behind him in the summer twilight lay the large oval lawn, and the
gates which once had doubtless marked the end of Manor Lane – now
Oak Street. And actually he had an impulse to rush back upon his steps,
and bring on himself eternal shame. The servant, however, primly held
him with her eyes alone, and he submitted to her sway.

'Mr Charles in?' he inquired glumly, affecting nonchalance.

The servant bowed her head with a certain condescending deference,
as who should say : 'Do not let us pretend that they are not expecting
you.'

A door to the right opened. Janet was revealed, and, behind her,
Charlie. Both were laughing. There was a sound of a piano. As soon as
Charlie caught sight of Edwin he exclaimed to Janet –

'Where's my bob?'

'Charlie!' she protested, checking her laughter.

'Why! What have I said?' Charlie inquired, with mock innocence,
perceiving that he had been indiscreet and trying to remedy his rash
mistake. 'Surely I can say "bob"!'

Edwin understood nothing of this brief passage. Janet, ignoring Charlie and dismissing the servant with an imperceptible sign, advanced to
the visitor. She was dressed in white, and Edwin considered her to be
extraordinarily graceful, dignified, sweet, and welcoming. There was a
peculiar charm in the way in which her skirts half-reluctantly followed
her along the carpet, causing beautiful curves of drapery from the waist.
And her smile was so warm and so sincere! For the moment she really
felt that Edwin's presence in the house satisfied the keenest of her desires, and of course her face generously expressed what she felt.

'Well, Miss Orgreave,' Edwin grinned. 'Here I am, you see!'

'And we're delighted,' said Janet simply, taking his hand. She might
have amiably teased him about the protracted difficulties of getting him.
She might have hinted an agreeable petulance against the fact that the
brother had succeeded where the sister had failed. Her sisterly manner

to Charlie a little earlier had perhaps shown flashes of such thoughts in her mind. But no. In the presence of Edwin, Janet's extreme good-nature forgot everything save that he was there, a stranger to be received and cherished.

'Here! Give us that tile,' said Charlie.

'Beautiful evening,' Edwin observed.

'Oh! Isn't it!' breathed Janet, in ecstasy, and gazed from the front door into the western sky. 'We were out on the lawn, but mother said it was damp. It wasn't,' she laughed. 'But if you think it's damp, it is damp, isn't it? Will you come and see mother? Charlie, you can leave the front door open.'

Edwin said to himself that she had all the attractiveness of a girl and of a woman. She preceded him towards the door to the right. Charlie hovered behind, on springs. Edwin, nervously pulling out his handkerchief and putting it back, had a confused vision of the hall full of little pictures, plates, stools, rugs, and old sword-sheaths. There seemed to him to be far more knick-knacks in that hall than in the whole of his father's house; Mr Orgreave's ingeniously contrived bookshelves were simply overlaid and smothered in knick-knacks. Janet pushed at the door, and the sound of the piano suddenly increased in volume.

II

There was no cessation of the music as the three entered. As it were beneath the music, Mrs Orgreave, a stout and faded calm lady, greeted him kindly: 'Mr Edwin!' She was shorter than Janet, but Edwin could see Janet in her movements and in her full lips. 'Well, Edwin!' said Osmond Orgreave with lazy and distinguished good-nature, shaking hands. Jimmie and Johnnie, now aged nineteen and eighteen respectively, were in the room; Johnnie was reading; their blushing awkwardness in salutation and comic efforts to be curtly benevolent in the manner of clubmen somewhat eased the tension in Edwin. They addressed him as 'Clayhanger'. The eldest and the youngest child of the family sat at the piano in the act of performing a duet. Tom, pale, slight, near-sighted, and wearing spectacles, had reached the age of thirty-two, and was junior partner in a firm of solicitors at Hanbridge; Bursley seldom saw him. Alicia had the delightful gawkiness of twelve years. One only of the seven children was missing, Marian, aged thirty, and married in London, with two little babies; Marian was adored by all her brothers and sisters, and most by Janet, who, during visits of the married sister, fell back with worshipping joy into her original situation of second daughter.

Edwin, Charles, and Janet sat down on a sofa. It was not until after a moment that Edwin noticed an ugly young woman who sat behind the players and turned over the pages of music for them. 'Surely that can't be his wonderful Hilda!' Edwin thought. In the excitement of arrival he had forgotten the advertised Hilda. Was that she? The girl could be no other. Edwin made the reflection that all men make : 'Well, it's astonishing what other fellows like!' And, having put down Charlie several points in his esteem, he forgot Hilda.

Evidently loud and sustained conversation was not expected nor desired while the music lasted. And Edwin was glad of this. It enabled him to get his breath and his bearings in what was to him really a tremendous ordeal. And in fact he was much more agitated than even he imagined. The room itself abashed him.

Everybody, including Mr Orgreave, had said that the Clayhanger drawing-room with its bay-window was a fine apartment. But the Or-greave drawing-room had a bay-window and another large window; it was twice as big as the Clayhangers' and of an interesting irregular shape. Although there were in it two unoccupied expanses of carpet, it nevertheless contained what seemed to Edwin immense quantities of furniture of all sorts. Easy-chairs were common, and everywhere. Several bookcases rose to the low ceiling; dozens and dozens of pictures hid the walls; each corner had its little society of objects; cushions and candle-sticks abounded; the piano was a grand, and Edwin was astounded to see another piano, a small upright, in the farther distance; there were even two fireplaces, with two mirrors, two clocks, two sets of orna-ments, and two embroidered screens. The general effect was of extra-ordinary lavish profusion – of wilful, splendid, careless extravagance.

Yet the arm of the sofa on which Edwin leaned was threadbare in two different places. The room was faded and worn, like its mistress. Like its mistress it seemed to exhale a silent and calm authority, based on historic tradition.

And the room was historic; it had been the theatre of history. For twenty-five years – ever since Tom was seven – it had witnessed the adventurous domestic career of the Orgreaves, so quiet superficially, so exciting in reality. It was the drawing-room of a man who had con-sistently used immense powers of industry for the satisfaction of his prodigal instincts; it was the drawing-room of a woman whose placidity no danger could disturb, and who cared for nothing if only her hus-band was amused. Spend and gain! And, for a change, gain and spend! That was the method. Work till sheer exhaustion beat you. Plan, scheme, devise! Satisfy your curiosity and your other instincts! Ex-periment! Accept risks! Buy first, order first, pledge yourself first; and then split your head in order to pay and to redeem! When chance aids you to accumulate, let the pile grow, out of mere perversity, and then scatter it royally! Play heartily! Play with the same intentness as you work! Live to the uttermost instant and to the last flicker of energy! Such was the spirit of Osmond Orgreave, and the spirit which reigned in the house generally, if not in every room of the house.

III

For each child had its room – except Jimmie and Johnnie, who shared one. And each room was the fortress of an egoism, the theatre of a separate drama, mysterious, and sacred from the others. Jimmie could not remember having been in Janet's room – it was forbidden by Alicia, who was jealous of her sole right of *entrée* – and nobody would have dreamed of violating the chamber of Jimmie and Johnnie to discover the origin of peculiar noises that puzzled the household at seven o'clock in the morning. As for Tom's castle – it was a legend to the younger children; it was supposed to be wondrous.

All the children had always cost money, and a great deal of money, until Marian had left the family in deep gloom for her absence, and Tom, with a final wrench of a vast sum from the willing but wincing father, had settled into a remunerative profession. Tom was now keeping himself and repaying the weakened parent. The rest cost more and more every year as their minds and bodies budded and flowered. It was endless, it was staggering, it would not bear thinking about. The long and varied chronicle of it was somehow written on the drawing-room as well as on the faces of the father and mother – on the drawing-room which had the same dignified, childlike, indefatigable, invincible, jolly expression as its owners. Threadbare in places? And why not? The very identical Turkey carpet at which Edwin gazed in his self-consciousness – on that carpet Janet the queenly and mature had sprawled as an infant while her mother, a fresh previous Janet of less than thirty, had cooed and said incomprehensible foolishness to her. Tom was patriarchal because he had vague memories of an earlier drawing-room, misted in far antiquity. Threadbare? By heaven, its mere survival was magnificent! I say that it was a miraculous drawing-room. Its chairs were humanized. Its little cottage piano that nobody ever opened now unless Tom had gone mad on something for two pianos, because it was so impossibly tinny – the cottage piano could humanly recall the touch of a perfect baby when Marian the wife sat down on it. Marian was one of your silly sentimental nice things; on account of its associations, she really preferred the cottage piano to the grand. The two carpets were both resigned, grim old humanities, used to dirty heels, and not caring, or pretending not to care. What did the curtains know of history? Naught. They were always new; they could not last. But even the newest curtains would at once submit to the influence of the room, and take on something of its physiognomy, and help to express its comfortableness. You could not hang a week in front of one of those windows without being subtly informed by the tradition of adventurous happiness that presided over the room. It was that : a drawing-room in which a man and a women, and boys and girls, had been on the whole happy, if often apprehensive.

IV

The music began to engage Edwin's attention. It was music of a kind quite novel to him. Most of it had no meaning for him, but at intervals some fragment detached itself from the mass, and stood out beautiful. It was as if he were gazing at a stage in gloom, but lighted momentarily by fleeting rays that revealed a lovely detail and were bafflingly cut off. Occasionally he thought he noticed a recurrence of the same fragment. Murmurs came from behind the piano. He looked cautiously. Alicia was making faces of alarm and annoyance. She whispered : 'Oh dear ! . . . It's no use ! . . . We're all wrong, I'm sure !' Tom kept his eyes on the page in front of him, doggedly playing. Then Edwin was conscious of dissonances. And then the music stopped.

'Now, Alicia,' her father protested mildly, 'you mustn't be nervous.'

'Nervous !' exclaimed Alicia. 'Tom's just as nervous as I am ! So *he* needn't talk.' She was as red as a cock's crest.

Tom was not talking. He pointed several times violently to a place on Alicia's half of the open book – she was playing the bass part. 'There ! There !' The music recommenced.

'She's always nervous like that,' Janet whispered kindly, 'when anyone's here. But she doesn't like to be told.'

'She plays splendidly,' Edwin responded. 'Do you play?'

Janet shook her head.

'Yes, she does,' Charlie whispered.

'Keep on, darling. You're at the end now.' Edwin heard a low, stern voice. That must be the voice of Hilda. A second later, he looked across, and surprised her glance, which was intensely fixed on himself. She dropped her eyes quickly; he also.

Then he felt by the nature of the chords that the piece was closing. The music ceased. Mr Orgreave clapped his hands. 'Bravo ! Bravo !'

'Why,' cried Charlie to the performers, 'you weren't within ten bars of each other !' And Edwin wondered how Charlie could tell that. As for him, he did not know enough of music to be able to turn over the pages for others. He felt himself to be an ignoramus among a company of brilliant experts.

'Well,' said Mr Orgreave, 'I suppose we may talk a bit now. It's more than our place is worth to breathe aloud while these Rubinsteins are doing Beethoven !' He looked at Edwin, who grinned.

158

'Oh! My word!' smiled Mrs Orgreave, supporting her hand.

'Beethoven, is it?' Edwin muttered. He was acquainted only with the name, and had never heard it pronounced as Mr Orgreave pronounced it.

'One symphony a night!' Mr Orgreave said, with irony. 'And we're only at the second, it seems. Seven more to come. What do you think of that, Edwin?'

'Very fine!'

'Let's have the 'Lost Chord', Janet,' Mr Orgreave suggested.

There was a protesting chorus of 'Oh, dad!'

'Very well! Very well!' the father murmured, acting humility. 'I'm snubbed!'

Tom had now strolled across the room, smiling to himself, and looking at the carpet, in an effort to behave as one who had done nothing in particular.

'How d'ye do, Clayhanger?' He greeted Edwin, and grasped his hand in a feverish clutch. 'You must excuse us. We aren't used to audiences. That's the worst of being rotten amateurs.'

Edwin rose. 'Oh!' he deprecated. He had never spoken to Tom Orgreave before, but Tom seemed ready to treat him at once as an established acquaintance.

Then Alicia had to come forward and shake hands. She could not get a word out.

'Now, baby!' Charlie teased her.

She tossed her mane, and found refuge by her mother's side. Mrs Orgreave caressed the mane into order.

'This is Miss Lessways. Hilda – Mr Edwin Clayhanger.' Janet drew the dark girl towards her as the latter hovered uncertainly in the middle of the room, her face forced into the look of elaborate negligence conventionally assumed by every self-respecting person who waits to be introduced. She took Edwin's hand limply, and failed to meet his glance. Her features did not soften. Edwin was confirmed in the impression of her obdurate ugliness. He just noticed her olive skin and black eyes and hair. She was absolutely different in type from any of the Clayhangers. The next instant she and Charlie were talking together.

Edwin felt the surprised relief of one who has plunged into the sea and discovers himself fairly buoyant on the threatening waves.

'Janet,' asked Mrs Orgreave, 'will supper be ready?'

In the obscurer corners of the room grey shadows gathered furtively, waiting their time.

V

'Seen my latest, Charlie?' asked Tom, in his thin voice.

'No, what is it?' Charlie replied. The younger brother was flattered by this proof of esteem from the elder, but he did his best by casualness of tone to prevent the fact from transpiring.

All the youths were now standing in a group in the middle of the drawing-room. Their faces showed pale and more distinct than their bodies in the darkening twilight. Mrs Orgreave, her husband, and the girls had gone into the dining-room.

Tom Orgreave, with the gestures of a precisian, drew a bunch of keys from his pocket, and unlocked a rosewood bookcase that stood between the two windows. Jimmy winked to Johnnie, and included Edwin in the fellowship of the wink, which meant that Tom was more comic than Tom thought, with his locked bookcases and his simple vanities of a collector. Tom collected books. As Edwin gazed at the bookcase he perceived that it was filled mainly with rich bindings. And suddenly all his own book-buying seemed to him petty and pitiful. He saw books in a new aspect. He had need of no instruction, of no explanation. The amorous care with which Tom drew a volume from the bookcase was enough in itself to enlighten Edwin completely. He saw that a book might be more than reading matter, might be a bibelot, a curious jewel, to satisfy the lust of the eye and of the hand. He instantly condemned his own few books as being naught; he was ashamed of them. Each book in that bookcase was a separate treasure.

'See this, my boy?' said Tom, handing to Charlie a calf-bound volume, with a crest on the sides. 'Six volumes. Picked them up at Stafford – Assizes, you know. It's the Wilbraham crest. I never knew they'd been selling their library.'

Charlie accepted the book with respect. Its edges were gilt, and the paper thin and soft. Edwin looked over his shoulder, and saw the title-page of Victor Hugo's *Notre-Dame de Paris*; in French. The volume had a most romantic, foreign, even exotic air. Edwin desired it fervently, or something that might rank equal with it.

'How much did they stick you for this lot?' asked Charlie.

Tom held up one finger.

'Quid?' Charlie wanted to be sure. Tom nodded.

'Cheap as dirt, of course!' said Tom. 'Binding's worth more than that. Look at the other volumes. Look at them!'

'Pity it's only a second edition,' said Charlie.

'Well, damn it, man! One can't have everything.'

Charlie passed the volume to Edwin, who fingered it with the strangest delight. Was it possible that this exquisitely delicate and uncustomary treasure, which seemed to exhale all the charm of France and the savour of her history, had been found at Stafford? He had been to Stafford himself. He had read *Notre-Dame* himself, but in English, out of a common book like any common book – not out of a bibelot.

'You've read it, of course, Clayhanger?' Tom said.

'Oh!' Edwin answered humbly. 'Only in a translation.' Yet there was a certain falseness in his humility, for he was proud of having read the work. What sort of a duffer would he have appeared had be been obliged to reply 'No'?

'You ought to read French *in* French,' said Tom, kindly authoritative.

'Can't,' said Edwin.

'Bosh!' Charlie said. 'You were always spiffing in French. You could simply knock spots off me.'

'And do you read French in French, the Sunday?' Edwin asked.

'Well,' said Charlie, 'I must say it was Thomas put me up to it. You simply begin to read, that's all. What you don't understand, you miss. But you soon understand. You can always look at a dictionary if you feel like it. I usually don't.'

'I'm sure *you* could read French easily in a month,' said Tom. 'They always gave a good grounding at Oldcastle. There's simply nothing in it.'

'Really!' Edwin murmured, relinquishing the book. 'I must have a shot, I never thought of it.' And he had never thought of reading French for pleasure. He had construed Xavier de Maistre's *Voyage autour de ma chambre* for marks, assuredly not for pleasure. 'Are there any books in this style to be got on that bookstall in Hanbridge Market?' he inquired of Tom.

'Sometimes,' said Tom, wiping his spectacles. 'Oh yes!'

It was astounding to Edwin how blind he had been to the romance of existence in the Five Towns.

'It's all very well,' observed Charlie reflectively, fingering one or two of the other volumes – 'it's all very well, and Victor Hugo is Victor Hugo; but you can say what you like – there's a lot of this that'll bear skipping, your worships.'

'Not a line!' said a passionate, vibrating voice.

The voice so startled and thrilled Edwin that he almost jumped, as he looked round. To Edwin it was dramatic; it was even dangerous and threatening. He had never heard a quiet voice so charged with intense emotion. Hilda Lessways had come back to the room, and she stood near the door, her face gleaming in the dusk. She stood like an Amazonian defender of the aged poet. Edwin asked himself, 'Can anyone be so excited as that about a book?' The eyes, lips, and nostrils were a revelation to him. He could feel his heart beating. But the girl strongly repelled him. Nobody else appeared to be conscious that anything singular had occurred. Jimmie and Johnnie sidled out of the room.

'Oh! Indeed!' Charlie directed his candid and yet faintly ironic smile upon Hilda Lessways. 'Don't *you* think that some of it's dullish, Teddy?'

Edwin blushed. 'Well, ye-es,' he answered, honestly judicial.

'Mrs Orgreave wants to know when you're coming to supper,' said Hilda, and left.

Tom was relocking the bookcase.

CHAPTER 8 : *The Family Supper*

I

'Now, father, let's have a bottle of wine, eh?' Charlie vociferously suggested.

Mr Orgreave hesitated : 'You'd better ask your mother.'

'Really, Charlie —' Mrs Orgreave began.

'Oh yes!' Charlie cut her short. 'Right you are, Martha!'

The servant, who had stood waiting for a definite command during this brief conflict of wills, glanced interrogatively at Mrs Orgreave and, perceiving no clear prohibition in her face, departed with a smile to get the wine. She was a servant of sound prestige, and had the inexpressible privilege of smiling on duty. In her time she had fought lively battles of repartee with all the children from Charlie downwards. Janet humoured Martha, and Martha humoured Mrs Orgreave.

The whole family (save absent Marian) was now gathered in the dining-room, another apartment on whose physiognomy were written in cipher the annals of the vivacious tribe. Here the curtains were drawn, and all the interest of the room centred on the large white gleaming table, about which the members stood or sat under the downward radiance of a chandelier. Beyond the circle illuminated by the shaded chandelier could be discerned dim forms of furniture and of pictures, with a glint of high light here and there burning on the corner of some gold frame. Mr and Mrs Orgreave sat at either end of the table. Alicia stood by her father, with one arm half round his neck. Tom sat near his mother. Janet and Hilda sat together, flanked by Jimmie and Johnnie, who stood, having pushed chairs away. Charlie and Edwin stood opposite. The table seemed to Edwin to be heaped with food : cold and yet rich remains of bird and beast; a large fruit pie, opened; another intact; some puddings; cheese; sandwiches; raw fruit; at Janet's elbow were cups and saucers and a pot of coffee; a large glass jug of lemonade shone near by; plates, glasses, and cutlery were strewn about irregularly. The effect upon Edwin was one of immense and careless prodigality; it intoxicated him; it made him feel that a grand profuseness was the finest thing in life. In his own home the supper consisted of cheese, bread, and water, save on Sundays, when cold sausages were generally added, to make a feast. But the idea of the price of living as the Orgreaves lived seriously startled the prudence in him. Imagine that expense always persisting day after day, night after night! There were certainly at least four in the family who bought clothes at Shillitoe's, and everybody looked elaborately costly, except Hilda Lessways, who did not flatter the eye. But equally, they all seemed quite unconscious of their costliness.

'Now, Charlie darling, you must look after Mr Edwin,' said Mrs Orgreave.

'She never calls *us* darling,' said Johnnie, affecting disgust.

'She will, as soon as you've left home,' said Janet, ironically soothing.

'I *do*, I often do!' Mrs Orgreave asserted. 'Much oftener than you deserve.'

'Sit down, Teddy,' Charlie enjoined.

'Oh! I'm all right, thanks,' said Edwin.

'Sit *down*!' Charlie insisted, using force.

'Do you talk to your poor patients in that tone?' Alicia inquired, from the shelter of her father.

'Here I come down specially to see them,' Charlie mused aloud, as he twisted the corkscrew into the cork of the bottle, unceremoniously handed to him by Martha, 'and not only they don't offer to pay my fares, but they grudge me a drop of claret! Plupp!' He grimaced as the cork came out. 'And my last night, too!' Hilda, this is better than coffee, as St Paul remarked on a famous occasion. Pass your glass.'

'Charlie!' his mother protested. 'I'll thank you to leave St Paul out.'

'Charlie! Your mother will be boxing your ears if you don't mind,' his father warned him.

'I'll not have it!' said his mother, shaking her head in a fashion that she imagined to be harsh and forbidding.

II

Towards the close of the meal, Mr Orgreave said –

'Well, Edwin, what does your father say about Bradlaugh?'

'He doesn't say much,' Edwin replied.

'Let me see, does he call himself a Liberal?'

'He calls himself a Liberal,' said Edwin, shifting on his chair. 'Yes, he calls himself a Liberal. But I'm afraid he's a regular old Tory.'

Edwin blushed, laughing, as half the family gave way to more or less violent mirth.

'Father's a regular old Tory, too!' Charlie grinned.

'Oh! I'm sorry,' said Edwin.

'Yes, father's a regular old Tory,' agreed Mr Orgreave. 'Don't apologize! Don't apologize! I'm used to these attacks. I've been nearly kicked out of my own house once. But someone has to keep the flag flying.'

It was plain that Mr Orgreave enjoyed the unloosing of the hurricane which he had brought about. Mrs Orgreave used to say that he employed that particular tone from a naughty love of mischief. In a moment all the boys were upon him, except Jimmie, who, out of sheer intellectual snobbery, as the rest averred, supported his father. Atheistical Bradlaugh had been exciting the British public to disputation for a long time, and the Bradlaugh question happened then to be acute. In that very week the Northampton member had been committed to custody for outraging Parliament, and released. And it was known that Gladstone meant immediately to bring in a resolution for permitting members to affirm, instead of taking oath by appealing to God. Than this complication of theology and politics nothing could have been better devised to impassion an electorate which had but two genuine interests – theology and politics. The rumour of the feverish affair had spread to the most isolated communities. People talked theology, and people talked politics, who had till then only felt silently on these subjects. In loquacious families Bradlaugh caused dissension and division, more real perhaps than apparent, for not all Bradlaugh's supporters had the courage to avow themselves such. It was not easy, at any rate it was not easy in the Five Towns, for a timid man in reply to the question, 'Are you in favour of a professed Freethinker sitting in the House of Commons?' to reply, 'Yes, I am.' There was something shameless in that word 'professed'. If the Freethinker had been ashamed of his freethinking, if he had sought to conceal it in phrases – the implication was that the case might not have been so bad. This was what astonished Edwin : the candour with which Bradlaugh's position was upheld in the dining-room of the Orgreaves. It was as if he were witnessing deeds of wilful perilous daring.

But the conversation was not confined to Bradlaugh, for Bradlaugh was not a perfect test for separating Liberals and Tories. Nobody in the room, for example, was quite convinced that Mr Orgreave was anti-Bradlaugh. To satisfy their instincts for father-baiting, the boys had to include other topics, such as Ireland and the proposal for Home Rule. As for Mr Orgreave, he could and did always infuriate them by refusing to answer seriously. The fact was that this was his device for maintaining his prestige among the turbulent mob. Dignified and brilliantly clever as Osmond Orgreave had the reputation of being in the town, he was somehow outshone in cleverness at home, and he never put the bar of his dignity between himself and his children. Thus he could only keep the upper hand by allowing hints to escape from him of the secret amusement roused in him by the comicality of the spectacle of his filial enemies. He had one great phrase, which he would drawl out at them with the accents of a man who is trying politely to hide his contempt : 'You'll learn better as you get older.'

III

Edwin, who said little, thought the relationship between father and sons utterly delightful. He had not conceived that parents and children ever were or could be on such terms.

'Now what do you say, Edwin?' Mr Orgreave asked. 'Are you a – Charlie, pass me that bottle.'

Charlie was helping himself to another glass of wine. The father, the two eldest sons, and Edwin alone had drunk of the wine. Edwin had never tasted wine in his life, and the effect of half a glass on him was very agreeable and strange.

'Oh, dad! I just want a –' Charlie objected, holding the bottle in the air above his glass.

'Charlie,' said his mother, 'do you hear your father?'

'Pass me that bottle,' Mr Orgreave repeated.

Charlie obeyed, proclaiming himself a martyr. Mr Orgreave filled his own glass, emptying the bottle, and began to sip.

'This will do me more good than you, young man,' he said. Then turning again to Edwin : 'Are you a Bradlaugh man?'

And Edwin, uplifted, said : 'All I say is – you can't help what you believe. You can't make yourself believe anything. And I don't see why you should, either. There's no virtue in believing.'

'Hooray!' cried the sedate Tom.

'No virtue in believing! Eh, Mr Edwin! Mr Edwin!'

This sad expostulation came from Mrs Orgreave.

'Don't you see what I mean?' he persisted vivaciously, reddening. But he could not express himself further.

'Hooray!' repeated Tom.

Mrs Orgreave shook her head, with grieved good-nature.

'You mustn't take mother too seriously,' said Janet, smiling. 'She only puts on that expression to keep worse things from being said. She's only pretending to be upset. Nothing could upset her, really. She's past being upset – she's been through so much – haven't you, you poor dear?'

In looking at Janet, Edwin caught the eyes of Hilda blazing on him fixedly. Her head seemed to tremble, and he glanced away. She had added nothing to the discussion. And indeed Janet herself had taken no part in the politics, content merely to advise the combatants upon their demeanour.

'So you're against me too, Edwin!' Mr Orgreave said with mock melancholy. 'Well, this is no place for me.' He rose, lifted Alicia and put her into his arm-chair, and then went towards the door.

'You aren't going to work, are you, Osmond?' his wife asked, turning her head.

'I am,' said he.

He disappeared amid a wailing chorus of 'Oh, dad!'

CHAPTER 9 : *In the Porch*

I

When the front door of the Orgreaves interposed itself that night between Edwin and a little group of gas-lit faces, he turned away towards the warm gloom of the garden in a state of happy excitement. He had left fairly early, despite protests, because he wished to give his father no excuse for a spectacular display of wrath; Edwin's desire for a tranquil existence was growing steadily. But now that he was in the open air, he did not want to go home. He wanted to be in full possession of himself, at leisure and in freedom, and to examine the treasure of his sensations. 'It's been rather quiet,' the Orgreaves had said. 'We generally have people dropping in.' Quiet! It was the least quiet evening he had ever spent.

He was intoxicated; not with wine, though he had drunk wine. A group of well-intentioned philanthropists, organized into a powerful society for combating the fearful evils of alcoholism, had seized Edwin at the age of twelve and made him bind himself with solemn, childish signature and ceremonies never to taste alcohol save by doctor's orders. He thought of this pledge in the garden of the Orgreaves. 'Damned rot,' he murmured, and dismissed the pledge from his mind as utterly unimportant, if not indeed fatuous. No remorse! The whole philosophy of asceticism inspired him, at that moment, with impatient scorn. It was the hope of pleasure that intoxicated him, the vision which he had had of the possibilities of being really interested in life. He saw new avenues towards joy, and the sight thereof made him tingle, less with the desire to be immediately at them than with the present ecstasy of contemplating them. He was conscious of actual physical tremors and agreeable smartings in his head; electric disturbances. But he did not reason;

he felt. He was passive, not active. He would not even, just then, attempt to make new plans. He was in a beatitude, his mouth unaware that it was smiling.

II

Behind him was the lighted house; in front the gloom of the lawn ended in shrubberies and gates, with a street-lamp beyond. And there was silence, save for the vast furnace-breathings, coming over undulating miles, which the people of the Five Towns, hearing them always, never hear. A great deal of diffused light filtered through the cloudy sky. The warm, wandering airs were humid on the cheek. He must return home. He could not stand dreaming all the night in the garden of the Orgreaves. To his right uprose the great rectangular mass of his father's new house, entirely free of scaffoldings, having all the aspect of a house inhabited. It looked enormous. He was proud of it. In such an abode, and so close to the Orgreaves, what could he not do?

Why go to gaze on it again? There was no common sense in doing so. And yet he felt: 'I must have another glance at it before I go home.' From his attitude towards it, he might have been the creator of that house. That house was like one of his more successful drawings. When he had done a drawing that he esteemed, he was always looking at it. He would look at it before running down to breakfast; and after breakfast, instead of going straight to the shop, he would rush upstairs to have still another look at it. The act of inspection gave him pleasure. So with the house. Strange, superficially; but the simple explanation was that for some things he had the eyes of love ... Yes, in his dancing and happy brain the impulse to revisit the house was not to be conquered.

The few battered yards of hedge between his father's land and that of Mr Orgreaves seemed more passable in the night. He crunched along the gravel, stepped carefully with noiseless foot on the flower-bed, and then pushed himself right through the frail bushes, forgetting the respect due to his suit. The beginning of summer had dried the sticky clay of the new garden; paths had already been traced on it, and trenches cut for the draining of the lawn that was to be. Edwin in the night saw the new garden finished, mellow, blooming with such blossoms as were sold in St Luke's Market; he had scarcely ever seen flowers growing in the mass. He saw himself reclining in the garden with a rare and beautiful book in his hand, while the sound of Beethoven's music came to him through the open window of the drawing-room. In so far as he saw Maggie at all, he saw her somehow mysteriously elegant and vivacious. He did not see his father. His fancy had little relation to reality. But this did not mar his pleasure. ... Then he saw himself talking over the hedge, wittily, to amiable and witty persons in the garden of the Orgreaves.

III

He had not his key to the new house, but he knew a way of getting into it through the cellar. No reason in doing so; nevertheless he must get into it, must localize his dream in it! He crouched down under the blank east wall, and, feet foremost, disappeared slowly, as though the house were swallowing him. He stood on the stillage of the cellar, and struck a match. Immense and weird, the cellar; and the doorless doorway, leading to the cellar steps, seemed to lead to affrighting matters. He was in the earth, in it, with the smells of damp mortar and of bricks and of the earth itself about him, and above him rose the house, a room over him, and a room over that and another over that, and then the chimney-cowl up in the sky. He jumped from the stillage, and went quickly to the doorway and saw the cellar steps. His heart was beating. He trembled, he was afraid, exquisitely afraid, acutely conscious of himself amid the fundamental mysteries of the universe. He reached the top of the steps as the match expired. After a moment he could distinguish the forms of things in the hall, even the main features of the pattern of the tiles. The small panes in the glazed front door, whose varied tints repeated those of the drawing-room window in daytime, now showed a uniform dull grey, lifeless. The cellar was formidable below, and the stairs curved upwards into the formidable. But he climbed them. The house seemed full of inexplicable noises. When he stopped to listen he could hear scores of different infinitesimal sounds. His spine thrilled, as if a hand delicate and terrible had run down it in a caress. All the unknown of the night and of the universe was pressing upon him, but it was he alone who had created the night and the universe. He reached his room, the room in which he meant to inaugurate the new life and the endeavour towards perfection. Already, after his manner, he had precisely settled where the bed was to be, and where the table, and all the other objects of his world. There he would sit and read rare and beautiful books in the original French! And there he would sit to draw. And to the right of the hearth, over the bookshelves, would be such and such a picture, and to the left of the hearth, over bookshelves, would be such and such another picture. . . . Only, now, he could not dream in the room as he had meant to dream; because beyond the open door was the empty landing and the well of the stairs and all the terror of the house. The terror came and mingled with the delicious sensations that had seized him in the solitude of the garden of the Orgreaves. No! Never had he been so intensively alive as then!

He went cautiously to the window and looked forth. Instantly the

terror of the house was annihilated. It fell away, was gone. He was not alone in his fancy-created universe. The reassuring illusion of reality came back like a clap of thunder. He could see a girl insinuating herself through the gap in the hedge which he had made ten minutes earlier.

IV

'What the deuce is she after?' he muttered. He wondered whether, if she happened to glance upwards, she would be able to see him. He stood away a little from the window, but as in the safer position he could no longer distinguish her he came again close to the glass. After all, there could be no risk of her seeing him. And if she did see him – the fright would be hers, not his.

Having passed through the hedge, she stopped, bent down, leaning backward and to one side, and lifted the hem of her skirt to examine it; possibly it was torn; then she dropped it. By that black, tight skirt and something in her walk he knew she was Hilda; he could not decipher her features. She moved towards the new house, very slowly, as if she had emerged for an aimless nocturnal stroll. Strange and disquieting creature! He peered as far as he could leftwards, to see the west wall of Lane End House. In a window of the upper floor a light burned. The family had doubtless gone to bed, or were going. . . . And she had wandered forth solitary and was trespassing in his garden. 'Cheek!' If ever he got an opportunity he should mysteriously tease her on the subject of illegal night excursions! Yes, he should be very witty and ironic. 'Nothing but cheek!' He was confirmed in his hostility to her. She had no charm, and yet the entire Orgreave family was apparently infatuated about her. Her interruption on behalf of Victor Hugo seemed to be savage. Girls ought not to use that ruthless tone. And her eyes were hard, even cruel. She was less feminine than masculine. Her hair was not like a girl's hair.

She still came on, until the projecting roof of the bay-window beneath him hid her from sight. He would have opened his window and leaned out to glimpse her, could he have done so without noise. Where was she? In the garden porch? She did not reappear. She might be capable of getting into the house! She might even then actually be getting into the house! She was queer, incalculable. Supposing that she was in the habit of surreptitiously visiting the house, and had found a key to fit one of the doors, or supposing that she could push up a window – she would doubtless mount the stairs and trap him! Absurd, these speculations; as absurd as a nightmare! But they influenced his conduct. He felt himself forced to provide against the wildest hazards. Abruptly he departed from the bedroom and descended the stairs, stamping, clumping, with all possible noise; in addition he whistled. This was to warn her to fly. He

stopped in the hall until she had had time to fly, and then he lit a match as a signal which surely no carelessness could miss. He could have gone direct by the front door into the street, so leaving her to her odd self; but, instead, he drew back the slipcatch of the garden door and opened it, self-consciously humming a tune.

She was within the porch. She turned deliberately to look at him. He could feel his heart-beats. His cheeks burned and yet he was chilled.

'Who's there?' he asked. But he did not succeed to his own satisfaction in acting alarmed surprise.

'Me!' said Hilda, challengingly, rudely.

'Oh!' he murmured, at a loss. 'Did you want me? Did anyone want me?'

'Yes,' she said. 'I just wanted to ask you something.' She paused. He could not see her scowling, but it seemed to him that she must be. He remembered that she had rather thick eyebrows, and that when she brought them nearer together by a frown, they made almost one continuous line, the effect of which was not attractive.

'Did you know I was in here?'

'Yes. That's my bedroom window over there – I've left the gas up – and I saw you get through the hedge. So I came down. They'd all gone off to bed except Tom, and I told him I was just going for a walk in the garden for a bit. They never worry me, you know. They let me alone. I knew you'd got into the house, by the light.'

'But I only struck a match a second ago,' he protested.

'Excuse me,' she said coldly; 'I saw a light quite five minutes ago.'

'Oh yes!' he apologized. 'I remember. When I came up the cellar steps.'

'I dare say you think it's very queer of me,' she continued.

'Not at all,' he said quickly.

'Yes, you do,' she bitterly insisted. 'But I want to know. Did you mean it when you said – you know, at supper – that there's no virtue in believing?'

'Did I say there was no virtue in believing?' he stammeringly demanded.

'Of course you did!' she remonstrated. 'Do you mean to say you can say a thing like that and then forget about it? If it's true, it's one of the most wonderful things that were ever said. And that's why I wanted to know if you meant it or whether you were only saying it because it sounded clever. That's what they're always doing in that house, you know – being clever!' Her tone was invariably harsh.

'Yes,' he said simply, 'I meant it. Why?'

'You did?' Her voice seemed to search for insincerity. 'Well, thank

you. That's all. It may mean a new life to me. I'm always trying to believe; always! Aren't you?'

'I don't know,' he mumbled. 'How do you mean?'

'Well – you know!' she said, as if impatiently smashing his pretence of not understanding her. 'But perhaps you do believe?'

He thought he detected scorn for a facile believer. 'No,' he said, 'I don't.'

'And it doesn't worry you? Honestly? Don't be clever! I hate that!'

'No,' he said.

'Don't you ever think about it?'

'No. Not often.'

'Charlie does.'

'Has he told you?' ('So she talks to the Sunday too!' he reflected.)

'Yes; but of course I quite see why it doesn't worry you – if you honestly think there's no virtue in believing.'

'Well,' said Edwin. '*Is* there?' The more he looked at it through her eyes, the more wonderful profundities he discovered in that remark of his, which at the time of uttering it had appeared to him a simple platitude. It went exceedingly deep in many directions.

'I hope you are right,' she replied. Her voice shook.

V

There was silence. To ease the strain of his self-consciousness Edwin stepped down from the stone floor of the porch to the garden. He felt rain. And he noticed that the sky was very much darker.

'By jove!' he said. 'It's beginning to rain, I do believe.'

'I thought it would,' she answered.

A squall of wind suddenly surged rustling through the high trees in the garden of the Orgreaves, and the next instant threw a handful of wild raindrops on his cheek.

'You'd better stand against the other wall,' he suggested. 'You'll catch it there, if it keeps on.'

She obeyed. He returned to the porch, but remained in the exposed portion of it.

'Better come here,' she said, indicating somehow her side.

'Oh! I'm all right.'

'You needn't be afraid of me,' she snapped.

He grinned awkwardly, but said nothing, for he could not express his secret resentment. He considered the girl to be of exceedingly unpleasant manners.

'Would you mind telling me the time?' she asked.

He took out his watch, but peer as he might, he could not discern the position of the hands.

'Half a second,' he said, and struck a match. The match was blown out before he could look at the dial, but by its momentary flash he saw Hilda pressed against the wall. Her lips were tight, her eyes blazing, her hands clenched. She frowned; she was pale, and expecially pale by contrast with the black of her plain, austere dress.

'If you'll come into the house,' he said, 'I can get a light there.' The door was ajar.

'No, thanks,' she declined. 'It doesn't really matter what time it is, does it? Good night!'

He divined that she was offering her hand. He clasped it blindly in the dark. He could not refuse to shake hands. Her hand gave his a feverish and lingering squeeze, which was like a contradicting message in the dark night; as though she were sending through her hand a secret denial of her spoken accents and her frown. He forgot to answer her 'good night'. A trap rattled furiously up the road. (Yes; only six yards off, on the other side of the boundary wall, was the public road! And he standing hidden there in the porch with this girl whom he had seen for the first time that evening!) It was the mail-cart, rushing to Knype.

She did not move. She had said 'good night' and shaken hands; and yet she remained. They stood speechless.

Then, without warning, after perhaps a minute that seemed like ten minutes, she walked away, slowly, into the rain. And as she did so, Edwin could just see her straightening her spine and throwing back her shoulders with a proud gesture.

'I say, Miss Lessways!' he called in a low voice. But he had no notion of what he wanted to say. Only her departure had unlocked his throat.

She made no sign. Again he grinned awkwardly, a little ashamed of her and a little ashamed of himself, because neither had behaved as woman or man of the world.

After a short interval he followed in her steps as far as the gap in the hedge, which he did not find easily. There was no sign of her. The gas burned serenely in her bedroom, and the window was open. Then he saw the window close up a little, and an arm in front of the drawn blind. The rain had apparently ceased.

VI

'Well, that's an eye-opener, that is!' he murmured, and thereby expressed the situation. 'Of all the damned impudence ...!' He somewhat overstated his feelings, because he was posing a little to himself : an accident that sooner or later happens to every man! 'And she'll go back and make out to Master Tom that she's just had a stroll in the garden! ... Garden, indeed! And yet they're all so fearfully stuck on her.'

172

He nodded his head several times reflectively, as if saying, 'Well, well! What next?' And he murmured aloud : 'So that's how they carry on, is it!' He meant, of course, women. . . . He was very genuinely astounded.

But the chief of all his acute sensations in that moment was pride : sheer pride. He thought, what ninety-nine men out of a hundred would have thought in such circumstances : 'She's taken a fancy to me!' Useless to call him a conceited coxcomb, from disgust that he did not conform to a sentimentally idealistic standard! He thought : 'She's taken a fancy to me!' And he was not a conceited coxcomb. He exulted in the thought. Nothing had ever before so startled and uplifted him. It constituted the supreme experience of his career as a human being. The delightful and stimulating experience of his evening in the house of the Orgreaves sank into unimportance by the side of it. The new avenues towards joy which had been revealed to him appeared now to be quite unexciting paths; he took them for granted. And he forgot the high and serious mood of complex emotion in which he had entered the new house. Music and the exotic flavours of a foreign language seemed a little thing, in comparison with the feverish hand-clasp of the girl whom he so peculiarly disliked. The lifeless hand which he had taken in the drawing-room of the Orgreaves could not be the same hand as that which had closed intimately on his under the porch. She must have two right hands!

And, even more base than his coxcombry, he despised her because it was he, Edwin, to whom she had taken a fancy. He had not sufficient self-confidence to justify her fancy in his own eyes. His argument actually was that no girl worth having could have taken a fancy to him at sight. Thus he condemned her for her faith in him. As for his historic remark about belief – well, there might or might not be something in that; perhaps there was something in it. One instant he admired it, and the next he judged it glib and superficial. Moreover, he had conceivably absorbed it from a book. But even if it were an original epigrammic pearl – was that an adequate reason for her following him to an empty house at dead of night? Of course, an overwhelming passion *might* justify such behaviour! He could recall cases in literature. . . . Yes, he had got so far as to envisage the possibility of overwhelming passion. . . . Then all these speculations disconcertingly vanished, and Hilda presented herself to his mind as a girl intensely religious, who would shrink from no unconventionality in the pursuit of truth. He did not much care for this theory of Hilda, nor did it convince him.

'Imagine marrying a girl like that!' he said to himself disdainfully. And he made a catalogue of her defects of person and of character. She was severe, satiric, merciless. 'And I suppose – if I were to put my finger up – !' Thus ran on his despicable ideas. 'Janet Orgreave, now – !' Janet had every quality he could desire, that he could even think of. Janet was balm.

'You needn't be afraid,' that unpleasant girl had said. And he had ony been able to grin in reply !

Still, pride ! Intense, masculine pride !

There was one thing he had liked about her : that straightening of the spine and setting back of the shoulders as she left him. She had in her some tinge of the heroic.

He quitted the garden, and as soon as he was in the street he remembered that he had not pulled-to the garden door of the house. 'Dash the confounded thing !' he exploded, returning. But he was not really annoyed. He would not have been really annoyed even if he had had to return from halfway down Trafalgar Road. Everything was a trifle save that a girl had run after him under such romantic circumstances. The circumstances were not strictly romantic, but they so seemed to him.

Going home, he did not meet a soul; only in the middle distance of one of the lower side streets he espied a policeman. Trafalgar Road was a solitude of bright and forlorn gas-lamps and dark, excluding façades.

Suddenly he came to the corner of Wedgwood Street. He had started from Bleakridge; he had arrived at home : the interval between these two events was a perfect blank, save for the policeman. He could not recall having walked all the way down the road. And as he put the key into the door he was not in the least disturbed by the thought that his father might not have gone to bed. He went upstairs with a certain swaggering clatter, as who should say to all sleepers and bullies : 'You be damned ! I don't care for any of you ! Something's happened to me.'

And he mused : 'If anybody had told me this afternoon that before midnight I should –'

CHAPTER 10 : *The Centenary*

I

It was immediately after this that the 'Centenary' – mispronounced in every manner conceivable – began to obsess the town. Superior and aloof persons, like the Orgreaves, had for weeks heard a good deal of vague talk about the Centenary from people whom intellectually they despised, and had condescended to the Centenary as an amiable and excusable affair which lacked interest for them. They were wrong. Edwin had gone further, and had sniffed at the Centenary, to everybody except his father. And Edwin was especially wrong. On the ante-penultimate day of June he first uneasily suspected that he had committed a fault of appraisement. That was when his father brusquely announced that by request of the Mayor all places of business in the town would be closed in honour of the Centenary. It was the Centenary of the establishment of Sunday schools.

Edwin hated Sunday schools. Nay, he venomously resented them, though they had long ceased to incommode him. They were connected in his memory with atrocious tedium, pietistic insincerity, and humiliating contacts. At the bottom of his mind he still regarded them as a malicious device of parents for wilfully harassing and persecuting inoffensive, helpless children. And he had a particular grudge against them because he alone of his father's offspring had been chosen for the nauseating infliction. Why should his sisters have been spared and he doomed? He became really impatient when Sunday schools were under discussion, and from mere irrational annoyance he would not admit that Sunday schools had any good qualities whatever. He knew nothing of their history, and wished to know nothing.

Nevertheless, when the day of the Centenary dawned – and dawned in splendour – he was compelled, even within himself, to treat Sunday schools with more consideration. And, in fact, for two or three days previously the gathering force of public opinion had been changing his attitude from stern hatred to a sort of half-hearted derision. Now, the derision was mysteriously transformed into an inimical respect. By what? By he knew not what. By something without a name in the air which the mind breathes. He felt it at six o'clock, ere he arose. Lying in bed he felt it. The day was to be a festival. The shop would not open, nor the printing office. The work of preparing for the removal would be suspended. The way of daily life would be quite changed. He was free – that was, nearly free. He said to himself that of course his excited father would expect him to witness the celebrations and to wear his best clothes, and that was a bore. But therein he was not quite honest. For he secretly wanted to witness the celebrations and to wear his best clothes. His curiosity was hungry. He admitted, what many had been asserting for weeks, that the Centenary was going to be a big thing; and his social instinct wished him to share in the pride of it.

'It's a grand day!' exclaimed his father, cheerful and all glossy, as he looked out upon Duck Square before breakfast. 'It'll be rare and hot!' And it was a grand day; one of the dazzling spectacular blue-and-gold days of early summer. And Maggie was in finery. And Edwin too! Useless for him to pretend that a big thing was not afoot – and his father in a white waistcoat! Breakfast was positively talkative, though the conversation was naught but a repeating and repeating of what the arrangements were, and of what everybody had decided to do. The three lingered over breakfast, because there was no reason to hurry. And then even Maggie left the sitting-room without a care, for though Clara was coming for dinner Mrs Nixon could be trusted. Mrs Nixon, if she had time, would snatch half an hour in the afternoon to see what remained to be seen of the show. Families must eat. And if Mrs Nixon was stopped by duty from assisting at this Centenary, she must hope to be more at liberty for the next.

II

At nine o'clock, in a most delicious mood of idleness, Edwin strolled into the shop. His father had taken down one shutter from the doorway, and slanted it carelessly against another on the pavement. A blind man or a drunkard might have stumbled against it and knocked it over. The letters had been hastily opened. Edwin could see them lying in disorder on the desk in the little office. The dust-sheets thought the day was Sunday. He stood in the narrow aperture and looked forth. Duck Square was a shimmer of sunshine. The Dragon and the Duck and the other public-house at the top corner seemed as usual, stolidly confident in the thirst of populations. But the Borough Dining Rooms, next door but one to the corner of Duck Square and Wedgwood Street, were not as usual. The cart of Doy, the butcher, had halted laden in front of the Borough Dining Rooms, and the anxious proprietor, attended by his two little daughers (aproned and sleeved for hard work in imitation of their stout, perspiring mother), was accepting unusual joints from it. Ticklish weather for meat – you could see that from the man's gestures. Even on ordinary days those low-ceiled dining-rooms, stretching far back from the street in a complicated vista of interiors, were apt to be crowded; for the quality of the eightpenny dinner could be relied upon. Edwin imagined what a stifling, deafening inferno of culinary odours and clatter they would be at one o'clock, at two o'clock.

Three hokey-pokey ice-cream hand-carts, one after another, turned the corner of Trafalgar Road and passed in front of him along Wedgwood Street. Three! The men pushing them, one an Italian, seemed to wear nothing but shirt and trousers, with a straw hat above and vague slippers below. The steam-car lumbered up out of the valley of the road and climbed Duck Bank, throwing its enormous shadow to the left. It was half full of bright frocks and suits. An irregular current of finery was setting in to the gates of the Wesleyan School yard at the top of the Bank. And ceremoniously bedecked individuals of all ages hurried in this direction and in that, some with white handkerchiefs over flowered hats, a few beneath parasols. All the town's store of Sunday clothes was in use. The humblest was crudely gay. Pawnbrokers had full tills and empty shops, for twenty-four hours.

Then a procession appeared, out of Moorthorne Road, from behind the Wesleyan Chapel-keeper's house. And as it appeared it burst into music. First a purple banner, upheld on crimson poles with gilded lance-points; then a brass band in full note; and then children, children, children – little, middling, and big. As the procession curved down into Trafalgar Road, it grew in stature, until, towards the end of it, the children were as tall as the adults who walked fussily as hens, proudly as peacocks, on its flank. And last came a railway lorry on which dozens of tiny infants had been penned; and the horses of the lorry were ribboned and their manes and tails tightly plaited; on that grand day they could not be allowed to protect themselves against flies; they were sacrificial animals.

A power not himself drew Edwin to the edge of the pavement. He could read on the immense banner : 'Moorthorne St John's Sunday School'. These, then, were church folk. And indeed the next moment he descried a curate among the peacocks. The procession made another curve into Wedgwood Street, on its way to the supreme rendezvous in St Luke's Square. The band blared; the crimson cheeks of the trumpeters sucked in and out; the drummer leaned backwards to balance his burden, and banged. Every soul of the variegated company, big and little, was in a perspiration. The staggering bearers of the purple banner, who held the great poles in leathern sockets slung from the shoulders, and their acolytes before and behind who kept the banner upright by straining at crimson halyards, sweated most of all. Every foot was grey with dust, and the dark trousers of boys and men showed dust. The steamy whiff of humanity struck Edwin's nostrils. Up hill and down dale the procession had already walked over two miles. Yet it was alert, joyous, and expectant : a chattering procession. From the lorry rose a continuous faint shriek of infantile voices. Edwin was saddened as by pathos. I believe that as he gazed at the procession waggling away along Wedgwood Street he saw Sunday schools in a new light.

And that was the opening of the day. There were to be dozens of such processions. Some would start only in the town itself; but others were coming from the villages like Red Cow, five sultry miles off.

III

A young woman under a sunshade came slowly along Wedgwood Street. She was wearing a certain discreet amount of finery, but her clothes did not fit well, and a thin mantle was arranged so as to lessen as much as possible the obviousness of the fact that she was about to become a mother. The expression of her face was discontented and captious. Edwin did not see her until she was close upon him, and then he immediately became self-conscious and awkward.

'Hello, Clara!' he greeted her, with his instinctive warm, transient smile, holding out his hand sheepishly. It was a most extraordinary and amazing thing that he could never regard the ceremony of shaking hands with a relative as other than an affectation of punctilio. Happily he was not wearing his hat; had it been on his head he would never have taken it off, and yet would have cursed himself for not doing so.

'We *are* grand!' exclaimed Clara, limply taking his hand and dropping it as an article of no interest. In her voice there was still some echo of former sprightliness. The old Clara in her had not till that moment beheld the smart and novel curves of Edwin's Shillitoe suit, and the satiric cry came unbidden from her heart.

Edwin gave an uneasy laugh, which was merely the outlet for his disgust. Not that he was specially disgusted with Clara, for indeed marriage had assuaged a little the tediousness of some of her mannerisms, even if it had taken away from her charm. He was disgusted more comprehensively by the tradition, universal in his class and in most classes, according to which relatives could not be formally polite to one another. He obeyed the tradition as slavishly as anyone, but often said to himself that he would violate the sacred rule if only he could count on a suitable response; and he had no mind to be in the excruciating position of one who, having started 'God save the Queen' at a meeting, finds himself alone in the song. Why could not he and Clara behave together as, for instance, he and Janet Orgreave would behave together, with dignity, with worldliness, with mutual deference? But no! It was impossible, and would ever be so. They had been too brutally intimate, and the result was irremediable.

'*She's* got no room to talk about personal appearance, anyway!' he thought sardonically.

There was another extraordinary and amazing thing. He was ashamed of her condition! He could not help the feeling. In vain he said to himself that her condition was natural and proper. In vain he remembered the remark of the sage that a young woman in her condition was the most beautiful sight in the world. He was ashamed of it. And he did not think it beautiful; he thought it ugly. It worried him. What – his sister? Other men's sisters, yes; but his! He forgot that he himself had been born. He could scarcely bear to look at Clara. Her face was thin, and changed in colour; her eyes were unnaturally lustrous and large, bold and fatigued; she looked ill, really ill; and she was incredibly unornamental. And this was she whom he could remember as a graceful child! And it was all perfectly correct and even laudable! So much so that Clara undoubtedly looked down, now, as from a superior height, upon both himself and Maggie!

'Where's father?' she asked. 'Just shut my sunshade.'

'Oh! Somewhere about, I expect he'll be along in a minute. Albert coming?' He followed her into the shop.

'Albert!' she protested, shocked. 'Albert can't possibly come till one o'clock. Didn't you know he's one of the principal stewards in St Luke's Square? He says we aren't to wait dinner for him if he isn't prompt.'

'Oh!' Edwin replied, and put the sunshade on the counter.

Clara sat down heavily on a chair, and began to fan herself with a handkerchief. In spite of the heat of exercise her face was of a pallid yellow.

'I suppose you're going to stay here all morning?' Edwin inquired.

'Well,' said Clara, 'you don't see me walking up and down the streets all morning, do you? Albert said I was to be sure and go upstairs at once and not move. He said there'd be plenty to see for a long time yet from the sitting-room window, and then afterwards I could lie down.'

Albert said! Albert said! Clara's intonation of this frequent phrase always jarred on Edwin. It implied that Albert was the supreme front of wisdom and authority in Bursley. Whereas, to Edwin, Albert was in fact a mere tedious, self-important manufacturer in a small way, with whom he had no ideas in common. 'A decent fellow at bottom,' the fastidious Edwin was bound to admit to himself by reason of slight glimpses which he had had of Albert's uncouth good-nature; but pietistic, overbearing, and without humour.

'Where's Maggie?' Clara demanded.

'I think she's putting her things on,' said Edwin.

'But didn't she understand I was coming early?' Clara's voice was querulous, and she frowned.

'I don't know,' said Edwin.

He felt that if they remained together for hours, he and Clara would never rise above this plane of conversation – personal, factual, perfectly devoid of wide interest. They would never reach an exchange of general ideas; they never had done. He did not think that Clara had any general ideas.

'I hear you're getting frightfully thick with the Orgreaves,' Clara observed, with a malicious accent and smile, as if to imply that he was getting frightfully above himself and – simultaneously – that the Orgreaves were after all no better than other people.

'Who told you that?' He walked towards the doorway uneasily. The worst was that he could not successfully pretend that these sisterly attacks were lost on him.

179

'Never mind who told me,' said Clara.

Her voice took on a sudden charming roguish quality, and he could hear again the girl of fourteen. His heart at once softened to her. The impartial and unmoved spectator that sat somewhere in Edwin, as in everybody who possesses artistic sensibility, watching his secret life as from a conning tower, thought how strange this was. He stared out into the street. And then a face appeared at the aperture left by the removed shutter. It was Janet Orgreave's, and it hesitated. Edwin gave a nervous start.

IV

Janet was all in white again, and her sunshade was white, with regular circular holes in it to let through spots of sunlight which flecked her face. Edwin had not recovered from the blow of her apparition just at that moment, when he saw Hilda Lessways beyond her. Hilda was slate-coloured, and had a black sunshade. His heart began to thump; it might have been a dramatic and dangerous crisis that had suddenly come about. And to Edwin the situation did in fact present itself as critical : his sister behind, and these two so different girls in front. Yet there was nothing critical in it whatsoever. He shook hands as in a dream, wondering what he should do, trying to summon out of himself the man of the world.

'Do come in,' he urged them, hoping they would refuse.

'Oh no. We mustn't come in,' said Janet, smiling gratefully. Hilda did not smile; she had not even smiled in shaking hands; and she had shaken hands without conviction.

Edwin heard a hurried step in the shop, and then the voice of Maggie, maternal and protective, in a low exclamation of surprise : 'You, dear !' And then the sound of a smacking kiss, and Clara's voice, thin, weak, and confiding : 'Yes, I've come.' 'Come upstairs, do !' said Maggie imploringly. 'Come and be comfortable.' Then steps, ceasing to be heard as the sisters left the shop at the back. The solicitude of Maggie for Clara during the last few months had seemed wonderful to Edwin, as also Clara's occasional childlike acceptance of it.

'But you must come in !' he said more boldly to the visitors, asking himself whether either Janet or Hilda had caught sight of his sisters in the gloom of the shop.

They entered, Hilda stiffly. Each with the same gesture closed her parasol before passing through the slit between the shutters into the deep shade. But whereas Janet smiled with pleasant anticipation as though she was going into heaven, Hilda wrinkled her forehead when her parasol would not subside at the first touch.

Janet talked of the Centenary; said they had decided only that morning to come down into the town and see whatever was to be seen; said with an angelic air of apologizing to the Centenary that up at Lane End House they had certainly been under-estimating its importance and its interest as a spectacle; said that it was most astonishing to see all the shops closed. And Edwin interjected vague replies, pulling the chair out of the little ebonized cubicle so that they could both sit down. And Hilda remained silent. And Edwin's thoughts were driving darkly beneath Janet's chatter as in a deep sea beneath light waves. He heard and answered Janet with a minor part of his being that functioned automatically.

'She's a caution!' reflected the main Edwin, obsessed in secret by Hilda Lessways. Who could have guessed, by looking at her, that only three evenings before she had followed him in the night to question him, to squeeze his hand, and to be rude to him? Did Janet know? Did anyone? No! He felt sure that he and she had the knowledge of that interview to themselves. She sat down glum, almost glowering. She was no more worldly than Maggie and Clara were worldly. Than they, she had no more skill to be sociable. And in appearance she was scarcely more stylish. But she was not as they, and it was useless vindictively to disparage her by pretending that she was. She could be passionate concerning Victor Hugo. She was capable of disturbing herself about the abstract question of belief. He had not heard her utter a single word in the way of common girlish conversation.

The doubt again entered his mind whether indeed her visit to the porch of the new house had been due to a genuine interest in abstract questions and not to a fancy for himself. 'Yes,' he reflected, 'that must have been it.'

In two days his pride in the affair had lost its first acuteness, though it had continued to brighten every moment of his life, and though he had not ceased to regret that he had no intimate friend to whom he could recount it in solemn and delicious intimacy. Now, philosophically, he stamped on his pride as on a fire. And he affected to be relieved at the decision that the girl had been moved by naught but a sort of fanaticism. But he was not relieved by the decision. The decision itself was not genuine. He still clung to the notion that she had followed him for himself. He preferred that she should have taken a fancy to him, even though he discovered no charm in her, no beauty, no solace, nothing but matter for repulsion. He wanted her to think of him, in spite of his distaste for her; to think of him hopelessly. 'You are an ass!' murmured the impartial watcher in the conning tower. And he was. But he did not care. It was agreeable thus to be an ass. . . . His pride flared up again, and instead of stamping he blew on it.

'By Jove!' he thought, eyeing her slyly, 'I'll make you show your hand – you see if I don't! You think you can play with me, but you can't!' He was as violent against her as if she had done him an injury instead of having squeezed his hand in the dark. Was it not injurious to have snapped at him, when he refused her invitation to stand by her against the wall in the porch, 'You needn't be afraid'? Janet would never have said such a thing. If only she resembled Janet...!

During all this private soliloquizing, Edwin's mien of mild nervousness never hardened to betray his ferocity, and he said nothing that might not have been said by an innocuous idiot.

The paper boy, arrayed richly, slipped apologetically into the shop. He had certain packets to take out for delivery, and he was late. Edwin nodded to him distantly. The conversation languished.

Then the head of Mr Orgreave appeared in the aperture. The architect seemed amused. Edwin could not understand how he had ever stood in awe of Mr Orgreave, who, with all his distinction and expensiveness, was the most companionable person in the world.

'Oh! Father!' cried Janet. 'What a deceitful thing you are! Do you know, Mr Edwin, he pooh-poohed us coming down : he said he was far too busy for such childish things as Centenaries! And look at him!'

Mr Orgreave, whose suit, hat, and necktie were a harmony of elegant greys, smiled with paternal ease, and swung his cane. 'Come along, now! Don't let's miss anything. Come along. Now, Edwin, you're coming, aren't you?'

'Did you ever see such a child?' murmured Janet, adoring him.

Edwin turned to the paper boy. 'Just find my father before you go,' he commanded. 'Tell him I've gone, and ask him if you are to put the shutter up.' The paper boy respectfully promised obedience. And Edwin was glad that the forbidding Hilda was there to witness his authority.

Janet went out first. Hilda hesitated; and Edwin, having taken his hat from its hook in the cubicle, stood attending her at the aperture. He was sorry that he could not run upstairs for a walking-stick. At last she seemed to decide to leave, yet left with apparent reluctance. Edwin followed, giving a final glance at the boy, who was tying a parcel hurriedly. Mr Orgreave and his daughter were ten yards off, arm-in-arm. Edwin fell into step with Hilda Lessways. Janet looked round, and smiled and beckoned. 'I wonder,' said Edwin to himself, 'what the devil's going to happen now? I'll take my oath she stayed behind on purpose! Well. . . .' This swaggering audacity was within. Without, even a skilled observer could have seen nothing but a faint, sheepish smile. And his heart was thumping again.

CHAPTER 11 : *The Bottom of the Square*

I

Another procession – that of the Old Church Sunday school – came up, with standards floating and drums beating, out of the steepness of Woodisun Bank, and turned into Wedgwood Street, which thenceforward was loosely thronged by procession and sightseers. The importance of the festival was now quite manifest, for at the end of the street could be seen St Luke's Square, massed with human beings in movement. Osmond Orgreave and his daughter were lost to view in the brave crowd; but after a little, Edwin distinctly saw Janet's sunshade leave Wedgwood Street at the corner of the Wedgwood Institution and bob slowly into the Cock Yard, which was a narrow thoroughfare leading to the market-place and the Town Hall, and so to the top of St Luke's Square. He said nothing, and kept straight on along Wedgwood Street past the Covered Market.

'I hope you didn't catch cold in the rain the other night,' he remarked – grimly, as he thought.

'I should have thought it would have been you who were more likely to catch cold,' Hilda replied, in her curt manner. She looked in front of her. The words seem to him to carry a double meaning. Suddenly she moved her head, glanced full at him for an instant, and glanced behind her. 'Where are they?' she inquired.

'The others? Aren't they in front? They must be somewhere about.'

Unless she also had marked their deviation into the Cock Yard, why had she glanced behind her in asking where they were? She knew as well as he that they had started in front. He could only deduce that she had been as willing as himself to lose Mr Orgreave and Janet. Just then an acquaintance raised his hat to Edwin in acknowledgement of the lady's presence, and he responded with pride. Whatever his private attitude to Hilda, he was undeniably proud to be seen in the streets with a disdainful, aloof girl unknown to the town. It was an experience entirely new to him, and it flattered him. He desired to look long at her face, to examine her expression, to make up his mind about her; but he could not, because they were walking side by side. The sole manifestation of her that he could judge was her voice. It was a remarkable voice, rather deep, with a sort of chiselled intonation. The cadences of it fell on the ear softly and yet ruthlessly, and when she had finished speaking you became aware of silence, as after a solemn utterance of destiny. What she happened to have been saying seemed to be immaterial to the effect, which was physical, vibratory.

II

At the border of St Luke's Square, junction of eight streets, true centre of the town's traffic, and the sole rectangular open space enclosed completely by shops, they found a line of constables which yielded only to processions and to the bearers of special rosettes. 'The Square', as it was called by those who inhabited it, had been chosen for the historic scene of the day because of its pre-eminent claim and suitability; the least of its advantages – its slope, from the top of which it could be easily dominated by a speaker on a platform – would alone have secured for it the honours of the Centenary.

As the police cordon closed on the procession from the Old Church, definitely dividing the spectators from the spectacle, it grew clear that the spectators were in the main a shabby lot; persons without any social standing : unkempt idlers, good-for-nothings, wastrels, clay-whitened pot-girls who had to work even on that day, and who had run out for a few moments in their flannel aprons to stare, and a few score raga-muffins, whose parents were too poor or too careless to make them superficially presentable enough to figure in a procession. Nearly the whole respectability of the town was either fussily marshalling processions or gazing down at them in comfort from the multitudinous open windows of the Square. The 'leads' over the projecting windows of Baines's, the chief draper's, were crowded with members of the ruling caste.

And even within the Square, it could be seen, between the towering backs of constables, that the spectacle itself was chiefly made up of indigence bedecked. The thousands of perspiring children, penned like sheep, and driven to and fro like sheep by anxious and officious rosettes, nearly all had the air of poverty decently putting the best face on itself; they were nearly all, beneath their vague sense of importance, wistful with the resigned fatalism of the young and of the governed. They knew not precisely why they were there : but merely that they had been commanded to be there, and that they were hot and thirsty, and that for weeks they had been learning hymns by heart for this occasion, and that the occasion was glorious. Many of the rosettes themselves had a poor, driven look. None of these bought suits at Shillitoe's, or millinery at Baines's. None of them gave orders for printing, or had preferences in the form of ledgers, or held views on Victor Hugo, or drank wine, or yearned for perfection in the art of social intercourse. To Edwin, who was just beginning to touch the planes of worldliness and of dilettantism in art, to Edwin, with the mysterious and haughty creature at his elbow, they seemed to have no more in common with himself and her than animals had. And he wondered by virtue of what decree he, in the Shillitoe suit, and the grand house waiting for him up at Bleakridge, had been lifted up to splendid ease above the squalid and pitiful human welter.

III

Such musings were scarcely more than subconscious in him. He stood now a few inches behind Hilda, and, above these thoughts, and beneath the stir and strident glitter and noise of the crawling ant-heap, his mind was intensely occupied with Hilda's ear and her nostril. He could watch her now at leisure, for the changeful interest of the scene made conversation unnecessary and even inept. What a lobe! What nostril! Every curve of her features seemed to express a fine arrogant acrimony and harsh truculence. At any rate she was not half alive; she was alive in every particle of herself. She gave off antipathies as a liquid gives off vapour. Moods passed across her intent face like a wind over a field. Apparently she was so rapt as to be unaware that her sunshade was not screening her. Sadness prevailed among her moods.

The mild Edwin said secretly :

'By Jove! If I had you to myself, my lady, I'd soon teach you a thing or two!' He was quite sincere, too.

His glance, roving, discovered Mrs Hamps above him, ten feet over his head, at the corner of the Baines balcony. He flushed, for he perceived that she must have been waiting to catch him. She was at her most stately and most radiant, wonderful in lavender, and she poured out on him the full opulence of a proud recognition.

Everybody should be made aware that Mrs Hamps was greeting her adored nephew, who was with a lady friend of the Orgreaves.

She leaned slightly from her cane chair.

'Isn't it a beautiful sight?' she cried. Her voice sounded thin and weak against the complex din of the Square.

He nodded, smiling.

'Oh! I think it's a beautiful sight!' she cried once more, ecstatic. People turned to see whom she was addressing.

But though he nodded again he did not think it was a beautiful sight. He thought it was a disconcerting sight, a sight vexatious and troublesome. And he was in no way tranquillized by the reflection that every town in England had the same sight to show at that hour.

And moreover, anticipating their next interview, he could, in fancy, plainly hear his Aunt Clara saying, with hopeless, longing benignancy, 'Oh, Edwin, how I *do* wish I could have seen you in the Square, bearing your part!'

Hilda seemed to be oblivious of Mrs Hamps's ejaculations, but immediately afterwards she straightened her back, with a gesture that Edwin knew, and staring into his eyes said, as it were resentfully –

'Well, they evidently aren't here!'

And looked with scorn among the sightseers. It was clear that the crowd contained nobody of the rank and stamp of the Orgreaves.

'They may have gone up the Cock Yard – if you know where that is,' said Edwin.

'Well, don't you think we'd better find them somehow?'

CHAPTER 12 : *The Top of the Square*

I

In making the detour through the Cock Yard to reach St Luke's Square again at the top of it, the only members of the Orgreave clan whom they encountered were Jimmie and Johnnie, who, on hearing of the disappearance of their father and Janet, merely pointed out that their father and Janet were notoriously always getting themselves lost, owing to gross carelessness about whatever they happened to be doing. The youths then departed, saying that the Bursley show was nothing, and that they were going to Hanbridge; they conveyed the idea that Hanbridge was the only place in the world for self-respecting men of fashion. But before leaving they informed Edwin that a fellow at the corner of the Square was letting out rather useful barrels on lease. This fellow proved to be an odd-jobman who had been discharged from the Duke of Wellington Vaults in the market-place for consistently intemperate language, but whose tongue was such that he had persuaded the landlord on this occasion to let him borrow a dozen stout empty barrels, and the police to let him dispose them on the pavement. Every barrel was occupied, and, perceiving this, Edwin at once became bold with the barrelman. He did not comfortably fancy himself perched prominent on a barrel with Hilda Lessways by his side, but he could enjoy talking about it, and he wished to show Hilda that he could be as dashing as those young sparks, Jimmie and Johnnie.

'Now, master!' shouted the barrel-man thickly, in response to Edwin's airy remark. 'These 'ere two chaps 'll shunt off for th' price of a quart!' He indicated a couple of barrel-tenants of his own tribe, who instantly jumped down, touching their soiled caps. They were part of the barrel-man's machinery for increasing profits. Edwin could not withdraw. His very cowardice forced him to be audacious. By the time he had satisfied the clawing greed of three dirty hands, the two barrels had cost him a shilling. Hilda's only observation was, as Edwin helped her to the plateau of the barrel : 'I do wish they wouldn't spit on their money.' All barrels being now let to *bona fide* tenants and paid for, the three men sidled hastily away in order to drink luck to Sunday schools in the Duke of Wellington's Entire. And Edwin, mounting the barrel next to Hilda's, was thinking : 'I've been done over that job. I ought to have got them for sixpence.' He saw how expensive it was, going about with delicately nurtured women. Never would he have offered a barrel to Maggie, and even had he done so Maggie would assuredly have said that she could make shift well enough without one.

'It's simply perfect for seeing,' exclaimed Hilda, as he achieved her altitude. Her tone was almost cordial. He felt surprisingly at ease.

II

The whole Square was now suddenly revealed as a swarming mass of heads, out of which rose banners and pennons that were cruder in tint even than the frocks and hats of the little girls and the dresses and bonnets of their teachers; the men, too, by their neckties, scarves, and rosettes, added colour to colour. All the windows were chromatic with the hues of bright costumes, and from many windows and from every roof that had a flagstaff flags waved heavily against the gorgeous sky. At the bottom of the Square the lorries with infants had been arranged, and each looked like a bank of variegated flowers. The principal bands – that is to say, all the bands that could be trusted – were collected round the red baize platform at the top of the Square, and the vast sun-reflecting euphoniums, trumpets, and cornets made a glittering circle about the officials and ministers and their wives and women. All denominations, for one day only, fraternized effusively together on that platform; for princes of the royal house, and the Archbishop of Canterbury and the Lord Mayor of London had urged that it should be so. The Primitive Methodists' parson discovered himself next but one to Father Milton, who on any other day would have been a Popish priest, and whose wooden substitute for a wife was the queen on a chessboard. And on all these the sun blazed torridly.

And almost in the middle of the Square an immense purple banner bellied in the dusty breeze, saying in large gold letters, 'The Blood of the Lamb', together with the name of some Sunday school, which Edwin from his barrel could not decipher.

Then a hoary white-tied notability on the platform raised his right arm very high, and a bugle called, and a voice that had filled fields in exciting times of religious revival floated in thunder across the enclosed Square, easily dominating it –

'Let us sing.'

And the conductor of the eager massed bands set them free with a gesture, and after they had played a stave, a small stentorian choir at the back of the platform broke forth, and in a moment the entire multitude, at first raggedly, but soon in good unison, was singing –

> Rock of Ages, cleft for me,
> Let me hide myself in Thee;
> Let the water and the blood,
> From Thy riven side which flowed,
> Be of sin the double cure:
> Cleanse me from its guilt and power.

The volume of sound was overwhelming. Its crashing force was enough to sweep people from barrels. Edwin could feel moisture in his eyes, and he dared not look at Hilda. 'Why the deuce do I want to cry?' he asked himself angrily, and was ashamed. And at the beginning of the second verse, when the glittering instruments blared forth anew, and the innumerable voices, high and loud, infantile and aged, flooded swiftly over their brassy notes, subduing them, the effect on Edwin was the same again : a tightening of the throat, and a squeezing down of the eyelids. Why was it? Through a mist he read the words 'The Blood of the Lamb', and he could picture the riven trunk of a man dying, and a torrent of blood flowing therefrom, and people like his Auntie Clara and his brother-in-law Albert plunging ecstatically into the liquid in order to be white. The picture came again in the third verse – the red fountains and the frantic bathers.

Then the notability raised his arm once more, and took off his hat, and all the males on the platform took off their hats, and presently every boy and man in the Square had uncovered his head to the strong sunshine; and at last Edwin had to do the same, and only the policemen, by virtue of their high office, could dare to affront the majesty of God. And the reverberating voice cried –

'Oh, most merciful Lord! Have pity upon us. We are brands plucked from the burning.' And continued for several minutes to descant upon the theme of everlasting torture by incandescence and thirst. Nominally addressing a deity, but in fact preaching to his audience, he announced that, even for the veriest infant on a lorry, there was no escape from the eternal fires save by complete immersion in the blood. And he was so convinced and convincing that an imaginative nose could have detected the odour of burnt flesh. And all the while the great purple banner waved insistently; 'The Blood of the Lamb.'

III

When the prayer was finished, for the benefit of the little ones, another old and favourite hymn had to be sung. (None but the classical lyrics of British Christianity had found a place in the programme of the great day.) Guided by the orchestra, the youth of Bursley and the maturity thereof chanted with gusto –

> There is a fountain filled with blood
> Drawn from Emmanuel's veins;
> And sinners, plunged beneath that flood,
> Lose all their guilty stains.
>
> . . . .
>
> Dear dying Lamb, Thy precious blood –

Edwin, like everybody, knew every line of the poem. With the purple banner waving there a bloody motto, he foresaw each sanguinary detail of the verse ere it came to him from the shrill childish throats. And a phrase from another hymn jumped from somewhere in his mind just as William Cowper's ended and a speech commenced. The phrase was 'India's coral strand'. In thinking upon it he forgot to listen to the speech. He saw the flags, banners, and pennons floating in the sunshine and in the heavy breeze; he felt the reverberation of the tropic sun on his head; he saw the crowded humanity of the Square attired in its crude, primary colours; he saw the great brass serpentine instruments gleaming; he saw the red dais; he saw, bursting with infancy, the immense cars to which were attached the fantastically plaited horses; he saw the venerable zealots on the dais raving lest after all the institutions whose centenary they had met to honour should not save these children from hopeless and excruciating torture for ever and ever; he saw those majestic purple folds in the centre embroidered with the legend of the blood of the mystic Paschal Lamb; he saw the meek, stupid, and super-stitious faces, all turned one way, all for the moment under the em-pire of one horrible idea, all convinced that the consequences of sins could be prevented by an act of belief, all gloating over inexhaustable tides of blood. And it seemed to him that he was not in England any longer. It seemed to him that in the dim cellars under the shambles behind the Town Hall, where he had once been, there dwelt, squatting, a strange and savage god who would blast all those who did not enter his presence dripping with gore, be they child or grandfather. It seemed to him that the drums were tom-toms, and Baines's a bazaar. He could fit every detail of the scene to harmonize with a vision of India's coral strand.

There was no mist before his eyes now. His sight was so clear that he could distinguish his father at a window of the Bank, at the other top corner of the Square. Part of his mind was so idle that he could wonder how his father had contrived to get there, and whether Maggie was staying at home with Clara. But the visualization of India's coral strand in St Luke's Square persisted. A phrase in the speech loosened some catch in him, and he turned suddenly to Hilda, and in an intimate half-whisper murmured –

'More blood!'

'What?' she harshly questioned. But he knew that she understood.

'Well,' he said audaciously, 'look at it! It only wants the Ganges at the bottom of the Square –'

No one heard save she. But she put her hand on his arm protestingly. 'Even if we don't believe,' said she – not harshly, but imploringly, 'we needn't make fun.'

'*We* don't believe'! And that new tone of entreaty! She had comprehended without explanation. She was a weird woman. Was there another creature, male or female, to whom he would have dared to say what he had said to her? He had chosen to say it to her because he despised her, because he wished to trample on her feelings. She roused the brute in him, and perhaps no one was more astonished than himself to witness the brute stirring. Imagine saying to the gentle and sensitive Janet: 'It only wants the Ganges at the bottom of the Square –' He could not.

They stood silent, gazing and listening. And the sun went higher in the sky and blazed down more cruelly. And then the speech ended, and the speaker wiped his head with an enormous handkerchief. And the multitude, led by the brazen instruments, which in a moment it overpowered, was singing to a solemn air –

> When I survey the wondrous cross
>   On which the Prince of Glory died,
> My richest gain I count but loss,
>   And pour contempt on all my pride.

Hilda shook her head.

'What's the matter?' he asked, leaning towards her from his barrel.

'That's the most splendid religious verse ever written!' she said passionately. 'You can say what you like. It's worth while believing anything, if you can sing words like that and mean them!'

She had an air of restrained fury.

But fancy exciting herself over a hymn!

'Yes, it is fine, that is!' he agreed.

'Do you know who wrote it?' she demanded menacingly.

'I'm afraid I don't remember,' he said. The hymn was one of his earliest recollections, but it had never occurred to him to be curious as to its authorship.

Her lips sneered. 'Dr Watts, of course!' she snapped.

He could hear her, beneath the tremendous chanting from the Square, repeating the words to herself with her precise and impressive articulation.

CHAPTER 13 : *The Oldest Sunday-school Teacher*

I

From the elevation of his barrel Edwin could survey, in the lordly and negligent manner of people on a height, all the detail of his immediate surroundings. Presently, in common with Hilda and the other aristocrats of barrels, he became aware of the increased vivacity of a scene which was passing at a little distance, near a hokey-pokey barrow. The chief actors in the affair appeared to be a young policeman, the owner of the hokey-pokey barrow, and an old man. It speedily grew into one of those episodes which, occurring on the outskirts of some episode immensely greater, draw too much attention to themselves and thereby outrage the sense of proportion residing in most plain men, and especially in most policemen.

'Give him a ha'porth o' hokey,' said a derisive voice. 'He hasn't got a tooth in his head, but it wants no chewing, hokey does na'.' There was a general guffaw from the little rabble about the barrow.

'Aye! Give us some o' that!' said the piping, silly voice of the old man. 'But I mun' get to that there platform, I'm telling ye. I'm telling all of ye.' He made a senile plunge against the body of the policeman, as against a moveless barricade, and then his hat was awry and it fell off, and somebody lifted it into the air with a neat kick so that it dropped on the barrow. All laughed. The old man laughed.

'Now, old sodger,' said the hot policeman curtly. 'None o' this! I advise ye civilly to be quiet; that's what I advise ye. You can't go on th' platform without a ticket.'

'Nay!' piped the old man. 'Don't I tell ye I lost it down th' Sytch!'

'And where's your rosette?'

'Never had any rosette,' the old man replied. 'I'm th' oldest Sunday-schoo' teacher i' th' Five Towns. Aye! Fifty years and more since I was Super at Turnhill Primitive Sunday schoo', and all Turnhill knows on it. And I've got to get on that there platform. I'm th' oldest Sunday-schoo' teachter i' th' Five Towns. And I was Super –'

Two ribald youngsters intoned 'Super, Super', and another person unceremoniously jammed the felt hat on the old man's head.

'It's nowt to me if ye was forty Supers,' said the policeman, with menacing disdain. 'I've got my orders, and I'm not here to be knocked about. Where did ye have yer last drink?'

'No wine, no beer, nor spirit-uous liquors have I tasted for sixty-one years from Martinmas,' whimpered the old man. And he gave another lurch against the policeman. 'My name's Shushions!' And he repeated in a frantic treble, 'my name's Shushions!'

'Go and bury thysen, owd gaffer!' a Herculean young collier advised him.

'Why,' murmured Hilda, with a sharp frown, 'that must be poor old Mr Shushions from Turnhill, and they're guying him! You must stop it. Something must be done at once.'

She jumped down feverishly, and Edwin had to do likewise. He wondered how he should conduct himself so as to emerge creditably from the situation. He felt himself, and had always felt himself, to be the last man in the world capable of figuring with authority in a public altercation. He loathed public altercations. The name of Shushions meant nothing to him; he had forgotten it, if indeed he had ever wittingly heard it. And he did not at first recognize the old man. Descended from the barrel, he was merely an item in the loose-packed crowd. As, in the wake of Hilda, he pushed with false eagerness between stubborn shoulders, he heard the band striking up again.

II

Approaching, he saw the old man was very old. And then memory stirred. He began to surmise that he had met the wizened face before, that he knew something about it. And the face brought up a picture of the shop door and of his father standing beside it, a long time ago. He recalled his last day at school. Yes, of course! This was the old man named Shushions, some sort of an acquaintance of his father's. This was the old man who had wept a surprising tear at sight of him, Edwin. The incident was so far off that it might have been recorded in history books. He had never seen Mr Shushions since. And the old man was changed, nearly out of recognition. The old man had lived too long; he had survived his dignity; he was now nothing but a bundle of capricious and obstinate instincts set in motion by ancient souvenirs remembered at hazard. The front of his face seemed to have given way in general collapse. The lips were in a hollow; the cheeks were concave; the eyes had receded; and there were pits in the forehead. The pale silvery straggling hairs might have been counted. The wrinkled skin was of a curious brown yellow, and the veins, instead of being blue, were outlined in Indian red. The impression given was that the flesh would be unpleasant and uncanny to the touch. The body was bent, and the neck eternally cricked backward in the effort of the eyes to look up. Moreover the old man was in a state of neglect. His beard alone proved that. His clothes were dirty and had the air of concealing dirt. And he was dressed with striking oddness. He wore boots that were not a pair. His collar was only fastened with one button, behind; the ends oscillated like wings; he had forgotten to fasten them in front; he had forgotten to put on a necktie; he had forgotten the use of buttons on all his garments. He had grown down into a child again, but Providence had not provided him with a nurse.

Worse than these merely material phenomena was the mumbling toothless gibber of his shrill protesting; the glassy look of idiocy from his fatigued eyes; and the inane smile and impotent frown that alternated on his features. He was a horrible and offensive old man. He was Time's obscene victim. Edwin was revolted by the spectacle of the younger men baiting him. He was astonished that they were so short-sighted as not to be able to see the image of themselves in the old man, so imprudent as not to think of their own future, so utterly brutalized. He wanted, by the simple force of desire, to seclude and shelter the old man, to protect the old man not only from the insults of stupid and crass bullies, but from the old man himself, from his own fatuous senility. He wanted to restore to him, by a benevolent system of pretences, the dignity and the self-respect which he had innocently lost, and so to keep him decent to the eye, if not to the ear until death came to repair its omission. And it was for his own sake, for the sake of his own image, as much as for the sake of the old man, that he wanted to do this.

III

All that flashed through his mind and heart in a second.

'I know this old gentleman, at least I know him by sight,' Hilda was saying to the policeman. 'He's very well known in Turnhill as an old Sunday-school teacher, and I'm sure he ought to be on that platform.'

Before her eye, and her precise and haughty voice, which had no trace of the local accent, the young policeman was secretly abashed, and the louts fell back sheepishly.

'Yes, he's a friend of my father's – Mr Clayhanger, printer,' said Edwin, behind her.'

The old man stood blinking in the glare.

The policeman, ignoring Hilda, glanced at Edwin, and touched his cap.

'His friends hadn't ought to let him out like this, sir. Just look at him.' He sneered, and added : 'I'm on point duty. If you ask me, I should say his friends ought to take him home.' He said this with a peculiar mysterious emphasis, and looked furtively at the louts for moral support in sarcasm. They encouraged him with grins.

'He must be got on to the platform, somehow,' said Hilda and glanced at Edwin as if counting absolutely on Edwin. 'That's what he's come for. I'm sure it means everything to him.'

'Aye!' the old man droned. 'I was Super when we had to teach 'em their alphabet and give 'em a crust to start with. Many's the man walking about in these towns i' purple and fine raiment as I taught his letters to, and his spelling, aye, and his multiplication table – in them days!'

'That's all very well, miss,' said the policeman, 'but who's going to get him to the platform? He'll be dropping in a sunstroke afore ye can say knife.'

'Can't *we*?' She gazed at Edwin appealingly.

'Tak' him into a pub!' growled the collier, audacious.

At the same moment two rosettes bustled up authoritatively. One of them was the burly Albert Benbow. For the first time Edwin was conscious of genuine pleasure at the sight of his brother-in-law. Albert was a born rosette.

'What's all this? What's this? What is it?' he asked sharply. 'Hello! What? Mr Shushions!' He bent down and looked close at the old man. 'Where you been, old gentleman?' He spoke loud in his ear. 'Everybody's been asking for you. Service is well-nigh over, but ye must come up.'

The old man did not appear to grasp the significance of Albert's patronage. Albert turned to Edwin and winked, not only for Edwin's benefit but for that of the policeman, who smiled in a manner that infuriated Edwin.

'Queer old stick!' Albert murmured. 'No doing anything with him. He's quarrelled with everybody at Turnhill. That's why he wanted to come to us. And of course we weren't going to refuse the oldest Sunday-school teacher in th' Five Towns. He's a catch . . . Come along, old gentleman!'

Mr Shushions did not stir.

'Now, Mr Shushions,' Hilda persuaded him in a voice exquisitely mild, and with a lovely gesture she bent over him. 'Let these gentlemen take you up to the platform. That's what you've come for, you know.'

The transformation in her amazed Edwin, who could see the tears in her eyes. The tableau of the little, silly old man looking up, and Hilda looking down at him, with her lips parted in a heavenly invitation, and one gloved hand caressing his greenish-black shoulder and the other mechanically holding the parasol aloft – this tableau was imprinted for ever on Edwin's mind. It was a vision blended in an instant and in an instant dissolved, but for Edwin it remained one of the epochal things of his experience.

Hilda gave Edwin her parasol and quickly fastened Mr Shushions's collar, and the old man consented to be led off between the two rosettes. The bands were playing the Austrian hymn.

'Like to come up with your young lady friend?' Albert whispered to Edwin importantly as he went.

'Oh no, thanks.' Edwin hurriedly smiled.

'Now, old gentleman,' he could hear Albert adjuring Mr Shushions, and he could see him broadly winking to the other rosettes and embracing the yielding crowd in his wink.

Thus was the doddering old fool who had given his youth to Sunday schools when Sunday schools were not patronized by princes, archbishops, and lord mayors, when Sunday schools were the scorn of the intelligent, and had sometimes to be held in public-houses for lack of better accommodation – thus was he taken off for a show and a museum curiosity by indulgent and shallow Samaritans who had not even the wit to guess that he had sown what they were reaping. And Darius Clayhanger stood oblivious at a high window of the sacred Bank. And Edwin, who, all unconscious, owed the very fact of his existence to the doting imbecile, regarded him chiefly as a figure in a tableau, as the chance instrument of a woman's beautiful revelation. Mr Shushions's sole crime against society was that he had forgotten to die.

IV

Hilda Lessways would not return to the barrels. She was taciturn, and the only remark which she made bore upon the advisability of discovering Janet and Mr Orgreave. They threaded themselves out of the moving crowd and away from the hokey-pokey stall and the barrels into the tranquillity of the market-place, where the shadow of the gold angel at the top of the Town Hall spire was a mere squat shapeless stain on the irregular paving-stones. The sound of the Festival came diminished from the Square.

'You're very fond of poetry, aren't you?' Edwin asked her, thinking, among many other things, of her observation upon the verse of Isaac Watts.

'Of course,' she replied disagreeably. 'I can't imagine anybody wanting to read anything else.' She seemed to be ashamed of her kindness to Mr Shushions, and to wish to efface any impression of amiability that she might have made on Edwin. But she could not have done so.

'Well,' he said to himself, 'there's no getting over it. You're the biggest caution I've ever come across!' His condition was one of various agitation.

Then, just as they were passing the upper end of the Cock Yard, which was an archway, Mr Orgreave and Janet appeared in the archway.

'We've been looking for you everywhere.'

'And so have we.'

'What have you been doing?'

'What have *you* been doing?'

Father and daughter were gay. They had not seen much, but they were gay. Hilda Lessways and Edwin were not gay, and Hilda would characteristically make no effort to seem that which she was not. Edwin, therefore, was driven by his own diffidence into a nervous light loquacity. He began the tale of Mr Shushions, and Hilda punctuated it with stabs of phrases.

Mr Orgreave laughed. Janet listened with eager sympathy.

'Poor old thing! What a shame!' said Janet.

But to Edwin, with the vision of Hilda's mercifulness in his mind, even the sympathy of Janet for Mr Shushions had a quality of uncomprehending, facile condescension which slightly jarred on him.

The steam-car loitered into view, discharged two passengers, and began to manoeuvre for the return journey.

'Oh! Do let's go home by car, father!' cried Janet. 'It's too hot for anything!'

Edwin took leave of them at the car steps. Janet was the smiling incarnation of loving-kindness. Hilda shook hands grudgingly. Through the windows of the car he saw her sternly staring at the advertisements of the interior. He went down the Cock Yard into Wedgwood Street, whence he could hear the bands again and see the pennons. He thought : 'This is a funny way of spending a morning!' and wondered what he should do with himself till dinner-time. It was not yet a quarter past twelve. Still, the hours had passed with extraordinary speed. He stood aimless at the corner of the pavement, and people who, having had their fill of the sun and the spectacle in the Square, were strolling slowly away, saw a fair young man, in a stylish suit, evidently belonging to the aloof classes, gazing at nothing whatever, with his hands elegantly in his pockets.

CHAPTER 14 : *Money*

I

Things sometimes fall out in a surprising way, and the removal of the Clayhanger household from the corner of Duck Square to the heights of Bleakridge was diversified by a circumstance which Edwin, the person whom alone it concerned, had not in the least anticipated.

It was the Monday morning after the Centenary. Foster's largest furniture-van, painted all over with fine pictures of the van itself travelling by road, rail, and sea, stood loaded in front of the shop. One van had already departed, and this second one, in its crammed interior, on its crowded roof, on a swinging platform beneath its floor, and on a posterior ledge supported by rusty chains, contained all that was left of the furniture and domestic goods which Darius Clayhanger had collected in half a century of ownership. The moral effect of Foster's activity was always salutary, in that Foster would prove to any man how small a space the acquisitions of a lifetime could be made to occupy when the object was not to display but to pack them. Foster could put all your pride on to four wheels, and Foster's driver would crack a whip and be off with the lot of it as though it were no more than a load of coal.

The pavement and the road were littered with straw, and the straw straggled into the shop, and heaped itself at the open side door. One large brass saucepan lay lorn near the doorstep, a proof that Foster was human. For everything except that saucepan a place had been found. That saucepan had witnessed sundry ineffectual efforts to lodge it, and had also suffered frequent forgetfulness. A tin candlestick had taken refuge within it, and was trusting for safety to the might of the obstinate vessel. In the sequel, the candlestick was pitched by Edwin on to the roof of the van, and Darius Clayhanger, coming fussily out of the shop, threw a question at Edwin and then picked up the saucepan and went off to Bleakridge with it, thus making sure that it would not be forgotten, and demonstrating to the town that he, Darius, was at last 'flitting' into his grand new house. Even weighted by the saucepan, in which Mrs Nixon had boiled hundredweights of jam, he still managed to keep his arms slanted outwards and motionless, retaining his appearance of a rigid body that swam smoothly along on mechanical legs. Darius, though putting control upon himself, was in a state of high complex emotion, partly due to apprehensiveness about the violent changing of the habits of a quarter of a century, and partly due to nervous pride.

Maggie and Mrs Nixon had gone to the new house half an hour earlier, to devise encampments therein for the night; for the Clayhangers would definitely sleep no more at the corner of Duck Square; the rooms in which they had eaten and slept and lain awake, and learnt what life and what death was, were to be transformed into workshops and stores for an increasing business. The premises were not abandoned empty. The shop had to function as usual on that formidable day, and the printing had to proceed. This had complicated the affair of the removal; but it had helped everybody to pretend, in an adult and sedate manner, that nothing in the least unusual was afoot.

Edwin loitered on the pavement, with his brain all tingling, and excitedly incapable of any consecutive thought whatever. It was his duty to wait. Two of Foster's men were across in the vaults of the Dragon; the rest were at Bleakridge with the first and smaller van. Only one of Foster's horses was in the dropped double-shafts, and even he had his nose towards the van, and in a nosebag; two others were to come down soon from Bleakridge to assist.

II

A tall, thin, grey-bearded man crossed Trafalgar Road from Aboukir Street. He was very tall and very thin, and the peculiarity of his walk was that the knees were never quite straightened, so that his height was really greater even than it seemed. His dark suit and his boots and hat were extraordinarily neat. You could be sure at once that he was a person of immutable habits. He stopped when, out of the corner of his eye, whose gaze was always precisely parallel to the direction of his feet, he glimpsed Edwin. Deflecting his course, he went close to Edwin, and, addressing the vacant air immediately over Edwin's pate, he said in a mysterious, confidential whisper –

'When are you coming in for that money?'

He spoke as though he was anxious to avoid, by a perfect air of nonchalance, arousing the suspicions of some concealed emissary of the Russian secret police.

Edwin started. 'Oh!' he exclaimed. 'Is it ready?'

'Yes. Waiting.'

'Are you going to your office now?'

'Yes.'

Edwin hesitated. 'It won't take a minute, I suppose. I'll slip along in two jiffs. I'll be there almost as soon as you are.'

'Bring a receipt stamp,' said the man, and resumed his way.

He was secretary of the Bursley and Turnhill Permanent £50 Benefit Building Society, one of the most solid institutions of the district. And he had been its secretary for decades. No stories of the defalcation of other secretaries of societies, no rumours as to the perils of the system of the more famous Starr-Bowkett Building Societies, ever bred a doubt in Bursley or Turnhill of the eternal soundness of the Bursley and Turnhill Permanent £50 Benefit Building Society. You could acquire a share in it by an entrance fee of one shilling, and then you paid eighteenpence per week for ten years, making something less than £40, and then, after an inactive period of three months, the Society gave you £50 and you began therewith to build a house, if you wanted a house, and, if you were prudent, you instantly took out another share. You could have as many shares as you chose. Though the Society was chiefly nourished by respectable artisans with stiff chins, nobody in the district would have considered membership to be beneath him. The Society was an admirable device for strengthening an impulse towards thrift, because, once you had put yourself into its machinery, it would stand no nonsense. Prosperous tradesmen would push their children into it, and even themselves. This was what had happened to Edwin in the dark past, before he had left school. Edwin had regarded the trick with indifference at first, because, except the opening half-crown, his father had paid the subscriptions for him until he left school and became a wage-earner. Thereafter he had regarded it as simple parental madness.

His whole life seemed to be nothing but a vista of Friday evenings on which he went to the Society's office, between seven and nine, to 'pay the Club'. The social origin of any family in Bursley might have been decided by the detail whether it referred to the Society as the 'Building Society' or as 'the Club'. Artisans called it the Club, because it did resemble an old-fashioned benefit club. Edwin had invariably heard it called 'Club' at home, and he called it 'Club', and he did not know why.

III

On ten thousand Friday evenings, as it seemed to him, he had gone into the gas-lit office with the wire-blinds, in the Cock Yard. And the procedure never varied. Behind a large table sat two gentlemen, the secretary and a subordinate, who was, however, older than the secretary. They had enormous ledgers in front of them, and at the lower corners of the immense pages was a transverse crease, like a mountain range on the left and like a valley on the right, caused by secretarial thumbs in turning over. On the table were also large metal inkstands and wooden money-coffers. The two officials both wore spectacles, and they both looked above their spectacles when they talked to members across the table. They spoke in low tones; they smiled with the most scrupulous politeness; they never wasted words. They counted money with prim and efficient gestures, ringing gold with the mein of judges inaccessible to human emotions. They wrote in the ledgers, and on the membership-cards, in a hand astoundingly regular and discreetly flourished; the pages of the ledgers had the mystic charm of ancient manuscripts, and the finality of decrees of fate. Apparently the scribes never made mistakes, but sometimes they would whisper in colloquy, and one, without leaning his body, would run a finger across the ledger of the other; their fingers knew intimately the geography of the ledgers, and moved as though they could have found a desired name, date, or number, in the dark. The whole ceremony was impressive. It really did impress Edwin, as he would wait his turn among the three or four proud and respectable members that the going and coming seemed always to leave in the room. The modest blue-yellow gas, the vast table and ledgers, and the two sober heads behind; the polite murmurings, the rustle of leaves, the chink of money, the smooth sound of elegant pens : all this made something not merely impressive but beautiful; something that had a true if narrow dignity; something that ministered to an ideal if a low one.

But Edwin had regarded the operation as a complete loss of the money whose payment it involved. Ten years! It was an eternity! And even then his father would have some preposterous suggestion for rendring useless the unimaginable fifty pounds! Meanwhile the weekly deduction of eighteenpence from his miserable income was an exasperating strain. And then one night the secretary had told him that he was entering on his last month. If he had possessed any genuine interest in money, he would have known for himself; but he did not. And then the payments had ceased. He had said nothing to his father.

And now the share had matured, and there was the unimaginable sum waiting for him! He got his hat and a stamp, and hurried to the Cock Yard. The secretary, in his private room now, gave him five notes as though the notes had been naught but tissue paper, and he accepted them in the same inhuman manner. The secretary asked him if he meant to take out another share, and from sheer moral cowardice he said that he did mean to do so; and he did so, on the spot. And in less than ten minutes he was back at the shop. Nothing had happened there. The other horses had not come down from Bleakridge, and the men had not come out of the Dragon. But he had fifty pounds in his pocket, and it was lawfully his. A quarter of an hour earlier he positively could not have conceived the miracle.

IV

Two days later, on the Wednesday evening, Edwin was in his new bed-room, overlooking his father's garden with a glimpse of the garden of Lane End House. His chamber, for him, was palatial and it was at once the symbol and the scene of his new life. A stranger entering would have beheld a fair-sized room, a narrow bed, two chairs, an old-fashioned table, a new wardrobe, an old dressing-table, a curious carpet and hearthrug, low bookshelves on either side of the fireplace, and a few prints and drawings, not all of them framed, on the distempered walls. A stranger might have said in its praise that it was light and airy. But a stranger could not have had the divine vision that Edwin had. Edwin looked at it and saw clearly, and with the surest conviction, that it was wonderful. He stood on the hearthrug, with his back to the hearth, bending his body concavely and then convexly with the idle, easy sinuousness of youth, and he saw that it was wonderful. As an organic whole it was wonderful. Its defects were qualities. For instance, it had no convenience for washing; but with a bathroom a few yards off, who would encumber his study (it was a study) with washing apparatus? He had actually presented his old, ramshackle washstand to the attic which was to be occupied by Mrs Nixon's niece, a girl engaged to aid her aunt in the terrible work of keeping clean a vast mansion.

And the bedroom could show one or two details that in a bedroom were luxurious. Chief of these were the carpet, the hearthrug, and the table. Edwin owed them to a marvellous piece of good fortune. He had feared, and even Maggie had feared, that their father would impair the practical value and the charm of the new house by parsimony in the matter of furniture. The furniture in the domestic portion of the old dwelling was quite inadequate for the new one, and scarcely fit for it either. Happily Darius had heard of a houseful of furniture for sale at Oldcastle by private treaty, and in a wild, adventurous hour he had purchased it, exceedingly cheap. Edwin had been amazed at his luck (he accepted the windfall as his own private luck) when he first saw the bought furniture in the new house before the removal. Out of it he had selected the table, the carpet, and the rug for his bedroom, and none had demurred. He noticed that his father listened to him, in affairs of the new house, as to an individuality whose views demanded some trifle of respect. Beyond question his father was proving himself to possess a mind equal to the grand situation. What with the second servant and the furniture, Edwin felt that he would not have to blush for the house no matter who might enter it to spy it out. As for his own room, he would not object to the Sunday seeing it. Indeed he would rather like the Sunday to see it, on his next visit. Already it was in nearly complete order, for he had shown a singular, callous disregard for the progress of the rest of the house : against which surprising display of selfishness both Maggie and Mrs Nixon had glumly protested. The truth was that he was entirely obsessed by his room; it had disabled his conscience.

When he had oscillated on his heels and toes for a few moments with his gaze on the table, he faced about, and stared in a sort of vacant beatitude at the bookshelves to the left hand; those to the right hand were as yet empty. Twilight was deepening.

V

He heard his father's heavy and clumsy footstep on the landing. The old man seemed to wander uncertainly a little, and then he pushed open Edwin's door with a brusque movement and entered the room. The two exchanged a look. They seldom addressed each other, save for an immediate practical purpose, and they did not address each other now. But Darius ejaculated 'um!' as he glanced around. They had no intimacy. Darius never showed any interest in his son as an independent human being with a developing personality, though he might have felt such an interest; and Edwin was never conscious of a desire to share any of his ideas or ideals with his father, whom he was content to accept as a creature of inscrutable motives. Now, he resented his father's incursion. He considered his room as his castle, whereof his rightful exclusive dominion ran as far as the door-mat; and to placate his pride Darius should have indicated by some gesture or word that he admitted being a visitor on sufferance. It was nothing to Edwin that Darius owned the room and nearly everything in it. He was generally nervous in his father's presence, and his submissiveness only hid a spiritual independence that was not less fierce for being restrained. He thought Darius a gross, fleshy organism, as he indeed was, and he privately objected to many paternal mannerisms, of eating, drinking, breathing, eructation, speech, deportment, and garb. Further, he had noted and felt the increasing moroseness of his father's demeanour. He could remember a period when Darius had moods of grim gaiety, displaying rough humour; these moods had long ceased to occur.

'So this is how ye've fixed yerself up!' Darius observed.

'Yes,' Edwin smiled, not moving from the hearthrug, and not ceasing to oscillate on heels and toes.

'Well, I'll say this. Ye've got a goodish notion of looking after yerself. When ye can spare a few minutes to do a bit downstairs —' This sentence was sarcastic and required no finishing.

'I was just coming,' said Edwin. And to himself, 'What on earth does he want here, making his noises?'

With youthful lack of imagination and of sympathy, he quite failed to perceive the patent fact that his father had been drawn into the room by the very same instinct which had caused Edwin to stand on the hearth-rug in an idle bliss of contemplation. It did not cross his mind that his father too was during those days going through wondrous mental experiences, that his father too had begun a new life, that his father

too was intensely proud of the house and found pleasure in merely looking at it, and looking at it again, and at every corner of it.

A glint of gold attracted the eye of Darius to the second shelf of the
left-hand bookcase, and he went towards it with the arrogance of an
autocrat whose authority recognizes no limit. Fourteen fine calf-backed
volumes stood on that shelf in a row; twelve of them were uniform, the
other two odd. These books were taller and more distinguished than
any of their neighbours. Their sole possible rivals were half a dozen
garishly bound Middle School prizes, machine-tooled, and to be mistaken for treasures only at a distance of several yards.

Edwin trembled, and loathed himself for trembling. He walked to the
window.

'What be these?' Darius inquired.

'Oh! Some books I've been picking up.'

VI

That same morning Edwin had been to the St Luke's Covered Market
to buy some apples for Maggie, who had not yet perfected the organiza-
tion necessary to a house-mistress who does not live within half a minute
of a large central source of supplies. And, to his astonishment, he had
observed that one of the interior shops was occupied by a second-hand
bookseller with an address at Hanbridge. He had never noticed the shop
before, or, if he had noticed it, he had despised it. But the chat with Tom
Orgreave had awakened in him the alertness of a hunter. The shop
was not formally open – Wednesday's market being only half a market.
The shopkeeper, however, was busy within. Edwin loitered. Behind the
piles of negligible sermons, pietisms, keepsakes, schoolbooks, and *Aris-
totles* (tied up in red twine, these last), he could descry, in the farther
gloom, actual folios and quartos. It was like seeing the gleam of nuggets
on the familiar slopes of Mow Cop, which is the Five Towns' mountain.
The proprietor, an extraordinarily grimy man, invited him to examine.
He could not refuse. He found Byron's *Childe Harold* in one volume and
Don Juan in another, both royal octavo editions, slightly stained, but
bound in full calf. He bought them. He knew that to keep his resolutions he must read a lot of poetry. Then he saw Voltaire's prose tales
in four volumes, in French – an enchanting Didot edition, with ink as
black as Hades and paper as white as snow; also bound in full calf. He
bought them. And then the proprietor showed him, in eight similar
volumes, Voltaire's *Dictionnarie Philosophique*. He did not want it; but
it matched the tales and it was impressive to the eye. And so he bought
the other eight volumes. The total cost was seventeen shillings. He was
intoxicated and he was frightened. What a nucleus for a collection of
real books, of treasures! Those volumes would do no shame even to Tom

203

Orgreave's bookcase. And they had been lying in the Covered Market, of all places in the universe. . . . Blind! How blind he had been to the possibilities of existence! Laden with a bag of apples in one hand and a heavy parcel of books in the other, he had had to go up to dinner in the car. It was no matter; he possessed riches. The car stopped specially for him at the portals of the new house. He had introduced the books into the new house surreptitiously, because he was in fear, despite his acute joy. He had pushed the parcel under the bed. After tea, he had passed half an hour in gazing at the volumes as at precious contraband. Then he had ranged them on the shelf, and had gazed at them for perhaps another quarter of an hour. And now his father, with the infallible nose of fathers for that which is no concern of theirs, had lighted upon them and was peering into them, and fingering them with his careless, brutal hands – hands that could not differentiate between a ready reckoner and a treasure. As the light failed, he brought one of them and then another to the window.

'Um!' he muttered. 'Voltaire!'

'Um! Byron!'

And : 'How much did they ask ye for these?'

'Fifteen shillings,' said Edwin, in a low voice.

'Here! Take it!' said his father, relinquishing a volume to him. He spoke in a queer, hard voice; and instantly left the room. Edwin followed him shortly, and assisted Maggie to hang pictures in that wilderness, the drawing-room. Supper was eaten in silence; and Maggie looked askance from her father to her brother, both of whom had a strained demeanour.

CHAPTER 15 : *The Insult*

I

The cold bath, the early excursion into the oblong of meadow that was beginning to be a garden, the brisk, stimulating walk down Trafalgar Road to business – all these novel experiences, which for a year Edwin had been anticipating with joyous eagerness as bliss final and sure, had lost their savour on the following morning. He had been ingenuous enough to believe that he would be happy in the new house – that the new house somehow meant the rebirth of himself and his family. Strange delusion! The bath-splashings and the other things gave him no pleasure, because he was saying to himself all the time, 'There's going to be a row this morning. There's going to be a regular shindy this morning!' Yet he was accustomed to his father's scenes. . . . Not a word at breakfast, for which indeed Darius was very late. But a thick cloud over the breakfast-table! Maggie showed that she felt the cloud. So did even Mrs Nixon. The niece alone, unskilled in the science of meteorology, did not notice it, and was pertly bright. Edwin departed before his father, hurrying. He knew that his father, starting from the luxurious books, would ask him brutally what he meant by daring to draw out his share from the Club without mentioning the affair, and particularly without confiding to his safe custody the whole sum withdrawn. He knew that his father would persist in regarding the fifty pounds as sacred, as the ark of the covenant, and on the basis of the alleged outrage would build one of those cold furies that seemed to give him so perverse a delight. On the other hand, despite his father's peculiar intonation of the names of Edwin's authors – Voltaire and Byron – he did not fear to be upbraided for possessing himself of loose and poisonous literature. It was a point to his father's credit that he never attempted any kind of censorship. Edwin never knew whether this attitude was the result of indifference or due to a grim sporting instinct.

There was no sign of trouble in the shop until noon. Darius was very busy superintending the transformation of the former living-rooms upstairs into supplementary workshops, and also the jobbing builder was at work according to the plans of Osmond Orgreave. But at five minutes past twelve – just before Stifford went out to his dinner – Darius entered the ebonized cubicle, and said curtly to Edwin, who was writing there –

'Show me your book.'

This demand surprised Edwin. 'His' book was the shop-sales book. He was responsible for it, and for the petty cash-book, and for the shop till. His father's private cash-book was utterly unknown to him, and he had no trustworthy idea of the financial totality of the business; but the management of the shop till gave him the air of being in his father's confidence, accustomed to the discipline of anxiety, and also somewhat flattered him.

He produced the book. The last complete page had not been added up.

'Add this,' said his father.

Darius himself added up the few lines on the incomplete page.

'Stiff,' he shouted, 'bring me the sales-slip.'

The amounts of sales conducted by Stifford himself were written on a slip of paper from which Edwin transferred the items at frequent intervals to the book.

'Go to yer dinner,' said Darius to Stifford, when he appeared at the door of the cubicle with the slip.

'It's not quite time yet, sir.'

'Go to yer dinner, I tell ye.'

Stifford had three-quarters of an hour for his dinner.

II

Darius combined the slip with the book and made a total.

'Petty cash,' he muttered shortly.

Edwin produced the petty cash-book, a volume of very trifling importance.

'Now bring me the till.'

Edwin went out of the cubicle and brought the till, which was a large and battered japanned cash-box with a lid in two independent parts, from its well-concealed drawer behind the fancy counter. Darius counted the coins in it and made calculations on blotting-paper, breathing stertorously all the time.

'What on earth are you trying to get at?' Edwin asked with innocent familiarity. He thought that the Club-share crisis had been postponed by one of his father's swift, strange caprices.

Darius turned on him glaring : 'I'm trying to get at where ye got the brass from to buy them there books as I saw last night. Where *did* ye get it from? There's nowt wrong here unless ye're a mighty lot cleverer than I take ye for. Where did ye get it from? Ye don't mean to tell me as ye saved it up !'

Edwin had had some shocks in his life. This was the greatest. He could feel his cheeks and his hands growing dully hot, and his eyes smarting; and he was suddenly animated by an almost murderous hatred and an inexpressible disgust for his father, who in the grossness of his perceptions and his notions had imagined his son to be a thief. 'Loathsome beast !' he thought savagely.

'I'm waiting,' said his father.

'I've drawn my Club money,' said Edwin.

For an instant the old man was at a loss; then he understood. He had entirely forgotten the maturing of the club share, and assuredly he had not dreamed that Edwin would accept and secrete so vast a sum as fifty pounds without uttering a word. Darius had made a mistake, and a bad one; but in those days fathers were never wrong; above all they never apologized. In Edwin's wicked act of concealment Darius could choose new and effective ground, and he did so.

'And what dost mean by doing that and saying nowt? Sneaking –'

'What do you mean by calling me a thief?' Edwin and Darius were equally startled by this speech. Edwin knew not what had come over him, and Darius, never having been addressed in such a dangerous tone by his son, was at a loss.

'I never called ye a thief.'

'Yes, you did! Yes, you did!' Edwin nearly shouted now. 'You starve me for money, until I haven't got sixpence to bless myself with. You couldn't get a man to do what I do for twice what you pay me. And then you call me a thief. And then you jump down my throat because I spend a bit of money of my own.' He snorted. He knew that he was quite mad, but there was a strange drunken pleasure in this madness.

'Hold yer tongue, lad!' said Darius, as stiffly as he could. But Darius, having been unprepared, was intimidated. Darius vaguely comprehended that a new and disturbing factor had come into his life. 'Make a less row!' he went on more strongly. 'D'ye want all th' street to hear ye?'

'I won't make a less row. You make as much noise as you want, and I'll make as much noise as I want!' Edwin cried louder and louder. And then in bitter scorn, 'Thief, indeed!'

'I never called ye a—'

'Let me come out!' Edwin shouted. They were very close together. Darius saw that his son's face was all drawn. Edwin snatched his hat off its hook, pushed violently past his father and, sticking his hands deep in his pockets, strode into the street.

III

In four minutes he was hammering on the front door of the new house. Maggie opened, in alarm. Edwin did not see how alarmed she was by his appearance.

'What—'

'Father thinks I've been stealing his damned money!' Edwin snapped, in a breaking voice. The statement was not quite accurate, but it suited his boiling anger to put it in the present tense instead of in the past. He hesitated an instant in the hall, throwing a look behind at Maggie, who stood entranced with her hand on the latch of the open door. Then he bounded upstairs, and shut himself in his room with a tremendous bang that shook the house. He wanted to cry, but he would not.

Nobody disturbed him till about two o'clock, when Maggie knocked at the door, and opened it, without entering.

'Edwin, I've kept your dinner hot.'

'No, thanks.' He was standing with his legs wide apart on the hearthrug.

'Father's had his dinner and gone.'

'No, thanks.'

She closed the door again.

CHAPTER 16 : *The Sequel*

I

'I say, Edwin,' Maggie called through the door.

'Well, come in, come in,' he replied gruffly. And as he spoke he sped from the window, where he was drumming on the pane, to the hearth-rug, so that he should have the air of not having moved since Maggie's previous visit. He knew not why he made this manoeuvre, unless it was that he thought vaguely that Maggie's impression of the seriousness of the crisis might thereby be intensified.

She stood in the doorway, evidently placatory and sympathetic, and behind her stood Mrs Nixon, in a condition of great mental turmoil.

'I think you'd better come and have your tea,' said Maggie firmly, and yet gently. She was soft and stout, and incapable of asserting herself with dignity; but she was his elder, and there were moments when an unusual, scarce-perceptible quality in her voice would demand from him a particular attention.

He shook his head, and looked sternly at his watch, in the manner of one who could be adamant. He was astonished to see that the hour was a quarter past six.

'Where is he?' he asked.

'Father? He's had his tea and gone back to the shop. Come along.'

'I must wash myself first,' said Edwin gloomily. He did not wish to yield, but he was undeniably very hungry indeed.

Mrs Nixon could not leave him alone at tea, worrying him with offers of specialities to tempt him. He wondered who had told the old thing about the affair. Then he reflected that she had probably heard his outburst when he entered the house. Possibly the pert, nice niece also had heard it. Maggie remained sewing at the bow-window of the dining-room while he ate a plenteous tea.

'Father said I could tell you that you could pay yourself an extra half-crown a week wages from next Saturday,' said Maggie suddenly, when she saw he had finished. It was always Edwin who paid wages in the Clayhanger establishment.

He was extremely startled by this news, with all that it implied of surrender and of pacific intentions. But he endeavoured to hide what he felt, and only snorted.

'He's been talking, then? What did he say?'

'O! Not much! He told me I could tell you if I liked.'

208

'It would have looked better of him, if he'd told me himself,' said Edwin, determined to be ruthless. Maggie offered no response.

II

After about a quarter of an hour he went into the garden, and kicked stones in front of him. He could not classify his thoughts. He considered himself to be perfectly tranquillized now, but he was mistaken. As he idled in the beautiful August twilight near the garden-front of the house, catching faintly the conversation of Mrs Nixon and her niece as it floated through the open window of the kitchen, round the corner, together with quiet soothing sounds of washing-up, he heard a sudden noise in the garden-porch, and turned swiftly. His father stood there. Both of them were off guard. Their eyes met.

'Had your tea?' Darius asked, in an unnatural tone.

'Yes,' said Edwin.

Darius, having saved his face, hurried into the house, and Edwin moved down the garden, with heart sensibly beating. The encounter renewed his agitation.

And at the corner of the garden, over the hedge, which had been repaired, Janet entrapped him. She seemed to have sprung out of the ground. He could not avoid greeting her, and in order to do so he had to dominate himself by force. She was in white. She appeared always to wear white on fine summer days. Her smile was exquisitely benignant.

'So you're installed?' she began.

They talked of the removal, she asking questions and commenting, and he giving brief replies.

'I'm all alone tonight,' she said, in a pause, 'except for Alicia. Father and mother and the boys are gone to a fête at Longshaw.'

'And Miss Lessways?' he inquired self-consciously.

'Oh! She's gone,' said Janet. 'She's gone back to London. Went yesterday.'

'Rather sudden, isn't it?'

'Well, she had to go.'

'Does she live in London?' Edwin asked, with an air of indifference.

'She does just now.'

'I only asked because I thought from something she said she came from Turnhill way.'

'Her people do,' said Janet. 'Yes, you may say she's a Turnhill girl.'

'She seems very fond of poetry,' said Edwin.

'You've noticed it!' Janet's face illuminated the dark. 'You should hear her recite!'

'Recite, does she?'

'You'd have heard her that night you were here. But when she knew you were coming, she made us all promise not to ask her.'

'Really!' said Edwin. 'But why? She didn't know me. She'd never seen me.'

'Oh! She might have just seen you in the street. In fact I believe she had. But that wasn't the reason,' Janet laughed. 'It was just that you were a stranger. She's very sensitive, you know.'

'Ye—es,' he admitted.

III

He took leave of Janet, somehow, and went for a walk up to Toft End, where the wind blows. His thoughts were more complex than ever in the darkness. So she had made them all promise not to ask her to recite while he was at the Orgreaves'! She had seen him, previous to that, in the street, and had obviously discussed him with Janet . . . And then, at nearly midnight, she had followed him to the new house! And on the day of the Centenary she had manoeuvred to let Jane and Mr Orgreave go in front. . . . He did not like her. She was too changeable, too dark, and too light. . . .But it was exciting. It was flattering. He saw again and again her gesture as she bent to Mr Shushions; and the straightening of her spine as she left the garden-porch on the night of his visit to the Orgreaves. . . . Yet he did not like her. Her sudden departure, however, was a disappointment; it was certainly too abrupt. . . . Probably very characteristic of her. . . . Strange day! He had been suspected of theft. He had stood up to his father. He had remained away from the shop. And his father's only retort was to give him a rise of half a crown a week!

'The old man must have had a bit of a shock!' he said to himself, grimly vain. 'I lay I don't hear another word about that fifty pounds.'

Yes, amid his profound resentment, there was some ingenuous vanity at the turn which things had taken. And he was particularly content about the rise of half a crown a week, because that relieved him from the most difficult of all the resolutions the carrying out of which was to mark the beginning of the new life. It settled the financial question, for the present at any rate. It was not enough, but it was a great deal – from his father. He was ashamed that he could not keep his righteous resentment pure from this gross satisfaction at an increase of income. The fineness of his nature was thereby hurt. But the gross satisfaction would well up in his mind.

And in the night, with the breeze on his cheek, and the lamps of the Five Towns curving out below him, he was not unhappy, despite what he had suffered and was still suffering. He had a tingling consciousness of being unusually alive.

IV

Later, in his bedroom, shut in, and safe and independent, with the new blind drawn, and the gas fizzing in its opaline globe, he tried to read *Don Juan*. He could not. He was incapable of fixity of mind. He could not follow the sense of a single stanza. Images of his father and of Hilda Lessways mingled with reveries of the insult he had received and the triumph he had won, and all the confused wonder of the day and evening engaged his thoughts. He dwelt lovingly on the supreme disappointment of his career. He fancied what he would have been doing, and where he would have been then, if his appalling father had not made it impossible for him to be an architect. He pitied himself. But he saw the material of happiness ahead, in the faithful execution of his resolves for self-perfecting. And Hilda had flattered him. Hilda had given him a new conception of himself. . . . A tiny idea arose in his brain that there was perhaps some slight excuse for his father's suspicion of him. After all, he had been secretive. He trampled on that idea, and it arose again.

He slept very heavily, and woke with a headache. A week elapsed before his agitation entirely disappeared, and hence before he could realize how extreme that agitation had been. He was ashamed of having so madly and wildly abandoned himself to passion.

CHAPTER 17 : *Challenge and Response*

I

Time passed, like a ship across a distant horizon, which moves but which does not seem to move. One Monday evening Edwin said that he was going round to Lane End House. He had been saying so for weeks, and hesitating. He thoroughly enjoyed going to Lane End House; there was no reason why he should not go frequently and regularly, and there were several reasons why he should. Yet his visitings were capricious because his nature was irresolute. That night he went, sticking a hat carelessly on his head, and his hands deep into his pockets. Down the slope of Trafalgar Road, in the biting November mist, between the two rows of gas-lamps that flickered feebly into the pale gloom, came a long straggling band of men who also, to compensate for the absence of overcoats, stuck hands deep into pockets, and strode quickly. With reluctance they divided for the passage of the steam-car, and closed growling together again on its rear. The potters were on strike, and a Bursley contingent was returning in embittered silence from a mass meeting at Hanbridge. When the sound of the steam-car subsided, as the car dipped over the hill-top on its descent towards Hanbridge, nothing could be heard but the tramp-tramp of the procession on the road.

Edwin hurried down the side street, and in a moment rang at the front door of the Orgreaves'. He nodded familiarly to the servant who opened, stepped on to the mat, and began contorting his legs in order to wipe the edge of his boot-soles.

'Quite a stranger, sir!' said Martha, bridling, and respectfully aware of her attractiveness for this friend of the house.

'Yes,' he laughed. 'Anybody in?'

'Well, sir, I'm afraid Miss Janet and Miss Alicia are out.'

'And Mr Tom?'

'Mr Tom's out, sir. He pretty nearly always is now, sir.' The fact was that Tom was engaged to be married, and the servant indicated, by a scarcely perceptible motion of the chin, that fiancés were and ever would be all the same. 'And Mr John and Mr James are out too, sir.' They also were usually out. They were both assisting their father in business, and sought relief from his gigantic conception of a day's work by evening's diversions at Hanbridge. These two former noisy Liberals had joined the Hanbridge Conservative Club because it *was* a club, and had a billiard-table that could only be equalled at the Five Towns Hotel at Knype.

'And Mr Orgreave?'

'He's working upstairs, sir. Mrs Orgreave's got her asthma, and so he's working upstairs.'

'Well, tell them I've called.' Edwin turned to depart.

'I'm sure Mr Orgreave would like to know you're here, sir,' said the maid firmly. 'If you'll just step into the breakfast-room.' That maid did as she chose with visitors for whom she had a fancy.

II

She conducted him to the so-called breakfast-room and shut the door on him. It was a small chamber behind the drawing-room, and shabbier than the drawing-room. In earlier days the children had used it for their lessons and hobbies. And now it was used as a sitting-room when mere cosiness was demanded by a decimated family. Edwin stooped down and amended the fire. Then he went to the wall and examined a framed water-colour of the old Sytch Pottery, which was signed with his initials. He had done it, aided by a photograph, and by Johnnie Orgreave in details of perspective, and by dint of preprandial frequentings of the Sytch, as a gift for Mrs Orgreave. It always seemed to him to be rather good.

Then he bent to examine bookshelves. Like the hall, the drawing-room, and the dining-room, this apartment too was plenteously full of everything, and littered over with the apparatus of various personalities. Only from habit did Edwin glance at the books. He knew their backs by heart. And books in quantity no longer intimidated him. Despite his grave defects as a keeper of resolves, despite his paltry trick of picking up a newspaper or periodical and reading it all through, out of sheer vacillation and mental sloth, before starting serious perusals, despite the human disinclination which he had to bracing himself, and keeping up the tension, in a manner necessary for the reading of long and difficult works, and despite sundry ignominious backslidings into original – sluggishness – still he had accomplished certain literary adventures. He could not enjoy *Don Juan*. Expecting from it a voluptuous and daring grandeur, he had found in it nothing whatever that even roughly fitted into his idea of what poetry was. But he had had a passion for *Childe Harold*, many stanzas of which thrilled him again and again, bringing back to his mind what Hilda Lessways had said about poetry. And further, he had a passion for Voltaire. In Voltaire, also, he had been deceived, as in Byron. He had expected something violent, arid, closely argumentative; and he found gaiety, grace, and really the funniest jokes. He could read *Candide* almost without a dictionary, and he had intense pride in doing so, and for some time afterwards *Candide* and *La Princesse de Babylone*, and a few similar witty trifles, were the greatest stories in the world for him. Only a faint reserve in Tom Orgreave's responsive enthusiasm made him cautiously reflect.

He could never be intimate with Tom, because Tom somehow never came out from behind his spectacles. But he had learnt much from him, and in especial a familiarity with the less difficult of Bach's preludes and fuges, which Tom loved to play. Edwin knew not even the notes of music, and he was not sure that Bach gave him pleasure. Bach affected him strangely. He would ask for Bach out of a continually renewed curiosity, so that he could examine once more and yet again the sensations which the music produced; and the habit grew. As regards the fugues, there could be no doubt that, the fugue begun, a desire was thereby set up in him for the resolution of the confusing problem created in the first few bars, and that he waited, with a pleasant and yet a trying anxiety, for the indications of that resolution, and that the final reassuring and utterly tranquillizing chords gave him deep joy. When he innocently said that he was 'glad when the end came of a fugue', all the Orgreaves laughed heartily, but after laughing, Tom said that he knew what Edwin meant and quite agreed.

III

It was while he was glancing along the untidy and crowded shelves with sophisticated eye that the door brusquely opened. He looked up mildly, expecting a face familiar, and saw one that startled him, and heard a voice that aroused disconcerting vibrations in himself. It was Hilda Lessways. She had in her hand a copy of the *Signal*. Over fifteen months had gone since their last meeting, but not since he had last thought of her. Her features seemed strange. His memory of them had not been reliable. He had formed an image of her in his mind, and had often looked at it, and he now saw that it did not correspond with the reality. The souvenir of their brief intimacy swept back upon him. Incredible that she should be there, in front of him; and yet there she was! More than once, after reflecting on her, he had laughed, and said lightly to himself : 'Well, the chances are I shall never see *her* again! Funny girl!' But the recollection of her gesture with Mr Shushions prevented him from dismissing her out of his head with quite that lightness. . . .

'I'm ordered to tell you that Mr Orgreave will be down in a few minutes,' she said.

'*Hello!*' he exclaimed. 'I'd no idea you were in Bursley!'

'Came today!' she replied.

'How odd,' he thought, 'that I should call like this on the very day she comes!' But he pushed away that instinctive thought with the rational thought that such a coincidence could not be regarded as in any way significant.

They shook hands in the middle of the room, and she pressed his hand, while looking downwards with a smile. And his mind was suddenly filled with the idea that during all those months she had been existing somewhere, under the eye of someone, intimate with someone, and constantly conducting herself with a familiar freedom that doubtless she would not use to him. And so she was invested, for him, with mysteriousness. His interest in her was renewed in a moment, and in a form much more acute than its first form. Moreover, she presented herself to his judgement in a different aspect. He could scarcely comprehend how he had ever dreamed her habitual expression to be forbidding. In fact, he could persuade himself now that she was beautiful, and even nobly beautiful. From one extreme he flew to the other. She sat down on an old sofa; he remained standing. And in the midst of a little conversation about Mrs Orgreave's indisposition, and the absence of the members of the family (she said she had refused an invitation to go with Janet and Alicia to Hillport), she broke the thread, and remarked –

'You would have known I was coming if you'd been calling here recently.' She pushed her feet near the fender, and gazed into the fire.

'Ah! But you see I haven't been calling recently.'

She raised her eyes to his. 'I suppose you've never thought about me once since I left!' she fired at him. An audacious and discomposing girl!

'Oh yes, I have,' he said weakly. What could you reply to such speeches? Nevertheless he was flattered.

'Really? But you've never inquired about me.'

'Yes, I have.'

'Only once.'

'How do you know?'

'I asked Janet.'

'Damn her!' he said to himself, but pleased with her. And aloud, in a tone suddenly firm, 'That's nothing to go by.'

'What isn't?'

'The number of *times* I've inquired.' He was blushing.

IV

In the smallness of the room, sitting as it were at his feet on the sofa, surrounded and encaged by a hundred domestic objects and by the glow of the fire and the radiance of the gas, she certainly did seem to Edwin to be an organism exceedingly mysterious. He could follow with his eye every fold of her black dress, he could trace the waving of her hair, and watch the play of light in her eyes. He might have physically hurt her, he might have killed her, she was beneath his hand – and yet she was most bafflingly withdrawn, and the essence of her could not be touched nor got at. Why did she challenge him by her singular attitude? Why was she always saying such queer things to him? No other girl (he thought, in the simplicity of his inexperience) would ever talk as she talked. He wanted to test her by being rude to her. 'Damn her!' he said to himself again. 'Supposing I took hold of her and kissed her – I wonder what sort of a face she'd pull then! . . .' (And a moment ago he had been appraising her as nobly beautiful! A moment ago he had been dwelling on the lovely compassion of her gesture with Mr Shushions!) This quality of daring and naughty enterprise had never before shown itself in Edwin, and he was surprised to discover in himself such impulses. But then the girl was so provocative. And somehow the sight of the girl delivered him from an excessive fear of consequences. He said to himself, 'I'll do something or I'll say something, before I leave her tonight, just to show her! . . .' He screwed up his resolution to the point of registering a private oath that he would indeed do or say something. Without a solemn oath he could not rely upon his valour. He knew that whatever he said or did in the nature of a bold advance would be accomplished clumsily. He knew that it would be unpleasant. He knew that inaction suited much better his instinct for tranquillity. No matter! All that was naught. She had challenged, and he had to respond. Besides, she allured. . . . And, after her scene with him in the porch of the new house, had he not the right? . . . A girl who had behaved as she did that night cannot effectively contradict herself!

'I was just reading about this strike,' she said, rustling the newspaper.

'You've soon got into local politics.'

'Well,' she said, 'I saw a lot of the men as we were driving from the station. I should think I saw two thousand of them. So of course I was interested. I made Mr Orgreave tell me all about it. Will they win?'

'It depends on the weather.' He smiled.

She remained silent, and grave. 'I see!' she said, leaning her chin on her hand. At her tone he ceased smiling. She said 'I see,' and she actually had seen.

'You see,' he repeated. 'If it was June instead of November! But then it isn't June. Wages are settled every year in November. So if there is to be a strike it can only begin in November.'

'But didn't the men ask for the time of the year to be changed?'

'Yes,' he said. 'But you don't suppose the masters were going to agree to that, do you?' He sneered masculinely.

'Why not?'

'Because it gives them such a pull.'

'What a shame!' Hilda exclaimed passionately. 'And what a shame it is that the masters want to make the wages depend on selling prices! Can't they see that selling prices ought to depend on wages?'

Edwin said nothing. She had knocked suddenly out of his head all ideas of flirting, and he was trying to reassemble them.

'I suppose you're like all the rest?' she questioned gloomily.

'How like all the rest?'

'Against the men. Mr Orgreave is, and he says your father is very strongly against them.'

'Look here,' said Edwin, with an air of resentment as to which he himself could not have decided whether it was assumed or genuine, 'what earthly right have you to suppose that I'm like all the rest?'

'I'm very sorry,' she surrendered. 'I knew all the time you weren't.' With her face still bent downwards, she looked up at him, smiling sadly, smiling roguishly.

'Father's against them,' he proceeded, somewhat deflated. And he thought of all his father's violent invective, and of Maggie's bland acceptance of the assumption that workmen on strike were rascals – how different the excellent simple Maggie from this feverish creature on the sofa! 'Father's against them, and most people are, because they broke the last arbitration award. But I'm not my father. If you ask me, I'll tell you what I think – workmen on strike are always in the right; at bottom I mean. You've only got to look at them in a crowd together. They don't starve themselves for fun.'

He was not sure if he was convinced of the truth of these statements; but she drew them out of him by her strange power. And when he had uttered them, they appeared fine to him.

'What does your father say to that?'

'Oh!' said Edwin uneasily. 'Him – and me – we don't argue about these things.'

'Why not?'

'Well, we don't.'

'You aren't ashamed of your own opinion, are you?' she demanded, with a hint in her voice that she was ready to be scornful.

'You know all the time I'm not.' He repeated the phrase of her previous confession with a certain acrimonious emphasis. 'Don't you?' he added curtly.

She remained silent.

'Don't you?' he said more loudly. And as she offered no reply, he went on, marvelling at what was coming out of his mouth. 'I'll tell you what I am ashamed of. I'm ashamed of seeing my father lose his temper. So you know!'

She said –

'I never met anybody like you before. No, never!'

At this he really was astounded, and most exquisitely flattered.

'I might say the same of you,' he replied, sticking his chin out.

'Oh no!' she said. 'I'm nothing.'

The fact was that he could not foretell their conversation even ten seconds in advance. It was full of the completely unexpected. He thought to himself, 'You never know what a girl like that will say next.' But what would *he* say next?

v

They were interrupted by Osmond Orgreave, with his 'Well, Edwin,' jolly, welcoming, and yet slightly quizzical. Edwin could not look him in the face without feeling self-conscious. Nor dared he glance at Hilda to see what her demeanour was like under the good-natured scrutiny of her friend's father.

'We thought you'd forgotten us,' said Mr Orgreave. 'But that's always the way with neighbours.' He turned to Hilda. 'It's true,' he continued, jerking his head at Edwin. 'He scarcely ever comes to see us, except when you're here.'

'Steady on!' Edwin murmured. 'Steady on, Mr Orgreave!' And

217

hastily he asked a question about Mrs Orgreave's asthma; and from that the conversation passed to the doings of the various absent members of the family.

'You've been working, as usual, I suppose,' said Edwin.

'Working!' laughed Mr Orgreave. 'I've done what I could, with Hilda there! Instead of going up to Hillport with Janet, she would stop here and chatter about strikes.'

Hilda smiled at him benevolently as at one to whom she permitted everything.

'Mr Clayhanger agrees with me,' she said.

'Oh! You needn't tell me!' protested Mr Orgreave. 'I could see you were as thick as thieves over it.' He looked at Edwin. 'Has she told you she wants to go over a printing works?'

'No,' said Edwin. 'But I shall be very pleased to show her over ours, any time.'

She made no observation.

'Look here,' said Edwin suddenly, 'I must be off. I only slipped in for a minute, really.' He did not know why he said this, for his greatest wish was to probe more deeply into the tantalizing psychology of Hilda Lessways. His tongue, however, had said it, and his tongue reiterated it when Mr Orgreave urged that Janet and Alicia would be back soon and that food would then be partaken of. He would not stay. Desiring to stay, he would not. He wished to be alone, to think. Clearly Hilda had been talking about him to Mr Orgreave, and to Janet. Did she discuss him and his affairs with everybody?

Nor would he, in response to Mr Orgreave's suggestion, promise definitely to call again on the next evening. He said he would try. Hilda took leave of him nonchalantly. He departed.

And as he made the half-circuit of the misty lawn, on his way to the gates, he muttered in his heart, where even he himself could scarcely hear: 'I swore I'd do something, and I haven't. Well, of course, when she talked seriously like that, what could I do?' But he was disgusted with himself and ashamed of his namby-pambiness.

He strolled thoughtfully up Oak Street, and down Trafalgar Road; and when he was near home, another wayfarer saw him face right about and go up Trafalgar Road and disappear at the corner of Oak Street.

The Orgreave servant was surprised to see him at the front door again when she answered a discreet ring.

'I wish you'd tell Miss Lessways I want to speak to her a moment, will you?'

'Miss Lessways?'

'Yes.' What an adventure!

'Certainly, sir. Will you come in?' She shut the door.

'Ask her to come here,' he said, smiling with deliberate confidential persuasiveness. She nodded, with a brighter smile.

The servant vanished, and Hilda came. She was as red as fire. He began hurriedly.

'When will you come to look over our works? Tomorrow? I should like you to come.' He used a tone that said : 'Now don't let's have any nonsense ! You know you want to come.'

She frowned frankly. There they were in the hall, like a couple of conspirators, but she was frowning; she would not meet him half-way. He wished he had not permitted himself this caprice. What importance had a private oath? He felt ridiculous.

'What time?' she demanded, and in an instant transformed his disgust into delight.

'Any time.' His heart was beating with expectation.

'Oh no ! You must fix the time.'

'Well, after tea. Say between half past six and a quarter to seven. That do?'

She nodded.

'Good,' he murmured. 'That's all ! Thanks. Good night !'

He hastened away, with a delicate photograph of the palm of her hand printed in minute sensations on the palm of his.

'I did it, anyhow !' he muttered loudly, in his heart. At any rate he was not shamed. At any rate he was a man. The man's face was burning, and the damp noxious chill of the night only caressed him agreeably.

CHAPTER 18 : *Curiosity*

I

He was afraid that, from some obscure motive of propriety or self-protection, she would bring Janet with her, or perhaps Alicia. On the other hand, he was afraid that she would come alone. That she should come alone seemed to him, in spite of his reason, too brazen. Moreover, if she came alone would he be equal to the situation? Would he be able to carry the things off in a manner adequate? He lacked confidence. He desired the moment of her arrival, and yet he feared it. His heart and his brain were all confused together in a turmoil of emotion which he could not analyse nor define.

He was in love. Love had caught him, and had affected his vision so that he no longer saw any phenomenon as it actually was; neither himself, nor Hilda, nor the circumstances which were uniting them. He could not follow a train of thought. He could not remain of one opinion nor in one mind. Within himself he was perpetually discussing Hilda, and her attitude. She was marvellous! But was she? She admired him! But did she? She had shown cunning! But was it not simplicity? He did not even feel sure whether he liked her. He tried to remember what she looked like, and he positively could not. The one matter upon which he could be sure was that his curiosity was hotly engaged. If he had to state the case in words to another he would not have gone farther than the word 'curiosity'. He had no notion that he was in love. He did not know what love was; he had not had sufficient opportunity of learning. Nevertheless the processes of love were at work within him. Silently and magically, by the force of desire and of pride, the refracting glass was being specially ground which would enable him, which would compel him, to see an ideal Hilda when he gazed at the real Hilda. He would not see the real Hilda any more unless some cataclysm should shatter the glass. And he might be likened to a prisoner on whom the gate of freedom is shut for ever, or to a stricken sufferer of whom it is known that he can never rise again and go forth into the fields. He was as somebody to whom the irrevocable had happened. And he knew it not. None knew. None guessed. All day he went his ways, striving to conceal the whirring preoccupation of his curiosity (a curiosity which he thought showed a fine masculine dash), and succeeded fairly well. The excellent, simple Maggie alone remarked in secret that he was slightly nervous and unnatural. But even she, with all her excellent simplicity, did not divine his victimhood.

At six o'clock he was back at the shop from his tea. It was a wet, chill night. On the previous evening he had caught cold, and he was beginning to sneeze. He said to himself that Hilda could not be expected to come on such a night. But he expected her. When the shop clock showed half past six, he glanced at his watch, which also showed half past six. Now at any instant she might arrive. The shop door opened, and simultaneously his heart ceased to beat. But the person who came in, puffing and snorting, was his father, who stood within the shop while shaking his soaked umbrella over the exterior porch. The draught from the shiny dark street and square struck cold, and Edwin responsively sneezed; and Darius Clayhanger upbraided him for not having worn his overcoat, and he replied with foolish unconvincingness that he had got a cold, that it was nothing. Darius grunted his way into the cubicle. Edwin remained in busy idleness at the right-hand counter; Stifford was tidying the contents of drawers behind the fancy-counter. And the fizzing gas-burners, inevitable accompaniment of night at the period, kept watch above. Under the heat of the stove, the damp marks of Darius Clayhanger's entrance disappeared more quickly than the minutes ran.

It grew almost impossible for Edwin to pass the time. At moments when his father was not stirring in the cubicle, and Stifford happened to be in repose, he could hear the ticking of the clock, which he could not remember ever having heard before, except when he mounted the steps to wind it.

At a quarter to seven he said to himself that he gave up hope, while pretending that he never had hoped, and that Hilda's presence was indifferent to him. If she came not that day she would probably come some other day. What could it matter? He was very unhappy. He said to himself that he should have a long night's reading, but the prospect of reading had no savour. He said : 'No, I shan't go in to see them tonight, I shall stay in and nurse my cold, and read.' This was mere futile bravado, for the impartial spectator in him, though far less clear-sighted and judicial now than formerly, foresaw with certainty that if Hilda did not come he would call at the Orgreaves'. At five minutes to seven he was miserable : he had decided to hope until five minutes to seven. He made it seven in despair. Then there were signs of a figure behind the misty glass of the door. The door opened. It could not be she! Impossible that it should be she! But it was she; she had the air of being a miracle.

II

His feelings were complex and contradictory, flitting about and crossing each other in his mind with astounding rapidity. He wished she had not come, because his father was there, and the thought of his father would intensify his self-consciousness. He wondered why he should care whether she came or not; after all she was only a young woman who wanted to see a printing works; at best she was not so agreeable as Janet, at worst she was appalling, and moreover he knew nothing about her. He had a glimpse of her face as, with a little tightening of the lips, she shut her umbrella. What was there in that face, judged impartially? Why should he be to so absurd a degree curious about her? He thought how exquisitely delicious it would be to be walking with her by the shore of a lovely lake on a summer evening, pale hills in the distance. He had this momentary vision by reason of a coloured print of the 'Silver Strand' of a Scottish loch which was leaning in a gilt frame against the artists' materials cabinet and was marked twelve-and-six. During the day he had imagined himself with her in all kinds of beautiful spots and situations. But the chief of his sensations was one of exquisite relief. . . . She had come. He could wreak his hungry curiosity upon her.

Yes, she was alone. No Janet! No Alicia! How had she managed it? What had she said to the Orgreaves? That she should have come alone, and through the November rain, in the night, affected him deeply. It gave her the quality of a heroine of high adventure. It was as though she had set sail unaided, in a frail skiff, on a formidable ocean, to meet him. It was inexpressibly romantic and touching. She came towards him, her face sedately composed. She wore a small hat, a veil, and a mackintosh, and black gloves that were splashed with wet. Certainly she was a practical woman. She had said she would come, and she had come, sensibly, but how charmingly, protected against the shocking conditions of the journey. There is naught charming in a mackintosh. And yet there was, in this mackintosh ! . . . Something in the contrast between its harshness and her fragility. . . . The veil was supremely charming. She had lifted it, exposing her mouth; the upper part of her flushed face was caged behind the bars of the veil; behind those bars her eyes mysteriously gleamed. . . . Spanish ! . . . No exaggeration in all this ! He felt every bit of it honestly, as he stood at the counter in thrilled expectancy. By virtue of his impassioned curiosity, the terraces of Granada and the mantillas of *señoritas* were not more romantic than he had made his father's shop and her dripping mackintosh. He tried to see her afresh; he tried to see her as though he had never seen before; he tried desperately once again to comprehend what it was in her that piqued him. And he could not. He fell back from the attempt. Was she the most wondrous? Or was she commonplace? Was she deceiving him? Or did he alone possess the true insight? . . . Useless ! He was baffled. Far from piercing her soul, he could scarcely even see her at all; that is, with intelligence. And it was always so when he was with her : he was in a dream, a vapour; he had no helm, his faculties were not under control. She robbed him of judgement.

And then the clear tones of her voice fell on the listening shop : 'Good evening, Mr Clayhanger. What a night, isn't it? I hope I'm not too late.'

Firm, business-like syllables. . . . And she straightened her shoulders. He suffered. He was not happy. Whatever his feelings, he was not happy in that instant. He was not happy because he was wrung between hope and fear, alike divine. But he would not have exchanged his sensations for the extremest felicity of any other person.

They shook hands. He suggested that she should remove her mackintosh. She consented. He had no idea that the effect of the removal of the mackintosh would be so startling as it was. She stood intimately revealed in her frock. The mackintosh was formal and defensive; the frock was intimate and acquiescent.

Darius blundered out of the cubicle and Edwin had a dreadful moment introducing her to Darius and explaining their purpose. Why had he not prepared the ground in advance? His pusillanimous cowardice again ! However, the directing finger of God sent a customer into the shop, and Edwin escaped with his Hilda through the aperture in the counter.

The rickety building at the back of the premises, which was still the main theatre of printing activities, was empty save for Big James, the hour of seven being past. Big James was just beginning to roll his apron round his waist, in preparation for departure. This happened to be one of the habits of his advancing age. Up till a year or two previously he would have taken off his apron and left it in the workshop; but now he could not confide it to the workshop; he must carry it about him until he reached home and a place of safety for it. When he saw Edwin and a young lady appear in the doorway, he let the apron fall over his knees again. As the day was only the second of the industrial week, the apron was almost clean; and even the office towel, which hung on a roller somewhat conspicuously near the door, was not offensive. A single gas jet burned. The workshop was in the languor of repose after toil which had officially commenced at 8 a.m.

The perfection of Big James's attitude, an attitude symbolized by the letting down of his apron, helped to put Edwin at ease in the original and difficult circumstances. 'Good evening, Mr Edwin. Good evening, miss,' was all that the man actually said with his tongue, but the formality of his majestic gestures indicated in the most dignified way his recognition of a sharp difference of class and his exact comprehension of his own rôle in the affair. He stood waiting : he had been about to depart, but he was entirely at the disposal of the company.

'This is Mr Yarlett, our foreman,' said Edwin, and to Big James : 'Miss Lessways has just come to look round.'

Hilda smiled. Big James suavely nodded his head.

'Here are some of the types,' said Edwin, because a big case was the object nearest him, and he glanced at Big James.

In a moment the foreman was explaining to Hilda, in his superb voice, the use of the composing-stick, and he accompanied the theory by a beautiful exposition of the practice; Edwin could stand aside and watch. Hilda listened and looked with an extraordinary air of sympathetic interest. And she was so serious, so adult. But it was the quality of sympathy, he thought, that was her finest, her most attractive. It was either that or her proud independence, as of a person not accustomed to bend to the will of others or to go to others for advice. He could not be sure. . . . No ! Her finest quality was her mystery. Even now, as he gazed at her comfortably, she baffled him; all her exquisite little movement and intonations baffled him. Of one thing, however, he was convinced : that she was fundamentally different from other women. There was she, and there was the rest of the sex.

For appearance's sake he threw in short phrases now and then, to which Big James, by his mere deportment, gave the importance of the words of a master.

'I suppose you printers did something special among yourselves to celebrate the four-hundredth anniversary of the invention of printing?' said Hilda suddenly, glancing from Edwin to Big James. And Big James and Edwin glanced at one another. Neither had ever heard of the four-hundredth anniversary of the invention of printing. In a couple of seconds Big James's downcast eye had made it clear that he regarded this portion of the episode as master's business.

'When was that? – let me see,' Edwin foolishly blurted out.

'Oh! Some years ago. Two or three – perhaps four.'

'I'm afraid we didn't,' said Edwin, smiling.

'Oh!' said Hilda slowly. 'I think they made a great fuss of it in London.' She relented somewhat. 'I don't really know much about it. But the other day I happened to be reading the new history of printing, you know – Cranswick's, isn't it?'

'Oh yes!' Edwin concurred, though he had never heard of Cranswick's new history of printing either.

He knew that he was not emerging creditably from this portion of the episode. But he did not care. The whole of his body went hot and then cold as his mind presented the simple question : 'Why had she been reading the history of printing?' Could the reason be any other than her interest in himself? Or was she a prodigy among young women, who read histories of everything in addition to being passionate about verse? He said that it was ridiculous to suppose that she would read a history of printing solely from interest in himself. Nevertheless he was madly happy for a few moments, and as it were staggered with joy. He decided to read a history of printing at once.

Big James came to the end of his expositions of the craft. The stove was dying out, and the steam-boiler cold. Big James regretted that the large machines could not be seen in action, and that the place was getting chilly. Edwin began to name various objects that were lying about, with their functions, but it was evident that the interest of the workshop was now nearly exhausted. Big James suggested that if Miss could make it convenient to call, say, on the next afternoon, she could see the large new Columbia in motion. Edwin seized the idea and beautified it. And on this he wavered towards the door, and she followed, and Big James in dignity bowed them forth to the elevated porch, and began to rewind his flowing apron once more. They pattered down the dark steps (now protected with felt roofing) and ran across six feet of exposed yard into what had once been Mrs Nixon's holy kitchen.

IV

After glancing at sundry minor workshops in delicious propinquity and solitude, they mounted to the first floor, where there was an account-book ruling and binding shop : the site of the old sitting-room and the girls' bedroom. In each chamber Edwin had to light a gas, and the corridors and stairways were traversed by the ray of matches. It was excitingly intricate. Then they went to the attics, because Edwin was determined that she should see all. There he found a forgotten candle.

'I used to work here,' he said, holding high the candle. 'There was no other place for me to work in.'

They were in his old work attic, now piled with stocks of paper wrapped up in posters.

'Work? What sort of work?'

'Well – reading, drawing, you know. . . . At that very table.' To be sure, there the very table was, thick with dust! It had been too rickety to deserve removal to the heights of Bleakridge. He was touched by the sight of the table now, though he saw it at least once every week. His existence at the corner of Duck Square seemed now to have been beautiful and sad, seemed to be far off and historic. And the attic seemed unhappy in its present humiliation.

'But there's no fireplace,' murmured Hilda.

'I know,' said Edwin.

'But how did you do in winter?'

'I did without.'

He had in fact been less of a martyr than those three telling words would indicate. Nevertheless it appeared to him that he really had been a martyr; and he was glad. He could feel her sympathy and her quiet admiration vibrating through the air towards him. Had she not said that she had never met anybody like him? He turned and looked at her. Her eyes glittered in the candle-light with tears too proud to fall. Solemn and exquisite bliss! Profound anxiety and apprehension! He was an arena where all the sensations of which a human being is capable struggled in blind confusion.

Afterwards, he could recall her visit only in fragments. The next fragment that he recollected was the last. She stood outside the door in her mackintosh. The rain had ceased. She was going. Behind them he could feel his father in the cubicle, and Stifford arranging the toilette of the shop for the night.

'Please don't come out here,' she enjoined, half in entreaty, half in command. Her solicitude thrilled him. He was on the step, she was on the pavement : so that he looked down at her, with the sodden, light-reflecting slope of Duck Square for a background to her.

'Oh! I'm all right. Well, you'll come tomorrow afternoon?'

'No, you aren't all right. You've got a cold and you'll make it worse, and this isn't the end of winter, it's the beginning; I think you're very liable to colds.'

'N-no!' he said, enchanted, beside himself in ecstasy of pleasure. 'I shall expect you tomorrow about three.'

'Thank you,' she said simply. 'I'll come.'

They shook hands.

'Now do go in!'

She vanished round the corner.

All evening he neither read nor spoke.

CHAPTER 19 : *A Catastrophe*

I

At half past two on the following afternoon he was waiting for the future in order to recommence living. During this period, to a greater extent even than the average individual in average circumstances, he was incapable of living in the present. Continually he looked either forward or back. All that he had achieved, or that had been achieved for him – the new house with its brightness and its apparatus of luxury, his books, his learning, his friends, his experience : not long since regarded by him as the precious materials of happiness – all had become negligible trifles, nothings, devoid of import. The sole condition precedent to a tolerable existence was now to have sight and speech of Hilda Lessways. He was intensely unhappy in the long stretches of time which separated one contact with her from the next. And in the brief moments of their companionship he was far too distraught, too apprehensive, too desirous, too puzzled, to be able to call himself happy. Seeing her apparently did naught to assuage the pain of his curiosity about her – not his curiosity concerning the details of her life and of her person, for these scarcely interested him, but his curiosity concerning the very essence of her being. At seven o'clock on the previous day, he had esteemed her visit as possessing a decisive importance which covered the whole field of his wishes. The visit had occurred, and he was not a whit advanced; indeed he had retrograded, for he was less content and more confused, and more preoccupied. The medicine had aggravated the disease. Nevertheless, he awaited a second dose of it in the undestroyed illusion of its curative property.

In the interval he had behaved like a very sensible man. Without appetite, he had still forced himself to eat, lest his relatives should suspect. Short of sleep, he had been careful to avoid yawning at breakfast, and had spoken in a casual tone of Hilda's visit. He had even said to his father : 'I suppose the big Columbia will be running off those overseer notices this afternoon?' And on the old man asking why he was thus interested, he had answered : 'Because that girl, Miss Lessways, thought of coming down to see it. For some reason or other she's very keen on printing, and as she's such a friend of the Orgreaves —'

Nobody, he considered, could have done that better than he had done it.

And now that girl, Miss Lessways, was nearly due. He stood behind the counter again, waiting, waiting. He could scarcely wait. He was in a state that approached fever, if not agony. To exist from half past two to three o'clock equalled in anguish the dreadful inquietude that comes before a surgical operation.

He said to himself : 'If I keep on like this I shall be in love with her one of these days.' He would not and could not believe that he already was in love with her, though the possibility presented itself to him. 'No,' he said, 'you don't fall in love in a couple of days. You mustn't tell me —' in a wise, superior, slightly scornful manner. 'I dare say there's nothing in it at all,' he said uncertainly, after having strongly denied throughout that there was anything in it.

The recollection of his original antipathy to Hilda troubled him. She was the same girl. She was the same girl who had followed him at night into his father's garden and merited his disdain. She was the same girl who had been so unpleasant, so sharp, so rudely disconcerting in her behaviour. And he dared not say that she had altered. And yet now he could not get her out of his head. And although he would not admit that he constantly admired her, he did admit that there were moments when he admired her passionately and deemed her unique and above all women. Whence the change in himself? How to justify it? The problem was insoluble, for he was intellectually too honest to say lightly that originally he had been mistaken. He did not pretend to solve the problem. He looked at it with perturbation, and left it. The consoling thing was that the Orgreaves had always expressed high esteem for Hilda. He leaned on the Orgreaves.

He wondered how the affair would end. It could not indefinitely continue on its present footing. How, indeed, would it end? Marriage. . . . He apologized to himself for the thought. . . . But just for the sake of argument . . . supposing . . . well, supposing the affair went so far that one day he told her . . . men did such things, young men ! No ! . . . Besides, she wouldn't . . . it was absurd. . . . No such idea, really ! . . . And then the frightful worry there would be with his father about money, and so on. . . . And the telling of Clara, and of everybody. No! He simply could not imagine himself married, or about to be married. Marriage might happen to other young men, but not to him. His case was special, somehow. . . . He shrank from such formidable enterprises. The mere notion of them made him tremble.

II

He brushed all that away impatiently, pettishly. The intense and terrible longing for her arrival persisted. It was now twenty-five to three. His father would be down soon from his after-dinner nap. Suddenly the door opened, and he saw the Orgreaves' servant, with a cloak over her white apron, and hands red with cold. And also he saw disaster like a ghostly figure following her. His heart sickeningly sank. Martha smiled and gave him a note, which he smilingly accepted. 'Miss Lessways asked me to come down with this,' she said confidentially. She was a little breathless, and she had absolutely the manner of a singing chambermaid in light opera. He opened the note, which said: 'Dear Mr Clayhanger, so sorry I can't come today. – Yours, H. L.' Nothing else. It was scrawled. 'It's all right, thanks,' he said, with an even brighter smile to the messenger, who nodded and departed.

It all occurred in an instant.

III

A catastrophe! He suffered then as he had never suffered.

His was no state approaching agony; it was agony itself, black and awful. She was not coming. She had not troubled herself to give a reason, nor to offer an excuse. She merely was not coming. She had showed no consideration for his feelings. It had not happened to her to reflect that she would be causing him disappointment. Disappointment was too mild a word. He had been building a marvellously beautiful castle, and with a thoughtless, careless stroke of the pen she had annihilated all his labour; she had almost annihilated him. Surely she owed him some reason, some explanation! Had she the right to play fast and loose with him like that? 'What a shame!' he sobbed violently in his heart, with an excessive and righteous resentment. He was innocent; he was blameless; and she tortured him thus! He supposed that all women were like her . . . 'What a shame!' He pitied himself for a victim. And there was no glint of hope anywhere. In half an hour he would have been near her, with her, guiding her to the workshop, discussing the machine with her; and savouring her uniqueness; feasting on her delicious and adorable personality! . . . 'So sorry I can't come today!' She doesn't understand. She can't understand!' he said to himself. 'No woman, however cruel, would ever knowingly be so cruel as she has been. It isn't possible!' Then he sought excuse for her, and then he cast the excuse away angrily. She was not coming. There was no ground beneath his feet. He was so exquisitely miserable that he could not face a future of even ten hours ahead. He could not look at what his existence would be till bedtime. The blow had deprived him of all force, all courage. It was a wanton blow. He wished savagely that he had never seen her . . . No! no! He could not call on the Orgreaves that night. He could not do it. She might be out. And then . . .

His father entered, and began to grumble. Both Edwin and Maggie had known since the beginning of dinner that Darius was quaking on the precipice of a bad bilious attack. Edwin listened to the rising storm of words. He had to resume the thread of his daily life. He knew what affliction was.

CHAPTER 20 : *The Man*

I

But he was young. Indeed to men of fifty, men just twice his age, he seemed a mere boy and incapable of grief. He was so slim, and his limbs were so loose, and his hair so fair, and his gestures often so naïve, that few of the mature people who saw him daily striding up and down Trafalgar Road could have believed him to be acquainted with sorrow like their sorrows. The next morning, as it were in justification of these maturer people, his youth arose and fought with the malady in him, and, if it did not conquer, it was not defeated. On the previous night, after hours of hesitation, he had suddenly walked forth and gone down Oak Street, and pushed open the garden gates of the Orgreaves, and gazed at the façade of the house – not at her window, because that was at the side – and it was all dark. The Orgreaves had gone to bed : he had expected it. Even this perfectly futile reconnaissance had calmed him. While dressing in the bleak sunrise he had looked at the oval lawn of the Orgreaves' garden, and had seen Johnnie idly kicking a football on it. Johnnie had probably spent the evening with her; and it was nothing to Johnnie! She was there, somewhere between him and Johnnie, within fifty yards of both of them, mysterious and withdrawn as ever, busy at something or other. And it was naught to Johnnie! By the thought of all this the woe in him was strengthened and embittered. Nevertheless his youth, aided by the astringent quality of the clear dawn, still struggled sturdily against it. And he ate six times more breakfast than his suffering and insupportable father.

At half past one – it was Thursday, and the shop closed at two o'clock – he had put on courage like a garment, and decided that he would see her that afternoon or night, 'or perish in the attempt'. And as the remembered phrase of the Sunday passed through his mind, he inwardly smiled and thought of school; and felt old and sure.

II

At five minutes to two, as he stood behind the eternal counter in his eternal dream, he had the inexpressible and delectable shock of seeing her. He was shot by the vision of her as by a bullet. She came in, hurried and preoccupied, apparently full of purpose.

'Have you got a Bradshaw?' she inquired, after the briefest greeting, gazing at him across the counter through her veil, as though imploring him for Bradshaw.

'I'm afraid we haven't one left,' he said. 'You see it's getting on for the end of the month. I could – No, I suppose you want it at once?'

'I want it now,' she replied. 'I'm going to London by the six express, and what I want to know is whether I can get on to Brighton tonight. They actually haven't a Bradshaw up there,' half in scorn and half in levity, 'and they said you'd probably have one here. So I ran down.'

'They'd be certain to have one at the Tiger,' he murmured, reflecting.

'The Tiger!' Evidently she did not care for the idea of the Tiger. 'What about the railway station?'

'Yes, or the railway station. I'll go up there with you now if you like, and find out for you. I know the head porter. We're just closing. Father's at home. He's not very well.'

She thanked him, relief in her voice.

In a minute he had put his hat and coat on and given instructions to Stifford, and he was climbing Duck Bank with Hilda at his side. He had forgiven her. Nay, he had forgotten her crime. The disaster, with all its despair, was sponged clean from his mind like writing off a slate, and as rapidly. It was effaced. He tried to collect his faculties and savour the new sensations. But he could not. Within him all was incoherent, wild, and distracting. Five minutes earlier, and he could not have conceived the bliss of walking with her to the station. Now he was walking with her to the station; and assuredly it was bliss, and yet he did not fully taste it. Though he would not have loosed her for a million pounds, her presence gave an even crueller edge to his anxiety and apprehension. London! Brighton! Would she be that night in Brighton? He felt helpless, and desperate. And beneath all this was the throbbing of a strange, bitter joy. She asked about his cold and about his father's indisposition. She said nothing of her failure to appear on the previous day, and he

230

knew not how to introduce it neatly : he was not in control of his intelligence.

They passed Snaggs' Theatre, and from its green, wooden walls came the obscure sound of humanity in emotion. Before the mean and shabby portals stood a small crowd of ragged urchins. Posters printed by Darius Clayhanger made white squares on the front.

'It's a meeting of the men,' said Edwin.

'They're losing, aren't they?'

He shrugged his shoulders. 'I expect they are.'

She asked what the building was, and he explained.

'They used to call it the Blood Tub,' he said.

She shivered. 'The Blood Tub?'

'Yes. Melodrama and murder and gore – you know.'

'How horrible!' she exclaimed. 'Why are people like – like that in the Five Towns?'

'It's our form of poetry, I suppose,' he muttered, smiling at the pavement, which was surprisingly dry and clean in the feeble sunshine.

'I suppose it *is*!' she agreed heartily, after a pause.

'But you belong to the Five Towns, don't you?' he asked.

'Oh yes! I used to.'

At the station the name of Bradshaw appeared to be quite unknown. But Hilda's urgency impelled them upwards from the head porter to the ticket clerk, and from the ticket clerk to the stationmaster; and at length they discovered, in a stuffy, stoveheated room with a fine view of a shawd-ruck and a pit-head, that on Thursday evenings there was a train from Victoria to Brighton at eleven-thirty. Hilda seemed to sigh relief, and her demeanour changed. But Edwin's uneasiness was only intensified. Brighton, which he had never seen, was in another hemisphere for him. It was mysterious, like her. It was part of her mystery. What could he do? His curse was that he had no initiative. Without her relentless force, he would never have penetrated even as far as the stuffy room where the unique Bradshaw lay. It was she who had taken him to the station, not he her. How could he hold her back from Brighton?

III

When they came again to the Blood Tub, she said –

'Couldn't we just go and look in? I've got plenty of time, now I know exactly how I stand.'

She halted, and glanced across the road. He could only agree to the proposition. For himself, a peculiar sense of delicacy would have made it impossible for him to intrude his prosperity upon the deliberations of starving artisans on strike and stricken; and he wondered what the potters might think or say about the invasion by a woman. But he had to traverse the street with her and enter, and he had to do so with an air of masculine protectiveness. The urchins stood apart to let them in.

Snaggs', dimly lit by a few glazed apertures in the roof, was nearly crammed by men who sat on the low benches and leaned standing against the sidewalls. In the small and tawdry proscenium, behind a worn picture of the Bay of Naples, were silhouetted the figures of the men's leader and of several other officials. The leader was speaking in a quiet, mild voice, the other officials were seated on Windsor chairs. The smell of the place was nauseating, and yet the atmosphere was bitingly cold. The warm-wrapped visitors could see rows and rows of discoloured backs and elbows, and caps, and stringy kerchiefs. They could almost feel the contraction of thousands of muscles in an involuntary effort to squeeze out the chill from all these bodies; not a score of overcoats could be discerned in the whole theatre, and many of the jackets were thin and ragged; but the officials had overcoats. And the visitors could almost see, as it were in rays, the intense fixed glances darting from every part of the interior, and piercing the upright figure in the centre of the stage.

'. . . Some method of compromise,' the leader was saying in his persuasive tones.

A young man sprang up furiously from the middle benches.

'To hell wi' compromise!' he shouted in a tigerish passion. 'Haven't us had forty pound from Ameriky?'

'Order! Order!' some protested fiercely. But one voice cried : 'Pitch the b— awt, neck and crop!'

Hands clawed at the interrupter and dragged him with extreme violence to the level of the bench, where he muttered like a dying volcano. Angry howls shot up here and there, snappish, menacing, and bestial.

'It is quite true,' said the leader soothingly, 'that our comrades at Trenton have collected forty pounds for us. But forty pounds would scarcely pay for a loaf of bread for one man in every ten on strike.'

There was more interruption. The dangerous growls continued in running explosions along the benches. The leader, ignoring them, turned to consult with his neighbour, and then faced his audience, and called out more loudly —

'The business of the meeting is at an end.'

The entire multitude jumped up, and there was stretching of arms and stamping of feet. The men nearest to the door now perceived Edwin and Hilda, who moved backwards as before a flood. Edwin seized Hilda's arm to hasten her.

'Lads,' bawled an old man's voice from near the stage, 'let's sing "Rock of Ages".'

A frowning and hirsute fellow near the door, with the veins prominent on his red forehead, shouted hoarsely, ' "Rock af Ages" be b–d !' and shifting his hands into his pockets he plunged for the street, head foremost and chin sticking out murderously. Edwin and Hilda escaped at speed and recrossed the road. The crowd came surging out of the narrow neck of the building and spread over the pavements like a sinister liquid. But from within the building came the lusty song of 'Rock of Ages'.

'It's terrible !' Hilda murmured, after a silence, 'Just to see them is enough. I shall never forget what you said.'

'What was that ?' he inquired. He knew what it was, but he wished to prolong the taste of her appreciation.

'That you've only got to see the poor things to know they're in the right ! Oh ! I've lost my handkerchief, unless I've left it in your shop. It must have dropped out of my muff.'

IV

The shop was closed. As with his latchkey he opened the private door and then stood on one side for her to precede him into the corridor that led to the back of the shop, he watched the stream of operatives scattering across Duck Bank and descending towards the Square. It was as if he and Hilda, being pursued, were escaping. And as Hilda, stopping an instant on the step, saw what he saw, her face took a troubled expression. They both went in and he shut the door.

'Turn to the left,' he said, wondering whether the big Columbia machine would be running, for her to see if she chose.

'Oh ! This takes you to the shop, does it ? How funny to be behind the counter !'

He thought she spoke self-consciously, in the way of small talk : which was contrary to her habit.

'Here's my handkerchief !' she cried with pleasure. It was on the counter, a little white wisp in the grey-sheeted gloom. Stifford must have found it on the floor and picked it up.

The idea flashed through Edwin's head : 'Did she leave her handkerchief on purpose, so that we should have to come back here ?'

The only illumination of the shop was from three or four diamond-shaped holes in the upper part of as many shutters. No object was at first quite distinct. The corners were very dark. All merchandise not in drawers or on shelves was hidden in pale dust-cloths. A chair wrong side up was on the fancy-counter, its back hanging over the front of the counter. Hilda had wandered behind the other counter, and Edwin was in the middle of the shop. Her face in the twilight had become more mysterious than ever. He was in a state of emotion, but he did not know to what category the emotion belonged. They were alone. Stifford had

233

gone for the half-holiday. Darius, sickly, would certainly not come near. The printers were working as usual in their place, and the clanking whirr of a treadle-machine overhead agitated the ceiling. But nobody would enter the shop. His excitement increased, but did not define itself. There was a sudden roar in Duck Square, and then cries.

'What can that be?' Hilda asked, low.

'Some of the strikers,' he answered, and went through the doors to the letter-hole in the central shutter, lifted the flap, and looked through.

A struggle was in progress at the entrance to the Duck Inn. One man was apparently drunk; others were jeering on the skirts of the lean crowd.

'It's some sort of a fight among them,' said Edwin loudly, so that she could hear in the shop. But at the same instant he felt the wind of the door swinging behind him, and Hilda was silently at his elbow.

'Let me look,' she said.

Assuredly her voice was trembling. He moved, as little as possible, and held the flap up for her. She bent and gazed. He could hear various noises in the Square, but she described nothing to him. After a long while she withdrew from the hole.

'A lot of them have gone into the public-house,' she said. 'The others seem to be moving away. There's a policeman. What a shame,' she burst out passionately, 'that they have to drink to forget their trouble!' She made no remark upon the strangeness of starving workmen being able to pay for beer sufficient to intoxicate themselves. Nor did she comment, as a woman, on the misery of the wives and children at home in the slums and the cheap cottage-rows. She merely compassioned the men in that they were driven to brutishness. Her features showed painful pity masking disgust.

She stepped back into the shop.

'Do you know,' she began, in a new tone, 'you've quite altered my notion of poetry – what you said as we were going up to the station.'

'Really!' He smiled nervously. He was very pleased. He would have been astounded by this speech from her, a professed devotee of poetry, if in those instants the capacity for astonishment had remained to him.

'Yes,' she said, and continued, frowning and picking at her muff: 'But you *do* alter my notions, I don't know how it is. . . . So this is your little office!'

The door of the cubicle was open.

'Yes, go in and have a look at it.'

'Shall I?' She went in.

He followed her.

And no sooner was she in than she muttered, 'I must hurry off now.' Yet a moment before she seemed to have infinite leisure.

'Shall you be at Brighton long?' he demanded, and scarcely recognized his own accents.

'Oh! I can't tell! I've no idea. It depends.'

'How soon shall you be down our way again?'

She only shook her head.

'I say – you know –' he protested.

'Good-bye,' she said, quavering. 'Thanks very much.' She held out her hand.

'But –' He took her hand.

His suffering was intolerable. It was torture of the most exquisite kind. Her hand pressed his. Something snapped in him. His left hand hovered shaking over her shoulder, and then touched her shoulder, and he could feel her left hand on his arm. The embrace was clumsy in its instinctive and unskilled violence, but its clumsiness was redeemed by all his sincerity and all hers. His eyes were within six inches of her eyes, full of delicious shame, anxiety, and surrender. They kissed. . . . He had amorously kissed a woman. All his past life sank away, and he began a new life on the impetus of that supreme and final emotion. It was an emotion that in its freshness, agitating and divine, could never be renewed. He had felt the virgin answer of her lips on his. She had told him everything, she had yielded up her mystery, in a second of time. Her courage in responding to his caress ravished and amazed him. She was so unaffected, so simple, so heroic. And the cool, delicate purity of those lips! And the faint feminine odour of her flesh and even of her stuffs! Dreams and visions were surpassed. He said to himself, in the flood-tide of masculinity –

'My God! She's mine.'

And it seemed incredible.

V

She was sitting in the office chair; he on the desk. She said in a trembling voice – 'I should never have come to the Five Towns again, if you hadn't . . .'

'Why not?'

'I couldn't have stood it. I couldn't.' She spoke almost bitterly, with a peculiar smile on her twitching lips.

To him it seemed that she had resumed her mystery, that he had only really known her for one instant, that he was bound to a woman entrancing, noble, but impenetrable. And this, in spite of the fact that he was close to her, touching her, tingling to her in the confined, crepuscular intimacy of the cubicle. He could trace every movement of her breast as she breathed, and yet she escaped the inward searching of his gaze. But he was happy. He was happy enough to repel all anxieties and inquietudes about the future. He was steeped in the bliss of the miracle. This was but the fourth day, and they were vowed.

'It was only Monday –' he began.

'Monday!' she exclaimed. 'I have thought of you for over a year.' She leaned towards him. 'Didn't you know? Of course you did! . . , You couldn't bear me at first.'

He denied this, blushing, but she insisted.

'You don't know how awful it was for me yesterday when you didn't come!' he murmured.

'Was it?' she said, under her breath. 'I had some very important letters to write.' She clasped his hand.

There it was again! She spoke just like a man of business, immersed in secret schemes.

'It's awfully funny,' he said. 'I scarcely know anything about you and yet –'

'I'm Janet's friend!' she answered. Perhaps it was the delicatest reproof of imagined distrust.

'And I don't want to,' he went on. 'How old are you?'

'Twenty-four,' she answered sweetly, acknowledging his right to put such questions.

'I thought you were.'

'I suppose you know I've got no relatives,' she said, as if relenting from her attitude of reproof. 'Fortunately, father just left enough money for me to live on.'

'Must you go to Brighton?'

She nodded.

'Where can I write to?'

'It will depend,' she said. 'But I shall send you the address tomorrow. I shall write you before I go to bed whether it's tonight or tomorrow morning.'

'I wonder what people will say!'

'Please tell no one, yet,' she pleaded. 'Really, I should prefer not! Later on, it won't seem so sudden; people are so silly.'

'But shan't you tell Janet?'

She hesitated. 'No! Let's keep it to ourselves till I come back.'

'When shall you come back?'

'Oh! Very soon. I hope in a few days, now. But I must go to this friend at Brighton. She's relying on me.'

It was enough for him, and indeed he liked the idea of a secret. 'Yes, yes,' he agreed eagerly.

There was the sound of another uproar in Duck Square. It appeared to roll to and fro thunderously.

She shivered. The fire was dead out in the stove, and the chill of night crept in from the street.

'It's nearly dark,' she said. 'I must go! I have to pack.... Oh dear, dear – those poor men! Somebody will be hurt!'

'I'll walk up with you,' he whispered, holding her, in ownership.

'No. It will be better not. Let me out.'

'Really?'

'Really!'

'But who'll take you to Knype Station?'

'Janet will go with me.'

She rose reluctantly. In the darkness they were now only dim forms to each other. He struck a match, that blinded them and expired as they reached the passage ...

When she had gone, he stood hatless at the open side door. Right at the top of Duck Bank, he could discern under the big lamp there, a knot of gesticulating and shouting strikers, menacing two policemen; and farther off, in the direction of Moorthorne Road, other strikers were running. The yellow-lit blinds of the Duck Inn across the Square seemed to screen a house of impenetrable conspiracies and debaucheries. And all that grim, perilous background only gave to his emotions a further intensity, troubling them to still stranger ecstasy. He thought : 'It has happened to me, too, now – this thing that is at the bottom of everybody's mind! I've kissed her! I've got her! She's marvellous, marvellous! I couldn't have believed it. But is it true? Has it happened?' It passed his credence.... 'By jove! I absolutely forgot about the ring! That's a nice how d'ye do!' ... He saw himself married. He thought of Clara's grotesque antics with her tedious babe. And he thought of his father and of vexations. But that night he was a man. She, Hilda, with her independence and her mystery, had inspired him with a full pride of manhood. And he discovered that one of the chief attributes of a man is an immense tenderness.

CHAPTER 21 : *The Marriage*

I

He was more proud and agitated than happy. The romance of the affair, and its secrecy made him proud; the splendid qualities of Hilda made him proud. It was her mysteriousness that agitated him, and her absence rendered him unhappy in his triumph. During the whole of Friday he was thinking : 'Tomorrow is Saturday and I shall have her address and a letter from her.' He decided that there was no hope of a letter by the last post on Friday, but as the hour of the last post drew nigh he grew excited, and was quite appreciably disappointed when it brought nothing. The fear, which had always existed in little, then waxed into enormous dread, that Saturday's post also would bring nothing. His manoeuvres in the early twilight of Saturday morning were complicated by the fact that it had not been arranged whether she should write to the shop or to the house. However, he prepared for either event by having his breakfast at seven o'clock, on the plea of special work in the shop. He had finished it at half past seven, and was waiting for the postman, whose route he commanded from the dining-room window. The postman arrived. Edwin with false calm walked into the hall, saying to himself that if the letter was not in the box it would be at the shop. But the letter was in the box. He recognized her sprawling hand on the envelope through the wirework. He snatched the letter and slipped upstairs with it like a fox with a chicken. It had come, then! The letter safely in his hand he admitted more frankly that he had been very doubtful of its promptitude.

'59 PRESTON STREET, BRIGHTON, 1 a.m.
'DEAREST, – This is my address. I love you. Every bit of me is absolutely yours. Write me. – H. L.'

That was all. It was enough. Its tone enchanted him. Also it startled him. But it reminded him of her lips. He had begun a letter to her. He saw now that what he had written was too cold in the expression of his feelings. Hilda's note suddenly and completely altered his views upon the composition of love-letters. 'Every bit of me is absolutely yours.' How fine, how untrammelled, how like Hilda! What other girl could or would have written such a phrase? More than ever was he convinced that she was unique. The thrill divine quickened in him again, and he rose eagerly to her level of passion. The romance, the secrecy, the mystery, the fever! He walked down Trafalgar Road with the letter in his pocket, and once he pulled it out to read it in the street. His discretion objected to this act, but Edwin was not his own master. Stifford, hurrying in exactly at eight, was somewhat perturbed to find his employer's son already installed in the cubicle, writing by the light of gas, as the shutters were not removed. Edwin had finished and stamped his first love-letter just as his father entered the cubicle. Owing to dyspeptic accidents Darius had not set foot in the cubicle since it had been sanctified by Hilda. Edwin, leaving it, glanced at the old man's back and thought disdainfully. 'Ah! You little know, you rhinoceros, that less than two days ago, she and I, on that very spot –'

As soon as his father had gone to pay the morning visit to the printing shops, he ran out to post the letter himself. He could not be contented until it was in the post. Now, when he saw men of about his own class and age in the street, he would speculate upon their experiences in the romance of women. And it did genuinely seem to him impossible that anybody else in a town like Bursley could have passed through an episode so exquisitely strange and beautiful as that through which he was passing. Yet his reason told him that he must be wrong there. His reason, however, left him tranquil in the assurance that no girl in Bursley had ever written to her affianced : 'I love you. Every bit of me is absolutely yours.'

Hilda's second letter did not arrive till the following Tuesday, by which time he had become distracted by fears and doubts. Yes, doubts! No rational being could have been more loyal than Edwin, but these little doubts would keep shooting up and withering away. He could not control them. The second letter was nearly as short as the first. It told him nothing save her love and that she was very worried by her friend's situation, and that his letters were a joy. She had had a letter from him each day. In his reply to her second he gently implied, between two lines, that her letters lacked quantity and frequency. She answered : 'I simply cannot write letters. It isn't in me. Can't you tell that from my handwriting? Not even to you! You must take me as I am.' She wrote each day for three days. Edwin was one of those who learn quickly, by the acceptance of facts. And he now learnt that profound lesson that an individual must be taken or left in entirety, and that you cannot change an object merely because you love it. Indeed he saw in her phrase, 'You must take me as I am', the accents of original and fundamental wisdom, springing from the very roots of life. And he submitted. At intervals he would resentfully say : 'But surely she could find five minutes each day to drop me a line ! What's five minutes?' But he submitted. Submission was made easier when he co-ordinated with Hilda's idiosyncrasy the fact that Maggie his own unromantic sister, could never begin to write a letter with less than from twelve to twenty-four hours' bracing of herself to the task. Maggie would be saying and saying : 'I really must write that letter. . . . Dear me! I haven't written that letter yet.'

His whole life seemed to be lived in the post, and postmen were the angels of the creative spirit. His unhappiness increased with the deepening of the impression that the loved creature was treating him with cruelty. Time dragged. At length he had been engaged a fortnight. On Thursday a letter should have come. It came not. Nor on Friday nor Saturday. On Sunday it must come. But it did not come on Sunday. He determined to telegraph to her on the Monday morning. His loyalty, though valorous, needed aid against all those prickling battalions of ephemeral doubts. On the Sunday evening he suddenly had the idea of strengthening himself by a process that resembled boatburning. He would speak to his father. His father's mentality was the core of a difficulty that troubled him exceedingly, and he took it into his head to attack the difficulty at once, on the spot.

II

For years past Darius Clayhanger had not gone to chapel on Sunday evening. In the morning he still went fairly regularly but in the evening he would now sit in the drawing-room, generally alone, to read. On weekdays he never used the drawing-room, where indeed there was seldom a fire. He had been accustomed to only one living-room, and save on Sunday, when he cared to bend the major part of his mind to the matter, he scorned to complicate existence by utilizing all the resources of the house which he had built. His children might do so; but not he. He was proud enough to see to it that his house had a drawing-room, and too proud to employ the drawing-room except on the ceremonious day. After tea, at about a quarter to six, when chapel-goers were hurriedly pulling gloves on, he would begin to establish himself in a saddle-backed, ear-flapped easy-chair with *The Christian News* and an ivory paper-knife as long and nearly as deadly as a scimitar. *The Christian News* was a religious weekly of a new type. It belonged to a Mr James Bott, and it gave to God and to the mysteries of religious experience a bright and breezy actuality. Darius's children had damned it for ever on its first issue, in which Clara had found, in a report of a very important charitable meeting, the following words : 'Among those present were the Prince of Wales and Mr James Bott'. Such is the hasty and unjudicial nature of children that this single sentence finished the career of *The Christian News* with the younger generation. But Darius liked it, and continued to like it. He enjoyed it. He would spend an hour and a half in reading it. And further, he enjoyed cutting open the morsel. Once when Edwin, in hope of more laughter, had cut the pages on a Saturday afternoon, and his father had found himself unable to use the paper-knife on Sunday evening, there had been a formidable inquiry : 'Who's been meddling with my paper?' Darius saved the paper even from himself until Sunday evening; not till then would he touch it. This habit had flourished for several years. It appeared never to lose its charm. And Edwin did not cease to marvel at his father's pleasure in a tedious monotony.

It was the hallowed rite of reading *The Christian News* that Edwin disturbed in his sudden and capricious resolve. Maggie and Mrs Nixon had gone to chapel, for Mrs Nixon, by reason of her years, bearing, mantle, and reputation, could walk down Trafalgar Road by the side of her mistress on a Sunday night without offence to the delicate instincts of the town. The niece, engaged to be married at an age absurdly youthful, had been permitted by Mrs Nixon the joy of attending evensong at the Bleakridge Church on the arm of a male, but under promise to be back at a quarter to eight to set supper. The house was perfectly still when Edwin came all on fire out of his bedroom and slid down the stairs. The gas burnt economically low within its stained-glass cage in the hall. The drawing-room door was unlatched. He hesitated a moment on the mat, and he could hear the calm ticking of the clock in the kitchen and see the red glint of the kitchen fire against the wall. Then he entered, looking and feeling apologetic.

His father was all curtained in; his slippered feet on the fender of the blazing hearth, his head cushioned to a nicety, the long paper-knife across his knees. And the room was really hot and in a glow of light. Darius turned and, lowering his face, gazed at Edwin over the top of his new gold-rimmed spectacles.

'Not gone to chapel?' he frowned.

'No! ... I say, father, I just wanted to speak to you.'

Darius made no reply, but shifted his glance from Edwin to the fire, and maintained his frown. He was displeased at the interruption. Edwin failed to shut the door at the first attempt, and then banged it in his nervousness. In spite of himself he felt like a criminal. Coming forward, he leaned his loose, slim frame against a corner of the old piano.

III

'Well?' Darius growled impatiently, even savagely. They saw each other, not once a week, but at nearly every hour of every day, and they were surfeited of the companionship.

'Supposing I wanted to get married?' This sentence shot out of Edwin's mouth like a bolt. And as it flew, he blushed very red. In the privacy of his mind he was horribly swearing.

'So that's it, is it?' Darius growled again. And he leaned forward and picked up the poker, not as a menace, but because he too was nervous. As an opposer of his son he had never had quite the same confidence in himself since Edwin's historic fury at being suspected of theft, though apparently their relations had resumed the old basis of bullying and submission.

'Well –' Edwin hesitated. He thought, 'after all, people do get married. It won't be a crime.'

'Who'st been running after?' Darius demanded inimically. Instead of being softened by this rumour of love, by this hint that his son had been passing through wondrous secret hours, he instinctively and without any reason hardened himself and transformed the news into an offence. He felt no sympathy and it did not occur to him to recall that he too had once thought of marrying. He was a man whom life had brutalized about half a century earlier.

'I was only thinking,' said Edwin clumsily – the fool had not sense enough even to sit down – 'I was only thinking, suppose *I did* want to get married.'

'Who'st been running after?'

'Well, I can't rightly say there's anything – what you may call settled. In fact, nothing was to be said about it all at present. But it's Miss Lessways, father – Hilda Lessways, you know.'

'Her as came in the shop the other day?'

'Yes.'

'How long's this been going on?'

Edwin thought of what Hilda had said. 'Oh! Over a year.' He could not possibly have said 'four days'. 'Mind you this is strictly q.t.! Nobody knows a word about it, nobody! But of course I thought I'd better tell you. You'll say nothing.' He tried wistfully to appeal as one loyal man to another. But he failed. There was no ray of response on his father's gloomy features, and he slipped back insensibly into the boy whose right to an individual existence had never been formally admitted.

Something base in him – something of that baseness which occasionally actuates the oppressed – made him add : 'She's got an income of her own. Her father left money.' He conceived that this would placate Darius.

'I know all about her father,' Darius sneered, with a short laugh. 'And her father's father! . . . Well, lad, ye'll go your own road.' He appeared to have no further interest in the affair, Edwin was not surprised, for Darius was seemingly never interested in anything except his business; but he thought how strange, how nigh to the incredible, the old man's demeanour was.

'But about money, I was thinking,' he said, uneasily shifting his pose.

'What about money?'

'Well,' said Edwin, endeavouring, and failing, to find courage to put a little sharpness into his tone, 'I couldn't marry on seventeen-and-six a week, could I?'

At the age of twenty-five, at the end of nine years' experience in the management and the accountancy of a general printing and stationery business, Edwin was receiving seventeen shillings and sixpence for a sixty-five-hour week's work, the explanation being that on his father's death the whole enterprise would be his, and that all money saved was saved for him. Out of this sum he had to pay ten shillings a week to Maggie towards the cost of board and lodging, so that three half-crowns remained for his person and his soul. Thus he could expect no independence of any kind until his father's death. Moreover, all his future, and all unpaid reward of his labours in the past, hung hazardous on his father's goodwill. If he quarrelled with him, he might lose everything. Edwin was one of a few odd-minded persons who did not regard this arrangement as perfectly just, proper, and in accordance with sound precedent. But he was helpless. His father would tell him, and did tell him, that he had fought no struggles, suffered no hardship, had no responsibility, and that he was simply coddled from head to foot in cottonwool.

'I say you must go your own road,' said his father.

'But at this rate I should never be able to marry!'

'Do you reckon,' asked Darius, with mild cold scorn, 'as you getting married will make your services worth one penny more to my business?' And he waited an answer with the august calm of one who is aware that he is unanswerable. But he might with equal propriety have tied his son's hands behind him and then diverted himself by punching his head.

'I do all I can,' said Edwin meekly.

'And what about getting orders?' Darius questioned grimly. 'Didn't I offer you two and a half per cent on all new customers you got yourself? And how many have you got? Not one. I give you a chance to make extra money and you don't take it. Ye'd sooner go running about after girls.'

This was a particular grievance of the father against the son : that the son brought no grist to the mill in the shape of new orders.

'But how can I get orders?' Edwin protested.

'How did I get 'em? How do I get 'em? Somebody has to get 'em.' The old man's lips were pressed together, and he waved *The Christian News* slightly in his left hand.

IV

In a few minutes both their voices had risen. Darius, savage, stooped to replace with the shovel a large burning coal that had dropped on the tiles and was sending up a column of brown smoke.

'I tell you what I shall do,' he said, controlling himself bitterly. 'It's against my judgement, but I shall put you up to a pound a week at the New Year, if all goes well, of course. And it's good money, let me add.'

He was entirely serious, and almost sincere. He loathed paying money over to his son. He was convinced that in an ideal world sons would toil gratis for their fathers who lodged and fed them and gifted them with the reversion of excellent businesses.

'But what good's a pound a week?' Edwin demanded, with the querulousness of one who is losing hope.'

'What good's a pound a week!' Darius repeated, hurt and genuinely hurt. 'Let me tell you that in my time young men married on a pound a week, and glad to! A pound a week!' He finished with a sardonic exclamation.

'I couldn't marry Miss Lessways on a pound a week,' Edwin murmured, in despair, his lower lip hanging. 'I thought you might perhaps be offering me a partnership by this time!' Possibly in some mad hour a thought so wild had indeed flitted through his brain.

'Did you?' rejoined Darius. And in the fearful grimness of the man's accents was concealed all his intense and egoistic sense of possessing in absolute ownership the business which the little boy out of the Bastille had practically created. Edwin did not and could not understand the fierce strength of his father's emotion concerning the business. Already in tacitly agreeing to leave Edwin the business after his own death, Darius imagined himself to be superbly benevolent.

'And then there would be house-furnishing, and so on,' Edwin continued.

'What about that fifty pounds?' Darius curtly inquired.

Edwin was startled. Never since the historic scene had Darius made the slightest reference to the proceeds of the Building Society share.

'I haven't spent all of it,' Edwin muttered.

Do what he would with his brain, the project of marriage and house-tenancy and a separate existence obstinately presented itself to him as fantastic and preposterous. Who was he to ask so much from destiny? He could not feel that he was a man. In his father's presence he never could feel that he was a man. He remained a boy, with no rights, moral or material.

'And if as ye say she's got money of her own –' Darius remarked, and was considerably astonished when the boy walked straight out of the room and closed the door.

It was his last grain of common sense that took Edwin in silence out of the room.

Miserable, despicable baseness! Did the old devil suppose that he would be capable of asking his wife to find the resources which he himself could not bring? He was to say to his wife : 'I can only supply a pound a week, but as you've got money it won't matter.' The mere notion outraged him so awfully that if he had stayed in the room there would have been an altercation and perhaps a permanent estrangement.

As he stood furious and impotent in the hall, he thought, with his imagination quickened by the memory of Mr Shushions : 'When you're old, and I've *got* you' – he clenched his fists and his teeth – 'when I've *got* you and you can't help yourself, by God it'll be my turn!'

And he meant it.

V

He seized his overcoat and hat, and putting them on anyhow, strode out. The kitchen clock struck half past seven as he left. Chapel-goers would soon be returning in a thin procession of twos and threes up Trafalgar Road. To avoid meeting acquaintances he turned down the side street, towards the old road which was a continuation of Aboukir Street. There he would be safe. Letting his overcoat fly open, he thrust his hands into the pockets of his trousers. It was a cold night of mist. Humanity was separated from him by the semi-transparent blinds of the cottage windows, bright squares in the dark and enigmatic façades of the street. He was alone.

All along he had felt and known that this disgusting crisis would come to pass. He had hoped against it, but not with faith. And he had no remedy for it. What could he immediately and effectively do? He was convinced that his father would not yield. There were frequent occasions when his father was proof against reason, when his father seemed genuinely unable to admit the claim of justice, and this occasion was one of them. He could tell by certain peculiarities of tone and gesture. A pound a week! Assuming that he cut loose from his father, in a formal and confessed separation, he might not for a long time be in a position to earn more than a pound a week. A clerk was worth no more. And, except as responsible manager of a business, he could only go into the market as a clerk. In the Five Towns how many printing offices were there that might at some time or another be in need of a manager? Probably not one. They were all of modest importance, and directed personally by their proprietary heads. His father's was one of the largest. . . . No! His father had nurtured and trained, in him, a helpless slave.

And how could he discuss such a humiliating question with Hilda? Could he say to Hilda: 'See here, my father won't allow me more than a pound a week. What are we to do?' In what terms should he telegraph to her tomorrow?

He heard the rapid footsteps of a wayfarer overtaking him. He had no apprehension of being disturbed in his bitter rage. But a hand was slapped on his shoulder, and a jolly voice said –

'Now, Edwin, where's this road leading you to on a Sunday night?'

It was Osmond Orgreave who, having been tramping for exercise in the high regions beyond the Loop railway line, was just going home.

'Oh! Nowhere particular,' said Edwin feebly.

'Working off Sunday dinner, eh?'

'Yes.' And Edwin added casually, to prove that there was nothing singular in his mood : 'Nasty night !'

'You must come in a bit,' said Mr Orgreave.

'Oh no !' He shrank away.

'Now, now !' said Mr Orgreave masterfully. 'You've got to come in, so you may as well give up first as last. Janet's in. She's like you and me, she's a bad lot – hasn't been to church.' He took Edwin by the arm, and they turned into Oak Street at the lower end.

Edwin continued to object, but Mr Orgreave, unable to scrutinize his face in the darkness, and not dreaming of an indiscretion, rode over his weak negative, horse and foot, and drew him by force into the garden; and in the hall took his hat away from him and slid his overcoat from his shoulders. Mr Orgreave, having accomplished a lot of forbidden labour on that Sabbath, was playful in his hospitality.

'Prisoner ! Take charge of him !' exclaimed Mr Orgreave shortly, as he pushed Edwin into the breakfast-room and shut the door from the outside. Janet was there, exquisitely welcoming, unconsciously pouring balm from her eyes. But he thought she looked graver than usual. Edwin had to enact the part of a man to whom nothing had happened. He had to behave as though his father was the kindest and most reasonable of fathers, as though Hilda wrote fully to him every day, as though he were not even engaged to Hilda. He must talk, and he scarcely knew what he was saying.

'Heard lately from Miss Lessways?' he asked lightly, or as lightly as he could. It was a splendid effort. Impossible to expect him to start upon the weather or the strike ! He did the best he could.

Janet's eyes became troubled. Speaking in a low voice she said, with a glance at the door –

'I suppose you've not heard. She's married.'

He did not move.

VI

'Married?'

'Yes. It is rather sudden, isn't it?' Janet tried to smile, but she was exceedingly self-conscious. 'To a Mr Cannon. She's known him for a very long time, I think.'

'When?'

'Yesterday. I had a note this morning. It's quite a secret yet. I haven't told father and mother. But she asked me to tell you if I saw you.'

He thought her eyes were compassionate.

Mrs Orgreave came smiling into the room.

'Well, Mr Edwin, it seems we can only get you in here by main force.'

'Are you quite better, Mrs Orgreave?' He rose to greet her.

He had by some means or other to get out.

'I must just run in home a second,' he said, after a moment. 'I'll be back in three minutes.'

But he had no intention of coming back. He would have told any lie in order to be free.

In his bedroom, looking at himself in the glass, he could detect on his face no sign whatever of suffering or of agitation. It seemed just an ordinary mild, unmoved face.

And this, too, he had always felt and known would come to pass: that Hilda would not be his. All that romance was unreal; it was not true; it had never happened. Such a thing could not happen to such as he was . . . He could not reflect. When he tried to reflect, the top of his head seemed as though it would fly off . . . Cannon! She was with Cannon somewhere at that very instant . . . She had specially asked that he should be told. And indeed he had been told before even Mr and Mrs Orgreave . . . Cannon! She might at that very instant be in Cannon's arms.

It could be said of Edwin that he fully lived that night. Fate had at any rate roused him from the coma which most men called existence.

Simple Maggie was upset because, from Edwin's absence and her father's demeanour at supper, she knew that her menfolk had had another terrible discussion. And since her father offered no remark as to it, she guessed that this one must be even more serious than the last.

There was one thing that Edwin could not fit into any of his theories of the disaster which had overtaken him, and that was his memory of Hilda's divine gesture as she bent over Mr Shushions on the morning of the Centenary.

BOOK THREE : HIS FREEDOM

I

Four and a half years later, on a Tuesday night in April 1886, Edwin was reading in an easy-chair in his bedroom. He made a very image of solitary comfort. The easy-chair had been taken from the dining-room, silently, without permission, and Darius had apparently not noticed its removal. A deep chair designed by someone learned in the poses natural to the mortal body, it was firm where it ought to be firm, and where it ought to yield, there it yielded. By its own angles it threw the head slightly back, and the knees slightly up. Edwin's slippered feet rested on a hassock, and in front of the hassock was a red-glowing gas-stove. That stove, like the easy-chair, had been acquired by Edwin at his father's expense without his father's cognizance. It consumed gas whose price swelled the quarterly bill three times a year, and Darius observed nothing. He had not even entered his son's bedroom for several years. Each month seemed to limit further his interest in surrounding phenomena, and to centralize more completely all his faculties in his business. Over Edwin's head the gas jet flamed through one of Darius's special private burners, lighting the page of a little book, one of Cassell's *National Library*, a new series of sixpenny reprints which had considerably excited the book-selling and the book-reading worlds, but which Darius had apparently quite ignored, though confronted in his house and in his shop by multitudinous examples of it. Sometimes Edwin would almost be persuaded to think that he might safely indulge any caprice whatever under his father's nose, and then the old man would notice some unusual trifle, of no conceivable importance, and go into a passion about it, and Maggie would say quietly, 'I told you what would be happening one of these days', which would annoy Edwin. His annoyance was caused less by Maggie's 'I told you so,' than by her lack of logic. If his father had ever overtaken him in some large and desperate caprice, such as the purchase of the gas-stove on the paternal account, he would have submitted in meekness to Maggie's triumphant reminder; but his father never did. It was always upon some perfectly innocent nothing, which the timidest son might have permitted himself, that the wrath of Darius overwhelmingly burst.

Maggie and Edwin understood each other on the whole very well. Only in minor points did their sympathy fail. And as Edwin would be exasperated because Maggie's attitude towards argument was that of a woman, so would Maggie resent a certain mulishness in him characteristic of the unfathomable stupid sex. Once a week, for example, when his room was 'done out', there was invariably a skirmish between them, because Edwin really did hate anybody to 'meddle among his things'. The derangement of even a brush on the dressing-table would rankle in his mind. Also he was very 'crotchety about his meals', and on the subject of fresh air. Unless he was sitting in a perceptible draught, he thought he was being poisoned by nitrogen : but when he could see the curtain or blind trembling in the wind he was hygienically at ease. His existence was a series of catarrhal colds, which, however, as he would learnedly explain to Maggie, could not be connected, in the brain of a reasonable person, with currents of fresh air. Maggie mutely disdained his science. This, too, fretted him. Occasionally she would somewhat tartly assert that he was a regular old maid. The accusation made no impression on him at all. But when, more than ordinarily exacerbated, she sang out that he was 'exactly like his father', he felt wounded.

II

The appearance of his bedroom, and the fact that he enjoyed being in it alone, gave some ground for Maggie's first accusation. A screen hid the bed, and this screen was half covered with written papers of memoranda; roughly, it divided the room into dormitory and study. The whole chamber was occupied by Edwin's personal goods, great and small, ranged in the most careful order; it was full; in the occupation of a young man who was not precociously an old maid, it would have been littered. It was a complex and yet practical apparatus for daily use, completely organized for the production of comfort. Edwin would move about in it with the loving and assured gestures of a creator; and always he was improving its perfection. His bedroom was his passion.

Often, during the wilderness of the day, he would think of his bedroom as of a refuge, to which in the evening he should hasten. Ascending the stairs after the meal, his heart would run on in advance of his legs, and be within the room before his hand had opened the door. And then he would close the door, as upon the whole tedious world, and turn up the gas, and light the stove with an explosive *plop*, and settle himself. And in the first few minutes of reading he would with distinct, conscious pleasure, allow his attention to circle the room, dwelling upon piled and serried volumes, and delighting in orderliness and in convenience. And he would reflect : 'This is my life. This is what I shall always live for. This is the best. And why not?' It seemed to him when he was alone in his bedroom and in the night, that he had respectably well solved the problem offered to him by destiny. He insisted to himself sharply that he was not made for marriage, that he had always known marriage to be impossible for him, that what had happened was bound to have happened. For a few weeks he had lived in a fool's paradise : that was all . . . Fantastic scheme, mad self-deception ! In such wise he thought of his love-affair. His profound satisfaction was that none except his father knew of it, and even his father did not know how far it had gone. He felt that if the town had been aware of his jilting, he could not have borne the humiliation. To himself he had been horribly humiliated; but he had recovered in his own esteem.

It was only by very slow processes, by insensible degrees, that he had arrived at the stage of being able to say to his mirror, 'I've got over that !' And who could judge better than he? He could trace no mark of the episode in his face. Save for the detail of a moustache, it seemed to him that he had looked on precisely the same unchangeable face for a dozen years. Strange, that suffering had left no sign ! Strange, that, in the months just after Hilda's marriage, no acquaintance had taken him on one side and said, 'What is the tragedy I can read on your features?'

And indeed the truth was that no one suspected. The vision of his face would remain with people long after he had passed them in the street, or spoken to them in the shop. The charm of his sadness persisted in their memory. But they would easily explain it to themselves by saying that his face had a naturally melancholy cast – a sort of accident that had happened to him in the beginning ! He had a considerable reputation, of which he was imperfectly aware, for secretiveness, timidity, gentleness, and intellectual superiority. Sundry young women thought of him wistfully when smiling upon quite other young men, and would even kiss him while kissing them, according to the notorious perversity of love.

III

He was reading Swift's *Tale of a Tub* eagerly, tasting with a palate consciously fastidious and yet catholic, the fine savour of a masterpiece. By his secret enthusiasm, which would escape from him at rare intervals in a word to a friend, he was continuing the reputation of the *Tale of a Tub* from one century towards the next. A classic remains a classic only because a few hundred Edwins up and down England enjoy it so heartily that their pleasure becomes religious. Edwin, according to his programme, had no right to be amusing himself with Swift at that hour. The portly Hallam, whom he found tedious, ought to have been in his hands. But Swift had caught him and would not let him go. Herein was one of the consequences of the pocketableness of Cassell's new series. Edwin had been obliged to agree with Tom Orgreave (now a married

251

man) that the books were not volumes for a collector; but they were so cheap, and they came from the press so often – once a week, and they could be carried so comfortably over the heart, that he could not resist most of them. His professed idea was that by their aid he could read smaller works in odd moments, at any time, thus surpassing his programme. He had not foreseen that Swift would make a breach in his programme, which was already in a bad way.

But he went on reading tranquilly, despite the damage to it; for in the immediate future shone the hope of the new life, when programmes would never be neglected. In less than a month he would be thirty years of age. At twenty, it had seemed a great age, an age of absolute maturity. Now, he felt as young and as boyish as ever, especially before his father, and he perceived that his vague early notion about the finality of such an age as thirty had been infantile. Nevertheless, the entry into another decade presented itself to him as solemn, and he meant to signalize it by new and mightier resolutions to execute vaster programmes. He was intermittently engaged, during these weeks, in the delicious, the enchanting business of constructing the ideal programme and scheming the spare hours to ensure its achievement. He lived in a dream and illusion of ultimate perfection.

Several times, despite the spell of Swift, he glanced at his watch. The hand went from nine to ten minutes past ten. And then he thought he heard the sound for which he had been listening. He jumped up, abandoned the book with its marker, opened the window wide, and lifting the blind by its rod, put his head out. Yes, he could hear the yelling afar off, over the hill, softened by distance into something gentle and attractive.

'*Signal! Signal!* Special edition! *Signal!*' And then words incomprehensible.

It came nearer in the night.

He drew down the window, and left the room. The mere distant sound of the newsboys' voices had roused him to a pleasing excitement. He fumbled in his pockets. He had neither a halfpenny nor a penny – it was just like him – and those newsboys with their valuable tidings would not care to halt and weigh out change with a balance.

'Got a halfpenny? Quick!' he cried, running into the kitchen, where Maggie and Mrs Nixon were engaged in some calm and endless domestic occupation amid linen that hung down whitely.

'What for?' Maggie mechanically asked, feeling the while under her apron.

'Paper,' he said.

'At this time of night? You'll never get one at this time of night!' she said, in her simplicity.

'Come *on* !'

He stamped his foot with impatience. It was absolutely astonishing, the ignorance in which Maggie lived, and lived efficiently and in content. Edwin filled the house with newspapers, and she never looked at them, never had the idea of looking at them, unless occasionally at the *Signal* for an account of a wedding or a bazaar. In which case she would glance at the world for an instant with mild *naïveté*, shocked, by the horrible things that were apparently going on there, and in five minutes would forget all about it again. Here the whole of England, Ireland, and Scotland was at its front doors that night waiting for newsboys, and to her the night was like any other night ! Yet she read many books.

'Here's a penny,' she said. 'Don't forget to give it me back.'

He ran out bareheaded. At the corner of the street somebody else was expectant. He could distinguish all the words now –

'*Signal!* Special edition ! Mester Gladstone's Home Rule Bill. Full report. Gladstone's speech. Special !'

The dark running figures approached, stopping at frequent gates, and their hoarse voices split the night. The next moment they had gone by, in a flying column, and Edwin and the other man found themselves with fluttering paper in their hands, they knew not how ! It was the most unceremonious snatch-and-thrust transaction that could be imagined. Bleakridge was silent again, and its gates closed, and the shouts were descending violently into Bursley.

'Where's father?' Maggie called out when she heard Edwin in the hall.

'Hasn't he come in yet?' Edwin replied negligently, as he mounted the stairs with his desire.

In his room he settled himself once more under the gas, and opened the flimsy newspaper with joy. Yes, there it was – columns, columns, in small type ! An hour or two previously Gladstone had been speaking in Parliament, and by magic the whole of his speech, with all the little convolutions of his intricate sentences, had got into Edwin's bedroom. Edwin began to read, as it were, voluptuously. Not that he had any peculiar interest in Irish politics ! What he had was a passion for great news, for news long expected. He could thrill responsively to a fine event. I say that his pleasure had the voluptuousness of an artistic sensation.

Moreover, the attraction of politics in general was increasing in him. Politics occupied his mind, often obsessing it. And this was so in spite of the fact that he had done almost nothing in the last election, and that the pillars of the Liberal Club were beginning to suspect him of being a weakling who might follow his father into the wilderness between two frontiers.

As he read the speech, slowly disengaging its significance from the thicket of words, it seemed incredible. A parliament in Dublin! The Irish taxing themselves according to their own caprices! The Irish controlling the Royal Irish Constabulary! The Irish members withdrawn from Westminster! A separate nation! Surely Gladstone could not mean it! The project had the same air of unreality as that of his marriage with Hilda. It did not convince. It was too good to be true. It could not materialize itself. And yet, as his glance, flitting from left to right and right to left, eagerly, reached the bottom of one column and jumped with a crinkling of paper to the top of the next, and then to the next after that, the sense of unreality did depart. He agreed with the principles of the Bill, and with all its details. Whatever Gladstone had proposed would have received his sympathy. He was persuaded in advance; he concurred in advance. All he lacked was faith. And those sentences, helped by his image of the aged legislator dominating the House, and by the wondrous legend of the orator's divine power – those long-stretching, majestic, misty sentences gave him faith. Henceforward he was an ardent Home Ruler. Reason might or might not have entered into the affair had the circumstances of it been other; but in fact reason did not. Faith alone sufficed. For ever afterwards argument about Home Rule was merely tedious to him, and he had difficulty in crediting that opponents of it were neither stupid nor insincere. Home Rule was part of his religion, beyond and above argument.

He wondered what they were saying at the Liberal Club, and smiled disdainfully at the thought of the unseemly language that would animate the luxurious heaviness of the Conservative Club, where prominent publicans gathered after eleven o'clock to uphold the State and arrange a few bets with sporting clients. He admitted, as the supreme importance of the night leaped out at him from the printed page, that, if only for form's sake, he ought to have been at the Liberal Club that evening. He had been requested to go, but had refused, because on Tuesdays, Thursdays, and Saturdays, he always spent the evening in study – or in the semblance of study. He would not break that rule even in honour of the culmination of the dazzling career of his political idol. Perhaps another proof of the justice of Maggie's assertion that he was a regular old maid!

He knew what his father would say. His father would be furious. His father in his uncontrolled fury would destroy Gladstone. And such was his father's empire over him that he was almost ready on Gladstone's behalf to adopt an apologetic and slightly shamed attitude to his father concerning this madness of Home Rule – to admit by his self-conscious blushes that it was madness. He well knew that at breakfast the next morning, in spite of any effort to the contrary, he would have a guilty air when his father began to storm. The conception of a separate parliament in Dublin, and of separate taxation, could not stand before his father's anger.

Beneath his window, in the garden, he suddenly heard a faint sound as of somebody in distress.

'What the deuce –!' he exclaimed. 'If that isn't the old man I'm –!' Startled, he looked at his watch. It was after midnight.

IV

As he opened the garden door, he saw, in the porch where had passed his first secret interview with Hilda, the figure of his father as it were awkwardly rising from the step. The gas had not been turned out in the hall, and it gave a feeble but sufficient illumination to the porch and the nearest parts of the garden. Darius stood silent and apparently irresolute, with a mournful and even despairing face. He wore his best black suit, and a new silk hat and new black gloves, and in one hand he carried a copy of the *Signal* that was very crumpled. He ignored Edwin.

'Hello, father!' said Edwin persuasively. 'Anything wrong?'

The heavy figure moved itself into the house without a word, and Edwin shut and bolted the door.

'Funeral go off all right?' Edwin inquired with as much nonchalance as he could. (The thought crossed his mind : 'I suppose he hasn't been having a drop too much, for once in a way? Why did he come round into the garden?')

Darius loosed a really terrible sigh. 'Yes,' he answered, expressing with a single word the most profound melancholy.

Four days previously Edwin and Maggie had seen their father considerably agitated by an item of gossip, casually received, to which it seemed to them he attached an excessive importance. Namely, that old Shushions, having been found straying and destitute by the authorities appointed to deal with such matters, had been taken to the workhouse and was dying there. Darius had heard the news as though it had been a message brought on horseback in a melodrama. 'The Bastille!' he exclaimed in a whisper, and had left the house on the instant. Edwin, while the name of Shushions reminded him of moments when he had most intensively lived, was disposed to regard the case of Mr Shushions philosophically. Of course it was a pity that Mr Shushions should be in the workhouse; but after all, from what Edwin remembered and could surmise, the workhouse would be very much the same as any other house to that senile mentality. Thus Edwin had sagely argued, and Maggie had agreed with him. But to them the workhouse was absolutely nothing but a name. They were no more afraid of the workhouse than of the Russian secret police; and of their father's early history they knew naught.

Mr Shushions had died in the workhouse, and Darius had taken his body out of the workhouse, and had organized for it a funeral which was to be rendered impressive by a procession of Turnhill Sunday-school teachers. Edwin's activity in connexion with the funeral had been limited to the funeral cards, in the preparation of which his father had shown an irritability more than usually offensive. And now the funeral was over. Darius had devoted to it the whole of Home Rule Tuesday, and had returned to his house at a singular hour and in a singular condition.

And Edwin, loathing sentimentality and full of the wisdom of nearly thirty years, sedately pitied his father for looking ridiculous and grotesque. He knew for a fact that his father did not see Mr Shushions from one year's end to the next : hence they could not have been intimate friends, or even friends : hence his father's emotion was throughout exaggerated and sentimental. His acquaintance with history and with biography told him that tyrants often carried sentimentality to the absurd, and he was rather pleased with himself for being able thus to correlate the general past and the particular present. What he did not suspect was the existence of circumstances which made the death of Mr Shushions in the workhouse the most distressing tragedy that could by any possibility have happened to Darius Clayhanger.

'Shall I put the gas out, or will you?' he asked, with kindly secret superiority, unaware, with all his omniscience, that the being in front of him was not a successful steam-printer and tyrannical father, but a tiny ragged boy who could still taste the Bastille skilly and still see his mother weeping round the knees of a powerful god named Shushions.'

'I – I don't know,' said Darius, with another sigh.

The next instant he sat down heavily on the stairs and began openly to blubber. His hat fell off and rolled about undecidedly.

'By jove !' said Edwin to himself, 'I shall have to treat this man like a blooming child !' He was rather startled, and interested. He picked up the hat.

'Better not sit there,' he advised. 'Come into the dining-room a bit.'

'What?' Darius asked feebly.

'Is he deaf?' Edwin thought, and half shouted : 'Better not sit there. It's chilly. Come into the dining-room a bit. Come on.'

Darius held out a hand, with a gesture inexpressibly sad; and Edwin, almost before he realized what he was doing, took it and assisted his father to his feet and helped him to the twilit dining-room, where Darius fell into a chair. Some bread and cheese had been laid for him on a napkin, and there was a gleam of red in the grate. Edwin turned up the gas, and Darius blinked. His coarse cheeks were all wet.

'Better have your overcoat off, hadn't you?'

Darius shook his head.

'Well, will you eat something?'

Darius shook his head again; then hid his face and violently sobbed.

Edwin was not equal to this situation. It alarmed him, and yet he did not see why it should alarm him. He left the room very quietly, went upstairs, and knocked at Maggie's door. He had to knock several times.

'Who's there?'

'I say, Mag!'

'What is it?'

'Open the door,' he said.

'You can come in.'

He opened the door, and within the darkness of the room he could vaguely distinguish a white bed.

'Father's come. He's in a funny state.'

'How?'

'Well, he's crying all over the place, and he won't eat, or do anything!'

'All right,' said Maggie – and a figure sat up in the bed. 'Perhaps I'd better come down.'

She descended immediately in an ulster and loose slippers. Edwin waited for her in the hall.

'Now, father,' she said brusquely, entering the dining-room, 'what's amiss?'

Darius gazed at her stupidly. 'Nothing,' he muttered.

'You're very late, I think. When did you have your last meal?'

He shook his head.

'Shall I make you some hot tea?'

He nodded.

'Very well,' she said comfortingly.

Soon, with her hair hanging about her face and hiding it, she was bending over the gleam of fire, and insinuating a small saucepan into the middle of it, and encouraging the gleam with a pair of bellows. Meanwhile Edwin uneasily ranged the room, and Darius sat motionless.

'Seen Gladstone's speech, I suppose?' Edwin said, daring a fearful topic in the extraordinary circumstances.

Darius paid no heed. Edwin and Maggie exchanged a glance. Maggie made the tea direct into a large cup, which she had previously warmed by putting it upside down on the saucepan lid. When it was infused and sweetened, she tasted it, as for a baby, and blew on it, and gave the cup to her father, who, by degrees, emptied it, though not exclusively into his mouth.

'Will you eat something now?' she suggested.

He would not.

'Very well, then, Edwin will help you upstairs.'

From her manner Darius might have been a helpless and half-daft invalid for years.

The ascent to bed was processional; Maggie hovered behind. But at the dining-room door Darius, giving no explanation, insisted on turning back : apparently he tried to speak but could not. He had forgotten his *Signal.* Snatching at it, he held it like a treasure. All three of them went into the father's bedroom. Maggie turned up the gas. Darius sat on the bed, looking dully at the carpet.

'Better see him into bed,' Maggie murmured quickly to Edwin, and Edwin nodded – the nod of capability – as who should say, 'Leave all that to me!' But in fact he was exceedingly diffident about seeing his father into bed.

Maggie departed.

'Now then,' Edwin began the business. 'Let's get that overcoat off, eh?' To his surprise Darius was most pliant. When the great clumsy figure, with its wet cheeks, stood in trousers, shirt, and socks, Edwin said, 'You're all right now, aren't you?' And the figure nodded.

'Well, good night.'

Edwin came out on to the landing, shut the door, and walked about a little in his own room. Then he went back to his father's room. Maggie's door was closed. Darius was already in bed, but the gas was blazing at full.

'You've forgotten the gas,' he said lightly and pleasantly, and turned it down to a blue point.

'I say, lad,' the old man stopped him, as he was finally leaving.

'Yes?'

'What about that Home Rule?'

The voice was weak, infantile. Edwin hesitated. The *Signal* made a patch of white on the ottoman.

'Oh!' he answered soothingly, and yet with condescension, 'it's much about what everybody expected. Better leave that till tomorrow.'

He shut the door. The landing received light through the open door of his bedroom and from the hall below. He went downstairs, bolted the front door, and extinguished the hall gas. Then he came softly up, and listened at his father's door. Not a sound! He entered his own room and began to undress, and then, half-clothed, crept back to his father's door. Now he could hear a heavy, irregular snoring.

'Devilish odd, all this!' he reflected, as he got into bed. Assuredly he had disconcerting thoughts, not all unpleasant. His excitement had even an agreeable, zestful quality.

CHAPTER 2 : *The Conclave*

I

The next morning Edwin overslept himself. He seldom rose easily from his bed, and his first passage down Trafalgar Road to business was notoriously hurried; the whole thoroughfare was acquainted with its special character. Often his father arrived at the shop before him, but Edwin's conscience would say that of course if Darius went down early for his own passion and pleasure, that was Darius's affair. Edwin's official time for beginning work was half-past eight. And at half-past eight, on this morning, he was barely out of the bath. His lateness, however, did not disturb him; there was an excuse for it. He hoped that his father would be in bed, and decided that he must go and see, and, if the old man was still sufficiently pliant, advise him to stay where he was until he had had some food.

But, looking out of the window over a half-buttoned collar, he saw his father dressed and in the garden. Darius had resumed the suit of broadcloth, for some strange reason, and was dragging his feet with painful, heavy slowness along the gravel at the south end of the garden. He carried in his left hand the *Signal*, crumpled. A cloth cap, surmounting the ceremonious suit, gave to his head a ridiculous appearance. He was gazing at the earth with an expression of absorbed and acute melancholy. When he reached the end of the path, he looked round, at a loss, then turned, as if on an inefficient pivot, and set himself in motion again. Edwin was troubled by this singular episode. And yet his reason argued with his instinct to the effect that he ought not to be troubled. Evidently the sturdy Darius was not ill. Nothing serious could be the matter. He had been harrowed and fatigued by the funeral; no more. In another day, doubtless, he would be again the harsh employer astoundingly concentrated in affairs and impervious to the emotional appeal of aught else. Nevertheless he made a strange sight, parading his excessive sadness there in the garden.

A knock at Edwin's door! He was startled. 'Hold on!' he cried, went to the door, and cautiously opened it. Maggie was on the mat.

'Here's Auntie Clara!' she said in a whisper, perturbed. 'She's come about father. Shall you be long?'

'About father? What about father?'

'It seems she saw him last night. He called there. And she was anxious.'

'Oh! I see!' Edwin affected to be relieved. Maggie nodded, also affecting, somewhat eagerly, to be relieved. But neither of them was relieved. Auntie Clara calling at half past eight! Auntie Clara neglecting that which she never neglected – the unalterable and divinely appointed rites for the daily cleansing and ordering of her abode!

'I shall be down in ten secs,' said he. 'Father's in the garden,' he added, almost kindly. 'Seems all right.'

'Yes,' said Maggie, with cheerfulness, and went. He closed the door.

II

Mrs Hamps was in the drawing-room. She had gone into the drawing-room because it was more secret, better suited to conversation of an exquisite privacy than the dining-room – a public resort at that hour. Edwin perceived at once that she was savouring intensely the strangeness of the occasion, inflating its import and its importance to the largest possible.

'Good morning, dear,' she greeted him in a low and significant tone. 'I felt I must come up at once. I couldn't fancy any breakfast till I'd been up, so I put on my bonnet and mantle and just came. It's no use fighting against what you feel you must do.'

'But –'

'Hasn't Maggie told you? Your father called to see me last night just after I'd gone upstairs. In fact I'd begun to get ready for bed. I heard the knocking and I came down and lit the gas in the lobby. "Who's there?" I said. There wasn't any answer, but I made sure I heard someone crying. And when I opened the door, there was your father. "Oh!" he said. "Happen you've gone to bed, Clara?" "No," I said. "Come in do!" But he wouldn't. And he looked so queer. I never saw him look like that before. He's such a strong self-controlled man. I knew he'd been to poor Mr Shushions's funeral. "I suppose you've been to the funeral, Darius," I said. And as soon as I said that he burst out crying, and half tumbled down the steps, and off he went! I couldn't go after him, as I was. I didn't know *what* to do. If anything happened to your father, I don't know *what* I should do.'

'What time was that?' Edwin asked, wondering what on earth she meant – 'if anything happened to your father!'

'Half past ten or hardly. What time did he come home? Very, very late, wasn't it?'

'A little after twelve,' he said carelessly. He was sorry that he had inquired as to the hour of the visit of his aunt. Obviously she was ready to build vast and terrible conjectures upon the mysterious interval between half-past ten and midnight.

'You've cut yourself, my dear,' she said, indicating with her gloved hand Edwin's chin. 'And I'm not surprised. How upsetting it is for you! Of course Maggie's the eldest, and we think a great deal of her, but you're the son – the only son!'

'I know,' he said, meaning that he knew he had cut himself, and he pressed his handkerchief to his chin. Within, he was blasphemously fuming. The sentimental accent with which she had finally murmured 'the only son' irritated him extremely. What in the name of God was she driving at? The fact was that, enjoying a domestic crisis with positive sensuality, she was trying to manufacture one! That was it! He knew her. There were times when he could share all Maggie's hatred of Mrs Hamps, and this was one of those times. The infernal woman, with her shaking plumes and her odour of black kid, was enjoying herself! In the thousandth part of a second he invented horrible and grotesque punishments for her, as that all the clothes should suddenly fall off that prim, widowed, odious modesty. Yet, amid the multitude of his sensations – the smarting of his chin, the tingling of all his body after the bath, the fresh vivacity of the morning, the increased consciousness of his own ego, due to insufficient sleep, the queerness of being in the drawing-room at such an hour in conspiratorial talk, the vague disquiet caused at midnight, and now intensified despite his angry efforts to avoid the contagion of Mrs Hamp's mood, and above all the thought of his father gloomily wandering in the garden – amid these confusing sensations, it was precisely an idea communicated to him by his annoying aunt, an obvious idea, an idea not worth uttering, that emerged clear and dramatic : he was the only son.

'There's no need to worry,' he said as firmly as he could. 'The funeral got on his nerves, that's all. He certainly did seem a bit knocked about last night, and I shouldn't have been surprised if he'd stayed in bed today. But you see he's up and about.' Both of them glanced at the window, which gave on the garden.

'Yes,' murmured Mrs Hamps, unconvinced. 'But what about his crying? Maggie tells me he was –'

'Oh!' Edwin interrupted her almost roughly. 'That's nothing. I've known him cry before.'

'Have you?' She seemed taken aback.

'Yes. Years ago. That's nothing fresh.'

'It's true he's very sensitive,' Mrs Hamps reflected. 'That's what we don't realize, maybe, sometimes. Of course if you think he's all right –'

She approached the window, and, leaning over the tripod which held a flower-pot enveloped in pink paper, she drew the white curtain aside, and gazed forth in silence. Darius was still pacing up and down the short path at the extremity of the garden; his eyes were still on the ground, and his features expressive of mournful despair, and at the end of the path he still turned his body round with slow and tedious hesitations. Edwin also could see him through the window. They both watched him; it was as if they were spying on him.

Maggie entered, and said, in an unusual flutter –

'Here's Clara and Albert!'

III

Clara and her husband came immediately into the drawing-room. The wife, dressed with a certain haste and carelessness, was carrying in her arms her third child, yet unweaned, and she expected a fourth in the early autumn. Clara had matured, she had grown stronger; and despite the asperity of her pretty pale face there was a charm in the free gestures and the large body of the young and prolific mother. Albert Benbow wore the rough, clay-dusted attire of the small earthenware manufacturer who is away from the works for half an hour. Both of them were electrically charged with importance.

Amid the general self-consciousness Maggie took the baby, and Clara and Mrs Hamps kissed each other tenderly, as though saying,'Affliction is upon us'. It was impossible, in the circumstances, to proceed to minute inquiry about the health of the children, but Mrs Hamps expressed all her solicitude in a look, a tone, a lingering of lip on lip. The years were drawing together Mrs Hamps and her namesake. Edwin was often astonished at the increasing resemblance of Clara to her aunt, with whom, thanks to the unconscious intermediacy of babies, she was even indeed quite intimate. The two would discuss with indefatigable gusto all the most minute physical details of motherhood and infancy : and Auntie's Clara's presents were worthy of her reputation.

As soon as the kiss was accomplished – no other greeting of any kind occurred – Clara turned sharply to Edwin –

'What's this about father?'

'Oh! He's had a bit of a shock. He's pretty much all right today.'

'Because Albert's just heard –' She looked at Albert.

Edwin was thunderstruck. Was the tale of his father's indisposition spread all over the Five Towns? He had thought that the arrival of Clara and her husband must be due to Auntie Hamps having called at their house on her way up to Bleakridge. But now he could see, even from his auntie's affrighted demeanour alone, that the Benbows' visit was an independent affair.

'Are you sure he's all right?' Albert questioned, in his superiorly

262

sagacious manner, which mingled honest bullying with a little good-nature.

'Because Albert just heard –' Clara put in again.

The company then heard what Albert had just heard. At his works before breakfast an old hollowware-presser, who lived at Turnhill, had casually mentioned that his father-in-law, Mr Clayhanger, had been cutting a very peculiar figure on the previous evening at Turnhill. The hollowware-presser had seen nothing personally; he had only been told. He could not or would not particularize. Apparently he possessed in a high degree the local talent for rousing an apprehension by the offer of food, and then under ingenious pretexts refusing the food. At any rate, Albert had been startled, and had communicated his alarm to Clara. Clara had meant to come up a little later in the morning, but she wanted Albert to come with her, and Albert, being exceedingly busy, had only the breakfast half-hour of liberty. Hence they had set out instantly, although the baby required sustenance; Albert having suggested that Clara could feed the baby just as well at her father's as at home.

Before the Benbow story was quite finished it became entangled with the story of Mrs Hamps, and then with Edwin's story. They were all speaking at once, except Maggie, who was trying to soothe the baby.

Holding forth her arms, Clara, without ceasing to talk rapidly and anxiously to Mrs Hamps, without even regarding what she did, took the infant from her sister, held it with one hand, and with the other loosed her tight bodice, and boldly exposed to the greedy mouth the magnificent source of life. As the infant gurgled itself into silence, she glanced with a fleeting ecstatic smile at Maggie, who smiled back. It was strange how Maggie, now midway between thirty and forty, a tall, large-boned, plump, mature woman, efficient, kindly, and full of common sense – it was strange how she always failed to assert herself. She listened now, not seeking notice and assuredly not receiving it.

Edwin felt again the implication, first rendered by his aunt, and now emphasized by Clara and Albert, that the responsibility of the situation was upon him, and that everybody would look to him to discharge it. He was expected to act, somehow, on his own initiative, and to do something.

'But what is there to do?' he exclaimed, in answer to a question.

'Well, hadn't he better see a doctor?' Clara asked, as if saying ironically, 'Hasn't it occurred to you even yet that a doctor ought to be fetched?'

Edwin protested with a movement of impatience –

'What on earth for? He's walking about all right.'

They had all been surreptitiously watching Darius from behind the curtains.

'Doesn't seem to be much the matter with him now! That I must say!' agreed Albert, turning from the window.

Edwin perceived that his brother-in-law was ready to execute one of those changes of front which lent variety to his positiveness, and he addressed himself particularly to Albert, with the persuasive tones and gesture of a man to another man in a company of women –

'Of course there doesn't! No doubt he was upset last night. But he's getting over it. *You* don't think there's anything in it, do you, Maggie?'

'I don't,' said Maggie calmly.

These two words had a great effect.

'Of course if we're going to listen to every tale that's flying about a potbank –' said Edwin.

'You're right there, Teddy!' the brother-in-law heartily concurred. 'But Clara thought we'd better –'

'Certainly,' said Edwin pacifically, admitting the entire propriety of the visit.

'Why's he wearing his best clothes?' Clara demanded suddenly. And Mrs Hamps showed a sympathetic appreciation of the importance of the question.

'Ask me another!' said Edwin. 'But you can't send for a doctor because a man's wearing his best clothes.'

Maggie smiled, scarce perceptibly. Albert gave a guffaw. Clara was slight irritated.

'Poor little dear!' murmured Mrs Hamps, caressing the baby. 'Well, I must be going,' she sighed.

'We shall see how he goes on,' said Edwin, in his rôle of responsible person.

'Perhaps it will be as well if you say nothing about us calling,' whispered Mrs Hamps. 'We'll just go quietly away. You can give a hint to Mrs Nixon. Much better he shouldn't know.'

'Oh! much better!' said Clara.

Edwin could not deny this. Yet he hated the chicane. He hated to observe on the face of the young woman and of the old their instinctive impulses towards chicane, their pleasure in it. The whole double visit was subtly offensive to him. Why should they gather like this at the first hint that his father was not well? A natural affectionate anxiety . . . Yes, of course, that motive could not be denied. Nevertheless, he did not like the tones and the gestures and the whisperings and oblique glances of their gathering.

IV

In the middle of a final miscellaneous conversation, Albert said –

'We'd better be off.'

'Wait a moment,' said Clara, with a nod to indicate the still busy infant.

Then the door opened, very slowly and cautiously, and as they all observed the movement of the door, they all fell into silence. Darius himself appeared. Unobserved, he had left the garden and come into the house. He stood in the doorway, motionless, astounded, acutely apprehensive, and with an expression of the most poignant sadness on his harsh, coarse, pimpled face. He still wore the ridiculous cap and held the newspaper. The broadcloth suit was soiled. His eye wandered among his family, and it said, terrorized, and yet feebly defiant, 'What are they plotting against me? Why are they all here like this?'

Mrs Hamps spoke first –

'Well, father, we just popped into see how you were after all that dreadful business yesterday. Of course I quite understand you didn't want to come in last night. You weren't equal to it.' The guilty crude sweetness of her cajoling voice grated excruciatingly on both Edwin and Maggie. It would not have deceived even a monarch.

Darius screwed himself round, and silently went forth again.

'Where are you going, father?' asked Clara.

He stopped, but his features did not relax.

'To the shop,' he muttered. His accents were of the most dreadful melancholy.

Everybody was profoundly alarmed by his mere tone and look. This was not the old Darius. Edwin felt intensely the futility and the hollowness of all those reassurances which he had just been offering.

'You haven't had your breakfast, father,' said Maggie quietly.

'Please, father! Please don't go like that. You aren't fit,' Clara entreated, and rushed towards him, the baby in her arms, and with one hand took his sleeve. Mrs Hamps followed, adding persuasions. Albert said bluffly, 'Now, dad? Now, dad!'

Edwin and Maggie were silent in the background.

Darius gazed at Clara's face, and then his glance fell, and fixed itself on her breast and on the head of the powerfully sucking infant, and then it rose to the plumes of Mrs Hamps. His expression of tragic sorrow did not alter in the slightest degree under the rain of sugared remonstrances and cajoleries that the two women directed upon him. And then, without any warning, he burst into terrible tears, and staggering, leaned against the wall. He was half carried to the sofa, and sat there, ineffably humiliated. One after another looked reproachfully at Edwin, who had made light of his father's condition. And Edwin was abashed and frightened.

'You or I had better fetch th' doctor,' Albert muttered.

CHAPTER 3 : *The Name*

I

'He mustn't go near business,' said Mr Alfred Heve, the doctor, coming to Edwin, who was waiting in the drawing-room, after a long examination of Darius.

Mr Heve was not wearing that gentle and refined smile which was so important a factor in the treatment of his patients and their families, and which he seemed to have caught from his elder brother, the vicar of St Peter's. He was a youngish man, only a few years older than Edwin himself, and Edwin's respect for his ability had limits. There were two other doctors in the town whom Edwin would have preferred, but Mr Heve was his father's choice, notable in the successful soothing of querulous stomachs, and it was inevitably Mr Heve who had been summoned. He had arrived with an apprehensive, anxious air. There had been a most distinct nervousness in his voice when, in replying to Edwin's question, he had said, 'Perhaps I'd better see him quite alone.' Edwin had somehow got it into his head that he would be present at the interview. In shutting the dining-room door upon Edwin, Mr Heve had nodded timidly in a curious way, highly self-conscious. And that dining-room door had remained shut for half an hour. And now Mr Heve had emerged with the same embarrassment.

'Whether he wants to or not?' Edwin suggested, with a faint smile.

'On no account whatever!' said the doctor, not answering the smile, which died.

They were standing together near the door. Edwin had his fingers on the handle. He wondered how he would prevent his father from going to business, if his father should decide to go.

'But I don't think he'll be very keen on business,' the doctor added.

'You don't?'

Mr Heve slowly shook his head. One of Mr Heve's qualities that slightly annoyed Edwin was his extraordinary discretion. But then Edwin had always regarded the discreetness of doctors as exaggerated. Why could not Heve tell him at once fully and candidly what was in his mind? He had surely the right to be told! . . . Curious! And yet far more curious than Mr Heve's unwillingness to tell, was Edwin's unwillingness to ask. He could not bring himself to demand bluntly of Heve : 'Well, what's the matter with him?'

'I suppose it's shock,' Edwin adventured.

266

Mr Heve lifted his chin. 'Shock may have had a little to do with it,' he answered doubtfully.

'And how long must he be kept off business?'

'I'm afraid there's not much chance of him doing any more business,' said Mr Heve.

'Really!' Edwin murmured. 'Are you sure?'

'Quite.'

Edwin did not feel the full impact of this prophecy at the moment. Indeed, it appeared to him that he had known since the previous midnight of his father's sudden doom; it appeared to him that the first glimpse of his father after the funeral had informed him of it positively. What impressed him at the moment was the unusual dignity which characterized Mr Heve's embarrassment. He was beginning to respect Mr Heve.

'I wouldn't care to give him more than two years,' said Mr Heve, gazing at the carpet, and then lifting his eyes to Edwin's.

Edwin flushed. And this time his 'Really!' was startled.

'Of course you may care to get other advice,' the doctor went on. 'I shall be delighted to meet a specialist. But I tell you at once my opinion.' This was a gesture of candour.

'Oh!' said Edwin. 'If you're sure –'

Strange that the doctor would not give a name to the disease! Most strange that Edwin even now could not demand the name.

'I suppose he's in his right *mind*?' said Edwin.

'Yes,' said the doctor. 'He's in his right *mind*.' But he gave the reply in a tone so peculiar that the affirmative was almost as disconcerting as a negative would have been.

'Just rest he wants?' said Edwin.

'Just rest. And looking after. I'll send up some medicine. He'll like it.' Mr Heve glanced absently at his watch. 'I must be going.'

'Well –' Edwin opened the door.

Then with a sudden movement Mr Heve put out his hand.

'You'll come again, soon?'

'Oh yes.'

In the hall they saw Maggie about to enter the dining-room with a steaming basin.

'I'm going to give him this,' she said simply in a low voice. 'It's so long to dinner-time.'

'By all means,' said Mr Heve, with his little formal bow. 'You've finished seeing him then, doctor?' He nodded.

'I'll be back soon,' said Edwin to Maggie, taking his hat from the rack. 'Tell father if he asks I've run down to the shop.'

She nodded and disappeared.

'I'll walk down a bit of the way with you,' said Mr Heve.

His trap, which was waiting at the corner, followed them down the road. Edwin could not begin to talk. And Mr Heve kept silence. Behind him, Edwin could hear the jingling of metal on Mr Heve's sprightly horse. After a couple of hundred yards the doctor stopped at a house-door.

'Well –' He shook hands again, and at last smiled with sad sweetness.

'He'll be a bit difficult to manage, you know,' said Edwin.

'I don't think so,' said the doctor.

'I'll let you know about the specialist. But if you're sure –'

The doctor waved a deprecating hand. It might have been the hand of his brother, the Vicar.

II

Edwin proceeded towards the town, absorbed in a vision of his father seated in the dining-room, inexpressibly melancholy, and Maggie with her white apron bending over him to offer some nice soup. It was a desolating vision – and yet he wondered why it should be! Whenever he reasoned he was always inimical to his father. His reason asked harshly why he should be desolated, as he undoubtedly was. The prospect of freedom, of release from a horrible and humiliating servitude – this prospect ought to have dazzled and uplifted him, in the safe, inviolable privacy of his own heart. But it did not . . . What a chump the doctor was, to be so uncommunicative! And he himself! . . . By the way, he had not told Maggie. It was like her to manifest no immediate curiosity, to be content to wait . . . He supposed he must call at his aunt's, and even at Clara's. But what should he say when they asked him why he had not asked the doctor for a name?

Suddenly an approaching man whose face was vaguely familiar but with whom he had no acquaintance whatever, swerved across the foot-path and stopped him.

'What's amiss with th' old gentleman?'

It was astounding how news flew in the town!

'He's not very well. Doctor's ordered him a rest.'

'Not in bed, is he?'

'Oh no!' Edwin lightly scorned the suggestion.

'Well, I hope it's nothing serious. Good morning.'

III

Edwin was detained a long time in the shop by a sub-manager from Bostocks in Hanbridge who was waiting, and who had come about an estimate for a rather considerable order. This man desired a decrease of the estimate and an increased speed in execution. He was curt. He was one business firm offering an ultimatum to another business firm. He asked Edwin whether Edwin could decide at once. Edwin said 'Certainly', using a tone that he had never used before. He decided. The man departed, and Edwin saw him spring on to the Hanbridge car as it swept down the hill. The man would not have been interested in the news that Darius Clayhanger had been to business for the last time. Edwin was glad of the incident because it had preserved him from embarrassed conversation with Stifford. Two hours earlier he had called for a few moments at the shop, and even then, ere Edwin had spoken, Stifford's face showed that he knew something sinister had occurred. With a few words of instruction to Stifford, he now went through towards the workshops to speak with Big James about the Bostock order.

All the workmen and apprentices were self-conscious. And Edwin could not speak naturally to Big James. When he had come to an agreement with Big James as to the execution of the order, the latter said –

'Would you step down a minute, Mr Edwin?'

Edwin shuffled. But Big James's majestic politeness gave to his expressed wish the force of a command. Edwin preceded Big James down the rough wooden stairs to the ground floor, which was still pillared with supporting beams. Big James, with deliberate, careful movements, drew the trap-door horizontal as he descended.

'Might I ask, sir, if Master's in a bad way?' he inquired, with solemn and delicate calm. But he would have inquired about the weather in the same fashion.

'I'm afraid he is,' said Edwin, glancing nervously about at the litter, and the cobwebs, and the naked wood, and the naked earth. The vibration of a treadle-machine above them put the place in a throb.

Astounding! Everybody knew or guessed everything! How?

Big James wagged his head and his grandiose beard, now more grey than black, and he fingered his apron.

'I believe in herbs myself,' said Big James. 'But this here softening of the brain – well –'

That was it! Softening of the brain! What the doctor had not told him he had learned from Big James. How it happened that Big James was in a position to tell him he could not comprehend. But he was ready now to believe that the whole town had acquired by magic the information which fate or original stupidity had kept from him alone . . . Softening of the brain!

'Perhaps I'm making too bold, sir,' Big James went on. 'Perhaps it's not so bad as that. But I did hear –'

Edwin nodded confirmingly.

269

'You needn't talk about it,' he murmured, indicating the first floor by an upward movement of the head.

'That I shall not, sir,' Big James smoothly replied, and proceeded in the same bland tone : 'And what's more, never will I raise my voice in song again ! James Yarlett has sung his last song.'

There was silence. Edwin, accustomed though he was to the mildness of Big James's deportment, did not on the instant grasp that the man was seriously anouncing a solemn resolve made under deep emotion. But as he understood, tears came into Edwin's eyes and he thrilled at the swift and dramatic revelation of the compositor's feeling for his employer. Its impressiveness was overwhelming and it was humbling. Why this excess of devotion?

'I don't say but what he had his faults like other folk,' said Big James. 'And far be it from me to say that you, Mr Edwin, will not be a better master than your esteemed father. But for over twenty years I've worked for him, and now he's gone, never will I lift my voice in song again !'

Edwin could not reply.

'I know what it is,' said Big James, after a pause.

'What is it?'

'This ce-re-bral softening. You'll have trouble, Mr Edwin.'

'The doctor says not.'

'You'll have trouble, if you'll excuse me saying so. But it's a good thing he's got you. It's a good thing for Miss Maggie as she isn't alone with him. It's a providence, Mr Edwin, as you're not a married man.'

'I very nearly *was* married once !' Edwin cried, with a sudden uncontrollable outburst of feeling which staggered while it satisfied him. Why should he make such a confidence to Big James? Between his pleasure in the relief, and his extreme astonishment at the confession, he felt as it were lost and desperate, as if he did not care what might occur.

'Were you now !' Big James commented, with an ever intensified blandness. 'Well, sir, I thank you.'

CHAPTER 4 : *The Victim of Sympathy*

I

On the same evening, Edwin, Albert Benbow, and Darius were smoking Albert's cigarettes in the dining-room. Edwin sat at the end of a disordered supper-table, Albert was standing, hat in hand, near the sideboard, and Darius leaned against the mantelpiece. Nobody could have supposed from his appearance that a doctor had responsibly prophesied this man's death within two years. Except for a shade of sadness upon his face, he looked the same as he had looked for a decade. Though regarded by his children as an old man, he was not old, being in fact still under sixty. His grey hair was sparse; his spectacles were set upon his nose with the negligence characteristic of age; but the downpointing moustache, which, abetted by his regular teeth, gave him that curious facial resemblance to a seal, showed great force, and the whole of his stiff and sturdy frame showed force. His voice, if not his mouth, had largely recovered from the weakness of the morning. Moreover, the fashion in which he smoked a cigarette had somehow the effect of rejuvenating him. It was Albert who had induced him to smoke cigarettes occasionally. He was not an habitual smoker, consuming perhaps half an ounce a week of pipe-tobacco : and assuredly he would never of his own accord have tried a cigarette. For Darius cigarettes were aristocratic and finicking; they were an affectation. He smoked a cigarette with the self-consciousness which usually marks the consumption of champagne in certain strata of society. His gestures, as he examined from time to time the end of the cigarette, or audibly blew forth spreading clouds, seemed to signify that in his opinion he was going the pace, cutting a dash, and seeing life. This *naïveté* had its charm.

The three men, left alone by their women, were discussing politics, which meant nothing but the subject of Home Rule. Darius agreed almost eagerly with everything that Albert Benbow said. Albert was a calm and utterly sound Conservative. He was one of those politicians whose conviction of rightness is so strong that they cannot help condescending towards an opponent. Albert would say persuasively to Liberal acquaintances : 'Now just *think* a moment !' apparently sure that the only explanation of their misguided views was that they never had thought for a moment. Or he would say : 'Surely all patriotic Liberals —' But one day when Edwin had said to him with a peculiar accent : 'Surely all patriotic Conservatives —' he had been politely offended for the rest of the evening, and Edwin and he had not mentioned politics to each other for a long time. Albert had had much influence over his father-in-law. And now Albert said, after Darius had concurred and concurred –

'You're one of the right sort, after all, old gentleman.'

Throughout the evening he had spoken to Darius in an unusually loud voice, as though it was necessary to shout to a man who had only two years to live.

'All I say is,' said Darius, 'country before party!'

'Why, of course!' Albert smiled, confident and superior. 'Haven't I been telling you for years you're one of us?'

Edwin, too, smiled, as superiorly as he could, but unhappily not with sufficient superiority to wither Albert's smile. He said nothing, partly from timid discretion, but partly because he was preoccupied with the thought of the malignant and subtle power working secretly in his father's brain. How could the doctor tell? What was the process of softening? Did his father know, in that sick brain of his, that he was condemned; or did he hope to recover? Now, as he leaned against the mantelpiece, protruding his body in an easy posture, he might have been any ordinary man, and not a victim; he might have been a man of business relaxing after a long day of hard and successful cerebral activity.

It seemed strange to Edwin that Albert could talk as he did to one whom destiny had set apart, to one whose being was the theatre of a drama so mysterious and tragic. Yet it was the proper thing for Albert to do, and Albert did it perfectly, better than anybody, except possibly Maggie.

'Those women take a deuce of a time putting their bonnets on!' Albert exclaimed.

II

The women came downstairs at last. At last, to Edwin's intense relief, everyone was going. Albert went into the hall to meet the women. Edwin rose and followed him. And Darius came as far as the door of the dining-room. Less than twenty-four hours had passed since Edwin had begun even to suspect any sort of disaster to his father. But the previous night seemed an age away. The day had been interminable, and the evening exasperating in the highest degree. What an evening! Why had Albert and Clara and Auntie Hamps all of them come up just at supper-time? At first they would not be persuaded! No! They had just called – sheer accident! – nothing abnormal! And yet the whole of the demeanour of Auntie Hamps and Clara was abnormal. Maggie herself, catching the infection, had transformed the meal into a kind of abnormal horrible feast by serving cold beef and pickles – flesh-meat being unknown to the suppers of the Clayhangers save occasionally on Sundays.

Edwin could not comprehend why the visitors had come. That is to say, he understood the reason quite well, but hated to admit it. They had come from a mere gluttony of curiosity. They knew all that could be known – but still they must come and gaze and indulge their lamentable hearts, and repeat the same things again and again, ten million times! Auntie Hamps, indeed, probably knew more than Edwin did, for she had thought fit to summon Dr Heve that very afternoon for an ailment of her own, and Clara, with an infant or so, had by a remarkable coincidence called at Mrs Hamps's house just after the doctor left. 'Odious,' thought Edwin.

These two had openly treated Darius as a martyr, speaking to him in soft and pitiful voices, urging him to eat, urging him to drink, caressing him, soothing him, humouring him; pretending to be brave and cheerful and optimistic, but with a pretence so poor, so wilfully poor, that it became an insult. When they said fulsomely, 'You'll be perfectly all right soon if only you'll take care and do as the doctor says,' Edwin could have risen and killed them both with hearty pleasure. They might just as well have said, 'You're practically in your grave'. And assuredly they were not without influence on Maggie's deportment. The curious thing was that it was impossible to decide whether Darius loathed, or whether he liked, to be so treated. His face was an enigma. However, he was less gloomy.

Then also the evening had necessarily been full of secret conferences. What would you? Each had to relate privately the things that he or she knew or had heard or had imagined. And there were questions of urgency to be discussed. For example the question of the specialist. They were all positively agreed, Edwin found, that a specialist was unnecessary. Darius was condemned beyond hope or argument. There he sat, eating and talking, in the large, fine house that he had created out of naught, looking not at all like a corpse; but he was condemned. The doctor had convinced them. Besides, did not everybody know what softening of the brain was? 'Of course, if he thinks he would prefer to have a specialist, if he has the slightest wish –' This from Auntie Hamps. There was the question, further, of domestic service. Mrs Nixon's niece had committed the folly of marriage, and for many months Maggie and the old servant had been 'managing'; but with a crochety invalid always in the house, more help would be indispensable. And still further – should Darius be taken away for a period to the sea, or Buxton, or somewhere? Maggie said that nothing would make him go, and Clara agreed with her. All these matters, and others, had to be kept away from the central figure; they were all full of passionate interest, and they had to be debated, in tones hushed but excited, in the hall, in the kitchen, upstairs, or anywhere except in the dining-room. The excuses invented by the conspiring women for quitting and entering the dining-room, their fatuous air of innocent simplicity, disgusted Edwin. And he became curter and curter, as he noticed the new deference which even Clara practised towards him.

III

The adieux were distressing. Clara, with her pale sharp face and troubled eyes, clasped Darius round the neck, and almost hung on it. And Edwin thought : 'Why doesn't she tell him straight out he's done for?' Then she retired and sought her husband's arm with the conscious pride of a wife fruitful up to the limits set by nature. And then Auntie Hamps shook hands with the victim. These two of course did not kiss. Auntie Hamps bore herself bravely. 'Now *do* do as the doctor advises !' she said, patting Darius on the shoulder. 'And *do* be guided by these dear children !'

Edwin caught Maggie's eye, and held it grimly.

'And you, my pet,' said Auntie Hamps, turning to Clara, who with Albert was now at the door. 'You must be getting back to your babies ! It's a wonder how you manage to get away ! But you're a wonderful arranger ! ... Only don't overdo it. Don't overdo it !'

Clara gave a fatigued smile, as of one whom circumstances often forced to overdo it.

They departed, Albert whistling to the night. Edwin observed again, in their final glances, the queer, new, ingratiating deference for himself. He bolted the door savagely.

Darius was still standing at the entrance to the dining-room. And as he looked at him Edwin thought of Big James's vow never to lift his voice in song again. Strange ! It was the idea of the secret strangeness of life that was uppermost in his mind : not grief, not expectancy. In the afternoon he had been talking again to Big James, who, it appeared, had known intimately a case of softening of the brain. He did not identify the case – it was characteristic of him to name no names – but clearly he was familiar with the course of the disease.

He had begun revelations which disconcerted Edwin, and had then stopped. And now as Edwin furtively examined his father, he asked himself : 'Will *that* happen to him, and *that*, and those still worse things that Big James did not reveal?' Incredible ! There he was, smoking a cigarette, and the clock striking ten in its daily, matter-of-fact way.

Darius let fall the cigarette, which Edwin picked up from the mat, and offered to him.

'Throw it away,' said Darius, with a deep sigh.

274

'Going to bed?' Edwin asked.

Darius shook his head, and Edwin debated what he should do. A moment later, Maggie came from the kitchen and asked –

'Going to bed, father?'

Again Darius shook his head. He then went slowly into the drawing-room and lit the gas there.

'What shall you do? Leave him?' Maggie whispered to Edwin in the dining-room, as she helped Mrs Nixon to clear the table.

'I don't know,' said Edwin. 'I shall see.'

In ten minutes both Maggie and Mrs Nixon had gone to bed. Edwin hesitated in the dining-room. Then he extinguished the gas there, and went into the drawing-room. Darius not having lowered the blinds, was gazing out of the black window.

'You needn't wait down here for me,' said he, a little sharply. And his tone was so sane, controlled, firm, and ordinary that Edwin could do nothing but submit to it.

'I'm not going to,' he answered quietly.

Impossible to treat a man of such demeanour like a child.

CHAPTER 5 : *The Slave's Fear*

I

Edwin closed the door of his bedroom with a sense of relief and of pleasure far greater than he would have admitted; or indeed could honestly have admitted, for it surpassed his consciousness. The feeling recurred that he was separated from the previous evening by a tremendous expanse of time. He had been flung out of his daily habits. He had forgotten to worry over the execution of his private programmes. He had forgotten even that the solemn thirtieth birthday was close upon him. It seemed to him as if his own egoism was lying about in scattered pieces, which he must collect in the calm of his cloister, and reconstruct. He wanted to resume possession of himself, very slowly, without violent effort. He wound up his watch; the hour was not yet half-past ten. The whole exquisite night was his.

He had brought with him, from the shop, almost mechanically, a copy of *Harper's Magazine*, not the copy which regularly once a month he kept from a customer during the space of twenty-four hours for his own uses, but a second copy which had been sent down by the wholesale agents in mistake, and which he could return when he chose. He had already seen the number, but he could not miss the chance of carefully going through it at leisure. Despite his genuine aspirations, despite his taste which was growing more and more fastidious, he found it exceedingly difficult to proceed with his regular plan of reading while there was an illustrated magazine unexplored. Besides, the name of *Harper's* was august. To read *Harper's* was to acquire merit; even the pictures in *Harper's* were too subtle for the uncultivated.

He turned over the pages, and they all appeared to promise new and strange joys. Such preliminary moments were the most ecstatic in his life, as in the lives of many readers. He had not lost sight of the situation created by his father's illness, but he could only see it very dimly through the semi-transparent pages.

II

The latch clicked and the door opened slightly. He jumped, supposing that his father had crept upstairs. And the first thought of the slave in him was that his father had never seen the gas-stove and would now infallibly notice it. But Maggie's face showed. She came in very quietly – she too had caught the conspiratorial manner.

'I thought you wouldn't be ready for bed just yet,' she said, in mild excuse of her entry. 'I didn't knock, for fear he might be wandering about and hear.'

'Oh!' muttered Edwin. 'What's up?' Instinctively he resented the invasion, and was alarmed for the privacy of his sacred room, although he knew that Maggie, and Mrs Nixon also, had it at their mercy every day. Nobody ever came into that room while he was in it.

Maggie approached the hearth.

'I think I ought to have a stove too,' she said pleasantly.

'Well, why don't you?' he replied. 'I can get it for you any time.' If Clara had envied his stove, she would have envied it with scoffing rancour, and he would have used sarcasm in response.

'Oh no!' said Maggie quickly. 'I don't really want one.'

'What's up?' he repeated. He could see she was hesitating.

'Do you know what Clara and auntie are saying?'

'No! What now? I should have thought they'd both said enough to last them for a few days at any rate.'

'Did Albert say anything to you?'

'What about?'

'Well – both Clara and auntie said I must tell you. Albert says he ought to make his will – they all think so.'

Edwin's lips curled.

'How do they know he hasn't made it?'

'Has he made it?'

276

'How do I know? You don't suppose he ever talks to me about his affairs, do you? Not much!'

'Well – they meant he ought to be asked.'

'Well, let 'em ask him, then. I shan't.'

'Of course what they say is – you're the –'

'What do I care for that?' he interrupted her. 'So that's what you were yarning so long about in your room!'

'I can tell you,' said Maggie, 'they're both of them very serious about it. So's Albert, it seems.'

'They disgust me,' he said briefly. 'Here the thing isn't a day old, and they begin worrying about his will! They go slobbering all over him downstairs, and upstairs it's nothing but his will they think about . . . You can't rush at a man and talk to him about his will like that. At least, I can't – it's altogether too thick! I expect some people could. But I can't. Damn it, you must have some sense of decency.

Maggie remained calm and benevolent. After a pause she said –

'You see – their point is that later on he mayn't be able to make a will.'

'Look here,' he questioned amicably, meeting her eyes, 'what do you think? What do you think yourself?'

'Oh!' she said, 'I should never dream of bothering about it. I'm only telling you what –'

'Of course you wouldn't!' he exclaimed. 'No decent person would. Later on, perhaps, if one could put in a word casually! But not now! . . . If he doesn't make a will he doesn't make one – that's all.'

Maggie leaned against the mantelpiece.

'Mind your skirt doesn't catch fire,' he warned her, in a murmur.

'I told them what you'd say,' she answered his outburst, perfectly unmoved. 'I knew what you'd say. But what they say is – it's all very well for *you*. You're the son, and it seems that if there isn't a will, if it's left too late –'

This aspect of the case had absolutely not presented itself to Edwin.

'If they think,' he muttered, with cold acrimony – 'if they think I'm the sort of person to take the slightest advantage of being the son – well, they must think it – that's all! Besides, they can always talk to him themselves – if they're so desperately anxious.'

'You have charge of everything.'

'Have I! . . . And I should like to know what it's got to do with auntie!'

Maggie lifted her head. 'Oh, auntie and Clara, you know – you can't separate them . . . Well, I've told you.'

She moved to leave.

'I say,' he stopped her, with a confidential appeal. 'Don't you agree with me?'

'Yes,' she replied simply. 'I think it ought to be left for a bit, perhaps he's made it, after all. Let's hope so. I'm sure it will save a lot of trouble if he has.'

'Naturally it ought to be left for a bit! Why – just look at him! . . . He might be on his blooming dying bed, to hear the way some people talk! Let 'em mention it to me, and I'll tell 'em a thing or two!'

Maggie raised her eyebrows. She scarcely recognized Edwin.

'I suppose he'll he all right, downstairs?'

'Right? Of course he'll be all right!' Then he added, in a tone less pugnacious – for, after all, it was not Maggie who had outraged his delicacy, 'Don't latch the door. Pull it to. I'll listen out.' She went silently away.

III

Searching with his body for the most comfortable deeps of the easy-chair, he set himself to savour *Harper's*. This monthly reassurance that nearly all was well with the world, and that what was wrong was not seriously wrong, waited on his knees to be accepted and to do its office. Unlike the magazines of his youth, its aim was to soothe and flatter, not to disconcert and impeach. He looked at the refined illustrations of South American capitals and of picturesque corners in Provence, and at the smooth or the rugged portraits of great statesmen and great bridges; all just as true to reality as the brilliant letterpress; and he tried to slip into the rectified and softened world offered by the magazine. He did not criticize the presentment. He did nothing so subtle as to ask himself whether if he encountered the reality he would recognize it from the presentment. He wanted the illusions of *Harper's*. He desired the comfort, the distraction, and the pleasant ideal longings which they aroused. But they were a medicine which he discovered he was not in a condition to absorb, a medicine therefore useless. There was no effective medicine for his trouble.

His trouble was that he objected to being disturbed. At first he had been pleasantly excited, but now he shrank away at the call to freedom, to action, to responsibility. All the slave in him protested against the knocking off of irons, and the imperative kick into the open air. He saw suddenly that in the calm of regular habit and of subjection, he had arrived at something that closely resembled happiness. He wished not to lose it, knowing that it was already gone. Actually, for his own sake, and quite apart from his father, he would have been ready, were it possible, to cancel the previous twenty-four hours. Everything was ominous, and he wandering about, lost, amid menaces . . . Why, even his cherished programmes of reading were smashed . . . Hallam ! . . . True, tonight was not a night appointed for reading, but tomorrow night was. And would he be able to read tomorrow night? No, a hundred new complications would have arisen to harass him and dispossess him of his tranquillity !

Destiny was demanding from him a huge effort, unexpected and formidable, and the whole of his being weakly complained, asking to be exempted, but asking without any hope of success; for all his faculties and his desires knew that his conscience was ultimately their master.

Talk to his father about making a will, eh ! Besides being disgusting, it was laughable. Those people did not know his father as he did. He foresaw that, even in conducting the routine of business, he would have difficulties with his father over the simplest details. In particular there was one indispensable preliminary to the old man's complete repose, and his first duty on the morrow would be to endeavour to arrange this preliminary with his father : but he scarcely hoped to succeed.

On the portion of the mantelpiece reserved for books in actual use lay the *Tale of a Tub*, last night so enchanting. And now he had positively forgotten it. He yawned, and prepared for bed. If he could not read *Harper's*, perhaps he could read Swift.

IV

He lay in bed. The gas was out, the stove was out, and according to his custom he was reading himself to sleep by the light of a candle in a sconce attached to the bed's head. His eyes ran along line after line and down page after page, and transmitted nothing coherent to his brain.

Then there were steps on the stair. His father was at last coming to bed. He was a little relieved, though he had been quite prepared to go to sleep and leave his father below. Why not? The steps died at the top of the stair, but an irregular creaking continued. After a pause the door was pushed open; and after another pause the figure of his father came into view, breathing loudly.

'Edwin, are you asleep?' Darius asked anxiously. Edwin wondered what could be the matter, but he answered with lightness, 'Nearly.'

'I've not put th' light out down yon ! Happen you'd better put it out.' There was in his father's voice a note of dependence upon him, of appeal to him.

'Funny !' he thought, and said aloud, 'All right.'

He jumped up. His father thudded off deliberately to his own room, apparently relieved of a fearful oppression, but still fixed in sadness.

On the previous night Edwin had extinguished the hall-gas and come last to bed; and again tonight. But tonight with what a different sentiment of genuine, permanent responsibility ! The appealing feebleness of his father's attitude seemed to give him strength. Surely a man so weak and fallen from tyranny could not cause much trouble! Edwin now had some hope that the unavoidable preliminary to the invalid's retirement might be achieved without too much difficulty. He braced himself.

CHAPTER 6 : *Keys and Cheques*

I

Coming up Trafalgar Road at twenty minutes past nine in the bright, astringent morning, Edwin carried by a string a little round parcel which for him contained the inspiring symbol of his new life. By mere accident he had awakened and had risen early, arriving at the shop before half past seven. He had deliberately lifted on to his shoulders the whole burden of the shop and the printing business, and as soon as he felt its weight securely lodged he became extraordinarily animated and vigorous; even gay. He had worked with a most agreeable sense of energy until nearly nine o'clock; and then, having first called at the ironmonger's, had stepped into the bank at the top of St Luke's Square a moment after its doors opened, and had five minutes' exciting conversation with the manager. After which, with righteous hunger in his belly and the symbol in his hand, he had come home to breakfast. The symbol was such as could be obtained at any ironmonger's : an alarm clock. Mrs Nixon had grown less reliable than formerly as an alarm clock; machinery was now supplanting her.

Dr Heve came out of the house, and Dr Heve too seemed gay with fine resolutions. The two met on the doorstep, each full of a justifiable self-satisfaction. The doctor explained that he had come thus early because Mr Clayhanger was one of those cases upon which he could look in casually at any time. In the sunshine they talked under the porch of early rising, as men who understood the value of that art. Edwin could see that Dr Heve's life was a series of little habits which would never allow themselves to be interfered with by any large interest, and he despised the man's womanish smile. Nevertheless his new respect for him did not weaken; he decided that he was a very decent fellow in his way, and he was more impressed than he would admit by the amount of work that the doctor had for years been doing in the morning before his intellectual superiors had sat up in bed. And he imagined that it might be even more agreeable to read in the fresh stillness of the morning than in the solitary night.

Then they returned to the case of Darius. The doctor was more communicative, and they were both cheerfully matter-of-fact concerning it. There it was, to be made the best of! And that Darius could never handle business again, and that in about two years his doom would be accomplished – these were basic feats, axiomatic. The doctor had seen his patient in the garden, and he suggested that if Darius could be persuaded to interest himself in gardening . . . ! They discussed his medicine, his meals, his digestion, and the great, impossible dream of 'taking him away', 'out of it all'. And every now and then Dr Heve dropped some little hint as to the management of Darius.

The ticking parcel drew the discreet attention of the doctor. The machine was one guaranteed to go in any position, and was much more difficult to stop than to start.

'It's only an alarm,' said Edwin, not without self-consciousness.

The doctor went, tripping neatly and optimistically, off towards his own breakfast. He got up earlier than his horse.

II

Darius was still in the garden when Edwin went to him. He had put on his daily suit, and was leisurely digging in an uncultivated patch of ground. He stuck the spade into the earth perpendicularly and deep, and when he tried to prise it up and it would not yield because of a concealed half-brick, he put his tongue between his teeth and then bit his lower lip, controlling himself, determined to get the better of the spade and the brick by persuasively humouring them. He took no notice whatever of Edwin.

'I see you aren't losing any time,' said Edwin, who felt as though he were engaging in small-talk with a stranger.

'Are *you*?' Darius replied, without turning his head.

'I've just come up for a bit of breakfast. Everything's all right,' he said. He would have liked to add: 'I was in the shop before seven-thirty,' but he was too proud.

After a pause, he ventured, essaying the casual –

'I say, father, I shall want the keys of the desk, and all that.'

'Keys o' th' desk!' Darius muttered, leaning on the spade, as though demanding in stupefaction, 'What on earth can you want the keys for?'

'Well –' Edwin stammered.

But the proposition was too obvious to be denied. Darius left the spade to stand by itself, and stared.

'Got 'em in your pocket?' Edwin inquired.

Slowly Darius drew forth a heavy, glittering bunch of keys, one of the chief insignia of his dominion, and began to fumble at it.

'You needn't take any of them off. I expect I know which is which,' said Edwin, holding out his hand.

Darius hesitated, and then yielded up the bunch.

'Thanks,' said Edwin lightly.

But the old man's reluctance to perform this simple and absolutely necessary act of surrender, the old man's air of having done something tremendous – these signs frightened Edwin and shook his courage for the demand compared to which the demand for the keys was naught. Still, the affair had to be carried through.

'And I say,' he proceeded, jingling the keys, 'about signing and endorsing cheques. They tell me at the bank that if you sign a general authority to me to do it for you, that will be enough.'

He could not avoid looking guilty. He almost felt guilty, almost felt as if he were plotting against his father's welfare. And as he spoke his words seemed unreal and his suggestion fantastic. At the Bank the plan had been simple, easy, and perfectly natural. But there could be no doubt, that as he had walked up Trafalgar Road, receding from the Bank and approaching his father, the plan had gradually lost those attractive qualities. And now in the garden it was merely monstrous.

Silent, Darius resumed the spade.

'Well,' said Edwin desperately. 'What about it?'

'Do you think' – Darius glowered upon him with heavy desolating scorn – 'do you think as I'm going to let you sign my cheques for me? You're taking too much on yourself, my lad.'

'But –'

'I tell ye you're taking too much on yourself!' he began to shout menacingly. 'Get about your business and don't act the fool! You needn't think you're going to be God A'mighty because you've got up a bit earlier for once in a way and been down to th' shop before breakfast.'

III

In all his demeanour there was not the least indication of weakness. He might never have sat down on the stairs and cried! He might never have submitted feebly and perhaps gladly to the caresses of Clara and the soothings of Auntie Hamps! Impossible to convince him that he was cut off from the world! Impossible even to believe it! Was this the man that Edwin and the Bank manager and the doctor and all the others had been disposing of as though he were an automaton accurately responsive to external suggestion?

'Look here,' Edwin knew what he ought to say. 'Let it be clearly understood once for all – I'm the boss now! I have the authority in my pocket and you must sign it, and quick too! I shall do my best for you, but I don't mean to be bullied while I'm doing it!'

But he could not say it. Nor could his heart emotionally feel it.

He turned away sheepishly, and then he faced his father again, with a distressed, apologetic smile.

'Well, then,' he asked, 'who *is* going to sign cheques?'

'I am,' said Darius.

'But you know what the doctor said! You know what you promised him!'

'What did the doctor say?'

'He said you weren't to do anything at all. And you said you wouldn't. What's more, you said you didn't want to.'

Darius sneered.

'I reckon I can sign cheques,' he said. 'And I reckon I can endorse cheques. . . . So it's got to that! I can't sign my own name now. I shall show some of you whether I can't sign my own name!'

'You know it isn't simply signing them. You know if I bring cheques up for you to sign you'll begin worrying about them at once, and – and there'll be no end to it. You'd much better –'

'Shut up!' It was like a clap of thunder.

Edwin hesitated an instant and then went towards the house. He could hear his father muttering, 'Whippersnapper!'

'And I'll tell you another thing,' Darius bawled across the garden – assuredly his voice would reach the street. 'It was like your impudence to go to the Bank like that without asking me first! "They tell you at the Bank!" "They tell you at the Bank!" Anything else they told you at the Bank?' Then a snort.

Edwin was humiliated and baffled. He knew not what he could do. The situation became impossible immediately it was faced. He felt also very resentful, and resentment was capturing him, when suddenly an idea seemed to pull him by the sleeve : 'All this is part of his disease. It's part of his disease that he can't see the point of a thing.' And the idea was insistent, and under its insistence Edwin's resentment changed to melancholy. He said to himself that he must think of his father as a child. He blamed himself, in a sort of pleasurable luxury of remorse, for all the anger which during all his life he had felt against his father. His father's unreasonableness had not been a fault, but a misfortune. His father had not been a tyrant, but a victim. His brain must always have been wrong! And now he was doomed, and the worst part of his doom was that he was unaware of it. And in the thought of Darius ignorantly blustering within the walled garden, in the spring sunshine, condemned, cut off, helpless at the last, pitiable at the last, there was something inexpressibly poignant. And the sunshine seemed a shame; and Edwin's youth and mental vigour seemed a shame. Nevertheless Edwin knew not what to do.

'Master Edwin,' said Mrs Nixon, who was rubbing the balustrade of the stairs, 'you munna' cross him like that.' She jerked her head in the direction of the garden. The garden door stood open.

If he had not felt solemn and superior, he could have snapped off that head of hers.

'Is my breakfast ready?' he asked. He hung up his hat, and absently took the little parcel which he had left on the marble ledge of the umbrella-stand.

CHAPTER 7 : *Laid Aside*

I

The safe, since the abandonment of the business premises by the family, had stood in a corner of a small nondescript room, sometimes vaguely called the safe-room, between the shop and what had once been the kitchen. It was a considerable safe, and it had the room practically to itself. As Edwin unlocked it, and the prodigious door swung with silent smoothness to his pull, he was aware of a very romantic feeling of exploration. He had seen the inside of the safe before; he had even opened the safe, and taken something from it, under his father's orders. But he had never had leisure, nor licence, to inspect its interior. From his boyhood had survived the notion that it must contain many marvels. In spite of himself his attitude was one of awe.

The first thing that met his eye was his father's large, black-bound private cash-book, which constituted the most sacred and mysterious document in the accountancy of the business. Edwin handled, and kept, all the books save that. At the beginning of the previous week he and Stifford had achieved the task of sending out the quarterly accounts, and of one sort or another there were seven hundred quarterly accounts. Edwin was familiar with every detail of the printer's work-book, the daybook, the combined book colloquially called 'invoice and ledger', the 'bought' ledger, and the shop cash-book. But he could form no sure idea of the total dimensions and results of the business, because his father always kept the ultimate castings to himself, and never displayed his private cash-book under any circumstances. By ingenuity and perseverance Edwin might have triumphed over Darius's mania for secrecy; but he did not care to do so; perhaps pride even more than honour caused him to refrain.

Now he held the book, and saw that only a portion of it was in the nature of a cash-book; the rest comprised summaries and general statements. The statement for the year 1885, so far as he could hastily decipher its meaning, showed a profit of £821. He was not surprised, and yet the sight of the figures in his father's heavy, scratchy hand was curiously impressive.

His father could keep nothing from him now. The interior of the safe was like a city that had capitulated; no law ran in it but his law, and he was absolute; he could commit infamies in the city and none might criticize. He turned over piles of dusty cheque-counterfoils, and old pass-books and other old books of account. He saw a linen bag crammed with four-shilling pieces (whenever Darius obtained a double florin he put it aside), and one or two old watches of no value. Also the title-deeds of the house at Bleakridge, their latest parchment still white with pounce; the mortgage, then, had been repaid, a fact which Darius had managed on principle to conceal from his son. Then he came to the four drawers, and in some of these he discovered a number of miscellaneous share-certificates with their big seals. He knew that his father had investments – it was impossible to inhabit the shop-cubicle with his father and not know that – but he had no conception of their extent or their value. Always he had regarded all those matters as foreign to himself, refusing to allow curiosity in regard to them to awake. Now he was differently minded, owing to the mere physical weight in his pocket of a bunch of keys! In a hasty examination he gathered that the stock was chiefly in railways and shipping, and that it amounted to large sums – anyhow quite a number of thousands. He was frankly astonished. How had his father's clumsy, slow intellect been able to cope with the dangerous intricacies of the Stock Exchange? It seemed incredible; and yet he had known quite well that his father was an investor!

'Of course he isn't keen on giving it all up!' Edwin exclaimed aloud suddenly. 'I wonder he even forked out the keys as easily as he did!'

The view of the safe enabled him to perform a feat which very few children ever achieve; he put himself in his father's place. And it was with benevolence, not with exasperation, that he puzzled his head to invent some device for defeating the old man's obstinacy about cheque-signing.

One drawer was evidently not in regular use. Often, in a series of drawers, one of them falls into the idle habit of being overlooked, slipping gradually by custom into desuetude, though other drawers may overflow. This drawer held merely a few scraps of sample paper, and a map, all dusty. He drew forth the map. It was coloured, and in shaky Roman characters underneath it ran the legend, 'The County of Staffordshire'. He seemed to recognize the map. On the back he read, in his father's handwriting: 'Drawn and coloured without help by my son Edwin, aged nine.'

He had utterly forgotten it. He could in no detail recall the circumstances in which he had produced the wonderful map. A childish, rude effort! ... Still, rather remarkable that at the age of nine (perhaps even before he had begun to attend the Oldcastle Middle School) he should have chosen to do a county map instead of a map of that country beloved by all juvenile map-drawers, Ireland! He must have copied it from the map in Lewis's Gazeteer of England and Wales. ... Twenty-one years ago, nearly! He might, from the peculiar effect on him, have just discovered the mummy of the boy that once had been Edwin. ... And his father had kept the map for over twenty years. The old cock must have been deuced proud of it once! Not that he ever said so – Edwin was sure of that!

'Now you needn't get sentimental!' he told himself. Like Maggie he had a fearful, an almost morbid, horror of sentimentality. But he could not arrest the softening of his heart, as he smiled at the *naïveté* of the map and at his father's parental simplicity.

As he was closing the safe, Stifford, agitated, hurried into the room.

'Please, sir, Mr Clayhanger's in the Square. I thought I'd better tell you.'

'What? Father?'

'Yes, sir. He's standing opposite the chapel and he keeps looking this way. I thought you'd like –'

Edwin turned the key, and ran forth, stumbling, as he entered the shop, against the step-ladder which, with the paper-boy at the summit of it, overtopped the doorway. He wondered why he should run, and why Stifford's face was so obviously apprehensive.

II

Darius Clayhanger was standing at the north-east corner of the little Square, half-way up Duck Bank, at the edge of the pavement. And his gaze, hesitant and feeble, seemed to be upon the shop. He merely stood there, moveless, and yet the sight of him was most strangely disconcerting. Edwin, who kept within the shelter of the doorway, comprehended now the look on Stifford's face. His father had the air of ranging round about the shop in a reconnaissance, like an Indian or a wild animal, or like a domestic animal violently expelled. Edwin almost expected him to creep round by the Town Hall into St Luke's Square, and then to reappear stealthily at the other end of Wedgwood Street, and from a western ambush stare again at his own premises.

A man coming down Duck Bank paused an instant near Darius, and with a smile spoke to him, holding out his hand. Darius gave a slight nod. The man, snubbed and confused, walked on, the smile still on his face but meaningless now and foolish.

At length Darius walked up the hill, his arms stiff and outpointing,

LAID ASIDE

as of old. Edwin got his hat and ran after him. Instead of turning to the left along the market-place, Darius kept on farther up the hill, past the Shambles, towards the old playground and the vague cinder-wastes where the town ended in a few ancient cottages. It was at the playground that Edwin, going slowly and cautiously, overtook him.

'Hello, father!' he began nervously. 'Where are you off to?'

Darius did not seem to be at all startled to see him at his side. Nevertheless he behaved in a queer fashion. Without saying a word he suddenly turned at right-angles and apparently aimed himself towards the market-place, by the back of the Town Hall. When he had walked a few paces, he stopped and looked round at Edwin, who could not decide what ought to be done.

'If ye want to know,' said Darius, with overwhelming sadness and embittered disgust, 'I'm going to th' Bank to sign that authority about cheques.'

'Oh!' Edwin responded. 'Good! I'll go with you if you like.'

'Happen it'll be as well,' said Darius, resigning himself.

They walked together in silence.

The old man was beaten. The old man had surrendered, unconditionally. Edwin's heart lightened as he perceived more and more clearly what his surprising victory meant. It meant that always in future he would have the upper hand. He knew now, and Darius knew, that his father had no strength to fight, and that any semblance of fighting could be treated as bluster. Probably nobody realized as profoundly as Darius himself his real and yet mysterious inability to assert his will against the will of another. The force of his individuality was gone. He who had meant to govern tyrannically to his final hour, to die with a powerful and grim gesture of command, had to accept the ignominy of submission. Edwin had not even insisted, had used no kind of threat. He had merely announced his will, and when the first fury had waned Darius had found his son's will working like a chemical agent in his defenceless mind, and had yielded. It was astounding. And always it would be thus, until the time when Edwin would say 'Do this' and Darius would do it, and 'Do that' and Darius would do it, meekly, unreasoningly, anxiously.

Edwin's relief was so great that it might have been mistaken for positive ecstatic happiness. His mind ranged exultingly over the future of the business. In a few years, if he chose, he could sell the business and spend the whole treasure of his time upon programmes. The entire world would be his, and he could gather the fruits of every art. He would utterly belong to himself. It was a formidable thought. The atmosphere of the market-place contained too much oxygen to be quite grateful to his lungs . . . In the meantime there were things he would do. He would raise Stifford's wages. Long ago they ought to have been raised. And he would see that Stifford had for his dinner a full hour; which in practice Stifford had never had. And he would completely give up the sale and delivery of newspapers and weeklies, and would train the paper-boy to the shop, and put Stifford in his own place and perhaps get another clerk. It struck him hopefully that Stifford might go forth for orders. Assuredly he himself had not one quality of a commercial traveller. And, most inviting prospect of all, he would stock new books. He cared not whether new books were unremunerative. It should be known throughout the Five Towns that at Clayhanger's in Bursley a selection of new books could always be seen. And if people would not buy them people must leave them. But he would have them. And so his thoughts flew.

III

And at the same time he was extremely sad, only less sad than his father. When he allowed his thoughts to rest for an instant on his father he was so moved that he could almost have burst into a sob – just one terrific sob. And he would say in his mind, 'What a damned shame! What a damned shame!' Meaning that destiny had behaved ignobly to his father, after all. Destiny had no right to deal with a man so faithlessly. Destiny should do either one thing or the other. It seemed to him that he was leading his father by a string to his humiliation. And he was ashamed : ashamed of his own dominance and of his father's craven submissiveness. Twice they were stopped by hearty and curious burgesses, and at each encounter Edwin, far more than Darius, was anxious to pretend that the harsh hand of Darius still firmly held the sceptre.

When they entered the shining mahogany interior of the richest Bank in the Five Towns, hushed save for a discreet shovelling of coins, Edwin waited for his father to speak, and Darius said not a word, but stood glumly quiescent, like a victim in a halter. The little wiry dancing cashier looked; every clerk in the place looked; from behind the third counter, in the far recesses of the Bank, clerks looked over their ledgers; and they all looked in the same annoying way; as at a victim in a halter; in their glance was all the pitiful gloating baseness of human nature, mingled with a little of its compassion.

Everybody of course knew that 'something had happened' to the successful steam-printer.

'Can we see Mr Lovatt?' Edwin demanded curtly. He was abashed and he was resentful.

The cashier jumped on all his springs into a sudden activity of deference.

Presently the manager emerged from the glazed door of his room, pulling his long whiskers.

'Oh, Mr Lovatt,' Edwin began nervously. 'Father's just come along –'

They were swallowed up into the manager's parlour. It might have been a court of justice, or a dentist's surgery, or the cabinet of an insurance doctor, or the room at Fontainebleau where Napoleon signed his abdication – anything but the thing it was. Happily Mr Lovatt had a manner which never varied; he had only one manner for all men and all occasions. So that Edwin was not distressed either by the deficiencies of amateur acting or by the exhibition of another's self-conscious awkwardness. Nevertheless when his father took the pen to write he was obliged to look studiously at the window and inaudibly hum an air. Had he not done so, that threatening sob might have burst its way out of him.

IV

'I'm going this road,' said Darius, when they were safely out of the Bank, pointing towards the Sytch.

'What for?'

'I'm going this road,' he repeated, gloomily obstinate.

'All right,' said Edwin cheerfully. 'I'll trot round with you.'

He did not know whether he could safely leave his father. The old man's eyes resented his assiduity and accepted it.

They passed the Old Sytch Pottery, the smoke of whose kilns now no longer darkened the sky. The senior partner of the firm which leased it had died, and his sons had immediately taken advantage of his absence to build a new and efficient works down by the canal-side at Shawport – a marvel of everything save architectural dignity. Times changed. Edwin remarked on the desolation of the place and received no reply. Then the idea occurred to him that his father was bound for the Liberal Club. It was so. They both entered. In the large room two young men were amusing themselves at the billiard-table which formed the chief attraction of the naked interior, and on the ledges of the table were two glasses. The steward in an apron watched them.

'Aye!' grumbled Darius, eyeing the group. 'That's Rad, that is! That's Rad! Not twelve o'clock yet!'

If Edwin with his father had surprised two young men drinking and playing billiards before noon in the Conservative Club, he would have been grimly pleased. He would have taken it for a further proof of the hollowness of the opposition to the great Home Rule Bill; but the spectacle of a couple of wastrels in the Liberal Club annoyed and shamed him. His vague notion was that at such a moment of high crisis the two wastrels ought to have had the decency to refrain from wasting.

'Well, Mr Clayhanger,' said the steward, in his absurd boniface way, 'you're quite a stranger.'

'I want my name taken off this Club,' said Darius shortly. 'Ye understand me! And I reckon I'm not the only one, these days.'

The steward did in fact understand. He protested in a low, amiable voice, while the billiard-players affected not to hear; but he perfectly understood. The epidemic of resignations had already set in, and there had been talk of a Liberal-Unionist Club. The steward saw that the grand folly of a senile statesman was threatening his own future prospects. He smiled. But at Edwin, as they were leaving, he smiled in a quite peculiar way, and that smile clearly meant : 'Your father goes potty, and the first thing he does is to change his politics.' This was the steward's justifiable revenge.

'*You* aren't leaving us?' the steward questioned Edwin in a half-whisper.

Edwin shook his head. But he could have killed the steward for that nauseating suggestive smile. The outer door swung to, cutting off the delicate click of billiard balls.

At the top of Duck Bank, Darius silently and without warning mounted the steps of the Conservative Club. Doubtless he knew how to lay his hand instantly on a proposer and seconder. Edwin did not follow him.

v

That evening, conscious of responsibility and of virtue, Edwin walked up Trafalgar Road with a less gawky and more dignified mien than ever he had managed to assume before. He had not only dismissed programmes of culture, he had forgotten them. After twelve hours as head of a business, they had temporarily ceased to interest him. And when he passed, or was overtaken by, other men of affairs, he thought to himself naïvely in the dark, 'I am the equal of these men.' And the image of Florence Simcox the clog-dancer floated through his mind.

He found Darius alone in the drawing-room, in front of an uncustomary fire, garden-clay still on his boots, and *The Christian News* under his spectacles. The Sunday before the funeral of Mr Shushions had been so unusual and so distressing that Darius had fallen into arrears with his perusals. True, he had never been known to read *The Christian News* on any day but Sunday, but now every day was Sunday.

Edwin nodded to him and approached the fire, rubbing his hands.

'What's this as I hear?' Darius began, with melancholy softness.

'Eh?'

'About Albert wanting to borrow a thousand pounds?' Darius gazed at him over his spectacles.

'Albert wanting to borrow a thousand pounds!' Edwin repeated, astounded.

'Aye! Have they said naught to you?'

'No,' said Edwin. 'What is it?'

'Clara and your aunt have both been at me since tea. Some tale as Albert can amalgamate into partnership with Hope & Carter's if he can put down a thousand. Then Albert's said naught to ye?'

'No, he hasn't!' Edwin exclaimed, emphasizing each word with a peculiar fierceness. It was as if he had said, 'I should like to catch him saying anything to me about it!'

He was extremely indignant. It seemed to him monstrous that those two women should thus try to snatch an advantage from his father's weakness, pitifully mean and base. He could not understand how people could bring themselves to do such things, nor how, having done them, they could ever look their fellows in the face again. Had they no shame? They would not let a day pass; but they must settle on the old man instantly, like flies on a carcase! He could imagine the plottings, the hushed chatterings; the acting-for-the-best demeanour of that cursed woman Auntie Hamps (yes, he now cursed her), and the candid greed of his sister.

'You wouldn't do it, would ye?' Darius asked, in a tone that expected a negative answer; but also with a rather plaintive appeal, as though he were depending on Edwin for moral support against the formidable forces of attack.

'I should not,' said Edwin stoutly, touched by the strange wistful note and by the glance. 'Unless of course you really want to.'

He did not care in the least whether the money would or would not be really useful and reasonably safe. He did not care whose enmity he was risking. His sense of fair play was outraged, and he would salve it at any cost. He knew that had his father not been struck down and defenceless, these despicable people would never have dared to demand money from him. That was the only point that mattered.

The relief of Darius at Edwin's attitude in the affair was painful. Hoping for sympathy from Edwin, he had yet feared in him another enemy. Now he was reassured, and he could not hide his feelings no better than a child.

'Seemingly they can't wait till my will's opened!' he murmured, with a scarcely successful affectation of grimness.

'Made a will, have you?' Edwin remarked, with an elaborate casualness to imply that he had never till then given a thought to his father's will, but that, having thought of the question, he was perhaps a very little surprised that his father had indeed made a will.

Darius nodded, quite benevolently. He seemed to have forgotten his deep grievance against Edwin in the matter of cheque-signing.

'Duncalf's got it,' he murmured after a moment. Duncalf was the town clerk and a solicitor.

So the will was made! And he had submissively signed away all control over all monetary transactions. What more could he do, except expire with the minimum of fuss? Truly Darius, in a local phrase, was now 'laid aside'! And of all the symptoms of his decay the most striking and the most tragic, to Edwin, was that he showed no curiosity whatever about business. Not one single word of inquiry had he uttered.

'You'll want shaving,' said Edwin in a friendly way.

Darius passed a hand over his face. He had ceased years ago to shave himself, and had a subscription at Dick Jones's in Aboukir Street, close by the shop.

'Aye!'

'Shall I send the barber up, or shall you let it grow?'

'What do you think?'

'Oh!' Edwin drawled, characteristically hesitating. Then he remembered that he was the responsible head of the family of Clayhanger. 'I think you might let it grow,' he decided.

And when he had issued the verdict, it seemed to him like a sentence of sequestration and death on his father.... 'Let it grow! What does it matter?' Such was the innuendo.

'You used to grow a full beard once, didn't you?' he asked.

'Yes,' said Darius.

That made the situation less cruel.

CHAPTER 8 : *A Change of Mind*

I

One evening, a year later, in earliest summer of 1887, Edwin and Mr Osmond Orgreave were walking home together from Hanbridge. When they reached the corner of the street leading to Lane End House, Osmond Orgreave said, stopping –

'Now you'll come with us?' And he looked Edwin hard in the eyes, and there was a most flattering appeal in his voice. It was some time since their eyes had met frankly, for Edwin had recently been having experience of Mr Orgreave's methods in financial controversy, and it had not been agreeable.

After an instant Edwin said heartily –

'Yes, I think I'll come. Of course I should like to. But I'll let you know.'

'Tonight?'

'Yes, tonight.'

'I shall tell my wife you're coming.'

Mr Orgreave waved a hand, and passed with a certain decorative gaiety down the street. His hair was now silvern, but it still curled in the old places, and his gestures had apparently not aged at all.

Mr and Mrs Orgreave were going to London for the Jubilee celebrations. So far as their family was concerned, they were going alone, because Osmond had insisted humorously that he wanted a rest from his children. But he had urgently invited Edwin to accompany them. At first Edwin had instinctively replied that it was impossible. He could not leave home. He had never been to London; a journey to London presented itself to him as an immense enterprise, almost as a piece of culpable self-indulgence. And then, under the stimulus of Osmond's energetic and adventurous temperament, he had said to himself, 'Why not? Why shouldn't I?'

The arguments favoured his going. It was absurd and scandalous that he had never been to London : he ought for his self-respect to depart thither at once. The legend of the Jubilee, spectacular, processional, historic, touched his imagination. Whenever he thought of it, his fancy saw pennons and corselets and chargers winding through stupendous streets, and, somewhere in the midst, the majesty of England in the frail body of a little old lady, who had many children and one supreme misfortune. Moreover, he could incidentally see Charlie. Moreover, he had been suffering from a series of his customary colds, and from overwork, and Heve had told him that he 'could do with a change'. Moreover, he had a project for buying paper in London : he had received, from London, overtures which seemed promising. He had never been able to buy paper quite as cheaply as Darius had bought paper, for the one reason that he could not haggle over sixteenths of a penny with efficient ruthlessness; he simply could not do it, being somehow ashamed to do it. In Manchester, where Darius had bought paper for thirty years, they were imperceptibly too brutal for Edwin in the harsh realities of a bargain; they had no sense of shame. He thought that in letters from London he detected a softer spirit.

And above all he desired, by accepting Mr Orgreave's invitation, to show to the architect that the differences between them were really expunged from his mind. Among many confusions in his father's flourishing but disorderly affairs, Edwin had been startled to find the Orgreave transactions. There were accounts and contra-accounts, and quantities of strangely contradictory documents. Never had a real settlement occurred between Darius and Osmond. And Osmond did not seem to want one. Edwin, however, with his old-maid's passion for putting and keeping everything in its place, insisted on one. Mr Orgreave had to meet him on his strongest point, his love of order. The process of settlement had been painful to Edwin; it had seriously marred some of his illusions. Nearly the last of the entanglements in his father's business, the Orgreave matter was straightened and closed now; and the projected escapade to London would bury it deep, might even restore agreeable illusions. And Edwin was incapable of nursing malice.

The best argument of all was that he had a right to go to London. He had earned London, by honest and severe work, and by bearing firmly the huge weight of his responsibility. So far he had offered himself no reward whatever, not even an increase of salary, not even a week of freedom or the satisfaction of a single caprice.

'I shall go, and charge it to the business,' he said to himself. He became excited about going.

II

As he approached his house, he saw the elder Heve, vicar of St Peter's, coming away from it, a natty clerical figure in a straw hat of peculiar shape. Recently this man had called once or twice; not professionally, for Darius was neither a churchman nor a parishioner, but as a brother of Dr Heve's, as a friendly human being, and Darius had been flattered. The vicar would talk about Jesus with quiet half-humorous enthusiasm. For him at any rate Christianity was grand fun. He seemed never to be solemn over his religion, like the Wesleyans. He never, with a shamed, defiant air, said, 'I am not ashamed of Christ', like the Wesleyans. He might have known Christ slightly at Cambridge. But his relations with Christ did not make him conceited, nor condescending. And if he was concerned about the welfare of people who knew not Christ, he hid his concern in the politest manner. Edwin, after being momentarily impressed by him, was now convinced of his perfect mediocrity; the Vicar's views on literature had damned him eternally in the esteem of Edwin, who was still naïve enough to be unable to comprehend how a man who had been to Cambridge could speak enthusiastically of *Uncle Tom's Cabin*. Moreover, Edwin despised him for his obvious pride in being a bachelor. The vicar would not say that a priest should be celibate, but he would, with delicacy, imply as much. Then also, for Edwin's taste, the parson was somewhat too childishly interested in the culture of cellar-mushrooms, which was his hobby. He would recount the tedious details of all his experiments to Darius, who, flattered by these attentions from the Established Church, took immense delight in the vicar and in the sample mushrooms offered to him from time to time.

Maggie stood in the porch, which commanded the descent into Bursley; she was watching the vicar as he receded. When Edwin appeared at the gate, she gave a little jump, and he fancied that she also blushed.

'Look here!' he exclaimed to himself, in a flash of suspicion. 'Surely she's not thinking of the vicar! Surely Maggie isn't after all . . .!' He did not conceive it possible that the vicar, who had been to Cambridge and had notions about celibacy, was thinking of Maggie. 'Women are queer,' he said to himself. (For him, this generalization from facts was quite original.) Fancy her staring after the vicar! She must have been doing it quite unconsciously! He had supposed that her attitude towards the vicar was precisely his own. He took it for granted that the vicar's attitude was the same to both of them, based on a polite and kindly but firm recognition that there could be no genuine sympathy between him and them.

'The vicar's just been,' said Maggie.

'Has he? . . . Cheered the old man up at all?'

'Not much.' Maggie shook her head gloomily.

Edwin's conscience seemed to be getting ready to hint that he ought not to go to London.

'I say, Mag,' he said quietly, as he inserted his stick in the umbrella-stand. She stopped on her way upstairs, and then approached him.

'Mr Orgreave wants me to go to London with him and Mrs Orgreave.' He explained the whole project to her.

She said at once, eagerly and benevolently –

'Of course you ought to go. It'll do you all the good in the world. I shall be all right here. Clara and Albert will come for Jubilee Day, anyhow. But haven't you driven it late? . . . The day after tomorrow, isn't it? Mr Heve was only saying just now that the hotels were all crammed.'

'Well, you know what Orgreave is! I expect he'll look after all that.'

'You go!' Maggie enjoined him.

'Won't upset him?' Edwin nodded vaguely to wherever Darius might be.

'Can't be helped if it does,' she said calmly.

'Well then, I'm dashed if I don't go! What about my collars?'

III

Those three – Darius, Maggie, and Edwin – sat down to tea in silence. The window was open, and the weather very warm and gay. During the previous twelve months they had sat down to hundreds of such meals. Save for a few brief periods of cheerfulness, Darius had steadily grown more taciturn, heavy, and melancholy. In the winter he had of course abandoned his attempts to divert himself by gardening – attempts at the best half-hearted and feeble – and he had not resumed them in the spring. Less than half a year previously he had often walked across the fields to Hillport and back, or up the gradual slopes to the height of Toft End – he never went townwards, had not once visited the Conservative Club. But now he could not even be persuaded to leave the garden. An old wicker arm-chair had been placed at the end of the garden, and he would set out for that arm-chair as upon a journey, and, having reached it, would sink into it with a huge sigh, and repose before bracing himself to the effort of return.

And now it seemed marvellous that he had ever had the legs to get to Hillport and to Toft End. He existed in a stupor of dull reflection, from pride pretending to read and not reading, or pretending to listen and not listening, and occasionally making a remark which was inapposite but which had to be humoured. And as the weeks passed his children's manner of humouring him became increasingly perfunctory, and their movements in putting right the negligence of his attire increasingly brusque. Vainly they tried to remember in time that he was a victim and not a criminal; they would remember after the careless remark and after the curt gesture, when it was too late. His malady obsessed them : it was in the air of the house, omnipresent; it weighed upon them, corroding the nerve and exasperating the spirit. Now and then, when Darius had vented a burst of irrational anger, they would say to each other with casual bitterness that really he was too annoying. Once, when his demeanour towards the new servant had strongly suggested that he thought her name was Bathsheba, Mrs Nixon herself had 'flown out' at him, and there had been a scene which the doctor had soothed by discreet professional explanations. Maggie's difficulty was that he was always there, always on the spot. To be free of him she must leave the house; and Maggie was not fond of leaving the house.

Edwin meant to inform him briefly of his intention to go to London, but such was the power of habit that he hesitated; he could not bring himself to announce directly this audacious and unprecedented act of freedom, though he knew that his father was as helpless as a child in his hands. Instead, he began to talk about the renewal of the lease of the premises in Duck Square, as to which it would be necessary to give notice to the landlord at the end of the month.

'I've been thinking I'll have it made out in my own name,' he said. 'It'll save you signing, and so on.' This in itself was a proposal sufficiently startling, and he would not have been surprised at a violent instinctive protest from Darius; but Darius seemed not to heed.

Then both Edwin and Maggie noticed that he was trying to hold a sausage firm on his plate with his knife, and to cut it with his fork.

'No, no, father !' said Maggie gently. 'Not like that !'

He looked up, puzzled, and then bent himself again to the plate. The whole of his faculties seemed to be absorbed in a great effort to resolve the complicated problem of the plate, the sausage, the knife, and the fork.

'You've got your knife in the wrong hand,' said Edwin impatiently, as to a wilful child.

Darius stared at the knife and at the fork, and he then sighed, and his sigh meant, 'This business is beyond me!' Then he endeavoured to substitute the knife for the fork, but he could not.

'See,' said Edwin, leaning over. 'Like this!' He took the knife, but Darius would not loose it. 'No, leave go!' he ordered. 'Leave go! How can I show you if you don't leave go?'

Darius dropped both knife and fork with a clatter. Edwin put the knife into his right hand, and the fork into his left; but in a moment they were wrong again. At first Edwin could not believe that his father was not indulging deliberately in naughtiness.

'Shall I cut it up for you, father?' Maggie asked, in a mild, persuasive tone.

Darius pushed the plate towards her.

When she had cut up the sausage, she said —

'There you are! I'll keep the knife. Then you can't get mixed up.'

And Darius ate the sausage with the fork alone. His intelligence had failed to master the original problem presented to it. He ate steadily for a few moments, and then the tears began to roll down his cheeks, and he ate no more.

This incident, so simple, so unexpected, and so dramatic, caused the most acute distress. And its effect was disconcerting in the highest degree. It reminded everybody that what Darius suffered from was softening of the brain. For long he had been a prisoner in the house and garden. For long he had been almost mute. And now, just after a visit which usually acted upon him as a tonic, he had begun to lose the skill to feed himself. Little by little he was demonstrating, by his slow declension from it, the wonder of the standard of efficiency maintained by the normal human being.

Edwin and Maggie avoided one another, even in their glances. Each affected the philosophical, seeking to diminish the significance of the episode. But neither succeeded. Of the two years allotted to Darius, one had gone. What would the second be?

IV

In his bedroom, after tea, Edwin fought against the gloomy influence, but uselessly. The inherent and appalling sadness of existence enveloped and chilled him. He gazed at the rows of his books. He had done no regular reading of late. Why read? He gazed at the screen in front of his bed, covered with neat memoranda. How futile! Why go to London? He would only have to come back from London! And then he said resistingly, 'I *will* go to London.' But as he said it aloud, he knew well that he would not go. His conscience would not allow him to depart. He could not leave Maggie alone with his father. He yielded to his conscience unkindly, reluctantly, with no warm gust of unselfishness; he yielded because he could not outrage his abstract sense of justice.

From the window he perceived Maggie and Janet Orgreave talking together over the low separating wall. And he remembered a word of Janet's to the effect that she and Maggie were becoming quite friendly and that Maggie was splendid. Suddenly he went downstairs into the garden. They were talking in attitudes of intimacy; and both were grave and mature, and both had a little cleft under the chin. Their pale frocks harmonized in the evening light. As he approached, Maggie burst into a girlish laugh. 'Not really?' she murmured, with the vivacity of a young girl. He knew not what they were discussing, nor did he care. What interested him, what startled him, was the youthful gesture and tone of Maggie. It pleased and touched him to discover another Maggie in the Maggie of the household. Those two women had put on for a moment the charming, chattering silliness of schoolgirls. He joined them. On the lawn of the Orgreaves. Alicia was battling fiercely at tennis with an elegant young man whose name he did not know. Croquet was deposed; tennis reigned.

Even Alicia's occasional shrill cry had a mournful quality in the languishing beauty of the evening.

'I wish you'd tell your father I shan't be able to go tomorrow,' Edwin said to Janet.

'But he's told all of us you *are* going!' Janet exclaimed.

'Shan't you go?' Maggie questioned, low.

'No,' he murmured. Glancing at Janet, he added, 'It won't do for me to go.'

'What a pity!' Janet breathed.

Maggie did not say, 'Oh! But you ought to! There's no reason whatever why you shouldn't!' By her silence she contradicted the philosophic nonchalance of her demeanour during the latter part of the meal.

CHAPTER 9 : *The Ox*

I

Edwin walked idly down Trafalgar Road in the hot morning sunshine of Jubilee Day. He had left his father tearfully sentimentalizing about the Queen. 'She's a good 'un !' Then a sob. 'Never was one like her !' Another sob. 'No, and never will be again !' Then a gush of tears on the newspaper, which the old man laboriously scanned for details of the official programme in London. He had not for months read the newspaper with such a determined effort to understand; indeed, since the beginning of his illness, no subject, except mushroom-culture, had interested him so much as the Jubilee. Each time he looked at the sky from his shady seat in the garden he had thanked God that it was a fine day, as he might have thanked Him for deliverance from a grave personal disaster.

Except for a few poor flags, there was no sign of gaiety in Trafalgar Road. The street, the town, and the hearts of those who remained in it, were wrapped in that desolating sadness which envelops the provinces when a supreme spectacular national rejoicing is centralized in London. All those who possessed the freedom, the energy, and the money had gone to London to witness a sight that, as everyone said to everyone, would be unique, and would remain unique for ever – and yet perhaps less to witness it than to be able to recount to their grandchildren that they had witnessed it. Many more were visiting nearer holiday resorts for a day or two days. Those who remained, the poor, the spiritless, the afflicted, and the captive, felt with mournful keenness the shame of their utter provinciality, envying the crowds in London with a bitter envy, and picturing London as the paradise of fashion and splendour.

It was from sheer aimless disgust that Edwin went down Trafalgar Road; he might as easily have gone up. Having arrived in the town, a wilderness of shut shops, he gazed a moment at his own, and then entered it by the side door. He had naught else to do. Had he chosen he could have spent the whole day in reading, or he might have taken again to his long-neglected water-colours. But it was not in him to put himself to the trouble of seeking contentment. He preferred to wallow in utter desolation, thinking of all the unpleasant things that had ever happened to him, and occasionally conjecturing what he would have been doing at a given moment had he accompanied the jolly, the distinguished, and the enterprising Osmond Orgreave to London.

He passed into the shop, sufficiently illuminated by the white rays that struck through the diamond holes in the shutters. The morning's letters – a sparse company – lay forlorn on the floor. He picked them up and pitched them down in the cubicle. Then he went into the cubicle, and with the negligent gesture of long habit unlocked a part of the desk, the part which had once been his father's privacy, and of which he had demanded the key more than a year ago. It was all now under his absolute dominion. He could do exactly as he pleased with a commercial apparatus that brought in some eight hundred pounds a year net. He was the unquestioned regent, and yet he told himself that he was no happier than when a slave.

He drew forth his books of account, and began to piece figures together on backs of envelopes, using a shorthand of accounts such as a principal will use when he is impatient and not particular to a few pounds. A little wasp of curiosity was teasing Edwin, and to quicken it a comparison was necessary between the result of the first six months of that year and the first six months of the previous year. True, June had not quite expired, but most of the quarterly accounts were ready, and he could form a trustworthy estimate. Was he, with his scorn of his father, his brains, his orderliness, doing better or worse than his father in the business? At the election of 1886, there had been considerably fewer orders than was customary at elections; he had done nothing whatever for the Tories, but that was a point that affected neither period of six months. Sundry customers had assuredly been lost; on the other hand, Stifford's travelling had seemed to be very satisfactory. Nor could it be argued that money had been dropped on the new-book business, because he had not yet inaugurated the new-book business, preferring to wait; he was afraid that his father might after all astoundingly walk in one day, and see new books on the counter, and rage. He had stopped the supplying of newspapers, and would deign to nothing lower than a sixpenny magazine; but the profit on newspapers was negligible.

The totals ought surely to compare in a manner favourable to himself, for he had been extremely and unremittingly conscientious. Nevertheless he was afraid. He was afraid because he knew, vaguely and still deeply, that he could neither buy nor sell as well as his father. It was not a question of brains; it was a question of individuality. A sense of honour, of fairness, a temperamental generosity, a hatred of meanness, often prevented him from pushing a bargain to the limit. He could not bring himself to haggle desperately. And even when price was not the main difficulty, he could not talk to a customer, or to a person whose customer he was, with the same rough, gruff, cajoling, bullying skill as his father. He could not, by taking thought, do what his father had done naturally, by the mere blind exercise of instinct. His father, with all his clumsiness, and his unscientific methods, had a certain quality, unseizable, unanalysable, and Edwin had not that quality.

He caught himself, in the rapid calculating, giving himself the benefit of every doubt; somehow he could not help it, childish as it was. And even so, he could see, or he could feel, that the comparison was not going to be favourable to the regent. It grew plainer that the volume of business had barely been maintained, and it was glaringly evident that the expenses, especially wages, had sensibly increased. He abandoned the figures not quite finished, partly from weary disgust, and partly because Big James most astoundingly walked into the shop, from the back. He was really quite glad to encounter Big James, a fellow-creature.

II

'Seeing the door open, sir,' said Big James cheerfully, through the narrow doorway of the cubicle, 'I stepped in to see as it was no one unlawful.'

'Did I leave the side door open?' Edwin murmured. It was surprising even to himself, how forgetful he was at times, he with his mania for orderliness!

Big James was in his best clothes, and seemed, with his indestructible blandness, to be perfectly happy.

'I was just strolling up to have a look at the ox,' he added.

'Oh!' said Edwin. 'Are they cooking it?'

'They should be, sir. But my fear is it may turn, in this weather.'

'I'll come out with you,' said Edwin, enlivened.

He locked the desk, and hurriedly straightened a few things, and then they went out together, by Wedgwood Street and the Cock Yard up to the market-place. No breeze moved, and the heat was tremendous. And there at the foot of the Town Hall tower, and in its scanty shadow, a dead ox, slung by its legs from an iron construction, was frizzling over a great primitive fire. The vast flanks of the animal, all rich yellows and browns, streamed with grease, some of which fell noisily on the almost invisible flames, while the rest was ingeniously caught in a system of runnels. The spectacle was obscene, nauseating to the eye, the nose, and the ear, and it powerfully recalled to Edwin the legends of the Spanish Inquisition. He speculated whether he would ever be able to touch beef again. Above the tortured and insulted corpse the air quivered in large waves. Mr Doy, the leading butcher of Bursley, and now chief executioner, regarded with anxiety the operation which had been entrusted to him, and occasionally gave instructions to a myrmidon. Round about stood a few privileged persons, whom pride helped to bear the double heat; and farther off on the pavements, a thin scattered crowd. The sublime spectacle of an ox roasted whole had not sufficed to keep the townsmen in the town. Even the sages who had conceived and commanded this peculiar solemnity for celebrating the Jubilee of a Queen and Empress had not stayed in the borough to see it enacted, though some of them were to return in time to watch the devouring of the animal by the aged poor at a ceremonial feast in the evening.

'It's a grand sight!' said Big James, with simple enthusiasm. 'A grand sight! Real old English! And I wish her well!' He meant the Queen and Empress. Then suddenly, in a different tone, sniffing the air, 'I doubt it's turned! I'll step across and ask Mr Doy.'

He stepped across, and came back with the news that the greater portion of the ox, despite every precaution, had in fact very annoyingly 'turned', and that the remainder of the carcase was in serious danger.

'What'll the old people say?' he demanded sadly. 'But it's a grand sight, turned or not!'

Edwin stared and stared, in a sort of sinister fascination. He thought that he might stare for ever. At length, after ages of ennui, he loosed himself from the spell with an effort and glanced at Big James.

'And what are you going to do with yourself today, James?'

Big James smiled. 'I'm going to take my walks abroad, sir. It's seldom as I get about in the town nowadays.'

'Well, I must be off!'

'I'd like you to give my respects to the old gentleman, sir.'

Edwin nodded and departed, very slowly and idly, towards Trafalgar Road and Bleakridge. He pulled his straw hat over his forehead to avoid the sun, and then he pushed it backwards to his neck to avoid the sun. The odour of the shrivelling ox remained with him; it was in his nostrils for several days. His heart grew blacker with intense gloom; and the contentment of Big James at the prospect of just strolling about the damnable dead town for the rest of the day surpassed his comprehension. He abandoned himself to misery voluptuously. The afternoon and evening stretched before him, an arid and appalling Sahara. The Benbows, and their babies, and Auntie Hamps were coming for dinner and tea, to cheer up grandfather. He pictured the repasts with savage gloating detestation – burnt ox, and more burnt ox, and the false odious brightness of a family determined to be mutually helpful and inspiring. Since his refusal to abet the project of a loan to Albert, Clara had been secretly hostile under her superficial sisterliness, and Auntie Hamps had often assured him, in a manner extraordinarily exasperating, that she was convinced he had acted conscientiously for the best. Strange thought, that after eight hours of these people and his father, he would still be alive!

CHAPTER 10 : *Mrs Hamps as a Young Man*

I

On the Saturday afternoon of the week following the Jubilee, Edwin and Mrs Hamps were sunning themselves in the garden, when Janet's face and shoulders appeared suddenly at the other side of the wall. At the sight of Mrs Hamps she seemed startled and intimidated, and she bowed somewhat more ceremoniously than usual.

'Good afternoon!'

Then Mrs Hamps returned the bow with superb extravagance, like an Oriental monarch who is determined to outvie magnificently the gifts of another. Mrs Hamps became conscious of the whole of her body and every article of her summer apparel, and nothing of it all was allowed to escape from contributing to the completeness of the bow. She bridled. She tossed proudly as it were against the bit. And the rich ruins of her handsomeness adopted new and softer lines in the over-powering sickly blandishment of a smile. Thus she always greeted any merely formal acquaintance whom she considered to be above herself in status – provided, of course, that the acquaintance had done nothing to offend her.

'Good after*n*oon, Miss Orgreave!'

Reluctantly she permitted her features to relax from the full effort of the smile; but they might not abandon it entirely.

'I thought Maggie was there,' said Janet.

'She was, a minute ago,' Edwin answered. 'She's just gone in to father. She'll be out directly. Do you want her?'

'I only wanted to tell her something,' said Janet, and then paused.

She was obviously very excited. She had the little quick movements of a girl. In her cream-tinted frock she looked like a mere girl. And she was beautiful in her maturity; a challenge to the world of males. As she stood there, rising from behind the wall, flushed, quivering, abandoned to an emotion and yet unconsciously dignified by that peculiar stateliness that never left her – as she stood there it seemed as if she really was offering a challenge.

'I'll fetch Mag, if you like,' said Edwin.

'Well,' said Janet, lifting her chin proudly, 'it isn't a secret. Alicia's engaged.' And pride was in every detail of her bearing.

'Well, I never!' Edwin exclaimed.

Mrs Hamps's features resumed the full smile.

303

'Can you imagine it? I can't! It seems only last week that she left school!'

And indeed it seemed only last week that Alicia was nothing but legs, gawkiness, blushes, and screwed-up shoulders. And now she was a destined bride. She had caught and enchanted a youth by her mysterious attractiveness. She had been caught and enchanted by the mysterious attractiveness of the male. She had known the dreadful anxiety that precedes the triumph, and the ecstasy of surrender. She had kissed as Janet had never kissed, and gazed as Janet had never gazed. She knew infinitely more than Janet. She had always been a child to Janet, but now Janet was the child. No wonder that Janet was excited.

'Might one ask who is the fortunate young gentleman?' Mrs Hamps dulcetly inquired.

'It's Harry Hesketh, from Oldcastle. . . . You've met him here,' she added, glancing at Edwin.

Mrs Hamps nodded, satisfied, and the approving nod indicated that she was aware of all the excellences of the Hesketh family.

'The tennis man!' Edwin murmured.

'Yes, of course! You aren't surprised, are you?'

The fact was that Edwin had not given a thought to the possible relations between Alicia and any particular young man. But Janet's thrilled air so patently assumed his interest that he felt obliged to make a certain pretence.

'I'm not what you'd call staggered,' he said roguishly. 'I'm keeping my nerve.' And he gave her an intimate smile.

'Father-in-law and son-in-law have just been talking it over,' said Janet archly, 'in the breakfast-room! Alicia thoughtfully went out for a walk. I'm dying for her to come back.' Janet laughed from simple joyous expectation. 'When Harry came out of the breakfast-room he just put his arms round me and kissed me. Yes! That was how I was told about it. He's a dear! Don't you think so? I mean really! I felt I must come and tell someone.'

Edwin had never seen her so moved. Her emotion was touching, it was beautiful. She need not have said that she had come because she must. The fact was in her rapt eyes. She was under a spell.

'Well, I must go!' she said, with a curious brusqueness. Perhaps she had a dim perception that she was behaving in a manner unusual with her. 'You'll tell your sister.'

Her departing bow to Mrs Hamps had the formality of courts, and was equalled by Mrs Hamps's bow. Just as Mrs Hamps, having re-created her elaborate smile, was allowing it finally to expire, she had to bring it into existence once more, and very suddenly, for Janet re-turned to the wall.

'You won't forget tennis after tea,' said Janet shortly.
Edwin said that he should not.

II

'Well, well!' Mrs Hamps commented, and sat down in the wicker-chair of Darius.

'I wonder she doesn't get married herself,' said Edwin idly, having nothing in particular to remark.

'You're a nice one to say such a thing!' Mrs Hamps exclaimed.

'Why?'

'Well, you really are!' She raised the structure of her bonnet and curls, and shook it slowly at him. And her gaze had an extraordinary quality of fleshly naughtiness that half pleased and half annoyed him.

'Why?' he repeated.

'Well,' she said again, 'you aren't a ninny, and you aren't a simpleton. At least I hope not. You must know as well as anybody the name of the young gentleman that *she's* waiting for.'

In spite of himself, Edwin blushed : he blushed more and more. Then he scowled.

'What nonsense!' he muttered viciously. He was entirely sincere. The notion that Janet was waiting for him had never once crossed his mind. It seemed to him fantastic, one of those silly ideas that a woman such as Auntie Hamps would be likely to have, or more accurately would be likely to pretend to have. Still, it did just happen that on this occasion his auntie's expression was more convincing than usual. She seemed more human than usual, to have abandoned, at any rate partially, the baffling garment of effusive insincerity in which she hid her soul. The Eve in her seemed to show herself and, looking forth from her eyes, to admit that the youthful dalliance of the sexes was alone interesting in this life of strict piety. The revelation was uncanny.

'You needn't talk like that,' she retorted calmly, 'unless you want to go down in my good opinion. You don't mean to tell me honestly that you don't know what's been the talk of the town for years and years!'

'It's ridiculous,' said Edwin. 'Why – what do you know of her – you don't know the Orgreaves at all!'

'I know *that*, anyway,' said Auntie Hamps.

'Oh! Stuff!' He grew impatient.

And yet, in his extreme astonishment, he was flattered and delighted.

'Of course,' said Auntie Hamps, 'you're so difficult to talk to –'

'Difficult to talk to! – Me?'

'Otherwise your auntie might have given you a hint long ago. I believe you are a simpleton after all! I cannot understand what's come over the young men in these days. Letting a girl like that wait and wait!' She implied, with a faint scornful smile, that if she were a young man she would be capable of playing the devil with the maidenhood of the town. Edwin was rather hurt. And though he felt that he ought not to be ashamed, yet he was ashamed. He divined that she was asking him how he had the face to stand there before her, at his age, with his youth unspilled. After all, she was an astounding woman. He remained silent.

'Why – look how splendid it would be!' she murmured. 'The very thing! Everybody would be delighted!'

He still remained silent.

'But you can't keep on philandering for ever!' she said sharply. 'She'll never see thirty again! . . . Why does she ask you to go and play at tennis? Can you tell me that? . . . Perhaps I'm saying too much, but this I *will* say –'

She stopped.

Darius and Maggie appeared at the garden door. Maggie offered her hand to aid her father, but he repulsed it. Calmly she left him, and came up the garden, out of the deep shadow into the sunshine. She had learnt the news of the engagement, and had fully expressed her feelings about it before Darius arrived at his destination and Mrs Hamps vacated the wicker-chair.

'I'll get some chairs,' said Edwin gruffly. He could look nobody in the eyes. As he turned away he heard Mrs Hamps say –

'Great news, father! Alicia Orgreave is engaged!'

The old man made no reply. His mere physical presence deprived the betrothal of all its charm. The news fell utterly flat and lay unregarded and insignificant.

Edwin did not get the chairs. He sent the servant out with them.

CHAPTER 11 : *An Hour*

I

Janet called out –

'Play – no, I think perhaps you'll do better if you stand a little farther back. Now – play!'

She brought down her lifted right arm, and smacked the ball into the net.

'Double fault!' she cried, lamenting, when she had done this twice. 'Oh dear! Now you go over to the other side of the court.'

Edwin would not have kept the rendezvous could he have found an excuse satisfactory to himself for staying away. He was a beginner of tennis, and a very awkward one, having little aptitude for games, and being now inelastic in the muscles. He possessed no flannels, though for weeks he had been meaning to get at least a pair of white pants. He was wearing Jimmie Orgreave's india-rubber pumps, which admirably fitted him. Moreover, he was aware that he looked better in his jacket than in his shirt-sleeves. But these reasons against the rendezvous were naught. The only genuine reason was that he had felt timid about meeting Janet. Could he meet her without revealing by his mere guilty glance that his aunt had half convinced him that he had only to ask nicely in order to receive? Could he meet her without giving her the impression that he was a conceited ass? He had met her. She was waiting for him in the garden, and by dint of starting the conversation in loud tones from a distance, and fumbling a few moments with the tennis balls before approaching her, he had come through the encounter without too much foolishness.

And now he was glad that he had not been so silly as to stay away. She was alone; Mrs Orgreave was lying down, and all the others were out. Alicia and her Harry were off together somewhere. She was alone in the garden, and she was beautiful, and the shaded garden was beautiful, and the fading afternoon. The soft short grass was delicate to his feet, and round the oval of the lawn were glimpses of flowers, and behind her clear-tinted frock was the yellow house laced over with green. A column of thick smoke rose from a manufactory close behind the house, but the trees mitigated it. He played perfunctorily, uninterested in the game, dreaming.

She was a wondrous girl! She was the perfect girl! Nobody had ever been able to find any fault with her. He liked her exceedingly. Had it been necessary, he would have sacrificed his just interests in the altercation with her father in order to avoid a coolness in which she might have been involved. She was immensely distinguished and superior. And she was over thirty and had never been engaged, despite the number and variety of her acquaintances, despite her challenging readiness to flirt, and her occasional coquetries. Ten years ago he had almost regarded her as a madonna on a throne, so high did she seem to be above him. His ideas had changed, but there could be no doubt that in an alliance between an Orgreave and a Clayhanger, it would be the Clayhanger who stood to gain the greater advantage. There she was! If she was not waiting for him, she was waiting – for someone! Why not for him as well as for another?

He said to himself –

'Why shouldn't I be happy? That other thing is all over!'

It was, in fact, years since the name of Hilda had ever been mentioned between them. Why should he not be happy? There was nothing to prevent her from being happy. His father's illness could not endure for ever. One day soon he would be free in theory as well as in practice. With no tie and no duty (Maggie was negligible) he would have both money and position. What might his life not be with a woman like Janet, brilliant, beautiful, elegant, and faithful? He pictured that life, and even the vision of it dazzled him. Janet his! Janet always there, presiding over a home which was his home, wearing hats that he had paid for, appealing constantly to his judgement, and meaning *him* when she said: 'My husband.' He saw her in the close and tender intimacy of marriage, acquiescent, exquisite, yielding, calmly accustomed to him, modest, but with a different modesty! It was a vision surpassing visions. And there she was on the other side of the net!

With her he could be his finest self. He would not have to hide his finest self from ridicule, as often now, among his own family.

She was a fine woman! He watched the free movement of her waist, and the curvings and flyings of her short tennis skirt. And there was something strangely feminine about the neck of her blouse, now that he examined it.

Your game!' she cried. 'That's four double faults I've served. I can't play! I really don't think I can. There's something the matter with me! Or else it's the net that's too high. Those boys will keep screwing it up!'

She had a pouting, capricious air, and it delighted him. Never had he seen her so enchantingly girlish as, by a curious hazard, he saw her now. Why should he not be happy? Why should he not wake up out of his nightmare and begin to live? In a momentary flash he seemed to see his past in a true perspective, as it really was, as some well-balanced person not himself would have seen it. . . . Mere morbidity to say, as he had been saying privately for years, that marriage was not for him! Marriage emphatically was for him, if only because he had fine ideals of it. Most people who married were too stupid to get the value of their adventure. Celibacy was grotesque, cowardly, and pitiful – no matter how intellectual the celibate – and it was no use pretending the contrary.

A masculine gesture, an advance, a bracing of the male in him . . . probably nothing else was needed.

'Well,' he said boldly, 'if you don't want to play, let's sit down and rest.' And then he gave a nervous little laugh.

II

They sat down on the bench that was shaded by the old elderberry tree. Visually, the situation had all the characteristics of an idyllic courtship.

'I suppose it's Alicia's engagement,' she said, smiling reflectively, 'that's put me off my game. They do upset you, those things do, and you don't know why. . . . It isn't as if Ailcia was the first – I mean of us girls. There was Marian; but then, of course, that was so long ago, and I was only a chit.'

'Yes,' he murmured vaguely; and though she seemed to be waiting for him to say more, he merely repeated, 'Yes.'

Such was his sole contribution to this topic, so suitable to the situation, so promising, so easy of treatment. They were so friendly that he was under no social obligation to talk for the sake of talking.

That was it : they were too friendly. She sat within a foot of him, reclining against the sloping back of the bench, and idly dangling one white-shod foot; her long hands lay on her knees. She was there in all her perfection. But by some sinister magic, as she had approached him and their paths had met at the bench, his vision had faded. Now, she was no longer a woman and he a man. Now, the curvings of her drapery from the elegant waistband were no longer a provocation. She was immediately beneath his eye, and he recognized her again for what she was – Janet! Precisely Janet – no less and no more! But her beauty, her charm, her faculty for affection – surely . . . No! His instinct was deaf to all 'buts'. His instinct did not argue; it cooled. Fancy had created a vision in an instant out of an idea, and in an instant the vision had died. He remembered Hilda with painful intensity. He remembered the feel of her frock under his hand in the cubicle, and the odour of her flesh that was like fruit. His cursed constancy ! . . . Could he not get Hilda out of his bones? Did she sleep in his bones like a malady that awakes whenever it is disrespectfully treated?

He grew melancholy. Accustomed to savour the sadness of existence, he soon accepted the new mood without resentment. He resigned himself to the destruction of his dream. He was like a captive whose cell has been opened in mistake, and who is too gentle to rave when he sees it shut again. Only in secret he poured an indifferent, careless scorn upon Auntie Hamps.

They played a whole interminable set, and then Edwin went home, possibly marvelling at the variety of experience that a single hour may contain.

CHAPTER 12 : *Revenge*

I

Edwin re-entered his home with a feeling of dismayed resignation. There was then no escape, and never could be any escape, from the existence to which he was accustomed; even after his father's death, his existence would still be essentially the same – incomplete and sterile. He accepted the destiny, but he was daunted by it.

He quietly shut the front door, which had been ajar, and as he did so he heard voices in the drawing-room.

'I tell ye I'm going to grow mushrooms,' Darius was saying. 'Can't I grow mushrooms in my own cellar,' Then a snort.

'I don't think it'll be a good thing,' was Maggie's calm reply.

'Ye've said that afore. Why won't it be a good thing? And what's it got to do with you?' The voice of Darius, ordinarily weak and languid, was rising and becoming strong.

'Well, you'd be falling up and down the cellar steps. You know how dark they are. Supposing you hurt yourself?'

'Ye'd only be too glad if I killed mysen!' said Darius, with a touch of his ancient grimness.

There was a pause.

'And it seems they want a lot of attention, mushrooms do,' Maggie went on with unperturbed placidity. 'You'd never be able to do it.'

'Jane could help me,' said Darius, in the tone of one who is rather pleased with an ingenious suggestion.

'Oh no, she couldn't!' Maggie exclaimed, with a peculiar humorous dryness which she employed only on the rarest occasions. Jane was the desired Bathsheba.

'And I say she could!' the old man shouted with surprising vigour. 'Her does nothing! What does Mrs Nixon do? What do you do? Three great strapping women in the house and doing naught! I say she shall!' The voice dropped and snarled. 'Who's master here? Is it me, or is it the cat? D'ye think as I can't turn ye all out of it neck and crop, if I've a mind? You and Edwin, and the lot of ye! And tonight too! Give me some money now, and quicker than that! I've got nought but sovereigns and notes. I'll go down and get the spawn myself – ay! and order the earth too! I'll make it my business to show my childer – But I mun have some change for my car fares.' He breathed heavily.

'I'm sure Edwin won't like it,' Maggie murmured.

'Edwin! Hast told Edwin?' Darius also murmured, but it was a murmur of rage.

'No, I haven't. Edwin's got quite enough on his hands as it is, without any other worries.'

There was the noise of a sudden movement, and of a chair falling.

'B– you all!' Darius burst out with a fury whose restraint showed that he had suspected reserves of strength. And then he began to swear. Edwin, like many timid men, often used forbidden words with much ferocity in private. Once he had had a long philosophic argument with Tom Orgreave on the subject of profanity. They had discussed all aspects of it, from its religious origin to its psychological results, and Edwin's theory had been that it was only improper by a purely superstitious convention, and that no man of sense could possibly be offended, in himself, by the mere sound of words that had been deprived of meaning. He might be offended on behalf of an unreasoning fellow-listener, such as a woman, but not personally. Edwin now discovered that his theory did not hold. He was offended. He was almost horrified. He had never in his life till that moment heard Darius swear. He heard him now. He considered himself to be a fairly first-class authority on swearing; he thought that he was familiar with all the sacred words and with all the combinations of them. He was mistaken. His father's profanity was a brilliant and appalling revelation. It comprised words which were strange to him, and strange perversions that renewed the vigour of decrepit words. For Edwin, it was a whole series of fresh formulae, brutal and shameless beyond his experience, full of images and similes of the most startling candour, and drawing its inspiration always from the sickening bases of life. Darius had remembered with ease the vocabulary to which he was hourly accustomed when he began life as a man of seven. For more than fifty years he had carried within himself these vestigies of a barbarism which his children had never even conceived, and now he threw them out in all their crudity at his daughter. And when she did not blench, he began to accuse her as men used to accuse their daughters in the bright days of the Sailor King. He invented enormities which she had committed, and there would have been no obscene infamy of which Maggie was not guilty, if Edwin – more by instinct than by volition – had not pushed open the door and entered the drawing-room.

II

He was angry, and the sight of the flushed meekness of his sister, as she leaned quietly with her back against an easy-chair, made him angrier.

'Enough of this!' he said gruffly and peremptorily.

Darius, with scarcely a break, continued.

'I say enough of this!' Edwin cried, with increased harshness.

The old man paused, half intimidated. With his pimpled face and glaring eyes, his gleaming gold teeth, his frowziness of a difficult invalid, his grimaces and gestures which were the results of a lifetime devoted to gain, he made a loathsome object. Edwin hated him, and there was a bitter contempt in his hatred.

'I'm going to have that spawn, and I'm going to have some change! Give me some money!' Darius positively hissed.

Edwin grew nearly capable of homicide. All the wrongs that he had suffered leaped up and yelled.

'You'll have no money!' he said, with brutal roughness. 'And you'll grow no mushrooms! And let that be understood once for all! You've got to behave in this house.'

Darius flickered up.

'Do you hear?' Edwin stamped on the conflagration.

It was extinguished. Darius, cowed, slowly and clumsily directed himself towards the door. Once Edwin had looked forward to a moment when he might have his father at his mercy, when he might revenge himself for the insults and the bullying that had been his. Once he had clenched his fist and his teeth, and had said, 'When you're old, and I've *got* you, and you can't help yourself . . . !' That moment had come, and it had even enabled and forced him to refuse money to his father – refuse money to his father! . . . As he looked at the poor figure fumbling towards the door, he knew the humiliating paltriness of revenge. As his anger fell, his shame grew.

Maggie lifted her eyebrows when Darius banged the door.

'He can't help it,' she said.

'Of course he can't help it,' said Edwin, defending himself, less to Maggie than to himself. 'But there must be a limit. He's got to be kept in order, you know, even if he is an invalid.' His heart was perceptibly beating.

'Yes, of course.'

'And evidently there's only one way of doing it. How long's he been on this mushroom tack?'

'Oh, not long.'

'Well, you ought to have told me,' said Edwin, with the air of a master of the house who is displeased. Maggie accepted the reproof.

'He'd break his neck in the cellar before he knew where he was,' Edwin resumed.

'Yes, he would,' said Maggie, and left the room.

Upon her placid features there was not the slightest trace of the onslaught of profanity. The faint flush had paled away.

III

The next morning, Sunday, Edwin came downstairs late, to the sound of singing. In his soft carpet-slippers he stopped at the foot of the stairs and tapped the weather-glass, after the manner of his father; and listened. It was a duet for female voices that was being sung, composed by Balfe to the words of the good Longfellow's *Excelsior*. A pretty thing, charming in its thin sentimentality; one of the few pieces that Darius in former days really understood and liked. Maggie and Clara had not sung it for years. For years they had not sung it at all.

Edwin went to the doorway of the drawing-room and stood there. Clara, in Sunday bonnet, was seated at the ancient piano; it had always been she who had played the accompaniments. Maggie, nursing one of the babies, sat on another chair, and leaned towards the page in order to make out the words. She had half-forgotten the words, and Clara was no longer at ease in the piano part, and their voices were shaky and unruly, and the piano itself was exceedingly bad. A very indifferent performance of indifferent music! And yet it touched Edwin. He could not deny that by its beauty and by the sentiment of old times it touched him. He moved a little forward in the doorway. Clara glanced at him, and winked. Now he could see his father. Darius was standing at some distance behind his daughters and his grandchild, and staring at them. And the tears rained down from his red eyes, and then his emotion overcame him and he blubbered, just as the duet finished.

'Now, father,' Clara protested cheerfully, 'this won't do. You know you asked for it. Give me the infant, Maggie.'

Edwin walked away.

CHAPTER 13 : *The Journey Upstairs*

I

Late on another Saturday afternoon in the following March, when Darius had been ill nearly two years, he and Edwin and Albert were sitting round the remains of high tea together in the dining-room. Clara had not been able to accompany her husband on what was now the customary Saturday visit, owing to the illness of her fourth child. Mrs Hamps was fighting chronic rheumatism at home. And Maggie had left the table to cosset Mrs Nixon, who of late received more help than she gave.

Darius sat in dull silence. The younger men were talking about the

Bursley Society for the Prosecution of Felons, of which Albert had just been made a member. Whatever it might have been in the past, the Society for the Prosecution of Felons was now a dining-club and little else. Its annual dinner, admitted to be the chief oratorical event of the year, was regarded as strictly exclusive, because no member, except the president, had the right to bring a guest to it. Only 'Felons', as they humorously named themselves, and the reporters of the *Signal*, might listen to the eloquence of Felons. Albert Benbow, who for years had been hearing about the brilliant funniness of the American Consul at these dinners, was so flattered by his Felonry that he would have been ready to put the letters S.P.F. after his name.

'Oh, you'll have to join!' said he to Edwin, kindly urgent, like a man who, recently married, goes about telling all bachelors that they positively must marry at once. 'You ought to get it fixed up before the next feed.'

Edwin shook his head. Though he, too, dreamed of the Felons' Dinner as a repast really worth eating, though he wanted to be a Felon, and considered that he ought to be a Felon, and wondered why he was not already a Felon, he repeatedly assured Albert that Felonry was not for him.

'You're a Felon, aren't you, dad?' Albert shouted at Darius.

'Oh yes, father's a Felon,' said Edwin. 'Has been ever since I can remember.'

'Did ye ever speak there?' asked Albert, with an air of good-humoured condescension.

Darius's elbow slipped violently off the tablecloth, and a knife fell to the floor and a plate after it. Darius went pale.

'All right! All right! Don't be alarmed, dad!' Albert reassured him, picking up the things. 'I was asking ye, did ye ever speak there – make a speech?'

'Yes,' said Darius heavily.

'Did you now!' Albert murmured, staring at Darius. And it was exactly as if he had said, 'Well, it's extraordinary that a foolish physical and mental wreck such as you are now, should ever have had wit and courage enough to rise and address the glorious Felons!'

Darius glanced up at the gas, with a gesture that was among Edwin's earliest recollections, and then he fixed his eyes dully on the fire, with head bent and muscles lax.

'Have a cigarette – that'll cheer ye up,' said Albert.

Darius made a negative sign.

'He's very tired, seemingly,' Albert remarked to Edwin, as if Darius had not been present.

'Yes,' Edwin muttered, examining his father. Darius appeared ten years older than his age. His thin hair was white, though the straggling beard that had been allowed to grow was only grey. His face was sunken and pale, but even more striking was the extreme pallor of the hands with their long clean fingernails, those hands that had been red and rough, tools of all work. His clothes hung somewhat loosely on him, and a shawl round his shoulders was awry. The comatose melancholy in his eyes was acutely painful to see – so much so that Edwin could not bear to look long at them. 'Father,' Edwin asked him suddenly, 'wouldn't you like to go to bed?'

And to his surprise Darius said, 'Yes.'

'Well, come on then.'

Darius did not move.

'Come on,' Edwin urged. 'I'm sure you're overtired, and you'll be better in bed.'

He took his father by the arm, but there was no responsive movement. Often Edwin noticed this capricious, obstinate attitude; his father would express a wish to do a certain thing, and then would make no effort to do it. 'Come!' said Edwin more firmly, pulling at the lifeless arm. Albert sprang up, and said that he would assist. One on either side, they got Darius to his feet, and slowly walked him out of the room. He was very exasperating. His weight and his inertia were terrible. The spectacle suggested that either Darius was pretending to be a carcase, or Edwin and Albert were pretending that a carcase was alive. On the stairs there was not room for the three abreast. One had to push, another to pull : Darius seemed wilfully to fall backwards if pressure were released. Edwin restrained his exasperation; but though he said nothing, his sharp half-vicious pull on that arm seemed to say, 'Confound you! Come up – will you!' The last two steps of the stair had a peculiar effect on Darius. He appeared to shy at them, and then finally to jib. It was no longer a reasonable creature that they were getting upstairs, but an incalculable and mysterious beast. They lifted him on to the landing, and he stood on the landing as if in his sleep. Both Edwin and Albert were breathless. This was the man who since the beginning of his illness had often walked to Hillport and back! It was incredible that he had ever walked to Hillport and back. He passed more easily along the landing. And then he was in his bedroom.

'Father going to bed?' Maggie called out from below.

'Yes,' said Albert. 'We've just been getting him upstairs.'

'Oh! That's right,' Maggie said cheerfully. 'I thought he was looking very tired tonight.'

'He gave us a doing,' said the breathless Albert in a low voice at the door of the bedroom, smiling, and glancing at his cigarette to see if it was still alight.

'He does it on purpose, you know,' Edwin whispered casually. 'I'll just get him to bed, and then I'll be down.'

Albert went, with a 'good night' to Darius that received no answer.

II

In his bedroom, Darius had sunk on to the cushioned ottoman. Edwin shut the door.

'Now then !' said Edwin encouragingly, yet commandingly. 'I can tell you one thing – you aren't losing weight.' He had recovered from his annoyance, but he was not disposed to submit to any trifling. For many months now he had helped Darius to dress, when he came up from the shop for breakfast, and to undress in the evening. It was not that his father lacked the strength, but he would somehow lose himself in the maze of his garments, and apparently he could never remember the proper order of doffing or donning them. Sometimes he would ask, 'Am I dressing or undressing?' And he would be capable of so involving himself in a shirt, if Edwin were not there to direct, that much patience was needed for his extrication. His misapprehensions and mistakes frequently reached the grotesque. As habit threw them more and more intimately together, the trusting dependence of Darius on Edwin increased. At morning and evening the expression of that intensely mournful visage seemed to be saying as its gaze met Edwin's, 'Here is the one clear-sighted, powerful being who can guide me through this complex and frightful problem of my clothes.' A suit, for Darius, had become as intricate as a quadratic equation. And, in Edwin, compassion and irritation fought an interminable guerilla. Now one obtained the advantage, now the other. His nerves demanded relief from the friction, but he could offer them no holiday, not one single day's holiday. Twice every day he had to manoeuvre and persuade that ponderous, irrational body in his father's bedroom. Maggie helped the body to feed itself at table. But Maggie apparently had no nerves.

'I shall never go down them stairs again,' said Darius, as if in fatigued disgust, on the ottoman.

'Oh, nonsense !' Edwin exclaimed.

Darius shook his head solemnly, and looked at vacancy.

'Well, we'll talk about that tomorrow,' said Edwin, and with the skill of regular practice drew out the ends of the bow of his father's necktie. He had gradually evolved a complete code of rules covering the entire process of the toilette, and he insisted on their observance. Every article had its order in the ceremony and its place in the room. Never had the room been so tidy, nor the rites so expeditious, as in the final months of Darius's malady.

III

The cumbrous body lay in bed. The bed was in an architecturally contrived recess, sheltered from both the large window and the door. Over its head was the gas-bracket and the bell-knob. At one side was a night-table, and at the other a chair. In front of the night-table were Darius's slippers. On the chair were certain clothes. From a hook near the night-table, and almost over the slippers, hung his dressing-gown. Seen from the bed, the dressing-table, at the window, appeared to be a long way off, and the wardrobe was a long way off in another direction. The gas was turned low. It threw a pale illumination on the bed, and gleamed on a curve of mahogany here and there in the distances.

Edwin looked at his father, to be sure that all was in order, that nothing had been forgotten. The body seemed monstrous and shapeless beneath the thickly piled clothes; and from the edge of the eiderdown, making a valley in the pillow, the bearded face projected, in a manner grotesque and ridiculous. A clock struck seven in another part of the house.

'What time's that?' Darius murmured.

'Seven,' said Edwin, standing close to him.

Darius raised himself slowly and clumsily on one elbow.

'Here! But look here!' Edwin protested. 'I've just fixed you up . . .'

The old man ignored him, and one of those unnaturally white hands stretched forth to the night-table, which was on the side of the bed opposite to Edwin. Darius's gold watch and chain lay on the night-table.

'I've wound it up! I've wound it up!' said Edwin, a little crossly. 'What are you worrying at?'

But Darius, silent, continued to manoeuvre his flannelled arm so as to possess the watch. At length he seized the chain, and, shifting his weight to the other elbow, held out the watch and chain to Edwin, with a most piteous expression. Edwin could see in the twilight that his father was ready to weep.

'I want ye –' the old man began, and then burst into violent sobs; and the watch dangled dangerously.

'Come now!' Edwin tried to soothe him, forcing himself to be kindly. 'What is it? I tell you I've wound it up all right. And it's correct time to a tick.' He consulted his own silver watch.

With a tremendous effort, Darius mastered his sobs, and began once more, 'I want ye –'

He tried several times, but his emotion overcame him each time before he could force the message out. It was always too quick for him.

Silent, he could control it, but he could not simultaneously control it and speak.

'Never mind,' said Edwin. 'We'll see about that tomorrow.' And he wondered what bizarre project affecting the watch had entered his father's mind. Perhaps he wanted it set a quarter of an hour fast.

Darius dropped the watch on the eiderdown, and sighed in despair, and fell back on the pillow and shut his eyes. Edwin restored the watch to the night-table.

Later, he crept into the dim room. Darius was snoring under the twilight of the gas. Like an unhappy child, he had found refuge in sleep from the enormous, infantile problems of his existence. And it was so pathetic, so distressing, that Edwin, as he gazed at that beard and those gold teeth, could have sobbed too.

CHAPTER 14 : *The Watch*

I

When Edwin the next morning, rather earlier than usual on Sundays, came forth from his bedroom to go into the bathroom, he was startled by a voice from his father's bedroom calling him. It was Maggie's. She had heard him open his door, and she joined him on the landing.

'I was waiting for you to be getting up,' she said in a quiet tone. 'I don't think father's so well, and I was wondering whether I hadn't better send Jane down for the doctor. It's not certain he'll call today if he isn't specially fetched.'

'Why?' said Edwin. 'What's up?'

'Oh, nothing,' Maggie answered. 'Nothing particular, but – you didn't hear him ringing in the night?'

'Ringing? No! What time?'

'About one o'clock. Jane heard the bell, and she woke me. So I got up to him. He said he couldn't do with being alone.'

'What did you do?'

'I made him something hot and stayed with him.'

'What? All night?'

'Yes,' said Maggie.

'But why didn't you call me?'

'What was the good?'

'You ought to have called me,' he said with curt displeasure, not really against Maggie, but against himself for having heard naught of

all these happenings. Maggie had no appearance of having passed the
night by her father's bedside.

'Oh,' she said lightly, 'I dozed a bit now and then. And as soon
as the girl was up I got her to come and sit with him while I spruced
myself.'

'I'll have a look at him,' said Edwin, in another tone.

'Yes, I wish you would. 'Now, as often, he was struck by Maggie's
singular deference to him, her submission to his judgement. In the past
her attitude had been different; she had exercised the moral rights of
an elder sister; but latterly she had mysteriously transformed herself
into a younger sister.

He went towards his father, drawing his dressing-gown more closely
round him. The chamber had an aspect of freshness and tidiness that
made it almost gay – until he looked at the object in the smooth and
rectified bed. He nodded to his father, who merely gazed at him. There
was no definite, definable change in the old man's face, but his bearing,
even as he lay, was appreciably more melancholy and impotent. The
mere sight of a man so broken and so sad was humiliating to the
humanity which Edwin shared with him.

'Well, father,' he nodded familiarly. 'Don't feel like getting up, eh?'
And, remembering that he was the head of the house, the source of
authority and of strength, he tried to be cheerful, casual, and invigorat-
ing, and was disgusted by the futile inefficiency of the attempt. He had
not, like Auntie Hamps, devoted a lifetime to the study of the trick.

Darius feebly moved his hopeless head to signify a negative.

And Edwin thought, with a lancinating pain, of what the old man
had mumbled on the previous evening : 'I shall never go down these
stairs again.' Perhaps the old man never would go down those stairs
again ! He had paid no serious attention to the remark at the moment,
but now it presented itself to him as a solemn and prophetic utterance,
of such as are remembered with awe for years and continue to jut up
clear in the mind when all minor souvenirs of the time have crumbled
away. And he would have given much of his pride to be able to go back
and help the old man upstairs once more, and do it with a more loving
patience.

'I've sent Jane,' said Maggie, returning to the bedroom. 'You'd
better go and finish dressing.'

On coming out of the bathroom he discovered Albert on the landing, waiting.

'The missus would have me come up and see how he was,' said Albert.
'So I've run in between school and chapel. When I told her what a
doing he gave us, getting him upstairs, she was quite in a way, and she
would have me come up. The kid's better.' He was exceedingly and

quite genuinely fraternal, not having his wife's faculty for nourishing a feud.

II

The spectacular developments were rapid. In the afternoon Auntie Hamps, Clara, Maggie, and Edwin were grouped around the bed of Darius. A fire burned in the grate; flowers were on the dressing-table. An extra table had been placed at the foot of the bed. The room was a sick-room.

Dr Heve had called, and had said that the patient's desire not to be left alone was a symptom of gravity. He suggested a nurse, and when Maggie, startled, said that perhaps they could manage without a nurse, he inquired how. And as he talked he seemed to be more persuaded that a nurse was necessary, if only for night duty, and in the end he went himself to the new Telephone Exchange and ordered a nurse from the Pirehill Infirmary Nursing Home. And the dramatic thing was that within two hours and a half the nurse had arrived. And in ten minutes after that it had been arranged that she should have Maggie's bedroom and that she should take night duty, and in order that she might be fresh for the night she had gone straight off to bed.

Then Clara had arrived, in spite of the illness of her baby, and Auntie Hamps had forced herself up Trafalgar Road, in spite of her rheumatism. And a lengthy confabulation between the women had occurred in the dining-room, not about the invalid, but about what 'she' had said, and about the etiquette of treating 'her', and about what 'she' looked like and shaped like; 'her' and 'she' being the professional nurse. With a professional nurse in it, each woman sincerely felt that the house was no longer itself, that it had become the house of the enemy.

Darius lay supine before them, physically and spiritually abased, accepting, like a victim who is too weak even to be ashamed, the cooings and strokings and prayers and optimistic mendacities of Auntie Hamps, and the tearful tendernesses of Clara.

'I've made my will,' he whimpered.

'Yes, yes,' said Auntie Hamps. 'Of course you have!'

'Did I tell you I'd made my will?' he feebly insisted.

'Yes, father,' said Clara. 'Don't worry about your will.'

'I've left th' business to Edwin, and all th' rest's divided between you two wenches.' He was weeping gently.

'Don't worry about that, father,' Clara repeated. 'Why are you thinking so much about your will?' She tried to speak in a tone that was easy and matter-of-fact. But she could not. This was the first authentic information that any of them had had as to the dispositions of the will, and it was exciting.

Then Darius began to try to sit up, and there were protests against such an act. Though he sat up to take his food, the tone of these apprehensive remonstrances implied that to sit up at any other time was to endanger his life. Darius, however, with a weak scowl, continued to lift himself, whereupon Maggie aided him, and Auntie Hamps like lightning put a shawl round his shoulders. He sighed, and stretched out his hand to the night-table for his gold watch and chain, which he dangled towards Edwin.

'I want ye –' He stopped, controlling the muscles of his face.

'He wants you to wind it up,' said Clara, struck by her own insight.

'No, he doesn't,' said Edwin. 'He knows it's wound up.'

'I want ye –' Darius recommenced. But he was defeated again by his insidious foe. He wept loudly and without restraint for a few moments, and then suddenly ceased, and endeavoured to speak, and wept anew, agitating the watch in the direction of Edwin.

'Take it, Edwin,' said Mrs Hamps. 'Perhaps he wants it put away,' she added, as Edwin obeyed.

Darius shook his head furiously. 'I want him –' Sobs choked him.

'I know what he wants,' said Auntie Hamps. 'He wants to give dear Edwin the watch, because Edwin's been so kind to him, helping him to dress every day, and looking after him just like a professional nurse – don't you, dear?'

Edwin secretly cursed her in the most horrible fashion. But she was right.

'Ye – hes,' Darius confirmed her, on a sob.

'He wants to show his gratitude,' said Auntie Hamps.

'Ye – hes,' Darius repeated, and wiped his eyes.

Edwin stood foolishly holding the watch with its massive Albert chain. He was very genuinely astonished, and he was profoundly moved. His father's emotion concerning him must have been gathering force for months and months, increasing a little and a little every day in those daily, intimate contacts, until at length gratitude had become, as it were, a spirit that possessed him, a monstrous demon whose wild eagerness to escape defeated itself. And Edwin had never guessed, for Darius had mastered the spirit till the moment when the spirit mastered him. It was out now, and Darius, delivered, breathed more freely. Edwin was proud, but his humiliation was greater than his pride. He suffered humiliation for his father. He would have preferred that Darius should never have felt gratitude, or at any rate, that he should never have shown it. He would have preferred that Darius should have accepted his help nonchalantly, grimly, thanklessly, as a right. And if, through disease, the old man could not cease to be a tyrant with dignity, could not become human without this appalling ceremonial abasement –

better that he should have excercised harshness and oppression to the very end! There was probably no phenomenon of human nature that offended Edwin's instincts more than an open conversion.

Maggie turned nervously away and busied herself with the grate.

'You must put it on,' said Auntie Hamps sweetly. 'Mustn't he, father?' Darius nodded.

The outrage was complete. Edwin removed his own watch and dropped it into the pocket of his trousers, substituting for it the gold one.

'There, father!' exclaimed Auntie Hamps proudly, surveying the curve of the Albert on her nephew's waistcoat.

'Ay!' Darius murmured, and sank back on the pillow with a sigh of relief.

'Thanks, father,' Edwin muttered, reddening. 'But there was no occasion.'

'Now you see what it is to be a good son!' Auntie Hamps observed.

Darius murmured indistinctly.

'What is it?' she asked, bending down.

'I must have his,' said Darius. 'I must have a watch here.'

'He wants your old one in exchange,' Clara explained eagerly.

Edwin smiled, discovering a certain alleviation in this shrewd demand of his father's, and he drew out the silver Geneva.

III

Shortly afterwards the nurse surprised them all by coming into the room. She carried a writing-case. Edwin introduced her to Auntie Hamps and Clara. Clara blushed and became mute. Auntie Hamps adopted a tone of excessive deference, of which the refrain was 'Nurse will know best'. Nurse seemed disinclined to be professional. Explaining that as she was not able to sleep she thought she might as well get up, she took a seat near the fire and addressed herself to Maggie. She was a tall and radiant woman of about thirty. Her aristocratic southern accent proved that she did not belong to the Five Towns, and to Maggie, in excuse for certain questions as to the district, she said that she had only been at Pirehill a few weeks. Her demeanour was extraordinarily cheerful. Auntie Hamps remarked aside to Clara what a good thing it was that Nurse was so cheerful; but in reality she considered such cheerfulness exaggerated in a sick-room, and not quite nice. The nurse asked about the posts, and said she had a letter to write and would write it there if she could have pen and ink. Auntie Hamps, telling her eagerly about the posts, thought that these professional nurses certainly did make themselves at home in a house. The nurse's accent intimidated all of them.

'Well, nurse, I suppose we mustn't tire our patient,' said Auntie Hamps at last, after Edwin had brought ink and paper.

Edwin, conscious of the glory of a gold watch and chain, and conscious also of freedom from future personal service on his father, preceded Auntie Hamps and Clara to the landing, and Nurse herself sped them from the room, in her quality of mistress of the room. And when she and Maggie and Darius were alone together she went to the bedside and spoke softly to her patient. She was so neat and bright and white and striped, and so perfect in every detail, that she might have been a model taken straight from a shop-window. Her figure illuminated the dusk. An incredible luxury for the little boy from the Bastille! But she was one of the many wonderful things he had earned.

CHAPTER 15 : *The Banquet*

I

It was with a conscience uneasy that Edwin shut the front door one night a month later, and issued out into Trafalgar Road. Since the arrival of Nurse Shaw, Darius had not risen from his bed, and the household had come to accept him as bed-ridden and the nurse a permanency. The sick-room was the centre of the house, and Maggie and Edwin and the servants lived, as it were, in a camp round about it, their days uncomfortably passing in suspense, in expectation of developments which tarried. 'How is he this morning?' 'Much the same.' 'How is he this evening?' 'Much the same.' These phrases had grown familiar and tedious. But for three days Darius had been noticeably worse, and the demeanour of Nurse Shaw had altered, and she had taken less sleep and less exercise. Osmond Orgreave had even called in person to inquire after the invalid, doubtless moved by Janet to accomplish this formality, for he could not have been without news. Janet was constantly in the house, helping Maggie; and Alicia also sometimes. Since her engagement, Alicia had been striving to prove that she appreciated the gravity of existence.

Still, despite the change in the patient's condition, everybody had insisted that Edwin should go to the annual dinner of the Society for the Prosecution of Felons, to which he had been duly elected with flattering dispatch. Why should he not go? Why should he not enjoy himself? What could he do if he stayed at home? Would not the change be good for him? At most the absence would be for a few hours, and if he could absent himself during ten hours for business, surely for healthful distraction he might absent himself during five hours! Maggie grew elder-sisterly at the last moment of decision, and told him he must go, and that if he didn't she should be angry. When he asked her 'What about *her* health? What about her needing a change?' she said curtly that that had nothing to do with it.

He went. The persuaders were helped by his own desire. And in spite of his conscience, when he was fairly in the street he drew a sigh of relief, and deliberately turned his heart towards gaiety. It seemed inexpressibly pathetic that his father was lying behind those just-lighted blinds above, and would never again breathe the open air, never again glide along those pavements with his arms fixed and slightly outwards. But Edwin was determined to listen to reason and not to be morbid.

The streets were lively with the red and the blue colours of politics. The Liberal member for the Parliamentary borough of Hanbridge, which included Bursley, had died very suddenly, and the seat was being disputed by the previously defeated Conservative candidate and a new Labour candidate officially adopted by the Liberal party. The Tories had sworn not to be beaten again in the defence of the integrity of the Empire. And though they had the difficult and delicate task of persuading a large industrial constituency that an industrial representative would not further industrial interests, and that they alone were actuated by unselfish love for the people, yet they had made enormous progress in a very brief period, and publicans were jubilant and bars sloppy.

The aspect of the affair that did not quite please the Society for the Prosecution of Felons was that the polling had been fixed for the day after its annual dinner instead of the day before. Powerful efforts had been made 'in the proper quarter' to get the date conveniently arranged, but without success; after all, the seat of authority was Hanbridge and not Bursley. Hanbridge, sadly failing to appreciate the importance of Bursley's Felonry, had suggested that the feast might be moved a couple of days. The Felonry refused. If its dinner clashed with the supreme night of the campaign, so much the worse for the campaign! Moreover, the excitement of the campaign would at any rate give zest to the dinner.

Ere he reached Duck Bank, the vivacity of the town, loosed after the day's labour to an evening's orgy of oratory and horseplay and beer, had communicated itself to Edwin. He was most distinctly aware of pleasure in the sight of the Tory candidate driving past, at a pace to overtake steam-cars, in a coach-and-four, with amateur postilions and an orchestra of horns. The spectacle, and the speed of it, somehow thrilled him, and for an instant made him want to vote Tory. A procession of illuminated carts, bearing white potters apparently engaged in the handicraft which the Labour candidate had practised in humbler days, also pleased him, but pleased him less. As he passed up Duck Bank the Labour candidate himself was raising loud enthusiastic cheers from a railway lorry in Duck Square, and Edwin's spirits went even higher, and he elbowed through the laughing, joking throng with fraternal good-humour, feeling that an election was in itself a grand thing, apart from its result, and apart from the profit which it brought to steam-printers.

In the porch of the Town Hall, a man turned from an eagerly smiling group of hungry Felons and, straightening his face, asked with quiet concern, 'How's your father?' Edwin shook his head. 'Pretty bad,' he answered. 'Is he?' murmured the other sadly. And Edwin suddenly saw his father again behind the blind, irrevocably prone.

II

But by the time the speeches were in progress he was uplifted high once more into the joy of life. He had been welcomed by acquaintances and by strangers with a deferential warmth that positively startled him. He realized, as never before, that the town esteemed him as a successful man. His place was not many moves from the chair. Osmond Orgreave was on his right, and Albert Benbow on his left. He had introduced an impressed Albert to his friend, Mr Orgreave, recently made a Justice of the Peace.

And down the long littered tables stretched the authority and the wealth of the town – aldermen, councillors, members of the school board, guardians of the poor, magistrates, solid tradesmen, and solid manufacturers, together with higher officials of the borough and some members of the learned professions. Here was the oligarchy which, behind the appearances of democratic government, effectively managed, directed, and controlled the town. Here was the handful of people who settled between them whether rates should go up or down, and to whom it did not seriously matter whether rates went up or down, provided that the interests of the common people were not too sharply set in antagonism to their own interests. Here were the privileged, who did what they liked on the condition of not offending each other. Here the populace was honestly and cynically and openly regarded as a restless child, to be humoured and to be flattered, but also to be ruled firmly, to be kept in its place, to be ignored when advisable, and to be made to pay.

For the feast, the court-room had been transformed into a banqueting hall, and the magistrates' bench, where habitual criminals were created and families ruined and order maintained, was hidden in flowers. Osmond Orgreave was dryly facetious about that bench. He exchanged comments with other magistrates, and they all agreed, with the same dry facetiousness, that most of the law was futile and some of it mischievous; and they all said, 'But what can you do?' and by their tone indicated that you could do nothing. According to Osmond Orgreave's wit, the only real use of a magistrate was to sign the necessary papers for persons who had lost pawn-tickets. It appeared that such persons in distress came to Mr Orgreave every day for the august signature. 'I had an old woman come to me this morning at my office,' he said. 'I asked her how it was they were always losing their pawn-tickets. I told her I never lost mine.' Osmond Orgreave was encircled with laughter. Edwin laughed heartily. It was a good joke. And even mediocre jokes would convulse the room.

Jos Curtenty, the renowned card, a jolly old gentleman of sixty, was in the chair, and therefore jollity was assured in advance Rising to inaugurate the oratorical section of the night, he took an enormous red flower from a bouquet behind him, and sticking it with a studiously absent air in his button-hole, said blandly, 'Gentlemen, no politics, please!' The uproarious effect was one of his very best He knew his audience. He could have taught Edwin a thing or two. For Edwin in his simplicity was astonished to find the audience almost all of one colour, frankly and joyously and optimistically Tory. There were not ten Liberals in the place, and there was not one who was vocal. The cream of the town, of its brains, its success, its respectability, was assembled together, and the Liberal party was practically unrepresented. It seemed as if there was no Liberal party. It seemed impossible that a Labour candidate could achieve anything but complete disaster at the polls. It seemed incredible that in the past a Liberal candidate had ever been returned. Edwin began, even in the privacy of his own heart, to be apologetic for his Liberalism. All these excellent fellows could not be wrong. The moral force of numbers intimidated him. He suspected that there was, after all, more to be said for Conservatism than he had hitherto allowed himself to suppose.

III

And the Felons were so good-humoured and kindly and so freehanded, and, with it all, so boyish! They burst into praise of one another on the slenderest excuse. They ordered more champagne as carelessly as though champagne were ginger-beer (Edwin was glad that by an excess of precaution he had brought two pounds in his pocket – the scale of expenditure was staggering); and they nonchalantly smoked cigars that would have made Edwin sick. They knew all about cigars and about drinks, and they implied by their demeanour, though they never said it, that a first-class drink and a first-class smoke were the 'good things' of life, the ultimate rewards; the references to women were sly . . . Edwin was like a demure cat among a company of splendid curly dogs.

The toasts, every one of them, called forth enthusiasm. Even in the early part of the evening much good-nature had bubbled out when, at intervals, a slim young bachelor of fifty, armed with a violent mallet, had rapped authoritatively on the table and cried : 'Mr President wishes to take wine with Mr Vice,' 'Mr President wishes to take wine with the bachelors on the right', 'Mr President wishes to take wine with the married Felons on the left', and so on till every sort and condition and geographical situation had been thus distinguished. But the toasts proper aroused displays of the most affectionate loving-kindness. Each reference to a Felon was greeted with warm cheers, and each reference touched the superlative of laudation. Every stroke of humour was noisily approved, and every exhibition of tender feeling effusively endorsed. And all the estates of the realm, and all the institutions of the realm and of the town, and all the services of war and peace, and all the official castes were handsomely and unreservedly praised, and their health and prosperity pledged with enthusiastic fervour. The organism of the Empire was pronounced to be essentially perfect. Nobody of importance, from the Queen's Majesty to the 'ministers of the Established Church and other denominations', was omitted from the certificate of supreme excellence and efficiency. And even when an alderman, proposing the toast of the 'town and trade of Bursley', mentioned certain disturbing symptoms in the demeanour of the lower classes, he immediately added his earnest conviction that the 'heart of the country beat true', and was comforted with grave applause.

Towards the end of the toast-list one of the humorous vocal quartets, which were designed to relieve the seriousness of the programme, was interrupted by the formidable sound of the governed proletariat beyond the walls of the Town Hall. And Edwin's memory, making him feel very old, leapt suddenly back into another generation of male glee-singers that did not disport humorously and that would not have permitted themselves to be interrupted by the shouting of populations; and he recalled 'Loud Ocean's Roar', and the figure of Florence Simcox flitted in front of him. The proletariat was cheering somebody. The cheers died down. And in another moment the Conservative candidate burst into the room, and was followed by two of his friends (the latter in evening-dress), whom he presented to the President. The ceremonious costume impressed the President himself, for at this period of ancient history Felons dined in frock-coats or cutaways; it proved that the wearers were so accustomed to wearing evening-dress of a night that they put it on by sheer habit and inadvertence even for electioneering. The candidate only desired to shake hands with a few supporters and to assure the President that nothing but hard necessity had kept him away from the dinner. Amid inspiriting bravos and hurrahs he fled, followed by his friends, and it became known that one of these was a baronet.

After this the vote of thanks to the President scarcely escaped being an anticlimax. And several men left, including Albert Benbow, who had once or twice glanced at his watch. 'She won't let you be out after half past ten, eh, Benbow?' said jocularly a neighbour. And Albert, laughing at the joke, nevertheless looked awkward. And the neighbour perceived that he had been perhaps a trifle clumsy. Edwin, since the mysterious influence in the background was his own sister, had to share Albert's confusion. He too would have departed. But Osmond Orgreave absolutely declined to let him go, and to prevent him from going used the force which good wine gives.

IV

The company divided itself into intimate groups, leaving empty white spaces at the disordered tables. The attendants now served whisky, and more liqueurs and coffee. Those guests who knew no qualm lighted fresh cigars; a few produced beloved pipes; the others were content with cigarettes. Someone ordered a window to be opened, and then, when the fresh night air began to disturb the curtains and scatter the fumes of the banquet, someone else crept aside and furtively closed it again.

Edwin found himself with Jos Curtenty and Osmond Orgreave and a few others. He felt gay and enheartened; he felt that there was a great deal of pleasure to be had on earth with very little trouble. Politics had been broached, and he made a mild joke about the Tory candidate. And amid the silence that followed it he mistily perceived that the remainder of the group, instead of becoming more jolly, had grown grave. For them the political situation was serious. They did not trouble to argue against the Labour candidate. All their reasoning was based on the assumption, which nobody denied or questioned, that at any cost the Labour candidate must be defeated. The success of the Labour candidate was regarded as a calamity. It would jeopardize the entire social order. It would deliver into the destroying hands of an ignorant, capricious, and unscrupulous rabble all that was best in English life. It would even mean misery for the rabble itself. The tones grew more solemn. And Edwin, astonished, saw that beneath the egotism of their success, beneath their unconscious arrogance due to the habit of authority, there was a profound and genuine patriotism and sense of duty. And he was abashed. Nevertheless, he had definitely taken sides, and out of mere self-respect he had gently to remind them of the fact. Silence would have been cowardly.

'Then what about "trusting to the people"?' he murmured, smiling.

'If trusting the people means being under the thumb of the British working man, my boy,' said Osmond Orgreave, 'you can scratch me out, for one.'

Edwin had never heard him speak so colloquially.

'I've always found 'em pretty decent,' said Edwin, but lamely.

Jos Curtenty fixed him with a grim eye.

'How many hands do you employ, Mr Clayhanger?'

'Fourteen,' said Edwin.

'Do you?' exclaimed another voice, evidently surprised and impressed.

Jos Curtenty pulled at his cigar. 'I wish I could make as much money as you make out of fourteen hands!' said he. 'Well, I've got two hundred of 'em at my place. And I know 'em! I've known 'em for forty years and more. There's not ten of 'em as I'd trust to do an honest day's work, of their own accord . . . And after the row in '80, when they'd agreed to arbitration – fifteen thousand of 'em – did they accept the award, or didn't they? Tell me that, if it isn't troubling ye too much.'

Only in the last phase did the irrepressible humorous card in him assert itself.

Edwin mumbled inarticulately. His mind was less occupied by politics than by the fact that in the view of all these men he had already finally and definitely taken the place of his father. But for the inquiries made at intervals during the evening, he might have supposed that Darius, lying in helpless obscurity up there at Bleakridge, had been erased from the memory of the town.

A crony who had not hitherto spoken began to give sarcastic and apparently damning details of the early record of the Labour candidate. Among other delinquencies the fellow had condoned the inexcusable rejection of the arbitrators' award long ago. And then someone said :

'Hello ! Here's Benbow back again !'

Albert, in overcoat and cap, beckoned to Edwin, who sprang up, pricked into an exaggerated activity by his impatient conscience.

'It's nothing particular,' said Albert at the door. 'But the missus has been round to your father's tonight, and it seems the nurse had knocked up. She thought I'd perhaps better come along and tell you, in case you hadn't gone.'

'Knocked up, has she?' said Edwin. 'Well, it's not to be wondered at. Nurse or no nurse, she's got no more notion of looking after herself than anybody else has. I was just going. It's only a little after eleven.'

The last thing he heard on quitting the precincts of the banqueting chamber was the violent sound of the mallet. Its wielder seemed to have developed a slight affection for the senseless block of wood.

CHAPTER 16 : *After the Banquet*

I

'Yes, yes,' said Edwin impatiently, in reply to some anxious remark of Maggie's, 'I shall be all right with him. Don't you worry till morning.'

They stood at the door of the sick-room, Edwin in an attitude almost suggesting that he was pushing her out.

He had hurried home from the festival and found the doctor just leaving and the house in a commotion. Dr Heve said mildly that he was glad Edwin had come, and he hinted that some general calming influence was needed. Nurse Shaw had developed one of the sudden abscesses in the ear which troubled her from time to time. This radiant and apparently strong creature suffered from an affection of the ear. Once her left had kept her in bed for six weeks, and she had risen with the drum pierced. Since which episode there had always been the danger, when the evil recurred, of the region of the brain being contaminated through the tiny orifice in the drum. Hence, even if the acute pain which she endured had not forced her to abandon other people's maladies for the care of her own, the sense of her real peril would have done so. This masterful, tireless woman, whom no sadness nor abomination of her habitual environment could depress or daunt, lived under a menace, and was sometimes laid low, like a child. She rested now in Maggie's room, with a poultice for a pillow. A few hours previously no one in the house had guessed that she had any weakness whatever. Her collapse gave to Maggie an excellent opportunity, such as Maggie loved, to prove that she was equal to a situation. Maggie would not permit Mrs Hamps to be sent for. Nor would she permit Mrs Nixon to remain up. She was excited and very fatigued, and she meant to manage the night with the sole aid of Jane. It was even part of her plan that Edwin should go to bed as usual – poor Edwin, with all the anxieties of business upon his head! But she had not allowed for Edwin's conscience, nor foreseen what the doctor would say to him privately. Edwin had learnt from the doctor – a fact which the women had not revealed to him – that his father during the day had shown symptoms of 'Cheyne-Stokes breathing', the final and the worst phenomenon of his disease; a phenomenon, too, interestingly rare. The doctor had done all that could be done by injections, and there was absolutely nothing else for anybody to do except watch.

'I shall come in in the night,' Maggie whispered.

Behind them the patient vaguely stirred and groaned in his recess.

'You'll do no such thing,' said Edwin shortly. 'Get all the sleep you can.'

'But Nurse has to have a fresh poultice every two hours,' Maggie protested.

'Now, look here!' Edwin was cross. 'Do show a little sense. Get – all – the – sleep – you – can. We shall be having you ill next, and then there'll be a nice kettle of fish. I won't have you coming in here. I shall be perfectly all right. Now!' He gave a gesture that she should go at once.

'You won't be fit for the shop tomorrow.'

'Damn the shop!'

'Well, you know where everything is.' She was resigned. 'If you want to make some tea –'

'All right, all right!' He forced himself to smile.

She departed, and he shut the door.

'Confounded nuisance women are!' he thought, half indulgently, as he turned towards the bed. But it was his conscience that was a confounded nuisance. He ought never to have allowed himself to be persuaded to go to the banquet. When his conscience annoyed him, it was usually Maggie who felt the repercussion.

II

Darius was extremely ill. Every part of his physical organism was deranged and wearied out. His features combined the expression of intense fatigue with the sinister liveliness of an acute tragic apprehension. His failing faculties were kept horribly alert by the fear of what was going to happen to him next. So much that was appalling had already happened to him! He wanted repose; he wanted surcease; he wanted nothingness. He was too tired to move, but he was also too tired to lie still. And thus he writhed faintly on the bed; his body seemed to have that vague appearance of general movement which a multitude of insects will give to a piece of decaying matter. His skin was sick, and his hair, and his pale lips. The bed could not be kept tidy for five minutes.

'He's bad, no mistake!' thought Edwin, as he met his father's anxious and intimidated gaze. He had never seen anyone so ill. He knew now what disease could do.

'Where's Nurse?' the old man murmured, with excessive feebleness, his voice captiously rising to a shrill complaint.

'She's not well. She's lying down. I'm going to sit with you tonight. Have a drink?' As Edwin said these words in his ordinary voice, it seemed to him that in comparison with his father he was a god of miraculous proud strength and domination.

Darius nodded.

'Her's a Tartar!' Darius muttered. 'But her's just! Her will have her own way!' He often spoke thus of the nurse, giving people to understand that during the long nights, when he was left utterly helpless to the harsh mercy of the nurse, he had to accept many humiliations. He seemed to fear and love her as a dog its master. Edwin, using his imagination to realize the absoluteness of the power which the nurse had over Darius during ten hours in every twenty-four, was almost frightened by it. 'By Jove!' he thought, 'I wouldn't be in his place with any woman on earth!' The old man's lips closed clumsily round the funnel of the invalid's cup that Edwin offered. Then he sank back, and shut his eyes, and appeared calmer.

Edwin smoothed the clothes, stared at him a long time, and finally sat down in the arm-chair by the fire. He wound up his watch. It was not yet midnight. He took off his boots and put on the slippers which now Darius had not worn for over a week and would not wear again. He yawned heavily. The yawn surprised him. He perceived that his head was throbbing and his mouth dry, and that the meats and liquors of the banquet, having ceased to stimulate, were incommoding him. His mind and body were in reaction. He reflected cynically upon the facile self-satisfactions of those successful men in whose company he had been. The whole dinner grew unreal. Nothing was real except imprisonment on a bed night and day, day and night for weeks. Everyone could have change and rest save his father. For his father there was no relief, not a moment's. He was always there, in the same recess, prone, in subjection, helpless, hopeless, and suffering. Politics! What were they?

III

He closed his eyes because it occurred to him that to do so would be agreeable. And he was awakened from a doze by a formidable stir on the bed. Darius's breathing was quick and shallow, and growing more so. He lifted his head from the pillow in order to breathe, and leaned on one elbow. Edwin sprang up and went to him.

'Clara! Clara! Don't leave me!' the old man cried in tones of agonized apprehension.

'It's all right; I'm here,' said Edwin reassuringly. And he took the sick man's hot, crackling hand and held it.

Gradually the breathing went slower and deeper, and at length Darius sighed very deeply as at a danger past, and relaxed his limbs, and Edwin let go his hand. But he had not been at ease more than a few seconds when the trouble recommenced, and he was fighting again, and with appreciably more difficulty, to get air down into his lungs. It entered in quantities smaller and smaller, until it seemed scarcely to reach his throat before it was expelled again. The respirations were as rapid as the ticking of a watch. Despite his feebleness Darius wrenched his limbs into contortions, and gripped fiercely Edwin's hands.

'Clara! Clara!' he cried once more.

'It's all right. You're all right. There's nothing to be afraid of,' said Edwin, soothing him.

And that paroxysm also passed, and the old man moaned in the melancholy satisfaction of deep breaths. But the mysterious disturbing force would not leave him in peace. In another moment yet a fresh struggle was commencing. And each was worse than the last. And it was always Clara to whom he turned for succour. Not Maggie, who had spent nearly forty years in his service, and never spoke ill-naturedly of him; but Clara, who was officious rather than helpful, who wept for him in his presence, and said harsh things behind his back; and who had never forgiven him since the refusal of the loan to Albert.

After he had passed through a dozen crises of respiration Edwin said to himself that the next one could not be worse. But it was worse. Darius breathed like a blown dog that has fallen. He snatched furiously at breath like a tiger snatching at meat. He accomplished exertions that would have exhausted an athlete, and when he had saved his life in the very instant of its loss, calling on Clara as on God, he would look at Edwin for confirmation of his hope that he had escaped again. The paroxysms continued, still growing more critical. Edwin was aghast at his own helplessness. He could do absolutely naught. It was even useless to hold the hand or to speak sympathy and reassurance. Darius at the keenest moment of battle was too occupied with his enemy to hear or feel the presence of a fellow-creature. He was solitary with his unseen enemy, and if the room had been full of ministering angels he would still have been alone and unsuccoured. He might have been sealed up in a cell with his enemy who, incredibly cruel, withheld from him his breath; and Edwin outside the cell trying foolishly to get in. He asked for little; he would have been content with very little; but it was refused him until despair had reached the highest agony.

IV

'He's dying, I do believe,' thought Edwin, and the wonder of this nocturnal adventure sent tremors down his spine. He faced the probability that at the next bout his father would be worsted. Should he fetch Maggie and then go for the doctor? Heve had told him that it would be 'pretty bad', and that nothing on earth could be done. No! He would not fetch Maggie, and he would not go for the doctor. What use? He would see the thing through. In the solemnity of the night he was glad that an experience tremendous and supreme had been vouchsafed to him. He knew now what the will to live was. He saw life naked, stripped of everything unessential. He saw life and death together. What caused his lip to curl when the thought of the Felons' dinner flashed through his mind was the damned complacency of the Felons. Did any of them ever surmise that they had never come within ten miles of life itself, that they were attaching importance to the most futile trifles? Let them see a human animal in a crisis of Cheyne-Stokes breathing, and they would know something about reality! ... So this was Cheyne-Stokes breathing, that rare and awful affliction! What was it? What caused it? What controlled its frequency? No answer! Not only could he do naught, he knew naught! He was equally useless and ignorant before the affrighting mystery.

Darius no longer sat up and twisted himself in the agony of the struggles. He lay flat, resigned but still obstinate, fighting with the only muscles that could fight now, those of his chest and throat. The enemy had got him down, but he would not surrender. Time after time he won a brief armistice in the ruthless altercation, and breathed deep and long, and sighed as if he would doze, and then his enemy was at him again, and Darius, aroused afresh to the same terror, summoned Clara in the extremity of his anguish.

Edwin moved away, and surveyed the bed from afar. The old man was perfectly oblivious of him. He looked at his watch, and timed the crises. They recurred fairly regularly about every hundred seconds. Thirty-six times an hour Darius, growing feebler, fought unaided and without hope of aid an enemy growing stronger, and would not yield. He was dragged to his death thirty-six times every hour, and thirty-six times managed to scramble back from the edge of the chasm. Occasionally his voice, demanding that Clara should not desert him, made a shriek which seemed loud enough to wake the street. Edwin listened for any noise in the house, but heard nothing.

v

A curious instinct drove him out of the room for a space on to the landing. He shut the door on the human animal in its lonely struggle. The gas was burning on the landing and also in the hall, for this was not a night on which to extinguish lights. The clock below ticked quietly, and then struck three. He had passed more than three hours with his father. The time had gone quickly. He crept to Maggie's door. No sound! Utter silence! He crept upstairs to the second storey. No sound there! Coming down again to the first floor he noticed that the door of his own bedroom was open. He crept in there, and started violently to see a dim form on the bed. It was Maggie, dressed, but fast asleep under a rug. He left her. The whole world was asleep, and he was awake with his father.

'What an awful shame!' he thought savagely. 'Why couldn't we have let him grow his mushrooms if he wanted to? What harm would it have done us? Supposing it *had* been a nuisance, supposing he *had* tried to kiss Jane, supposing he *had* hurt himself, what then? Why couldn't we let him do what he wanted?'

And he passionately resented his own harshness and that of Maggie as he might have resented the cruelty of some national injustice.

He listened. Nothing but the ticking of the clock disturbed the calm of the night. Could his father have expired in one of those frantic bouts with his enemy? Brusquely, with false valiance, he re-entered the chamber, and saw again the white square of the blind and the expanse of carpet and the tables littered with nursing apparatus, and saw the bed and his father on it, panting in a new and unsurpassable despair, but still unbeaten, under the thin gas-flame. The crisis eased as he went in. He picked up the arm-chair and carried it to the bedside and sat down facing his father, and once more took his father's intolerably pathetic hand.

'All right!' he murmured, and never before had he spoken with such tenderness. 'All right! I'm here. I'm not leaving you.'

The victim grew quieter.

'Is it Edwin?' he whispered, scarcely articulate, out of a bottomless depth of weakness.

'Yes,' said Edwin cheerfully; 'you're a bit better now, aren't you?'

'Aye!' sighed Darius in hope.

And almost immediately the rumour of struggle recommenced, and in a minute the crisis was at its fiercest.

Edwin became hardened to the spectacle. He reasoned with himself about suffering. After all, what was its importance? Up to a point it could be borne, and when it could not be borne it ceased to be suffering. The characteristic grimness of those latitudes showed itself in him. There was nothing to be done. They who were destined to suffer, must suffer; and no more could be said. The fight must come to an end sooner or later. Fortitude alone could meet the situation. Nevertheless, the night seemed eternal, and at intervals fortitude lacked.

'By jove!' he would mutter aloud, under the old man's constant appeals to Clara, 'I shan't be sorry when this is over.'

Then he would interest himself in the periodicity of the attacks, timing them by his watch with care. Then he would smooth the bed. Once he looked at the fire. It was out. He had forgotten it. He immediately began to feel chilly, and then he put on his father's patched dressing-gown and went to the window, and, drawing aside the blind, glanced forth. All was black and utterly silent. He thought with disdain of Maggie and the others unconscious in sleep. He returned to the chair.

VI

He was startled, at a side glance, by something peculiar in the appearance of the window. It was the first messenger of the dawn. Yes, a faint greyness, very slowly working in secret against the power of the gaslight: timid, delicate, but brightening by imperceptible degrees into strength.

'Some of them will be getting up soon, now,' he said to himself. The hour was between four and half past. He looked forward to release. Maggie was sure to come and release him shortly. And even as he held the sick man's arm, comforting him, he yawned.

But no one came. Five o'clock, half past five! The first car rumbled down. And still the victim, unbroken, went through his agony every two minutes or oftener, with the most frightful regularity.

He extinguished the gas, and lo! there was enough daylight to see clearly. He pulled up the blind. The night had gone. He had been through the night. The entire surface of his head was tingling. Now he would look at the martyrdom of the victim as at a natural curiosity, having no capacity left for feeling. And now his sympathy would gush forth anew, and he would cover with attentions his father, who, fiercely preoccupied with the business of obtaining breath, gave no heed to them. And now he would stand impressed, staggered, by the magnificence of the struggle.

The suspense from six to seven was the longest. When would somebody come? Had the entire household taken laudanum? He would go and rouse Maggie. No, he would not. He was too proud.

At a quarter past seven the knob of the door clicked softly. He could scarcely believe his ears. Maggie entered. Darius was easier between two crises.

'Well,' she said tranquilly, 'how is he?' She was tying her apron.

'Pretty bad,' Edwin answered, with affected nonchalance.

'Nurse is a bit better. I've given her three fresh poultices since midnight. You'd better go now, hadn't you?'

'All right. I've let the fire out.'

'I'll tell Jane to light it. She's just making some tea for you.'

He went. He did not need twice telling. As he went, carelessly throwing off the dressing-gown and picking up his boots, Darius began to pant afresh, to nerve himself instinctively afresh for another struggle. Edwin, strong and healthy, having done nothing but watch, was completely exhausted. But Darius, weakened by disease, having fought a couple of hundred terrific and excruciating encounters, each a supreme battle, in the course of a single night, was still drawing upon the apparently inexhaustible reserves of his volition.

'I couldn't have stood that much longer,' said Edwin, out on the landing.

CHAPTER 17 : *The Chain Broken*

I

Shortly after eight o'clock Edwin was walking down Trafalgar Road on his way to the shop. He had bathed, and drunk some tea, and under the stimulation he felt the factitious vivacity of excessive fatigue. Rain had fallen quietly and perseveringly during the night, and though the weather was now fine the streets were thick with black mire. Paintresses with their neat gloves and their dinner-baskets and their thin shoes were trudging to work, and young clerks and shop-assistants and the upper classes of labour generally. Everybody was in a hurry. The humbler mass had gone long ago. Miners had been in the earth for hours. Later, and more leisurely, the magnates would pass by.

There were carriages about. An elegant wagonette, streaming with red favours, dashed down the road behind two horses. Its cargo was a handful of clay-soiled artisans, gleeful in the naïve pride of their situation, wearing red and shouting red, and hurrahing for the Conservative candidate.

'Asses!' murmured Edwin, with acrid and savage disdain. 'Do you think he'd drive you anywhere tomorrow?' He walked on a little, and broke forth again, all to himself : 'Of course he's doing it solely in your interest, isn't he? Why doesn't he pick some of these paintresses out of the mud and give them a drive?'

He cultivated an unreasoning anger against the men who had so impressed him at the banquet. He did not try to find answers to their arguments. He accused them stoutly of wilful blindness, of cowardice, of bullying, of Pharisaism, and of other sins. He had no wish to hear their defence. He condemned them, and as it were ordered them to be taken away and executed. He had a profound conviction that argument was futile, and that nothing would serve but a pitched battle, in which each fighting man should go to the poll and put a cross against a name in grim silence. Argue with these gross self-satisfied fellows about the turpitude of the artisans! Why, there was scarcely one of them whose grandfather had not been an artisan! Curse their patriotism! Then he would begin bits of argument to himself, and stop them, too

337

impatient to continue. . . . The shilling cigars of those feasters disgusted him. . . . In such wise his mind ran. And he was not much kinder to the artisan. If scorn could have annihilated, there would have been no proletariat left in the division. . . . Men? Sheep rather! Letting themselves be driven up and down like that, and believing all the yarns that were spun to them! Gaping idiots, they would swallow any mortal thing! There was simply naught that they were not stupid enough to swallow with a glass of beer. It would serve them right if – However, that could not happen. Idiocy had limits. At least he presumed it had.

Early as it was, the number of carriages was already considerable. But he did not see one with the blue of the Labour candidate. Blue rosettes there were, but the red rosettes bore them down easily. Even dogs had been adorned with red rosettes, and nice clean infants! And on all the hoardings were enormous red posters exhorting the shrewd common-sense potter not to be misled by paid agitators, but to plump for his true friend, for the man who was anxious to devote his entire career and goods to the welfare of the potter and the integrity of the Empire.

II

'If you can give me three days off, sir,' said Big James, in the majestic humility of his apron, 'I shall take it kindly.'

Edwin had gone into the composing room with the copy for a demy poster, consisting of four red words to inform the public that the true friend of the public was 'romping in'. A hundred posters were required within an hour. He had nearly refused the order, in his feverish fatigue and his disgust, but some remnant of sagacity had asserted itself in him and saved him from this fatuity.

'Why?' he asked roughly. 'What's up now, James?'

'My old comrade Abraham Harracles is dead, sir, at Glasgow, and I'm wishful for to attend the interment, far as it is. He was living with his daughter, and she's written to me. If you could make it convenient to spare me –'

'Of course, of course!' Edwin interrupted him hastily. In his present mood, it revolted him that a man of between fifty and sixty should be humbly asking as a favour to be allowed to fulfil a pious duty.

'I'm very much obliged to you, sir,' said Big James simply, quite unaware that captious Edwin found his gratitude excessive and servile. 'I'm the last now, sir, of the old glee-party,' he added.

'Really!'

Big James nodded, and said quietly, 'And how's the old gentleman, sir?'

Edwin shook his head.

'I'm sorry, sir,' said Big James.

'I've been up with him all night,' Edwin told him.

'I wonder if you'd mind dropping me a line to Glasgow, sir, if anything happens. I can give you the address. If it isn't –'

'Certainly, if you like.' He tried to be nonchalant. 'When are you going?'

'I did think of getting to Crewe before noon, sir. As soon as I've seen to this –' He cocked his eye at the copy for the poster.

'Oh, you needn't bother about that,' said Edwin carelessly. 'Go now if you want to go.'

'I've got time, sir. Mr Curtenty's coming for me at nine o'clock to drive me to th' polling-booth.'

This was the first time that Edwin had ever heard Big James talk of his private politics. The fact was that Big James was no more anxious than Jos Curtenty and Osmond Orgreave to put himself under the iron heel of his fellow working-man.

'And what's *your* colour, James?' His smile was half a sneer.

'If you'll pardon me for saying so, sir, I'm for Her Most Gracious,' Big James answered with grave dignity.

Three journeymen, pretending to be busy, were listening with all ears from the other side of a case.

'Oh!' exclaimed Edwin, dashed. 'Well, that's all right!'

He walked straight out, put on his hat, and went to the Bleakridge polling-station and voted Labour defiantly, as though with a personal grievance against the polling-clerk. He had a vote, not as lessee of the business premises, but as his father's lodger. He despised Labour; he did not care what happened to Labour. In voting for Labour, he seemed to have the same satisfaction as if from pique he had voted against it because its stupidity had incensed him.

Then, instead of returning him to the shop, his legs took him home and upstairs, and he lay down in his own room.

III

He was awakened by the presence of someone at his bedside, and the whole of his body protested against the disturbance.

'I couldn't make you hear with knocking,' said Dr Heve, 'so I came into the room.'

'Hello, doctor, is that you?' Edwin sat up, dazed, and with a sensation of large waves passing in slow succession through his head. 'I must have dropped asleep.'

'I hear you had a pretty bad night with him,' the doctor remarked.

'Yes. It's a mystery to me how he could keep it up.'

339

'I was afraid you would. Well, he's quieter now. In fact, he's unconscious.'

'Unconscious, is he?'

'You'll have no more trouble with the old gentleman,' said the doctor. He was looking at the window, as though at some object of great interest to be seen thence. His tone was gentle and unaffected. For the twentieth time Edwin privately admitted that in spite of the weak, vacuous smile which seemed to delight everybody except himself, there was a sympathetic quality in this bland doctor. In common moments he was common, but in the rare moments when a man with such a smile ought to be at his worst, a certain soft dignity would curiously distinguish his bearing.

'Um!' Edwin muttered, also looking at the window. And then, after a pause, he asked : 'Will it last long?'

'I don't know,' said the doctor. 'The fact is, this is the first case of Cheyne-Stokes breathing I've ever had. It may last for days.'

'How's the nurse?' Edwin demanded.

They talked about the nurse, and then Dr Heve said that, his brother the Vicar and he having met in the street, they had come in together, as the Vicar was anxious to have news of his old acquaintance's condition. It appeared that the Vicar was talking to Maggie and Janet in the drawing-room.

'Well,' said Edwin, 'I shan't come down. Tell him I'm only presentable enough for doctors.'

With a faint smile and a nod, the doctor departed. As soon as he had gone, Edwin jumped off the bed and looked at his watch, which showed two o'clock. No doubt dinner was over. No doubt Maggie had decided that it would be best to leave him alone to sleep. But that day neither he nor anybody in the household had the sense of time, the continuous consciousness of what the hour was. The whole systemized convention of existence was deranged, and all values transmuted. Edwin was aware of no feeling whatever except an intensity of curiosity to see again in tranquillity the being with whom he had passed the night. Pushing his hand through his hair, he hurried into the sick-room. It was all tidy and fresh, as though nothing had ever happened in it. Mrs Nixon, shrivelled and deaf, sat in the arm-chair, watching. No responsibility now attached to the vigil, and so it could be left to the aged and almost useless domestic. She gave a gesture which might have meant anything – despair, authority, pride, grief.

Edwin stood by the bedside and gazed. Darius lay on his back, with eyes half-open, motionless, unseeing, unhearing, and he breathed faintly, with the soft regularity of an infant. The struggle was finished, and he had emerged from it with the right to breath. His hair had been brushed, and his beard combed. It was uncanny, this tidiness, this calm, this passivity. The memory of the night grew fantastic and remote. Surely the old man must spring up frantically in a moment, to beat off his enemy! Surely his agonized cry for Clara must be ringing through the room! But nothing of him stirred. Air came and went through those parted and relaxed lips with the perfect efficiency of a healthy, natural function. And yet he was not asleep. His obstinate and tremendous spirit was now withdrawn somewhere, into some fastness more recondite than sleep; not far off, not detached, not dethroned; but undiscoverably hidden, and beyond any summons. Edwin gazed and gazed, until his heart could hold no more of the emotion which this mysteriously impressive spectacle at once majestic and poignant, distilled into it. Then he silently left the old woman sitting dully by the spirit concealed in its ruined home.

IV

In the evening he was resting on the sofa in the drawing-room. Auntie Hamps was near him, at work on some embroidery. In order that her dear Edwin might doze a little if he could, she refrained from speech; from time to time she stopped her needle and looked reflectively at the morsel of fire, or at the gas. She had been in the house since before tea. Clara also had passed most of the day there, with a few intervals at her own home; but now Clara was gone, and Janet too had gone. Darius was tiring them all out, in his mild and senseless repose. He remained absolutely still, and the enigma which he so indifferently offered to them might apparently continue for ever; at any rate the doctor's statement that he might keep as he was for days and days, beyond help, hung over the entire household, discouraging and oppressive. The energy of even Auntie Hamps was baffled. Only Alicia, who had come in, as she said, to take Janet's place, insisted on being occupied. This was one of the nights dedicated by family arrangement to her betrothed, but Alicia had found pleasure in sacrificing herself, and him, to her very busy sense of duty.

Suddenly the drawing-room door was pushed open, without a sound, and Alicia, in all the bursting charm of her youthfulness and the delicious *naïveté* of her self-importance, stood in the doorway. She made no gesture; she just looked at Edwin with a peculiar, ominous, and excited glance, and Edwin rose quickly and left the room. Auntie Hamps had noticed nothing.

'Maggie wants you upstairs,' said Alicia to Edwin.

He made no answer. He did not ask where Maggie was. They went upstairs together. But at the door of the sick-room Alicia hung back, intimidated, and Edwin entered and shut the door on that beautiful image of proud, throbbing life.

Maggie, standing by the bed under the gas which blazed at full, turned to him as he approached.

'Just come and look at him,' she said quietly.

Darius lay in exactly the same position; except that his mouth was open a little wider, he presented exactly the same appearance as in the afternoon. His weary features, pitiful and yet grim, had exactly the same expression. But there was no sign of breathing. Edwin bent and listened.

'Oh! He's dead!' he murmured.

Maggie nodded, her eyes glittering as though set with diamonds. 'I think so,' she said.

'When was it?'

'Scarcely a minute ago. I was sitting there, by the fire, and I thought I noticed something –'

'What did you notice?'

'I don't know . . . I must go and tell nurse.'

She went, wiping her eyes.

Edwin, now alone, looked again at the residue of his father. The spirit, after hiding within so long, had departed and left no trace. It had done with that form and was away. The vast and forlorn adventure of the little boy from the Bastille was over. Edwin did not know that the little boy from the Bastille was dead. He only knew that his father was dead. It seemed intolerably tragic that the enfeebled wreck should have had to bear so much, and yet intolerably tragic also that death should have relieved him. But Edwin's distress was shot through and enlightened by his solemn satisfaction at the fact that destiny had allotted to him, Edwin, an experience of such profound and overwhelming grandeur. His father was, and lo! he was not. That was all, but it was ineffable.

Maggie returned to the room, followed by Nurse Shaw, whose head was enveloped in various bandages. Edwin began to anticipate all the tedious formalities, as to which he would have to inform himself, of registration and interment. . . .

v

Ten o'clock. The news was abroad in the house. Alicia had gone to spread it. Maggie had startled everybody by deciding to go down and tell Clara herself, though Albert was bound to call. The nurse had laid out the corpse. Auntie Hamps and Edwin were again in the drawing-room together; the ageing lady was making up her mind to go. Edwin, in search of an occupation, prepared to write letters to one or two distant relatives of his mother. Then he remembered his promise to Big James, and decided to write that letter first.

'What a mercy he passed away peacefully!' Auntie Hamps exclaimed not for the first time.

Edwin, at a rickety fancy desk, began to write: 'Dear James, my father passed peacefully away at –' Then, with an abrupt movement, he tore the sheet in two and threw it in the fire, and began again: 'Dear James, my father died quietly at eight o'clock tonight.'

Soon afterwards, when Mrs Hamps had departed with her genuine but too spectacular grief, Edwin heard an immense commotion coming down the road from Hanbridge: cheers, shouts, squeals, penny whistles, and trumpets. He opened the gate.

'Who's in?' he asked a stout, shabby man, who was gesticulating in glee with a little Tory flag on the edge of the crowd.

'Who do *you* think, mister?' replied the man drunkenly.

'What majority?'

'Four hundred and thirty-nine.'

The integrity of the empire was assured, and the paid agitator had received a proper rebuff.

'Miserable idiots!' Edwin murmured, with the most extraordinary violence of scorn, as he re-entered the house, and the blare of triumph receded. He was very much surprised. He had firmly expected his own side to win, though he was reconciled to a considerable reduction of the old majority. His lips curled.

It was in his resentment, in the hard setting of his teeth as he confirmed himself in the rightness of his own opinions, that he first began to realize an individual freedom. 'I don't care if we're beaten forty times,' his thoughts ran. 'I'll be a more out-and-out Radical than ever! I don't care, and I don't care!' And he felt sturdily that he was free. The chain was at last broken that had bound together those two beings so dissimilar, antagonistic, and ill-matched – Edwin Clayhanger and his father.

BOOK FOUR : HIS START IN LIFE

CHAPTER I : *The Birthday Visit*

I

It was Auntie Hamps's birthday.

'She must be quite fifty-nine,' said Maggie.

'Oh, stuff!' Edwin contradicted her curtly. 'She can't be anything like as much as that.'

Having by this positive and sharp statement disposed of the question of Mrs Hamps's age, he bent again with eagerness to his newspaper. The *Manchester Examiner* no longer existing as a Radical organ, he read the *Manchester Guardian*, of which that morning's issue contained a long and vivid obituary of Charles Stewart Parnell.

Brother and sister were at breakfast. Edwin had changed the character of this meal. He went fasting to business at eight o'clock, opened correspondence, and gave orders to the wonderful Stifford, a person now of real importance in the firm, and at nine o'clock, flew by car back to the house to eat bacon and eggs and marmalade leisurely, like a gentleman. It was known that between nine and ten he could not be seen at the shop.

'Well,' Maggie continued, with her mild persistence, 'Aunt Spenser told me –'

'Who's Aunt Spenser, in God's name?'

'You know – mother's and auntie's cousin – the fat old thing!'

'Oh! Her!' He recalled one of the unfamiliar figures that had bent over his father's coffin.

'She told me auntie was either fifty-five or fifty-six, at father's funeral. And *that's* nearly three and a half years ago. So she must be –'

'Two and a half, you mean.' Edwin interrupted with a sort of savageness.

'No, I don't. It's nearly three years since Mrs Nixon died.'

Edwin was startled to realize the passage of time. But he said nothing. Partly he wanted to read in peace, and partly he did not want to admit his mistake. Bit by bit he was assuming the historic privileges of the English master of the house. He had the illusion that if only he could maintain a silence sufficiently august his error of fact and of manner would cease to be an error.

'Yes; she must be fifty-nine,' Maggie resumed placidly.

'I don't care if she's a hundred and fifty-nine!' snapped Edwin. 'Any more coffee? Hot, that is.'

Without moving his gaze from the paper, he pushed his cup a little way across the table.

Maggie took it, her chin slightly lifting, and her cheeks showing a touch of red.

'I hope you didn't forget to order the inkstand, after all,' she said stiffly. 'It's not been sent up yet, and I want to take it down to auntie's myself this morning. You know what a lot she thinks of such things!'

It had been arranged that Auntie Hamps should receive that year a cut-glass double inkstand from her nephew and niece. The shop occasionally dealt in such articles. Edwin had not willingly assented to the choice. He considered that a cut-glass double inkstand was a vicious concession to Mrs Hamps's very vulgar taste in knicknacks, and, moreover, he always now discouraged retail trade at the shop. But still, he had assented, out of indolence.

'Well, it won't come till tomorrow,' he said.

'But Edwin, how's that?'

'How's that? Well, if you want to know, I didn't order it till yesterday. I can't think of everything.'

'It's very annoying!' said Maggie sincerely.

Edwin put on the martyr's crown. 'Some people seem to think I've nothing else to do down at my shop but order birthday presents,' he remarked with disagreeable sarcasm.

'I think you might be a little more polite,' said Maggie.

'Do you!'

'Yes; I do!' Maggie insisted stoutly. 'Sometimes you get positively unbearable. Everybody notices it.'

'Who's everybody?'

'You never mind!'

II

Maggie tossed her head, and Edwin knew that when she tossed her head – a gesture rare with her – she was tossing the tears back from her eyes. He was more than startled, he was intimidated, by that feminine movement of the head. She was hurt. It was absurd of her to be so susceptible, but he had undoubtedly hurt her. He had been clumsy enough to hurt her. She was nearing forty and he also was close behind her on the road to forty; she was a perfectly decent sort, and yet they lacked the skill not to bicker. They no longer had the somewhat noisy altercations of old days concerning real or fancied interferences with the order and privacy of Edwin's sacred chamber, but their general demeanour to one another had dully soured. It was as if they tolerated one another, from motives of self-interest. Why should this be so? They were, at bottom, affectionate and mutually respectful. In a crisis they could and would rely on one another utterly. Why should their demeanour be so false an index to their real feelings? He supposed it was just the fault of loose habit. He did not blame her. From mere pride he blamed himself. He knew himself to be cleverer, more perceptive, wilier, than she; and he ought to have been able to muster the diplomatic skill necessary for smooth and felicitous intercourse. Any friction, whether due to her stupidity or not, was a proof of his incompetence in the art of life . . .

'Everybody notices it!' The phrase pricked him. An exaggeration, of course! Still, a phrase that would not be dismissed by a superior curl of the lips. Maggie was not Clara, and she did not invent allegations. His fault! Yes, his fault! Beyond doubt he was occasionally gruff, he was churlish, he was porcupinish. He did not mean to be so – indeed he most honestly meant not to be so – but he was. He must change. He must turn over a new leaf. He wished it had been his own birthday, or, better still, the New Year, instead of his auntie's birthday, so that he might have turned over a new leaf at once with due solemnity. He actually remembered a pious saw uttered over twenty years earlier by that wretch in a white tie who had damnably devised the Saturday afternoon Bible-class, a saw which he furiously scorned – 'Every day begins a New Year'. Well, every day did begin a New Year! So did every minute. Why not begin a New Year then, in that minute? He had only to say in a cajoling, goodnatured tone, 'All right, all right! Keep your hair on, my child. I grovel!' He had only to say some such words, and the excellent, simple, unresentful Maggie would at once be appeased. It would be a demonstration of his moral strength to say them.

But he could not say them.

III

Nevertheless he did seriously determine to turn over a new leaf at the very next occasion. His eyes were now following the obituary of Parnell mechanically, without transmitting any message that his preoccupied brain would seize. He had been astonished to find that Parnell was only forty-five. He thought : 'Why, at my age Parnell was famous – a great man and a power!' And there was he, Edwin, eating bacon and eggs opposite his sister in the humdrum dining-room at Bleakridge. But after all, what was the matter with the dining-room? It was not the dining-room that his father had left. He had altered and improved it to suit his own taste. He was free to do so, and he had done so. He was free in every way. The division of his father's estate according to the will had proved unjust to himself; but he had not cared in the least. He had let Albert do as Albert and Clara pleased. In the settlement Maggie had taken the house (at a figure too high), and he paid her an adequate rent for it, while she in turn paid him for her board and lodging. They were all in clover, thanks to the terrible lifelong obstinacy of the little boy from the Bastille. And Edwin had had the business unburdened. It was not growing, but it brought in more than twice as much as he spent. Soon he would be as rich as either of the girls, and that without undue servitude. He bought books surpassing those books of Tom Orgreave which had once seemed so hopelessly beyond his reach. He went to the theatre. He went to concerts. He took holidays. He had been to London, and more than once. He had a few good friends. He was his own master. Nobody dreamed of saying him nay, and no bad habits held him in subjection. Everywhere he was treated with quite notable respect. Even when, partly from negligence, and partly to hide recurring pimples, he had allowed his beard to grow, Clara herself had not dared to titter. And although he suffered from certain disorders of the blood due to lack of exercise and to his condition, his health could not be called bad. The frequency of his colds had somewhat diminished. His career, which to others probably seemed dull and monotonous, presented itself to him as almost miraculously romantic in its development.

And withal he could uneasily ask himself, 'Am I happy?' Maggie did not guess that, as he bent unseeing over his precious *Manchester Guardian*, he was thinking : 'I must hold an inquisition upon my whole way of existence. I must see where I stand. If ever I am to be alive, I ought to be alive now. And I'm not at all sure whether I am.' Maggie never put such questions to herself. She went on in placidness from hour to hour, ruffled occasionally.

IV

An unusual occurrence gave him the opportunity to turn over a new leaf immediately. The sounds of the front-door bell and of voices in the hall were followed by the proud entrance of Auntie Hamps herself into the dining-room.

'Now don't disturb yourselves, please,' Mrs Hamps entreated. She often began with this phrase.

Maggie sprang up and kissed her, somewhat effusively for Maggie, and said in a quiet, restrained tone –

'A long life and a merry one, auntie !'

Then Edwin rose, scraping his arm-chair backwards along the floor, and shook hands with her, and said with a guilty grin –

'A long life and a merry one, auntie !'

'Eh !' she exclaimed, falling back with a sigh of satisfaction into a chair by the table. 'I'm sure everybody's very kind. Will you believe me, those darling children of Clara's were round at my house before eight o'clock this morning !'

'Is Amy's cough better?' Maggie interjected, as she and Edwin sat down.

'Bless ye!' cried Auntie Hamps, 'I was in such a fluster I forgot to ask the little toddler. But I didn't hear her cough. I do hope it is. October's a bad time for coughs to begin. I ought to have asked. But I'm getting an old woman.'

'We were just arguing whether you were thirty-eight or thirty-nine, auntie,' said Edwin.

'What a tease he is – with his beard!' she archly retorted. 'Well, your old aunt is sixty this day.'

'Sixty!' the nephew and niece repeated together in astonishment.

Auntie Hamps nodded.

'You're the finest sixty I ever saw!' said Edwin, with unaffected admiration.

And she was fine. The pride in her eye as she made the avowal – probably the first frank avowal of her age that had passed those lips for thirty years – was richly justified. With her clear, rosy complexion, her white regular teeth, her straight spine, her plump figure, her brilliant gaze, her rapid gestures, and that authentic hair of hers falling in Victorian curls, she offered to the world a figure that no one could regard without a physical pleasure and stimulation. And she was so shiningly correct in her black silk and black velvet, and in the massive jet at her throat, and in the slenderness of her shoe! It was useless to recall her duplicities, her mendacities, her hypocrisies, her meannesses. At any rate she could be generous at moments, and the splendour of her vitality sometimes, as now, hid all her faults. She would confess to aches and pains like other folk, bouts of rheumatism for example – but the high courage of her body would not deign to ratify such miserable statements; it haughtily repelled the touch of time; it kept at least the appearance of victory. If you did not like Auntie Hamps willingly, in her hours of bodily triumph, you had to like her unwillingly. Both Edwin and Maggie had innumerable grievances against her, but she held their allegiance, and even their warm instinctive affection, on the morning of her sixtieth birthday. She had been a lone widow ever since Edwin could remember, and yet she had continued to bloom. Nothing could desiccate nor wither her. Even her sins did not find her out. God and she remained always on the best terms, and she thrived on insincerity.

V

'There's a little parcel for you, auntie,' said Edwin, with a particular effort to make his voice soft and agreeable. 'But it's in Manchester. It won't be here till tomorrow. My fault entirely! You know how awful I am for putting off things.'

'We quite expected it would be here today,' said the loyal Maggie, when most sisters – and Clara assuredly – would have said in an eager, sarcastic tone : 'Yes, it's just like Edwin, and yet I reminded him I don't know how many times !' (Edwin felt with satisfaction that the new leaf was already turned. He was glad that he had said 'My fault entirely.' He now said to himself : 'Maggie's all right, and so am I. I must keep this up. Perfect nonsense, people hinting that she and I can't get on together !')

'Please, *please* !' Auntie Hamps entreated. 'Don't talk about parcels !' And yet they knew that if they had not talked about a parcel the ageing lady would have been seriously wounded. 'All I want is your love. You children are all I have now. And if you knew how proud I am of you all, seeing you all so nice and good, and respected in the town, and Clara's little darlings beginning to run about, and such strong little things. If only your poor mother – !'

Impossible not to be impressed by those accents ! Edwin and Maggie might writhe under Auntie Hamps's phraseology ; they might remember the most horrible examples of her cant. In vain ! They were impressed. They had to say to themselves : 'There's something very decent about her, after all.'

Auntie Hamps looked from one to the other, and at the quiet opulence of the breakfast-table, and the spacious solidities of the room. Admiration and respect were in that eye, always too masculine to weep under emotion. Undoubtedly she was proud of her nephew and nieces. And had she not the right to be ? The bearded Edwin, one of the chief tradesmen in the town, and so fond of books, such a reader, and so quiet in his habits ! And the two girls, with nice independent fortunes : Clara so fruitful and so winning, and Maggie so dependable, so kind ! Auntie Hamps had scarce anything else to wish for. Her ideals were fulfilled. Undoubtedly since the death of Darius her attitude towards his children had acquired even a certain humility.

'Shall you be in tomorrow morning, auntie ?' Maggie asked, in the constrained silence that followed Mrs Hamps's protestations.

'Yes, I shall,' said Mrs Hamps, with assurance. 'I shall be mending curtains.'

'Well, then, I shall call. About eleven.' Maggie turned to Edwin benevolently. 'It won't be too soon if I pop in at the shop a little before eleven ?'

'No,' said Edwin with equal benevolence. 'It's not often Sutton's delivery is after ten. That'll be all right. I'll have it unpacked.'

VI

He lit a cigarette.

'Have one?' he suggested to Mrs Hamps, holding out the case.

'I shall give you a rap over the knuckles in a minute,' smiled Mrs Hamps, who was now leaning an elbow on the table, in easy intimacy. And she went on in a peculiar tone, low, mysterious, and yet full of vivacity : 'I can't quite make out who that little nephew is that Janet Orgreave is taking about.'

'Little nephew that Janet's taking about!' murmured Maggie, in surprise; and to Edwin, 'Do you know?'

Edwin shook his head. 'When?' he asked.

'Well, this morning,' said Mrs Hamps. 'I met them as I was coming up. She was on one side of the road, and the child was on the other – just opposite Howson's. My belief is she'd lost all control over the little jockey. Oh ! A regular little jockey ! You could see that at once. "Now, George, come along", she called to him. And then he shouted, "I want you to come on this side, auntie". Of course I couldn't stop to see it out. She was so busy with him she only just moved to me.'

'George? George?' Maggie consulted her memory. 'How old was he, about?'

'Seven or eight, I should say.'

'Well, it couldn't be one of Tom's children. Nor Alicia's.'

'No,' said Auntie Hamps. 'And I always understood that the eldest daughter – what's her name?'

'Marian.'

'Marian's were all girls.'

'I believe they are. Aren't they, Edwin?'

'How can I tell?' said Edwin. It was a marvel to him how his auntie collected her information. Neither she nor Clara had ever been in the slightest degree familiar with the Orgreaves, and Maggie, so far as he knew, was not a gossiper. He thought he perceived, however, the explanation of Mrs Hamps's visit. She had encountered in the street a phenomenon which would not harmonize with facts of her own knowledge, and the discrepancy had disturbed her to such an extent that she had been obliged to call in search of relief. There was that, and there was also her natural inclination to show herself off on her triumphant sixtieth birthday.

'Charles Orgreave isn't married, is he?' she inquired.

'No,' said Maggie.

VII

Silence fell upon this enigma of Janet's entirely unaccountable nephew.

'Charlie *may* be married,' said Edwin humorously, at length. 'You never know! It's a funny world! I suppose you've seen,' he looked particularly at his auntie, 'that your friend Parnell's dead?'

She affected to be outraged.

'I've seen that Parnell is dead,' she rebuked him, with solemn quietness. 'I saw it on a poster as I came up. I don't want to be uncharitable, but it was the best thing he could do. I do hope we've heard the last of all this Home Rule now!'

Like many people Mrs Hamps was apparently convinced that the explanation of Parnell's scandalous fall and of his early death was to be found in the inherent viciousness of the Home Rule cause, and also that the circumstances of his end were a proof that Home Rule was cursed of God. She reasoned with equal power forwards and backwards. And she was so earnest and so dignified that Edwin was sneaped into silence. Once more he could not keep from his face a look that seemed to apologize for his opinions. And all the heroic and passionate grandeur of Parnell's furious career shrivelled up to mere sordidness before the inability of one narrow-minded and ignorant but vigorous woman to appreciate its quality. Not only did Edwin feel apologetic for himself, but also for Parnell. He wished he had not tried to be funny about Parnell; he wished he had not mentioned him. The brightness of the birthday was for an instant clouded.

'I don't know what's coming over things!' Auntie Hamps murmured sadly, staring out of the window at the street gay with October sunshine. 'What with that! And what with those terrible baccarat scandals. And now there's this free education, that we ratepayers have to pay for. They'll be giving the children of the working classes free meals next!' she added, with remarkably intelligent anticipation.

'Oh well! Never mind!' Edwin soothed her.

She gazed at him in loving reproach. And he felt guilty because he only went to chapel about once in two months, and even then from sheer moral cowardice.

'Can you give me those measurements, Maggie?' Mrs Hamps asked suddenly. 'I'm on my way to Brunt's.'

The women left the room together. Edwin walked idly to the window. After all, he had been perhaps wrong concerning the motive of her visit. The next moment he caught sight of Janet and the unaccountable nephew, breasting the hill from Bursley, hand in hand.

CHAPTER 2 : *Janet's Nephew*

I

Edwin was a fairly conspicuous object at the dining-room window. As Janet and the child drew level with the corner her eye accidentally caught Edwin's. He nodded, smiling, and took the cigarette out of his mouth and waved it. They were old friends. He was surprised to notice that Janet blushed and became self-conscious. She returned his smile awkwardly, and then, giving a gesture to signify her intention, she came in at the gate. Which action surprised Edwin still more. With all her little freedoms of manner, Janet was essentially a woman stately and correct, and time had emphasized these qualities in her. It was not in the least like her to pay informal, capricious calls at a quarter to ten in the morning.

He went to the front door and opened it. She was persuading the child up the tiled steps. The breeze dashed gaily into the house.

· 'Good morning. You're out early.'

'Good morning. Yes. We've just been down to the post-office to send off a telegram, haven't we, George?'

She entered the hall, the boy following, and shook hands, meeting Edwin's gaze fairly. Her esteem for him, her confidence in him, shone in her troubled, candid eyes. She held herself proudly, mastering her curious constraint. 'Now just see that!' she said, pointing to a fleck of black mud on the virgin elegance of her pale brown costume. Edwin thought anew, as he had often thought, that she was a distinguished and delightful piece of goods. He never ceased to be flattered by her regard. But with harsh masculine impartiality he would not minimize to himself the increasing cleft under her chin, nor the deterioration of her once brilliant complexion.

'Well, young man!' Edwin greeted the boy with that insolent familiarity which adults permit themselves to children who are perfect strangers.

'I thought I'd just run in and introduce my latest nephew to you,' said Janet quickly, adding, 'and then that would be over.'

'Oh!' Edwin murmured. 'Come into the drawing-room, will you? Maggie's upstairs.'

They passed into the drawing-room, where a servant in striped print was languidly caressing the glass of a bookcase with a duster. 'You can leave this a bit,' Edwin said curtly to the girl, who obsequiously acquiesced and fled, forgetting a brush on a chair.

'Sit down, will you?' Edwin urged awkwardly. 'And which particular nephew is this? I may tell you he's already raised a great deal of curiosity in the town.'

Janet most unusually blushed again.

'Has he?' she replied. 'Well, he isn't my nephew at all really, but we pretend he is, don't we, George? It's cosier. This is Master George Cannon.'

'Cannon? You don't mean –'

'You remember Mrs Cannon, don't you? Hilda Lessways? Now, Georgie, come and shake hands with Mr Clayhanger.'

But George would not.

II

'Indeed!' Edwin exclaimed, very feebly. He knew not whether his voice was natural or unnatural. He felt as if he had received a heavy blow with a sandbag over the heart : not a symbolic, but a real physical blow. He might, standing innocent in the street, have been staggeringly assailed by a complete stranger of mild and harmless appearance, who had then passed tranquilly on. Dizzy astonishment held him, to the exclusion of any other sentiment. He might have gasped, foolish and tottering : 'Why – what's the meaning of this? What's happened?' He looked at the child uncomprehendingly, idiotically. Little by little – it seemed an age, and was in fact a few seconds – he resumed his faculties, and remembered that in order to keep a conventional self-respect he must behave in such a manner as to cause Janet to believe that her revelation of the child's identity had in no way disturbed him. To act a friendly indifference seemed to him, then, to be the most important duty in life. And he knew not why.

'I thought,' he said in a low voice, and then he began again, 'I thought you hadn't been seeing anything of her, of Mrs Cannon, for a long time now.'

The child was climbing on a chair at the window that gave on the garden, absorbed in exploration and discovery, quite ignoring the adults. Either Janet had forgotten him, or she had no hope of controlling him, and was trusting to chance that the young wild stag would do nothing too dreadful.

'Well,' she admitted, 'we haven't.' Her constraint recurred. Very evidently she had to be careful about what she said. There were reasons why even to Edwin she would not be frank. 'I only brought him down from London yesterday.'

Edwin trembled as he put the question –

'Is she here too – Mrs Cannon?'

Somehow he could only refer to Mrs Cannon as 'her' and 'she'.

'Oh *no*!' said Janet, in a tone to indicate that there was no possibility of Mrs Cannon being in Bursley.

He was relieved. Yes, he was glad. He felt that he could not have endured the sensation of her nearness, of her actually being in the next house. Her presence at the Orgreaves' would have made the neighbourhood, the whole town, dangerous. It would have subjected him to the risk of meeting her suddenly at any corner. Nay, he would have been forced to go in cold blood to encounter her. The constraint of such an interview would have been torture too acute. Strange, that though he was absolutely innocent, though he had done naught but suffer, he should feel like a criminal, should have the criminal's shifting downcast glance!

III

'Auntie!' cried the boy. 'Can't I go into this garden? There's a swing there.'

'Oh no!' said Janet. 'This isn't our garden. We must go home. We only just called in. And big boys who won't shake hands –'

'Yes, yes!' Edwin dreamily stopped her. 'Let him go into the garden for a minute if he wants to. You can't run off like that! Come along, my lord.'

He saw an opportunity of speaking to her out of the child's hearing. Janet consented, perhaps divining his wish. The child turned and stared deliberately at Edwin, and then plunged forward, too eager to await guidance, towards the conquest of the garden.

Standing silent and awkward in the garden porch, they watched him violently agitating the swing, a contrivance erected by a good-natured Uncle Edwin for the diversion of Clara's offspring.

'How old is he?' Edwin demanded, for the sake of saying something.

'About nine,' said Janet.

'He doesn't look it.'

'No, but he talks it – sometimes.'

George did not in fact look his age. He was slight and small, and he seemed to have no bones – nothing but articulations that functioned with equal ease in all possible directions. His skin was pale and unhealthy. His eyes had an expression of fatigue, or he might have been ophthalmic. He spoke loudly, his gestures were brusque, and his life was apparently made up of a series of intense, absolute absorptions. The general effect of his personality upon Edwin was not quite agreeable, and Edwin's conclusion was that George, in addition to being spoiled, was a profound and rather irritating egoist by nature.

'By the way,' he murmured, 'what's *Mr* Cannon?'

'Oh!' said Janet, hesitating, with emotion, 'she's a widow.'

He felt sick. Janet might have been a doctor who had informed him that he was suffering from an unexpected disease, and that an operation severe and perilous lay in front of him. The impartial observer in him asked somewhat disdainfully why he should allow himself to be deranged in this physical manner, and he could only reply feebly and very meekly that he did not know. He felt sick.

Suddenly he said to himself, making a discovery –

'Of course she won't come to Bursley. She'd be ashamed to meet me.'

'How long?' he demanded of Janet.

'It was last year, I think,' said Janet, with emotion increased, her voice heavy with the load of its sympathy. When he first knew Janet an extraordinary quick generous concern for others had been one of her chief characteristics. But of late years, though her deep universal kindness had not changed, she seemed to have hardened somewhat on the surface. Now he found again the earlier Janet.

'You never told me.'

'The truth is, we didn't know,' Janet said, and without giving Edwin time to put another question, she continued : 'The poor thing's had a great deal of trouble, a very great deal. George's health, now! The sea air doesn't suit him. And Hilda couldn't possibly leave Brighton.'

'Oh! She's still at Brighton?'

'Yes.'

'Let me see – she used to be at – what was it? – Preston Street?'

Janet glanced at him with interest : 'What a memory you've got! Why, it's ten years since she was here!'

'Nearly!' said Edwin. 'It just happened to stick in my mind. You remember she came down to the shop to ask me about trains and things the day she left.'

'Did she?' Janet exclaimed, raising her eyebrows.

Edwin had been suspecting that possibly Hilda had given some hint to Janet as to the nature of her relations with him. He now ceased to suspect that. He grew easier. He gathered up the reins again, though in a rather limp hand.

'Why is she so bound to stay in Brighton?' he inquired with affected boldness.

'She's got a boarding-house.'

'I see. Well, it's a good thing she has a private income of her own.'

'That's just the point,' said Janet sadly. 'We very much doubt if she has any private income any longer.'

Edwin waited for further details, but Janet seemed to speak unwilling. She would follow him, but she would not lead.

Behind them he could hear the stir of Mrs Hamps's departure. She and Maggie were coming down the stairs. Guessing not the dramatic arrival of Janet Orgreave and the mysterious nephew, Mrs Hamps, having peeped into the empty dining-room, said : 'I suppose the dear boy has gone,' and forthwith went herself. Edwin smiled cruelly at the thought of what her joy would have been actually to inspect the mysterious nephew at close quarters, and to learn the strange suspicious truth that he was not a nephew after all.

'Auntie !' yelled the boy across the garden.

'Come along, we must go now,' Janet retorted.

'No ! I want you to swing me. Make me swing very high.'

'George !'

'Let him swing a bit,' said Edwin. 'I'll go and swing him.' And calling loud to the boy : 'I'll come and swing you.'

'He's dreadfully spoiled,' Janet protested. 'You'll make him worse.'

'I don't care,' said Edwin carelessly.

He seemed to understand, better than he had ever done with Clara's litter, how and why parents came to spoil their children. It was not because they feared a struggle of wills; but because of the unreasoning instinctive pleasure to be derived from the conferring of pleasure, especially when the pleasure thus conferred might involve doubtful consequences. He had not cared for the boy, did not care for him. In theory he had the bachelor's factitious horror of a spoiled child. Nevertheless he would now support the boy against Janet. His instinct said : 'He wants something. I can give it him. Let him have it. Never mind consequences. He shall have it.'

He crossed the damp grass, and felt the breeze and the sun. The sky was a moving medley of Chinese white and Prussian blue, that harmonized admirably with the Indian red architecture which framed it on all sides. The high trees in the garden of the Orgreaves were turning to rich yellows and browns, and dead leaves slanted slowly down from their summits, a few reaching even the Clayhanger garden, speckling its evergreen with ochre. On the other side of the west wall traps and carts rattled and rumbled and creaked along Trafalgar Road.

The child had stopped swinging and greeted him with a most heavenly persuasive grateful smile. A different child ! A sudden angel, with delicate, distinguished gestures ! . . . A wondrous screwing up of the eyes in the sun ! Weak eyes, perhaps ! The thick eyebrows recalled Hilda's. Possibly he had Hilda's look ! Or was that fancy ? Edwin was sure that he would never have guessed George's parentage.

'Now !' he warned. 'Hold tight.' And, going behind the boy, he strongly clasped his slim little waist in its blue sailor-cloth, and sent the whole affair – swing-seat and boy and all – flying to the skies. And the boy shrieked in the violence of his ecstasy, and his cap fell on the grass. Edwin worked hard without relaxing.

'Go on! Go on!' The boy shriekingly commanded.

And amid these violent efforts and brusque delicious physical contacts, Edwin was calmly penetrated and saturated by the mystic effluence that is disengaged from young children. He had seen his father dead, and had thought: 'Here is the most majestic and impressive enigma that the earth can show!' But the child George – aged nine and seeming more like seven – offered an enigma surpassing in solemnity that of death. This was Hilda's. This was hers, who had left him a virgin. With a singular thrilled impassivity he imagined, not bitterly, the history of Hilda. She who was his by word and by kiss, had given her mortal frame to be the unknown Cannon – yielded it. She had conceived. At some moment when he, Edwin, was alive and suffering, she had conceived. She had ceased to be a virgin. Quickly, with an astounding quickness – for was not George nine years old? – she had passed from virginity to motherhood. And he imagined all that too; all of it; clearly. And here, swinging and shrieking, exerting the powerful and unique charm of infancy, was the miraculous sequel! Another individuality; a new being; definitely formed, with character and volition of its own; unlike any other individuality in the universe! Something fresh! Something unimaginably created! A phenomenon absolutely original of the pride and the tragedy of life! George!

Yesterday she was a virgin, and today there was this! And this might have been his, ought to have been his! Yes, he thrilled secretly amid all those pushings and joltings! The mystery obsessed him. He had no rancour against Hilda. He was incapable of rancour, except a kind of wilful, fostered rancour in trifles. Thus he never forgave the inventor of Saturday afternoon Bible-classes. But rancour against Hilda! – No! Her act had been above rancour; like an act of Heaven. And she existed yet. On a spot of the earth's surface entitled Brighton, which he could locate upon a map. She existed: a widow, in difficulty, keeping a boarding-house. She ate, slept, struggled; she brushed her hair. He could see her brushing her hair. And she was thirty-four – was it? The wonder of the world amazed and shook him. And it appeared to him that his career was more romantic than ever.

George with dangerous abruptness wriggled his legs downwards and slipped off the seat of the swing, not waiting for Edwin to stop it. He rolled on the grass and jumped up in haste. He had had enough.

'Well, want any more?' Edwin asked, breathing hard.

The child made a shy, negative sign, twisting his tousled head down into his right shoulder. After all he was not really impudent, brazen. He could show a delicious timidity. Edwin decided that he was an enchanting child. He wanted to talk to him, but he could not think of anything natural and reasonable to say by way of an opening.

'You haven't told me your name, you know,' he began at length. 'How do I know what your name is? George, yes – but George what? George is nothing by itself, I know ten million Georges.'

The child smiled.

'George Edwin Cannon,' he replied shyly.

V

'Now, George!' came Janet's voice, more firmly than before. After all, she meant in the end to be obeyed. She was learning her business as aunt to this new and difficult nephew; but learn it she would, and thoroughly!

'Come on!' Edwin counselled the boy.

They went together to the house. Maggie had found Janet, and the two were conversing. Soon afterwards aunt and nephew departed.

'How very odd!' murmured Maggie, with an unusual intonation, in the hall, as Edwin was putting on his hat to return to the shop. But whether she was speaking to herself or to him, he knew not.

'What?' he asked gruffly.

'Well,' she said, 'isn't it?'

She was more like Auntie Hamps, more like Clara, than herself in that moment. He resented the suspicious implications of her tone. He was about to give her one of his rude, curt rejoinders, but happily he remembered in time that scarce half an hour earlier he had turned over a new leaf; so he kept silence. He walked down to the shop in a deep dream.

CHAPTER 3 : *Adventure*

I

It was when Edwin fairly reached the platform at Victoria Station and saw the grandiose express waiting its own moment to start, that the strange, irrational quality of his journey first fully impressed him and frightened him – so much that he was almost ready to walk out of the station again. To come gradually into London from the North, to pass from the Manchester train half-full of Midlanders through Bloomsbury into the preoccupied, struggling, and untidy Strand – this gave no shock, typified nothing definite. But, having spent a night in London, deliberately to leave it for the South, where he had never been, of which he was entirely ignorant – that was like an explicit self-committal, like turning the back on the last recognizable landmark in an ill-considered voyage of pure adventure.

The very character of Victoria Station and of this express was different from that of any other station and express in his experience. It was unstrenuous, soft; it had none of the busy harshness of the Midlands; it spoke of pleasure, relaxation, of spending free from all worry and humiliation of getting. Everybody who came towards this train came with an assured air of wealth and of dominion. Everybody was well dressed; many if not most of the women were in furs; some had expensive and delicate dogs; some had pale, elegant footmen, being too august even to speak to porters. All the luggage was luxurious; handbags could be seen that were worth fifteen or twenty pounds apiece. There was no question of first, second, or third class; there was no class at all on this train. Edwin had the apologetic air of the provincial who is determined to be as good as anybody else. When he sat down in the vast interior of one of those gilded vehicles he could not dismiss from his face the consciousness that he was an intruder, that he did not belong to that world. He was ashamed of his hand-baggage, and his gesture in tipping the porter lacked carelessness. Of course he pretended a frowning, absorbed interest in a newspaper – but the very newspaper was strange; he guessed not that unless he glanced first at the penultimate column of page one thereof he convicted himself of not knowing his way about.

He could not think consecutively, not even of his adventure. His brain was in a maze of anarchy. But at frequent intervals recurred the query: 'What the devil am I up to?' And he would uneasily smile to himself. When the train rolled with all its majesty out of the station and across the Thames, he said to himself, fearful, 'Well, I've done it now!'

II

On the Thursday he had told Maggie, with affected casualness, that on the Friday he might have to go to London, about a new machine. Sheer invention! Fortunately Maggie had been well drilled by her father in the manner proper to women in accepting announcements connected with 'business'. And Edwin was just as laconic and mysterious as Darius had been about 'business'. It was a word that ended arguments, or prevented them. On the Friday he had said that he should go in the afternoon. On being asked whether he should return on the Saturday, he had replied that he did not know, but that he would telegraph. Whereupon Maggie had said that if he stayed away for the week-end she should probably have all the children up for dinner and tea. At the shop, 'Stifford,' he had said, 'I suppose you don't happen to know a good hotel in Brighton? I might run down there for the week-end if I don't come back tomorrow. But you needn't say anything.' 'No, sir,' Stifford had discreetly concurred in this suggestion. 'They say there's really only one hotel in Brighton, sir – the Royal Sussex. But I've never been there.' Edwin had replied : 'Not the Metropole, then?' 'Oh *no*, sir !' Stifford had become a great and wonderful man, and Edwin's constant fear was that he might lose this indispensable prop to his business. For Stifford, having done a little irregular commercial travelling in Staffordshire and the neighbouring counties, had been seised of the romance of travelling; he frequented the society of real commercial travellers, and was gradually becoming a marvellous encyclopedia of information about hotels, routes, and topography.

Edwin having been to the Bank himself, instead of sending Stifford, had departed with the minimum of ostentation. He had in fact crept away. Since the visit of Janet and the child he had not seen either of them again, nor had he mentioned the child to anybody at all.

III

When, in an astounding short space of time, he stood in the King's Road at Brighton, it seemed to him that he was in a dream; that he was not really at Brighton, that town which for so many years had been to him naught but a romantic name. Had his adventurousness, his foolhardiness, indeed carried him so far? As for Brighton, it corresponded with no dream. It was vaster than any imagining of it. Edwin had only seen the pleasure cities of the poor and of the middling, such as Blackpool and Llandudno. He had not conceived what wealth would do when it organized itself for the purposes of distraction. The train had prepared him to a certain extent, but not sufficiently. He suddenly saw Brighton in its autumnal pride, Brighton beginning one of its fine week-ends, and he had to admit that the number of rich and idle people in the world surpassed his provincial notions. For miles westwards and miles eastwards, against a formidable background of high, yellow and brown architecture, persons the luxuriousness of any one of whom would have drawn remarks in Bursley, walked or drove or rode in thronging multitudes. Edwin could comprehend lolling by the sea in August, but in late October it seemed unnatural, fantastic. The air was full of the trot of glossy horses and the rattle of bits and the roll of swift wheels, and the fall of elegant soles on endless clean pavements; it was full of the consciousness of being correct and successful. Many of the faces were monstrously ugly, most were dissatisfied and querulous; but they were triumphant. Even the pale beings in enlarged perambulators, pulled solemnly to and fro by their aged fellow-beings, were triumphant. The scared, the maimed, yes, and the able-bodied blind trusting to the arms of friends, were triumphant. And the enormous policemen, respectfully bland, confident in the system which had chosen them and fattened them, gave as it were to the scene an official benediction.

The bricks and stucco which fronted the sea on the long embanked promenade never sank lower than a four-storey boarding-house, and were continually rising to the height of some gilt-lettered hotel, and at intervals rose sheer into the skies – six, eight, ten storeys – where a hotel, admittedly the grandest on any shore of ocean, sent terra-cotta chimneys to lose themselves amid the pearly clouds. Nearly every building was a lodgment waiting for the rich, and nearly every great bow-window, out of tens of thousands of bow-windows bulging forward in an effort to miss no least glimpse of the full prospect, exhibited the apparatus and the menials of gormandize. And the eye, following the interminable irregular horizontal lines of architecture, was foiled in the far distances, and, still farther off, after a break of indistinguishable brown, it would catch again the receding run of roofs, simplified by atmosphere into featureless rectangles of grey against sapphire or rose. There were two piers that strode and sprawled into the sea, and these also were laden with correctness and with domination. And, between the two, men were walking miraculously on the sea to build a third, that should stride farther and deeper than the others.

IV

Amid the crowd, stamping and tapping his way monotonously along with the assured obstinacy of a mendicant experienced and hardened, came a shabby man bearing on his breast a large label with these words : 'Blind through boy throwing mortar. Discharged from four hospitals. Incurable'. Edwin's heart seemed to be constricted. He thought of the ragged snarling touts who had fawned to him at the station, and of the creatures locked in the cellars whence came beautiful odours of confectionery and soup through the pavement gratings, and of the slatternly women who kept thrusting flowers under his nose, and the half-clad infants who skimmed before the wind yelling the names of newspapers. All was not triumph ! Where triumph was, there also must be the conquered.

She was there, she too ! Somewhere, close to him. He recalled the exact tone of Janet's voice as she had said : 'The poor thing's had a great deal of trouble.' A widow, trying to run a boarding-house and not succeeding ! Why, there were hundreds upon hundreds of boarding-houses, all large, all imposing, all busy at the end of October ! Where was hers hidden away, her pathetic little boarding-house? Preston Street! He knew not where Preston Street was, and he had purposely refrained from inquiring. But he might encounter it at any moment. He was afraid to look too closely at the street-signs as he passed them; afraid!

'What am I doing here?' he asked himself curiously, and sometimes pettishly. 'What's my object? Where's the sense of it? I'm nothing but a damned fool. I've got no plan. I don't know what I'm going to do.' It was true. He had no plan, and he did not know what he was going to do. What he did most intimately know was that the idea of her nearness made him tremble.

'I'd much better go back at once,' he said.

He walked miles, until he came to immense and silent squares of huge palatial houses, and wide transversal avenues running far up into the land and into the dusk. In the vast avenues and across these vast squares infrequent carriages sped like mechanical toys guided by mannikins. The sound of the sea waxed. And then he saw the twinkle of lights, and then fire ran slowly along the promenade : until the whole map of it was drawn out in flame; and he perceived that though he had walked a very long way, the high rampart of houses continued still interminably beyond him. He turned. He was tired. His face caught the full strength of the rising wind. Foam gleamed on the rising tide. In the profound violet sky to the east stars shone and were wiped out, in fields; but to the west, silver tarried. He had not seen Preston Street, and it was too dark now to decipher the signs. He was glad. He went on and on, with rapidly increasing fatigue, disgust, impatience. The thronging multitudes had almost disappeared; but many illuminated vehicles were flitting to and fro, and the shops were brilliant. He was so exhausted by the pavements that he could scarcely walk. And Brighton became for him the most sorrowful city on earth.

'What am I doing here?' he asked himself savagely. However, by dint of sticking doggedly to it he did in the end reach the hotel.

v

After dinner, and wine, both of which, by their surprising and indeed unique excellence, fostered the prestige of Stifford as an authority upon hotels, Edwin was conscious of new strength and cheerfulness. He left the crowded and rose-lit dining-room early, because he was not at ease amid its ceremoniousness of attire and of service, and went into the turkey-carpeted hall, whose porter suddenly sprang into propitiatory life on seeing him. He produced a cigarette, and with passionate haste the porter produced a match, and by his method of holding the flame to the cigarette, deferential and yet firm, proved that his young existence had not been wasted in idleness. When the cigarette was alight, the porter surveyed his work with a pleased smile.

'Another rare storm blowing up, sir,' said the porter.

'Yes,' said Edwin. 'It's been giving the window of my room a fine shake.'

The porter glanced at the clock. 'High tide in half an hour, sir.'

'I think I'll go out and have a look at it,' said Edwin.

'Yes, sir.'

'By the way,' Edwin added, 'I suppose you haven't got a map of Brighton?'

'Certainly, sir,' said the porter, and with a rebirth of passion began to search among the pile of time-tables and other documents on a table behind him.

Edwin wished he had not asked for the map. He had not meant to ask for it. The words had said themselves. He gazed unseeing at the map for a few instants.

'What particular street did you want, sir?' the porter murmured.

In deciding how to answer, it seemed to Edwin that he was deciding the hazard of his life.

'Preston Street!'

'Oh! Preston Street!' the porter repeated in a relieved tone, as if assuring Edwin that there was nothing very esoteric about Preston Street. 'It's just beyond the Metropole. You know Regency Street. Well, it's the next street after that. There's a club at the corner.'

In the afternoon, then, Edwin must have walked across the end of Preston Street twice. This thought made him tremble, as at the perception of a danger past but unperceived at the moment.

The porter gave his whole soul to the putting of Edwin's overcoat on Edwin's back; he offered the hat with an obeisance; and having ushered Edwin into the night so that the illustrious guest might view the storm, he turned with a sudden new mysterious supply of zeal to other guests who were now emerging from the dining-room.

VI

The hotel fronted north on an old sheltered square where no storm raged, but simultaneously with Edwin's first glimpse of the sea the wind struck him a tremendous blow, and continued to strike. He had the peculiar grim joy of the Midlander and Northerner in defying an element. All the lamps of the promenade were insecurely flickering. Grouped opposite a small jetty was a crowd of sightseers. The dim extremity of the jetty was wreathed in spray, and the waves ran along its side, making curved lines on the masonry like curved lines of a rope shaken from one end. The wet floor of the jetty shone like a mirror.

Edwin approached the crowd, and, peeping over black shoulders, could see down into the hollow of the corner between the jetty and the sea-wall, where boys on the steps dared the spent waves, amid jeering laughter. The crowd had the air of being a family intimately united. Farther on was another similiar crowd, near an irregular high fountain of spray that glittered in the dark. On the beach below, at vague distances were curious rows of apparently tiny people silhouetted like the edge of a black saw against an excessive whiteness. This whiteness was the sheet of foam that the sea made. It stretched everywhere, until the eye lost it seawards. Edwin descended to the beach, adding another tooth to the saw. The tide ran up absolutely white in wide chords of a circle, and then, to the raw noise of disturbed shingle, the chord vanished; and in a moment was recreated. This play went on endlessly, hypnotizing the spectators who, beaten by the wind and deafened by sound, stared and stared, safe, at the mysterious and menacing world of spray and foam and darkness. Before, was the open malignant sea. Close behind, on their eminence, the hotels rose in vast cubes of yellow light, moveless, secure, strangely confident that nothing sinister could happen to them.

Edwin was aware of emotion. The feel of his overcoat-collar up-turned against the chin was friendly to him amid that onset of the pathos of the human world. He climbed back to the promenade. Always at the bottom of his mind, the foundation of all the shifting structures in his mind, was the consciousness of his exact geographical relation to Preston Street. He walked westwards along the promenade. 'Why don't I go home? I must be mad to be doing this.' Still his legs carried him on, past lamp-post after lamp-post of the wind-driven promenade, now almost deserted. And presently the high lighted windows of the grandest hotels were to be seen, cut like square holes in the sky; and then the pier, which had flung a string of lanterns over the waves into the storm; and opposite the pier a dark empty space and a rectangle of gas-lamps : Regency Square. He crossed over, and passed up the Square, and out of it by a tiny side street, at hazard, and lo ! he was in Preston Street. He went hot and cold.

VII

Well, and what then? Preston Street was dark and lonely. The wind charged furiously through it, panting towards the downs. He was in Preston Street, but what could he do? She was behind the black walls of one of those houses. But what then? Could he knock at the door in the night and say : 'I've come. I don't know why?'

He said : 'I shall walk up and down this street once, and then I shall go back to the hotel. That's the only thing to do. I've gone off my head, that's what's the matter with me! I ought to have written to her. Why in the name of God didn't I begin by writing to her? . . . Of course I might write to her from the hotel . . . send the letter by messenger, to-night . . . or early tomorrow. Yes, that's what I'll do.'

He set himself to make the perambulation of the street. Many of the numbers were painted on the fanlights over the doors and showed plain against illumination. Suddenly he saw the large figures '59'. He was profoundly stirred. He had said that the matter with him was that he had gone off his head; but now, staring at that number on the opposite side of the street, he really did not know what was the matter with him. He might have been dying. The front of the house was dark save for the fanlight. He crossed over and peered down into the area and at the black door. A brass plate : 'Cannon's Boarding-House', he could read. He perspired. It seemed to him that he could see her within the house, mysteriously moving at her feminine tasks. Or did she lie in bed? He had come from Bursley to London, from London to Brighton, and now he had found her portal; it existed. The adventure seemed incredible in its result. Enough for the present! He could stand no more. He walked away, meaning not to return.

When he returned, five minutes later, the fanlight was dark. Had *she*, in the meantime, come into the hall of the house and extinguished the gas? Strange, that all lights should be out in a boarding establishment before ten o'clock! He stood hesitant quite near the house, holding himself against the wind. Then the door opened a little, as it were stealthily, and a hand and arm crept out and with a cloth polished the face of the brass plate. He thought, in his excited fancy, that it was her hand and arm. Within, he seemed to distinguish a dim figure. He did not move; could not. The door opened wider, and the figure stood revealed, a woman's. Surely it was she! She gazed at him suspiciously, duster in hand.

'What are you standing there for?' she questioned inimically. 'We've had enough of loiterers in this street. Please go away.'

She took him for a knave expectant of some chance to maraud. She was not fearful, however. It was she. It was her voice.

CHAPTER 4 : *In Preston Street*

I

He said, 'I happened to be in Brighton, so I thought I'd just call, and – I thought I'd just call.'

She stared at him, frowning, in the dim diffused light of the street.

'I've been seeing your little boy,' he said. 'I thought perhaps as I was here you'd like to know how he was getting on.'

'Why,' she exclaimed, with seeming bitterness, 'you've grown a beard!'

'Yes,' he admitted foolishly, apologetically.

'We can't stand here in this wind,' she said, angry with the wind, which was indeed blowing her hair about, and her skirts and her duster.

She did not in words invite him to enter, but she held the door more widely open and drew back for him to pass. He went in. She closed the door with a bang and rattle of large old-fashioned latches, locks, and chains, and the storm was excluded. They were in the dark of the hall. 'Wait till I put my hand on the matches,' she said. Then she struck a match, which revealed a common oil-lamp, with a reservoir of yellow glass and a paper shade. She raised the chimney and lit the lamp, and regulated the wick.

Edwin kept silence. The terrible constraint which had half paralysed him when Janet first mentioned Hilda, seized him again. He stood near the woman who without a word of explanation or regret had jilted, outraged, and ruined him ten years before; this was their first meeting after their kisses in his father's shop. And yet she was not on her knees, nor in tears, nor stammering an appeal for forgiveness. It was rather he who was apologetic, who sought excuses. He felt somehow like a criminal, or at least like one who commits an enormous indiscretion.

The harsh curves of her hair were the same. Her thick eyebrows were the same. Her blazing glance was the same. Her intensely clear intonation was the same. But she was a profoundly changed woman. Even in his extreme perturbation he could be sure of that. As, bending under the lamp shade to arrange the wick, she exposed her features to the bright light, Edwin saw a face marred by anxiety and grief and time, the face of a mature woman, with no lingering pretension to girlishness. She was thirty-four, and she looked older than Maggie, and much older than Janet. She was embittered. Her black dress was shabby and untidy, her finger-nails irregular, discoloured, and damaged. The

367

aspect of her pained Edwin acutely. It seemed to him a poignant shame that time and sorrow and misfortune could not pass over a young girl's face and leave no mark. When he recalled what she had been, comparing the woman with the delicious wistful freshness of the girl that lived unaltered in his memory, he was obliged to clear his throat. The contrast was too pathetic to be dwelt on. Only with the woman before him did he fully appreciate the exquisite innocent simplicity of the girl. In the day of his passion Hilda had not seemed to him very young, very simple, very wistful. On the contrary she had seemed to have much of the knowledge and the temper of a woman.

Having at length subjugated the wick, she straightened her back, with a gesture that he knew, and for one instant she was a girl again.

II

'Will you come this way?' she said coldly, holding the lamp in front of her, and opening a door.

At the same moment another door opened at the far end of the hall; there was a heavy footstep; a great hand and arm showed, and then Edwin had a glimpse of a man's head and shoulders emerging from an oblong flickering firelight.

Hilda paused. 'All right,' she called to the man, who at once disappeared, shutting the door and leaving darkness where he had been. The large shadows cast by Hilda's lamp now had the gaunt hall to themselves again.

'Don't be alarmed,' she laughed harshly. 'It's only the broker's man.'

Edwin was tongue-tied. If Hilda were joking, what answer could be made to such a pleasantry in such a situation? And if she were speaking the truth, if the bailiffs really were in possession . . .! His life seemed to him once again astoundingly romantic. He had loved this woman, conquered her. And now she was a mere acquaintance, and he was following her stiffly into the recesses of a strange and sinister abode peopled by mysterious men. Was this a Brighton boarding-house? It resembled nothing reputable in his experience. All was incomprehensible.

The room into which she led him was evidently the dining-room. Not spacious, perhaps not quite so large as his own dining-room, it was nearly filled by one long bare table. Eight or ten monotonous chairs were ranged round the grey walls. In the embrasure of the window was a wicker stand with a withered plant on its summit, and at the other end of the room a walnut sideboard in the most horrible taste. The mantelpiece was draped with dark knotted and rosetted cloth; within the fender stood a small paper screen. The walls were hung with ancient and with fairly modern engravings, some big, others little, some coloured, others in black-and-white, but all distressing in their fatuous ugliness. The ceiling seemed black. The whole room fulfilled pretty accurately the scornful scrupulous housewife's notion of a lodging-house interior. It was suspect. And in Edwin there was a good deal of the housewife. He was appalled. Obviously the house was small – he had known that from the outside – and the entire enterprise insignificant. This establishment was not in the King's Road, nor on the Marine Parade, nor at Hove; no doubt hundreds of such little places existed precariously in a vast town like Brighton. Widows, of course, were often in straits. And Janet had told him . . . Nevertheless he was appalled, and completely at a loss to reconcile Hilda with her environment. And then – 'the broker's man' !

At her bidding he sat down, in his overcoat, with his hat insecure on his knee, and observed under the lamp, the dust on the surface of the long table. Hilda seated herself opposite, so that the lamp was between them, hiding him from her by its circle of light. He wondered what Maggie would have thought, and what Clara would have said, could they have seen him in that obscurity.

III

'So you've seen my boy?' she began, with no softening of tone.

'Yes, Janet Orgreave brought him in one morning – the other day. He didn't seem to me to be so ill as all that.'

'Ill !' she exclaimed. 'He certainly wasn't ill when he left here. But he had been. And the doctor said that this air didn't suit him – it never had suited him. It doesn't suit some folks, you know – people can say what they like.'

'Anyhow, he's a lively piece – and no mistake about that !'

'When he's well, he's very well,' said George's mother. 'But he's up and down in a minute. And on the whole he's been on the poorly side.'

He noticed that, though there was no relapse from the correctness of her accent, she was using just such phrases as she might have used had she never quitted her native Turnhill. He looked round the lamp at her furtively, and seemed to see in her shadowed face a particular local quality of sincerity and downrightness that appealed strongly to his admiration. (Yet ten years earlier he had considered her markedly foreign to the Five Towns.) That this quality should have survived in her was a proof to him that she was a woman unique. Unique she had been, and unique she still remained. He did not know that he had long ago lost for ever the power of seeing her with a normal vision. He imagined in his simplicity, which disguised itself as chill critical impartiality, that he was adding her up with clear-sighted shrewdness . . . And then she was a mother ! That meant a mysterious, a mystic perfecting! For him, it was as if among all women she alone had been a mother – so special was his view of the influence of motherhood upon her. He drew together all the beauty of an experience almost universal, transcendentalized it, and centred it on one being. And he was disturbed, baffled, agitated by the effect of the secret workings of his own unsuspected emotion. He was made sad, and sadder. He wanted to right wrongs, to efface from hearts the memory of grief, to create bliss; and he knew that this could never be done. He now saw Hilda exclusively as a victim, whose misfortunes were innumerable. Imagine this creature, with her passion for Victor Hugo, obliged by circumstances to polish a brass door-plate surreptitiously at night! Imagine her solitary in the awful house – with the broken's man! Imagine her forced to separate herself from her child! Imagine the succession of disasters that had soured her and transformed seriousness into harshness and acridity! . . . And within that envelope, what a soul must be burning!

'And when he begins to grow – he's scarcely *begun* to grow yet,' Hilda continued about her offspring, 'then he will need all his strength!'

'Yes, he will,' Edwin concurred heartily.

He wanted to ask her, 'Why did you call him Edwin for his second name? Was it his father's name, or your father's, or did *you* insist on it yourself, because –?' But he could not ask. He could ask nothing. He could not even ask why she had jilted him without a word. He knew naught, and evidently she was determined to give no information. She might at any rate have explained how she had come to meet Janet and under what circumstances Janet had taken possession of the child. All was a mystery. Her face, when he avoided the lamp, shone in the midst of a huge dark cloud of impenetrable mystery. She was too proud to reveal anything whatever. The grand pride in her forbade her even to excuse her conduct to himself. A terrific woman!

IV

Silence fell. His constraint was excruciating. She too was nervous, tapping the table and creaking her chair. He could not speak.

'Shall you be going back to Bursley soon?' she demanded. In her voice was desperation.

'Oh yes!' he said, thankfully eager to follow up any subject. 'On Monday, I expect.'

'I wonder if you'd mind giving Janet a little parcel from me – some things of George's? I meant to send it by post, but if you –'

'Of course! With pleasure!' He seemed to implore her.

'It's quite small,' she said, rising and going to the sideboard, on which lay a little brown-paper parcel.

His eye followed her. She picked up the parcel, glanced at it, and offered it to him.

'I'll take it across on Monday night,' he said fervently.

'Thanks.'

She remained standing; he got up.

'No message or anything?' he suggested.

'Oh!' she said coldly, 'I write, you know.'

'Well –' He made the gesture of departing. There was no alternative.

'We're having very rough weather, aren't we?' she said, with careless conventionality, as she took the lamp.

In the hall, when she held out her hand, he wanted tremendously to squeeze it, to give her through his hand the message of sympathy which his tongue, intimidated by her manner, dared not give. But his hand also refused to obey him. The clasp was strictly ceremonious. As she was drawing the heavy latch of the door he forced himself to say, 'I'm in Brighton sometimes, off and on. Now I know where you are, I must look you up.'

She made no answer. She merely said good night as he passed out into the street and the wind. The door banged.

V

Edwin took a long breath. He had seen her! Yes, but the interview had been worse than his worst expectations. He had surpassed himself in futility, in fatuous lack of enterprise. He had behaved like a schoolboy. Now, as he plunged up the street with the wind, he could devise easily a dozen ways of animating and guiding and controlling the interview so that, even if sad, its sadness might have been agreeable. The interview had been hell, ineffable torture, a perfect crime of clumsiness. It had resulted in nothing. (Except, of course, that he had seen her – that fact was indisputable.) He blamed himself. He cursed himself with really extraordinary savageness.

'Why did I go near her?' he demanded. 'Why couldn't I keep away? I've simply made myself look a blasted fool! Creeping and crawling round her! . . . After all, she *did* throw me over! And now she asks me to take a parcel to her confounded kid! The whole thing's ridiculous! And what's going to happen to her in that hole! I don't suppose she's got the least notion of looking after herself. Impossible – the whole thing! If anybody had told me that I should – that she's –' Half of which talk was simple bluster. The parcel was bobbing on its loop against his side.

When he reached the top of the street he discovered that he had been going up it instead of down it. 'What am I thinking of?' he grumbled impatiently. However, he would not turn back. He adventured forward, climbing into latitudes whose geography was strange to him, and scarcely seeing a single fellow-wanderer beneath the gas-lamps. Presently, after a steep hill, he came to a churchyard, and then he redescended, and at last tumbled into a street alive with people who had emerged from a theatre, laughing, lighting cigarettes, linking arms. Their existence seemed shallow, purposeless, infantile, compared to his. He felt himself superior to them. What did they know about life? He would not change with any of them.

Recognizing the label on an omnibus, he followed its direction, and arrived almost immediately in the vast square which contained his hotel, and which was illuminated by the brilliant façades of several hotels. The doors of the Royal Sussex were locked, because eleven o'clock had struck. He could not account for the period of nearly three hours which had passed since he left the hotel. The zealous porter, observing his shadow through the bars, had sprung to unfasten the door before he could ring.

VI

Within the hotel reigned gaiety, wine, and the dance. Small tables had been placed in the hall, and at these sat bald-headed men, smoking cigars and sharing champagne with ladies of every age. A white carpet had been laid in the large smoking-room, and through the curtained archway that separated it from the hall, Edwin could see couples revolving in obedience to the music of a piano and a violin. One of the Royal Sussex's Saturday Cinderellas was in progress. The self-satisfied gestures of men inspecting their cigars or lifting glasses, of simpering women glancing on the sly at their jewels, and of youths pulling straight their white waistcoats as they strolled about with the air of Don Juans, invigorated his contempt for the average existence. The tinkle of the music appeared exquisitely tedious in its superficiality. He could not remain in the hall because of the incorrectness of his attire, and the staircase was blocked, to a timid man, by elegant couples apparently engaged in the act of flirtation. He turned, through a group of attendant waiters, into the passage leading to the small smoking-room which adjoined the discreetly situated bar. This smoking-room, like a club, warm and bright, was empty, but in passing he had caught sight of two mutually affectionate dandies drinking at the splendid mahogany of the bar. He lit a cigarette. Seated in the smoking-room he could hear their conversation; he was forced to hear it.

'I'm really a very quiet man, old chap, *very* quiet,' said one, with a wavering drawl, 'but when they get at me – I was at the Club at one o'clock. I wasn't drunk, but I had a top on.'

'You were just gay and cheerful,' the other flatteringly and soothingly suggested, in an exactly similar wavering drawl.

'Yes. I felt as if I wanted to go out somewhere and have another drink. So I went to Willis's Rooms. I was in evening-dress. You know you have to get a domino for those things. Then, of course, you're a mark at once. I also got a nose. A girl snatched it off me. I told her what I thought of *her* and I got another nose. Then five fellows tried to snatch my domino off me. Then I *did* get angry. I landed out with my right at the nearest chap – right on his heart. Not his face. His heart. I lowered him. He asked me afterwards, "Was that your right?" "Yes", I said, "and my left's worse!" I couldn't use my left because they were holding it. You see? You *see*?'

'Yes,' said the other impatiently, and suddenly cantankerous. 'I see that all right! Damned awful rot those Willis's Rooms affairs are getting, if you ask me!'

'Asses!' Edwin exploded within himself. 'Idiots!' He could not tolerate their crassness. He had a hot prejudice against them because they were not as near the core of life as he was himself. It appeared to him that most people died without having lived. Willis's Rooms! Girls! Nose! Heart! ... Asses!

He surged again out of the small room, desolating the bar with one scornful glance as he went by. He braved the staircase, leaving those scenes of drivelling festivity. In his bedroom, with the wind crashing against the window, he regarded meditatively the parcel. After all, if she had meant to have nothing to do with him, she would not have charged him with parcel. The parcel was a solid fact. The more he thought about it, the more significant a fact it seemed to him. His ears sang with the vibrating intensity of his secret existence, but from the wild confusion of his heart he could disentangle no constant idea.

CHAPTER 5 : *The Bully*

I

The next morning he was early, preternaturally awake. When he descended the waiters were waiting for him, and the zealous porter stood ready to offer a Sunday paper, just as though in the night they had refreshed themselves magically, without going to bed. No sign nor relic of the Cinderella remained. He breakfasted in an absent mind, and then went idly into the lounge, a room with one immense circular window, giving on the Square. Rain was falling heavily. Already from the porter, and in the very mien of the waiters, he had learnt that the Brighton Sunday was ruined. He left the window. On a round table in the middle of the room were ranged, with religious regularity, all the most esoteric examples of periodical literature in our language, from *The Iron-Trades Review* to *The Animals' Guardian*. With one careless movement he destroyed the balanced perfection of a labour into which some menial had put his soul, and then dropped into a gigantic easy-chair near the fire, whose thin flames were just rising through the interstices of great black lumps of coal.

The housekeeper, stiff with embroidered silk, swam majestically into the lounge, bowed with a certain frigid and deferential surprise to the early guest, and proceeded to an inquiry into dust. In a moment she called, sharp and low –

'Arthur !'

And a page ran eagerly in, to whom, in the difficult corners of upholstery and of sculptured wood, she pointed out his sins of omission, lashing him with a restrained voice that Edwin could scarcely hear. Passing her hand carelessly along the beading of a door panel and then examining her fingers, she departed. The page fetched a duster.

'I see why this hotel has such a name,' said Edwin to himself. And suddenly the image of Hilda in that dark and frowzy tenement in Preston Street, on that wet Sunday morning, filled his heart with a revolt capricious and violent. He sprang to his feet, unreflecting, wilful, and strode into the hall.

'Can I have a cab?' he asked the porter.

'Certainly, sir,' said the porter, as if saying, 'You ask me too little. Why will you not ask for a white elephant so that I may prove my devotion?' And within five seconds the screech of a whistle sped through the air to the cabstand at the corner.

II

'Why am I doing this?' he once more asked himself, when he heard the bell ring, in answer to his pull, within the house in Preston Street. The desire for a tranquil life had always been one of his strongest instincts, and of late years the instinct had been satisfied, and so strengthened. Now he seemed to be obstinately searching for tumult; and he did not know why. He trembled at the sound of movement behind the door. 'In a moment,' he thought, 'I shall be right in the thick of it !'

As he was expecting, she opened the door herself; but only a little, with the gesture habitual to women who live alone in apprehension, and she kept her hand on the latch.

'Good morning,' he said curtly. 'Can I speak to you?'

374

His eyes could not blaze like hers, but all his self-respect depended on his valour now, and with desperation he affronted her. She opened the door wider, and he stepped in, and at once began to wipe his boots on the mat with nervous particularity.

'Frightful morning!' he grinned.

'Yes,' she said. 'Is that your cab outside?'

He admitted that it was.

'Perhaps if we go upstairs,' she suggested.

Thanking her, he followed her upwards into the gloom at the head of the narrow stairs, and then along a narrow passage. The house appeared quite as unfavourably by day as by night. It was shabby. All its tints had merged by use and by time into one tint, nondescript and unpleasant, in which yellow prospered. The drawing-room was larger than the dining-room by the poor width of the hall. It was a heaped, confused mass of chairs, sofas, small tables, draperies, embroideries, and valueless knick-knacks. There was no peace in it for the eye, neither on the walls nor on the floor. The gaze was driven from one ugliness to another without rest.

The fireplace was draped; the door was draped; the back of the piano was draped; and none of the dark suspicious stuffs showed a clear pattern. The faded chairs were hidden by faded antimacassars; the little futile tables concealed their rickets under vague needlework, on which were displayed in straw or tinsel frames pale portraits of dowdy people who had stood like sheep before fifteenth-rate photographers. The mantelpiece and the top of the piano were thickly strewn with fragments of coloured earthenware. At the windows hung heavy dark curtains from great rings that gleamed gilt near the ceiling; and lest the light which they admitted should be too powerful it was further screened by greyish white curtains within them. The carpet was covered in most places by small rugs or bits of other carpets, and in the deep shadows beneath sofas and chairs and behind the piano it seemed to slip altogether out of existence into black nothingness. The room lacked ventilation, but had the appearance of having been recently dusted.

III

Hilda closed the draped door with a mysterious, bitter, cynical smile.

'Sit down,' she said coldly.

'Last night,' Edwin began, without sitting down, 'when you mentioned the broker's man, were you joking, or did you meant it?'

She was taken aback.

'Did I say "broker's man"?'

'Well,' said Edwin, 'you've not forgotten, I suppose.'

She sat down, with some precision of pose, on the principal sofa.

'Yes,' she said at length. 'As you're so curious. The landlords are in possession.'

'The bailiffs still here?'

'Yes.'

'But what are you going to do?'

'I'm expecting them to take the furniture away tomorrow, or Tuesday at the latest,' she replied.

'And then what?'

'I don't know.'

'But haven't you got any money?'

She took a purse from her pocket, and opened it with a show of impartial curiosity. 'Two-and-seven,' she said.

'Any servant in the house?'

'What do you think?' she replied. 'Didn't you see me cleaning the door-plate last night? I *do* like that to look nice at any rate!'

'I don't see much use in that looking nice, when you've got the bailiffs in, and no servant and no money,' Edwin said roughly, and added, still more roughly : 'What should you do if anyone came inquiring for rooms?' He tried to guess her real mood, but her features would betray nothing.

'I was expecting three old ladies – sisters – next week,' she said. 'I'd been hoping I could hold out till they came. They're horrid women, though they don't know it; but they've stayed a couple of months in this house every winter for I don't know how many years, and they're firmly convinced it's the best house in Brighton. They're quite enough to keep it going by themselves when they're here. But I shall have to write and tell them not to come this time.'

'Yes,' said Edwin. 'But I keep asking you – what then?'

'And I keep saying I don't know.'

'You must have some plans?'

'I haven't.' She put her lips together, and dimpled her chin, and again cynically smiled. At any rate she had not resented his inquisition.

'I suppose you know you're behaving like a perfect fool?' he suggested angrily. She did not wince.

'And what if I am? What's that got to do with you?' she asked, as if pleasantly puzzled.

'You'll starve. You can't live on two-and-seven.'

'Well?'

'And the boy? Is he going to starve?'

'Oh,' said Hilda, 'Janet will look after him till something turns up. The fact is, that's one reason why I allowed her to take him.'

' "Something turns up", "something turns up" !' Edwin repeated deliberately, letting himself go. 'You make me absolutely sick! It's

376

absolutely incredible how some people will let things slide! What in the name of God Almighty do you think will turn up?'

'I don't know,' she said, with a certain weakness, still trying to be placidly bitter, and not now succeeding.

'Where is the bailiff-johnny?'

'He's in the kitchen with one of his friends, drinking.'

Edwin with bravado flopped his hat down forcefully on a table, pushed a chair aside, and strode towards the door.

'Where are you going?' she asked in alarm, standing up.

'Where do you suppose I'm going? I'm going to find out from that chap how much will settle it. If you can't show any common sense for yourself, other folks must show some for you – that's all. The brokers in the house! I never heard of such work!'

And indeed, to a respected and successful tradesman, the entrance of the bailiffs into a house did really seem to be the very depth of disaster and shame for the people of that house. Edwin could not remember that he had ever before seen a bailiff. To him a bailiff was like a bug – something heard of, something known to exist, but something not likely to enter the field of vision of an honest and circumspect man.

He would deal with the bailiff. He would have a short way with the bailiff. Secure in the confidence of his bankers, he was ready to bully the innocent bailiff. He would not reflect, would not pause. He had heated himself. His steam was up, and he would not let the pressure be weakened by argumentative hesitations. His emotion was not disagreeable.

When he was in the passage he heard the sound of a sob. Prudently, he had not banged the door after him. He stopped, and listened. Was it a sob? Then he heard another sob. He went back to the drawing-room.

IV

Yes! She stood in the middle of the room weeping. Save Clara, and possibly once or twice Maggie, he had never seen a woman cry – that is, in circumstances of intimacy; he had seen women crying in the street, and the spectacle usually pained him. On occasion he had very nearly made Maggie cry, and had felt exceedingly uncomfortable. But now, as he looked at the wet eyes and the shaken bosom of Hilda Cannon, he was aware of acute joy. Exquisite moment! Damn her! He could have taken her and beaten her in his sudden passion – a passion not of revenge, not of punishment! He could have made her scream with the pain that his love would inflict.

She tried to speak, and failed, in a storm of sobs. He had left the door open. Half blind with tears she dashed to the door and shut it, and then turned and fronted him, with her hands hovering near her face.

377

'I can't let you do it!' she murmured imploringly, plaintively, and yet with that still obstinate bitterness in her broken voice.

'Then who is to do it?' he demanded, less bitterly than she had spoken, nevertheless not softly. 'Who is to keep you if I don't? Have you got any other friends who'll stand by you?'

'I've got the Orgreaves,' she answered.

'And do you think it would be better for the Orgreaves to keep you, or for me?' As she made no response, he continued : 'Anybody else besides the Orgreaves?'

'No,' she muttered sulkily. 'I'm not the sort of woman that makes a lot of friends. I expect people don't like me, as a rule.'

'You're the sort of woman that behaves like a blooming infant!' he said. 'Supposing I don't help you? What then – I keep asking you? How shall you get money? You can only borrow it – and there's nobody but Janet, and she'd have to ask her father for it. Of course, if you'd sooner borrow from Osmond Orgreave than from me . . .'

'I don't want to borrow from anyone,' she protested.

'Then you want to starve! And you want your boy to starve – or else live on charity! Why don't you look facts in the face? You'll have to look them in the face sooner or later, and the sooner the better. You think you're doing a fine thing by sitting tight and bearing it, and saying nothing, and keeping it all a secret, until you get pinched into the street! Let me tell you you aren't.'

v

She dropped into a chair by the piano, and rested her elbows on the curved lid of the piano.

'You're frightfully cruel!' she sobbed, hiding her face.

He fidgeted away to the larger of the two windows, which was bayed, so that the room could boast a view of the sea. On the floor he noticed an open book, pages downwards. He picked it up. It was the poems of Crashaw, an author he had never read but had always been intending to read. Outside, the driver of his cab was bunching up his head and shoulders together under a large umbrella, upon which the rain spattered. The flanks of the resigned horse glistened with rain.

'You needn't talk about cruelty!' he remarked, staring hard at the signboard of an optician opposite. He could hear the faint clanging of church bells.

After a pause she said, as if apologetically –

'Keeping a boarding-house isn't my line. But what could I do? My sister-in-law had it, and I was with her. And when she died. . . . Besides, I dare say I can keep a boarding-house as well as plenty of other people. But – well, it's no use going into that!'

Edwin abruptly sat down near her.

'Come, now,' he said less harshly, more persuasively. 'How much do you owe?'

'Oh!' she cried, pouting and shifting her feet. 'It's out of the question! They've distrained for seventy-five pounds.'

'I don't care if they've distrained for seven hundred and seventy-five pounds!' She seemed just like a girl to him again now, in spite of her face and her figure. 'If that was cleared off, you could carry on, couldn't you? This is just the season. Could you get a servant in, in time for these three sisters?'

'I could get a charwoman, anyhow,' she said unwillingly.

'Well, do you owe anything else?'

'There'll be the expenses.'

'Of the distraint?'

'Yes.'

'That's nothing. I shall lend you a hundred pounds. It just happens that I've got fifty pounds on me in notes. That and a cheque'll settle the bailiff person, and the rest of the hundred I'll send you by post. It'll be a bit of working capital.'

She rose and threaded between chairs and tables to the sofa, several feet from Edwin. With a vanquished and weary sigh, she threw herself on the sofa.

'I never knew there was anybody like you in the world,' she breathed, flicking away some fluff from her breast. She seemed to be regarding him, not as a benefactor, but as a natural curiosity.

VI

He looked at her like a conquerer. He had taught her a thing or two. He had been a man. He was proud of himself. He was proud of all sorts of details in his conduct. The fifty pounds in notes, for example, was not an accident. Since the death of his father, he had formed the habit of never leaving his base of supplies without a provision far in excess of what he was likely to need. He was extravagant in nothing, but the humiliations of his penurious youth and early manhood had implanted in him a morbid fear of being short of money. He had fantastically sur- mised circumstances in which he might need a considerable sum at Brighton. And lo! the sequel had transformed his morbidity into prudence.

'This time yesterday,' he reflected, in his triumph, 'I hadn't even seen her, and didn't know where she was. Last night I was a fool. Half an hour ago she herself hadn't a notion that I was going to get the upper hand of her. . . . Why, it isn't two days yet since I left home! . . . And look where I am now!'

With pity and with joy he watched her slowly wiping her eyes. Thirty-four, perhaps; yet a child – compared to him! But if she did not give a natural ingenuous smile of relief, it was because she could not. If she acted foolishly it was because of her tremendous haughtiness. However, he had lowered that. He had shown her her master. He felt that she had been profoundly wronged by destiny, and that gentleness must be lavished upon her.

In a casual tone he began to talk about the most rapid means of getting rid of the bailiff. He could not tolerate the incubus of the bailiff a moment longer than was absolutely unavoidable. At intervals a misgiving shot like a thin flying needle through the solid satisfaction of his sensations : 'She is a strange and an incalculable woman – why am I doing this?' Shot, and was gone, almost before perceived!

CHAPTER 6 : *The Rendezvous*

I

In the afternoon the weather cleared somewhat. Edwin, vaguely blissful, but with nothing to occupy him save reflection, sat in the lounge drinking tea at a Moorish table. An old Jew, who was likewise drinking tea at a Moorish table, had engaged him in conversation and was relating the history of a burglary in which he had lost from his flat in Bolton Street, Piccadilly, nineteen gold cigarette-cases and thirty-seven jewelled scarf-pins, tokens of esteem and regard offered to him by friends and colleagues at various crises of his life. The lounge was crowded, but not with tea-drinkers. Despite the horrid dismalness of the morning, hope had sent down from London trains full of people whose determination was to live and to see life in a grandiose manner. And all about the lounge of the Royal Sussex were groups of elegant youngish men and flaxen, uneasily stylish women, inviting the assistance of flattered waiters to decide what liqueurs they should have next. Edwin was humanly trying to publish in nonchalant gestures the scorn which he really felt for these nincompoops, but whose free expression was hindered by a layer of envy.

The hall-porter appeared, and his eye ranged like a condor's over the field until it discovered Edwin, whom he approached with a mien of joy and handed to him a letter.

Edwin took the letter with an air of custom, as if he was anxious to convince the company that his stay at the Royal Sussex was frequently punctuated by the arrival of special missives.

'Who brought this?' he asked.

'An oldish man, sir,' said the porter, and bowed and departed.

The handwriting was hers. Probably the broker's man had offered to bring the letter. In the short colloquy with him in the morning, Edwin had liked the slatternly, coarse fellow. The bailiff could not, un-authorized, accept cheques, but his tone in suggesting an immediate visit to his employers had shown that he had bowels, that he sympathized with the difficulties of careless tenants in a harsh world of landlords. It was Hilda who, furnished with notes and cheque, had gone, in Edwin's cab, to placate the higher powers. She had preferred to go herself, and to go alone. Edwin had not insisted. He had so mastered her that he could afford to yield to her in trifles.

II

The letter said exactly this : 'Everything is all right and settled. I had no trouble at all. But I should like to speak to you this afternoon. Will you meet me on the West Pier at six? – H. C.' No form of greeting! No thanks! The bare words necessary to convey a wish! On leaving her in the morning no arrangement had been made for a further interview. She had said nothing, and he had been too proud to ask – the terrible pride of the benefactor! It was only by chance that it had even oc-curred to him to say : 'By the way, I am staying at the Royal Sussex.' She had shown no curiosity whatever about him, his doings, his move-ments. She had not put to him a single question. He had intended to call at Preston Street on the Monday morning. And now a letter from her! Her handwriting had scarcely changed. He was to meet her on the pier. At her own request he now had a rendezvous with her on the pier! Why not at her house? Perhaps she was afraid of his power over her in the house. (Curious, how she, and she almost alone, roused the mas-culine force in him!) Perhaps she wanted to thank him in surroundings which would compel both of them to be calm. That would be like her! Essentially modest, restrained! And did she not know how to be meek, she who was so headstrong and independent!

He looked at the clock. The hour was not yet five. Nevertheless he felt obliged to go out, to bestir himself. On the misty, crowded, darken-ing promenade he abandoned himself afresh to indulgence in the souvenance of the great critical scene of the morning. Yes, he had done marvels; and fate was astoundingly kind to him also. But there was one aspect of the affair that intrigued and puzzled him, and weakened his self-satisfaction. She had been defeated, yet he was baffled by her. She was a mystery within folds of mysteries. He was no nearer – he secretly felt – to the essential Her than he had been before the short struggle and his spectacular triumph. He wanted to reconstruct in his fancy all her emotional existence; he wanted to get *at* her – to possess her intimate mind – and lo! he could not even recall the expressions of her face from minute to minute during the battle. She hid herself from him. She eluded him . . . Strange creature! The polishing of the door-plate in the night! That volume of Crashaw – on the floor! Her cold, almost daemonic smile! Her sobs! Her sudden retreats! What was at the back of it all? He remembered her divine gesture over the fond Shushions. He remembered the ecstatic quality of her surrender in the shop. He remembered her first love-letter : 'Every bit of me is absolutely yours.' And yet the ground seemed to be unsure beneath his feet, and he wondered whether he had ever in reality known her, ever grasped firmly the secret of her personality, even for an instant.

He said to himself that he would be seeing her face to face in an hour, and that then he would, by the ardour of his gaze, get behind those enigmatic features to the arcana they concealed.

III

Before six o'clock it was quite dark. He thought it a strange notion, to fix a rendezvous at such an hour, on a day in autumn, in the open air. But perhaps she was very busy, doing servant's work in the preparation of her house for visitors. When he reached the pier gates at five minutes to six, they were closed, and the obscure vista of the pier as deserted as some northern pier in mid-winter. Naturally it was closed! There was a notice prominently displayed that the pier would close that evening at dusk. What did she mean! The truth was, he decided, that she lived in the clouds, ordering her existence by means of sudden and capricious decisions in which facts were neglected – and herein probably lay the explanation of her misfortunes. He was very philosophical : rather amused than disturbed, because her house was scarcely a stone's-throw away : she could not escape him.

He glanced up and down the lighted promenade, and across the broad muddy road towards the opening of Preston Street. The crowds had disappeared; only scattered groups and couples, and now and then a solitary, passed quickly in the gloom. The hotels were brilliant, and carriages with their flitting lamps were continually stopping in front of them; but the blackness of the shop-fronts produced the sensation of melancholy proper to the day even in Brighton, and the renewed sound of church bells intensified this arid melancholy.

Suddenly he saw her, coming not across the road from Preston Street, but from the direction of Hove. He saw her before she saw him. Under the multiplicity of lamps her face was white and clear. He had a chance to read in it. But he could reach nothing in it save her sadness, save that she had suffered. She seemed querulous, preoccupied, worried, and afflicted. She had the look of one who is never free from apprehension. Yet for him that look of hers had a quality that he had never found in another, but which he was completely unable to define. He wanted acutely to explain to himself what it was, and he could not.

'You are frightfully cruel,' she had said. And he admitted that he had been. Yes, he had bullied her, her who, he was convinced, had always been the victim. In spite of her vigorous individuality she was destined to be a victim. He was sure that she had never deserved anything but sympathy and respect and affection. He was sure she was the very incarnation of honesty – possibly she was too honest for the actual world. Did not the Orgreaves worship her? And could he himself have been deceived in his estimate of her character?

She recognized him only when she was close upon him. A faint, transient, wistful smile lightened her brooding face, pale and stern.

IV

'Oh! There you are!' she exclaimed, in her clear voice. 'Did I say six, or five, in my note?'

'Six.'

'I was afraid I had done, when I came here at five and didn't find you. I'm so sorry.'

'No!' he said. 'I think *I* ought to be sorry. It's you who've had the waiting to do. The pier's closed now.'

'It was just closing at five,' she answered. 'I ought to have known. But I didn't. The fact is, I scarcely ever go out. I remembered once seeing the pier open at night, and I thought it was always open.' She shrugged her shoulders as if stopping a shiver.

'I hope you haven't caught cold,' he said. 'Suppose we walk along a bit.'

They walked westwards in silence. He felt as though he were by the side of a stranger, so far was he from having pierced the secret of that face.

As they approached one of the new glazed shelters, she said –

'Can't we sit down a moment? I – I can't talk standing up. I must sit down.'

They sat down, in an enclosed seat designed to hold four. And Edwin could feel the wind on his calves, which stretched beyond the screened side of the structure. Odd people passed dimly to and fro in front of them, glanced at them with nonchalant curiosity, and glanced away. On the previous evening he had observed couples in those shelters, and had wondered what could be the circumstances or the preferences which led them to accept such a situation. Certainly he could not have dreamed that within twenty-four hours he would be sitting in one of them with her, by her appointment, at her request. He thrilled with excitement – with delicious anxieties.

'Janet told you I was a widow,' Hilda began, gazing at the ferrule of her umbrella, which gleamed on the ground.

'Yes.' Again she was surprising him.

'Well, we arranged she should tell everyone that. But I think you ought to know that I'm not.'

'No?' he murmured weakly. And in one small unimportant region of his mind he reflected with astonishment upon the hesitating but convincing air with which Janet had lied to him. Janet!

'After what you've done' – she paused, and went on with unblurred clearness – 'after what you've insisted on doing, I don't want there to be any misunderstanding. I'm not a widow. My husband's in prison. He'll be in prison for another six or seven years. That's all I wanted to tell you.'

'I'm very sorry,' he breathed. 'I'd no idea you'd had this trouble.' What could he say? What could anybody have said?

'I ought to have told you at once,' she said. 'I ought to have told you last night.' Another pause. 'Then perhaps you wouldn't have come again this morning.'

'Yes, I should!' he asserted eagerly. 'If you're in a hole, you're in a hole. What difference could it possibly make whether you were a widow or not?'

'Oh!' she said. 'The wife of a convict ... you know!'

He felt that she was evading the point.

She went on : 'It's a good thing my three old ladies don't know, anyhow! . . . I'd no chance to tell you this morning. You were too much for me.'

'I don't care whose wife you are!' he muttered, as though to himself, as though resenting something said by someone who had gone away and left him. 'If you're in a hole, you're in a hole.'

She turned and looked at him. His eyes fell before hers.

'Well,' she said. 'I've told you. I must go. I haven't a moment. Good night.' She held out her hand. 'You don't want me to thank you a lot, do you?'

'That I don't!' he exclaimed.

'Good night.'

'But –'

'I really must go.'

He rose and gave his hand. The next instant she was gone.

There was a deafening roar in his head. It was the complete destruction by earthquake of a city of dreams. A calamity which left nothing – even to be desired! A tremendous silence reigned after the event.

V

On the following evening, when from the windows of the London-to-Manchester express he saw in the gloom the high-leaping flames of the blast-furnaces that seem to guard eternally the southern frontier of the Five Towns, he felt that he had returned into daily reality out of an impossible world. Waiting for the loop-line train in the familiar tedium of Knype platform, staring at the bookstall, every item on which he knew by heart and despised, surrounded once more by local physiognomies, gestures, and accent, he thought to himself: '*This* is my lot. And if I get messing about, it only shows what a damned fool I am!' He called himself a damned fool because Hilda had proved to have a husband; because of that he condemned the whole expedition to Brighton as a piece of idiocy. His dejection was profound and bitter. At first, after Hilda had quitted him on the Sunday night, he had tried to be cheerful, had persuaded himself indeed that he was cheerful; but gradually his spirit had sunk, beaten and miserable. He had not called at Preston Street again. Pride forbade, and the terror of being misunderstood.

And when he sat at his own table, in his own dining-room, and watched the calm incurious Maggie dispensing to him his elaborate tea-supper with slightly more fuss and more devotion than usual, his thoughts, had they been somewhat less vague, might have been summed up thus: 'The right sort of women don't get landed as the wives of convicts. Can you imagine such a thing happening to Maggie, for instance! Or Janet?' (And yet Janet was in the secret! This disturbed the flow of his reflections.) Hilda was too mysterious. Now she had half disclosed yet another mystery. But what? Why was her husband a convict! Under what circumstances? For what crime? Where? Since when? He knew the answer to none of these questions. More deeply than ever was that woman embedded in enigmas.

'What's this parcel on the sideboard?' Maggie inquired.

'Oh! I want you to send it in to Janet. It's from her particular friend, Mrs Cannon – something for the kid, I believe. I ran across her in Brighton, and she asked me if I'd bring the parcel along.'

The innocence of his manner was perfectly acted. He wondered that he could do it so well. But really there was no danger. Nobody in Bursley, or in the world, had the least suspicion of his past relations with Hilda. The only conceivable danger would have been in hiding the fact that he had met her in Brighton.

'Of course,' said Maggie, mildly interested. 'I was forgetting she

385

lived at Brighton. Well?' and she put a few casual questions, to which Edwin casually replied.

'You look tired,' she said later.

He astonished her by admitting that he was. According to all precedent her statement ought to have drawn forth a quick contradiction.

The sad image of Hilda would not be dismissed. He had to carry it about with him everywhere, and it was heavy enough to fatigue a stronger man than Edwin Clayhanger. The pathos of her situation overwhelmed him, argue as he might about the immunity of 'the right sort of women' from a certain sort of disaster. On the Tuesday he sent her a post-office order for twenty pounds. It rather more than made up the agreed sum of hundred pounds. She returned it, saying she did not need it. 'Little fool!' he said. He was not surprised. He was, however, very much surprised, a few weeks later, to receive from Hilda her own cheque for eighty pounds odd! More mystery! An absolutely incredible woman! Whence had she obtained that eighty pounds? Needless to say, she offered no explanation. He abandoned all conjecture. But he could not abandon the image. And first Auntie Hamps said, and then Clara, and then even Maggie admitted, that Edwin was sticking too close to business and needed a change, needed rousing. Auntie Hamps urged openly that a wife ought to be found for him. But in a few days the great talkers of the family, Auntie Hamps and Clara, had grown accustomed to Edwin's state, and some new topic supervened.

CHAPTER 7 : *The Wall*

I

One morning – towards the end of November – Edwin, attended by Maggie, was rearranging books in the drawing-room after breakfast, when there came a startling loud tap at the large central pane of the window. Both of them jumped.

'Who's throwing?' Edwin exclaimed.

'I expect it's that boy,' said Maggie, almost angrily.

'Not Georgie?'

'Yes. I wish you'd go and stop him. You've no idea what a tiresome little thing he is. And so rough too !'

This attitude of Maggie towards the mysterious nephew was a surprise for Edwin. She had never grumbled about him before. In fact they had seen little of him. For a fortnight he had not been abroad, and the rumour ran that he was unwell, that he was 'not so strong as he ought to be.' And now Maggie suddenly charged him with a whole series of misdoings! But it was Maggie's way to keep unpleasant things from Edwin for a time, in order to save her important brother from being worried, and then in a moment of tension to fling them full in his face, like a wet clout.

'What's he been up to?' Edwin inquired for details.

'Oh! I don't know,' answered Maggie vaguely. At the same instant came another startling blow on the window. 'There!' Maggie cried, in triumph, as if saying: 'That's what he's been up to!' After all, the windows were Maggie's own windows.

Edwin left on the sofa a whole pile of books that he was sorting, and went out into the garden. On the top of the wall separating him from the Orgreaves a row of damaged earthenware objects – jugs and jars chiefly – at once caught his eye. He witnessed the smashing of one of them, and then he ran to the wall, and taking a spring, rested on it with his arms, his toes pushed into crevices. Young George, with hand outstretched to throw, in the garden of the Orgreaves, seemed rather diverted by this apparition.

'Hello!' said Edwin. 'What are you up to?'

'I'm practising breaking crocks,' said the child. That he had acquired the local word gave Edwin pleasure.

'Yes, but do you know you're practising breaking my windows too? When you aim too high you simply can't miss one of my windows.'

George's face was troubled, as he examined the facts, which had hitherto escaped his attention, that there was a whole world of consequences on the other side of the wall, and that a missile which did not prove its existence against either the wall or a crock had not necessarily ceased to exist. Edwin watched the face with a new joy, as though looking at some wonder of nature under a microscope. It seemed to him that he now saw vividly why children were interesting.

'I can't see any windows from here,' said George, in defence.

'If you climb up here you'll see them all right.'

'Yes, but I can't climb up. I've tried to, a lot of times. Even when I stood on my toes on this stump I could only just reach to put the crocks on the top.'

'What did you want to get on the wall for?'

'I wanted to see that swing of yours.'

'Well,' said Edwin, laughing, 'if you could remember the swing why couldn't you remember the windows?'

George shook his head at Edwin's stupidity, and looked at the ground. 'A swing isn't windows,' he said. Then he glanced up with a diffident smile: 'I've often been wanting to come and see you.'

Edwin was tremendously flattered. If he had made a conquest, the child by this frank admission had made a greater

'Then why didn't you come?'

'I couldn't by myself. Besides, my back hasn't been well. Did they tell you?'

George was so naturally serious that Edwin decided to be serious too.

'I did hear something about it,' he replied, with the grave confidential tone that he would have used to a man of his own age. This treatment was evidently appreciated by George, and always afterwards Edwin conversed with him as with an equal, forbearing from facetiousness.

Damp though it was, Edwin twisted himself round and sat on the wall next to the crocks, and bent over the boy beneath, who gazed with upturned face.

'Why didn't you ask Auntie Janet to bring you?'

'I don't generally ask for things that I really want,' said the boy, with a peculiar glance.

'I see,' said Edwin, with an air of comprehension. He did not, however, comprehend. He only felt that the boy was wonderful. Imagine the boy saying that! He bent lower. 'Come on up,' he said. 'I'll give you a hand. Stick your feet into that nick there.'

II

In an instant George was standing on the wall, light as fluff. Edwin held him by the legs, and his hand was on Edwin's cap. The feel of the boy was delightful; he was so lithe and so yielding, and yet firm. And his glance was so trustful and admiring. 'Rough!' thought Edwin, remembering Maggie's adjective. 'He isn't a bit rough! Unruly? Well, I dare say he can be unruly if he cares to be. It all depends how you handle him.' Thus Edwin reflected in the pride of conquest, holding close to the boy, and savouring intimately his charm. Even the boy's slightness attracted him. Difficult to believe that he was nine years old! His body was indeed backward. So, too, it appeared, was his education. And yet was there not the wisdom of centuries in 'I don't generally ask for things that I really want'?

Suddenly the boy wriggled, and gave a sound of joy that was almost a yell. 'Look!' he cried.

The covered top of the steam-car could just be seen gliding along above the high wall that separated Edwin's garden from the street.

'Yes,' Edwin agreed. 'Funny, isn't it?' But he considered that such glee at such a trifle was really more characteristic of six or seven than of nine years. George's face was transformed by ecstasy.

'It's when things move like that – horizontal!' George explained, pronouncing the word carefully.

388

Edwin felt that there was no end to the surpassing strangeness of this boy. One moment he was aged six, and the next he was talking about horizontality.

'Why? What do you mean?'

'I don't know!' George sighed. 'But somehow . . .' Then, with fresh vivacity : 'I tell you – when Auntie Janet comes to wake me up in the morning the cat comes in too, with its tail up in the air – you know!' Edwin nodded. 'Well, when I'm lying in bed I can't see the cat, but I can see the top of its tail sailing along the edge of the bed. But if I sit up I can see all the cat, and that spoils it, so I don't sit up at first.'

The child was eager for Edwin to understand his pleasure in horizontal motion that had no apparent cause, like the tip of a cat's tail on the horizon of a bed, or the roof of a tram-car on the horizon of the wall. And Edwin was eager to understand, and almost persuaded himself that he did understand; but he could not be sure. A marvellous child – disconcerting ! He had a feeling of inferiority to the child, because the child had seen beauty where he had not dreamed of seeing it.

'Want a swing,' he suggested, 'before I have to go off to business?'

III

When it occurred to him that he had had as much violent physical exercise as was good for his years, and that he had left his books in disarray, and that his business demanded him, Edwin apologetically announced that he must depart, and the child admitted that Aunt Janet was probably waiting to give him his lessons.

'Are you going back the way you came? You'd better. It's always best,' said Edwin.

'Is it?'

'Yes.'

He lifted and pushed the writhing form on to the wall, dislodging a jar, which crashed dully on the ground.

'Auntie Janet told me I could have them to do what I liked with. So I break them,' said George, 'when they don't break themselves!'

'I bet she never told you to put them on this wall,' said Edwin.

'No, she didn't. But it was the best place for aiming. And she told me it didn't matter how many crocks I broke, because they make crocks here. Do they really?'

'Yes.'

'Why?'

'Because there's clay here,' said Edwin glibly.

'Where?'

'Oh ! Round about.'

'White, like that?' exclaimed George eagerly, handling a teapot without a spout. He looked at Edwin : 'Will you take me to see it? I should like to see white ground.'

'Well,' said Edwin, more cautiously, 'the clay they get about here isn't exactly white.

'Then do they make it white?'

'As a matter of fact the white clay comes from a long way off – Cornwall, for instance.'

'Then why do they make the things here?' George persisted, with the annoying obstinacy of his years. He had turned the teapot upside down. 'This was made here. It's got "Bursley" on it. Auntie Janet showed me.'

Edwin was caught. He saw himself punished for that intellectual sloth which leads adults to fob children off with any kind of a slipshod, dishonestly simplified explanation of phenomena whose adequate explanation presents difficulty. He remembered how nearly twenty years earlier he had puzzled over the same question and for a long time had not found the answer.

'I'll tell you how it is,' he said, determined to be conscientious. 'It's like this –' He had to pause. Queer, how hard it was to state the thing coherently! 'It's like this. In the old days they used to make crocks anyhow, very rough, out of any old clay. And crocks were first made here because the people found common yellow clay, and the coal to burn it with, lying close together in the ground. You see how handy it was for them.'

'Then the old crocks were yellow?'

'More or less. Then people got more particular, you see, and when white clay was found somewhere else they had it brought here, because everybody was used to making crocks here, and they had all the works and the tools they wanted, and the coal too. Very important, the coal! Much easier to bring the clay to the people and the works, than cart off all the people – and their families, don't forget – and so on, to the clay, and build fresh works into the bargain. . . . That's why. Now are you sure you see?'

George ignored the question. 'I suppose they used up all the yellow clay there was here, long ago?'

'Not much !' said Edwin. 'And they never will ! You don't know what a sagger is, I reckon?'

'What is a sagger?'

'Well, I can't stop to tell you all that now. But I will some time. They make saggers out of the yellow clay.'

'Will you show me the yellow clay?'

'Yes, and some saggers too.'

'When?'

'I don't know. As soon as I can.'

'Will you tomorrow?'

Tomorrow happened to be Thursday. It was not Edwin's free afternoon, but it was an afternoon to which a sort of licence attached. He yielded to the ruthless egotism of the child.

'All right!' he said.

'You won't forget?'

'You can rely on me. Ask your auntie if you may go, and if she says you may, be ready for me to pull you up over the wall here, about three o'clock.'

'Auntie will have to let me go,' said George, in a savage tone, as Edwin helped him to slip down into the garden of the Orgreaves. Edwin went off to business with a singular consciousness of virtue, and with pride in his successful manner of taming wayward children, and with a very strong new interest in the immediate future.

CHAPTER 8 : *The Friendship*

I

The next afternoon George's invincible energy took both himself and the great bearded man, Edwin, to a certain spot on the hollow confines of the town towards Turnhill, where there were several pits of marl and clay. They stared in silence at a vast ochreous-coloured, glistening cavity in the ground, on the high edges of which grew tufts of grass amid shards and broken bottles. In the bottom of the pit were laid planks, and along the planks men with pieces of string tied tight round their legs beneath the knees drew large barrows full or empty, sometimes insecurely over pools of yellow water into which the plank sagged under their weight and sometimes over little hillocks and through little defiles formed in the basin of the mine. They seemed to have no aim. The whole cavity had a sticky look which at first amused George, but on the whole he was not interested, and Edwin gathered that the clay-pit in some mysterious way fell short of expectations. A mineral line of railway which, nearby, ambled at random like a pioneer over rough country, was much more successful than the pit in winning his approval.

'Can we go and see the saggers now?' he suggested.

Edwin might have taken him to the manufactory in which Albert Benbow was a partner, but he preferred not to display to the father of Clara's offspring his avuncular patronage of George Cannon, and he chose the works of a customer down at Shawport for whom he was printing a somewhat ambitious catalogue. He would call at the works and talk about the catalogue, and then incidentally mention that his young friend desired to see saggers.

'I suppose God put that clay there so that people could practise on it first, before they tried the white clay,' George observed, as the pair descended Oldcastle Street.

Decidedly he had moments of talking like an infant, like a baby of three. Edwin recalled that Hilda used to torture herself about questions of belief when she was not three but twenty-three. The scene in the garden porch seemed to have happened after all not very long ago. Yet a new generation, unconceived on that exciting and unforgettable night, had since been born and had passed through infancy and was now trotting and arguing and dogmatizing by his side. It was strange, but it was certainly a fact, that George regarded him as a being immeasurably old. He still felt a boy.

How ought he to talk to the child concerning God? He was about to make a conventional response, when he stopped himself. 'Confound it! Why should I?' he thought.

'If I were you I shouldn't worry about God,' he said, aloud, in a casual and perhaps slightly ironic tone.

'Oh, I don't!' George answered positively. 'But now and then He comes into your head, doesn't He? I was only just thinking –' The boy ceased, being attracted by the marvellous spectacle of a man perilously balanced on a crate-float driving a long-tailed pony full tilt down the steep slope of Oldcastle Street : it was equal to a circus.

II

The visit to the works was a particular brilliant success. By good fortune an oven was just being 'drawn', and the child had sights of the finest, the most barbaric picture that the manufacture of earthenware, from end to end picturesque, offers to the imaginative observer. Within the dark and sinister bowels of the kiln, illuminated by pale rays that came down through the upper orifice from the smoke-soiled sky, half-naked figures moved like ghosts, strenuous and damned, among the saggers of ware. At rapid intervals they emerged, their hairy torsos glistening with sweat, carrying the fired ware, which was still too hot for any but inured fingers to touch : an endless procession of plates and saucers and cups and mugs and jugs and basins, thousands and thousands! George stared in an enchanted silence of awe. And presently one of the Herculeses picked him up, and held him for a moment within the portal of the torrid kiln, and he gazed at the high curved walls, like the walls of a gigantic tomb, and at the yellow saggers that held the ware. Now he knew what a sagger was.

'I'm glad you took me,' he said afterwards, clearly impressed by the authority of Edwin, who could stroll out and see such terrific goings-on whenever he chose. During all the walk home he did not speak.

On the Saturday, nominally in charge of his Auntie Janet, he called upon his chum with some water-colour drawings that he had done; they showed naked devils carrying cups and plates amid bright salmon-tinted flames: designs horrible, and horribly crude, interesting only because a child had done them. But somehow Edwin was obscurely impressed by them, and also he was touched by the coincidence that George painted in water-colours, and he, too, had once painted in water-colours. He was moreover expected to judge the drawing as an expert. On Monday he brought up the most complicated box of water-colours that his shop contained, and presented it to George, who astounded, dazed, bore it away to his bedroom without a single word. Their friendship was sealed and published; it became a fact recognized by the two families.

III

About a week later, after a visit of a couple of days to Manchester, Edwin went out into the garden as usual when breakfast was finished, and discovered George standing on the wall. The boy had learned how to climb the wall from his own side of it without help.

'I say!' George cried, in a loud, rough, angry voice, as soon as he saw Edwin at the garden door. 'I've got to go off in a minute, you know.'

'Go off? Where?'

'Home. Didn't they tell you in your house? Auntie Janet and I came to your house yesterday, after I'd waited on the wall for you I don't know how long, and you never came. We came to tell you but you weren't in. So we asked Miss Clayhanger to tell you. Didn't Miss Clayhanger tell you?'

'No,' said Edwin. 'She must have forgot.' It occurred to him that even the simple and placid Maggie had her personal prejudices, and that one of them might be against this child. For some reason she did not like the child. She positively could not have forgotten the child's visit with Janet. She had merely not troubled to tell him : a touch of that malice which, though it be as rare as radium, nevertheless exists even in the most benignant natures. Edwin and George exchanged a silent, puzzled glance.

'Well, that's a nice thing!' said the boy. It was.

'When are you going home?'

'I'm going *now*! Mr Orgreave has to go to London today, and mamma wrote to Auntie Janet yesterday to say that I must go with him, if he'd let me, and she would meet me at London. She wants me back. So Auntie Janet is taking me to Knype to meet Mr Orgreave there – he's gone to his office first. And the gardener has taken my luggage in the barrow up to Bleakridge Station. Auntie's putting her hat on. Can't you see I've got my other clothes on?'

'Yes,' said Edwin, 'I noticed that.'

'And my other hat?'

'Yes.'

'I've promised auntie I'll come and put my overcoat on as soon as she calls me. I say – you wouldn't believe how jammed my trunk is with that paint box and everything! Auntie Janet had to sit on it like anything! I say – shall you be coming to Brighton soon?'

Edwin shook his head.

'I never go to Brighton.'

'But when I asked you once if you'd been you said you had.'

'So I have, but that was an accident.'

'Was it long since?'

'Well,' said Edwin, 'you ought to know. It was when I brought that parcel for you.'

'Oh! Of course!'

Edwin was saying to himself : 'She's sent for him on purpose. She's heard that we're great friends, and she's sent for him! She means to stop it! That's what it is!' He had no rational basis for this assumption. It was instinctive. And yet why should she desire to interfere with the course of the friendship? How could it react unpleasantly on her? There obviously did not exist between mother and son one of those passionate attachments which misfortune and sorrow sometimes engender. She had been able to let him go. And as for George, he seldom mentioned his mother. He seldom mentioned anybody who was not actually present, or necessary to the fulfilment of the idea that happened to be reigning in his heart. He lived a life of absorption, hypnotized by the idea of the moment. These ideas succeeded each other like a dynasty of kings, like a series of dynasties, marked by frequent dynastic quarrels, by depositions and sudden deaths; but George's loyalty was the same to all of them; it was absolute.

'Well, anyhow,' said he, 'I shall come back here. Mother will have to let me.'

And he jumped down from the wall into Edwin's garden, carelessly, his hands in his pockets, with a familiar ease of gesture that implied practice. He had in fact often done it before. But just this time – perhaps he was troubled by the unaccustomed clothes – having lighted on his feet, he failed to maintain his balance and staggered back against the wall.

'Now, clumsy!' Edwin commented.

The boy turned pale, and bit his lip, and then Edwin could see the tears in his eyes. One of his peculiarities was that he had no shame whatever about crying. He could not, or he would not, suffer stoically. Now he put his hands to his back, and writhed.

'Hurt yourself?' Edwin asked.

George nodded. He was very white, and startled. At first he could not command himself sufficiently to be able to articulate. Then he spluttered, 'My back!' he subsided gradually into a sitting posture.

Edwin ran to him, and picked him up. But he screamed until he was set down. At the open drawing-room window, Maggie was arranging curtains. Edwin reluctantly left George for an instant and hurried to the window. 'I say, Maggie, bring a chair or something out, will you? This dashed kid's fallen and hurt himself.'

'I'm not surprised,' said Maggie calmly. 'What surprises me is that you should ever have given him permission to scramble over the wall and trample all about the flower-beds the way he does!'

However, she moved at once to obey.

He returned to George. Then Janet's voice was heard from the other garden, calling him: 'George! George! Nearly time to go!'

Edwin put his head over the wall.

'He's fallen and hurt his back,' he answered to Janet, without any prelude.

'His back!' she repeated in a frightened tone.

Everybody was afraid of that mysterious back. And George himself was most afraid of it.

'I'll get over the wall,' said Janet.

Edwin quitted the wall. Maggie was coming out of the house with a large cane easy-chair and a large cushion. But George was not standing up, though still crying. His beautiful best sailor hat lay on the winter ground.

'Now,' said Maggie to him, 'you mustn't be a baby!'

He glared at her resentfully. She would have dropped down dead on the spot if his wet and angry glance could have killed her. She was a powerful woman. She seized him carefully and set him in the chair, and supported the famous spine with the cushion.

'I don't think he's much hurt,' she decided. 'He couldn't make that noise if he was, and see how his colour's coming back!'

In another case Edwin would have agreed with her, for the tendency of both was to minimize an ill and to exaggerate the philosophical attitude in the first moments of any occurrence that looked serious. But now he honestly thought that her judgement was being influenced by her prejudice, and he felt savage against her. The worst was that it was all his fault. Maggie was odiously right. He ought never to have encouraged the child to be acrobatic on the wall. It was he who had even put the idea of the wall as a means of access into the child's head.

'Does it hurt?' he inquired, bending down, his hands on his knees.

'Yes,' said George, ceasing to cry.

'Much?' asked Maggie, dusting the sailor hat and sticking it on his head.

'No, not much,' George unwillingly admitted. Maggie could not at any rate say that he did not speak the truth.

Janet, having obtained steps, stood on the wall in her elaborate street-array.

'Who's going to help me down?' she demanded anxiously. She was not so young and sprightly as once she had been. Edwin obeyed the call.

Then the three of them stood round the victim's chair, and the victim, like a god, permitted himself to be contemplated. And Janet had to hear Edwin's account of the accident, and also Maggie's account of it, as seen from the window.

'I don't know what to do!' said Janet.

'It is annoying, isn't it?' said Maggie. 'And just as you were going to the station too!'

'I – I think I'm all right,' George announced.

Janet passed a hand down his back, as though expecting to be able to judge the condition of his spine through the thickness of all his clothes.

'Are you?' she questioned doubtfully.

'It's nothing,' said Maggie, with firmness.

'He'd be all right in the train,' said Janet. 'It's the walking to the station that I'm afraid of.... You never know.'

'I can carry him,' said Edwin quickly.

'Of course you can't!' Maggie contradicted. 'And even if you could you'd jog him far worse than if he walked himself.'

'There's no time to get a cab, now,' said Janet, looking at her watch. 'If we aren't at Knype, father will wonder what on earth's happened, and I don't know what his mother would say!'

'Where's that old pram?' Edwin demanded suddenly of Maggie.

'What? Clara's? It's in the outhouse.'

'I can run him up to the station in two jiffs in that.'

'Oh yes! Do!' said George. 'You must. And then lift me into the carriage!'

The notion was accepted.

'I hope it's the best thing to do,' said Janet, apprehensive and doubtful, as she hurried off to the other house in order to get the boy's overcoat and meet Edwin and the perambulator at the gates.

'I'm certain it is,' said Maggie calmly. 'There's nothing really the matter with that child.'

'Well, it's very good of Edwin, I'm sure,' said Janet.

Edwin had already rushed for the perambulator, an ancient vehicle which was sometimes used in the garden for infant Benbows.

In a few moments Trafalgar Road had the spectacle of the bearded and eminent master-printer, Edwin Clayhanger, steaming up its muddy pavement behind a perambulator with a grown boy therein. And dozens of persons who had not till then distinguished the boy from other boys, inquired about his identity, and gossip was aroused. Maggie was displeased.

In obedience to the command Edwin lifted George into the train; and the feel of his little slippery body, and the feel of Edwin's mighty arms, seemed to make them more intimate than ever. Except for dirty tear-marks on his cheeks, George's appearance was absolutely normal.

Edwin expected to receive a letter from him, but none came, and this negligence wounded Edwin.

CHAPTER 9 : *The Arrival*

I

On a Saturday in the early days of the following year, 1892, Edwin by special request had gone in to take afternoon tea with the Orgreaves. Osmond Orgreaves was just convalescent after an attack of influenza, and in the opinion of Janet wanted cheering up. The task of enlivening him had been laid upon Edwin. The guest, and Janet and her father and mother sat together in a group round the fire in the drawing-room.

The drawing-room alone had grown younger with years. Money had been spent on it rather freely. During the previous decade Osmond's family, scattering, had become very much less costly to him, but his habits of industry had not changed, nor his faculty for collecting money. Hence the needs of the drawing-room, which had been pressing for quite twenty years, had at last been satisfied; indeed Osmond was saving, through mere lack of that energetic interest in things which is necessary to spending. Possibly even the drawing-room would have remained untouched – both Janet and her elder sister Marian sentimentally preferred it as it was – had not Mrs Orgreave been 'positively ashamed' of it when her married children, including Marian, came to see her. They were all married now, except Janet and Charlie and Johnnie; and Alicia at any rate had a finer drawing-room than her mother. So far as the parents were concerned Charlie might as well have been married, for he had acquired a partnership in a practice at Ealing and seldom visited home. Johnnie, too, might as well have been married. Since

Jimmie's wedding he had used the house strictly as a hotel, for sleeping and eating, and not always for sleeping. He could not be retained at home. His interests were mysterious, and lay outside it. Janet alone was faithful to the changed drawing-room, with its new carpets and wall-papers and upholstery.

'I've got more grandchildren than children now,' said Mrs Orgreave to Edwin, 'and I never thought to have!'

'Have you really?' Edwin responded. 'Let me see —'

'I've got nine.'

'Ten, mother,' Janet corrected. 'She's forgetting her own grand-children now!'

'Bless me!' exclaimed Mrs Orgreave, taking off her eye-glasses and wiping them, 'I'd missed Tom's youngest.'

'You'd better not tell Emily that,' said Janet. (Emily was the mother of Tom's children.) 'Here, give me those eye-glasses, dear. You'll never get them right with a linen handkerchief. Where's your bit of chamois?'

Mrs Orgreave absently and in somewhat stiff silence handed over the pince-nez. She was now quite an old woman, small, shapeless, and delightfully easy-going, whose sense of humour had not developed with age. She could never see a joke which turned upon her relations with her grandchildren, and in fact the jocular members of the family had almost ceased to employ this subject of humour. She was undoubtedly rather foolish about her grandchildren – 'fond', as they say down there. The parents of the grandchildren did not object to this foolishness – that is, they only pretended to object. The task of preventing a pardonable weakness from degenerating into a tedious and mischievous mania fell solely upon Janet. Janet was ready to admit that the health of the grandchildren was a matter which could fairly be left to their fathers and mothers, and she stood passive when Mrs Orgreave's grandmotherly indulgences seemed inimical to their health; but Mrs Orgreave was apt to endanger her own health in her devotion to the profession of grand-mother – for example by sitting up to unchristian hours with a needle. Then there would be a struggle of wills, in which of course Mrs Or-greave, being the weaker, was defeated; though her belief survived that she and she alone, by watchfulness, advice, sagacity, and energy, kept her children's children out of the grave. On all other questions the harmony between Janet and her mother was complete and Mrs Or-greave undoubtedly considered that no mother had ever had a daughter who combined so many virtues and charms.

II

Mr Orgreave, forgetful of the company, was deciphering the *British Medical Journal* in the twilight of the afternoon. His doctor had lent him this esoteric periodical because there was an article therein on influenza, and Mr Orgreave was very much interested in influenza.

'You remember the influenza of '89, Edwin?' he asked suddenly, looking over the top of the paper.

'Do I?' said Edwin. 'Yes, I fancy I do remember a sort of epidemic.'

'I should think so indeed!' Janet murmured.

'Well,' continued Mr Orgreave, 'I'm like you. I thought it was an epidemic. But it seems it wasn't. It was a pandemic. What's a pandemic, now?'

'Give it up,' said Edwin.

'You might just look in the dictionary – Ogilvie there,' and while Edwin ferreted in the bookcase, Mr Orgreave proceeded, reading: ' "This pandemic of 1889 has been followed by epidemics, and by endemic prevalence in some areas!" So you see how many *demics* there are! I suppose they'd call it an epidemic we've got in the town now.'

His voice had changed on the last sentence. He had meant to be a little facetious about the Greek words; but it was the slowly prepared and rather exasperating facetiousness of an ageing man, and he had dropped it listlessly, as though he himself had perceived this. Influenza had weakened and depressed him; he looked worn, and even outworn. But not influenza alone was responsible for his appearance. The incredible had happened; Osmond Orgreave was getting older. His bald head was not the worst sign of his declension, nor the thickened veins in his hands, nor the deliberation of his gestures, nor even the unsprightliness of his wit. The worst sign was that he was losing his terrific zest in life; his palate for the intense savour of it was dulled. In his last attack of influenza he had not fought against the onset of the disease. He had been wise; he had obeyed his doctor, and laid down his arms at once; and he showed no imprudent anxiety to resume them. Yes, a changed Osmond! He was still one of the most industrious professional men in Bursley; but he worked from habit, not from passion.

When Edwin had found 'pandemic' in Ogilvie, Mr Orgreave wanted to see the dictionary for himself, and then he wanted the Greek dictionary, which could not be discovered, and then he began to quote further from the *British Medical Journal*.

' "It may be said that there are three well-marked types of the disease, attacking respectively the respiratory, the digestive, and the nervous system." Well, I should say I'd had 'em all three. "As a rule the attack –" '

399

Thus he went on. Janet made a *moue* at Edwin, who returned the signal. These youngsters were united in good-natured forbearing condescension towards Mr Orgreave. The excellent old fellow was prone to be tedious; they would accept his tediousness, but they could not disguise from each other their perception of it.

'I hear the Vicar of St Peter's is very ill indeed,' said Mrs Orgreave, blandly interrupting her husband.

'What? Heve? With influenza?'

'Yes. I wouldn't tell you before because I thought it might pull you down again.'

Mr Orgreave, in silence, stared at the immense fire.

'What about this tea, Janet?' he demanded.

Janet rang the bell.

'Oh! I'd have done that!' said Edwin, as soon as she had done it.

III

While Janet was pouring out the tea, Edwin restored Ogilvie to his place in the bookcase, feeling that he had had enough of Ogilvie.

'Not so many books here now as there used to be!' he said, vacuously amiable, as he shut the glass door which had once protected the treasures of Tom Orgreave.

For a man who had been specially summoned to the task of cheering up, it was not a felicitous remark. In the first place it recalled the days when the house, which was now a hushed retreat where settled and precise habits sheltered themselves from a changing world, had been an arena for the jolly, exciting combats of outspread individualities. And in the second place it recalled a slight difficulty between Tom and his father. Osmond Orgreave was a most reasonable father, but no father is perfect in reasonableness, and Osmond had quite inexcusably resented that Tom on his marriage should take away all Tom's precious books. Osmond's attitude had been that Tom might in decency have left, at any rate, some of the books. It was not that Osmond had a taste for book-collecting: it was merely that he did not care to see his house depleted and bookcases empty. But Tom had shown no compassion. He had removed not merely every scrap of a book belonging to himself, but also two bookcases which he happened to have paid for. The weight of public opinion was decidedly against Mr Orgreave, who had to yield and affect pleasantness. Nevertheless the books had become a topic which was avoided between father and son.

'Ah!' muttered Mr Orgreave, satirical, in response to Edwin's clumsiness.

'Suppose we have another gas lighted,' Janet suggested. The servant had already lighted several burners and drawn the blinds and curtains.

Edwin comprehended that he had been a blundering fool, and that Janet's object was to create a diversion. He lit the extra burner above her head. She sat there rather straight and rather prim between her parents, sticking to them, smoothing creases for them, bearing their weight, living for them. She was the kindliest, the most dignified, the most capable creature; but she was now an old maid. You saw it even in the way she poured tea and dropped pieces of sugar into the cups. Her youth was gone; her complexion was nearly gone. And though in one aspect she seemed indispensable, in another the chief characteristic of her existence seemed to be a tragic futility. Whenever she came seriously into Edwin's thoughts she saddened him. Useless for him to attempt to be gay and frivolous in that house!

IV

With the inevitable passionate egotism of his humanity he almost at once withdrew his aroused pity from her to himself. Look at himself! Was he not also to be sympathized with? What was the object or the use of his being alive? He worked, saved, improved his mind, voted right, practised philosophy, and was generally benevolent; but to what end? Was not his existence miserable and his career a respectable fiasco? He too had lost zest. He had diligently studied both Marcus Aurelius and Epictetus; he was enthusiastic, to others, about the merit of these two expert daily philosophers; but what had they done for him? Assuredly they had not enabled him to keep the one treasure of this world – zest. The year was scarcely a week old, and he was still young enough to have begun the year with resolutions and fresh hopes and inspirations, but already the New Year sensation had left him, and the year might have been dying in his heart.

And yet what could he have done that he had not done? With what could he reproach himself? Ought he to have continued to run after a married woman? Ought he to have set himself titanically against the conventions amid which he lived, and devoted himself either to secret intrigue or to the outraging of the susceptibilities which environed him? There was only one answer. He could not have acted otherwise than he had acted. His was not the temperament of a rebel, nor was he the slave of his desires. He could sympathize with rebels and with slaves, but he could not join them; he regarded himself as spiritually their superior.

And then the disaster of Hilda's career! He felt, more than ever, that he had failed in sympathy with her overwhelming misfortune. In the secrecy of his heart a full imaginative sympathy had been lacking. He had not realized, as he seemed to realize then, in front of the fire in the drawing-room of the Orgreaves, what it must be to be the wife of a convict. Janet, sitting there as innocent as a doe, knew that Hilda was the wife of a convict. But did her parents know? And was she aware that he knew? He wondered, drinking his tea.

V

Then the servant – not the Martha who had been privileged to smile on duty if she felt so inclined – came with a tawny gold telegram on a silver plate, and hesitated a moment as to where she should bestow it.

'Give it to me, Selina,' said Janet.

Selina impassively obeyed, imitating as well as she could the deportment of an automaton; and went away.

'That's my telegram,' said Mr Orgreave. 'How is it addressed?'

'Orgreave, Bleakridge, Bursley.'

'Then it's mine.'

'Oh no, it isn't!' Janet archly protested. 'If you have your business telegrams sent here you must take the consequences. I always open all telegrams that come here, don't I, mother?'

Mrs Orgreave made no reply, but waited with candid and fretful impatience, thinking of her five absent children, and her ten grandchildren, for the telegram to be opened.

Janet opened it.

Her lips parted to speak, and remained so in silent astonishment. 'Just read that!' she said to Edwin, passing the telegram to him; and she added to her father : 'It was for me, after all.'

Edwin read aloud : 'Am sending George down today. Please meet 6.30 train at Knype. Love. Hilda.'

'Well, I never!' exclaimed Mrs Orgreave. 'You don't mean to tell me she's letting that boy travel alone! What next?'

'Where's the telegram sent from?' asked Mr Orgreave.

Edwin examined the official indications : 'Victoria'.

'Then she's brought him up to London, and she's putting him in a train at Euston. That's it.'

'Only there is no London train that gets to Knype at half past six,' Edwin said. 'It's 7.12, or 7.14 – I forget.'

'Oh! That's near enough for Hilda,' Janet smiled, looking at her watch.

'She doesn't mean any other train?' Mrs Orgreave fearfully suggested.

'She can't mean any other train. There is no other. Only probably she's been looking at the wrong time-table,' Janet reassured her mother.

'Because if the poor little thing found no one to meet him at Knype –'

'Don't worry, dear,' said Janet. 'The poor little thing would soon be engaging somebody's attention. Trust him!'

'But has she been writing to you lately?' Mrs Orgreaves questioned.

'No.'

'Then why –'

'Don't ask *me*!' said Janet. 'No doubt I shall get a letter tomorrow, after George has come and told us everything! Poor dear, I'm glad she's doing so much better now.'

'Is she?' Edwin murmured, surprised.

'Oh yes!' said Janet. 'She's got a regular bustling partner, and they're that busy they scarcely know what to do. But they only keep one little servant.'

In the ordinary way Janet and Edwin never mentioned Hilda to one another. Each seemed to be held back by a kind of timid shame and by a cautious suspicion. Each seemed to be inquiring: 'What does *he* know?' 'What does *she* know?'

'If I thought it wasn't too cold, I'd go with you to Knype,' said Mr Orgreave.

'Now, Osmond!' Mrs Orgreave sat up.

'Shall I go?' said Edwin.

'Well,' said Janet, with much kindliness, 'I'm sure he'd be delighted to see *you*.'

Mrs Orgreave rang the bell.

'What do you want, mother?'

'There'll be the bed –'

'Don't you trouble with those things, dear,' said Janet, very calmly. 'There's heaps of time.'

But Janet was just as excited as her parents. In two minutes the excitement had spread through the whole house, like a piquant and agreeable odour. The place was alive again.

'I'll just step across and ask Maggie to alter supper,' said Edwin, 'and then I'll call for you. I suppose we'll go down by train.'

'I'm thankful he's had influenza,' observed Mrs Orgreave, implying that thus there would be less chance of George catching the disease under her infected roof.

That George had been down with influenza before Christmas was the sole information about him that Edwin obtained. Nobody appeared to consider it worth while to discuss the possible reasons for his sudden arrival. Hilda's caprices were accepted in that house like the visitations of heaven.

VI

Edwin and Janet stood together on the windy and bleak down-platform of Knype Station, awaiting the express, which had been signalled. Edwin was undoubtedly very nervous and constrained, and it seemed to him that Janet's demeanour lacked naturalness.

'It's just occurred to me how she made that mistake about the time of the train,' said Edwin, chiefly because he found the silence intolerably irksome. 'It stops at Lichfield, and in running her eye across the page she must have mixed up the Lichfield figures with the Knype figures – you know how awkward it is in a time-table. As a matter of fact, the train *does* stop at Lichfield about 6.30.'

'I see,' said Janet reflectively.

And Edwin was saying to himself –

'It's a marvel to me how I can talk to her at all. What made me offer to come with her? How much does she know about me and Hilda? Hilda may have told her everything. If she's told her about her husband why shouldn't she have told her about me? And here we are both pretending that there's never been anything at all between me and Hilda!'

Then the train appeared, obscure round the curve, and bore down formidable and dark upon them, growing at every instant in stature and in noise until it deafened and seemed to fill the station; and the platform was suddenly in an uproar.

And almost opposite Janet and Edwin, leaning forth high above them from the door of a third-class carriage, the head and the shoulders of George Cannon were displayed in the gaslight. He seemed to dominate the train and the platform. At the windows on either side of him were adult faces, excited by his excitement, of the people who had doubtless been friendly to him during the journey. He distinguished Janet and Edwin almost at once, and shouted, and then waved.

'Hello, young son of a gun!' Edwin greeted him, trying to turn the handle of the door. But the door was locked, and it was necessary to call a porter, who tarried.

'I *made* mamma let me come!' George cried victoriously. 'I told you I should!' He was far too agitated to think of shaking hands, and seemed to be in a state of fever. All his gestures were those of a proud, hysterical conqueror, and like a conqueror he gazed down at Edwin and Janet, who stood beneath him with upturned faces. He had absolutely forgotten the existence of his acquaintances in the carriage. 'Did you know I've had the influenza? My temperature was up to 104 once – but it didn't stay long,' he added regretfully.

When the door was at length opened, he jumped headlong, and Edwin caught him. He shook hands with Edwin and allowed Janet to kiss him.

'How hot you are!' Janet murmured.

The people in the compartment passed down his luggage, and after one of them shouted good-bye to him twice, he remembered them, as it were by an effort, and replied, 'Good-bye, good-bye,' in a quick, impatient tone.

It was not until his anxious and assiduous foster-parents had bestowed him and his goods in the tranquillity of an empty compartment of the Loop Line train that they began to appreciate the morbid unusualness of his condition. His eyes glittered with extraordinary brilliance. He talked incessantly, not listening to their answers. And his skin was burning hot.

'Why, whatever's the matter with you, my dear?' asked Janet, alarmed. 'You're like an oven!'

'I'm thirsty,' said George. 'If I don't have something to drink soon, I don't know what I shall do.'

Janet looked at Edwin.

'There won't be time to get something at the refreshment room?'

They both felt heavily responsible.

'I might—' Edwin said irresolutely.

But just then the guard whistled.

'Never mind!' Janet comforted the child. 'In twenty minutes we shall be in the house. . . . No! you must keep your overcoat buttoned.'

'How long have you been like that, George?' Edwin asked. 'You weren't like that when you started, surely?'

'No,' said George judicially. 'It came on in the train.'

After this, he appeared to go to sleep.

'He's certainly not well,' Janet whispered.

Edwin shrugged his shoulders. 'Don't you think he's grown?' he observed.

'Oh yes!' said Janet. 'It's astonishing, isn't it, how children shoot up in a few weeks!'

They might have been parents exchanging notes, instead of celibates playing at parenthood for a hobby.

'Mamma says I've grown an inch.' George opened his eyes. 'She says it's about time I had! I dare say I shall be very tall. Are we nearly there?' His high, curt, febrile tones were really somewhat alarming.

When the train threw them out into the sodden waste that surrounds Bleakridge Station, George could scarcely stand. At any rate he showed no wish to stand. His protectors took him strongly by either arm, and thus bore him to Lane End House, with irregular unwilling assistance from his own feet. A porter followed with the luggage. It was an extremely distressing passage. Each protector in secret was imagining for George some terrible fever, of swift onslaught and fatal effect. At length they entered the garden, thanking their gods.

'He's not well,' said Janet to her mother, who was fussily awaiting them in the hall. Her voice showed apprehension, and she was not at all convincing when she added : 'But it's nothing serious. I shall put him straight to bed and let him eat there.'

Instantly George became the centre of the house. The women disappeared with him, and Edwin had to recount the whole history of the arrival to Osmond Orgreave in the drawing-room. This recital was interrupted by Mrs Orgreave.

'Mr Edwin, Janet thinks if we sent for the doctor, just to be sure. As Johnnie isn't in, would you mind –'

'Stirling, I suppose?' said Edwin.

Stirling was the young Scottish doctor who had recently come into the town and taken it by storm.

When Edwin at last went home to a much-delayed meal, he was in a position to tell Maggie that young George Cannon had thought fit to catch influenza a second time in a couple of months. And Maggie, without a clear word, contrived to indicate that it was what she would have expected from a boy of George's violent temperament.

CHAPTER 10 : *George and the Vicar*

I

On the Tuesday evening Edwin came home from business at six o'clock, and found that he was to eat alone. The servant anxiously explained that Miss Clayhanger had gone across to the Orgreaves' to assist Miss Orgreave. It was evident that before going Miss Clayhanger had inspired the servant with a full sense of the importance of Mr Clayhanger's solitary meal, and of the terrible responsibility lying upon the person in charge of it. The girl was thrillingly alive; she would have liked some friend or other of the house to be always seriously ill, so that Miss Clayhanger might often leave her to the voluptuous savouring of this responsibility whose formidableness surpassed words. Edwin, as he went upstairs and as he came down again, was conscious of her excited presence somewhere near him, half-visible in the warm gas-lit house, spying upon him in order to divine the precise moment for the final service of the meal.

And in the dining-room the table was laid differently, so that he might be well situated, with regard to the light, for reading. And by the side of his plate were the newspaper, the magazines, and the book, among which Maggie had well guessed that he would make his choice for perusal. He was momentarily touched. He warmed his hands at the splendid fire, and then he warmed his back, watching the servant as with little flouncings and perkings she served, and he was touched by the placid and perfect efficiency of Maggie as a housekeeper. Maggie gave him something no money could buy.

The servant departed and shut the door.

When he sat down he minutely changed the situation of nearly everything on the table, so that his magazine might be lodged at exactly the right distance and angle, and so that each necessary object might be quite handy. He was in luxury, and he yielded himself to it absolutely. The sense that unusual events were happening, that the course of social existence was disturbed while his comfort was not disturbed, that danger hung cloudy on the horizon – this sense somehow intensified the appreciation of the hour, and positively contributed to his pleasure. Moreover, he was agreeably excited by a dismaying anticipation affecting himself alone.

II

The door opened again, and Auntie Hamps was shown in by the servant. Before he could move the old lady had with overwhelming sweet supplications insisted that he should not move – no, not even to shake hands! He rose only to shake hands, and then fell back into his comfort. Auntie Hamps fixed a chair for herself opposite him, and drummed her black-gloved hands on the white table-cloth. She was steadily becoming stouter, and those chubby little hands seemed impossibly small against the vast mountain of fur which was crowned by her smirking crimson face and the supreme peak of her bonnet.

'They keep very friendly – those two,' she remarked, with a strangely significant air, when he told her where Maggie was. She had shown no surprise at finding him alone, for the reason that she had already learnt everything from the servant in the hall.

'Janet and Maggie? They're friendly enough when they can be of use to each other.'

'How *kind* Miss Janet was when your father was ill! I'm sure Maggie feels she must do all she can to return her kindness,' Mrs Hamps murmured, with emotion. 'I shall always be grateful for her helpfulness! She's a grand girl, a grand girl!'

'Yes,' said Edwin awkwardly.

'She's still waiting for you,' said Mrs Hamps, not archly, but sadly.

Edwin restively poohed. At the first instant of her arrival he had been rather glad to see her, for unusual events create a desire to discuss them; but if she meant to proceed in that strain unuttered curses would soon begin to accumulate for her in his heart.

'I expect the kid must be pretty bad,' he said.

'Yes,' sighed Mrs Hamps. 'And probably poor Mrs Orgreave is more in the way than anything else. And Mr Orgreave only just out of bed, as you may say! . . . That young lady must have her hands full! My word! What a blessing it is she *has* made such friends with Maggie!'

Mrs Hamps had the peculiar gift, which developed into ever-increasing perfection as her hair grew whiter, of being able to express ideas by means of words which had no relation to them at all. Within three minutes, by three different remarks whose occult message no stranger could have understood but which forced itself with unpleasant clearness upon Edwin, Mrs Hamps had conveyed. 'Janet Orgreave only cultivates Maggie because Maggie is the sister of Edwin Clayhanger.'

'You're all very devoted to that child,' she said, meaning, 'There is something mysterious in that quarter which sooner or later is bound to come out.' And the meaning was so clear that Edwin was intimidated. What did she guess? Did she know anything? Tonight Auntie Hamps was displaying her gift at its highest.

'I don't know that Maggie's so desperately keen on the infant!' he said.

'She's not like you about him, that's sure!' Mrs Hamps admitted. And she went on, in a tone that was only superficially casual, 'I wonder the mother doesn't come down to him!'

Not 'his' mother – 'the' mother. Odd, the effect of that trifle! Mrs Hamps was a great artist in phrasing.

'Oh!' said Edwin. 'It's not serious enough for that.'

'Well, I'm not so sure,' Auntie Hamps gravely replied. '*The Vicar is dead.*'

The emphasis which she put on these words was tremendous.

'Is he?' Edwin stammered. 'But what's that got to do with it?'

He tried to be condescending towards her absurdly superstitious assumption that the death of the Vicar of St Peter's could increase the seriousness of George's case. And he feebly succeeded in being condescending. Nevertheless he could not meet his auntie's gaze without self-consciousness. For her emphasis had been double, and he knew it. It had implied, secondly, that the death of the Vicar was an event specially affecting Edwin's household. The rough sketch of a romance between the Vicar and Maggie had never been completed into a picture, but on the other hand it had never been destroyed. The Vicar and Maggie had been supposed to be still interested in each other, despite the Vicar's priestliness, which latterly had perhaps grown more marked, just as his church had grown more ritualistic. It was a strange affair, thin, elusive; but an affair it was. The Vicar and Maggie had seldom met of recent years; they had never – so far as anyone knew – met alone; and yet, upon the news of the Vicar's death, the first thought of nearly everybody was for Maggie Clayhanger.

Mrs Hamps's eyes, swimming in the satisfaction of several simultaneous woes, said plainly, 'What about poor Maggie?'

'When did you hear?' Edwin asked. 'It isn't in this afternoon's paper.'

'I've only just heard. He died at four o'clock.'

She had come up immediately with the news as fresh as orchard fruit.

'And the Duke of Clarence is no better,' she said, in a luxurious sighing gloom. 'And I'm afraid it's all over with Cardinal Manning.' She made a peculiar noise in her throat, not quite a sigh; rather a brave protest against the general fatality of things, stiffened by a determination to be strong though melancholy in misfortune.

III

Maggie suddenly entered, hatted, with a jacket over her arm.

'Hello, auntie, you here!'

They had already met that morning.

'I just called,' said Mrs Hamps guiltily. Edwin felt as though Maggie had surprised them both in some criminal act. They knew that Mr Heve was dead. She did not know. She had to be told. He wished violently that Auntie Hamps had been elsewhere.

'Everything all right?' Maggie asked Edwin, surveying the table. 'I gave particular orders about the eggs.'

'As right as rain,' said Edwin, putting into his voice a note of true appreciation. He saw that her sense of duty towards him had brought her back to the house. She had taken every precaution to ensure his well-being, but she could not be content without seeing for herself that the servant had not betrayed the trust.

'How are things – across?' he inquired.

'Well,' said Maggie, frowning, 'that's one reason why I came back sooner than I meant. The doctor's just been. His temperature is getting higher and higher. I wish you'd go over as soon as you've finished. If you ask me, I think they ought to telegraph to his mother. But Janet doesn't seem to think so. Of course it's enough when Mrs Orgreave begins worrying about telegraphing for Janet to say there's no need to telegraph. She's rather trying, Mrs Orgreave is, I must admit. All that *I've* been doing is to keep her out of the bedroom. Janet has everything on her shoulders. Mr Orgreave is just about as fidgety as Mrs. And of course the servants have their own work to do. Naturally Johnnie isn't in!' Her tone grew sarcastic and bitter.

'What does Stirling say about telegraphing?' Edwin demanded. He had intended to say 'telegraphing for Mrs Cannon', but he could not utter the last words; he could not compel his vocal organs to utter them. He became aware of the beating of his heart. For twenty-four hours he had been contemplating the possibility of a summons to Hilda. Now the possibility had developed into a probability. Nay, a certainty! Maggie was the very last person to be alarmist.

Maggie replied : 'He says it might be as well to wait till tomorrow. But then you know he is like that – a bit.'

'So they say,' Auntie Hamps agreed.

'Have you seen the kid?' Edwin asked.

'About two minutes,' said Maggie. 'It's pitiable to watch him.'

'Why? Is he in pain?'

'Not what you'd call pain. No! But he's so upset. Worried about himself. He's got a terrific fever on him. I'm certain he's delirious sometimes. Poor little thing!'

Tears gleamed in her eyes. The plight of the boy had weakened her prejudices against him. Assuredly he was not 'rough' now.

Astounded and frightened by those shimmering tears, Edwin exclaimed, 'You don't mean to say there's actual danger?'

'Well –' Maggie hesitated, and stopped.

There was silence for a moment. Edwin felt that the situation was now further intensified.

'I expect you've heard about the poor Vicar,' Mrs Hamps funereally insinuated. Edwin mutely damned her.

Maggie looked up sharply. 'No! ... He's not –'

Mrs Hamps nodded twice.

The tears vanished from Maggie's eyes, forced backwards by all the secret pride that was in her. It was obvious that not the news of the Vicar had originally caused those tears; but nevertheless there should be no shadow of misunderstanding. The death of the Vicar must be associated with no more serious sign of distress in Maggie than in others. She must be above suspicion. For one acute moment, as he read her thoughts and as the profound sacrificial tragedy of her entire existence loomed less indistinctly than usual before him, Edwin ceased to think about himself and Hilda.

She made a quick hysterical movement.

'I wish you'd go across, Edwin,' she said harshly.

'I'll go now,' he answered, with softness. And he was glad to go.

IV

It was Osmond Orgreave who opened to him the front door of Lane End House. Maggie had told the old gentleman that she should send Edwin over, and he was wandering vaguely about in nervous expectation. In an instant they were discussing George's case, and the advisability of telegraphing to Hilda. Mrs Orgreave immediately joined them in the hall. Both father and mother clearly stood in awe of the gentle but powerful Janet. And somehow the child was considered as her private affair, into which others might not thrust themselves save on sufferance. Perceiving that Edwin was slightly inclined to the course of telegraphing, they drew him towards them as a reinforcement, but while Mrs Orgreave frankly displayed her dependence on him, Mr Orgreave affected to be strong, independent, and judicial.

'I wish you'd go and speak to her,' Mrs Orgreave entreated.

'Upstairs?'

'It won't do any harm, anyhow,' said Osmond, finely indifferent.

They went up the stairs in a procession. Edwin did not wish to tell them about the Vicar. He could see no sense in telling them about the Vicar. And yet, before they reached the top of the stairs, he heard himself saying in a concerned whisper –

'You know about the Vicar of St Peter's?'

'No.'

'Died at four o'clock.'

'Oh dear me! Dear me!' murmured Mrs Orgreave, agonized.

Most evidently George's case was aggravated by the Vicar's death – and not only in the eyes of Mrs Orgreave and her falsely stoic husband, but in Edwin's eyes too! Useless for him to argue with himself about idiotic superstitiousness! The death of the Vicar had undoubtedly influenced his attitude towards George.

They halted on the landing, outside a door that was ajar. Near them burned a gas jet, and beneath the bracket was a large framed photograph of the bridal party at Alicia's wedding. Farther along the landing were other similar records of the weddings of Marion, Tom, and Jimmie.

Mr Orgreave pushed the door half open.

'Janet,' said Mr Orgreave conspirationally.

'Well?' from within the bedroom.

'Here's Edwin.'

Janet appeared in the doorway, pale. She was wearing an apron with a bib.

'I – I thought I'd just look in and inquire,' Edwin said awkwardly, fiddling with his hat and a pocket of his overcoat. 'What's he like now?'

Janet gave details. The sick-room lay hidden behind the face of the door, mysterious and sacred.

'Mr Edwin thinks you ought to telegraph,' said Mrs Orgreave timidly.

'Do you?' demanded Janet. Her eyes seemed to pierce him. Why did she gaze at him with such particularity, as though he possessed a special interest in Hilda?

'Well –' he muttered. 'You might just wire how things are, and leave it to her to come as she thinks fit.'

'Just so,' said Mr Orgreave quickly, as if Edwin had expressed his own thought.

'But the telegram couldn't be delivered tonight,' Janet objected. 'It's nearly half past seven now.'

It was true. Yet Edwin was more than ever conscious of a keen desire to telegraph at once.

'But it would be delivered first thing in the morning,' he said. 'So that she'd have more time to make arrangements if she wanted to.'

'Well, if you think like that,' Janet acquiesced.

The visage of Mrs Orgreave lightened.

'I'll run down and telegraph myself, if you like,' said Edwin. 'Of course you've written to her. She knows –'

'Oh yes!'

V

In a minute he was walking rapidly with his ungainly, slouching stride, down Trafalgar Road, his overcoat flying loose. Another crisis was approaching, he thought. As he came to Duck Square, he met a newspaper boy shouting shrilly and wearing the contents bill of a special edition of the *Signal* as an apron : 'Duke of Clarence. More serious bulletin'. The scourge and fear of influenza was upon the town, upon the community, tangible, oppressive, tragic.

In the evening calm of the shabby, gloomy post-office, holding a stubby pencil that was chained by a cable to the wall, he stood over a blank telegraph-form, hesitating how to word the message. Behind the counter an instrument was ticking unheeded, and far within could be discerned the vague bodies of men dealing with parcels. He wrote, 'Cannon, 59 Preston Street, Brighton. George's temperature 104'. Then he paused, and added, 'Edwin'. It was sentimental. He ought to have signed Janet's name. And, if he was determined to make the telegram personal, he might at least have put his surname. He knew it was sentimental, and he loathed sentimentality. But that evening he wanted to be sentimental.

He crossed to the counter, and pushed the form under the wire-netting.

A sleepy girl accepted it, and glanced mechanically at the clock, and then wrote the hour 7.42.

'It won't be delivered tonight,' she said, looking up, as she counted the words.

'No, I know,' said Edwin.

'Sixpence, please.'

As he paid the sixpence he felt as though he had accomplished some great, critical, agitating deed. And his heart asserted itself again, thunderously beating.

CHAPTER 11 : *Beginning of the Night*

I

The next day was full of strange suspense; it was coloured throughout with that quality of strangeness which puts a new light on all quotidian occupations and exposes their fundamental unimportance. Edwin arose to the fact that a thick grey fog was wrapping the town. When he returned home to breakfast at nine the fog was certainly more opaque than it had been an hour earlier. The steam-cars passed like phantoms, with a continuous clanging of bells. He breakfasted under gas – and alone. Maggie was invisible, or only to be seen momentarily, flying across the domestic horizon. She gave out that she was very busy in the attics, cleaning those shockingly neglected rooms. 'Please sir,' said the servant, 'Miss Clayhanger says she's been across to Mr Orgreave's, and Master George is about the same.' Maggie would not come and tell him herself. On the previous evening he had not seen her after the reception of the news about the Vicar. She had gone upstairs when he came back from the post-office. Beyond doubt, she was too disturbed emotionally, to be able to face him with her customary tranquillity. She was getting over the shock with brush and duster up in the attics. He was glad that she had not attempted to be as usual. The ordeal of attempting to be as usual would have tried him perhaps as severely as her.

He went forth again into the fog in a high state of agitation, constricted with sympathetic distress on Maggie's account, apprehensive for the boy, and painfully expectant of the end of the day. The whole day slipped away so, hour after monotonous hour, while people talked about influenza and about distinguished patients, and doctors hurried from house to house, and the fog itself seemed to be the visible mantle of the disease. And the end of the day brought nothing to Edwin save an acuter expectancy. George varied; on the whole he was worse; not much worse, but worse. Dr Stirling saw him twice. No message arrived from Hilda, nor did she come in person. Maggie watched George for five hours in the late afternoon and evening while Janet rested.

At eight o'clock, when there was no further hope of a telegram from Hilda, everybody pretended to concur in the view that Hilda, knowing her boy better than anybody else, and having already seen him through an attack of influenza, had not been unduly alarmed by the telegraphic news of his temperature, and was content to write. She might probably be arranging to come on the morrow. After all, George's temperature had reached 104 in the previous attack. Then there was the fog. The fog would account for anything.

Nevertheless, nobody was really satisfied by these explanations of Hilda's silence and absence. In every heart lay the secret and sinister thought of the queerness and the incalculableness of Hilda.

Edwin called several times on the Orgreaves. He finally left their house about ten o'clock, with some difficulty tracing his way home from gas lamp to gas lamp through the fog. Mr Orgreave himself had escorted him with a lantern round the wilderness of the lawn to the gates. 'We shall have a letter in the morning,' Mr Orgreave had said. 'Bound to!' Edwin had replied. And they had both superiorly puffed away into the fog the absurd misgivings of women.

Knowing that he was in no condition to sleep. Edwin mended the drawing-room fire, and settled down on the sofa to read. But he could no more read than sleep. He seemed to lie on the sofa for hours while his thoughts jigged with fatiguing monotony in his head. He was extraordinarily wakeful and alive, every sense painfully sharpened. At last he decided to go to bed. In his bedroom he gazed idly out at the blank density of the fog. And then his heart leapt as his eye distinguished a moving glimmer below in the garden of the Orgreaves. He threw up the window in a tumult of anticipation. The air was absolutely still. Then he heard a voice say, 'Good night.' It was undoubtedly Dr Stirling's voice. The Scotch accent was unmistakable. Was the boy worse? Not necessarily, for the doctor had said that he might look in again 'last thing', if chance favoured. And the Scotch significance of 'last thing' was notoriously comprehensive; it might include regions beyond midnight. Then Edwin heard another voice : 'Thanks ever so much!' At first it puzzled him. He knew it, and yet –! Could it be the Sunday's voice? Assuredly it was not the voice of Mr Orgreave, nor of any one living in the house. It reminded him of the Sunday's voice.

He went out of his bedroom, striking a match, and going downstairs lit the gas in the hall, which he had just extinguished. Then he put on a cap, found a candlestick in the kitchen, unbolted the garden door as quietly as he could, and passed into the garden. The flame of the candle stood upright in the fog. He blundered along to the dividing wall, placed the candle on the top of it, and managed to climb over. Leaving the candle on the wall to guide his return, he approached the house, which showed gleams at several windows, and rang the bell. And in fact it was Charlie Orgreave himself who opened the door. And a lantern, stuck carelessly on the edge of a chair, was still burning in the hall.

II

In a moment he had learnt the chief facts. Hilda had gone up to London, dragged Charlie out of Ealing, and brought him down with her to watch over her child. Once more she had done something which nobody could have foreseen. The train – not the London express, but the loop – was late. The pair had arrived about half past ten, and a little later Dr Stirling had fulfilled his promise to look in if he could. The two doctors had conferred across the child's bed, and had found themselves substantially in agreement. Moreover, the child was if anything somewhat better. The Scotsman had gone. Charles and Hilda had eaten. Hilda meant to sit up, and had insisted that Janet should go to bed; it appeared that Janet had rested but not slept in the afternoon.

Charlie took Edwin into the small breakfast-room, where Osmond Orgreave was waiting, and the three men continued to discuss the situation. They were all of them too excited to sit down, though Osmond and – in a less degree – Charlie affected the tranquillity of high philosophers. At first Edwin knew scarcely what he did. His speech and gestures were not the result of conscious volition. He seemed suddenly to have two individualities, and the new one, which was the more intimate one, watched the other as in a dim-lighted dream. . . . She was there in a room above! She had come in response to the telegram signed 'Edwin'! Last night she was far away. Tonight she was in the very house with him. Miracle! He asked himself : 'Why should I get myself into this state simply because she is here? It would have been mighty strange if she had not come. I must take myself in hand better than this. I mustn't behave like a blooming girl.' He frowned and coughed.

'Well,' said Osmond Orgreave to his son, thrusting out his coat-tails with his hand towards the fire, and swaying slightly to and fro on his heels and toes, 'so you've had your consultation, you eminent specialists! What's the result?'

He looked at his elegant son with an air half-quizzical and half-deferential.

'I've told you he's evidently a little better, dad,' Charlie answered casually. His London deportment was more marked than ever. The bracingly correct atmosphere of Ealing had given him a rather obvious sense of importance. He had developed into a man with a stake in the country, and he twisted his moustache like a man, and took out a cigarette like such a man.

'Yes, I know,' said Osmond, with controlled impatience. 'But what sort of influenza is it? I'm hoping to learn something now you've come. Stirling will talk about anything except influenza.'

'What sort of influenza is it? What do you mean?' And Charlie's twinkling glance said condescendingly : 'What's the old cock got hold of now? This is just like him.'

'But is there any real danger?' Edwin murmured.

'Well,' said Osmond bringing up his regiments, 'as I understand it, there are three types of influenza – the respiratory, the gastro-intestinal, and the nervous. Which one is it?'

Charlie laughed and prodded his father with a forefinger in a soft region near the shoulder, disturbing his balance. 'You've been reading the *B.M.J.*,' he said. 'And so you needn't pretend you haven't!'

Osmond paused an instant to consider the meaning of these initials.

'What if I have?' he demanded, raising his eyebrows, 'I say there are three types –'

'Thirty; you might be nearer the mark with thirty,' Charlie interrupted him. 'The fact is that this division into types is all very well in theory,' he proceeded, with easy disdain. 'But in practice it won't work out. Now for instance, what this kid has won't square with any of your three types. It's purely febrile, that's what it is. Rare, decidedly rare, but less rare in children than in adults – at any rate in my experience – in my experience. If his temperature wasn't so high, I should say the thing might last for days – weeks even. I've known it. The first question I put was – has he been in a stupor? He had. It may recur. That, and headache, *and* the absence of localized nervous symptoms –' He stopped, leaving the sentence in the air, grandiose and formidable, but of no purport.

Charlie shrugged his shoulders, allowing the beholder to choose his own interpretation of the gesture.

'You're a devilish wonderful fellow,' said Osmond grimly to his son. And Charlie winked grimly at Edwin, who grimly smiled.

'You and your *British Medical Journal*!' Charlie exclaimed, with an irony from which filial affection was not absent, and again prodded his father in the same spot.

'Of course I know I'm an old man,' said Osmond, condescendingly rejecting Charlie's condescension. He thought he did not mean what he said; nevertheless, it was the expression of the one idea which latterly beyond all other ideas had possessed him.

III

Janet came into the room, and was surprised to see Edwin. She was in a state of extreme fatigue – pale, with burning eyes, and hair that has lost the gracefulness of its curves.

'So you know?' she said.

Edwin nodded.

'It seems I've got to go to bed,' she went on. 'Father, you must go to bed too. Mother's gone. It's frightfully late. Come along now!'

She was insistent. She had been worried during the greater part of the day by her restless parents, and she was determined not to leave either of them at large.

'Charlie, you might run upstairs and see that everything's all right before I go. I shall get up again at four.'

'I'll be off,' said Edwin.

'Here! Hold on a bit,' Charlie objected. 'Wait till I come down. Let's have a yarn. You don't want to go to bed yet.'

Edwin agreed to the suggestion, and was left alone in the breakfast-room. What struck him was that the new situation created by Hilda's strange caprice had instantly been accepted by everybody, and had indeed already begun to seem quite natural. He esteemed highly the demeanour of all the Orgreaves. Neither he himself nor Maggie could have surpassed them in their determination not to exaggerate the crisis, in their determination to bear themselves simply and easily, and to speak with lightness, even with occasional humour. There were few qualities that he admired more than this.

And what was her demeanour, up there in the bedroom?

Suddenly the strangeness of Hilda's caprice presented itself to him as even more strange. She had merely gone to Ealing and captured Charlie. Charlie was understood to have a considerable practice. At her whim all his patients had been abandoned. What an idea, to bring him down like this! What tremendous faith in him she must have! And Edwin remembered distinctly that the first person who had ever spoken to him of Hilda was Charlie! And in what terms of admiration! Was there a long and secret understanding between these two? They must assuredly be far more intimate than he had ever suspected. Edwin hated to think that Hilda would depend more upon Charlie than upon himself in a grave difficulty. The notion caused him acute discomfort. He was resentful against Charlie as against a thief who had robbed him of his own, but who could not be apprehended and put to shame.

The acute discomfort was jealousy; but this word did not occur to him.

IV

'I say,' Edwin began, in a new intimate tone, when after what seemed a very long interval Charlie Orgreave returned to the breakfast-room with the information that for the present all had been done that could be done.

'What's up?' said Charlie, responding quite eagerly to the appeal for intimacy in Edwin's voice. He had brought in a tray with whisky and its apparatus, and he set this handily on a stool in front of the fire, and poked the fire, and generally made the usual ritualistic preparations for a comfortable talkative night.

'Rather delicate, wasn't it, you coming down and taking Stirling's case off him?'

Edwin smiled idly as he lolled far back in an old easy-chair. His two individualities had now merged into one.

'My boy,' Charlie answered, pausing impressively with his curly head forward, before dropping into an arm-chair by the stool, 'you may take it from me that "delicate" is not the word!'

Edwin nodded sympathetically, perceiving with satisfaction that beneath his Metropolitan mannerism, and his amusing pomposities, and his perfectly dandiacal clothes, Charlie still remained the Sunday, possibly more naïve than ever. This *naïveté* of Charlie's was particularly pleasing to him, for the reason that it gave him a feeling of superiority to the more brilliant being and persuaded him that the difference between London and the provinces was inessential and negligible. Charlie's hair still curled like a boy's, and he had not outgrown the *naïveté* of boyhood. Against these facts the fact that Charlie was a partner in a fashionable and dashing practice at Ealing simply did not weigh. The deference which in thought Edwin had been slowly acquiring for this Charlie, as to whom impressive news reached Bursley from time to time, melted almost completely away. In fundamentals he was convinced that Charlie was an infant compared to himself.

'Have a drop?'

'Well, it's not often I do, but I will tonight. Steady on with the whisky, old chap.'

Each took a charged glass and sipped. Edwin, by raising his arm, could just lodge his glass on the mantelpiece. Charlie then opened his large gun-metal cigarette-case, and with one match lighted two cigarettes.

'Yes, my boy,' Charlie resumed, as he meditatively blew out the match and threw it on the fire, 'you may well say "delicate". The truth is that if I hadn't seen at once that Stirling was a very decent sort of chap, and very friendly here, I might have funked it. Yes, I might. He came in just after we'd arrived. So I saw him alone – here. I made a clean breast of it, and put myself in his hands. Of course he appreciated the situation at once; and considering he'd never seen *her*, it was rather clever of him. . . . I suppose people rather like that Scotch accent of his down here?'

'They say he makes over a thousand a year already,' Edwin replied. He was thinking, 'Is she likely to be coming downstairs? No.'

'The deuce he does!' Charlie murmured, with ingenuous animation, foolishly betraying by an instant's lack of self-control the fact that

Ealing was not Utopia. Envy was in his voice as he continued : 'It's astonishing how some chaps can come along and walk straight into anything they want – whatever it happens to be !'

'What do you think of him as a doctor?' Edwin questioned.

'Seems all right,' said Charlie, with a fine brief effort to be patronizing.

'He's got a great reputation down here,' Edwin said quietly.

'Yes, yes. I should say he's quite all right.'

v

'How came it that Mrs Cannon came and rummaged *you* out?' Edwin knew that he would blush, and so he reached up for his whisky, and drank, adding : 'The old man still clings to his old brand of Scotch.'

'My dear fellow, I know no more than you. I was perfectly staggered – I can tell you that. I hadn't seen her since before she was married. Only heard of her again just lately through Janet. I suppose it was Janet who told her I was at Ealing. It's an absolute fact that just at the first blush I didn't even recognize her.'

'Didn't you?' Edwin wondered how this could be.

'I did not. She came into our surgery, as if she'd come out of the next room and I'd seen her only yesterday, and she just asked me to come away with her at once to Bursley. I thought she was off her nut, but she wasn't. She showed me your telegram.'

'The dickens she did !' Edwin was really startled.

'Yes. I told her there was nothing absolutely fatal in a temperature of 104. It happened in thousands of cases. Then she explained to me exactly how he'd been ill before, seemingly in the same way, and I could judge from what she said that he wasn't a boy who would stand a high temperature for very long.'

'By the way, what's his temperature tonight?' Edwin interrupted.

'102 point 7,' said Charlie. 'Yes,' he resumed, 'she did convince me it might be serious. But what then? I told her I couldn't possibly leave. She asked why not. She kept on asking me why not. I said, What about my patients here? She asked if any of them were dying. I said no, but I couldn't leave them all to my partner. I don't think she realized, before that, that I was in partnership. She stuck to it worse than ever then. I asked her why she wanted just me. I said all we doctors were much about the same, and so on. But it was no use. The fact is, you know, Hilda always had a great notion of me as a doctor. Can't imagine why! Kept it to herself of course, jolly close, as she did most things, but I'd noticed it now and then. You know – one of those tremendous beliefs she has. You're another of her beliefs, if you want to know.'

'How do you know? Give us another cigarette,' Edwin was exceed-

419

ingly uneasy, and yet joyous. One of his fears was that the Sunday might inquire how it was that he signed telegrams to Hilda with only his Christian name. The Sunday, however, made no such inquiry.

'How do I know!' Charlie exclaimed. 'I could tell in a second by the way she showed me your telegram. Oh! And besides, that's an old story, my young friend. You needn't flatter yourself it wasn't common property at one time.'

'Oh! Rot!' Edwin muttered. 'Well, go on!'

'Well, then I explained that there was such a thing as medical etiquette. . . . Ah! you should have heard Hilda on medical etiquette. You should just have heard her on that lay – medical etiquette versus the dying child. I simply had to chuck that. I said to her, "But suppose you hadn't caught me at home? I might have been out for the day – a hundred things." It was sheer accident she had caught me. At last she said : "Look here, Charlie, will you come, or won't you?" '

VI

'Well, and what did you say?'

'I should tell you she went down on her knees. What should you have said, eh, my boy? What could I say? They've got you when they put it that way. Especially a woman like she is! I tell you she was simply terrific. I tell you I wouldn't go through it again – not for something.'

Edwin responsively shook.

'I just threw up the sponge and came. I told Huskisson a thundering lie, to save my face, and away I came, and I've been with her ever since. Dashed if I haven't!'

'Who's Huskisson?'

'My partner. If anybody had told me beforehand that I should do such a thing I should have laughed. Of course, if you look at it calmly, it's preposterous. Preposterous – there's no other word – from my point of view. But when they begin to put it the way she put it – well, you've got to decide quick whether you'll be sensible and a brute, or whether you'll sacrifice yourself and be a damned fool. . . . What good am I here? No more good than anybody else. Supposing there *is* danger? Well, there may be. But I've left twenty or thirty influenza cases at Ealing. Every influenza case is dangerous, if it comes to that.'

'Exactly,' breathed Edwin.

'I wouldn't have done it for any other woman,' Charlie recommended. 'Not much!'

'Then why did you do it for her?'

Charlie shrugged his shoulders. 'There's something about her . . . I don't know. . . .' He lifted his nostrils fastidiously and gazed at the fire. 'There's not many women knocking about like *her*. . . . She gets hold

420

of you. She's nothing at all for about six months at a stretch, and then she has one minute of the grand style. . . . That's the sort of woman she is. Understand? But I expect you don't know her as we do.'

'Oh yes, I understand,' said Edwin. 'She must be tremendously fond of the kid.'

'You bet she is! Absolute passion. What sort is he?'

'Oh! He's all right. But I've never seen them together, and I never thought she was so particularly keen on him.'

'Don't you make any mistake,' said Charlie loftily. 'I believe women often are like that about an only child when they've had a rough time. And by the look of her she must have had a pretty rough time. I've never made out why she married that swine, and I don't think anyone else has either.'

'Did you know him?' Edwin asked, with sudden eagerness.

'Not a bit. But I've sort of understood he was a regular outsider. Do you know how long she's been a widow?'

'No,' said Edwin. 'I've barely seen her.'

At these words he became so constrained, and so suspicious of the look on his own face, that he rose abruptly and began to walk about the room.

'What's the matter?' demanded Charlie. 'Got pins and needles?'

'Only fidgets,' said Edwin.

'I hope this isn't one of your preliminaries for clearing out and leaving me alone,' Charlie complained. 'Here – where's that glass of yours? Have another cigarette.'

There was a sound that seemed to resemble a tap on the door.

'What's that noise,' said Edwin, startled. The whole of his epidermis tingled, and he stood still. They both listened.

The sound was repeated. Yes, it was a tap on the door; but in the night, and in the repose of the house, it had the characters of some unearthly summons.

Edwin was near the door. He hesitated for an instant afraid, and then with an effort, brusquely opened the door and looked forth beyond the shelter of the room. A woman's figure was disappearing down the passage in the direction of the stairs. It was she.

'Did you –' he began. But Hilda had gone. Agitated, he said to Charlie, his hand still on the knob : 'It's Mrs Cannon. She just knocked and ran off. I expect she wants you.'

Charlie jumped up and scurried out of the room exactly like a boy, despite his tall, mature figure of a man of thirty-five.

CHAPTER 12 : *End of the Night*

I

For the second time that night Edwin was left alone for a long period in the little breakfast-room. Charlie's phrase, 'You're another of her beliefs', shone like a lamp in his memory, beneficent. And though he was still jealous of Charlie, with whom Hilda's relations were obviously very intimate; although he said to himself, 'She never made any appeal to *me*, she would scarcely have *my* help at any price'; nevertheless he felt most singularly uplifted and, without any reason, hopeful. So much so that the fate of the child became with him a matter of secondary importance. He excused this apparent callousness by making sure in his own mind that the child was in no real danger. On the other hand he blamed himself for ever having fancied that Hilda was indifferent to George. She, indifferent to her own son! What a wretched, stupid slander! He ought to have known better than that. He ought to have known that a Hilda would bring to maternity the mightiest passions. All that Charlie had said confirmed him in his idolization of her. 'One minute of the grand style.' That was it. Charlie had judged her very well – damn him! And the one minute was priceless, beyond all estimation.

The fire sank, with little sounds of decay; and he stared at it, prevented as if by a spell from stooping to make it up, prevented even from looking at his watch. At length he shivered slightly, and the movement broke the trance. He wandered to the door, which Charlie had left ajar, and listened. No sign of life! He listened intently, but his ear could catch nothing whatever. What were those two doing upstairs with the boy? Cautiously he stepped out into the passage, and went to the foot of the stairs, where a gas-jet was burning. He was reminded of the nights preceding his father's death.

Another gas jet showed along the corridor at the head of the stairs. He put his foot on the first step; it creaked with a noise comparable to the report of a pistol in the dead silence. But there was no responsive sound to show that anyone had been alarmed by this explosion. Impelled by nervous curiosity, and growing careless, he climbed the reverberating, complaining stairs, and, entering the corridor, stood exactly in front of the closed door of the sick-room, and listened again, and heard naught. His heart was obstreperously beating. Part of the household slept; the other part watched; and he was between the two, like a thief, like a spy. Should he knock, discreetly, and ask if he could be of help? The strange romance of his existence, and of all existence, flowed around him in mysterious currents, obsessing him.

Suddenly the door opened, and Charlie, barely avoiding a collision, started back in alarm. Then Charlie recovered his self-possession and carefully shut the door.

'I was just wondering whether I could be any use,' Edwin stammered in a whisper.

Charlie whispered : 'It's all right, but I must run round to Stirling's, to get a drug I want.'

'Is he worse?'

'Yes. That is – yes. You never know with a child. They're up and down and all over the place inside of an hour.'

'Can I go?' Edwin suggested.

'No. I can explain to him quicker than you.'

'You'll never find your way in this fog.'

'Bosh, man! D'you think I don't know the town as well as you? Besides, it's lifted considerably.'

By a common impulse they tiptoed to the window at the end of the corridor. Across the lawn could be dimly discerned a gleam through the trees.

'I'll come with you,' said Edwin.

'You'd much better stay here – in case.'

'Shall I go into the bedroom?'

'Certainly.'

Charlie turned to descend the stairs.

'I say,' Edwin called after him in a loud whisper, 'when you get to the gate – you know the house – you go up the side entry. The night bell's rather high up on the left hand.'

'All right! All right!' Charlie replied impatiently. 'Just come and shut the front door after me. I don't want to bang it.'

II

When Edwin crept into the bedroom he was so perturbed by continually growing excitement that he saw nothing clearly except the central group of objects : that is to say, a narrow bed, whose burden was screened from him by its foot, a table, an empty chair, the gas-globe luminous against a dark-green blind, and Hilda in black, alert and erect beneath the down-flowing light. The rest of the chamber seemed to stretch obscurely away into no confines. Not for several seconds did he even notice the fire. This confusing excitement was not caused by anything external such as the real or supposed peril of the child; it had its source within.

As soon as Hilda identified him her expression changed from the intent frowning stare of inquiry to a smile. Edwin had never before seen her smile in that way. The smile was weak, resigned, almost piteous; and it was extraordinarily sweet. He closed the door quietly, and moved in silence towards the bed. She nodded an affectionate welcome. He returned her greeting eagerly, and all his constraint was loosed away, and he felt at ease, and happy. Her face was very pale indeed against the glittering blackness of her eyes, and her sombre disordered hair and untidy dress; but it did not show fatigue nor extreme anxiety; it was a face of calm meekness. The sleeves of her dress were reversed, showing the forearms, which gave her an appearance of dishabille, homely, intimate, confiding. 'So it was common property at one time,' Edwin thought, recalling a phrase of Charlie's in the breakfast-room. Strange : he wanted her in all her disarray, with all her woes, anxieties, solicitudes; he wanted her, piteous, meek, beaten by destiny, weakly smiling; he wanted her because she stood so, after the immense, masterful effort of the day, watching in acquiescence by that bed !

'Has he gone?' she asked, in a voice ordinarily loud, but, for her, unusually tender.

'Yes,' said Edwin. 'He's gone. He told me I'd better come in here. So I came.'

She nodded again. 'Have that chair.'

Without arguing, he took the chair. She remained standing.

The condition of George startled him. Evidently the boy was in a heavy stupor. His body was so feverish that it seemed to give off a perceptible heat. There was no need to touch the skin in order to know that it burned : one divined this. The hair was damp. About the pale lips an irregular rash had formed, purplish, patchy, and the rash seemed to be the mark and sign of some strange dreadful disease that nobody had ever named : a plague. Worse than all this was the profound, comprehensive discomfort of the whole organism, showing itself in the unnatural pose of the limbs, and in multitudinous faint instinctive ways of the inert but complaining body. And the child was so slight beneath the blanket, so young, so helpless, spiritually so alone. How could even Hilda communicate her sympathy to that spirit, withdrawn and inaccessible? During the illness of his father Edwin had thought that he was looking upon the extreme tragic limit of pathos, but this present spectacle tightened more painfully the heart. It was more shameful; a more excruciating accusation against the order of the universe. To think of George in his pride, strong, capricious, and dominant, while gazing at this victim of malady . . . the contrast was intolerable !

George was very ill. And yet Hilda, despite the violence of her nature, could stand there calm, sweet, and controlled. What power ! Edwin was humbled. 'This is the sort of thing that women of her sort can do,' he said to himself. 'Why, Maggie and I are simply nothing to her!' Maggie and he could be self-possessed in a crisis; they could stand a strain; but the strain would show itself either in a tense harshness, or in some unnatural lightness, or even flippancy. Hilda was the very image of soft caressing sweetness. He felt that he must emulate her.

'Surely his temperature's gone up?' he said quietly.

'Yes,' Hilda replied, fingering absently the clinical thermometer that with a lot of other gear lay on the table. 'It's nearly 105. It can't last like this. It won't. I've been through it with him before, but not quite so bad.'

'I didn't think anyone could have influenza twice, so soon,' Edwin murmured.

'Neither did I,' said she. 'Still, he must have been sickening for it before he came down here.' There was a pause. She wiped the boy's forehead. 'This change has come on quite suddenly,' she said, in a different voice. 'Two hours ago – less than two hours ago – there was scarcely a sign of that rash.'

'What is it?'

'Charlie says it's nothing particular.'

'What's Charlie gone for?'

'I don't know.' She shook her head; then smiled. '*Isn't* it a good thing I brought him?'

Indubitably it was. Her caprice, characterized as preposterous by males, had been justified. Thus chance often justifies women; setting at naught the high priests of reason.

III

Looking at the unconscious and yet tormented child, Edwin was aware of a melting protective pity for him, of an immense desire to watch over his rearing with all insight, sympathy, and help, so that in George's case none of the mistakes and cruelties and misapprehensions should occur which had occurred in his own. This feeling was intense to the point of being painful.

'I don't know whether you know or not,' he said, 'but we're great pals, the infant and I.'

Hilda smiled, and in the very instant of seeing the smile its effect upon him was such that he humiliated himself before her in secret for ever having wildly suspected that she was jealous of the attachment. 'Do you think I don't know all about that?' she murmured. 'He wouldn't be here now if it hadn't been for that.' After a silence she added: 'You're the only person that he ever has really cared for, and I can tell you he likes you better than he likes me.'

'How do you know that?'

'I know by the way he talks and looks.'

'If he takes after his mother, that's no sign,' Edwin retorted, without considering what he said.

'What do you mean – "if he takes after his mother"?' She seemed puzzled.

'Could anyone tell *your* real preferences from the way *you* talked and looked?' His audacious rashness astounded him. Nevertheless he stared her in the eyes, and her glance fell.

'No one but you could have said a thing like that,' she observed mildly, yieldingly.

And what he had said suddenly acquired a mysterious and wise significance and became oracular. She alone had the power of inspiring him to be profound. He had noticed that before, years ago, and first at their first meeting. Or was it that she saw in him an oracle, and caused him to see with her?

Slowly her face coloured, and she walked away to the fireplace, and cautiously tended it. Constraint had seized him again, and his heart was loud.

'Edwin,' she summoned him, from the fireplace.

He rose, shaking with emotion, and crossed the undiscovered spaces of the room to where she was. He had the illusion that they were by themselves not in the room but in the universe. She was leaning with one hand on the mantelpiece.

'I must tell you something,' she said, 'that nobody at all knows except George's father, and probably nobody ever will know. His sister knew, but she's dead.'

'Yes!' he muttered, in an exquisite rush of happiness. After all, it was not with Charlie, nor even with Janet, that she was most intimate; it was with himself!

'George's father was put in prison for bigamy. George is illegitimate.' She spoke with her characteristic extreme clearness of enunciation, in a voice that showed no emotion.

'You don't mean it!' He gasped foolishly.

She nodded. 'I'm not a married woman. I once thought I was, but I wasn't. That's all.'

'But –'

'But what?'

'You – said six or seven years, didn't you? Surely they don't give that long for bigamy?'

'Oh!' she replied mildly. 'That was for something else. When he came out of prison the first time they arrested him again instantly – so I was told. It was in Scotland.'

'I see.'

There was a rattle as of hailstones on the window. They both started. 'That must be Charlie!' she exclaimed, suddenly loosing her excitement under this pretext. 'He doesn't want to ring and wake the house.'

Edwin ran out of the room, sliding and slipping down the deserted stairs that waited patiently through the night for human feet.

'Forgot to take a key,' said Charlie, appearing, breathless, just as the door opened. 'I meant to take the big key, and then I forgot.' He had a little round box in his hand. He mounted the stairs two and three at a time.

Edwin slowly closed the door. He could not bring himself to follow Charlie and, after a moment's vacillation, he went back into the breakfast-room.

IV

Amazing, incalculable, woman, wrapped within fold after fold of mystery! He understood better now, but even now there were things that he did not understand; and the greatest enigma of all remained unsolved, the original enigma of her treachery to himself. . . . And she had chosen just that moment, just that crisis, to reveal to him that sinister secret which by some unguessed means he had been able to hide from her acquaintance. Naturally, if she wished to succeed with a boarding-house in Brighton she would be compelled to conceal somehow the fact that she was the victim of a bigamist and her child without a lawful name! The merest prudence would urge her to concealment so long as concealment was possible; yes, even from Janet! Her other friends deemed her a widow; Janet thought her the wife of a convict; he alone knew that she was neither wife nor widow. Though what scathing experience she must have passed! An unfamiliar and disconcerting mood gradually took complete possession of him. At first he did not correctly analyse it. It was sheer, exuberant, instinctive, unreasoning, careless joy.

Then, after a long period of beatific solitude in the breakfast-room, he heard stealthy noises in the hall, and his fancy jumped to the idea of burglary. Excited, unreflecting, he hurried into the hall. Johnnie Orgreave, who had let himself in with a latchkey, was shutting and bolting the front door. Johnnie's surprise was the greater. He started violently on seeing Edwin, and then at once assumed the sang-froid of a hero of romance. When Edwin informed him that Hilda had come, and Charlie with her, and that those two were watching by the boy, the rest of the household being in bed, Johnnie permitted himself a few verbal symptoms of astonishment.

'How is Georgie?' he asked with an effort, as if ashamed.

'He isn't much better,' said Edwin evasively.

Johnnie made a deprecatory sound with his tongue against his lips, and frowned, determined to take his proper share in the general anxiety.

With careful, dignified movements, he removed his silk hat and his heavy ulster, revealing evening-dress, and a coloured scarf that overhung a crumpled shirt-front.

'Where've you been?' Edwin asked.

'Tennis dance. Didn't you know?'

'No,' said Edwin.

'Really!' Johnnie murmured, with a falsely ingenuous air. After a pause he said : 'They've left you all alone, then?'

'I was in the breakfast-room,' said Edwin, when he had given further information.

They walked into the breakfast-room together. Charlie's cigarette-case lay on the tray.

'Those your cigarettes?' Johnnie inquired.

'No. They're Charlie's.'

'Oh! Master Charlie's, are they? I wonder if they're any good.' He took one fastidiously. Between two enormous out-blowings of smoke he said : 'Well, I'm dashed! So Charlie's come with her! I hope the kid'll soon be better. . . . I should have been back long ago, only I took Mrs Chris Hamson home.'

'Who's Mrs Chris Hamson?'

'Don't you know her? She's a ripping woman.'

He stood there in all the splendour of thirty years, with more than Charlie's *naïveté*, politely trying to enter into the life of the household, but failing to do so because of his pre-occupation with the rippingness of Mrs Chris Hamson. The sight of him gave pleasure to Edwin. It did not occur to him to charge the young man with being callous.

When the cigarette was burnt, Johnnie said –

'Well, I think I shall leave seeing Charlie till breakfast.'

And he went to bed. On reaching the first-floor corridor he wished that he had gone to bed half a minute sooner; for in the corridor he encountered Janet, who had risen and was returning to her post; and Janet's face, though she meant it not, was an accusation. Four o'clock had struck.

v

It was nearly half past seven before Edwin left the house. In the meantime he had seen Charlie briefly twice, and Janet once, but he had not revisited the sick-room nor seen Hilda again. The boy's condition was scarcely altered; if there was any change, it was for the better.

Dawn had broken. The fog was gone, but a faint mist hung in the trees over the damp lawn. The air was piercingly chill. Yawning and glancing idly about him, he perceived a curious object on the dividing wall. It was the candlestick which he had left there on the previous night. The candle was entirely consumed. 'I may as well get over the wall,' he said to himself, and he scrambled up it with adventurous cheerfulness, and took the candlestick with him; it was covered with drops of moisture. He deposited it in the kitchen, where the servant was cleaning the range. On the oak chest in the hall lay the *Manchester Guardian*, freshly arrived. He opened it with another heavy yawn. At the head of one column he read, 'Death of the Duke of Clarence,' and at the head of another, 'Death of Cardinal Manning'. The double news shocked him strangely. He thought of what those days had been to others beside himself. And he thought : 'Supposing after all the kid doesn't come through?'

CHAPTER 13 : *Her Heart*

I

After having been to business and breakfasted as usual, Edwin returned to the shop at ten o'clock. He did not feel tired, but his manner was very curt, even with Stifford, and melancholy had taken the place of his joy. The whole town was gloomy, and seemed to savour its gloom luxuriously. But Edwin wondered why he should be melancholy. There was no reason for it. There was less reason for it than there had been for ten years. Yet he was; and, like the town, he found pleasure in his state. He had no real desire to change it. At noon he suddenly went off home, thus upsetting Stifford's arrangements for the dinner-hour. 'I shall lie down for a bit,' he said to Maggie. He slept till a little after one o'clock, and he could have slept longer, but dinner was ready. He said to himself, with an extraordinary sense of satisfaction, '*I have had a sleep.*' After dinner he lay down again, and slept till nearly three o'clock. It was with the most agreeable sensations that he awakened. His melancholy was passing; it had not entirely gone, but he could foresee the end of it as of an eclipse. He made the discovery that he had only been tired. Now he was somewhat reposed. And as he lay in repose he was aware of an intensified perception of himself as a physical organism. He thought calmly, '*What a fine thing life is!*'

'I was just going to bring you some tea up,' said Maggie, who met him on the stairs as he came down. 'I heard you moving. Will you have some?'

He rubbed his eyes. His head seemed still to be distended with sleep, and this was a part of his well-being. 'Aye !' he replied, with lazy satisfaction. 'That'll just put me right.'

'George is much better,' said Maggie.

'Good !' he said heartily.

Joy, wild and exulting, surged through him once more; and it was of such a turbulent nature that it would not suffer any examination of its origin. It possessed him by its might. As he drank the admirable tea he felt that he still needed a lot more sleep. There were two points of pressure at the top of his head. But he knew that he could sleep, and sleep well, whenever he chose; and that on the morrow his body would be perfectly restored.

He walked briskly back to the shop, intending to work, and he was a little perturbed to find that he could not work. His head refused. He sat in the cubicle vaguely staring. Then he was startled by a tremendous yawn, which seemed to have its inception in the very centre of his being, and which by the pang of its escape almost broke him in pieces. 'I've never yawned like that before,' he thought, apprehensive. Another yawn of the same seismic kind succeeded immediately, and these frightful yawns continued one after another for several minutes, each leaving him weaker than the one before. 'I'd better go home while I can,' he thought, intimidated by the suddenness and the mysteriousness of the attack. He went home. Maggie at once said that he would be better in bed, and to his own astonishment he agreed. He could not eat the meal that Maggie brought to his room.

'There's something the matter with you,' said Maggie.

'No. I'm only tired.' He knew it was a lie.

'You're simply burning,' she said, but she refrained from any argument, and left him.

He could not sleep. His anticipations in that respect were painfully falsified.

Later, Maggie came back.

'Here's Dr Heve,' she said briefly, in the doorway. She was silhouetted against the light from the landing. The doctor, in mourning, stood behind her.

'Dr Heve? What the devil —' But he did not continue the protest.

Maggie advanced into the room and turned up the gas, and the glare wounded his eyes.

'Yes,' said Dr Heve, at the end of three minutes. 'You've got it. Not badly, I hope. But you've got it all right.'

Humiliating ! For the instinct of the Clayhangers was always to assume that by virtue of some special prudence, or immunity, or resisting power, peculiar to them alone, they would escape any popular affliction such as an epidemic. In the middle of the night, amid feverish tossings and crises of thirst, and horrible malaise, it was more than humiliating! Supposing he died? People did die of influenza. The strangest, the most monstrous things did happen. For the first time in his life he lay in the genuine fear of death. He had never been ill before. And now he was ill. He knew what it was to be ill. The stupid, blundering clumsiness of death aroused his angry resentment. No! It was impossible that he should die! People did not die of influenza.

The next day the doctor laughed. But Edwin said to himself: 'He may have laughed only to cheer me up. They never tell their patients the truth.' And every cell of his body was vitiated, poisoned, inefficient, profoundly demoralized. Ordinary health seemed the most precious and the least attainable boon.

II

After wildernesses of time that were all but interminable, the attack was completely over. It had lasted a hundred hours, of which the first fifty had each been an age. It was a febrile attack similar to George's but less serious. Edwin had possibly caught the infection at Knype Railway Station: yet who could tell? Now he was in the drawing-room, shaved, clothed, but wearing slippers for a sign that he was only convalescent, and because the doctor had forbidden him the street. He sat in front of the fire, in the easy-chair that had been his father's favourite. On his left hand were an accumulation of newspapers and a book; on his right, some business letters and documents left by the assiduous Stifford after a visit of sympathy and of affairs. The declining sun shone with weak goodwill on the garden.

'Please sir, there's a lady,' said the servant, opening the door.

He was startled. His first thought naturally was, 'It's Hilda!' in spite of the extreme improbability of it being Hilda. Hilda had never set foot in his house. Nevertheless, supposing it was Hilda, Maggie would assuredly come into the drawing-room – she could not do otherwise – and the three-cornered interview would, he felt, be very trying. He knew that Maggie, for some reason inexplicable by argument, was out of sympathy with Hilda, as with Hilda's son. She had given him regular news of George, who was now at about the same stage of convalescence as himself, but she scarcely mentioned the mother, and he had not dared to inquire. These thoughts flashed through his brain in an instant.

'Who is it?' he asked gruffly.

'I – I don't know, sir. Shall I ask?' replied the servant, blushing as she perceived that once again she had sinned. She had never before been in a house where aristocratic ceremony was carried to such excess as at Edwin's. Her unconquerable instinct, upon opening the front door to a

431

well-dressed stranger was to rush off and publish the news that some-body mysterious and grand had come, leaving the noble visitor on the doormat. She had been instructed in the ritual proper to these crises, but with little good result, for the crises took her unawares.

'Yes. Go and ask the name, and then tell my sister,' said Edwin shortly.

'Miss Clayhanger is gone out, sir.'

'Well, run along,' he told her impatiently.

He was standing anxiously near the door when she returned to the room.

'Please, sir, it's a Mrs Cannon, and it's you she wants.'

'Show her in,' he said, and to himself : 'My God !'

In the ten seconds that elapsed before Hilda appeared he glanced at himself in the mantel mirror, fidgeted with his necktie, and walked to the window and back again to his chair. She had actually called to see him ! . . . His agitation was extreme. . . . But how like her it was to call thus boldly ! . . . Maggie's absence was providential.

Hilda entered, to give him a lesson in blandness. She wore a veil, and carried a muff – outworks of her self-protective, impassive demeanour. She was pale, and as calm as pale. She would not take the easy-chair which he offered her. Useless to insist – she would not take it. He brushed away letters and documents from the small chair to his right, and she took that chair. . . . Having taken it, she insisted that he should resume the easy-chair.

'I called just to say good-bye,' she said. 'I knew you couldn't come out, and I'm going tonight.'

'But surely he isn't fit to travel?' Edwin exclaimed.

'George? Not yet. I'm leaving him behind. You see I musn't stay away longer than's necessary.'

She smiled, and lifted her veil as far as her nose. She had not smiled before.

'Charlie's gone back?'

'Oh yes. Two days ago. He left a message for you.'

'Yes. Maggie gave it me. By the way, I'm sorry she's not in.'

'I've just seen her,' said Hilda.

'Oh !'

'She came in to see Janet. They're having a cup of tea in George's bedroom. So I put my things on and walked round here at once.'

As Hilda made this surprising speech she gazed full at Edwin.

III

A blush slowly covered his face. They both sat silent. Only the fire crackled lustily. Edwin thought, as his agitation increased and entirely confused him, 'No other woman was ever like this woman!' He wanted to rise masterfully, to accomplish some gesture splendid and decisive, but he was held in the hollow of the easy-chair as though by paralysis. He looked at Hilda; he might have been looking at a stranger. He tried to read her face, and he could not read it. He could only see in it vague trouble. He was afraid of her. The idea even occurred to him that, could he be frank with himself, he would admit that he hated her. The moments were intensely painful; the suspense exasperating and excruciating. Ever since their last encounter he had anticipated this scene; his fancy had been almost continuously busy in fashioning this scene. And now the reality had swept down upon him with no warning, and he was overwhelmed.

She would not speak. She had withdrawn her gaze, but she would not speak. She would force him to speak.

'I say,' he began gruffly, in a resentful tone, careless as to what he was saying, 'you might have told me earlier – what you told me on Wednesday night. Why didn't you tell me when I was at Brighton?'

'I wanted to,' she said meekly. 'But I couldn't. I really couldn't bring myself to do it.'

'Instead of telling me a lie,' he went on. 'I think you might have trusted me more than that.'

'A lie?' she muttered. 'I told you the truth. I told you he was in prison.'

'You told me your husband was in prison,' he corrected her, in a voice meditative and judicial. He knew not in the least why he was talking in this strain.

She began to cry. At first he was not sure that she was crying. He glanced surreptitiously, and glanced away, as if guilty. But at the next glance he was sure. Her eyes glistened behind the veil, and tear-drops appeared at its edge and vanished under her chin.

'You don't know how much I wanted to tell you!' she wept.

She hid her half-veiled face in her hands. And then he was victimized by the blackest desolation. His one desire was that the scene should finish, somehow, anyhow.

'I never wrote to you because there was nothing to say. Nothing!' She sobbed, still covering her face.

'Never wrote to me – do you mean –'

She nodded violently twice. 'Yes. *Then!*' He divined that suddenly she had begun to talk of ten years ago. 'I knew you'd know it was because I couldn't help it.' She spoke so indistinctly through her emotion and her tears, and her hands, that he could not distinguish the words.

'What do you say?'

'I say I couldn't help doing what I did. I knew you'd know I couldn't

433

help it. I couldn't write. It was best for me to be silent. What else was there for me to do except be silent? I knew you'd know I couldn't help it. It was a –' Sobs interrupted her.

'Of course I knew that,' he said. He had to control himself very carefully, or he too would have lost command of his voice. Such was her power of suggestion over him that her faithlessness seemed now scarcely to need an excuse.

(Somewhere within himself he smiled as he reflected that he, in his father's place, in his father's very chair, was thus under the spell of a woman whose child was nameless. He smiled grimly at the thought of Auntie Hamps, of Clara, of the pietistic Albert! They were of a different race, a different generation! They belonged to a dead world!)

'I shall tell you,' Hilda recommenced mournfully, but in a clear and steady voice, at last releasing her face, which was shaken like that of a child in childlike grief. 'You'll never understand what I had to go through, and how I couldn't help myself' – she was tragically plaintive – 'but I shall tell you. . . . You *must* understand!'

She raised her eyes. Already for some moments his hands had been desiring the pale wrists between her sleeve and her glove. They fascinated his hands, which, hesitatingly, went out towards them. As soon as she felt his touch, she dropped to her knees, and her chin almost rested on the arm of his chair. He bent over a face that was transfigured.

'My heart never kissed any other man but you!' she cried. 'How often and often and often have I kissed you, and you never knew! . . . It was for a message that I sent George down here – a message to you! I named him after you. . . . Do you think that if dreams could make him your child – he wouldn't be yours?'

Her courage, and the expression of it, seemed to him to be sublime.

'You don't know me!' she sighed, less convulsively.

'Don't I!' he said, with lofty confidence.

After a whole decade his nostrils quivered again to the odour of her olive skin. Drowning amid the waves of her terrible devotion, he was recompensated in the hundredth part of a second for all that through her he had suffered or might hereafter suffer. The many problems and difficulties which marriage with her would raise seemed trivial in the light of her heart's magnificent and furious loyalty. He thought of the younger Edwin whom she had kissed into rapture, as of a boy too inexperienced in sorrow to appreciate this Hilda. He braced himself to the exquisite burden of life.

[In the autumn of 1911 the author will publish a novel dealing with the history of Hilda Lessways up to the day of her marriage with Edwin. This will be followed by a novel dealing with the marriage.]